James De Mille

The Cryptogram

A Novel

THE CRYPTOGRAM.

CHAPTER I.

TWO OLD FRIENDS.

CHETWYNDE CASTLE was a large baronial mansion, belonging to the Plantagenet period, and situated in Monmouthshire. It was a grand old place, with dark towers, and turrets, and gloomy walls surmounted with battlements, half of which had long since tumbled down, while the other half seemed tottering to ruin. That menacing ruin was on one side of the structure concealed beneath a growth of ivy, which contrasted the dark green of its leaves with the sombre hue of the ancient stones. Time with its defacing fingers had only lent additional grandeur to this venerable pile. As it rose there—" standing with half its battlements alone, and with five hundred years of ivy grown"—its picturesque magnificence and its air of hoar antiquity made it one of the noblest monuments of the past which England could show.

All its surroundings were in keeping with the central object. Here were no neat paths, no well-kept avenues, no trim lawns. On the con-trary, every thing bore the unmistakable marks of neglect and decay; the walks were overgrown, the terraces dilapidated, and the rose pleasaunce had degenerated into a tangled mass of bushes and briers. It seemed as though the whole domain were about to revert into its original state of nature; and every thing spoke either of the absence of a master, or else of something more important still—the absence of money.

The castle stood on slightly elevated ground; and from its gray stone ivy-covered portal so magnificent was the view that the most careless observer would be attracted by it, and stand wonder-struck at the beauty of the scene, till he forgot in the glories of nature the deficiencies of art. Below, and not far away, flowed the silvery Wye, most charming of English streams, winding tortuously through fertile meadows and wooded copses; farther off lay fruitful vales and rolling hills; while in the distance the prospect was bounded by the giant forms of the Welsh mountains.

At the moment when this story opens these beauties were but faintly visible through the fast-fading twilight of a summer evening; the shadows were rapidly deepening; and the only signs of life about the place appeared where from some of the windows at the eastern end faint rays of light stole out into the gloom.

The interior of the castle corresponded with the exterior in magnificence and in ruin—in its picturesque commingling of splendor and decay. The hall was hung with arms and armor of past generations, and ornamented with stags' heads, antlers, and other trophies of the chase; but rust, and mould, and dust covered them all. Throughout the house a large number of rooms were empty, and the whole western end was un-furnished. In the furnished rooms at the east-ern end every thing belonged to a past genera-tion, and all the massive and antiquated furni-ture bore painful marks of poverty and neglect. Time was every where asserting his power, and nowhere was any resistance made to his ravages.

Some comfort, however, was still to be found in the old place. There were rooms which were as yet free from the general touch of desolation. Among these was the dining-room, where at this time the heavy curtains were drawn, the lamps shone out cheerily, and, early June though it was, a bright wood-fire blazed on the ample hearth, lighting up with a ruddy glow the heavy panelings and the time-worn tapestries.

Dinner was just over, the dessert was on the table, and two gentlemen were sitting over their wine—though this is to be taken rather in a fig-urative sense, for their conversation was so engrossing as to make them oblivious of even the charms of the old ancestral port of rare vintage which Lord Chetwynde had produced to do honor to his guest. Nor is this to be wondered at. Friends of boyhood and early manhood, sharers long ago in each other's hopes and aspirations, they had parted last when youth and ambition were both at their height. Now, after the lapse of years, wayworn and weary from the strife, they had met again to recount how those hopes had been fulfilled.

The two men were of distinguished appearance. Lord Chetwynde was of about the medium size, with slight figure, and pale, aristocratic face. His hair was silver-white, his features were delicately chiseled, but wore habitually a sad and anxious expression. His whole physique betokened a nature of extreme refinement and sensibility, rather than force or strength of character. His companion, General Pomeroy, was a man of different stamp. He was tall, with a high receding brow, hair longer than is common with soldiers; thin lips, which spoke of resolution, around which, however, there always dwelt as he spoke a smile of inexpressible sweetness. He had a long nose, and large eyes that lighted up with every varying feeling. There was in his face both resolution and kindliness, each in extreme, as though he could remorselessly take vengeance on an enemy or lay down his life for a friend.

As long as the servants were present the conversation, animated though it was, referred to topics of a general character; but as soon as they had left the room the two friends began to refer more confidentially to the past.

"You have lived so very secluded a life," said General Pomeroy, "that it is only at rare intervals that I have heard any thing of you, and that was hardly more than the fact that you were alive. You were always rather reserved and secluded, you know; you hated, like Horace, the *profanum vulgus*, and held yourself aloof from them, and so I suppose you would not go into political life. Well, I don't know but that, after all, you were right."

"My dear Pomeroy," said Lord Chetwynde, leaning back in his chair, "my circumstances have been such that entrance into political life has scarcely ever depended on my own choice. My position has been so peculiar that it has hardly ever been possible for me to obtain advancement in the common ways, even if I had desired it. I dare say, if I had been inordinately ambitious, I might have done something; but, as it was, I have done nothing. You see me just about where I was when we parted, I don't know how many years ago."

"Well, at any rate," said the General, "you have been spared the trouble of a career of ambition. You have lived here quietly on your own place, and I dare say you have had far more real happiness than you would otherwise have had."

"Happiness!" repeated Lord Chetwynde, in a mournful tone. He leaned his head on his hand for a few moments, and said nothing. At last he looked up and said, with a bitter smile: "The story of my life is soon told. Two words will embody it all — disappointment and failure."

General Pomeroy regarded his friend earnestly for a few moments, and then looked away without speaking.

"My troubles began from the very first," continued Lord Chetwynde, in a musing tone, which seemed more like a soliloquy than any thing else. "There was the estate, saddled with debt handed down from my grandfather to my father. It would have required years of economy and good management to free it from encumbrance. But my father's motto was always *Dum vivimus vivamus*, and his only idea was to get what money he could for himself, and let his heirs look out for themselves. In consequence, heavier mortgages were added. He lived in Paris, enjoying himself, and left Chetwynde in charge of a factor, whose chief idea was to feather his own nest. So he let every thing go to decay, and oppressed the tenants in order to collect money for my father, and prevent his coming home to see the ruin that was going on. You may not have known this before. I did not until after our separation, when it all came upon me at once. My father wanted me to join him in breaking the entail. Overwhelmed by such a calamity, and indignant with him, I refused to comply with his wishes. We quarreled. He went back to Paris, and I never saw him again.

"After his death my only idea was to clear away the debt, improve the condition of the tenants, and restore Chetwynde to its former condition. How that hope has been realized you have only to look around you and see. But at that time my hope was strong. I went up to London, where my name and the influence of my friends enabled me to enter into public life. You were somewhere in England then, and I often used to wonder why I never saw you. You must have been in London.' I once saw your name in an army list among the officers of a regiment stationed there. At any rate I worked hard, and at first all my prospects were bright, and I felt confident in my future.

"Well, about that time I got married, trusting to my prospects. She was of as good a family as mine, but had no money."

Lord Chetwynde's tone as he spoke about his marriage had suddenly changed. It seemed as though he spoke with an effort. He stopped for a time, and slowly drank a glass of wine.

"She married me," he continued, in an icy tone, "for my prospects. Sometimes you know it is very safe to marry on prospects. A rising young statesman is often a far better match than a dissipated man of fortune. Some mothers know this; my wife's mother thought me a good match, and my wife thought so too. I loved her very dearly, or I would not have married—though I don't know, either: people often marry in a whim."

General Pomeroy had thus far been gazing fixedly at the opposite wall, but now he looked earnestly at his friend, whose eyes were downcast while he spoke, and showed a deeper attention.

"My office," said Lord Chetwynde, "was a lucrative one, so that I was able to surround my bride with every comfort; and the bright prospects which lay before me made me certain about my future. After a time, however, difficulties arose. You are aware that the chief point in my religion is Honor.. It is my nature, and was taught me by my mother. Our family motto is, *Noblesse oblige*, and the full meaning of this great maxim my mother had instilled into every fibre of my being. But on going into the world I found it ridiculed among my own class as obsolete and exploded. Every where it seemed to have given way to the mean doctrine of expediency. My sentiments were gayly ridiculed, and I soon began to fear that I was not suited for political life.

"At length a crisis arrived. I had either to sacrifice my conscience or resign my position. I chose the latter alternative, and in doing so I gave up my political life forever. I need not tell the bitterness of my disappointment. But the loss of worldly prospects and of hope was as nothing compared with other things. The worst of all was the reception which I met at home. My young, and as I supposed loving wife, to whom I went at once with my story, and from whom I expected the warmest sympathy, greeted me with nothing but tears and reproaches. She could only look upon my act with the world's eyes. She called it ridiculous Quixotism. She charged me with want of affection; denounced me for beguiling her to marry a pauper; and after a painful interview we parted in coldness."

Lord Chetwynde, whose agitation was now evident, here paused and drank another glass of wine. After some time he went on:

"After all, it was not so bad. I soon found employment. I had made many powerful friends, who, though they laughed at my scruples, still seemed to respect my consistency, and had confidence in my ability. Through them I obtained a new appointment where I could be more independent, though the prospects were poor. Here I might have been happy, had it not been for the continued alienation between my wife and me. She had been ambitious. She had relied on my future. She was now angry because I had thrown that future away. It was a death-blow to her hopes, and she could not forgive me. We lived in the same house, but I knew nothing of her occupations and amusements. She went much into society, where she was greatly admired, and seemed to be neglectful of her home and of her child. I bore my misery as best I could in silence, and never so much as dreamed of the tremendous catastrophe in which it was about to terminate."

Lord Chetwynde paused, and seemed overcome by his recollections.

"You have heard of it, I suppose?" he asked at length, in a scarce audible voice.

The General looked at him, and for a moment their eyes met; then he looked away. Then he shaded his eyes with his hand and sat as though awaiting further revelations.

Lord Chetwynde did not seem to notice him at all. Intent upon his own thoughts, he went on in that strange soliloquizing tone with which he had begun.

"She fled—" he said, in a voice which was little more than a whisper.

"Heavens!" said General Pomeroy.

There was a long silence.

"It was about three years after our marriage," continued Lord Chetwynde, with an effort. "She fled. She left no word of farewell. She fled. She forsook me. She forsook her child. My God! Why?"

He was silent again.

"Who was the man?" asked the General, in a strange voice, and with an effort.

"He was known as Redfield Lyttoun. He had been devoted for a long time to my wretched wife. Their flight was so secret and so skillfully managed that I could gain no clew whatever to it—and, indeed, it was better so—perhaps—yes—better so." Lord Chetwynde drew a long breath. "Yes, better so," he continued —"for if I had been able to track the scoundrel and take his life, my vengeance would have been gained, but my dishonor would have been proclaimed. To me that dishonor would have brought no additional pang. I had suffered all that I could. More were impossible; but as it was my shame was not made public—and so, above all—above all—my boy was saved. The frightful scandal did not arise to crush my darling boy."

The agitation of Lord Chetwynde overpowered him. His face grew more pallid, his eyes were fixed, and his clenched hands testified to the struggle that raged within him. A long silence followed, during which neither spoke a word.

At length Lord Chetwynde went on. "I left London forever," said he, with a deep sigh. "After that my one desire was to hide myself from the world. I wished that if it were possible my very name might be forgotten. And so I came back to Chetwynde, where I have lived ever since, in the utmost seclusion, devoting myself entirely to the education and training of my boy.

"Ah, my old friend, that boy has proved the one solace of my life. Well has he repaid me for my care. Never was there a nobler or a more devoted nature than his. Forgive a father's emotion, my friend. If you but knew my noble, my brave, my chivalrous boy, you would excuse me. That boy would lay down his life for me. In all his life his one thought has been to spare me all trouble and to brighten my dark life. Poor Guy! He knows nothing of the horror of shame that hangs over him—he has found out nothing as yet. To him his mother is a holy thought—the thought of one who died long ago, whose memory he thinks so sacred to me that I dare not speak of her. Poor Guy! Poor Guy!"

Lord Chetwynde again paused, overcome by deep emotion.

"God only knows," he resumed, "how I feel for him and for his future. It's a dark future for him, my friend. For in addition to this grief which I have told you of there is another which weighs me down. Chetwynde is not yet redeemed. I lost my life and my chance to save the estate. Chetwynde is overwhelmed with debt. The time is daily drawing near when I will have to give up the inheritance which has come down through so long a line of ancestors. All is lost. Hope itself has departed. How can I bear to see the place pass into alien hands?"

"Pass into alien hands?" interrupted the General, in surprise. "Give up Chetwynde? Impossible! It can not be thought of."

"Sad as it is," replied Lord Chetwynde, mournfully, "it must be so. Sixty thousand pounds are due within two years. Unless I can raise that amount all must go. When Guy comes of age he must break the entail and sell the estate. It is just beginning to pay again, too," he added, regretfully. "When I came into it it was utterly impoverished, and every available stick of timber had been cut down; but my expenses have been very small, and if I have fulfilled no other hope of my life, I have at least done something for my ground-down tenantry; for every penny which I have saved, after paying the interest, I have spent on improving their homes and farms, so that the place is now in very good condition, though I have been obliged to leave the pleasure-grounds utterly neglected."

"What are you going to do with your son?" asked the General.

"I have just got him a commission in the army," said Lord Chetwynde. "Some old friends, who had actually remembered me all these years, offered to do something for me in the diplomacy line; but if he entered that life I should feel that all the world was pointing the finger of scorn at him for his mother's sake; besides, my boy is too honest for a diplomat. No —he must go and make his own fortune. A viscount with neither money, land, nor position —the only place for him is the army."

A long silence followed. Lord Chetwynde seemed to lose himself among those painful recollections which he had raised, while the General, falling into a profound abstraction, sat with his head on one hand, while the other drummed mechanically on the table. As much as half an hour passed away in this manner. The General was first to rouse himself.

"I arrived in England only a few months ago," he began, in a quiet, thoughtful tone. "My life has been one of strange vicissitudes. My own country is almost like a foreign land to me. As soon as I could get Pomeroy Court in order I determined to visit you. This visit was partly for the sake of seeing you, and partly for the sake of asking a great favor. What you have just been saying has suggested a new idea, which I think may be carried out for the benefit of both of us. You must know, in the first place, I have brought my little daughter home with me. In fact, it was for her sake that I came home—"

"You were married, then?"

"Yes, in India. You lost sight of me early in life, and so perhaps you do not know that I exchanged from the Queen's service to that of the East India Company. This step I never regretted. My promotion was rapid, and after a year or two I obtained a civil appointment. From this I rose to a higher office; and after ten or twelve years the Company recommended me as Governor in one of the provinces of the Bengal Presidency. It was here that I found my sweet wife."

"It is a strange story," said the General, with a long sigh. "She came suddenly upon me, and changed all my life. Thus far I had so devoted myself to business that no idea of love or sentiment ever entered my head, except when I was a boy. I had reached the age of forty-five without having hardly ever met with any woman who had touched my heart, or even my head, for that matter.

"My first sight of her was most sudden and most strange," continued the General, in the tone of one who loved to linger upon even the smallest details of the story which he was telling

—"strange and sudden. I had been busy all day in the audience chamber, and when at length the cases were all disposed of, I retired thoroughly exhausted, and gave orders that no one should be admitted on any pretext whatever. On passing through the halls to my private apartment I heard an altercation at the door. My orderly was speaking in a very decided tone to some one.

"'It is impossible,' I heard him say. 'His Excellency has given positive orders to admit no one to-day.'

"I walked on, paying but little heed to this. Applications were common after hours, and my rules on this point were stringent. But suddenly my attention was arrested by the sound of a woman's voice. It affected me strangely, Chetwynde. The tones were sweet and low, and there was an agony of supplication in them which lent additional earnestness to her words.

"'Oh, do not refuse me!' the voice said. 'They say the Resident is just and merciful. Let me see him, I entreat, if only for one moment.'

"At these words I turned, and at once hastened to the door. A young girl stood there, with her hands clasped, and in an attitude of earnest entreaty. She had evidently come closely veiled, but in her excitement her veil had been thrown back, and her upturned face lent an unspeakable earnestness to her pleading. At the sight of her I was filled with the deepest sympathy.

"'I am the Resident,' said I. 'What can I do for you?'

"She looked at me earnestly, and for a time said nothing. A change came over her face. Her troubles seemed to have overwhelmed her. She tottered, and would have fallen, had I not supported her. I led her into the house, and sent for some wine. This restored her.

"She was the most beautiful creature that I ever beheld," continued the General, in a pensive tone, after some silence. "She was tall and slight, with all that litheness and grace of movement which is peculiar to Indian women, and yet she seemed more European than Indian. Her face was small and oval, her hair hung round it in rich masses, and her eyes were large, deep, and liquid, and, in addition to their natural beauty, they bore that sad expression which, it is said, is the sure precursor of an early death. Thank God!" continued the General, in a musing tone, "I at least did something to brighten that short life of hers.

"As soon as she was sufficiently recovered she told me her story. It was a strange one. She was the daughter of an English officer, who having fallen in love with an Indian Begum gave up home, country, and friends, and married her. Their daughter Aruna had been brought up in the European manner, and to the warm, passionate, Indian nature she added the refined intelligence of the English lady. When she was fourteen her father died. Her mother followed in a few years. Of her father's friends she knew nothing, and her mother's brother, who was the only one on whom she could rely. Her mother while dying charged her always to remember that she was the daughter of a British officer, and that if she were ever in need of protection she should demand it of the English authorities. After her mother's death the Rajah took her away, and assumed the control of all her inheritance. At the age of eighteen she was to come into possession, and as the time drew near the Rajah informed her that he wished her to marry his son. But this son was detestable to her, and to her English ideas the proposal was abhorrent. She refused to marry him. The Rajah swore that she should. At this she threatened that she would claim the protection of the British government. Fearful of this, and enraged at her firmness, he confined her in her rooms for several months, and at length threatened that if she did not consent he would use force. This threat reduced her to despair. She determined to escape and appeal to the British authorities. She bribed her attendants, escaped, and by good fortune reached my Residency.

"On hearing her story I promised that full justice should be done her, and succeeded in quieting her fears. I obtained a suitable home for her, and found the widow of an English officer who consented to live with her.

"Ah, Chetwynde, how I loved her! A year passed away, and she became my wife. Never before had I known such happiness as I enjoyed with her. Never since have I known any happiness whatever. She loved me with such devotion that she would have laid down her life for me. She looked on me as her savior as well as her husband. My happiness was too great to last.

"I felt it—I knew it," he continued, in a broken voice. "Two years my darling lived with me, and then—she was taken away.

"I was ill for a long time," continued the General, in a gentle voice. "I prayed for death, but God spared me for my child's sake. I recovered sufficiently to attend to the duties of my office, but it was with difficulty that I did so. I never regained my former strength. My child grew older, and at length I determined to return to England. I have come here to find all my relatives dead, and you, the old friend of my boyhood, are the only survivor. One thing there is, however, that imbitters my situation now. My health is still very precarious, and I may at any moment leave my child unprotected. She is the one concern of my life. I said that I had come here to ask a favor of you. It was this, that you would allow me to nominate you as her guardian in case of my death, and assist me also in finding any other guardian to succeed you in case you should pass away before she reached maturity. This was my purpose. But after what you have told me other things have occurred to my mind. I have been thinking of a plan which seems to me to be the best thing for both of us.

"Listen now to my proposal," he said, with greater earnestness. "That you should give up Chetwynde is not to be thought of for one moment. In addition to my own patrimony and my wife's inheritance I have amassed a fortune during my residence in India, and I can think of no better use for it than in helping my old friend in his time of need."

Lord Chetwynde raised his hand deprecatingly.

"Wait—no remonstrance. Hear me out," said the General. "I do not ask you to take this as a loan, or any thing of the kind. I only ask you to be a protector to my child. I could not rest in my grave if I thought that I had left her unprotected."

"What!" cried Lord Chetwynde, hastily interrupting him, "can you imagine that it is necessary to buy my good offices?"

"You don't understand me yet, Chetwynde; I want more than that. I want to secure a protector for her all her life. Since you have told me about your affairs I have formed a strong desire to see her betrothed to your son. True, I have never seen him, but I know very well the stock he comes from. I know his father," he went on, laying his hand on his friend's arm: "and I trust the son is like the father. In this way you see there will be no gift, no loan, no obligation. The Chetwynde debts will be all paid off, but it is for my daughter; and where could I get a better dowry?"

"But she must be very young," said Lord Chetwynde, "if you were not married until forty-five."

"She is only a child yet," said the General. "She is ten years old. That need not signify, however. The engagement can be made just as well. I free the estate from all its encumbrances; and as she will eventually be a Chetwynde, it will be for her sake as well as your son's. There is no obligation."

Lord Chetwynde wrung his friend's hand.

"I do not know what to say," said he. "It would add years to my life to know that my son is not to lose the inheritance of his ancestors. But of course I can make no definite arrangements until I have seen him. He is the one chiefly interested; and besides," he added, smilingly, "I can not expect you to take a father's estimate of an only son. You must judge him for yourself, and see whether my account has been too partial."

"Of course, of course. I must see him at once," broke in the General. "Where is he?"

"In Ireland. I will telegraph to him to-night, and he will be here in a couple of days."

"He could not come sooner, I suppose?" said the General, anxiously.

Lord Chetwynde laughed.

"I hardly think so—from Ulster. But why such haste? It positively alarms me, for I'm an idle man, and have had my time on my hands for half a lifetime."

"The old story, Chetwynde," said the General, with a smile; "petticoat government. I promised my little girl that I would be back to-morrow. She will be sadly disappointed at a day's delay. I shall be almost afraid to meet her. I fear she has been a little spoiled, poor child; but you can scarcely wonder, under the circumstances. After all, she is a good child though; she has the strongest possible affection for me, and I can guide her as I please through her affections."

After some further conversation Lord Chetwynde sent off a telegram to his son to come home without delay.

CHAPTER II.

THE WEIRD WOMAN.

THE morning-room at Chetwynde Castle was about the pleasantest one there, and the air of poverty which prevailed elsewhere was here lost in the general appearance of comfort. It was a large apartment, commensurate with the size of the castle, and the deep bay-windows commanded an extensive view.

On the morning following the conversation already mentioned General Pomeroy arose early, and it was toward this room that he turned his steps. Throughout the castle there was that air of neglect already alluded to, so that the morning-room afforded a pleasant contrast. Here all the comfort that remained at Chetwynde seemed to have centred. It was with a feeling of intense satisfaction that the General seated himself in an arm-chair which stood within the deep recess of the bay-window, and surveyed the apartment.

The room was about forty feet long and thirty feet wide. The ceiling was covered with quaint figures in fresco, the walls were paneled with oak, and high-backed, stolid-looking chairs stood around. On one side was the fire-place, so vast and so high that it seemed itself another room. It was the fine old fire-place of the Tudor or Plantagenet period—the unequaled, the unsurpassed—whose day has long since been done, and which in departing from the world has left nothing to compensate for it. Still, the fire-place lingers in a few old mansions; and here at Chetwynde Castle was one without a peer. It was lofty, it was broad, it was deep, it was well-paved, it was ornamented not carelessly, but lovingly, as though the hearth was the holy place, the altar of the castle and of the family. There was room in its wide expanse for the gathering of a household about the fire; its embrace was the embrace of love; and it was the type and model of those venerable and hallowed places which have given to the English language a word holier even than "Home," since that word is "Hearth."

It was with some such thoughts as these that General Pomeroy sat looking at the fire-place, where a few fagots sent up a ruddy blaze, when suddenly his attention was arrested by a figure which entered the room. So quiet and noiseless was the entrance that he did not notice it until the figure stood between him and the fire. It was a woman; and certainly, of all the women whom he had ever seen, no one had possessed so weird and mystical an aspect. She was a little over the middle height, but exceedingly thin and emaciated. She wore a cap and a gown of black serge, and looked more like a Sister of Charity than any thing else. Her features were thin and shrunken, her cheeks hollow, her chin peaked, and her hair was as white as snow. Yet the hair was very thick, and the cap could not conceal its heavy white masses. Her side-face was turned toward him, and he could not see her fully at first, until at length she turned toward a picture which hung over the fire-place, and stood regarding it fixedly.

It was the portrait of a young man in the dress of a British officer. The General knew that it was the only son of Lord Chetwynde, for whom he had written, and whom he was expecting; and now, as he sat there with his eyes riveted on this singular figure, he was amazed at the expression of her face.

Her eyes were large and dark and mysterious. Her face bore unmistakable traces of sorrow. Deep lines were graven on her pale forehead,

and on her wan, thin cheeks. Her hair was white as snow, and her complexion was of an unearthly grayish hue. It was a memorable face —a face which, once seen, might haunt one long afterward. In the eyes there was tenderness and softness, yet the fashion of the mouth and chin seemed to speak of resolution and force, in spite of the ravages which age or sorrow had made. She stood quite unconscious of the General's presence, looking at the portrait with a fixed and rapt expression. As she gazed her face changed in its aspect. In the eyes there arose unutterable longing and tenderness; love so deep that the sight of it thus unconsciously expressed might have softened the hardest and sternest nature; while over all her features the same yearning expression was spread. Gradually, as she stood, she raised her thin white hands and clasped them together, and so stood, intent upon the portrait, as though she found some spell there whose power was overmastering.

At the sight of so weird and ghostly a figure the General was strangely moved. There was something startling in such an apparition. At first there came involuntarily half-superstitious thoughts. He recalled all those mysterious beings of whom he had ever heard whose occupation was to haunt the seats of old families. He thought of the White Lady of Avenel, the Black Lady of Scarborough, the Goblin Woman of Hurst, and the Bleeding Nun. A second glance served to show him, however, that she could by no possibility fill the important post of Family Ghost, but was real flesh and blood. Yet even thus she was scarcely less impressive. Most of all was he moved by the sorrow of her face. She might serve for Niobe with her children dead; she might serve for Hecuba over the bodies of Polyxena and Polydore. The sorrows of woman have ever been greater than those of man. The widow suffers more than the widower; the bereaved mother than the bereaved father. The ideals of grief are found in the faces of women, and reach their intensity in the woe that meets our eyes in the Mater Dolorosa. This woman was one of the great community of sufferers, and anguish both past and present still left its traces on her face.

Besides all this there was something more; and while the General was awed by the majesty of sorrow, he was at the same time perplexed by an inexplicable familiarity which he felt with that face of woe. Where, in the years, had he seen it before? Or had he seen it before at all; or had he only known it in dreams? In vain he tried to recollect. Nothing from out his past life recurred to his mind which bore any resemblance to this face before him. The endeavor to recall this past grew painful, and at length he returned to himself. Then he dismissed the idea as fanciful, and began to feel uncomfortable, as though he were witnessing something which he had no business to see. She was evidently unconscious of his presence, and to be a witness of her emotion under such circumstances seemed to him as bad as eaves-dropping. The moment, therefore, that he had overcome his surprise he turned his head away, looked out of the window, and coughed several times. Then he rose from his chair, and after standing for a moment he turned once more.

As he turned he found himself face to face

"SHE TURNED TOWARD A PICTURE WHICH HUNG OVER THE FIRE-PLACE, AND STOOD
REGARDING IT FIXEDLY."

with the woman. She had heard him, and turned with a start, and turning thus their eyes met.

If the General had been surprised before, he was now still more so at the emotion which she evinced at the sight of himself. She started back as though recoiling from him: her eyes were fixed and staring, her lips moved, her hands clutched one another convulsively. Then, by a sudden effort, she seemed to recover herself, and the wild stare of astonishment gave place to a swift glance of keen, sharp, and eager scrutiny. All this was the work of an instant. Then her eyes dropped, and with a low courtesy she turned away, and after arranging some chairs she left the room.

The General drew a long breath, and stood looking at the doorway in utter bewilderment. The whole incident had been most perplexing. There was first her stealthy entry, and the suddenness with which she had appeared before him; then those mystic surroundings of her strange, weird figure which had excited his superstitious fancies; then the idea which had arisen, that somehow he had known her before; and, finally, the woman's own strong and unconcealed emotion at the sight of himself. What did it all mean? Had he ever seen her? Not that he knew. Had she ever known him? If so, when and where? If so, why such emotion? Who could this be that thus recoiled from him at encountering his glance? And he found all these questions utterly unanswerable.

In the General's eventful life there were many things which he could recall. He had wandered over many lands in all parts of the world, and had known his share of sorrow and of joy. Seating himself once more in his chair he tried to summon up before his memory the figures of the past, one by one, and compare them with this woman whom he had seen. Out of the gloom of that past the ghostly figures came, and passed on, and vanished, till at last from among them all two or three stood forth distinctly and vividly; the forms of those who had been associated with him in one event of his life; that life's first great tragedy; forms well remembered—never to be forgotten. He saw the form of one who had been betrayed and forsaken, bowed and crushed by grief, and staring with white face and haggard eyes; he saw the form of the false friend and foul traitor slinking away with averted face; he saw the form of the true friend, true as steel, standing up solidly in his loyalty between those whom he loved and the Ruin that was before them; and, lastly, he saw the central figure of all—a fair young woman with a face of dazzling beauty; high-born, haughty, with an air of high-bred grace and inborn delicacy; but the beauty was fading, and the charm of all that grace and delicacy was veiled under a cloud of shame and sin. The face bore all that agony of woe which looks at us now from the eyes of Guido's Beatrice Cenci—eyes which disclose a grief deeper than tears; eyes whose glance is never forgotten.

Suddenly there came to the General a Thought like lightning, which seemed to pierce to the inmost depths of his being. He started back as he sat, and for a moment looked like one transformed to stone. At the horror of that Thought his face changed to a deathly pallor, his features grew rigid, his hands clenched, his eyes fixed and staring with an awful look. For a few moments he sat thus, and then with a deep groan he sprang to his feet and paced the apartment.

The exercise seemed to bring relief.

"I'm a cursed fool!" he muttered. "The thing's impossible—yes, absolutely impossible."

Again and again he paced the apartment, and gradually he recovered himself.

"Pooh!" he said at length, as he resumed his seat, "she's insane, or, more probably, I am in-sane for having had such wild thoughts as I have had this morning."

Then with a heavy sigh he looked out of the window abstractedly.

An hour passed and Lord Chetwynde came down, and the two took their seats at the breakfast-table.

"By - the - way," said the General at length, after some conversation, and with an effort at indifference, "who is that very singular-looking woman whom you have here? She seems to be about sixty, dresses in black, has very white hair, and looks like a Sister of Charity."

"That?" said Lord Chetwynde, carelessly. "Oh, that must be the housekeeper, Mrs. Hart."

"Mrs. Hart—the housekeeper?" repeated the General, thoughtfully.

"Yes; she is an invaluable woman to one in my position."

"I suppose she is some old family servant."

"No. She came here about ten years ago. I wanted a housekeeper, she heard of it, and applied. She brought excellent recommendations, and I took her. She has done very well."

"Have you ever noticed how very singular her appearance is?"

"Well, no. Is it? I suppose it strikes you so as a stranger. I never noticed her particularly."

"She seems to have had some great sorrow," said the General, slowly.

"Yes, I think she must have had some troubles. She has a melancholy way, I think. I feel sorry for the poor creature, and do what I can for her. As I said, she is invaluable to me, and I owe her positive gratitude."

"Is she fond of Guy?" asked the General, thinking of her face as he saw it upturned toward the portrait.

"Exceedingly," said Lord Chetwynde. "Guy was about eight years old when she came. From the very first she showed the greatest fondness for him, and attached herself to him with a devotion which surprised me. I accounted for it on the ground that she had lost a son of her own, and perhaps Guy reminded her in some way of him. At any rate she has always been exceedingly fond of him. Yes," pursued Lord Chetwynde, in a musing tone, "I owe every thing to her, for she once saved Guy's life."

"Saved his life? How?"

"Once, when I was away, the place caught fire in the wing where Guy was sleeping. Mrs. Hart rushed through the flames and saved him. She nearly killed herself too—poor old thing! In addition to this she has nursed him through three different attacks of disease that seemed fatal. Why, she seems to love Guy as fondly as I do."

"And does Guy love her?"

"Exceedingly. The boy is most affectionate by nature, and of course she is prominent in his affections. Next to me he loves her."

The General now turned away the conversation to other subjects; but from his abstracted manner it was evident that Mrs. Hart was still foremost in his thoughts.

CHAPTER III.

THE BARTER OF A LIFE.

Two evenings afterward a carriage drove up to the door of Chetwynde Castle, and a young man alighted. The door was opened by the old butler, who, with a cry of delight, exclaimed:

"Master Guy! Master Guy! It's welcome ye are. They've been lookin' for you these two hours back."

"Any thing wrong?" was Guy's first exclamation, uttered with some haste and anxiety.

"Lord love ye, there's naught amiss; but ye're welcome home, right welcome, Master Guy," said the butler, who still looked upon his young master as the little boy who used to ride upon his back, and whose tricks were at once the torment and delight of his life.

The old butler himself was one of the heirlooms of the family, and partook to the full of the air of antiquity which pervaded the place. He looked like the relic of a by-gone generation. His queue, carefully powdered and plaited, stood out stiff from the back of his head, as if in perpetual protest against any new-fangled notions of hair-dressing; his livery, scrupulously neat and well brushed, was threadbare and of an antediluvian cut, and his whole appearance was that of highly respectable antediluvianism. As he stood there with his antique and venerable figure his whole face fairly beamed with delight at seeing his young master.

"I was afraid my father might be ill," said Guy, "from his sending for me in such a hurry."

"Ill?" said the other, radiant. "My lord be better and cheerfuler like than ever I have seen him since he came back from Lunnon—the time as you was in a small chap, Master Guy. There be a gentleman stopping here. He and my lord have been sittin' up half the night a-talkin'. I think there be summut up, Master Guy, and that he be connected with it; for when my lord told me to send you the telegram he said as it were on business he wanted you, but," he added, looking perplexed, "it's the first time as ever I heard of business makin' a man look cheerful."

Guy made a jocular observation and hurried past him into the hall. As he entered he saw a figure standing at the foot of the great staircase. It was Mrs. Hart. She was trembling from head to foot and clinging to the railing for support. Her face was pale as usual; on each cheek there was a hectic flush, and her eyes were fastened on him.

"My darling nurse!" cried Guy with the warm enthusiastic tone of a boy, and hurrying toward her he embraced her and kissed her.

The poor old creature trembled and did not say a single word.

"Now you didn't know I was coming, did you, you dear old thing?" said Guy. "But what is the matter? Why do you tremble so? Of course you're glad to see your boy. Are you not?"

Mrs. Hart looked up to him with an expression of mute affection, deep, fervent, unspeakable; and then seizing his warm young hand in her own wan and tremulous ones, she pressed it to her thin white lips and covered it with kisses.

"Oh, come now," said Guy, "you always break down this way when I come home; but you must not—you really must not. If you do I won't come home at all any more. I really

won't. Come, cheer up. I don't want to make you cry when I come home."

"But I'm crying for joy," said Mrs. Hart, in a faint voice. "Don't be angry."

"You dear old thing! Angry?" exclaimed Guy, affectionately. "Angry with my darling old nurse? Have you lost your senses, old woman? But where is my father? Why has he sent for me? There's no bad news, I hear, so that I suppose all is right."

"Yes, all is well," said Mrs. Hart, in a low voice. "I don't know why you were sent for, but there is nothing bad. I think your father sent for you to see an old friend of his."

"An old friend?"

"Yes. General Pomeroy," replied Mrs. Hart, in a constrained voice. "He has been here two or three days."

"General Pomeroy! Is it possible?" said Guy. "Has he come to England? I didn't know that he had left India. I must hurry up. Good-by, old woman," he added, affectionately, and kissing her again he hurried up stairs to his father's room.

Lord Chetwynde was there, and General Pomeroy also. The greeting between father and son was affectionate and tender, and after a few loving words Guy was introduced to the General. He shook him heartily by the hand.

"I'm sure," said he, "the sight of you has done my father a world of good. He looks ten years younger than he did when I last saw him. You really ought to take up your abode here, or live somewhere near him. He mopes dreadfully, and needs nothing so much as the society of an old friend. You could rouse him from his blue fits and ennui, and give him new life."

Guy then went on in a rattling way to narrate some events which had befallen him on the road. As he spoke in his animated and enthusiastic way General Pomeroy scanned him earnestly and narrowly. To the most casual observer Guy Molyneux must have been singularly prepossessing. Tall and slight, with a remarkably well-shaped head covered with dark curling hair, hazel eyes, and regular features, his whole appearance was eminently patrician, and bore the marks of high-breeding and refinement; but there was something more than this. Those eyes looked forth frankly and fearlessly; there was a joyous light in them which awakened sympathy; while the open expression of his face, and the clear and ringing accent of his fresh young voice, all tended to inspire confidence and trust. General Pomeroy noted all this with delight, for in his anxiety for his daughter's future he saw that Guy was one to whom he might safely intrust the dearest idol of his heart.

"Come, Guy," said Lord Chetwynde at last, after his son had rattled on for half an hour or more, "if you are above all considerations of dinner, we are not. I have already had it put off two hours for you, and we should like to see some signs of preparation on your part."

"All right, Sir. I shall be on hand by the time it is announced," said Guy, cheerily; "you don't generally have to complain of me in that particular, I think."

So saying, Guy nodded gayly to them and left the room, and they presently heard him whistling through the passages gems from the last new opera.

"A splendid fellow," said the General, as the door closed, in a tone of hearty admiration. "I see his father over again in him. I only hope he will come into our views."

"I can answer for his being only too ready to do so," said Lord Chetwynde, confidently.

"He exceeds the utmost hopes that I had formed of him," said the General. "I did not expect to see so frank and open a face, and such freshness of innocence and purity."

Lord Chetwynde's face showed all the delight which a fond father feels at hearing the praises of an only son.

Dinner came and passed. The General retired, and Lord Chetwynde then explained to his son the whole plan which had been made about him. It was a plan which was to affect his whole life most profoundly in its most tender part; but Guy was a thoughtless boy, and received the proposal like such. He showed nothing but delight. He never dreamed of objecting to any thing. He declared that it seemed to him too good to be true. His thoughts did not appear to dwell at all upon his own share in this transaction, though surely to him that share was of infinite importance, but only on the fact that Chetwynde was saved.

"And is Chetwynde really to be ours, after all?" he cried, at the end of a burst of delight, repeating the words, boy-like, over and over again, as though he could never tire of hearing the words repeated. After all, one can not wonder at his thoughtlessness and enthusiasm. Around Chetwynde all the associations of his life were twined. Until he had joined the regiment he had known no other home; and beyond this, to this high-spirited youth, in whom pride of birth and name rose very high, there had been from his earliest childhood a bitter humiliation in the thought that the inheritance of his ancestors, which had never known any other than a Chetwynde for its master, must pass from him forever into alien hands. Hitherto his love for his father had compelled him to refrain from all expression of his feelings about this, for he well knew that, bitter as it would be for him to give up Chetwynde, to his father it would be still worse—it would be like rending his very heart-strings. Often had he feared that this sacrifice to honor on his father's part would be more than could be endured. He had, for his father's sake, put a restraint upon himself; but this concealment of his feelings had only increased the intensity of those feelings; the shadow had been gradually deepening over his whole life, throwing gloom over the sunlight of his joyous youth; and now, for the first time in many years, that shadow seemed to be dispelled. Surely there is no wonder that a mere boy should be reckless of the future in the sunshine of such a golden present.

When General Pomeroy appeared again, Guy seized his hand in a burst of generous emotion, with his eyes glistening with tears of joy.

"How can I ever thank you," he cried, impetuously, "for what you have done for us! As you have done by us, so will I do by your daughter—to my life's end—so help me God!"

And all this time did it never suggest itself to the young man that there might be a reverse to the brilliant picture which his fancy was so busily sketching—that there was required from him something more than money or estate; something, indeed, in comparison with which even Chetwynde itself was as nothing? No. In his inexperience and thoughtlessness he would have looked with amazement upon any one who would have suggested that there might be a drawback to the happiness which he was portraying before his mind. Yet surely this thing came most severely upon him. He gave up the most, for he gave himself. To save Chetwynde, he was unconsciously selling his own soul. He was bartering his life. All his future depended upon this hasty act of a moment. The happiness of the mature man was risked by the thoughtless act of a boy. If in after-life this truth came home to him, it was only that he might see that the act was irrevocable, and that he must bear the consequences. But so it is in life.

That evening, after the General had retired, Guy and his father sat up far into the night, discussing the future which lay before them. To each of them the future marriage seemed but a secondary event, an accident, an episode. The first thing, and almost the only thing, was the salvation of Chetwynde. Those day-dreams which they had cherished for so many years seemed now about to be realized, and Chetwynde would be restored to all its former glory. Now, for the first time, each let the other see, to the full, how grievous the loss would have been to him.

It was not until after all the future of Chetwynde had been discussed, that the thoughts of Guy's engagement occurred to his father.

"But, Guy," said he, "you are forgetting one thing. You must not in your joy lose sight of the important pledge which has been demanded of you. You have entered upon a very solemn obligation, which we both are inclined to treat rather lightly."

"Of course I remember it, Sir; and I only wish it were something twenty times as hard that I could do for the dear old General," answered Guy, enthusiastically.

"But, my boy, this may prove a severe sacrifice in the future," said Lord Chetwynde, thoughtfully.

"What? To marry, father? Of course I shall marry some time; and as to the question of whom, why, so long as she is a lady (and General Pomeroy's daughter must be this), and is not a fright (I own I hate ugly women), I don't care who she is. But the daughter of such a man as that ought to be a little angel, and as beautiful as I could desire. I am all impatience to see her. By-the-way, how old is she?"

"Ten years old."

"Ten years!" echoed Guy, laughing boisterously. "I need not distress myself, then, about her personnel for a good many years at any rate. But, I say, father, isn't the General a little premature in getting his daughter settled? Talk of match-making mothers after this!"

The young man's flippant tone jarred upon his father. "He had good reasons for the haste to which you object, Guy," said Lord Chetwynde. "One was the friendlessness of his daughter in the event of any thing happening to him; and the other, and a stronger motive (for under any circumstances I should have been her guardian), was to assist your father upon the only terms upon which he could have accepted assistance with honor. By this arrangement his daughter reaps the full benefit of his money, and he has his own mind at ease. And, remember, Guy," continued Lord Chetwynde, solemnly, "from this time you must consider yourself as a married man; for, although no altar vow or priestly benediction binds you, yet by every law of that Honor by which you profess to be guided, you are bound *irrevocably.*"

"I know that," answered Guy, lightly. "I think you will never find me unmindful of that tie."

"I trust you, my boy," said Lord Chetwynde, "as I would trust myself."

CHAPTER IV.

A STARTLING VISITOR.

AFTER dinner the General had retired to his room, supposing that Guy and the Earl would wish to be together. He had much to think of. First of all there was his daughter Zillah, in whom all his being was bound up. Her miniature was on the mantle-piece of the room, and to this he went first, and taking it up in his hands he sat down in an arm-chair by the window, and feasted his eyes upon it. His face bore an expression of the same delight which a lover shows when looking at the likeness of his mistress. At times a smile lighted it up, and so wrapt up was he in this that more than an hour passed before he put the picture away. Then he resumed his seat by the window and looked out. It was dusk; but the moon was shining brightly, and threw a silvery gleam over the dark trees of Chetwynde, over the grassy slopes, and over the distant hills. That scene turned his attention in a new direction. The shadows of the trees seemed to suggest the shadows of the past. Back over that past his mind went wandering, encountering the scenes, the forms, and the faces of long ago—the lost, the never-to-be-forgotten. It was not that more recent past of which he had spoken to the Earl, but one more distant—one which intermingled with the Earl's past, and which the Earl's story had suggested. It brought back old loves and old hates; it suggested memories which had lain dormant for years, but now rose before him clothed in fresh power, as vivid as the events from which they flowed. There was trouble in these memories, and the General's mind was agitated, and in his agitation he left the chair and paced the room. He rang for lights, and after they came he seated himself at the table, took paper and pens, and began to lose himself in calculations.

Some time passed, when at length ten o'clock came, and the General heard a faint tap at the door. It was so faint that he could barely hear it, and at first supposed it to be either his fancy or else one of the death-watches making a somewhat louder noise than usual. He took no further notice of it, but went on with his occupation, when he was again interrupted by a louder knock. This time there was no mistake. He rose and opened the door, thinking that it was the Earl who had brought him some information as to his son's views.

Opening the door, he saw a slight, frail figure, dressed in a nun-like garb, and recognized the housekeeper. If possible she seemed paler than usual, and her eyes were fixed upon him with a strange wistful earnestness. Her appearance

was so unexpected, and her expression so peculiar, that the General involuntarily started back. For a moment he stood looking at her, and then, recovering with an effort his self-possession, he asked:

"Did you wish to see me about any thing, Mrs. Hart?"

"If I could speak a few words to you I should be grateful," was the answer, in a low, supplicating tone.

"Won't you walk in, then?" said the General, in a kindly voice, feeling a strange commiseration for the poor creature, whose face, manner, and voice exhibited so much wretchedness.

The General held the door open, and waited for her to enter. Then closing the door he offered her a chair, and resumed his former seat. But the housekeeper declined sitting. She stood looking strangely confused and troubled, and for some time did not speak a word. The General waited patiently, and regarded her earnestly. In spite of himself he found that feeling arising within him which had occurred in the morning-room —a feeling as if he had somewhere known this woman before. Who was she? What did it mean? Was he a precious old fool, or was there really some important mystery connected with Mrs. Hart? Such were his thoughts.

Perhaps if he had seen nothing more of Mrs. Hart the Earl's account of her would have been accepted by him, and no thoughts of her would have perplexed his brain. But her arrival now, her entrance into his room, and her whole manner, brought back the thoughts which he had before with tenfold force, in such a way that it was useless to struggle against them. He felt that there was a mystery, and that the Earl himself not only knew nothing about it, but could not even suspect it. But *what* was the mystery? That he could not, or perhaps dared not, conjecture. The vague thought which darted across his mind was one which was madness to entertain. He dismissed it and waited.

At last Mrs. Hart spoke.

"Pardon me, Sir," she said, in a faint, low voice, "for troubling you. I wished to apologize for intruding upon you in the morning-room. I did not know you were there."

She spoke abstractedly and wearily. The General felt that it was not for this that she had thus visited him, but that something more lay behind. Still he answered her remark as if he took it in good faith. He hastened to reassure her. It was no intrusion. Was she not the housekeeper, and was it not her duty to go there? What could she mean?

At this she looked at him, with a kind of solemn yet eager scrutiny. "I was afraid," she said, after some hesitation, speaking still in a dull monotone, whose strangely sorrowful accents were marked and impressive, and in a voice whose tone was constrained and stiff, but yet had something in it which deepened the General's perplexity—"I was afraid that perhaps you might have witnessed some marks of agitation in me. Pardon me for supposing that you could have troubled yourself so far as to notice one like me; but—but—I—that is, I am a little—eccentric; and when I suppose that I am alone that eccentricity is marked. I did not know that you were in the room, and so I was thrown off my guard."

Every word of this singular being thrilled

through the General. He looked at her steadily without speaking for some time. He tried to force his memory to reveal what it was that this woman suggested to him, or who it was that she had been associated with in that dim and shadowy past which but lately he had been calling up. Her voice, too—what was it that it suggested? That voice, in spite of its constraint, was woeful and sad beyond all description. It was the voice of suffering and sorrow too deep for tears—that changeless monotone which makes one think that the words which are spoken are uttered by some machine.

Her manner also by this time evinced a greater and a deeper agitation. Her hands mechanically clasped each other in a tight, convulsive grasp, and her slight frame trembled with irrepressible emotion. There was something in her appearance, her attitude, her manner, and her voice, which enchained the General's attention, and was nothing less than fascination. There was something yet to come, to tell which had led her there, and these were only preliminaries. This the General felt. Every word that she spoke seemed to be a mere formality, the precursor of the real words which she wished to utter. What was it? Was it her affection for Guy? Had she come to ask about the betrothal? Had she come to look at Zillah's portrait? Had she come to remonstrate with him for arranging a marriage between those who were as yet little more than children? But what reason had she for interfering in such an affair? It was utterly out of place in one like her. No; there was something else, he could not conjecture what.

All these thoughts swept with lightning speed through his mind, and still the poor stricken creature stood before him with her eyes lowered and her hands clasped, waiting for his answer. He roused himself, and sought once more to reassure her. He told her that he had noticed nothing, that he had been looking out of the window, and that in any case, if he had, he should have thought nothing about it. This he said in as careless a tone as possible, willfully misstating facts, from a generous desire to spare her uneasiness and set her mind at rest.

"Will you pardon me, Sir, if I intrude upon your kindness so far as to ask one more question?" said the housekeeper, after listening dreamily to the General's words. "You are going away, and I shall not have another opportunity."

"Certainly," said the General, looking at her with unfeigned sympathy. "If there is any thing that I can tell you I shall be happy to do so. Ask me, by all means, any thing you wish."

"You had a private interview with the Earl," said she, with more animation than she had yet shown.

"Yes."

"Pardon me, but will you consider it impertinence if I ask you whether it was about your past life? I know it is impertinent; but oh, Sir, I have my reasons." Her voice changed suddenly to the humblest and most apologetic accent.

The General's interest was, if possible, increased; and, if there were impertinence in such a question from a housekeeper, he was too excited to be conscious of it. To him this woman seemed more than this.

"We were talking about the past," said he, kindly. "We are very old friends. We were telling each other the events of our lives. We parted early in life, and have not seen one another for many years. We also were arranging some business matters."

Mrs. Hart listened eagerly, and then remained silent for a long time.

"His old friend," she murmured at last; "his old friend! Did you find him much altered?"

"Not more than I expected," replied the General, wonderingly. "His secluded life here has kept him from the wear and tear of the world. It has not made him at all misanthropical or even cynical. His heart is as warm as ever. He spoke very kindly of you."

Mrs. Hart started, and her hands involuntarily clutched each other more convulsively. Her head fell forward and her eyes dropped.

"What did he say of me?" she asked, in a scarce audible voice, and trembling visibly as she spoke.

The General noticed her agitation, but it caused no surprise, for already his whole power of wondering was exhausted. He had a vague idea that the poor old thing was troubled for fear she might from some cause lose her place, and wished to know whether the Earl had made any remarks which might affect her position. So with this feeling he answered in as cheering a tone as possible:

"Oh, I assure you, he spoke of you in the highest terms. He told me that you were exceedingly kind to Guy, and that you were quite indispensable to himself."

"'Kind to Guy'—'indispensable to him,'" she repeated in low tones, while tears started to her eyes. She kept murmuring the words abstractedly to herself, and for a few moments seemed quite unconscious of the General's presence. He still watched her, on his part, and gradually the thought arose within him that the easiest solution for all this was possible insanity. Insanity, he saw, would account for every thing, and would also give some reason for his own strange feelings at the sight of her. It was, he thought, because he had seen this dread sign of insanity in her face—that sign only less terrible than that dread mark which is made by the hand of the King of Terrors. And was she not herself conscious to some extent of this? he thought. She had herself alluded to her eccentricity. Was she not disturbed by a fear that he had noticed this, and, dreading a disclosure, had come to him to explain? To her a stranger would be an object of suspicion, against whom she would feel it necessary to be on her guard. The people of the house were doubtless accustomed to her ways, and would think nothing of any freak, however whimsical; but a stranger would look with different eyes. Few, indeed, were the strangers or visitors who ever came to Chetwynde Castle; but when one did come he would naturally be an object of suspicion to this poor soul, conscious of her infirmity, and struggling desperately against it. Such thoughts as these succeeded to the others which had been passing through the General's mind, and he was just beginning to think of some plan by which he could soothe this poor creature, when he was aware of a movement on her part which made him look up hastily. Her eyes were fastened on his. They were large, luminous, and earnest in their gaze, though dimmed by the grief of years. Tears were in them, and the look which they threw toward him was full

"BUT THE WOMAN, WITH A LOW MOAN, FLUNG HERSELF ON THE FLOOR BEFORE HIM."

of agony and earnest supplication. That emaciated face, that snow-white hair, that brow marked by the lines of suffering, that slight figure with its sombre vestments, all formed a sight which would have impressed any man. The General was so astonished that he sat motionless, wondering what it was now that the diseased fancy of one whom he still believed to be insane would suggest. It was to him that she was looking; it was to him that her shriveled hands were outstretched. What could she want with him?

She drew nearer to him while he sat thus wondering. She stooped forward and downward, with her eyes still fixed on his. He did not move, but watched her in amazement. Again that thought which the sight of her had at first suggested came to him. Again he thrust it away. But the woman, with a low moan, suddenly flung herself on the floor before him, and reaching out her hands clasped his feet, and he felt her feeble frame all shaken by sobs and shudders. He sat spell-bound. He looked at her for a moment aghast. Then he reached forth his hands, and without speaking a word took hers, and tried to lift her up. She let herself be raised till she was on her knees, and then raised her head once more. She gave him an indescribable look, and in a low voice, which was little above a whisper, but which penetrated to the very depths of his soul, pronounced one single solitary word, ——.

The General heard it. His face grew as pale and as rigid as the face of a corpse; the blood seemed to leave his heart; his lips grew white; he dropped her hands, and sat regarding her with eyes in which there was nothing less than horror. The woman saw it, and once more fell with a low moan to the floor.

"My God!" groaned the General at last, and said not another word, but sat rigid and mute while the woman lay on the floor at his feet. The horror which that word had caused for some time overmastered him, and he sat staring vacantly. But the horror was not against the woman who had called it up, and who lay prostrate before him. She could not have been personally abhorrent, for in a few minutes, with a start, he noticed her once more, and his face was overspread by an anguish of pity and sympathy. He raised her up, he led her to a couch, and made her sit down, and then sat in silence before her with his face buried in his hands. She reclined on the couch with her countenance turned toward him, trembling still, and panting for breath, with her right hand under her face, and her left pressed tightly against her heart. At times she looked at the General with mournful inquiry, and seemed to be patiently waiting for him to speak. An hour passed in silence. The General seemed to be struggling with recollections that overwhelmed him. At last he raised his head, and regarded her in solemn silence, and still his face and his eyes bore that expression of unutterable pity and sympathy which dwelt there when he raised her from the floor.

After a time he addressed her in a low voice, the tones of which were tender and full of sadness. She replied, and a conversation followed which lasted for hours. It involved things of fearful moment—crime, sin, shame, the perfidy of traitors, the devotion of faithful ones, the sharp pang of injured love, the long anguish of despair, the deathless fidelity of devoted affection. But the report of this conversation and the recital of these things do not belong to this place. It is enough to say that when at last Mrs. Hart arose it was with a serener face and a steadier step than had been seen in her for years.

That night the General did not close his eyes. His friend, his business, even his daughter, all were forgotten, as though his soul were overwhelmed and crushed by the weight of some tremendous revelation.

CHAPTER V.

THE FUTURE BRIDE.

IT had been arranged that Guy should accompany General Pomeroy up to London, partly for the sake of arranging about the matters relating to the Chetwynde estates, and partly for the purpose of seeing the one who was some day to be his wife. Lord Chetwynde was unable to undergo the fatigue of traveling, and had to leave every thing to his lawyers and Guy.

At the close of a wearisome day in the train they reached London, and drove at once to the General's lodgings in Great James Street. The door was opened by a tall, swarthy woman, whose Indian nationality was made manifest by the gay-colored turban which surmounted her head, as well as by her face and figure. At the sight of the General she burst out into exclamations of joy.

"Welcome home, sahib; welcome home!" she cried. "Little missy, her fret much after you."

"I am sorry for that, nurse," said the General, kindly.

As he was speaking they were startled by a piercing scream from an adjoining apartment, followed by a shrill voice uttering some words which ended in a shriek. The General entered the house, and hastened to the room from which the sounds proceeded, and Guy followed him. The uproar was speedily accounted for by the tableau which presented itself on opening the door. It was a tableau extremely vivant, and represented a small girl, with violent gesticulations, in the act of rejecting a dainty little meal which a maid, who stood by her with a tray, was vainly endeavoring to induce her to accept. The young lady's arguments were too forcible to admit of gainsaying, for the servant did not dare to venture within reach of either the hands or feet of her small but vigorous opponent. The presence of the tray prevented her from defending herself in any way, and she was about retiring, worsted, from the encounter, when the entrance of the gentlemen gave a new turn to the position of affairs. The child saw them at once; her screams of rage changed into a cry of joy, and the face which had been distorted with passion suddenly became radiant with delight.

" Papa ! papa !" she cried, and, springing forward, she darted to his embrace, and twined her arms about his neck with a sob which her joy had wrung from her.

" Darling papa !" she cried ; " I thought you were never coming back. How could you leave me so long alone ?" and, saying this, she burst into a passion of tears, while her father in vain tried to soothe her.

At this strange revelation of the General's daughter Guy stood perplexed and wondering. Certainly he had not been prepared for this. His *fiancée* was undoubtedly of a somewhat stormy nature, and in the midst of his bewilderment he was conscious of feeling deeply reconciled to her ten years.

At length her father succeeded in quieting her, and, taking her arms from his neck, he placed her on his knee, and said :

" My darling, here is a gentleman waiting all this time to speak to you. Come, go over to him and shake hands with him."

At this the child turned her large black eyes on Guy, and scanned him superciliously from head to foot. The result seemed to satisfy her, for she advanced a few steps to take the hand which he had smilingly held out; but a thought seemed suddenly to strike her which arrested her progress half-way.

" Did *he* keep you, papa ?" she said, abruptly, while a jerk of her head in Guy's direction signified the proper noun to which the pronoun referred.

" He had something to do with it," answered her father, with a smile.

" Then I sha'n't shake hands with him," she said, resolutely ; and, putting the aforesaid appendages behind her back to prevent any forcible appropriation of them, she hurried away, and clambered up on her father's knee. The General, knowing probably by painful experience the futility of trying to combat any determination of this very decided young lady, did not attempt to make any remonstrance, but allowed her to establish herself in her accustomed position. During this process Guy had leisure to inspect her. This he did without any feeling of the immense importance of this child's character to his own future life, without thinking that this little creature might be destined to raise him up to heaven or thrust him down to hell, but only with the idle, critical view of an uninterested spectator. Guy was, in fact, too young to estimate the future, and things which were connected with that future, at their right value. He was little more than a boy, and so he looked with a boy's eyes upon this singular child.

She struck him as the oddest little mortal that he had ever come across. She was very tiny, not taller than many children of eight, and so slight and fragile that she looked as if a breath might blow her away. But if in figure she looked eight, in face she looked fifty. In that face there

was no childishness whatever. It was a thin, peaked, sallow face, with a discontented expression; her features were small and pinched, her hair, which was of inky blackness, fell on her shoulders in long, straight locks, without a ripple or a wave in them. She looked like an elf, but still this elfish little creature was redeemed from the hideousness which else might have been her doom by eyes of the most wonderful brilliancy. Large, luminous, potent eyes—intensely black, and deep as the depths of ocean, they seemed to fill her whole face; and in moments of excitement they could light up with volcanic fires, revealing the intensity of that nature which lay beneath. In repose they were unfathomable, and defied all conjecture as to what their possessor might develop into.

All this Guy noticed, as far as was possible to one so young and inexperienced; and the general result of this survey was a state of bewilderment and perplexity. He could not make her out. She was a puzzle to him, and certainly not a very attractive one.

When she had finally adjusted herself on her father's knee, the General, after the fashion of parents from time immemorial, asked :

" Has my darling been a good child since papa has been away ?"

The question may have been a stereotyped one. Not so the answer, which came out full and decided, in a tone free alike from penitence or bravado, but giving only a simple statement of facts.

" No," she said, " I have not been a good girl. I've been very naughty indeed. I haven't minded any thing that was said to me. I scratched the ayah, and kicked Sarah. I bit Sarah too. Besides, I spilt my rice and milk, and broke the plates, and I was just going to starve myself to death."

At this recital of childish enormities, with its tragical ending, Guy burst into a loud laugh. The child raised herself from her father's shoulder, and, fixing her large eyes upon him, said slowly, and with set teeth:

" I hate you !"

She looked so uncanny as she said this, and the expression of her eyes was so intense in its malignity, that Guy absolutely started.

" Hush," exclaimed her father, more peremptorily than usual ; " you must not be so rude."

As he spoke she again looked at Guy, with a vindictive expression, but did not deign to speak. The face seemed to him to be utterly diabolical and detestable. She looked at him for a moment, and then her head sank down upon her father's shoulder.

The General now made an effort to turn the conversation to where it had left off, and reverting to Zillah's confession he said :

" I thought my little girl never broke her word, and that when she promised to be good while I was away, I could depend upon her being so."

This reproach seemed to touch her. She sprang up instantly and exclaimed, in vehement tones :

" It was you who broke your promise to me. You said you would come back in two days, and you staid four. I did keep my word. I was good the first two days. Ask the ayah. When I found that you had deceived me, then I did not care."

"But you should have trusted me, my child," said the General, in a tone of mild rebuke. "You should have known that I must have had some good reason for disappointing you. I had very important business to attend to—business, darling, which very nearly affects your happiness. Some day you shall hear about it."

"But I don't want to hear about any thing that will keep you away from me," said Zillah, peevishly. "Promise never to leave me again."

"Not if I can help it, my child," said the General, kissing her fondly.

"No; but promise that you won't at all," persisted Zillah. "Promise never to leave me at all. Promise, promise, papa; promise—promise."

"Well," said the General, "I'll promise to take you with me the next time. That will do, won't it?"

"But I don't want to go away," said this sweet child; "and I won't go away."

The General gave a despairing glance at Guy, who he knew was a spectator of this scene. He felt a vague desire to get Guy alone so as to explain to him that this was only occasional and accidental, and that Zillah was really one of the sweetest and most angelic children that ever were born. Nor would this good General have consciously violated the truth in saying so; for in his heart of hearts he believed all this of his loved but sadly spoiled child. The opportunity for such explanations did not occur, however, and the General had the painful consciousness that Guy was seeing his future bride under somewhat disadvantageous circumstances. Still he trusted that the affectionate nature of Zillah would reveal itself to Guy, and make a deep impression upon him.

While such thoughts as these were passing through his mind, and others of a very varied nature were occurring to Guy, the maid Sarah arrived to take her young charge to bed. The attempt to do so roused Zillah to the most active resistance. She had made up her mind not to yield. "I won't," she cried—"I won't go to bed. I will never go away from papa a single instant until that horrid man is gone. I know he will take you away again, and I hate him. Why don't you make him go, papa?"

At this remark, which was so flattering to Guy, the General made a fresh effort to appease his daughter, but with no better success than before. Children and fools, says the proverb, speak the truth; and the truth which was spoken in this instance was not very agreeable to the visitor at whom it was flung. But Guy looked on with a smile, and nothing in his face gave any sign of the feelings that he might have. He certainly had not been prepared for any approach to any thing of this sort. On the journey the General had alluded so often to that daughter, who was always uppermost in his mind, that Guy had expected an outburst of rapturous affection from her. Had he been passed by unnoticed, he would have thought nothing of it; but the malignancy of her look, and the venom of her words, startled him, yet he was too good-hearted and considerate to exhibit any feeling whatever.

Sarah's effort to take Zillah away had resulted in such a complete failure that she retired discomfited, and there was rather an awkward

period, in which the General made a faint effort to induce his daughter to say something civil to Guy. This, however, was another failure, and in a sort of mild despair he resigned himself to her wayward humor.

At last dinner was announced. Zillah still refused to leave her father, so that he was obliged, greatly to his own discomfort, to keep her on his knee during the meal. When the soup and fish were going on she was comparatively quiet; but at the first symptoms of entrées she became restive, and popping up her quaint little head to a level with the table, she eyed the edibles with the air of an habitué at the Lord Mayor's banquet. Kaviole was handed round. This brought matters to a crisis.

"A plate and a fork for me, Thomas," she ordered, imperiously.

"But, my darling," remonstrated her father, "this is much too rich for you so late at night."

"I like kaviole," was her simple reply, given with the air of one who is presenting an unanswerable argument, and so indeed it proved to be.

This latter scene was re-enacted, with but small variations, whenever any thing appeared which met with her ladyship's approval; and Guy found that in spite of her youth she was a decided connoisseur in the delicacies of the table. Now, to tell the truth, he was not at all fond of children; but this one excited in him a positive horror. There seemed to be something in her weird and uncanny; and he found himself constantly speculating as to how he could ever become reconciled to her; or what changes future years could make in her; and whether the lapse of time could by any possibility develop this impish being into any sort of a presentable woman. From the moment that he saw her he felt that the question of beauty must be abandoned forever; it would be enough if she could prove to be one with whom a man might live with any degree of domestic comfort. But the prospect of taking her at some period in the future to preside over Chetwynde Castle filled him with complete dismay. He now began to realize what his father had faintly suggested—namely, that his part of the agreement might hereafter prove a sacrifice. The prospect certainly looked dark, and for a short time he felt somewhat downcast; but he was young and hopeful, and in the end he put all these thoughts from him as in some sort treacherous to his kind old friend, and made a resolute determination, in spite of fate, to keep his vow with him.

After anticipating the dessert, and preventing her father from taking cheese, on the ground that she did not like it, nature at last took pity on that much enduring and long suffering man, and threw over the daughter the mantle of sweet unconsciousness. Miss Pomeroy fell asleep. In that helpless condition she was quietly conveyed from her father's arms to bed, to the unspeakable relief of Guy, who felt, as the door closed, as if a fearful incubus had been removed.

On the following morning he started by an early train for Dublin, so that on this occasion he had no further opportunity of improving his acquaintance with his lovely bride. Need it be said that the loss was not regretted by the future husband?

CHAPTER VI.

TWO IMPORTANT CHARACTERS.

ABOUT five years passed away since the events narrated in the last chapter. The General's household had left their London lodgings not long after Guy's visit, and had removed to the family seat at Pomeroy Court, where they had remained ever since. During these years Guy had been living the life common with young officers, moving about from place to place, going sometimes on a visit to his father, and, on the whole, extracting an uncommonly large amount of enjoyment out of life. The memory of his betrothal never troubled him; he fortunately escaped any affair of the heart more serious than an idle flirtation in a garrison town; the odd scene of his visit to General Pomeroy's lodgings soon faded into the remote past; and the projected marriage was banished in his mind to the dim shades of a remote future. As for the two old men, they only met once or twice in all these years. General Pomeroy could not manage very well to leave his daughter, and Lord Chetwynde's health did not allow him to visit Pomeroy. He often urged the General to bring Zillah with him to Chetwynde Castle, but this the young lady positively refused to consent to. Nor did the General himself care particularly about taking her there.

Pomeroy Court was a fine old mansion, with no pretensions to grandeur, but full of that solid comfort which characterizes so many country houses of England. It was irregular in shape, and belonged to different periods; the main building being Elizabethan, from which there projected an addition in that stiff Dutch style which William and Mary introduced. A wide, well-timbered park surrounded it, beyond which lay the village of Pomeroy.

One morning in June, 1856, a man came up the avenue and entered the hall. He was of medium size, with short light hair, low brow, light eyes, and thin face, and he carried a scroll of music in his hand. He entered the hall with the air of an habitué, and proceeded to the south parlor. Here his attention was at once arrested by a figure standing by one of the windows. It was a young girl, slender and graceful in form, dressed in black, with masses of heavy black hair coiled up behind her head. Her back was turned toward him, and he stood in silence for some time looking toward her.

At last he spoke: "Miss Krieff—"

The one called Miss Krieff turned and said, in an indifferent monotone: "Good-morning, Mr. Gualtier."

Turning thus she showed a face which had in it nothing whatever of the English type—a dark olive complexion, almost swarthy, in fact; thick, luxuriant black hair, eyes intensely black and piercingly lustrous, retreating chin, and retreating narrow forehead. In that face, with its intense eyes, there was the possibility of rare charm and fascination, and beauty of a very unusual kind; but at the present moment, as she looked carelessly and almost sullenly at her visitor, there was something repellent.

"Where is Miss Pomeroy?" asked Gualtier.

"About, somewhere," answered Miss Krieff, shortly.

"Will she not play to-day?"

"I think not."

"Why?"

"The usual cause."

"What?"

"Tantrums," said Miss Krieff.

"It is a pity," said Gualtier, dryly, "that she is so irregular in her lessons. She will never advance."

"The idea of her ever pretending to take lessons of any body in any thing is absurd," said Miss Krieff. "Besides, it is as much as a teacher's life is worth. You will certainly leave the house some day with a broken head."

Gualtier smiled, showing a set of large yellow teeth, and his small light eyes twinkled.

"It is nothing for me, but I sometimes think it must be hard for you, Miss Krieff," said he, insinuatingly.

"Hard!" she repeated, and her eyes flashed as she glanced at Gualtier; but in an instant it passed, and she answered in a soft, stealthy voice: "Oh yes, it is hard sometimes; but then dependents have no right to complain of the whims of their superiors and benefactors, you know."

Gualtier said nothing, but seemed to wait further disclosures. After a time Miss Krieff looked up, and surveyed him with her penetrating gaze.

"You must have a great deal to bear, I think," said he at last.

"Have you observed it?" she asked.

"Am I not Miss Pomeroy's tutor? How can I help observing it?" was the reply.

"Have I ever acted as though I was dissatisfied or discontented, or did you ever see any thing in me which would lead you to suppose that I was otherwise than contented?"

"You are generally regarded as a model of good-nature," said Gualtier, in a cautious, noncommittal tone. "Why should I think otherwise? They say that no one but you could live with Miss Pomeroy."

Miss Krieff looked away, and a stealthy smile crept over her features.

"Good-nature!" she murmured. A laugh that sounded almost like a sob escaped her. Silence followed, and Gualtier sat looking abstractedly at his sheet of music.

"How do you like the General?" he asked, abruptly.

"How could I help loving Miss Pomeroy's father?" replied Miss Krieff, with the old stealthy smile reappearing.

"Is he not just and honorable?"

"Both—more too—he is generous and tender. He is above all a fond father; so fond," she added, with something like a sneer, "that all his justice, his tenderness, and his generosity are exerted for the exclusive benefit of that darling child on whom he dotes. I assure you, you can have no idea how touching it is to see them together."

"Do you often feel this tenderness toward them?" asked Gualtier, turning his thin sallow face toward her.

"Always," said Miss Krieff, slowly. She rose from her chair, where she had taken her seat, and looked fixedly at him for some time without one word.

"You appear to be interested in this family," said she at length. Gualtier looked at her for a moment—then his eyes fell.

"How can I be otherwise than interested in one like you?" he murmured.

"The General befriended you. He found you in London, and offered you a large salary to teach his daughter."

"The General was very kind, and is so still."

Miss Krieff paused, and looked at him with keen and vigilant scrutiny.

"Would you be shocked," she asked at length, "if you were to hear that the General had an enemy?"

"That would altogether depend upon who the enemy might be."

"An enemy," continued Miss Krieff, with intense bitterness of tone—"in his own family?"

"That would be strange," said Gualtier; "but I can imagine an enemy with whom I would not be offended."

"What would you think," asked Miss Krieff, after another pause, during which her keen scrutinizing gaze was fixed on Gualtier, "if that enemy had for years been on the watch, and under a thin veil of good-nature had concealed the most vengeful feelings? What would you say if that enemy had grown so malignant that only one desire remained, and that was—to do some injury in some way to General Pomeroy?"

"You must tell me more," said Gualtier, "before I answer. I am fully capable of understanding all that hate may desire or accomplish. But has this enemy of whom you speak *done* any thing? Has she found out any thing? Has she ever discovered any way in which her hate may be gratified?"

"You seem to take it for granted that his enemy is a woman!"

"Of course."

"Well, then, I will answer you. She *has* found out something—or, rather, she is in the way toward finding out something—which may yet enable her to gratify her desires."

"Have you any objections to tell what that may be?" asked Gualtier.

Miss Krieff said nothing for some time, during which each looked earnestly at the other.

"No," said she at last.

"What is it?"

"It is something that I have found among the General's papers," said she, in a low voice.

"You have examined the General's papers, then?"

"What I said implied that much, I believe," said Miss Krieff, coolly.

"And what is it?"

"A certain mysterious document."

"Mysterious document?" repeated Gualtier.

"Yes."

"What?"

"It is a writing in cipher."

"And you have made it out?"

"No, I have not."

"Of what use is it, then?"

"I think it may be of some importance, or it would not have been kept where it was, and it would not have been written in cipher."

"What can you do with it?" asked Gualtier, after some silence.

"I do not yet see what I can do with it, but others may."

"What others?"

"I hope to find some friend who may have more skill in cryptography than I have, and may be able to decipher it."

"Can you not decipher it at all?"

"Only in part."

"And what is it that you have found out?"

"I will tell you some other time, perhaps."

"You object to tell me now?"

"Yes."

"When will you tell me?"

"When we are better acquainted."

"Are we not pretty well acquainted now?"

"Not so well as I hope we shall be hereafter."

"I shall wait most patiently, then," said Gualtier, earnestly, "till our increased intimacy shall give me some more of your confidence. But might you not give me some general idea of that which you think you have discovered?"

Miss Krieff hesitated.

"Do not let me force myself into your confidence," said Gualtier.

"No," said Miss Krieff, in that cold, repellent manner which she could so easily assume. "There is no danger of that. But I have no objection to tell you what seems to me to be the general meaning of that which I have deciphered."

"What is it?"

"As far as I can see," said Miss Krieff, "it charges General Pomeroy with atrocious crimes, and implicates him in one in particular, the knowledge of which, if it be really so, can be used against him with terrible—yes, fatal effect. I now can understand very easily why he was so strangely and frantically eager to betroth his child to the son of Lord Chetwynde—why he trampled on all decency, and bound his own daughter, little more than a baby, to a stranger—why he purchased Guy Molyneux, body and soul, for money. All is plain from this. But, after all, it is a puzzle. He makes so high a profession of honor that if his profession were real he would have thought of a betrothal any where except *there*. Oh, if Lord Chetwynde only had the faintest conception of this!"

"But what is it?" cried Gualtier, with eager curiosity, which was stimulated to the utmost by Miss Krieff's words and tones.

"I will tell you some other time," said Miss Krieff, resuming her repellent tone—"not now. If I find you worthy of my confidence, I will give it to you."

"I will try to show myself worthy of it," said Gualtier, and, after a time, took his departure, leaving Miss Krieff to her thoughts.

Now, who was this Miss Krieff? She was an important member of the numerous household which the General had brought with him from India. She had been under his guardianship since her infancy; who she was no one knew but the General himself. Her position was an honorable one, and the General always treated her with a respect and affection that were almost paternal. Thus her life had been passed, first as playmate to Zillah, whom she exceeded in age by about four years, and afterward as companion, friend, almost sister, to the spoiled child and wayward heiress.

Hilda Krieff was a person of no common character. Even in India her nature had exhibited remarkable traits. Child as she then was, her astuteness and self-control were such as might have excited the admiration of Macchiavelli himself. By persistent flattery, by the indulgence of every whim, and, above all, by the most'exaggerated protestations of devotion, she had obtained a powerful influence over Zillah's uncontrolled but loving nature; and thus she had gradually made herself so indispensable to her that Zillah could never bear to be separated from one who so humored all her whims, and bore her most ungovernable fits of passion with such unvarying sweetness. Hilda had evidently taken her lesson from the General himself; and thus Zillah was treated with equal servility by her father and her friend.

Personally, there was some general resemblance between the two girls; though in Hilda the sallow hue of ill health was replaced by a clear olive complexion; and her eyes, which she seldom raised, had a somewhat furtive manner at times, which was altogether absent from Zillah's clear frank gaze. Hilda's voice was low and melodious, never even in the abandon of childish play, or in any excitement, had she been known to raise its tones; her step was soft and noiseless, and one had no idea that she was in the room till she was found standing by one's side.

Zillah's maid Sarah described in her own way the characteristics of Hilda Krieff.

"That Injun girl," she said, "always giv her a turn. For her part she preferred Missy, who, though she did kick uncommon, and were awful cantankerous to manage, was always ready to make it up, and say as she had been naughty. For my part," concluded Sarah, "I am free to confess I have often giv Missy a sly shake when she was in one of them tantrums, and I got the chance, and however that girl can be always

meek spoken even when she has books a-shied at her head is more than I can tell, and I don't like it neither. I see a look in them eyes of hers sometimes as I don't like."

Thus we see that Hilda's Christian-like forgiveness of injuries met with but little appreciation in some quarters. But this mattered little, since with the General and Zillah she was always in the highest favor.

What had these years that had passed done for Zillah? In personal appearance not very much. The plain sickly child had developed into a tall ungainly girl, whose legs and arms appeared incessantly to present to their owner the insoluble problem—What is to be done with us? Her face was still thin and sallow, although it was redeemed by its magnificent eyes and wealth of lustrous, jet-black hair. As to her hair, to tell the truth, she managed its luxuriant folds in a manner as little ornamental as possible. She would never consent to allow it to be dressed, affirming that it would drive her mad to sit still so long, and it was accordingly tricked up with more regard to expedition than to neatness; and long untidy locks might generally be seen straggling over her shoulders. Nevertheless a mind possessed of lively imagination and great faith might have traced in this girl the possibility of better things.

In mental acquirements she was lamentably deficient. Her mind was a garden gone to waste; the weeds flourished, but the good seed refused to take root. It had been found almost impossible to give her even the rudiments of a good education. Governess after governess had come to Pomeroy Court; governess after governess after a short trial had left, each one telling the same story: Miss Pomeroy's abilities were good, even above the average, but her disinclination to learning was so great—such was the delicately expressed formula in which they made known to the General Zillah's utter idleness and selfishness—that she (the governess) felt that she was unable to do her justice; that possibly the fault lay in her own method of imparting instruction, and that she therefore begged to resign the position of Miss Pomeroy's instructress. Now, as each new teacher had begun a system of her own which she had not had time to develop, it may be easily seen that the little knowledge which Zillah possessed was of the most desultory character. Yet after all she had something in her favor. She had a taste for reading, and this led her to a familiarity with the best authors. More than this, her father had instilled into her mind a chivalrous sense of honor; and from natural instinct, as well as from his teachings, she loved all that was noble and pure. Medieval romance was most congenial to her taste; and of all the heroes who figure there she loved best the pure, the high-souled, the heavenly Sir Galahad. All the heroes of the Arthurian or of the Carlovingian epopee were adored by this wayward but generous girl. She would sit for hours curled up on a window-sill of the library, reading tales of Arthur and the knights of the Round Table, or of Charlemagne and his Paladins. Fairy lore, and whatever else our medieval ancestors have loved, thus became most familiar to her, and all her soul became imbued with these bright and radiant fancies. And through it all she learned the one great lesson which these romances teach—that the grandest and most heroic of all virtues is self-abnegation at the call of honor and loyalty.

The only trouble was, Zillah took too grand a view of this virtue to make it practically useful in daily life. If she had thus taken it to her heart, it might have made her practice it by giving up her will to those around her, and by showing from day to day the beauty of gentleness and courtesy. This, however, she never thought of; or, if it came to her mind, she considered it quite beneath her notice. Hers was simply a grand theory, to carry out which she never dreamed of any sacrifice but one of the grandest character.

The General certainly did all in his power to induce her to learn; and if she did not, it was scarcely his fault. But, while Zillah thus grew up in ignorance, there was one who did profit by the instructions which she had despised, and, in spite of the constant change of teachers which Zillah's impracticable character had rendered necessary, was now, at the age of nineteen, a refined, well-educated, and highly-accomplished young lady. This was Hilda Krieff. General Pomeroy was anxious that she should have every possible advantage, and Zillah was glad enough to have a companion in her studies. The result is easily stated. Zillah was idle, Hilda was studious, and all that the teachers could impart was diligently mastered by her.

CHAPTER VII.

THE SECRET CIPHER.

SOME time passed away, and Gualtier made his usual visits. Zillah's moods were variable and capricious. Sometimes she would languidly declare that she could not take her lesson; at other times she would take it for about ten minutes; and then, rising hastily from the piano, she would insist that she was tired, and refuse to study any more for that day. Once or twice, by an extreme effort, she managed to devote a whole half hour, and then, as though such exertion was superhuman, she would retire, and for several weeks afterward plead that half hour as an excuse for her negligence. All this Gualtier bore with perfect equanimity. Hilda said nothing; and generally, after Zillah's retirement, she would go to the piano herself and take a lesson.

These lessons were diversified by general conversation. Often they spoke about Zillah, but very seldom was it that they went beyond this. Miss Krieff showed no desire to speak of the subject which they once had touched upon, and Gualtier was too cunning to be obtrusive. So the weeks passed by without any renewal of that confidential conversation in which they had once indulged.

While Zillah was present, Hilda never in any instance showed any sign whatever of anger or impatience. She seemed not to notice her behavior, or if she did notice it she seemed to think it a very ordinary matter. On Zillah's retiring she generally took her place at the piano without a word, and Gualtier began his instructions. It was during these instructions that their conversation generally took place.

One day Gualtier came and found Hilda alone. She was somewhat *distrait*, but showed pleasure at seeing him, at which he felt both gratified and flattered. "Where is Miss Pomeroy?" he asked, after the usual greetings had been exchanged.

"You will not have the pleasure of seeing her to-day," answered Hilda, dryly.

"Is she ill?"

"Ill? She is never ill. No. She has gone out."

"Ah?"

"The General was going to take a drive to visit a friend, and she took it into her head to accompany him. Of course he had to take her. It was very inconvenient—and very ridiculous—but the moment she proposed it he assented, with only a very faint effort at dissuasion. So they have gone, and will not be back for some hours."

"I hope you will allow me to say," remarked Gualtier, in a low voice, "that I consider her absence rather an advantage than otherwise."

"You could hardly feel otherwise," said Hilda. "You have not yet got a broken head, it is true; but it is coming. Some day you will not walk out of the house. You will be carried out."

"You speak bitterly."

"I feel bitterly."

"Has any thing new happened?" he asked, following up the advantage which her confession gave him.

"No; it is the old story. Interminable troubles, which have to be borne with interminable patience."

There was a long silence. "You spoke once," said Gualtier at last, in a low tone, "of something which you promised one day to tell me—some papers. You said that you would show them some day when we were better acquainted. Are we not better acquainted? You have seen me now for many weeks since that time, and ought to know whether I am worthy to be trusted or not."

"Mr. Gualtier," said Hilda, frankly, and without hesitation, "from my point of view I have concluded that you are worthy to be trusted. I have decided to show you the paper."

Gualtier began to murmur his thanks. Hilda waved her hand. "There is no need of that," said she. "It may not amount to any thing, and then your thanks will be thrown away. If it does amount to something you will share the benefit of it with me—though you can not share the revenge," she muttered, in a lower tone. "But, after all," she continued, "I do not know that any thing can be gained by it. The conjectures which I have formed may all be unfounded."

"At any rate, I shall be able to see what the foundation is," said Gualtier.

"True," returned Hilda, rising; "and so I will go at once and get the paper."

"Have you kept it ever since?" he asked.

"What! the paper? Oh, you must not imagine that I have kept the original! No, no. I kept it long enough to make a copy, and returned the original to its place."

"Where did you find it?"

"In the General's private desk."

"Did it seem to be a paper of any importance?"

"Yes; it was kept by itself in a secret drawer. That showed its importance."

Hilda then left the room, and in a short time returned with a paper in her hand.

"Here it is," she said, and she gave it to Gualtier. Gualtier took it, and unfolding it, he saw this:

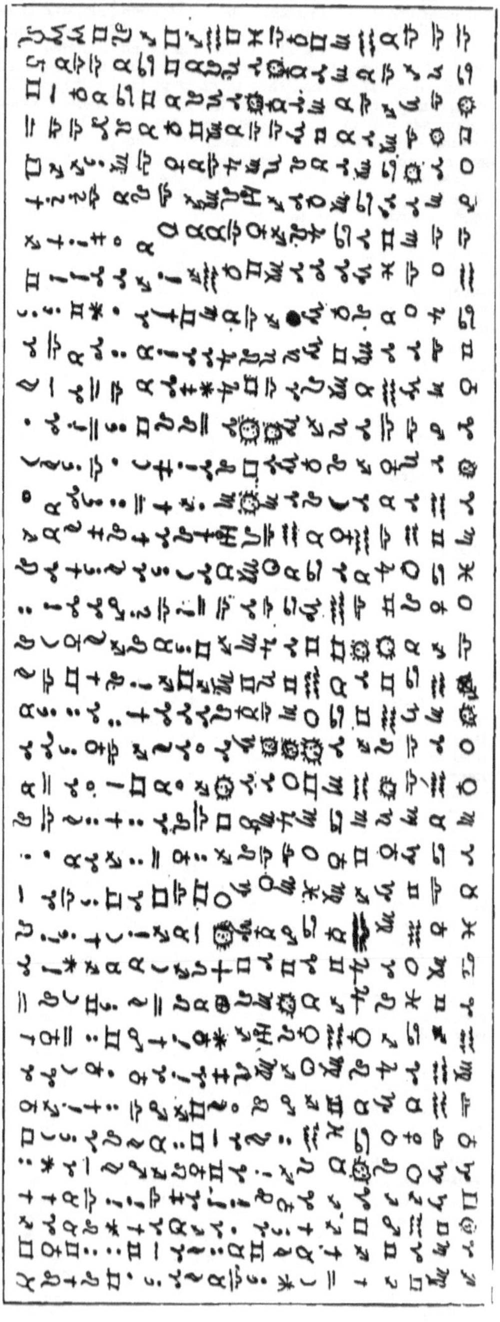

Gualtier took this singular paper, and examined it long and earnestly. Hilda had copied out the characters with painful minuteness and beautiful accuracy; but nothing in it suggested to him any revelation of its dark meaning, and he put it down with a strange, bewildered air.

"What is it all?" he asked.

"It seems to contain some mystery, beyond a doubt. I can gather nothing from the characters. They are all astronomical signs; and, so far as I can see, are the signs of the zodiac and of the planets. Here, said he, pointing to the character ☉, is the sign of the Sun; and here, pointing to ♎, is Libra; and here is Aries, pointing to the sign ♈.

"Yes," said Hilda; "and that occurs most frequently."

"What is it all?"

"I take it to be a secret cipher."

"How?"

"Why, this—that these signs are only used to represent letters of the alphabet. If such a simple mode of concealment has been used the solution is an easy one."

"Can you solve cipher alphabets?"

"Yes, where there is nothing more than a concealment of the letters. Where there is any approach to hieroglyphic writing, or syllabic ciphers, I am baffled."

"And have you solved this?"

"No."

"I thought you said that you had, and that it contained charges against General Pomeroy."

"That is my difficulty. I have tried the usual tests, and have made out several lines; but there is something about it which puzzles me; and though I have worked at it for nearly a year, I have not been able to get to the bottom of it."

"Are you sure that your deciphering is correct?"

"No."

"Why not?"

"Because it ought to apply to all, and it does not. It only applies to a quarter of it."

"Perhaps it is all hieroglyphic, or syllabic writing."

"Perhaps so."

"In that case can you solve it?"

"No; and that is one reason

"'WHAT IS IT ALL?' HE ASKED."

why I have thought of you. Have you ever tried any thing of the kind?"

"No; never. And I don't see how you have learned any thing about it, or how you have been able to arrive at any principle of action."

"Oh, as to that," returned Hilda, "the principle upon which I work is very simple; but I wish you to try the solution with your own unaided ingenuity. So, simple as my plan is, I will not tell you any thing about it just now."

Gualtier looked again at the paper with an expression of deep perplexity.

"How am I even to begin?" said he. "What am I to do? You might as well ask me to translate the Peschito version of the Syriac gospels, or the Rig-Veda."

"I think," said Hilda, coolly, "that you have sufficient ingenuity."

"I have," said Gualtier; "but, unfortunately, my ingenuity does not lie at all in this direction. This is something different from any thing that has ever come in my way before. See," he said, pointing to the paper, "this solid mass of letters. It is a perfect block, an exact rectangle. How do you know where to begin? Nothing on the letters shows this. How do you know whether you are to read from left to right, or from right to left, like Hebrew and Arabic; or both ways, like the old Greek Boustrephedon; or vertically, like the Chinese; or, for that matter, diagonally? Why, one doesn't know even how to begin!"

"That must all be carefully considered," said Hilda. "I have weighed it all, and know every letter by heart; its shape, its position, and all about it."

"Well," said Gualtier, "you must not be at all surprised if I fail utterly."

"At least you will try?"

"Try? I shall be only too happy. I shall devote to this all the time that I have. I will give up all my mind and all my soul to it. I will not only examine it while I am by myself, but I will carry this paper with me wherever I go, and occupy every spare moment in studying it. I'll learn every character by heart, and think over them all day, and dream about them all night. Do not be afraid that I shall neglect it. It is enough for me that you have given this for me to attempt its solution."

Gualtier spoke with earnestness and impetuosity, but Hilda did not seem to notice it at all.

"Recollect," she said, in her usual cool manner, "it is as much for your interest as for mine. If my conjecture is right, it may be of the utmost value. If I am wrong, then I do not know what to do."

"You think that this implicates General Pomeroy in some crime?"

"That is my impression, from my own attempt at solving it. But, as I said, my solution is only a partial one. I can not fathom the rest of it, and do not know how to begin to do so. That is the reason why I want your help."

CHAPTER VIII.

DECIPHERING.

MANY weeks passed away before Gualtier had another opportunity of having a confidential conversation with Miss Krieff. Zillah seemed to be perverse. She was as capricious as ever as to her music: some days attending to it for five minutes, other days half an hour; but now she did not choose to leave the room. She would quit the piano, and, flinging herself into a chair, declare that she wanted to see how Hilda stood it. As Hilda seated herself and wrought out elaborate combinations from the instrument, she would listen attentively, and when it was over she would give expression to some despairing words as to her own stupidity.

Yet Gualtier had opportunities, and he was not slow to avail himself of them. Confidential intercourse had arisen between himself and Miss

Krieff, and he was determined to avail himself of the great advantage which this gave him. They had a secret in common—she had admitted him to her intimacy. There was an understanding between them. Each felt an interest in the other. Gualtier knew that he was more than an ordinary music-teacher to her.

During those days when Zillah persistently staid in the room he made opportunities for himself. Standing behind her at the piano he had chances of speaking words which Zillah could not hear.

Thus: "Your fingering there is not correct, Miss Krieff," he would say in a low tone. "You must put the second finger on G. I have not yet deciphered it."

"But the book indicates the third finger on G. Have you tried?"

"It is a blunder of the printer. Yes, every day—almost every hour of every day."

"Yet it seems to me to be natural to put the third finger there. Are you discouraged?"

"Try the second finger once or twice, this way;" and he played a few notes. "Discouraged? no; I am willing to keep at it for an indefinite period."

"Yes, I see that it is better. You must succeed. I was three months at it before I discovered any thing."

"That passage is *allegro*, and you played it *andante*. I wish you would give me a faint hint as to the way in which you deciphered it."

"I did not notice the directions," responded Miss Krieff, playing the passage over again. "Will that do? No, I will give no hint. You would only imitate me then, and I wish you to find out for yourself on your own principle."

"Yes, that is much better. But I have no principle to start on, and have not yet found out even how to begin."

"I must pay more attention to 'expression,' I see. You say my 'time' is correct enough. If you are not discouraged, you will find it out yet."

"Your 'time' is perfect. If it is possible, I will find it out. I am not discouraged."

"Well, I will hope for something better the next time, and now don't speak about it any more. The 'brat' is listening."

"*Allegro, allegro;* remember, Miss Krieff. You always confound *andante* with *allegro.*"

"So I do. They have the same initials."

Such was the nature of Gualtier's musical instructions. These communications, however, were brief and hurried, and only served to deepen the intimacy between them. They had now mutually recognized themselves as two conspirators, and had thus become already indispensable to one another.

They waited patiently, however, and at length their patient waiting was rewarded. One day Gualtier came and found that Zillah was unwell, and confined to her room. It was the slightest thing in the world, but the General was anxious and fidgety, and was staying in the room with her trying to amuse her. This Miss Krieff told him with her usual bitterness.

"And now," said she, "we will have an hour. I want to know what you have done."

"Done! Nothing."

"Nothing?"

"No, nothing. My genius does not lie in

that direction. You might as well have expected me to decipher a Ninevite inscription. I can do nothing."

"Have you tried?"

"Tried! I assure you that for the last month the only thing that I have thought of has been this. Many reasons have urged me to decipher it, but the chief motive was the hope of bringing to you a complete explanation."

"Have you not made out at least a part of it?"

"Not a part—not a single word—if there are words in it—which I very much doubt."

"Why should you doubt it?"

"It seems to me that it must consist of hiero-glyphics. You yourself say that you have only made out a part of it, and that you doubt whether it is a valid interpretation. After all, then, your interpretation is only partial—only a conjecture. Now I have not begun to make even a conjecture. For see—what is this?" and Gualtier drew the well-thumbed paper from his pocket. "I have counted up all the different characters here, and find that they are forty in number. They are composed chiefly of astronomical signs; but six-teen of them are the ordinary punctuation marks, such as one sees every day. If it were merely a secret alphabet, there would be twenty-six signs only, not forty. What can one do with forty signs?

"I have examined different grammars of for-eign languages to see if any of them had forty letters, but among the few books at my command I can find none; and even if it were so, what then? What would be the use of trying to de-cipher an inscription in Arabic? I thought at one time that perhaps the writer might have adopted the short-hand alphabet, but changed the signs. Yet even when I go from this prin-ciple I can do nothing."

"Then you give it up altogether?"

"Yes, altogether and utterly, so far as I am concerned; but I still am anxious to know what you have deciphered, and how you have deci-phered it. I have a hope that I may gain some light from your discovery, and thus be able to do something myself."

"Well," said Miss Krieff, "I will tell you, since you have failed so completely. My principle is a simple one; and my deciphering, though only partial, seems to me to be so true, as far as it goes, that I can not imagine how any other re-sult can be found.

"I am aware," she continued, "that there are forty different characters in the inscription. I counted them all out, and wrote them out most carefully. I went on the simple principle that the writer had written in English, and that the number of the letters might be disregarded on a first examination.

"Then I examined the number of times in which each letter occurred. I found that the sign τ occurred most frequently. Next was π; next 8; and then ☾, and ਪ, and ⏾, and ƨ, and ȝ." Miss Krieff marked these signs down as she spoke.

Gualtier nodded.

"There was this peculiarity about these signs," said Miss Krieff, "that they occurred all through the writing, while the others occurred some in the first half and some in the second. For this inscription is very peculiar in this respect. It is only in the second half that the signs of punctua-

tion occur. The signs of the first half are all astronomical.

"You must remember," continued Miss Krieff, "that I did not think of any other language than the English. The idea of its being any dialect of the Hindustani never entered my head. So I went on this foundation, and naturally the first thought that came to me was, what letters are there in English which occur most frequently? It seemed to me if I could find this out I might obtain some key, partially, at any rate, to the letters which occurred so frequently in this writ-ing.

"I had plenty of time and unlimited patience. I took a large number of different books, written by standard authors, and counted the letters on several pages of each as they occurred. I think I counted more than two hundred pages in this way. I began with the vowels, and counted up the number of times each one occurred. Then I counted the consonants."

"That never occurred to me," said Gualtier. "Why did you not tell me?"

"Because I wanted you to decipher it your-self on your own principle. Of what use would it be if you only followed over my track? You would then have come only to my result. But I must tell you the result of my examination. After counting up the recurrence of all the letters on more than two hundred pages of standard authors, I made out an average of the times of their recurrence, and I have the paper here on which I wrote the average down."

And Miss Krieff drew from her pocket a paper which she unfolded and showed to Gualtier.

On it was the following:

AVERAGE OF LETTERS.

E......222 times per page.	N......90 times per page.
T......162 " " "	L......62 " " "
A......120 " " "	D......46 " " "
H. J....110 " " "	C......42 " " "
I. J....109 " " "	U. V...36 " " "
S......104 " " "	B......36 " " "
O......100 " " "	W......30 " " "
R......100 " " "	G......30 " " "

"The rest," said Miss Krieff, "occur on the average less than thirty times on a page, and so I did not mark them. 'F,' 'P,' and 'K' may be supposed to occur more frequently than some others; but they do not.

"'E,' then," she continued, "is the letter of first importance in the English language. 'A,' and 'T,' and 'H,' are the next ones. Now there are some little words which include these letters, such as 'the.' 'And' is another word which may be discovered and deciphered, it is of such fre-quent occurrence. If these words only can be found, it is a sign at least that one is on the right track. There are also terminations which seem to me peculiar to the English language; such as 'ng,' 'ing,' 'ed,' 'ly,' and so on. At any rate, from my studies of the Italian, French, and Ger-man, and from my knowledge of Hindustani, I know that there are no such terminations in any of the words of those languages. So you see," concluded Miss Krieff, with a quiet smile, "the simple principle on which I acted."

"Your genius is marvelously acute!" ex-claimed Gualtier, in undisguised admiration. "You speak of your principle as a simple one, but it is more than I have been able to arrive at."

"Men," said Miss Krieff, "reason too much.

You have been imagining all sorts of languages in which this may have been written. Now, women go by intuitions. I acted in that way."

"Intuitions!" exclaimed Gualtier. "You have reasoned out this thing in a way which might have done honor to Bacon. You have laid down a great principle as a foundation, and have gone earnestly to work building up your theory. Champollion himself did not surpass you."

Gualtier's tone expressed profound admiration. It was not idle compliment. It was sincere. He looked upon her at that moment as a superior genius. His intellect bowed before hers. Miss Krieff saw the ascendency which she had gained over him; and his expressions of admiration were not unwelcome. Admiration! Rare, indeed, was it that she had heard any expressions of that kind, and when they came they were as welcome as is the water to the parched and thirsty ground. Her whole manner softened toward him, and her eyes, which were usually so bright and hard, now grew softer, though none the less bright.

"You overestimate what I have done," said she, "and you forget that it is only partially effected."

"Whether partially or not," replied Gualtier, "I have the most intense curiosity to see what you have done. Have you any objections to show it to me? Now that I have failed by myself, the only hope that I have is to be able to succeed through your assistance. You can show your superiority to me here; perhaps, in other things, I may be of service to you."

"I have no objections," said Miss Krieff. "Indeed I would rather show you my results than not, so as to know what you have to say about them. I am not at all satisfied, for it is only partial. I know what you will say. You will see several reasons, all of which are very good, for doubting my interpretation of this writing."

"I can assure you that I shall doubt nothing. After my own disgraceful failure any interpretation will seem to me to be a work of genius. Believe me any interpretation of yours will only fill me with a sense of my own weakness."

"Well," said Miss Krieff, after a pause, "I will show you what I have done. My papers are in my room. Go and play on the piano till I come back."

Saying this she departed, and was absent for about a quarter of an hour or twenty minutes, and then returned.

"How is Miss Pomeroy?" asked Gualtier, turning round on the piano-stool and rising.

"About the same," said Miss Krieff. "The General is reading Puss in Boots to her, I believe. Perhaps it is Jack and the Bean Stalk, or Beauty and the Beast. It is one of them, however. I am not certain which."

She walked up to a centre-table and opened a paper which she held in her hand. Gualtier followed her, and took a seat by her side.

"You must remember," said Miss Krieff, "that this interpretation of mine is only a partial one, and may be altogether wrong. Yet the revelations which it seemed to convey were so startling that they have produced a very deep impression on my mind. I hoped that you would have done something. If you had arrived at a

solution similar to mine, even if it had been a partial one, I should have been satisfied that I had arrived at a part of the truth at least. As you have not done so, nothing remains but to show you what I have done."

Saying this, she opened the paper which she held and displayed it to Gualtier:

"In that writing," said she, "there are twenty lines. I have been able to do any thing with ten of them only, and that partially. The rest is beyond my conjecture."

The paper was written so as to show under each character the corresponding letter, or what Miss Krieff supposed to be the corresponding letter, to each sign.

"This," said Miss Krieff, "is about half of the signs. You see if my key is applied it makes intelligible English out of most of the signs in this first half. There seems to me to be a block of letters set into a mass of characters. Those triangular portions of signs at each end, and all the lower part, seem to me to be merely a mass of characters that mean nothing, but added to conceal and distract."

"It is possible," said Gualtier, carefully examining the paper.

"It must mean something," said Miss Krieff, "and it can mean nothing else than what I have written. That is what it was intended to express. Those letters could not have tumbled into that position by accident, so as to make up these words. See," she continued, "here are these sentences written out separately, and you can read them more conveniently."

She handed Gualtier a piece of paper, on which was the following:

Oh may God have mercy on my wretched soul Amen
O Pomeroy forged a hundred thousand dollars
O N Pomeroy eloped with poor Lady Chetwynde
She acted out of a mad impulse in flying
She listened to me and ran off with me
She was piqued at her husband's act
Fell in with Lady Mary Chetwynd
Expelled the army for gaming .
N Pomeroy of Pomeroy Berks
O I am a miserable villain

Gualtier read it long and thoughtfully.

"What are the initials 'O. N.?'"

"Otto Neville. It is the General's name."

Silence followed. "Here he is called O Pomeroy, O N Pomeroy, and N Pomeroy."

"Yes; the name by which he is called is Neville."

"Your idea is that it is a confession of guilt, written by this O. N. Pomeroy himself?"

"It reads so."

"I don't want to inquire into the probability of the General's writing out this and leaving it in his drawer, even in cipher, but I look only at the paper itself."

"What do you think of it?" .

"In the first place your interpretation is very ingenious."

"But—?"

"But it seems partial."

"So it does to me. That is the reason why I want your help. You see that there are several things about it which give it an incomplete character. First, the mixture of initials; then, the interchange of the first and third persons. At one moment the writer speaking of Pomeroy as a third person, running off with Lady Chetwynde, and again saying he himself fell in with her. Then there are incomplete sentences, such as, 'Fell in with Lady Mary Chetwynde—'"

"I know all that, but I have two ways of accounting for it."

"What?"

"First, that the writer became confused in writing the cipher characters and made mistakes."

"That is probable," said Gualtier. "What is another way?"

"That he wrote it this way on purpose to baffle."

"I think the first idea is the best: if he had wished to baffle he never would have written it at all."

"No; but somebody else might have written it in his name thus secretly and guardedly. Some one who wished for vengeance, and tried this way."

Gualtier said nothing in reply, but looked earnestly at Miss Krieff.

CHAPTER IX.

A SERIOUS ACCIDENT.

ABOUT this time an event took place which caused a total change in the lives of all at Pomeroy Court. One day, when out hunting, General Pomeroy met with an accident of a very serious nature. While leaping over a hedge the horse slipped and threw his rider, falling heavily on him at the same time. He was picked up bleeding and senseless, and in that condition carried home. On seeing her father thus brought back, Zillah gave way to a perfect frenzy of grief. She threw herself upon his unconscious form, uttering wild ejaculations, and it was with extreme difficulty that she could be taken away long enough to allow the General to be undressed and laid on his bed. She then took her place by her father's bedside, where she remained without food or sleep for two or three days, refusing all entreaties to leave him. A doctor had been sent for with all speed, and on his arrival did what he could for the senseless sufferer. It was a very serious case, and it was not till the third day that the General opened his eyes. The first sight that he saw, was the pale and haggard face of his daughter.

"What is this?" he murmured, confusedly, and in a faint voice. "What are you doing here, my darling?"

At the sight of this recognition, and the sound of his voice, Zillah uttered a loud cry of joy, and twined her arms about him in an eager hunger of affection.

"Oh, papa! papa!" she moaned, "you are getting better! You will not leave me—you will not—you will not!"

All that day the doctor had been in the house, and at this moment had been waiting in an adjoining apartment. The cry of Zillah startled him, and he hurried into the room. He saw her prostrate on the bed, with her arms around her father, uttering low, half-hysterical words of fondness, intermingled with laughter and weeping.

"Miss Pomeroy," he said, with some sternness, "are you mad? Did I not warn you above all things to restrain your feelings?"

Instantly Zillah started up. The reproof of the doctor had so stung her that for a moment she forgot her father, and regarded her reprover with a face full of astonishment and anger.

"How dare you speak so to me?" she cried, savagely.

The doctor looked fixedly at her for a few moments, and then answered, quietly:

"This is no place for discussion. I will explain afterward." He then went to the General's bedside, and surveyed his patient in thoughtful silence. Already the feeble beginnings of returning consciousness had faded away, and the sick man's eyes were closed wearily. The doctor administered some medicine, and after waiting for nearly an hour in silence, he saw the General sink off into a peaceful sleep.

"Now," said he, in a low voice, "Miss Pomeroy, I wish to say something to you. Come with me." He led the way to the room where he had been waiting, while Zillah, for the first time in her life, obeyed an order. She followed in silence.

"Miss Pomeroy," said the doctor, very gravely, "your father's case is very serious indeed, and I want to have a perfect understanding with you. If you have not thorough confidence in me, you have only to say so, and I will give you a list of physicians of good standing, into whose hands you may safely confide the General. But if, on the contrary, you wish me to continue my charge, I will only do so on the condition that I am to be the sole master in that room, and that my injunctions are to be implicitly attended to. Now, choose for yourself."

This grave, stern address, and the idea that he might leave her, frightened Zillah altogether out of her passion. She looked piteously at him, and grasped his hand as if in fear that he would instantly carry out his threat.

"Oh, doctor!" she cried, "pray forgive me; do not leave me when dear papa is so ill! It shall be all as you say, only you will not send me away from him, will you? Oh, say that you will not!"

The doctor retained her hand, and answered very kindly: "My dear child, I should be most sorry to do so. Now that your father has come back to consciousness, you may be the greatest

C

possible comfort to him if you will. But, to do this, you really must try to control yourself. The excitement which you have just caused him has overcome him, and if I had not been here I do not know what might have happened. Remember, my child, that love is shown not by words but by deeds; and it would be but a poor return for all your father's affection to give way selfishly to your own grief."

"Oh, what have I done?" cried Zillah, in terror.

"I do not suppose that you have done him very serious injury," said the doctor, reassuringly; "but you ought to take warning by this. You will promise now, won't you, that there shall be no repetition of this conduct?"

"Oh, I will! I will!"

"I will trust you, then," said the doctor, looking with pity upon her sad face. "You are his best nurse, if you only keep your promise. So now, my dear, go back to your place by his side." And Zillah, with a faint murmur of thanks, went back again.

On the following day General Pomeroy seemed to have regained his full consciousness. Zillah exercised a strong control over herself, and was true to her promise. When the doctor called he seemed pleased at the favorable change. But there was evidently something on the General's mind. Finally, he made the doctor understand that he wished to see him alone. The doctor whispered a few words to Zillah, who instantly left the room.

"Doctor," said the General, in a feeble voice, as soon as they were alone, "I must know the whole truth. Will you tell it to me frankly?"

"I never deceive my patients," was the answer.

"Am I dangerously ill?"

"You are."

"How long have I to live?"

"My dear Sir, God alone can answer that question. You have a chance for life yet. Your sickness may take a favorable turn, and we may be able to bring you around again."

"But the chances are against me, you think?"

"We must be prepared for the worst," said the doctor, solemnly. "At the same time, there is a chance."

"Well, suppose that the turn should be unfavorable, how long would it be, do you think, before the end? I have much to attend to, and it is of the greatest importance that I should know this."

"Probably a month—possibly less," answered the doctor, gravely, after a moment's thought; "that is, if the worst should take place. But it is impossible to speak with certainty until your symptoms are more fully developed."

"Thank you, doctor, for your frankness; and now, will you kindly send my daughter to me?"

"Remember," said the doctor, doubtfully, "that it is of the greatest possible moment that you should be kept free from all excitement. Any agitation of mind will surely destroy your last chance."

"But I must see her!" answered the General, excitedly. "I have to attend to something which concerns her. It is her future. I could not die easily, or rest in my grave, if this were neglected."

Thus far the General had been calm, but the thought of Zillah had roused him into a dangerous agitation. The doctor saw that discussion would only aggravate this, and that his only chance was to humor his fancies. So he went out, and found Zillah pacing the passage in a state of uncontrollable agitation. He reminded her of her promise, impressed on her the necessity of caution, and sent her to him. She crept softly to the bedside, and, taking her accustomed seat, covered his hand with kisses.

"Sit a little lower, my darling," said the General, "where I may see your face." She obeyed, still holding his hand, which returned with warmth her caressing pressure.

The agitation which the General had felt at the doctor's information had now grown visibly stronger. There was a kind of feverish excitement in his manner which seemed to indicate that his brain was affected. One idea only filled that half-delirious brain, and this, without the slightest warning, he abruptly began to communicate to his daughter.

"You know, Zillah," said he, in a rapid, eager tone which alarmed her, "the dearest wish of my heart is to see you the wife of Guy Molyneux, the son of my old friend. I betrothed you to him five years ago. You remember all about it, of course. He visited us at London. The time for the accomplishment of my desire has now arrived. I received a letter from Lord Chetwynde on the day of my, accident, telling me that his son's regiment was shortly to sail for India. I intended writing to ask him to pay us a visit before he left; but now," he added, in a dreamy voice, "of course he must come, and—he must marry you before he goes."

Any thing more horrible, more abhorrent, to Zillah than such language, at such a time, could not be conceived. She thought he was raving. A wild exclamation of fear and remonstrance started to her lips; but she remembered the doctor's warning, and by a mighty effort repressed it. It then seemed to her that this raving delirium, if resisted, might turn to madness and endanger his last chance. In her despair she found only one answer, and that was something which might soothe him.

"Yes, dear papa," she said, quietly; "yes, we will ask him to come and see us."

"No, no," cried the General, with feverish impatience. "That will not do. You must marry him at once—to-day—to-morrow—do you hear? There is no time to lose."

"But I must stay with you, dearest papa, you know," said Zillah, still striving to soothe him. "What would you do without your little girl? I am sure you can not want me to leave you."

"Ah, my child!" said the General, mournfully, "I am going to leave you. The doctor tells me that I have but a short time to live; and I feel that what he says is true. If I must leave you, my darling, I can not leave you without a protector."

At this Zillah's unaccustomed self-control gave way utterly. Overcome by the horror of that revelation and the anguish of that discovery, she flung her arms around him and clung to him passionately.

"You shall not go!" she moaned. "You shall not go; or if you do you must take me with you. I can not live without you. You know that I can not. Oh, papa! papa!"

The tones of her voice, which were wailed out in a wild, despairing cry, reached the ears of the doctor, who at once hurried in.

"What is this?" he said, sharply and sternly, to Zillah. "Is this keeping your promise?"

"Oh, doctor!" said Zillah, imploringly, "I did not mean to—I could not help it—but tell me —it is not true, is it? Tell me that my father is not going to leave me!"

"I will tell you this," said he, gravely. "You are destroying every chance of his recovery by your vehemence."

Zillah looked up at him with an expression of agony on her face such as, accustomed as he was to scenes of suffering, he had but seldom encountered.

"I've killed him, then!" she faltered.

The doctor put his hand kindly on her shoulder. "I trust not, my poor child," said he; "but it is my duty to warn you of the consequences of giving way to excessive grief."

"Oh, doctor! you are quite right, and I will try very hard not to give way again."

During this conversation, which was low and hurried, General Pomeroy lay without hearing any thing of what they were saying. His lips moved, and his hands picked at the bed-clothes convulsively. Only one idea was in his mind— the accomplishment of his wishes. His daughter's grief seemed to have no effect on him whatever. Indeed, he did not appear to notice it.

"Speak to her, doctor," said he, feebly, as he heard their voices. "Tell her I can not die happy unless she is married—I can not leave her alone in the world."

The doctor looked surprised. "What does he mean?" he said, taking Zillah aside. "What is this fancy? Is there any thing in it?"

"I'm sure I don't know," said Zillah. "It is certainly on his mind, and he can't be argued or humored out of it. It is an arrangement made some years ago between him and Lord Chetwynde that when I grew up I should marry his son, and he has just been telling me that he wishes it carried out now. Oh! what—what shall I do?" she added, despairingly. "Can't you do something, doctor?"

"I will speak to him," said the latter; and, approaching the bed, he bent over the General, and said, in a low voice:

"General Pomeroy, you know that the family physician is often a kind of father-confessor as well. Now I do not wish to intrude upon your private affairs; but from what you have said I perceive that there is something on your mind, and if I can be of any assistance to you I shall be only too happy. Have you any objection to tell me what it is that is troubling you?"

While the doctor spoke the General's eyes were fixed upon Zillah with feverish anxiety. "Tell her," he murmured, "that she must consent at once—at once," he repeated, in a more excited tone.

"Consent to what?"

"To this marriage that I have planned for her. She knows. It is with the son of my old friend, Lord Chetwynde. He is a fine lad, and comes of a good stock. I knew his father before him. I have watched him closely for the last five years. He will take care of her. He will make her a good husband. And I—shall be able to die—in peace. But it must be done—immediately—for he is going—to India."

The General spoke in a very feeble tone, and with frequent pauses.

"And do you wish your daughter to go with him? She is too young to be exposed to the dangers of Indian life."

This idea seemed to strike the General very forcibly. For some minutes he did not answer, and it was with difficulty that he could collect his thoughts. At last he answered, slowly:

"That is true—but she need not accompany him. Let her stay with me—till all is over—then she can go—to Chetwynde. It will be her natural home. She will find in my old friend a second father. She can remain with him—till her husband returns."

A long pause followed. "Besides," he resumed, in a fainter voice, "there are other things. I can not explain—they are private—they concern the affairs of others. But if Zillah were to refuse to marry him—she would lose one-half of her fortune. So you can understand my anxiety. She has not a relative in the world—to whom I could leave her."

Here the General stopped, utterly exhausted by the fatigue of speaking so much. As for the doctor, he sat for a time involved in deep thought. Zillah stood there pale and agitated, looking now at her father and now at the doctor, while a new and deeper anguish came over her heart. After a while he rose and quietly motioned to Zillah to follow him to the adjoining room.

"My dear child," said he, kindly, when they had arrived there, "your father is excited, but yet is quite sane. His plan seems to be one which he has been cherishing for years; and he has so thoroughly set his heart upon it that it now is evidently his sole idea. I do not see what else can be done than to comply with his wishes."

"What!" cried Zillah, aghast.

"To refuse," said the doctor, "might be fatal. It would throw him into a paroxysm."

"Oh, doctor!" moaned Zillah. "What do you mean? You can not be in earnest. What—to do such a thing when darling papa is—is dying!"

Sobs choked her utterance. She buried her face in her hands and sank into a chair.

"He is not yet so bad," said the doctor, earnestly, "but he is certainly in a critical state; and unless it is absolutely impossible—unless it is too abhorrent to think of—unless any calamity is better than this—I would advise you to try and think if you can not bring yourself to—to indulge his wish, wild as it may seem to you. There, my dear, I am deeply sorry for you; but I am honest, and say what I think."

For a long time Zillah sat in silence, struggling with her emotions. The doctor's words impressed her deeply; but the thing which he advised was horrible to her—abhorrent beyond words. But then there was her father lying so near to death—whom, perhaps, her self-sacrifice might save, and whom certainly her selfishness would destroy. She could not hesitate. It was a bitter decision, but she made it. She rose to her feet paler than ever, but quite calm.

"Doctor," said she, "I have decided. It is horrible beyond words; but I will do it, or any thing, for his sake. I would die to save him; and this is something worse than death."

She was calm and cold; her voice seemed unnatural; her eyes were tearless.

"It seems very hard," she murmured, after a pause; "I never saw Captain Molyneux but once, and I was only ten years old."

"How old are you now?" asked the doctor, who knew not what to say to this poor stricken heart.

"Fifteen."

"Poor child!" said he, compassionately; "the trials of life are coming upon you early; but," he added, with a desperate effort at condolence, "do not be so despairing; whatever may be the result, you are, after all, in the path of duty; and that is the safest and the best for us all in the end, however hard it may seem to be in the present."

Just then the General's voice interrupted his little homily, sounding querulously and impatiently: "Zillah! Zillah!"

She sprang to his bedside: "Here I am, dear papa."

"Will you do as I wish?" he asked, abruptly.

"Yes," said Zillah, with an effort at firmness which cost her dear. Saying this, she kissed him; and the beam of pleasure which at this word lighted up the wan face of the sick man touched Zillah to the heart. She felt that, come what might, she had received her reward.

"My sweetest, dutiful child," said the General, tenderly; "you have made me happy, my darling. Now get your desk and write for him at once. You must not lose time, my child."

This unremitting pressure upon her gave Zillah a new struggle, but the General exhibited such feverish impatience that she dared not resist. So she went to a Davenport which stood in the corner of the room, and saying, quietly, "I will write here, papa," she seated herself, with her back toward him.

"Are you ready?" he asked.

"Yes, papa."

The General then began to dictate to her what she was to write. It was as follows:

"My dear old Friend,—I think it will cause you some grief to hear that our long friendship is about to be broken up. My days, I fear, are numbered."

Zillah stifled the sobs that choked her, and wrote bravely on:

"You know the sorrow which has blighted my life; and I feel that I could go joyfully to my beloved, my deeply mourned wife, if I could feel that I was leaving my child—her child and mine—happily provided for. For this purpose I should like Guy, before he leaves for India, to fulfil his promise, and, by marrying my daughter, give me the comfort of knowing that I leave her in the hands of a husband upon whom I can confidently rely."

But at this point Zillah's self-control gave way. She broke down utterly, and, bowing her head in her hands on the desk, burst forth into a passion of sobs.

The poor child could surely not be blamed. Her nature was impassioned and undisciplined; from her birth every whim had been humored, and her wildest fancies indulged to the utmost; and now suddenly upon this petted idol, who had been always guarded so carefully from the slightest disappointment, there descended the storm-cloud of sorrow, and that too not gradually, but almost in one moment. Her love for her father was a passion; and he was to be taken from her, and she was to be given into the hands of entire strangers. The apparent calmness, almost indifference, with which her father made these arrangements, cut her to the quick. She was too young to know how much of this eagerness was attributable entirely to disease. He appeared to her as thinking of only his own wishes, and showing no consideration whatever for her own crushing grief, and no appreciation of the strength of her affection for him. The self-sacrificing father had changed into the most selfish of men, who had not one thought for her feelings.

"Oh, Zillah!" cried her father, reproachfully, in answer to her last outburst of grief. She rose and went to his bedside, struggling violently with her emotion.

"I can not write this, dearest papa," she said, in a tremulous voice; "I have promised to do just as you wish, and I will keep my word; but indeed, indeed, I can not write this letter. Will it not do as well if Hilda writes it?"

"To be sure, to be sure," said the General, who took no notice of her distress. "Hilda will do it, and then my little girl can come and sit beside her father."

Hilda was accordingly sent for. She glided noiselessly in and took her place at the Davenport; while Zillah, sitting by her father, buried her head in the bed-clothes, his feeble hands the while playing nervously with the long, straggling locks of her hair which scattered themselves over the bed. The letter was soon finished, for it contained little more than what has already been given, except the reiterated injunction that Guy should make all haste to reach Pomeroy Court. It was then sent off to the post, to the great delight of the General, whose mind became more wandering, now that the strain which had been placed upon it was removed.

"Now," said he, in a flighty way, and with an eager impetuosity which showed that his delirium had increased, "we must think of the wedding—my darling must have a grand wedding," he murmured to himself in a low whisper.

A shudder ran through Zillah as she sat by his side, but not a sound escaped her. She looked up in terror. Had every ray of reason left her father?. Was she to sacrifice herself on so hideous an altar without even the satisfaction of knowing that she had given him pleasure? Then she thought that perhaps her father was living again in the past, and confounding this fearful thing which he was planning for her with his own joyous wedding. Tears flowed afresh, but silently, at the thought of the contrast. Often had her ayah delighted her childish imagination by her glowing descriptions of the magnificence of that wedding, where the festivities had lasted for a week, and the arrangements were all made on a scale of Oriental splendor. She loved to descant upon the beauty of the bride, the richness of her attire, the magnificence of her jewels, the grandeur of the guests, the splendor of the whole display—until Zillah had insensibly learned to think all this the necessary adjuncts of a wedding, and had built many a day-dream about the pomp which should surround hers, when the glorious knight whom the fairy tales had led her to expect should come to claim her hand. But at this time it was not the sacrifice of all this that was wringing her heart. She gave it not even a

sigh. It was rather the thought that this marriage, which now seemed inevitable, was to take place here, while her heart was wrung with anxiety on his account—here in this room—by that bedside, which her fears told her might be a bed of death. There lay her father, her only friend —the one for whom she would lay down her life, and to soothe whose delirium she had consented to this abhorrent sacrifice of herself. The marriage thus planned was to take place thus; it was to be a hideous, a ghastly mockery—a frightful violence to the solemnity of sorrow. She was not to be married—she was to be sold. The circumstances of that old betrothal had never been explained to her; but she knew that money was in some way connected with it, and that she was virtually bought and sold like a slave, without any will of her own. Such bitter thoughts as these filled her mind as she sat there by her father's side.

Presently her father spoke again. "Have you any dresses, Zillah?"

"Plenty, papa."

"Oh, but I mean a wedding-dress—a fine new dress; white satin my darling wore; how beautiful she looked! and a veil you must have, and plenty of jewels — pearls and diamonds. My pet will be a lovely bride."

Every one of these words was a stab, and Zillah was dumb; but her father noticed nothing of this. It was madness, but, like many cases of madness, it was very coherent.

"Send for your ayah, dear," he continued; "I must talk to her — about your wedding-dress."

Zillah rang the bell. As soon as the woman appeared the General turned to her with his usual feverish manner.

"Nurse," said he, "Miss Pomeroy is to be married at once. You must see—that she has every thing prepared—suitably—and of the very best."

The ayah stood speechless with amazement. This feeling was increased when Zillah said, in a cold monotone:

"Don't look surprised, nurse. It's quite true. I am to be married within a day or two."

Her master's absurdities the ayah could account for on the ground of delirium; but was "Little Missy" mad too? Perhaps sorrow had turned her brain, she thought. At any rate, it would be best to humor them.

"Missy had a white silk down from London last week, Sir."

"Not satin? A wedding-dress should be of satin," said the General.

"It does not matter, so that it is all white," said the nurse, with decision.

"Doesn't it? Very well," said the General. "But she must have a veil, nurse, and plenty of jewels. She must look like my darling. You remember, nurse, how *she* looked.",

"Indeed I do, sahib, and you may leave all to me. I will see that Missy is as fine and grand as any of them."

The ayah began already to feel excited, and to fall in with this wild proposal. The very mention of dress had excited her Indian love of finery.

"That is right," said the General; "attend to it all. Spare no expense. Don't you go, my child," he continued, as Zillah rose and walked shudderingly to the window. "I think I can sleep, now that my mind is at ease. Stay by me, my darling child."

"Oh, papa, do you think I would leave you?" said Zillah, and she came back to the bed.

The doctor, who had been waiting until the General should become a little calmer, now administered an anodyne, and he fell asleep, his hand clasped in Zillah's, while she, fearful of making the slightest movement, sat motionless and despairing far into the night.

CHAPTER X.

A WEDDING IN EXTREMIS.

Two days passed; on the second Guy Molyneux arrived. Lord Chetwynde was ill, and could not travel. He sent a letter, however, full of earnest and hopeful sympathy. He would not believe that things were as bad as his old friend feared; the instant that he could leave he would come up to Pomeroy Court; or if by God's providence the worst should take place, he would instantly fetch Zillah to Chetwynde Castle; and the General might rely upon it that, so far as love and tenderness could supply a father's place, she should not feel her loss.

On Guy's arrival he was shown into the library. Luncheon was laid there, and the housekeeper apologized for Miss Pomeroy's absence. Guy took a chair and waited for a while, meditating on the time when he had last seen the girl who in a short time was to be tied to him for life. The event was excessively repugnant to him, even though he did not at all realize its full importance; and he would have given any thing to get out of it; but his father's command was sacred, and for years he had been bound by his father's word. Escape was utterly impossible. The entrance of the clergyman, who seemed more intent on the luncheon than any thing else, did not lessen Guy's feelings of repugnance. He said but little, and sank into a fit of abstraction, from which he was roused by a message that the General would like to see him. He hurried up stairs.

The General smiled faintly, and greeted him with as much warmth as his weak and prostrated condition would allow.

"Guy, my boy," said he, feebly, "I am very glad to see you."

To Guy the General seemed like a doomed man, and the discovery gave him a great shock, for he had scarcely anticipated any thing so bad as this. In spite of this, however, he expressed a hope that the General might yet recover, and be spared many years to them.

"No," said the General, sadly and wearily; "no; my days are numbered. I must die, my boy; but I shall die in peace, if I feel that I do not leave my child uncared for."

Guy, in spite of his dislike and repugnance, felt deeply moved.

"You need have no fear of that, Sir," he went on to say, in solemn, measured tones. "I solemnly promise you that no unhappiness shall ever reach her if I can help it. To the end of my life I will try to requite to her the kindness that you have shown to us. My father feels as I do, and he begged me to assure you, if he is

not able to see you again, as he hopes to do, that the instant your daughter needs his care he will himself take her to Chetwynde Castle, and will watch over her with the same care and affection that you yourself would bestow; and she shall leave his home only for mine."

The General pressed his hand feebly. "God bless you!" he said, in a faint voice.

Suddenly a low sob broke the silence which followed. Turning hastily, Guy saw in the dim twilight of the sick-room what he had not before observed. It was a girl's figure crouching at the foot of the bed, her head buried in the clothes. He looked at her—his heart told him who it was—but he knew not what to say.

The General also had heard that sob. It raised no pity and compassion in him; it was simply some new stimulus to the one idea of his distempered brain.

"What, Zillah!" he said, in surprise. "You here yet? I thought you had gone to get ready."

Still the kneeling figure did not move.

"Zillah," said the General, querulously, and with an excitement in his feeble voice which showed how readily he might lapse into complete delirium—"Zillah, my child, be quick. There is no time to lose. Go and get ready for your wedding. Don't you hear me? Go and dress yourself."

"Oh, papa!" moaned Zillah, in a voice which pierced to the inmost heart of Guy, "will it not do as I am? Do not ask me to put on finery at a time like this." Her voice was one of utter anguish and despair.

"A time like this?" said the General, rousing himself somewhat—"what do you mean, child? Does not the Bible say, Like as a bride adorneth herself—for her husband—and ever shall be —world without end—amen—yes—white satin and pearls, my child—oh yes—white pearls and satin—we are all ready—where are you, my darling?" Another sob was the only reply to this incoherent speech. Guy stood as if petrified. In his journey here he had simply tried to muster up his own resolution, and to fortify his own heart. He had not given one thought to this poor despairing child. Her sorrow, her anguish, her despair, now went to his heart. Yet he knew not what to do. How gladly he would have made his escape from this horrible mockery—for her sake as well as for his own! But for such escape he saw plainly there was no possibility. That delirious mind, in its frenzy, was too intent upon its one purpose to admit of this. He himself also felt a strange and painful sense of guilt. Was not he to a great extent the cause of this, though the unwilling cause? Ah! he thought, remorsefully, can wrong be right? and can any thing justify such a desecration as this both of marriage and of death? At that moment Chetwynde faded away, and to have saved it was as nothing. Willingly would he have given up every thing if he could now have said to this poor child—who thus crouched down, crushed by a woman's sorrow before she had known a woman's years—"Farewell. You are free. I will give you a brother's love and claim nothing in return. I will give back all, and go forth penniless into the battle of life."

But the General again interrupted them, speaking impatiently: "What are you waiting for? Is not Zillah getting ready?"

Guy scarcely knew what he was doing; but, obeying the instincts of his pity, he bent down and whispered to Zillah, "My poor child, I pity you, and sympathize with you more than words can tell. It is an awful thing for you. But can you not rouse yourself? Perhaps it would calm your father. He is getting too excited."

Zillah shrunk away as though he were pollution, and Guy at this resumed his former place in sadness and in desperation, with no other idea than to wait for the end.

"Zillah! Zillah!" cried the General, almost fiercely.

At this Zillah sprang up, and rushed out of the room. She hurried up stairs, and found the ayah in her dressing-room with Hilda. In the next room her white silk was laid out, her wreath and veil beside it.

"Here's my jewel come to be dressed in her wedding-dress," said the ayah, joyously.

"Be quiet!" cried Zillah, passionately. "Don't dare to say any thing like that to me; and you may put all that trash away, for I'm not going to be married at all. I can't do it, and I won't. I hate him! I hate him! I hate him! I hate him!"

These words she hissed out with the venom of a serpent. Her attendants tried remonstrance, but in vain. Hilda pointed out to her the handsome dress, but with no greater success. Vainly they tried to plead, to coax, and to persuade. All this only seemed to strengthen her determination. At last she threw herself upon the floor, like a passionate child, in a paroxysm of rage and grief.

The unwonted self-control which for the last few days she had imposed upon herself now told upon her in the violence of the reaction which had set in. When once she had allowed the barriers to be broken down, all else gave way to the onset of passion; and the presence and remonstrances of the ayah and Hilda only made it worse. She forgot utterly her father's condition; she showed herself now as selfish in her passion as he had shown himself in his delirium. Nothing could be done to stop her. The others, familiar with these outbreaks, retired to the adjoining room and waited.

Meanwhile the others were waiting also in the room below. The doctor was there, and sat by his patient, exerting all his art to soothe him and curb his eagerness. The General refused some medicine which he offered, and declared with passion that he would take nothing whatever till the wedding was over. To have used force would have been fatal; and so the doctor had to humor his patient. The family solicitor was there with the marriage settlements, which had been prepared in great haste. Guy and the clergyman sat apart in thoughtful silence.

Half an hour passed, and Zillah did not appear. On the General's asking for her the clergyman hazarded a remark intended to be pleasant, about ladies on such occasions needing some time to adorn themselves—a little out of place under the circumstances, but it fortunately fell in with the sick man's humor, and satisfied him for the moment.

Three-quarters of an hour passed. "Surely she must be ready now," said the General, who grew more excited and irritable every moment. A messenger was thereupon dispatched for her,

but she found the door bolted, and amidst the outcry and confusion in the room could only distinguish that Miss Pomeroy was not ready. This message she delivered without entering into particulars.

An hour passed, and another messenger went, with the same result. It then became impossible to soothe the General any longer. Guy also grew impatient, for he had to leave by that evening's train; and if the thing had to be it must be done soon. He began to hope that it might be postponed—that Zillah might not come —and then he would have to leave the thing unfinished. But then he thought of his father's command, and the General's desire—of his own promise—of the fact that it must be done—of the danger to the General if it were not done. Between these conflicting feelings—his desire to escape, and his desire to fulfill what he considered his obligations—his brain grew confused, and he sat there impatient for the end—to see what it might turn out to be.

Another quarter of an hour passed. The General's excitement grew worse, and was deepening into frenzy. Dr. Cowell looked more and more anxious, and at last, shrewdly suspecting the cause of the delay, determined himself to go and take it in hand. He accordingly left his patient, and was just crossing the room, when his progress was arrested by the General's springing up with a kind of convulsive start, and jumping out of bed, declaring wildly and incoherently that something must be wrong, and that he himself would go and bring Zillah. The doctor had to turn again to his patient. The effort was a spasmodic one, and the General was soon put back again to bed, where he lay groaning and panting; while the doctor, finding that he could not leave him even for an instant, looked around for some one to send in his place. Who could it be? Neither the lawyer nor the clergyman seemed suitable. There was no one left but Guy, who seemed to the doctor, from his face and manner, to be capable of dealing with any difficulty. So he called Guy to him, and hurriedly whispered to him the state of things.

"If the General has to wait any longer, he will die," said the doctor. "You'll have to go and bring her. You're the only person. You must. Tell her that her father has already had one fit, and that every moment destroys his last chance of life. She must either decide to come at once, or else sacrifice him."

He then rang the bell, and ordered the servant to lead Captain Molyneux to Miss Pomeroy. Guy was thus forced to be an actor where his highest desire was to be passive. There was no alternative. In that moment all his future was involved. He saw it; he knew it; but he did not shrink. Honor bound him to this marriage, hateful as it was. The other actor in the scene detested it as much as he did, but there was no help for it. Could he sit passive and let the General die? The marriage, after all, he thought, had to come off; it was terrible to have it now; but then the last chance of the General's life was dependent upon this marriage. What could he do?

What? A rapid survey of his whole situation decided him. He would perform what he considered his vow. He would do his part toward saving the General's life, though that part was so hard. He was calm, therefore, and self-possessed, as the servant entered and led the way to Zillah's apartments. The servant on receiving the order grinned in spite of the solemnity of the occasion. He had a pretty clear idea of the state of things; he was well accustomed to what was styled, in the servants' hall, "Missy's tantrums;" and he wondered to himself how Guy would ever manage her. He was too good a servant, however, to let his feelings be seen, and so he led the way demurely, and knocking at Zillah's door, announced:

"Captain Molyneux."

The door was at once opened by the ayah. At that instant Zillah sprang to her feet and looked at him in a fury of passion.

"You!" she cried, with indescribable malignancy. "You! You here! How dare you come here? Go down stairs this instant! If it is my money you want, take it all and begone. I will never, never, never, marry you!"

For a moment Guy was overcome. The taunt was certainly horrible. He turned pale, but soon regained his self-possession.

"Miss Pomeroy," said he, quietly, yet earnestly, "this is not the time for a scene. Your father is in the utmost danger. He has waited for an hour and a quarter. He is getting worse every moment. He made one attempt to get out of bed, and come for you himself. The doctor ordered me to come, and that is why I am here."

"I don't believe you!" screamed Zillah. "You are trying to frighten me."

"I have nothing to say," replied Guy, mournfully. "Your father is rapidly getting into a state of frenzy. If it lasts much longer he will die."

Guy's words penetrated to Zillah's inmost soul. A wild fear arose, which in a moment chased away the fury which had possessed her. Her face changed. She struck her hands against her brow, and uttered an exclamation of terror.

"Tell him — tell him — I'm coming. Make haste," she moaned. "I'll be down immediately. Oh, make haste!"

She hurried back, and Guy went down stairs again, where he waited at the bottom with his soul in a strange tumult, and his heart on fire. Why was it that he had been sold for all this — he and that wretched child?

But now Zillah was all changed. Now she was as excited in her haste to go down stairs as she had before been anxious to avoid it. She rushed back to the bedroom where Hilda was, who, though unseen, had heard every thing, and, foreseeing what the end might be, was now getting things ready.

"Be quick, Hilda!" she gasped. "Papa is dying! Oh, be quick — be quick! Let me save him!"

She literally tore off the dress that she had on, and in less than five minutes she was dressed. She would not stop for Hilda to arrange her wreath, and was rushing down stairs without her veil, when the ayah ran after her with it.

"You are leaving your luck, Missy darling," said she.

"Ay — that I am," said Zillah, bitterly.

"But you will put it on, Missy," pleaded the ayah. "Sahib has talked so much about it."

Zillah stopped. The ayah threw it over her, and enveloped her in its soft folds.

"It was your mother's veil, Missy," she added. "Give me a kiss for her sake before you go."

Zillah flung her arms around the old woman's neck.

"Hush, hush!" she said. "Do not make me give way again, or I can never do it."

At the foot of the stairs Guy was waiting, and they entered the room solemnly together — these two victims — each summoning up all that Honor and Duty might supply to assist in what each felt to be a sacrifice of all life and happiness. But to Zillah the sacrifice was worse, the task was harder, and the ordeal more dreadful. For it was her father, not Guy's, who lay there, with a face that already seemed to have the touch of death; it was she who felt to its fullest extent the ghastliness of this hideous mockery.

But the General, whose eyes were turned eagerly toward the door, found in this scene nothing but joy. In his frenzy he regarded them as blessed and happy, and felt this to be the full realization of his highest hopes.

"Ah!" he said, with a long gasp; "here she is at last. Let us begin at once."

So the little group formed itself around the bed, the ayah and Hilda being present in the back-ground.

In a low voice the clergyman began the marriage service. Far more solemn and impressive did it sound now than when heard under circumstances of gayety and splendor; and as the words sank into Guy's soul, he reproached himself more than ever for never having considered the meaning of the act to which he had so thoughtlessly pledged himself.

The General had now grown calm. He lay perfectly motionless, gazing wistfully at his daughter's face. So quiet was he, and so fixed was his gaze, that they thought he had sunk into some abstracted fit; but when the clergyman, with some hesitation, asked the question,

"Who giveth this woman to be married to this man?" the General instantly responded, in a firm voice, "I do." Then reaching forth, he took Zillah's hand, and instead of giving it to the clergyman, he himself placed it within Guy's, and for a moment held both hands in his, while he seemed to be praying for a blessing to rest on their union.

The service proceeded. Solemnly the priest uttered the warning: "Those whom God hath joined together, let no man put asunder." Solemnly, too, he pronounced the benediction — "May ye so live together in this life that in the world to come ye shall have life everlasting."

And so, for better or worse, Guy Molyneux and Zillah Pomeroy rose up — man and wife!

After the marriage ceremony was over the clergyman administered the Holy Communion — all who were present partaking with the General; and solemn indeed was the thought that filled the mind of each, that ere long, perhaps, one of their number might be — not figuratively, but literally — "with angels and archangels, and all the company of heaven."

After this was all over the doctor gave the General a soothing draught. He was quite calm now; he took it without objection; and it had the effect of throwing him soon into a quiet sleep.

The clergyman and the lawyer now departed; and the doctor, motioning to Guy and Zillah to

leave the room, took his place, with an anxious countenance, by the General's bedside. The husband and wife went into the adjoining room, from which they could hear the deep breathing of the sick man.

It was an awkward moment. Guy had to depart in a short time. That sullen stolid girl who now sat before him, black and gloomy as a thun-

der-cloud, was *his wife*. He was going away, perhaps forever. He did not know exactly how to treat her; whether with indifference as a willful child, or compassionate attention as one deeply afflicted. On the whole he felt deeply for her, in spite of his own forebodings of his future; and so he followed the more generous dictates of his heart. Her utter loneliness, and the thought that her father might soon be taken away, touched him deeply; and this feeling was evident in his whole manner as he spoke.

"Zillah," said he, "our regiment sails for India several days sooner than I first expected, and it is necessary for me to leave in a short time. You, of course, are to remain with your father, and I hope that he may soon be restored to you. Let me assure you that this whole scene has been, under the circumstances, most painful, for your sake, for I have felt keenly that I was the innocent cause of great sorrow to you."

He spoke to her calmly, and as a father would to a child, and at the same time reached out his hand to take hers. She snatched it away quickly.

"Captain Molyneux," said she, coldly, "I married you solely to please my father, and because he was not in a state to have his wishes opposed. It was a sacrifice of myself, and a bitter one. As to you, I put no trust in you, and take no interest whatever in your plans. But there is one thing which I wish you to tell me. What did papa mean by saying to the doctor, that if I did not marry you I should lose one-half of my fortune?"

Zillah's manner at once chilled all the warm feelings of pity and generosity which Guy had begun to feel. Her question also was an embarrassing one. He had hoped that the explanation might come later, and from his father. It was an awkward one for him to make. But Zillah was looking at him impatiently.

"Surely," she continued in a stern voice as she noticed his hesitation, "that is a question which I have a right to ask."

"Of course," said Guy, hastily. "I will tell you. It was because more than half your fortune was taken to pay off the debt on Chetwynde Castle."

A deep, angry, crimson flush passed over Zillah's face.

"So that is the reason why I have been sold?" she cried, impetuously. "Well, Sir, your manœuvring has succeeded nobly. Let me congratulate you. You have taken in a guileless old man, and a young girl."

Guy looked at her for a moment in fierce indignation. But with a great effort he subdued it, and answered, as calmly as possible:

"You do not know either my father or myself, or you would be convinced that such language could not apply to either of us. The proposal originally emanated entirely from General Pomeroy."

"Ah?" said Zilla, fiercely. "But you were base enough to take advantage of his generosity and his love for his old friend. Oh!" she cried, bursting into tears, "that is what I feel, that he could sacrifice me, who loved him so, for your sakes. I honestly believed once that it was his anxiety to find me a protector."

Guy's face had grown very pale.

"And so it was," he said, in a voice which was deep and tremulous from his strong effort at self-control. "He trusted my father, and trusted me, and wished to protect you from unprincipled fortune-hunters."

"Fortune-hunters!" cried Zillah, her face flushed, and with accents of indescribable scorn. "Good Heavens! What are you if you are not this very thing? Oh, how I hate you! how I hate you!"

Guy looked at her, and for a moment was on the point of answering her in the same fashion, and pouring out all his scorn and contempt. But again he restrained himself.

"You are excited," he said, coolly. "One of these days you will find out your mistake. You will learn, as you grow older, that the name of Chetwynde can not be coupled with charges like these. In the mean time allow me to advise you not to be quite so free in your language when you are addressing honorable gentlemen; and to suggest that your father, who loved you better than any one in the world, may possibly have had *some* cause for the confidence which he felt in us."

There was a coolness in Guy's tone which showed that he did not think it worth while to be angry with her, or to resent her insults. But Zillah did not notice this. She went on as before:

"There is one thing which I will never forgive."

"Indeed? Well, your forgiveness is so very important that I should like to know what it is that prevents me from gaining it."

"The way in which I have been deceived!" burst forth Zillah, fiercely. "If papa had wished to give you half of his money, or all of it, I should not have cared a bit. I do not care for that at all. But why did nobody tell me the truth? Why was I told that it was out of regard to *me* that this horror, this frightful mockery of marriage, was forced upon me, while my heart was breaking with anxiety about my father; when to you I was only a necessary evil, without which you could not hope to get my father's money; and the only good I can possibly have is, the future privilege of living in a place whose very name I loathe, with the man who has cheated me, and whom all my life I shall hate and abhor? Now go! and I pray God I may never see you again."

With these words, and without waiting for a reply, she left the room, leaving Guy in a state of mind by no means enviable.

He stood staring after her. "And that thing is mine for life!" he thought; "that she-devil! utterly destitute of sense and of reason! Oh, Chetwynde, Chetwynde! you have cost me dear. See you again, my fiend of a wife! I hope not. No, never while I live. Some of these days I'll give you back your sixty thousand with interest. And you, why you may go to the devil forever!"

Half an hour afterward Guy was seated in the dog-cart bowling to the station as fast as two thorough-breds could take him; every moment congratulating himself on the increasing distance which was separating him from his bride of an hour.

The doctor watched all that night. On the following morning the General was senseless. On the next day he died.

CHAPTER XI.

A NEW HOME.

DEARLY had Zillah paid for that frenzy of her dying father; and the consciousness that her whole life was now made over irrevocably to another, brought to her a pang so acute that it counterbalanced the grief which she felt for her father's death. Fierce anger and bitter indignation struggled with the sorrow of bereavement, and sometimes, in her blind rage, she even went so far as to reproach her father's memory. On all who had taken part in that fateful ceremony she looked with vengeful feelings. She thought, and there was reason in the thought, that they might have satisfied his mind without binding her. They could have humored his delirium without forfeiting her liberty. They could have had a mock priest, who might have read a service which would have had no authority, and imposed vows which would not be binding. On Guy she looked with the deepest scorn, for she believed that he was the chief offender, and that if he had been a man of honor he might have found many ways to avoid this thing. Possibly Guy as he drove off was thinking the same, and cursing his dull wit for not doing something to delay the ceremony or make it void. But to both it was now too late.

The General's death took place too soon for Zillah. Had he lived she might have been spared long sorrows. Had it not been for this, and his frantic haste in forcing on a marriage, her early betrothal might have had different results. Guy would have gone to India. He would have remained there for years, and then have come home. On his return he might possibly have won her love, and then they could have settled down harmoniously in the usual fashion. But now she found herself thrust upon him, and the very thought of him was a horror. Never could the remembrance of that hideous mockery at the bedside of one so dear, who was passing away forever, leave her mind. All the solemnities of death had been outraged, and all her memories of the dying hours of her best friend were forever associated with bitterness and shame.

For some time after her father's death she gave herself up to the motions of her wild and ungovernable temper. Alternations of savage fury and mute despair succeeded to one another. To one like her there was no relief from either mood; and, in addition to this, there was the prospect of the arrival of Lord Chetwynde. The thought of this filled her with such a passion of anger that she began to meditate flight. She mentioned this to Hilda, with the idea that of course Hilda would go with her.

Hilda listened in her usual quiet way, and with a great appearance of sympathy. She assented to it, and quite appreciated Zillah's position. But she suggested that it might be difficult to carry out such a plan without money.

"Money!" said Zillah, in astonishment. "Why, have I not plenty of money? All is mine now surely."

"Very likely," said Hilda, coolly; "but how do you propose to get it? You know the lawyer has all the papers, and every thing else under lock and key till Lord Chetwynde comes, and the will is read; besides, dear," she added with a soft smile, "you forget that a married woman can not possess property. Our charming English law gives her no rights. All that you nominally possess in reality belongs to your husband."

At this hated word "husband," Zillah's eyes flashed. She clenched her hands, and ground her teeth in rage.

"Be quiet!" she cried, in a voice which was scarce audible from passion. "Can you not let me forget my shame and disgrace for one moment? Why must you thrust it in my face?"

Hilda's little suggestion thus brought full before Zillah's mind one galling yet undeniable truth, which showed her an insurmountable obstacle in the way of her plan. To one utterly unaccustomed to control of any kind, the thought added fresh rage, and she now sought refuge in thinking how she could best encounter her new enemy, Lord Chetwynde, and what she might say to show how she scorned him and his son. She succeeded in arranging a very promising plan of action, and made up many very bitter and insulting speeches, out of which she selected one which seemed to be the most cutting, galling, and insulting which she could think of. It was very nearly the same language which she had used to Guy, and the same taunts were repeated in a somewhat more pointed manner.

At length Lord Chetwynde arrived, and Zillah, after refusing to see him for two days, went down. She entered the drawing-room, her heart on fire, and her brain seething with bitter words, and looked up to see her enemy. That enemy, however, was an old man whose sight was too dim to see the malignant glance of her dark eyes, and the fierce passion of her face. Knowing that she was coming, he was awaiting her, and Zillah on looking up saw him. That first sight at once quelled her fury. She saw a noble and refined face, whereon there was an expression of tenderest sympathy. Before she could recover from the shock which the sight of such a face had given to her passion he had advanced rapidly toward her, took her in his arms, and kissed her tenderly.

"My poor child," he said, in a voice of indescribable sweetness—"my poor orphan child, I can not tell how I feel for you; but you belong to me now. I will try to be another father."

The tones of his voice were so full of affection that Zillah, who was always sensitive to the power of love and kindness, was instantly softened and subdued. Before the touch of that kiss of love and those words of tenderness every emotion of anger fled away; her passion subsided; she forgot all her vengeance, and, taking his hand in both of hers, she burst into tears.

The Earl gently led her to a seat. In a low voice full of the same tender affection he began to talk of her father, of their friendship in the long-vanished youth, of her father's noble nature, and self-sacrificing character; till his fond eulogies of his dead friend awakened in Zillah, even amidst her grief for the dead, a thousand reminiscences of his character when alive, and she began to feel that one who so knew and loved her father must himself have been most worthy to be her father's friend.

It was thus that her first interview with the Earl dispelled her vindictive passion. At once she began to look upon him as the one who was best adapted to fill her father's place, if that place could ever be filled. The more she saw of him, the more her new-born affection for him strengthened, and during the week which he spent at Pomeroy Court she had become so greatly changed that she looked back to her old feelings of hate with mournful wonder.

In due time the General's will was read. It was very simple: Thirty thousand pounds were left to Zillah. To Hilda three thousand pounds were left as a tribute of affection to one who had been to him, as he said, "like a daughter." Hilda he recommended most earnestly to the care and affection of Lord Chetwynde, and desired that she and Zillah should never be separated unless they themselves desired it. To that last request of his dying friend Lord Chetwynde proved faithful. He addressed Hilda with kindness and affection, expressed sympathy with her in the loss of her benefactor, and promised to do all in his power to make good the loss which she had suffered in his death. She and Zillah, he told her, might live as sisters in Chetwynde Castle. Perhaps the time might come when their grief would be alleviated, and then they would both learn to look upon him with something of that affection which they had felt for General Pomeroy.

When Hilda and Zillah went with the Earl to Chetwynde Castle there was one other who was invited there, and who afterward followed. This was Gualtier. Hilda had recommended him; and as the Earl was very anxious that Zillah should not grow up to womanhood without further education, he caught at the idea which Hilda had thrown out. So before leaving he sought out Gualtier, and proposed that he should continue his instructions at Chetwynde.

"You can live very well in the village," said the Earl. "There are families there with whom you can lodge comfortably. Mrs. Molyneux is acquainted with you and your style of teaching, and therefore I would prefer you to any other."

Gualtier bowed so low that the flush of pleasure which came over his sallow face, and his smile of ill-concealed triumph, could not be seen.

"You are too kind, my lord," he said, obsequiously. "I have always done my best in my instructions, and will humbly endeavor to do so in the future."

So Gualtier followed them, and arrived at Chetwynde a short time after them, bearing with him his power, or perhaps his fate, to influence Zillah's fortunes and future.

Chetwynde Castle had experienced some changes during these years. The old butler had been gathered to his fathers, but Mrs. Hart still remained. The Castle itself and the grounds had changed wonderfully for the better. It had lost that air of neglect, decay, and ruin which had formerly been its chief characteristic. It was no longer poverty-stricken. It arose, with its antique towers and venerable ivy-grown walls, exhibiting in its outline all that age possesses of dignity, without any of the meanness of neglect. It seemed like one of the noblest remains which England possessed of the monuments of feudal times. The first sight of it elicited a cry of admiration from Zillah; and she found not the least of its attractions in the figure of the old Earl—himself a monument of the past—whose figure, as he stood on the steps to welcome them, formed a fore-ground which an artist would have loved to portray.

Around the Castle all had changed. What had once been little better than a wilderness was now a wide and well-kept park. The rose pleasaunce had been restored to its pristine glory. The lawns were smooth-shaven and glowing in their rich emerald-green. The lakes and ponds were no longer overgrown with dank rushes; but had been reclaimed from being little better than marshes into bright expanses of clear water, where fish swam and swans loved to sport. Long avenues and cool, shadowy walks wound far away through the groves; and the stately oaks and elms around the Castle had lost that ghostly and gloomy air which had once been spread about them.

Within the Castle every thing had undergone a corresponding change. There was no attempt at modern splendor, no effort to rival the luxuries of the wealthier lords of England. The Earl had been content with arresting the progress of decay, and adding to the restoration of the interior some general air of modern comfort. Within, the scene corresponded finely to that which lay without: and the medieval character of the interior made it attractive to Zillah's peculiar taste.

The white-faced, mysterious-looking housekeeper, as she looked sadly and wistfully at the new-comers, and asked in a tremulous voice which was Guy's wife, formed for Zillah a striking incident in the arrival. To her Zillah at once took a strong liking, and Mrs. Hart seemed to form one equally strong for her. From the very first her affection for Zillah was very manifest, and as the days passed it increased. She seemed to cling to the young girl as though her loving nature needed something on which to expend its love; as though there was a maternal instinct which craved to be satisfied, and sought such satisfaction in her. Zillah returned her tender affection with a fondness which would have satisfied the most exigeant nature. She herself had never known the sweetness of a mother's care, and it seemed as though she had suddenly found out all this. The discovery was delightful to so affectionate a nature as hers; and her enthusiastic disposition made her devotion to Mrs. Hart more marked. She often wondered to herself why Mrs. Hart had "taken such a fancy" to her. And so did the other members of the household. Perhaps it was because she was the wife of Guy, who was so dear to the heart of his affectionate old nurse. Perhaps it was something in Zillah herself which attracted Mrs. Hart, and made her seek in her one who might fill Guy's place.

Time passed away, and Gualtier arrived, in accordance with the Earl's request. Zillah had supposed that she was now free forever from all teachers and lessons, and it was with some dismay that she heard of Gualtier's arrival. She said nothing, however, but prepared to go through the form of taking lessons in music and drawing as before. She had begun already to have a certain instinct of obedience toward the Earl, and felt desirous to gratify his wishes. But whatever changes of feeling she had experienced toward her new guardian, she showed no change of manner toward Gualtier. To her, application to any thing was a thing as irksome as ever. Perhaps her fitful efforts to advance were more frequent; but after each effort she used invariably to relapse into idleness and tedium.

Her manner troubled Gualtier as little as ever. He let her have her own way quite in the old style. Hilda, as before, was always present at these instructions; and after the hour devoted to Zillah had expired she had lessons of her own. But Gualtier remarked that, for some reason or other, a great change had come over her. Her attitude toward him had relapsed into one of reti-

"THE WHITE-FACED, MYSTERIOUS-LOOKING HOUSEKEEPER ASKED IN A TREMULOUS VOICE WHICH WAS GUY'S WIFE."

cence and reserve. The approaches to confidence and familiarity which she had formerly made seemed now to be completely forgotten by her. The stealthy conversations in which they used to indulge were not renewed. Her manner was such that he did not venture to enter upon his former footing. True. Zillah was always in the room now, and did not leave so often as she used to do, but still there were times when they were alone; yet on these occasions Hilda showed no desire to return to that intimacy which they had once known in their private interviews.

This new state of things Gualtier bore meekly and patiently. He was either too respectful or too cunning to make any advances himself. Perhaps he had a deep conviction that Hilda's changed manner was but temporary, and that the purpose which she had once revealed might still be cherished in her heart. True, the General's death had changed the aspect of affairs; but he had his reasons for believing that it could not altogether destroy her plans. He had a deep conviction that the time would come one day when he would know what was on her mind. He was patient. He could wait. So the time went on.

As the time passed the life at Chetwynde Castle became more and more grateful, to Zillah. Naturally affectionate, her heart had softened under its new trials and experiences, and there was full chance for the growth of those kindly and generous emotions which, after all, were most natural and congenial to her. In addition to her own affection for the Earl and for Mrs. Hart, she found a constraint on her here which she had not known while living the life of a spoiled and indulged child in her own former home. The sorrow through which she had passed had made her less childish. The Earl began in reality to seem to her like a second father, one whom she could both revere and love.

Very soon after her first acquaintance with him she found out that by no possibility could he be a party to any thing dishonorable. Finding thus that her first suspicions were utterly unfounded, she began to think it possible that her marriage, though odious in itself, had been planned with a good intent. To think Lord Chetwynde mercenary was impossible. His character was so high-toned, and even so punctilious in its regard to nice points of honor, that he was not even worldly wise. With the mode in which her marriage had been finally carried out he had clearly nothing whatever to do. Of all her suspicions, her anger against an innocent and noble-minded man, and her treatment of him on his first visit to Pomeroy Court, she now felt thoroughly ashamed. She longed to tell him all about it—to explain why it was that she had felt so and done so—and waited for some favorable opportunity for making her confession.

At length an opportunity occurred. One day the Earl was speaking of her father, and he told Zillah about his return to England, and his visit to Chetwynde Castle; and finally told how the whole arrangement had been made between them by which she had become Guy's wife. He spoke with such deep affection about General Pomeroy, and so feelingly of his intense love for his daughter, that at last Zillah began to understand perfectly the motives of the actors in this matter. She saw that in the whole affair, from first to last, there was nothing but the fondest thought of herself, and that the very money itself, which she used to think had "purchased her," was in some sort an investment for her own benefit in the future. As the whole truth flashed suddenly into Zillah's mind she saw now most clearly not only how deeply she had wronged Lord Chetwynde, but also—and now for the first time—how foully she had insulted Guy by her malignant accusations. To a generous nature like hers the shock of this discovery was intensely painful. Tears started to her eyes, she twined her arms around Lord Chetwynde's neck, and told him the whole story, not excepting a single word of all that she had said to Guy.

"And I told him," she concluded, "all this— I said that he was a mean fortune-hunter; and

that you had cheated papa out of his money; and that I hated him—and oh! will you ever forgive me?"

This was altogether a new and unexpected disclosure to the Earl, and he listened to Zillah in unfeigned astonishment. Guy had told him nothing beyond the fact communicated in a letter—that "whatever his future wife might be remarkable for, he did not think that amiability was her forte." But all this revelation, unexpected though it was, excited no feeling of resentment in his mind.

"My child," said he, tenderly, though somewhat sadly, "you certainly behaved very ill. Of course you could not know us; but surely you might have trusted your father's love and wisdom. But, after all, there were a good many excuses for you, my poor little girl—so I pity you very much indeed—it was a terrible ordeal for one so young. I can understand more than you have cared to tell me."

"Ah, how kind, how good you are!" said Zillah, who had anticipated some reproaches. "But I'll never forgive myself for doing you such injustice."

"Oh, as to that," said Lord Chetwynde; "if you feel that you have done any injustice, there is one way that I can tell you of by which you can make full reparation. Will you try to make it, my little girl?"

"What do you want me to do?" asked Zillah, hesitatingly, not wishing to compromise herself. The first thought which she had was that he was going to ask her to apologize to Guy—a thing which she would by no means care about doing, even in her most penitent mood. Lord Chetwynde was one thing; but Guy was quite another. The former she loved dearly; but toward the latter she still felt resentment—a feeling which was perhaps strengthened and sustained by the fact that every one at Chetwynde looked upon her as a being who had been placed upon the summit of human happiness by the mere fact of being Guy's wife. To her it was intolerable to be valued merely for his sake. Human nature is apt to resent in any case having its blessings perpetually thrust in its face; but in this case what they called a blessing, to her seemed the blackest horror of her life; and Zillah's resentment was all the stronger; while all this resentment she naturally vented on the head of the one who had become her husband. She could manage to tolerate his praises when sounded by the Earl, but hardly so with the others. Mrs. Hart was most trying to her patience in this respect; and it needed all Zillah's love for her to sustain her while listening to the old nurse as she grew eloquent on her favorite theme. Zillah felt like the Athenian who was bored to death by the perpetual praise of Aristides. If she had no other complaint against him, this might of itself have been enough.

The fear, however, which was in her mind as to the reparation which was expected of her was dispelled by Lord Chetwynde's answer:

"I want you, my child," said he, "to try and improve yourself—to get on as fast as you can with your masters, so that when the time comes for you to take your proper place in society you may be equal to ladies of your own rank in education and accomplishments. I want to be proud of my daughter when I show her to the world."

"And so you shall," said Zillah, twining her arms again about his neck and kissing him fondly. "I promise you that from this time forward I will try to study."

He kissed her lovingly. "I am sure," said he, "that you will keep your word, my child; and now," he added, "one thing more: How much longer do you intend to keep up this 'Lord Chetwynde?' I must be called by another name by you—not the name by which you called your own dear father—that is too sacred to be given to any other. But have I not some claim to be called 'Father,' dear? Or does not my little Zillah care enough for me for that?"

At this the warm-hearted girl flung her arms around him once more and kissed him, and burst into tears.

"Dear father!" she murmured.

And from that moment perfect confidence and love existed between these two.

CHAPTER XII

CORRESPONDENCE.

TIME sped rapidly and uneventfully by. Guy's letters from India formed almost the only break in the monotony of the household. Zillah soon found herself, against her will, sharing in the general eagerness respecting these letters. It would have been a very strong mind indeed, or a very obdurate heart, which could have remained unmoved at Lord Chetwynde's delight when he received his boy's letters. Their advent was also the Hegira from which every thing in the family dated. Apart, however, from the halo which surrounded these letters, they were interesting in themselves. Guy wrote easily and well.

His letters to his father were half familiar, half filial; a mixture of love and good-fellowship, showing a sort of union, so to speak, of the son with the younger brother. They were full of humor also, and made up of descriptions of life in the East, with all its varied wonders. Besides this, Guy happened to be stationed at the very place where General Pomeroy had been Resident for so many years; and he himself had command of one of the hill stations where Zillah herself had once been sent to pass the summer. These places of which Guy's letters treated possessed for her a peculiar interest, surrounded as they were by some of the pleasantest associations of her life; and thus, from very many causes, it happened that she gradually came to take an interest in these letters which increased rather than diminished.

In one of these there had once come a note inclosed to Zillah, condoling with her on her father's death. It was manly and sympathetic, and not at all stiff. Zillah had received it when her bitter feelings were in the ascendant, and did not think of answering it until Hilda urged on her the necessity of doing so. It is just possible that if Hilda had made use of different arguments she might have persuaded Zillah to send some sort of an answer, if only to please the Earl. The arguments, however, which she did use happened to be singularly ill chosen. The "husband" loomed largely in them, and there were very many direct allusions to marital authority. As these were Zillah's sorest points, such references only served to excite fresh repugnance, and strengthen Zillah's determination not to write. Hilda, however, persisted in her efforts; and the result was that finally, at the end of one long and rather stormy discussion, Zillah passionately threw the letter at her, saying:

"If you are so anxious to have it answered, do it yourself. It is a world of pities he is not your husband instead of mine, you seem so wonderfully anxious about him."

"It is unkind of you to say that," replied Hilda, in a meek voice, "when you know so well that my sympathy and anxiety are all for you, and you alone. You argue with me as though I had some interest in it; but what possible interest can it be to me?"

"Oh, well, dearest Hilda," said Zillah, instantly appeased; "I'm always pettish; but you won't mind, will you?· You never mind my ways."

"I've a great mind to take you at your word," said Hilda, after a thoughtful pause, "and write it for you. It ought to be answered, and you won't; so why should I not do the part of a friend, and answer it for you?"

Zillah started, and seemed just a little nettled.

"Oh, I don't care," she said, with assumed indifference. "If you choose to take the trouble, why I am sure I ought to be under obligations to you. At any rate, I shall be glad to get rid of it so long as I have nothing to do with it. I suppose it must be done."

Hilda made some protestations of her devotion to Zillah, and some further conversation followed, all of which resulted in this—that *Hilda wrote the letter in Zillah's name*, and signed that name *in her own hand*, and under Zillah's own eye, and with Zillah's half-reluctant, half-pettish concurrence.

Out of this beginning there flowed results of an important character, which were soon perceived even by Zillah, though she was forced to keep her feelings to herself. Occasional notes came afterward from time to time for Zillah, and were answered in the same way by Hilda. All this Zillah endured quietly, but with real repugnance, which increased until the change took place in her feelings which has been mentioned at the beginning of this chapter, when she at length determined to put an end to such an anomalous state of things and assert herself. It was difficult to do so. She loved Hilda dearly, and placed perfect confidence in her. She was too guileless to dream of any sinister motive in her friend; and the only difficulty of which she was conscious was the fear that Hilda might suspect the change in her feelings toward Guy. The very idea of Hilda's finding this out alarmed her sensitive pride, and made her defer for a long time her intent. At length, however, she felt unable to do so any longer, and determined to run the risk of disclosing the state of her feelings.

So one day, after the receipt of a note to herself, a slight degree more friendly than usual, she hinted to Hilda rather shyly that she would like to answer it herself.

"Oh, I am so glad, darling!" cried Hilda, enthusiastically. "It will be so much nicer for you to do it yourself. It will relieve me from embarrassment, for, after all, my position was embarrassing—writing for you always—and then, you know, you will write far better letters than I can."

"It will be a Heaven-born gift, then," returned Zillah, laughing, "as I never wrote a letter in my life."

"That is nothing," said Hilda. "I write for another; but you will be writing for yourself, and that makes all the difference in the world, you know."

"Well, perhaps so. You see, Hilda, I have taken a fancy to try my hand at it," said Zillah, laughingly, full of delight at the ease with which she had gained her desire. "You see," she went on, with unusual sprightliness of manner, "I got hold of a 'Complete Letter-Writer' this morning; and the beauty, elegance, and even eloquence of those amazing compositions have so excited me that I want to emulate them. Now it happens that Guy is the only correspondent that I have, and so he must be my first victim."

So saying, Zillah laughingly opened her desk, while Hilda's dark eyes regarded her with sharp and eager watchfulness.

"You must not make it too eloquent, dear," said she. "Remember the very commonplace epistles that you have been giving forth in your name."

"Don't be alarmed," said Zillah. "If it is not exactly like a child's first composition we shall all have great cause for thankfulness."

So saying, she took out a sheet of paper.

"Here," said she, "is an opportunity of using some of this elaborately monogrammed paper which poor darling papa got for me, because I wanted to see how they could work my unpromising 'Z' into a respectable cipher. They have made it utterly illegible, and I believe that is the great point to be attained."

Thus rattling on, she dated her letter, and began to write. She wrote as far as "MY DEAR GUY."—Then she stopped, and read it aloud.—"This is really getting most exciting," she said, in high good-humor. "Now what comes next? To find a beginning—there's the rub. I must turn to my 'Complete Letter-Writer.' Let me see. 'Letter from a Son at School'—that won't do. 'From a Lady to a Lover returning a Miniature'—nor that. 'From a Suitor requesting to be allowed to pay his attentions to a Lady'—worse and worse. 'From a Father declining the application of a Suitor for his Daughter's hand'—absurd! Oh, here we are—'From a Wife to a Husband who is absent on urgent business.' Oh, listen, Hilda!" and Zillah read:

"'BELOVED AND HONORED HUSBAND,—The grief which wrung my heart at your departure has been mitigated by the delight which I experienced at the receipt of your most welcome letters.' Isn't that delightful? Unluckily his departure didn't wring my heart at all, and, worse still, I have no grief at his absence to be mitigated by his letters. Alas! I'm afraid mine must be an exceptional case, for even my 'Complete Letter-Writer,' my vade-mecum, which goes into such charming details, can not help me. After all I suppose I must use my own poor brains."

After all this nonsense Zillah suddenly grew serious. Hilda seemed to understand the cause of her extravagant volatility, and watched her closely. Zillah began to write, and went on rapidly, without a moment's hesitation; without any signs whatever of that childish inexperience at which she had hinted. Her pen flew over the paper with a speed which seemed to show that she had plenty to say, and knew perfectly well how to say it. So she went on until she had filled two pages, and was proceeding to the third. Then an exclamation from Hilda caused her to look up.

"My dear Zillah," cried Hilda, who was sitting in a chair a little behind her, "what in the world are you thinking of? From this distance I can distinguish your somewhat peculiar caligraphy—with its bold down strokes and decided 'character,' that people talk about. Now, as you know that I write a little, cramped, German hand, you will have to imitate my humble handwriting, or else I'm afraid Captain Molyneux will be thoroughly puzzled—unless, indeed, you tell him that you have been employing an amanuensis. That will require a good deal of explanation, but—" she added, after a thoughtful pause, "I dare say it will be the best in the end."

At these words Zillah started, dropped her pen, and sat looking at Hilda perfectly aghast.

"I never thought of that," she murmured, and sat with an expression of the deepest dejection. At length a long sigh escaped her.

"You are right, Hilda," she said. "Of course it will need explanation; but how is it possible to do that in a letter? It can't be done. At least I can't do it. What shall I do?"

She was silent, and sat for a long time, looking deeply vexed and disappointed.

"Of course," she said at last, "he will have to know all when he comes back; but that is nothing. How utterly stupid it was in me not to think of the difference in our writing! And now I suppose I must give up my idea of writing a letter. It is really hard—I have not a single correspondent."

Her deep disappointment, her vexation, and her feeble attempt to conceal her emotions, were not lost upon the watchful Hilda. But the latter showed no signs that she had noticed any thing.

"Oh, don't give it up!" she answered, with apparent eagerness. "I dare say you can copy my hand accurately enough to avoid detection. Here is a note I wrote yesterday. See if you can't imitate that, and make your writing as like mine as possible."

So saying she drew a note from her pocket and handed it to Zillah. The other took it eagerly, and began to try to imitate it, but a few strokes showed her the utter impossibility of such an undertaking. She threw down the pen, and leaning her head upon her hand, sat looking upon the floor in deeper dejection than ever.

"I can't copy such horrid cramped letters," she said, pettishly; "why should you write such a hand? Besides, I feel as if I were really forging, or doing something dreadful. I suppose," she added, with unconcealed bitterness of tone, "we shall have to go on as we began, and you must be *Zillah Molyneux* for some time longer."

Hilda laughed.

"Talk of forging!" she said. "What is forging if that is not? But really, Zillah, darling, you seem to me to show more feeling about this than I ever supposed you could possibly be capable of. Are you aware that your tone is somewhat bitter, and that if I were sensitive I might feel hurt? Do you mean by what you said to lay any blame to me?"

She spoke so sadly and reproachfully that Zillah's heart smote her. At once her disappointment and vexation vanished at the thought that she had spoken unkindly to her friend.

"Hilda!" she cried, "you can not think that I am capable of such ingratitude. You have most generously given me your services all this time. You have been right, from the very first, and I have been wrong. You have taken a world of trouble to obviate the difficulties which my own obstinacy and temper have caused. If any trouble could possibly arise, I only could be to blame. But, after all, none can arise. I'm sure Captain Molyneux will very readily believe that I disliked him too much when he first went away to dream of writing to him. He certainly had every reason for thinking so."

"Shall you tell him that?" said Hilda, mildly, without referring to Zillah's apologies.

"Certainly I shall," said Zillah, "if the opportunity ever arises. The simple truth is always the easiest and the best. I think he is already as well aware as he can be of that fact; and, after all, why should I, or how could I, have liked him under the circumstances? I knew nothing of him whatever; and every thing—yes, every thing, was against him."

"You know no more of him now," said Hilda; "and yet, though you are very reticent on the subject, I have a shrewd suspicion, my darling, that you do not dislike him."

As she spoke she looked earnestly at Zillah as if to read her inmost soul.

Zillah was conscious of that sharp, close scrutiny, and blushed crimson, as this question which

thus concerned her most sacred feelings was brought home to her so suddenly. But she answered, as lightly as she could:

"How can you say that, or even hint at it? How absurd you are, Hilda! I know no more of him now than I knew before. Of course I hear very much about him at Chetwynde, but what of that? He certainly pervades the whole atmosphere of the house. The one idea of Lord Chetwynde is Guy; and as for Mrs. Hart, I think if he wished to use her for a target she would be delighted. Death at such hands would be bliss to her. She treasures up every word he has ever spoken, from his earliest infancy to the present day."

"And I suppose that is enough to account for the charm which you seem to find in her society," rejoined Hilda. "It has rather puzzled me, I confess. For my own part I have never been able to break through the reserve which she chooses to throw around her. I can not get beyond the barest civilities with her, though I'm sure I've tried to win her good-will more than I ever tried before, which is rather strange, for, after all, there is no reason whatever why I should try any thing of the kind. She seems to have a very odd kind of feeling toward me. She looks at me sometimes so strangely that she positively gives me an uncomfortable feeling. She seems frightened to death if my dress brushes against hers. She shrinks away. I believe she is not sane. In fact, I'm sure of it."

"Poor old Mrs. Hart!" said Zillah. "I suppose she does seem a little odd to you; but I know her well, and I assure you she is as far removed from insanity as I am. Still she is undoubtedly queer. Do you know, Hilda, she seems to me to have had some terrible sorrow which has crushed all her spirit and almost her very life. I have no idea whatever of her past life. She is very reticent. She never even so much as hints at it."

"I dare say she has very good reasons," interrupted Hilda.

"Don't talk that way about her, dear Hilda. You are too ill-natured, and I can't bear to have ill-natured things said about the dear old thing. You don't know her as I do, or you would never talk so."

"Oh, Zillah—really—you feel my little pleasantries too much. It was only a thoughtless remark."

"She seems to me," said Zillah, musingly, after a thoughtful silence, "to be a very—very mysterious person. Though I love her dearly, I see that there is some mystery about her. Whatever her history may be she is evidently far above her present position, for when she does allow herself to talk she has the manner and accent of a refined lady. Yes, there is a deep mystery about her, which is utterly beyond my comprehension. I remember once when she had been talking for a long time about Guy and his wonderful qualities, I suddenly happened to ask her some trivial question about her life before she came to Chetwynde; but she looked at me so wild and frightened, that she really startled me. I was so terrified, that I instantly changed the conversation, and rattled on so as to give her time to recover herself, and prevent her from discovering my feelings."

"Why, how very romantic!" said Hilda, with

a smile. "You seem, from such circumstances, to have brought yourself to consider our very prosaic housekeeper as almost a princess in disguise. I, for my part, look upon her as a very common person, so weak-minded, to say the least, as to be almost half-witted. As to her accent, that is nothing. I dare say she has seen better days. I have heard more than once of ladies in destitute or reduced circumstances who have been obliged to take to housekeeping. After all, it is not bad. I'm sure it must be far better than being a governess."

"Well, if I am romantic, you are certainly prosaic enough. At all events I love Mrs. Hart dearly. But come, Hilda, if you are going to write you must do so at once, for the letters are to be posted this afternoon."

Hilda instantly went to the desk and began her task. Zillah, however, went away. Her chagrin and disappointment were so great that she could not stay, and she even refused afterward to look at the note which Hilda showed her. In fact, after that she would never look at them at all.

Some time after this Zillah and Mrs. Hart were together on one of those frequent occasions which they made use of for confidential interviews. Somehow Zillah had turned the conversation from Guy in person to the subject of her correspondence, and gradually told all to Mrs. Hart. At this she looked deeply shocked and grieved.

"That girl," she said, "has some secret motive."

She spoke with a bitterness which Zillah had never before noticed in her.

"Secret motive!" she repeated, in wonder; "what in the world do you mean?"

"She is bad and deceitful," said Mrs. Hart, with energy; "you are trusting your life and honor in the hands of a false friend."

Zillah started back and looked at Mrs. Hart in utter wonder.

"I know," said she at last, "that you don't like Hilda, but I feel hurt when you use such language about her. She is my oldest and dearest friend. She is my sister virtually. I have known her all my life, and know her to her heart's core. She is incapable of any dishonorable action, and she loves me like herself."

All Zillah's enthusiastic generosity was aroused in defending against Mrs. Hart's charge a friend whom she so dearly loved.

Mrs. Hart sadly shook her head.

"My dear child," said she, "you know I would not hurt your feelings for the world. I am sorry. I will say nothing more about her, since you love her. But don't you feel that you are in a very false position?"

"But what can I do? There is the difficulty about the handwriting. And then it has gone on so long."

"Write to him at all hazards," said Mrs. Hart, "and tell him every thing."

Zillah shook her head.

"Well, then—will you let me?"

"How can I? No; it must be done by myself—if it ever is done; and as to writing it myself—I can not."

Such a thought was indeed abhorrent. After all it seemed to her in itself nothing. She employed an amanuensis to compose those formal notes which went in her name. And what fault was there? To Mrs. Hart, whose whole life was bound up in Guy, it was impossible to look at this matter except as to how it affected him. But Zillah had other feelings—other memories. The very proposal to write a "confession" fired her heart with stern indignation. At once all her resentment was roused. Memory brought back again in vivid colors that hideous mockery of a marriage over the death-bed of her father, with reference to which, in spite of her changed feelings, she had never ceased to think that it might have been avoided, and ought to have been. Could she stoop to confess to this man any thing whatever? Impossible!

Mrs. Hart did not know Zillah's thoughts. She supposed she was trying to find a way to extricate herself from her difficulty. So she made one further suggestion.

"Why not tell all to Lord Chetwynde? Surely you can do that easily enough. He will understand all, and explain all."

"I can not," said Zillah, coldly. "It would be doubting my friend—the loving friend who is to me the same as a sister—who is the only companion I have ever had. She is the one that I love dearest on earth, and to do any thing apart from her is impossible. You do not know her—I do—and I love her. For her I would give up every other friend."

At this Mrs. Hart looked sadly away, and then the matter of the letters ended. It was never again brought up.

CHAPTER XIII.

POMEROY COURT REVISITED.

OVER a year had passed away since Zillah had come to live at Chetwynde Castle, and she had come at length to find her new home almost as dear to her as the old one. Still that old home was far from being forgotten. At first she never mentioned it; but at length, as the year approached its close, there came over her a great longing to revisit the old place, so dear to her heart and so well remembered. She hinted to Lord Chetwynde what her desires were, and the Earl showed unfeigned delight at finding that Zillah's grief had become so far mitigated as to allow her to think of such a thing. So he urged her by all means to go.

"But of course you can't go just yet," said he. "You must wait till May, when the place will be at its best. Just now, at the end of March, it will be too cold and damp."

"And you will go with me—will you not?" pleaded Zillah.

"If I can, my child; but you know very well that I am not able to stand the fatigue of traveling."

"Oh, but you must make an effort and try to stand it at this time. I can not bear to go away and leave you behind."

Lord Chetwynde looked affectionately down at the face which was upturned so lovingly toward his, and promised to go if he could. So the weeks passed away; but when May came he had a severe attack of gout, and though Zillah waited through all the month, until the severity of the disease had relaxed, yet the Earl did not

D

find himself able to undertake such a journey. Zillah was therefore compelled either to give up the visit or else to go without him. She decided to do the latter. Roberts accompanied her, and her maid Mathilde. Hilda too, of course, went with her, for to her it was as great a pleasure as to Zillah to visit the old place, and Zillah would not have dreamed of going any where without her.

Pomeroy Court looked very much as it had looked while Zillah was living there. It had been well and even scrupulously cared for. The grounds around showed marks of the closest attention. Inside, the old housekeeper, who had remained after the General's death, with some servants, had preserved every thing in perfect order, and in quite the same state as when the General was living. This perfect preservation of the past struck Zillah most painfully. As she entered, the intermediate period of her life at Chetwynde seemed to fade away. It was to her as though she were still living in her old home. She half expected to see the form of her father in the hall. The consciousness of her true position was violently forced upon her. With the sharpness of the impression which was made upon her by the unchanged appearance of the old home, there came another none less sharp. If Pomeroy Court brought back to her the recollection of the happy days once spent there, but now gone forever, it also brought to her mind the full consciousness of her loss. To her it was *infandum renovare dolorem*. She walked in a deep melancholy through the dear familiar rooms. She lingered in profound abstraction and in the deepest sadness over the mournful reminders of the past. She looked over all the old home objects, stood in the old places, and sat in the old seats. She walked in silence through all the

house, and finally went to her own old room, so loved, so well remembered. As she crossed the threshold and looked around she felt her strength give way. A great sob escaped her, and sinking into a chair where she once used to sit in happier days, she gave herself up to her recollections. For a long time she lost herself in these. Hilda had left her to herself, as though her delicacy had prompted her not to intrude upon her friend at such a moment; and Zillah thought of this with a feeling of grateful affection. At length she resumed to some degree her calmness, and summoning up all her strength, she went at last to the chamber where that dread scene had been enacted—that scene which seemed to her a double tragedy—that scene which had burned itself in her memory, combining the horror of the death of her dearest friend with the ghastly farce of a forced and unhallowed marriage. In that place a full tide of misery rushed over her soul. She broke down utterly. Chetwynde Castle, the Earl. Mrs. Hart, all were forgotten. The past faded away utterly. This only was her true home—this place darkened by a cloud which might never be dispelled.

"Oh, papa! Oh, papa!" she moaned, and flung herself upon the bed where he had breathed his last.

But her sorrow now, though overwhelming, had changed from its old vehemence. This change had been wrought in Zillah—the old, unreasoning passion had left her. A real affliction had brought out, by its gradual renovating and creative force, all the good that was in her. That the uses of adversity are sweet, is a hackneyed Shakspeareanism, but it is forever true, and nowhere was its truth more fully displayed than here. Formerly it happened that an ordinary check in the way of her desires was sufficient to send her almost into convulsions; but now, in the presence of her great calamity, she had learned to bear with patience all the ordinary ills of life. Her father had spoiled her; by his death she had become regenerate.

This tendency of her nature toward a purer and loftier standard was intensified by her visit to Pomeroy Court. Over her spirit there came a profounder earnestness, caught from the solemn scenes in the midst of which she found herself. Sorrow had subdued and quieted the wild impulsive motions of her soul. This renewal of that sorrow in the very place of its birth, deepened the effect of its first presence. This visit did more for her intellectual and spiritual growth than the whole past year at Chetwynde Castle.

They spent about a month here. Zillah, who had formerly been so talkative and restless, now showed plainly the fullness of the change that had come over her. She had grown into a life far more serious and thoughtful than any which she had known before. She had ceased to be a giddy and unreasoning girl. She had become a calm, grave, thoughtful woman. But her calmness and gravity and thoughtfulness were all underlaid and interpenetrated by the fervid vehemence of her intense Oriental nature. Beneath the English exterior lay, deep within her, the Hindu blood. She was of that sort which can be calm in ordinary life—so calm as to conceal utterly all ordinary workings of the fretful soul; but which, in the face of any great excitement, or in the presence of any great wrong, will be all overwhelmed and transformed into a furious tornado of passionate rage.

Zillah, thus silent and meditative, and so changed from her old self, might well have awakened the wonder of her friend. But whatever Hilda may have thought, and whatever wonder she may have felt, she kept it all to herself; for she was naturally reticent, and so secretive that she never expressed in words any feelings which she might have about things that went on around her. If Zillah chose to stay by herself, or to sit in her company without speaking a word, it was not in Hilda to question her or to remonstrate with her. She rather chose to accommodate herself to the temper of her friend. She could also be meditative and profoundly silent. While Zillah had been talkative, she had talked with her; now, in her silence, she rivaled her as well. She could follow Zillah in all her moods.

At the end of a month they returned to Chetwynde Castle, and resumed the life which they had been leading there. Zillah's new mood seemed to Hilda, and to others also, to last much longer than any one of those many moods in which she had indulged before. But this proved to be more than a mood. It was a change. The promise which had given to the Earl she had tried to fulfill most conscientiously. She really had striven as much as possible to "study." That better understanding, born of affection, which had arisen between them, had formed a new motive within her, and rendered her capable of something like application. But it was not until after her visit to Pomeroy Court that she showed any effort that was at all adequate to the purpose before her. The change that then came over her seemed to have given her a new control over herself. And so it was that, at last, the hours devoted to her studies were filled up by efforts that were really earnest, and also really effective.

Under these circumstances, it happened that Zillah began at last to engross Gualtier's attention altogether, during the whole of the time allotted to her; and if he had sought ever so earnestly, he could not have found any opportunity for a private interview with Hilda. What her wishes might be was not visible; for, whether she wished it or not, she did not, in any way, show it. She was always the same—calm, cool, civil, to her music-teacher, and devoted to her own share of the studies. Those little "asides" in which they had once indulged were now out of the question; and, even if a favorable occasion had arisen, Gualtier would not have ventured upon the undertaking. He, for his part, could not possibly know her thoughts: whether she was still cherishing her old designs, or had given them up altogether. He could only stifle his impatience, and wait, and watch, and wait. But how was it with her? Was she, too, watching and waiting for one opportunity? He thought so. But with what aim, or for what purpose? That was the puzzle. Yet that there was something on her mind which she wished to communicate to him he knew well; for it had at last happened that Hilda had changed in some degree from her cool and undemonstrative manner. He encountered sometimes—or thought that he encountered—an earnest glance which she threw at him, on greeting him, full of meaning, which

told him this most plainly. It seemed to him to say: Wait, wait, wait; when the time comes, I have that to say which you will be glad to learn. What it might be he knew not, nor could he conjecture; but he thought that it might still refer to the secret of that mysterious cipher which had baffled them both.

Thus these two watched and waited. Months passed away, but no opportunity for an interview arose. Of course, if Hilda had been reckless, or if it had been absolutely necessary to have one, she could easily have arranged it. The park was wide, full of lonely paths and sequestered retreats, where meetings could have been had, quite free from all danger of observation or interruption. She needed only to slip a note into his hand, telling him to meet her at some place there, and he would obey her will. But Hilda did not choose to do any thing of the kind. Whatever she did could only be done by her in strict accordance with *les convenances*. She would have waited for months before she would consent to compromise herself so far as to solicit a stolen interview. It was not the dread of discovery, however, that deterred her; for, in a place like Chetwynde, that need not have been feared, and if she had been so disposed, she could have had an interview with Gualtier every week, which no one would have found out. The thing which deterred her was something very different from this. It was her own pride. She could not humble herself so far as to do this. Such an act would be to descend from the position which she at present occupied in his eyes. To compromise herself, or in any way put herself in his power, was impossible for one like her.

It was not, however, from any thing like moral cowardice that she held aloof from making an interview with him; nor was it from any thing like conscientious scruples; nor yet from maidenly modesty. It arose, most of all, from pride, and also from a profound perception of the advantages enjoyed by one who fulfilled all that might be demanded by the proprieties of life. Her aim was to see Gualtier under circumstances that were unimpeachable—in the room where he had a right to come. To do more than this might lower herself in his eyes, and make him presumptuous.

CHAPTER XIV.

NEW DISCOVERIES.

AT last the opportunity came for which they had waited so long.

For many months Zillah's application to her studies had been incessant, and the Earl began to notice signs of weariness in her. His conscience smote him, and his anxiety was aroused. He had recovered from his gout, and as he felt particularly well he determined to take Zillah on a long drive, thinking that the change would be beneficial to her. He began to fear that he had brought too great a pressure to bear on her, and that she in her new-born zeal for study might carry her self-devotion too far, and do some injury to her health. Hilda declined going, and Zillah and the Earl started off for the day.

On that day Gualtier came at his usual hour. On looking round the room he saw no signs of

Zillah, and his eyes brightened as they fell on Hilda.

"Mrs. Molyneux," said she, after the usual civilities, "has gone out for a drive. She will not take her lesson to-day."

"Ah, well, shall I wait till your hour arrives, or will you take your lesson now?"

"Oh, you need not wait," said Hilda; "I will take my lesson now. I think I will appropriate both hours."

There was a glance of peculiar meaning in Hilda's eyes which Gualtier noticed, but he cast his eyes meekly upon the floor. He had an idea that the long looked for revelation was about to be given, but he did not attempt to hasten it in any way. He was afraid that any expression of eagerness on his part might repel Hilda, and, therefore, he would not endanger his position by asking for any thing, but rather waited to receive what she might voluntarily offer.

Hilda, however, was not at all anxious to be asked. Now that she could converse with Gualtier, and not compromise herself, she had made up her mind to give him her confidence. It was safe to talk to this man in this room. The servants were few. They were far away. No one would dream of trying to listen. They were sitting close together near the piano.

"I have something to say to you," said Hilda at last.

Gualtier looked at her with earnest inquiry, but said nothing.

"You remember, of course, what we were talking about the last time we spoke to one another?"

"Of course, I have never forgotten that."

"It was nearly two years ago," said Hilda, "At one time I did not expect that such a conversation could ever be renewed. With the General's death all need for it seemed to be destroyed. But now that need seems to have arisen again."

"Have you ever deciphered the paper?" asked Gualtier.

"Not more than before," said Hilda. "But I have made a discovery of the very greatest importance; something which entirely confirms my former suspicions gathered from the cipher. They are additional papers which I will show you presently, and then you will see whether I am right or not. I never expected to find any thing of the kind. I found them quite by chance, while I was half mechanically carrying out my old idea. After the General's death I lost all interest in the matter for some time, for there seemed before me no particular inducement to go on with it. But this discovery has changed the whole aspect of the affair."

"What was it that you found?" asked Gualtier, who was full of curiosity. "Was it the key to the cipher, or was it a full explanation, or was it something different?"

"They were certain letters and business papers. I will show them to you presently. But before doing so I want to begin at the beginning. The whole of that cipher is perfectly familiar to me, all its difficulties are as insurmountable as ever, and before I show you these new papers I want to refresh your memory about the old ones.

"You remember, first of all," said she, "the peculiar character of that cipher writing, and of my interpretation. The part that I deciphered

seemed to be set in the other like a wedge, and while this was decipherable the other was not."

Gualtier nodded.

"Now I want you to read again the part that I deciphered," said Hilda, and she handed him a piece of paper on which something was written. Gualtier took it and read the following, which the reader has already seen. Each sentence was numbered.

1. *Oh may God have mercy on my wretched soul Amen*
2. *O Pomeroy forged a hundred thousand dollars*
3. *O N Pomeroy eloped with poor Lady Chetwynde*
4. *She acted out of a mad impulse in flying*
5. *She listened to me and ran off with me*
6. *She was piqued at her husband's act*
7. *Fell in with Lady Mary Chetcynd*
8. *Expelled the army for gaming*
9. *N Pomeroy of Pomeroy Berks*
10. *O I am a miserable villain*

Gualtier looked over it and then handed it back.

"Yes," said he, "I remember, of course, for I happen to know every word of it by heart."

"That is very well," said Hilda, approvingly. "And now I want to remind you of the difficulties in my interpretation before going on any further.

"You remember that these were, first, the confusion in the way of writing the name, for here there is 'O Pomeroy,' 'O N Pomeroy,' and 'N Pomeroy,' in so short a document.

"Next, there is the mixture of persons, the writer sometimes speaking in the first person and sometimes in the third, as, for instance, when he says, 'O N Pomeroy eloped with poor Lady Chetwynde;' and then he says, 'She listened to me and ran off with me.'

"And then there are the incomplete sentences, such as, 'Fell in with Lady Mary Chetwynd'— 'Expelled the army for gaming.'

"Lastly, there are two ways in which the lady's name is spelled, 'Chetwynde,' and 'Chetwynd.'

"You remember we decided that these might be accounted for in one of two ways. Either, first, the writer, in copying it out, grew confused in forming his cipher characters; or, secondly, he framed the whole paper with a deliberate purpose to baffle and perplex."

"I remember all this," said Gualtier, quietly. "I have not forgotten it."

"The General's death changed the aspect of affairs so completely," said Hilda, "and made this so apparently useless, that I thought you might have forgotten at least these minute particulars. It is necessary for you to have these things fresh in your mind, so as to regard the whole subject thoroughly."

"But what good will any discovery be now?" asked Gualtier, with unfeigned surprise. "The General is dead, and you can do nothing."

"The General is dead," said Hilda; "but the General's daughter lives."

Nothing could exceed the bitterness of the tone in which she uttered these words.

"His daughter! Of what possible concern can all this be to her?" asked Gualtier, who wished to get at the bottom of Hilda's purpose.

"I should never have tried to strike at the General," said Hilda, "if he had not had a daughter. It was not him that I wished to harm. It was her."

"And now," said Gualtier, after a silence,

"she is out of your reach. She is Mrs. Moly-neux. She will be the Countess of Chetwynde. How can she be harmed?"

As he spoke he looked with a swift interrogative glance at Hilda, and then turned away his eyes.

"True," said Hilda, cautiously and slowly; "she is beyond my reach. Besides, you will observe that I was speaking of the past. I was telling what I wished—not what I wish."

"That is precisely what I understood," said Gualtier. "I only asked so as to know how your wishes now inclined. I am anxious to serve you in any way."

"So you have said before, and I take you at your word," said Hilda, calmly. "I have once before reposed confidence in you, and I intend to do so again."

Gualtier bowed, and murmured some words of grateful acknowledgment.

"My work now," said Hilda, without seeming to notice him, "is one of investigation. I merely wish to get to the bottom of a secret. It is to this that I have concluded to invite your assistance."

"You are assured of that already, Miss Krieff," said Gualtier, in a tone of deep devotion. "Call it investigation, or call it any thing you choose, if you deign to ask my assistance I will do any thing and dare any thing."

Hilda laughed harshly.

"In truth," said she, dryly, "this does not require much daring, but it may cause trouble—it may also take up valuable time. I do not ask for any risks, but rather for the employment of the most ordinary qualities. Patience and perseverance will do all that I, wish to have done."

"I am sorry, Miss Krieff, that there is nothing more than this. I should prefer to go on some enterprise of danger for your sake."

He laid a strong emphasis on these last words, but Hilda did not seem to notice it. She continued, in a calm tone:

"All this is talking in the dark. I must explain myself instead of talking round about the subject. To begin, then. Since our last interview I could find out nothing whatever that tended to throw any light on that mysterious cipher writing. Why it was written, or why it should be so carefully preserved, I could not discover. The General's death seemed to make it useless, and so for a long time I ceased to think about it. It was only on my last visit to Pomeroy Court that it came to my mind. That was six or eight months ago.

"On going there Mrs. Molyneux gave herself up to grief, and scarcely ever spoke a word. She was much by herself, and brooded over her sorrows. She spent much time in her father's room, and still more time in solitary walks about the grounds. I was much by myself. Left thus alone, I rambled about the house, and one day happened to go to the General's study. Here every thing remained almost exactly as it used to be. It was here that I found the cipher writing, and, on visiting it again, the circumstances of that discovery naturally suggested themselves to my mind."

Hilda had warmed with her theme, and spoke with something like recklessness, as though she was prepared at last to throw away every scruple

and make a full confidence. The allusion to the discovery of the cipher was a reminder to herself and to Gualtier of her former dishonorable conduct. Having once more touched upon this, it was easier for her to reveal new treachery upon her part. Nevertheless she paused for a moment, and looked with earnest scrutiny upon her companion. He regarded her with a look of silent devotion which seemed to express any degree of subserviency to her interests, and disarmed every suspicion. Reassured by this, she continued:

"It happened that I began to examine the General's papers. It was quite accidental, and arose merely from the fact that I had nothing else to do. It was almost mechanical on my part. At any rate I opened the desk, and found it full of documents of all kinds which had been apparently undisturbed for an indefinite period. Naturally enough I examined the drawer in which I had found the cipher writing, and was able to do so quite at my leisure. On first opening it I found only some business papers. The cipher was no longer there. I searched among all the other papers to find it, but in vain. I then concluded that he had destroyed it. For several days I continued to examine that desk, but with no result. It seemed to fascinate me. At last, however, I came to the conclusion that nothing more could be discovered.

"All this time Mrs. Molyneux left me quite to myself, and my search in the desk and my discouragement were altogether unknown to her. After about a week I gave up the desk and tore myself away. Still I could not keep away from it, and at the end of another week I returned to the search. This time I went with the intention of examining all the drawers, to see if there was not some additional place of concealment.

"It is not necessary for me to describe to you minutely the various trials which I made. It is quite enough for me now to say that I at last found out that in that very private drawer where I had first discovered the cipher writing there was a false bottom of very peculiar construction. It lay close to the real bottom, fitting in very nicely, and left room only for a few thin papers. The false bottom and the real bottom were so thin that no one could suspect any thing of the kind. Something about the position of the drawer led me to examine it minutely, and the idea of a false bottom came to my mind. I could not find out the secret of it, and it was only by the very rude process of prying at it with a knife that I at length made the discovery."

She paused.

"And did you find any thing?" said Gualtier, eagerly.

"I did."

"Papers?"

"Yes. The old cipher writing was there—shut up—concealed carefully, jealously—doubly concealed, in fact. Was not this enough to show that it had importance in the eyes of the man who had thus concealed it? It must be so. Nothing but a belief in its immense importance could possibly have led to such extraordinary pains in the concealment of it. This I felt, and this conviction only intensified my desire to get at the bottom of the mystery which it incloses. And this much I saw plainly—that the deciphering which I have made carries in itself so dread a confession, that the man who made it would willingly

"THE OLD CIPHER WRITING WAS THERE."

conceal it both in cipher writing and in secret drawers."

"But of course," said Gualtier, taking advantage of a pause, "you found something else besides the cipher. With that you were already familiar."

"Yes, and it is this that I am going to tell you about. There were some papers which had evidently been there for a long time, kept there in the same place with the cipher writing. When I first found them I merely looked hastily over them, and then folded them all up together, and took them away so as to examine them in my own room at leisure. On looking over them I found the names which I expected occurring frequently. There was the name of O. N. Pomeroy and the name of Lady Chetwynde. In addition to these there was another name, and a very singular one. The name is Obed Chute, and seems to me to be an American name. At any rate the owner of it lived in America."

"Obed Chute," repeated Gualtier, with the air of one who is trying to fasten something on his memory.

"Yes; and he seems to have lived in New York."

"What was the nature of the connection which he had with the others?"

"I should conjecture that he was a kind of guide, philosopher, and friend, with a little of the agent and commission-merchant," replied Hilda. "But it is impossible to find out any thing in particular about him from the meagre letters which I obtained. I found nothing else except these papers, though I searched diligently. Every thing is contained here. I have them, and I intend to show them to you without any further delay."

Saying this Hilda drew some papers from her pocket, and handed them to Gualtier.

On opening them Gualtier found first a paper covered with cipher writing. It was the same which Hilda had copied, and the characters were familiar to him from his former attempt to decipher them. The paper was thick and coarse, but Hilda had copied the characters very faithfully.

The next paper was a receipt written out on a small sheet which was yellow with age, while the ink had faded into a pale brown:

"$100,000.   New York, May 10, 1840.
"Received from O. N. Pomeroy the sum of one hundred thousand dollars in payment for my claim.
"Obed Chute."

It was a singular document in every respect; but the mention of the sum of money seemed to confirm the statement gathered from the cipher writing.

The next document was a letter:

"NEW YORK, *August* 23, 1840.

"DEAR SIR,—I take great pleasure in informing you that L. C. has experienced a change, and is now slowly recovering. I assure you that no pains shall be spared to hasten her cure. The best that New York can afford is at her service. I hope soon to acquaint you with her entire recovery. Until then, believe me,

"Yours truly, OBED CHUTE.

"Capt. O. N. POMEROY."

The next paper was a letter written in a lady's hand. It was very short:

"NEW YORK, *September* 20, 1840.

"Farewell, dearest friend and more than brother. After a long sickness I have at last recovered through the mercy of God and the kindness of Mr. Chute. We shall never meet again on earth; but I will pray for your happiness till my latest breath. MARY CHETWYNDE."

There was only one other. It was a letter also, and was as follows:

"NEW YORK, *October* 10, 1840.

"DEAR SIR,—I have great pleasure in informing you that your friend L. C. has at length entirely recovered. She is very much broken down, however; her hair is quite gray, and she looks twenty years older. She is deeply penitent and profoundly sad. She is to leave me to-morrow, and will join the Sisters of Charity. You will feel with me that this is best for herself and for all. I remain yours, very truly,

"OBED CHUTE.

"Capt. O. N. POMEROY."

Gualtier read these letters several times in deep and thoughtful silence. Then he sat in profound thought for some time.

"Well," said Hilda at length, with some impatience, "what do you think of these?"

"What do *you* think?" asked Gualtier.

"I?" returned Hilda. "I will tell you what I think; and as I have brooded over these for eight months now, I can only say that I am more confirmed than ever in my first impressions. To me, then, these papers seem to point out two great facts—the first being that of the forgery; and the second that of the elopement. Beyond this I see something else. The forgery has been arranged by the payment of the amount. The elopement also has come to a miserable termination. Lady Chetwynde seems to have been deserted by her lover, who left her perhaps in New York. She fell ill, very ill, and suffered so that on her recovery she had grown in appearance twenty years older. Broken-hearted, she did not dare to go back to her friends, but joined the Sisters of Charity. She is no doubt dead long ago. As to this Chute, he seems to me perhaps to have been a kind of tool of the lover, who employed him probably to settle his forgery business, and also to take care of the unhappy woman whom he had ruined and deserted. He wrote these few letters to keep the recreant lover informed about her fate. In the midst of these there is

the last despairing farewell of the unhappy creature herself. All these the conscience-stricken lover has carefully preserved. In addition to these, no doubt for the sake of easing his conscience, he wrote out a confession of his sin. But he was too great a coward to write it out plainly, and therefore wrote it in cipher. I believe that he would have destroyed them all if he had found time; but his accident came too quickly for this, and he has left these papers as a legacy to the discoverer."

As Hilda spoke Gualtier gazed at her with unfeigned admiration.

"You are right," said he. "Every word that you speak is as true as fate. You have penetrated to the very bottom of this secret. I believe that this is the true solution. Your genius has solved the mystery."

"The mystery," repeated Hilda, who showed no emotion whatever at the fervent admiration of Gualtier—"the mystery is as far from solution as ever."

"Have you not solved it?"

"Certainly not. Mine, after all, are merely conjectures. Much more remains to be done. In the first place, I must find out something about Lady Chetwynde. For months I have tried, but in vain. I have ventured as far as I dared to question the people about here. Once I hinted to Mrs. Hart something about the elopement, and she turned upon me with that in her eyes which would have turned an ordinary mortal into stone. Fortunately for me, I bore it, and survived. But since that unfortunate question she shuns me more than ever. The other servants know nothing, or else they will reveal nothing. Nothing, in fact, can be discovered here. The mystery is yet to be explained, and the explanation must be sought elsewhere."

"Where?"

"I don't know."

"Have you thought of any thing? You must have, or you would not have communicated with me. There is some work which you wish me to do. You have thought about it, and have determined it. What is it? Is it to go to America? Shall I hunt up Obed Chute? Shall I search through the convents till I find that Sister who once was Lady Chetwynde? Tell me. If you say so I will go."

Hilda mused; then she spoke, as though rather to herself than to her companion.

"I don't know. I have no plans—no definite aim, beyond a desire to find out what it all means, and what there is in it. What can I do? What could I do if I found out all? I really do not know. If General Pomeroy were alive, it might be possible to extort from him a confession of his crimes, and make them known to the world."

"If General Pomeroy were alive," interrupted Gualtier, "and were to confess all his crimes, what good would that do?"

"What good?" cried Hilda, in a tone of far greater vehemence and passion than any which had yet escaped her. "What good? Humiliation, sorrow, shame, anguish, for his daughter! It is not on his head that I wish these to descend, but on hers. You look surprised. You wonder why? I will not tell you—not now, at least. It is not because she is passionate and disagreeable; that is a trifle, and besides she has changed from that; it is not because she ever injured me—she never injured me; she loves me; but"—and Hilda's brow grew dark, and her eyes flashed as she spoke—"there are other reasons, deeper than all this—reasons which I will not divulge even to you, but which yet are sufficient to make me long and yearn and crave for some opportunity to bring down her proud head into the very dust."

"And that opportunity shall be yours," cried Gualtier, vehemently. "To do this it is only necessary to find out the whole truth. I will find it out. I will search over all England and all America till I discover all that you want to know. General Pomeroy is dead. What matter? He is nothing to you. But she lives, and is a mark for your vengeance."

"I have said more than I intended to," said Hilda, suddenly resuming her coolness. "At any rate, I take you at your word. If you want money, I can supply it."

"Money?" said Gualtier, with a light laugh. "No, no. It is something far more than that which I want. When I have succeeded in my search I will tell you. To tell it now would be premature. But when shall I start? Now?"

"Oh no," said Hilda, who showed no emotion one way or the other at the hint which he had thrown out. "Oh no, do nothing suddenly. Wait until your quarter is up. When will it be out?"

"In six weeks. Shall I wait?"

"Yes."

"Well, then, in six weeks I will go."

"Very well."

"And if I don't succeed I shall never come back."

Hilda was silent.

"Is it arranged, then?" said Gualtier, after a time.

"Yes; and now I will take my music lesson." And Hilda walked over to the piano.

After this interview no further opportunity occurred. Gualtier came every day as before. In a fortnight he gave notice to the Earl that pressing private engagements would require his departure. He begged leave to recommend a friend of his, Mr. Hilaire. The Earl had an interview with Gualtier, and courteously expressed his regret at his departure, asking him at the same time to write to Mr. Hilaire and get him to come. This Gualtier promised to do.

Shortly before the time of Gualtier's departure Mr. Hilaire arrived. Gualtier took him to the Castle, and he was recognized as the new teacher. In a few days Gualtier took his departure.

CHAPTER XV.

FROM GIRLHOOD TO WOMANHOOD.

ONE evening Zillah was sitting with Lord Chetwynde in his little sanctum. His health had not been good of late, and sometimes attacks of gout were superadded. At this time he was confined to his room.

Zillah was dressed for dinner, and had come to sit with him until the second bell rang. She had been with him constantly during his confinement to his room. At this time she was seated on a low stool near the fire, which threw its glow over her face, and lit up the vast masses of her jet-black hair. Neither of them had spoken for some time, when Lord Chetwynde, who had been looking steadily at her for some minutes, said, abruptly:

"Zillah, I'm sure Guy will not know you when he comes back."

She looked up laughingly.

"Why, father? I think every lineament on my face must be stereotyped on his memory."

"That is precisely the reason why I say that he will not know you. I could not have imagined that three years could have so thoroughly altered any one."

"It's only fine feathers," said Zillah, shaking her head. "You must allow that Mathilde is incomparable. I often feel that were she to have the least idea of the appearance which I presented, when I first came here, there would be nothing left for me but suicide. I could not survive her contempt. I was always fond of finery. I have Indian blood enough for that; but when I remember my combinations of colors, it really makes me shudder; and my hair was always streaming over my shoulders in a manner more negligé than becoming."

"I do Mathilde full justice," returned Lord Chetwynde. "Your toilette and coiffure are now irreprochable; but even her power has its limits, and she could scarcely have turned the sallow, awkward girl into a lovely and graceful woman."

Zillah, who was unused to flattery, blushed very red at this tribute to her charms, and answered, quickly:

"Whatever change there may be is entirely due to Monmouthshire. Devonshire never agreed with me. I should have been ill and delicate to this day if I had remained there; and as to sallowness, I must plead guilty to that. I remember a lemon-colored silk I had, in which it was impossible to tell where the dress ended and my neck began. But, after all, father, you are a very prejudiced judge. Except that I am healthy now, and well dressed, I think I am very much the same personally as I was three years ago. In character, however, I feel that I have altered."

"No," he replied; "I have been looking at you for the last few minutes with perfectly unprejudiced eyes, trying to see you as a stranger would, and as Guy will when he returns. And now," he added, laughingly, "you shall be punished for your audacity in doubting my powers of discrimination, by having a full inventory given you. We will begin with the figure—about the middle height, perhaps a little under it, slight and graceful; small and beautifully proportioned head; well set on the shoulders; complexion no longer sallow or lemon-colored, but clear, bright, transparent olive; hair, black as night, and glossy as—"

But here he was interrupted by Zillah, who suddenly flung her arms about his neck, and the close proximity of the face which he was describing impeded further utterance.

"Hush, father," said she; "I won't hear another word, and don't you dare to talk about ever looking at me with unprejudiced eyes. I want you to love me without seeing my faults."

"But would you not rather that I saw your failings, Zillah, than that I clothed you with an ideal perfection?"

"No; I don't care for the love that is always looking out for faults, and has a 'but' even at the tenderest moments. That is not the love I give. Perhaps strangers might not think dear papa, and you, and Hilda absolutely perfect; but I can not see a single flaw, and I should hate myself if I could."

Lord Chetwynde kissed her fondly, but sighed as he answered:

"My child, you know nothing of the world. I fear life has some very bitter lessons in store for you before you will learn to read it aright, and form a just estimate of the characters of the people among whom you are thrown."

"But you surely would not have me think people bad until I have proved them to be so. Life would not be worth having if one must live in a constant state of suspicion."

"No, nor would I have you think all whom you love to be perfect. Believe me, my child, you will meet with but few friends in the world. Honor is an exploded notion, belonging to a past generation."

"You may be right, father, but I do not like the doctrine; so I shall go on believing in people until I find them to be different from what I thought."

"I should say to you, do so, dear—believe as long as you can, and as much as you can; but the danger of that is when you find that those whom you have trusted do not come up to the standard which you have formed. After two or three disappointments you will fall into the opposite extreme, think every one bad, and not believe in any thing or any body."

"I should die before I should come to that," cried Zillah, passionately. "If what you say is true, I had better not let myself like any body." Then, laughing up in his face, she added: "By-the-way, I wonder if you are safe. You see you have made me so skeptical that I shall begin by suspecting my tutor. No, don't speak," she went on, in a half-earnest, half-mocking manner, and put her hand before his mouth. "The case is hopeless, as far as you are concerned. The warning has come too late. I love you as I thought I should never love any one after dear papa."

Lord Chetwynde smiled, and pressed her fondly to his breast.

The steady change which had been going on in Zillah, in mind and in person, was indeed sufficient to justify Lord Chetwynde's remark. Enough has been said already about her change in personal appearance. Great as this was, however, it was not equal to that more subtle change which had come over her soul. Her nature was intense, vehement, passionate; but its development was of such a kind that she was now earnest where she was formerly impulsive, and calm where she had been formerly weak. A profound depth of feeling already was made manifest in this rich nature, and the thoughtfulness of the West was added to the fine emotional sensibility of the East; forming by their union a being of rare susceptibility, and of quick yet deep feeling, who still could control those feelings, and smother them, even though the concealed passion should consume like a fire within her.

Three years had passed since her hasty and repugnant marriage, and those years had been eventful in many ways. They had matured the wild, passionate, unruly girl into the woman full of sensibility and passion. They had also been filled with events upon which the world gazed in awe, which shook the British empire to its centre, and sent a thrill of horror to the heart of that empire, followed by a fierce thirst for vengeance. For the Indian mutiny had broken out, the horrors of Cawnpore had been enacted, the stories of sepoy atrocity had been told by every English fireside, and the whole nation had roused itself to send forth armies for vengeance and for punishment. Dread stories were these for the quiet circle at Chetwynde Castle; yet they had been spared its worst pains. Guy had been sent to the north of India, and had not been witness of the scenes of Cawnpore. He had been joined with those soldiers who had been summoned together to march on Delhi, and he had shared in the danger and in the final triumph of that memorable expedition.

The intensity of desire and the agony of impatience which attended his letters were natural. Lord Chetwynde thought only of one thing for many months, and that was his son's letters. At the outbreak of the mutiny, a dread anxiety had taken possession of him lest his son might be in danger. At first the letters came regularly, giving details of the mutiny as he heard them. Then there was a long break, for the army was on the march to Delhi. Then a letter came from the British camp before Delhi, which roused Lord Chetwynde from the lowest depths of despair to joy and exultation and hope. Then there was another long interval, in which the Earl, sick with anxiety, began to anticipate the worst, and was fast sinking into despondency, until, at last, a letter came, which raised him up in an instant to the highest pitch of exultation and triumph. Delhi was taken. Guy had distinguished himself, and was honorably mentioned in the dispatches. He had been among the first to scale the walls and penetrate into the beleaguered city. All had fallen into their hands. The great danger which had impended had been dissipated, and vengeance had been dealt out to those whose hands were red with English blood. Guy's letter, from beginning to end, was one long note of triumph. Its enthusiastic tone, coming, as it did, after a long period of anxiety, completely overcame the Earl. Though naturally the least demonstrative of men, he was now overwhelmed by the full tide of his emotions. He burst into tears, and wept for some time tears of joy. Then he rose, and walking over to Zillah, he kissed her, and laid his hand solemnly upon her head.

"My daughter," said he, "thank God that your husband is preserved to you through the perils of war, and that he is saved to you, and will come to you in safety and in honor."

The Earl's words sank deeply into Zillah's heart. She said nothing, but bowed her head in silence.

Living, as she did, where Guy's letters formed the chief delight of him whom she loved as a father, it would have been hard indeed for a generous nature like hers to refrain from sharing his feelings. Sympathy with his anxiety and his joy was natural, nay, inevitable. In his sorrow she was forced to console him by pointing out all that might be considered as bright in his prospects; in his joy she was forced to rejoice with him, and listen to his descriptions of Guy's exploits, as his imagination enlarged upon the more meagre facts stated in the letters. This year of anxiety and of triumph, therefore, compelled her to think very much about Guy, and, whatever her feelings were, it certainly exalted him to a prominent place in her thoughts.

And so it happened that, as month succeeded to month, she found herself more and more compelled to identify herself with the Earl, to talk to him about the idol of his heart, to share his anxiety and his joy, while all that anxiety and all that joy referred exclusively to the man who was her husband, but whom, as a husband, she had once abhorred.

CHAPTER XVI.

THE AMERICAN EXPEDITION.

ABOUT three years had passed away since Zillah had first come to Chetwynde, and the life which she had lived there had gradually come to be grateful and pleasant and happy. Mr. Hilaire was attentive to his duty and devoted to his pupil, and Zillah applied herself assiduously to her music and drawing. At the end of a year Mr. Hilaire waited upon the Earl with a request to withdraw, as he wanted to go to the Continent. He informed the Earl, however, that Mr. Gualtier was coming back, and would like to get his old situation, if possible. The Earl consented to take back the old teacher; and so, in a few months more, after an absence of about a year and a half, Gualtier resumed his duties at Chetwynde Castle, *vice* Mr. Hilaire, resigned.

On his first visit after his return Hilda's face expressed an eagerness of curiosity which even her fine self-control could not conceal. No one noticed it, however, but Gualtier, and he looked at her with an earnest expression that might mean any thing or nothing. It might tell of success or failure; and so Hilda was left to conjecture. There was no chance of a quiet conversation, and she had either to wait as before, perhaps for months, until she could see him alone, or else throw away her scruples and arrange a meeting. Hilda was not long in coming to a conclusion. On Gualtier's second visit she slipped a piece of paper into his hand, on which he read, after he had left, the following:

"*I will be in the West Avenue, near the Lake, this afternoon at three o'clock.*"

That afternoon she made some excuse and went out, as she said to Zillah, for a walk through the Park. As this was a frequent thing with her, it excited no comment. The West Avenue led from the door through the Park, and finally, after a long detour, ended at the main gate. At its farthest point there was a lake, surrounded by a dense growth of Scotch larch-trees, which formed a very good place for such a tryst—although, for that matter, in so quiet a place as Chetwynde Park, they might have met on the main avenue without any fear of being noticed. Here, then, at three o'clock, Hilda went, and on reaching the spot found Gualtier waiting for her. She walked under the shadow of the trees before she said a word.

"You are punctual," said she at last.

"I have been here ever since noon."

"You did not go out, then?"

"No, I staid here for you."

His tone expressed the deepest devotion, and his eyes, as they rested on her for a moment, had the same expression.

Hilda looked at him benignantly and encouragingly.

"You have been gone long, and I dare say you have been gone far," she said. "It is this which I want to hear about. Have you found out any thing, and what have you found out?"

"Yes, I have been gone long," said Gualtier, "and have been far away; but all the time I have done nothing else than seek after what you wish to know. Whether I have discovered any thing of any value will be for you to judge. I can only tell you of the result. At any rate you will see that I have not spared myself for your sake."

"What have you done?" asked Hilda, who saw that Gualtier's devotion was irrepressible, and would find vent in words if she did not restrain him. "I am eager to hear."

Gualtier dropped his eyes, and began to speak in a cool business tone.

"I will tell you every thing, then, Miss Krieff," said he, "from the beginning. When I left here I went first to London, for the sake of making inquiries about the elopement. I hunted up all whom I could find whose memories embraced the last twenty years, so as to see if they could throw any light on this mystery. One or two had some faint recollection of the affair, but nothing of any consequence. At length I found out an old sporting character who promised at first to be what I wished. He remembered Lady Chetwynde, described her beauty, and said that she was left to herself very much by her husband. He remembered well the excitement that was caused by her flight. He remembered the name of the man with whom she had fled. It was *Redfield Lyttoun.*"

"*Redfield Lyttoun!*" repeated Hilda, with a peculiar expression.

"Yes; but he said that, for his part, he had good reason for believing that it was an assumed name. The man who bore the name had figured for a time in sporting circles, but after this event it was generally stated that it was not his true name. I asked whether any one knew his true name. He said some people had stated it, but he could not tell. I asked what was the name. He said Pomeroy."

As Gualtier said this he raised his eyes, and those small gray orbs seemed to burn and flash with triumph as they encountered the gaze of Hilda. She said not a word, but held out her hand. Gualtier tremblingly took it, and pressed it to his thin lips.

"This was all that I could discover. It was vague; it was only partially satisfactory; but it was all. I soon perceived that it was only a waste of time to stay in London; and after thinking of many plans, I finally determined to visit the family of Lady Chetwynde herself. Of course such an undertaking had to be carried out very cautiously. I found out where the family lived, and went there. On arriving I went to the Hall, and offered myself as music-teacher. It was in an out-of-the-way place, and Sir Henry Furlong, Lady Chetwynde's brother, happened to have two or three daughters who were studying under a governess. When I showed him a certificate which the Earl here was kind enough to

"'YOU ARE PUNCTUAL,' SAID SHE AT LAST."

give me, he was very much impressed by it. He asked me all about the Earl and Chetwynde, and appeared to be delighted to hear about these things. My stars were certainly lucky. He engaged me at once, and so I had constant access to the place.

"I had to work cautiously, of course. My idea was to get hold of some of the domestics. There was an old fellow there, a kind of butler, whom I propitiated, and gradually drew into conversations about the family. My footing in the house inspired confidence in him, and he gradually became communicative. He was an old gossip, in his dotage, and he knew all about the family, and remembered when Lady Chetwynde was born. He at first avoided any allusion to her, but I told him long stories about the Earl, and won upon his sympathies so that he told me at last all that the family knew about Lady Chetwynde.

"His story was this: Lord Chetwynde was busy in politics, and left his wife very much to herself. A coolness had sprung up between them, which increased every day. Lady Chetwynde was vain, and giddy, and weak. The Redfield Lyttoun of whom I had heard in London was much at her house, though her husband knew nothing about it. People were talking about them every where, and he only was in the dark. At last they ran away. It was known that they had fled to America. That is the last that was ever heard of her. She vanished out of sight, and her paramour also. Not one word has ever been heard about either of them since. From which I conjecture that Redfield Lyttoun, when he had become tired of his victim, threw her off, and came back to resume his proper name, to lead a life of honor, and to die in the odor of sanctity. What do you think of my iden?"

"It seems just," said Hilda, thoughtfully. "In the three months which I spent there I found out all that the family could tell; but still I was far enough away from the object of my search. I only had conjectures, I wanted certainty. I thought it all over; and, at length, saw that the only thing left to do was to go to America, and try to get upon their tracks. It was a desperate undertaking; America changes so that traces of fugitives are very quickly obliterated; and who could detect or discover any after a lapse of nearly twenty years? Still, I determined to go. There seemed to be a slight chance that I might find this Obed Chute, who figures in the correspondence. There was also a chance of tracing Lady Chetwynde among the records of the Sisters of Charity. Besides, there was the chapter of accidents, in which unexpected things often turn up. So I went to America. My first search was after Obed Chute. To my amazement, I found him at once. He is one of the foremost bankers of New York, and is well known all over the city. I waited on him without delay. I had documents and certificates which I presented to him. Among others, I had written out a very good letter from Sir Henry Furlong, commissioning me to find out about his beloved sister, and another from General Pomeroy, to the effect that I was his friend—"

"That was forgery," interrupted Hilda, sharply.

Gualtier bowed with a deprecatory air, and hung his head in deep abasement.

"Go on," said she.

"You are too harsh," said he, in a pleading voice. "It was all for your sake—"

"Go on," she repeated.

"Well, with these I went to see Obed Chute. He was a tall, broad-shouldered, square-headed man, with iron-gray hair, and a face—well, it was one of those faces that make you feel that the owner can do any thing he chooses. On entering his private office I introduced myself, and began a long explanation. He interrupted me by shaking hands with me vehemently, and pushing me into a chair. I sat down, and went on with my explanation. I told him that I had come out as representative of the Furlong family, and the friend of General Pomeroy, now dead. I told him that there were several things which I

wished to find out. First, to trace Lady Chetwynde, and find out what had become of her, and bring her back to her friends, if she were alive; secondly, to clear up certain charges relative to a forgery; and, finally, to find out about the fate of Redfield Lyttoun.

"Mr. Obed Chute at first was civil enough, after his rough way; but, as I spoke, he looked at me earnestly, eying me from head to foot with sharp scrutiny. He did not seem to believe my story.

"'Well,' said he, when I had ended, 'is that all?'

"'Yes,' said I.

"'So you want to find out about Lady Chetwynde, and the forgery, and Redfield Lyttoun?'

"'Yes.'

"'And General Pomeroy told you to apply to me?'

"'Yes. On his dying bed,' said I, solemnly, 'his last words were: "Go to Obed Chute, and tell him to explain all."'

"'To explain all!' repeated Obed Chute.

"'Yes,' said I. ''The confession," said the General, "can not be made by me. He must make it."'

"'The confession!' he repeated.

"'Yes. And I suppose that you will not be unwilling to grant a dying man's request.'

"Obed Chute said nothing for some time, but sat staring at me, evidently engaged in profound thought. At any rate, he saw through and through me.

"'Young man,' said he at last, 'where are you lodging?'

"'At the Astor House,' said I, in some surprise.

"'Well, then, go back to the Astor House, pack up your trunk, pay your bill, take your fare in the first steamer, and go right straight back home. When you get there, give my compliments to Sir Henry Furlong, and tell him if he wants his sister he had better hunt her up himself. As to that affecting message which you have brought from General Pomeroy, I can only say, that, as he evidently did not explain this business to you, I certainly will not. I was only his agent. Finally, if you want to find Redfield Lyttoun, you may march straight out of that door, and look about you till you find him.'

"Saying this, he rose, opened the door, and, with a savage frown, which forbade remonstrance, motioned me out.

"I went out. There was evidently no hope of doing any thing with Obed Chute."

"Then you failed," said Hilda, in deep disappointment.

"Failed? No. Do you not see how the reticence of this Obed Chute confirms all our suspicions? But wait till you hear all, and I will tell you my conclusions. You will then see whether I have discovered any thing definite or not.

"I confess I was much discouraged at first at my reception by Obed Chute. I expected every thing from this interview, and his brutality baffled me. I did not venture back there again, of course. I thought of trying other things, and went diligently around among the convents and religious orders, to see if I could find out any thing about the fate of Lady Chetwynde. My letters of introduction from Sir H. Furlong and from Lord Chetwynde led these simple-minded

"WITH A SAVAGE FROWN HE MOTIONED ME OUT."

people to receive me with confidence. They readily seconded my efforts, and opened their records to me. For some time my search was in vain; but, at last, I found what I wanted. One of the societies of the Sisters of Charity had the name of Sister Ursula, who joined them in the year 1840. She was Lady Chetwynde. She lived with them eight years, and then disappeared. Why she had left, or where she had gone, was equally unknown. She had disappeared, and that was the end of her. After this I came home."

"And you have found out nothing more?" said Hilda, in deep disappointment.

"Nothing," said Gualtier, dejectedly; "but are you not hasty in despising what I have found out? Is not this something?"

"I do not know that you have discovered any thing but what I knew before," said Hilda, coldly. "You have made some conjectures—that is all."

"Conjectures!—no, conclusions from additional facts," said Gualtier, eagerly. "What we suspected is now, at least, more certain. The very brutality of that beast, Obed Chute, proves this. Let me tell you the conclusions that I draw from this:

"First, General Pomeroy, under an assumed name, that of Redfield Lyttoun, gained Lady Chetwynde's love, and ran away with her to America.

"Secondly, he forged a hundred thousand dollars, which forgery he hushed up through this Obed Chute, paying him, no doubt, a large sum for hush-money.

"Thirdly, he deserted Lady Chetwynde when he was tired of her, and left her in the hands of

Obed Chute. She was ill, and finally, on her recovery, joined the Sisters of Charity.

"Fourthly, after eight years she ran away—perhaps to fall into evil courses and die in infamy.

"And lastly, all this must be true, or else Obed Chute would not have been so close, and would not have fired up so at the very suggestion of an explanation. If it were not true, why should he not explain? But if it be true, then there is every reason why he should not explain."

A long silence followed. Hilda was evidently deeply disappointed. From what Gualtier had said at the beginning of the interview, she had expected to hear something more definite. It seemed to her as though all his trouble had resulted in nothing. Still, she was not one to give way to disappointment, and she had too much good sense to show herself either ungrateful or ungracious.

"Your conclusions are, no doubt, correct," said she at last, in a pleasanter tone.than she had yet assumed; "but they are only inferences, and can not be made use of—in the practical way in which I hoped they would be. We are still in the attitude of inquirers, you see. The secret which we hold is of such a character that we have to keep it to ourselves until it be confirmed."

Gualtier's face lighted up with pleasure as Hilda thus identified him with herself, and classed him with her as the sharer of the secret.

"Any thing," said he, eagerly—"any thing that I can do, I will do. I hope you know that you have only to say the word—"

Hilda waved her hand.

"I trust you," said she. "The time will come when you will have something to do. But just now I must wait, and attend upon circumstances. There are many things in my mind which I will not tell you—that is to say, not yet. But when the time comes, I promise to tell you. You may be interested in my plans—or you may not. I will suppose that you are."

"Can you doubt it, Miss Krieff?"

"No, I do not doubt it, and I promise you my confidence when any thing further arises."

"Can I be of no assistance now—in advising, or in counseling?" asked Gualtier, in a hesitating voice.

"No—whatever half-formed plans I may have relate to people and to things which are altogether outside of your sphere, and so you could do nothing in the way of counseling or advising."

"At least, tell me this much—must I look upon all my labor as wasted utterly? Will you at least accept it, even if it is useless, as an offering to you?"

Gualtier's pale sallow face grew paler and more sallow as he asked this; his small gray eyes twinkled with a feverish light as he turned them anxiously upon Hilda. Hilda, for her part, regarded him with her usual calmness.

"Accept it?" said she. "Certainly, right gladly and gratefully. My friend, if I was disappointed at the result, do not suppose that I fail to appreciate the labor. You have shown rare perseverance and great acuteness. The next time you will succeed."

This approval of his labors, slight as it was, and spoken as it was, with the air of a queen, was eagerly and thankfully accepted by Gualtier. He hungered after her approval, and in his hunger he was delighted even with crumbs.

CHAPTER XVII.

A FRESH DISCOVERY.

SOME time passed away, and Hilda had no more interviews with Gualtier. The latter settled down into a patient, painstaking music-teacher once more, who seemed not to have an idea beyond his art. Hilda held herself aloof; and, even when she might have exchanged a few confidential words, she did not choose to do so. And Gualtier was content, and quiet, and patient.

Nearly eighteen months had passed away since Zillah's visit to Pomeroy Court, and she began to be anxious to pay another visit. She had been agitating the subject for some time; but it had been postponed from time to time, for various reasons, the chief one being the ill health of the Earl. At length, however, his health improved somewhat, and Zillah determined to take advantage of this to go.

This time, the sight of the Court did not produce so strong an effect as before. She did not feel like staying alone, but preferred having Hilda with her, and spoke freely about the past. They wandered about the rooms, looked over all the well-remembered places, rode or strolled through the grounds, and found, at every step, inside of the Court, and outside also, something which called up a whole world of associations.

Wandering thus about the Court, from one room to another, it was natural that Zillah should go often to the library, where her father formerly passed the greater part of his time. Here they chiefly staid, and looked over the books and pictures.

One day the conversation turned toward the desk, and Zillah casually remarked that her father used to keep this place so sacred from her intrusion that she had acquired a kind of awe of it, which she had not yet quite overcome. This led Hilda to propose, laughingly, that she should explore it now, on the spot; and, taking the keys, she opened it, and turned over some of the papers. At length she opened a drawer, and drew out a miniature. Zillah snatched it from her, and, looking at it for a few moments, burst into tears.

"It's my mother," she cried, amidst her sobs; "my mother! Oh, my mother!"

Hilda said nothing.

"He showed it to me once, when I was a little child, and I often have wondered, in a vague way, what became of it. I never thought of looking here."

"You may find other things here, also, if you look," said Hilda, gently. "No doubt your papa kept here all his most precious things."

The idea excited Zillah. She covered the portrait with kisses, put it in her pocket, and then sat down to explore the desk.

There were bundles of papers there, lying on the bottom of the desk, all neatly wrapped up and labeled in a most business-like manner. Outside there was a number of drawers, all of which were filled with papers. These were all wrapped in bundles, and were labeled, so as to show at the first glance that they referred to the business of the estate. Some were mortgages, others receipts, others letters, others returned checks and drafts. Nothing among these had any interest for Zillah.

Inside the desk there were some drawers, which Zillah opened. Once on the search, she kept it up most vigorously. The discovery of her mother's miniature led her to suppose that something else of equal value might be found here somewhere. But, after a long search, nothing whatever was found. The search, however, only became the more exciting, and the more she was baffled the more eager did she become to follow it out to the end. While she was investigating in this way, Hilda stood by her, looking on with the air of a sympathizing friend and interested spectator. Sometimes she anticipated Zillah in opening drawers which lay before their eyes, and in seizing and examining the rolls of papers with which each drawer was filled. The search was conducted by both, in fact, but Zillah seemed to take the lead.

"There's nothing more," said Hilda at last, as Zillah opened the last drawer, and found only some old business letters. "You have examined all, you have found nothing. At any rate, the search has given you the miniature; and, besides, it has dispelled that awe that you spoke of."

"But, dear Hilda, there ought to be something," said Zillah. "I hoped for something more. I had an idea that I might find something—I don't know what—something which I could keep for the rest of my life."

"Is not the miniature enough, dearest?" said Hilda, in affectionate tones. "What more could you wish for?"

"I don't know. I prize it most highly; but, still, I feel disappointed."

"There is no more chance," said Hilda.

"No; I have examined every drawer."

"You can not expect any thing more, so let us go away—unless," she added, "you expect to find some mysterious secret drawer somewhere, and I fancy there is hardly any room here for any thing of that kind."

"A secret drawer!" repeated Zillah, with visible excitement. "What an idea! But could there be one? Is there any place for one? I don't see any place. There is the open place where the books are kept, and, on each side, a row of drawers. No; there are no secret drawers here. But see—what is this?"

As Zillah said this she reached out her hand toward the lower part of the place where the books were kept. A narrow piece of wood projected there beyond the level face of the back of the desk. On this piece of wood there was a brass catch, which seemed intended to be fastened; but now, on account of the projection of the piece, it was not fastened. Zillah instantly pulled the wood, and it came out.

It was a shallow drawer, not more than half an inch in depth, and the catch was the means by which it was closed. A bit of brass, that looked like an ornamental stud, was, in reality, a spring, by pressing which the drawer sprang open. But when Zillah looked there the drawer was already open, and, as she pulled it out, she saw it all.

As she pulled it out her hand trembled, and her heart beat fast. A strange and inexplicable feeling filled her mind—a kind of anticipation of calamity—a mysterious foreboding of evil—which spread a strange terror through her. But her excitement was strong, and was not now to be quelled; and it would have needed something far more powerful than this vague fear to stop her in the search into the mystery of the desk.

When men do any thing that is destined to affect them seriously, for good or evil, it often happens that at the time of the action a certain unaccountable premonition arises in the mind. This is chiefly the case when the act is to be the cause of sorrow. Like the wizard with Lochiel, some dark phantom arises before the mind, and warns of the evil to come. So it was in the present case. The pulling out of that drawer was an eventful moment in the life of Zillah. It was a crisis fraught with future sorrow and evil and suffering. There was something of all this in her mind at that moment; and, as she pulled it out, and as it lay before her, a shudder passed through her, and she turned her face away.

'"Oh, Hilda, Hilda!" she murmured. "I'm afraid—"

"Afraid of what?" asked Hilda. "What's the matter? Here is a discovery, certainly. This secret drawer could never have been suspected. What a singular chance it was that you should have made such a discovery!"

But Zillah did not seem to hear her. Before she had done speaking she had turned to examine the drawer. There were several papers in it. All were yellow and faded, and the writing upon them was pale with age. These Zillah seized in a nervous and tremulous grasp. The first one which she unfolded was the secret cipher. Upon this she gazed for some time in bewilderment, and then opened a paper which was inclosed within it. This paper, like the other, was faded, and the ink was pale. It contained what seemed like a key to decipher the letters on the other. These Zillah placed on one side, not choosing to do any more at that time. Then she went on to examine the others. What these were has already been explained. They were the letters of Obed Chute, and the farewell note of Lady Chetwynde. But in addition to these there was another letter, with which the reader is not as yet acquainted. It was as brown and as faded as the other papers, with writing as pale and as illegible. It was in the handwriting of Obed Chute. It was as follows:

"New York, *October* 20, 1841.

"Dear Sir,—L. C. has been in the convent a year. The seventy thousand dollars will never again trouble you. All is now settled, and no one need ever know that the Redfield Lyttoun who ran away with L. C. was really Captain

Pomeroy. There is no possibility that any one can ever find it out, unless you yourself disclose your secret. Allow me to congratulate you on the happy termination of this unpleasant business.
"Yours, truly,   Obed Chute.
"Captain O. N. Pomeroy."

Zillah read this over many times. She could not comprehend one word of it as yet. Who was L. C. she knew not. The mention of Captain Pomeroy, however, seemed to implicate her father in some "unpleasant business." A darker anticipation of evil, and a profounder dread, settled over her heart. She did not say a word to Hilda. This, whatever it was, could not be made the subject of girlish confidence. It was something which she felt was to be examined by herself in solitude and in fear. Once only did she look at Hilda. It was when the latter asked, in a tone of sympathy:

"Dear Zillah, what is it?" And, as she asked this, she stooped forward and kissed her.

Zillah shuddered involuntarily. Why? Not because she suspected her friend. Her nature was too noble to harbor suspicion. Her shudder rather arose from that mysterious premonition which, according to old superstitions, arises warningly and instinctively and blindly at the approach of danger. So the old superstition says that this involuntary shudder will arise when any one steps over the place which is destined to be our grave. A pleasant fancy!

Zillah shuddered, and looked up at Hilda with a strange dazed expression. It was some time before she spoke.

"They are family papers," she said. "I—I don't understand them. I will look over them."

She gathered up the papers abruptly, and left the room. As the door closed after her Hilda sat looking at the place where she had vanished, with a very singular smile on her face.

For the remainder of that day Zillah continued shut up in her own room. Hilda went once to ask, in a voice of the sweetest and tenderest sympathy, what was the matter. Zillah only replied that she was not well, and was lying down. She would not open her door, however. Again, before bedtime, Hilda went. At her earnest entreaty Zillah let her in. She was very pale, with a weary, anxious expression on her face.

Hilda embraced her and kissed her.

"Oh, my darling," said she, "will you not tell me your trouble? Perhaps I may be of use to you. Will you not give me your confidence?"

"Not just yet, Hilda dearest. I do not want to trouble you. Besides, there may be nothing in it. I will speak to the Earl first, and then I will tell you."

"And you will not tell me now?" murmured Hilda, reproachfully.

"No, dearest, not now. Better not. You will soon know all, whether it is good or bad. I am going back to Chetwynde to-morrow."

"To-morrow?"

"Yes," said Zillah, mournfully. "I must go back to end my suspense. You can do nothing. Lord Chetwynde only can tell me what I want to know. I will tell him all, and he can dispel my trouble, or else deepen it in my heart forever."

"How terrible! What a frightful thing this

must be. My darling, my friend, my sister, tell me this—was it that wretched paper?"

"Yes," said Zillah. "And now, dearest, good-night. Leave me—I am very miserable."

Hilda kissed her again.

"Darling, I would not leave you, but you drive me away. You have no confidence in your poor Hilda. But I will not reproach you. Good-night, darling."

"Good-night, dearest."

CHAPTER XVIII.

A SHOCK.

THE discovery of these papers thus brought the visit to Pomeroy Court to an abrupt termination. The place had now become intolerable to Zillah. In her impatience she was eager to leave, and her one thought now was to apply to Lord Chetwynde for a solution of this dark mystery.

"Why, Zillah," he cried, as she came back; "what is the meaning of this? You have made but a short stay.. Was Pomeroy Court too gloomy, or did you think that your poor father was lonely here without you? Lonely enough he was—and glad indeed he is to see his little Zillah."

And Lord Chetwynde kissed her fondly, exhibiting a delight which touched Zillah to the heart. She could not say any thing then and there about the real cause of her sudden return. She would have to wait for a favorable opportunity, even though her heart was throbbing, in her fierce impatience, as though it would burst. She took refuge in caresses and in general remarks as to her joy on finding herself back again, leaving him to suppose that the gloom which hung around Pomeroy Court now had been too oppressive for her, and that she had hurried away from it.

The subject which was uppermost in Zillah's mind was one which she hardly knew how to introduce. It was of such delicacy that the idea of mentioning it to the Earl filled her with repugnance. For the first day she was distrait and preoccupied. Other days followed. Her nights were sleepless. The Earl soon saw that there was something on her mind, and taxed her with it. Zillah burst into tears and sat weeping.

"My child," said the Earl, tenderly. "This must not go on. There can not be any thing in your thoughts which you need hesitate to tell me. Will you not show some confidence toward me?"

Zillah looked at him, and his loving face encouraged her. Besides, this suspense was unendurable. Her repugnance to mention such a thing for a time made her silent; but at last she ventured upon the dark and terrible subject.

"Something occurred at Pomeroy Court," she said, and then stopped.

"Well?" said the Earl, kindly and encouragingly.

"It is something which I want very much to ask you about—"

"Well, why don't you?" said Lord Chetwynde. "My poor child, you can't be afraid of me, and yet it looks like it. You are very mysterious. This 'something' must have been very import-

ant to have sent you back so soon. Was it a discovery, or was it a fright? Did you find a dead body? But what is that you can want to ask me about? I have been a hermit for twenty years. I crept into my shell before you were born, and here I have lived ever since."

The Earl spoke playfully, yet with an uneasy curiosity in his tone. Zillah was encouraged to go on.

"It is something," said she, timidly and hesitatingly, "which I found among my father's papers."

Lord Chetwynde looked all around the room. Then he rose.

"Come into the library," said he. "Perhaps it is something very important; and if so, there need be no listeners."

Saying this he led the way in silence, followed by Zillah. Arriving there he motioned Zillah to a seat, and took a chair opposite hers, looking at her with a glance of perplexity and curiosity. Amidst this there was an air of apprehension about him, as though he feared that the secret which Zillah wished to tell might be connected with those events in his life which he wished to remain unrevealed. This suspicion was natural. His own secret was so huge, so engrossing, that when one came to him as Zillah did now, bowed down by the weight of another secret, he would naturally imagine that it was connected with his own. He sat now opposite Zillah, with this fear in his face, and with the air of a man who was trying to fortify himself against some menacing calamity.

"I have been in very deep trouble," began Zillah, timidly, and with downcast eyes. "This time I ventured into dear papa's study—and I happened to examine his desk."

She hesitated.

"Well?" said the Earl, in a low voice.

"In the desk I found a secret drawer, which I would not have discovered except by the merest chance; and inside of this secret drawer I found some papers, which—which have filled me with anxiety."

"A secret drawer?" said the Earl, as Zillah again paused. "And what were these papers that you found in it?" There was intense anxiety in the tones of his voice as he asked this question.

"I found there," said Zillah, "a paper written in cipher. There was a key connected with it, by means of which I was able to decipher it."

"Written in cipher? How singular!" said the Earl, with increasing anxiety. "What could it possibly have been?"

Zillah stole a glance at him fearfully and inquiringly. She saw that he was much excited and most eager in his curiosity.

"What was it?" repeated the Earl. "Why do you keep me in suspense? You need not be afraid of me, my child. Of course it is nothing that I am in any way concerned with; and even if it were—why—at any rate, tell me what it was."

The Earl spoke in a tone of feverish excitement, which was so unlike any thing that Zillah had ever seen in him before that her embarrassment was increased.

"It was something," she went on, desperately, and in a voice which trembled with agitation, "with which you are connected—something which I had never heard of before—something which filled me with horror. I will show it to you—but I want first to ask you one thing. Will you answer it?"

"Why should I not?" said the Earl, in a low voice.

"It is about Lady Chetwynde," said Zillah, whose voice had died away to a whisper.

The Earl's face seemed to turn to stone as he looked at her. He had been half prepared for this, but still, when it finally came, it was overwhelming. Once before, and once only in his life, had he told his secret. That was to General Pomeroy. But Zillah was different, and even she, much as he loved her, was not one to whom he could speak about such a thing as this.

"Well?" said he at last, in a harsh, constrained voice. "Ask what you wish."

Zillah started. The tone was so different from that in which Lord Chetwynde usually spoke that she was frightened.

"I—I do not know how to ask what I want to ask," she stammered.

"I can imagine it," said the Earl. "It is about my dishonor. I told General Pomeroy about it once, and it seems that he has kindly written it out for your benefit."

Bitterness indescribable was in the Earl's tones as he said this. Zillah shrank back into herself and looked with fear and wonder upon this man, who a few moments before had been all fondness, but now was all suspicion. Her first impulse was to go and caress him, and explain away the cipher so that it might never again trouble him in this way. But she was too frank and honest to do this, and, besides, her own desire to unravel the mystery had by this time become so intense that it was impossible to stop. The very agitation of the Earl, while it frightened her, still gave new power to her eager and feverish curiosity. But now, more than ever, she began to realize what all this involved. That face which caught her eyes, once all love, which had never before regarded her with aught but tenderness, yet which now seemed cold and icy—that face told her all the task that lay before her. Could she encounter it? But how could she help it? Dare she go on? Yet she could not go back now.

The Earl saw her hesitation.

"I know what you wish to ask," said he, "and will answer it. Child, she dishonored me—she dragged my name down into the dust! Do you ask more? She fled with a villain!"

That stern, white face, which was set in anguish before her, from whose lips these words seemed to be torn, as, one by one, they were flung out to her ears, was remembered by Zillah many and many a time in after years. At this moment the effect upon her was appalling. She was dumb. A vague desire to avert his wrath arose in her heart. She looked at him imploringly; but her look had no longer any power.

"Speak!" he said, impatiently, after waiting for a time. "Speak. Tell me what it is that you have found; tell me what this thing is that concerns me. Can it be any thing more than I have said?"

Zillah trembled. This sudden transformation—this complete change from warm affection to icy coldness—from devoted love to iron sternness—was something which she did not anticipate. Being thus taken unawares, she was all unnerved and overcome. She could no longer restrain herself.

"Oh, father!" she cried, bursting into tears, and flinging herself at his feet in uncontrollable emotion. "Oh, father! Do not look at me so—do not speak so to your poor Zillah. Have I any friend on earth but you?"

She clasped his thin, white hands in hers, while hot tears fell upon them. But the Earl sat unmoved, and changed not a muscle of his countenance. He waited for a time, taking no notice of her anguish, and then spoke, with no relaxation of the sternness of his tone.

"Daughter," said he, "do not become agitated. It was you yourself who brought on this conversation. Let us end it at once. Show me the papers of which you speak. You say that they are connected with me—that they filled you with horror. What is it that you mean? Something more than curiosity about the unhappy woman who was once my wife has driven you to ask explanations of me. Show me the papers."

His tone forbade denial. Zillah said not a word. Slowly she drew from her pocket those papers, heavy with fate, and, with a trembling hand, she gave them to the Earl. Scarcely had she done so than she repented. But it was too late. Beside, of what avail would it have been to have kept them? She herself had begun this conversation; she herself had sought for a revelation of this mystery. The end must come, whatever it might be.

"Oh, father!" she moaned, imploringly.

"What is it?" asked the Earl.

"You knew my dear papa all his life, did you not, from his boyhood?"

"Yes," said the Earl, mechanically, looking at the papers which Zillah had placed in his hand; "yes—from boyhood."

"And you loved and honored him?"

"Yes."

"Was there ever a time in which you lost sight of one another, or did not know all about one another?"

"Certainly. For twenty years we lost sight of one another completely. Why do you ask?"

"Did he ever live in London?" asked Zillah, despairingly.

"Yes," said the Earl; "he lived there for two years, and I scarcely ever saw him. I was in politics; he was in the army. I was busy every moment of my time; he had all that leisure which officers enjoy, and leading the life of gayety peculiar to them. But why do you ask? What connection has all this with the papers?"

Zillah murmured some inaudible words, and then sat watching the Earl as he began to examine the papers, with a face on which there were visible a thousand contending emotions. The Earl looked over the papers. There was the cipher and the key; and there was also a paper written out by Zillah, containing the explanation of the cipher, according to the key. On the paper which contained the key was a written statement to the effect that two-thirds of the letters had no meaning. Trusting to this, Zillah had written out her translation of the cipher, just as Hilda had before done.

The Earl read the translation through most carefully.

"What's this?" he exclaimed, in deeper agita-

E

tion. Zillah made no reply. In fact, at that moment her heart was throbbing so furiously that she could not have spoken a word. Now had come the crisis of her fate, and her heart, by a certain deep instinct, told her this. Beneath all the agitation arising from the change in the Earl ,there was something more profound, more dread. It was a continuation of that dark foreboding which she had felt at Pomeroy Court—a certain fearful looking for of some obscure and shadowy calamity.

The Earl, after reading the translation, took the cipher writing and held up the key beside it, while his thin hands trembled, and his eyes seemed to devour the sheet, as he slowly spelled out the frightful meaning. It was bad for Zillah that these papers had fallen into his hands in such a way. Her evil star had been in the ascendent when she was drawn on to this. Coming to him thus, from the hand of Zillah herself, there was an authenticity and an authority about the papers which otherwise might have been wanting. It was to him, at this time, precisely the same as if they had been handed to him by the General himself. Had they been discovered by himself originally, it is possible—in fact, highly probable—that he would have looked upon them with different eyes, and their effect upon him would have been far otherwise. As it was, however, Zillah herself had found them and given them to him. Zillah had been exciting him by her agitation and her suffering, and had, last of all, been rousing him gradually up to a pitch of the most intense excitement, by the conversation which she had brought forward, by her timidity, her reluctance, her strange questionings, and her general agitation. To a task which required the utmost coolness of feeling, and calm impartiality of judgment, he brought a feverish heart, a heated brain, and an unreasoning fear of some terrific disclosure. All this prepared him to accept blindly whatever the paper might reveal.

As he examined the paper he did not look at Zillah, but spelled out the words from the characters, one by one, and saw that the translation was correct. This took a long time ; and all the while Zillah sat there, with her eyes fastened on him ; but he did not give her one look. All his soul seemed to be absorbed by the papers before him. At last he ended with the cipher writing—or, at least, with as much of it as was supposed to be decipherable—and then he turned to the other papers. These he read through; and then, beginning again, he read them through once more. One only exclamation escaped him. It was while reading that last letter, where mention was made of the name *Redfield Lyttoun* being an assumed one. Then he said, in a low voice which seemed like a groan wrung out by anguish from his inmost soul :

"Oh, my God ! my God !"

At last the Earl finished examining the papers. He put them down feebly, and sat staring blankly at vacancy. He looked ten years older than when he had entered the dining-room. His face was as bloodless as the face of a corpse, his lips were ashen, and new furrows seemed to have been traced on his brow. On his face there was stamped a fixed and settled expression of dull, changeless anguish, which smote Zillah to her heart. He did not see her—he did not notice that other face, as pallid as his own,

which was turned toward his, with an agony in its expression which rivaled all that he was enduring. No—he noticed nothing, and saw no one. All his soul was taken up now with one thought. He had read the paper, and had at once accepted its terrific meaning. To him it had declared that in the tragedy of his young life, not only his wife had been false, but his friend also. More—that it was his friend who had betrayed his wife. More yet—and there was fresh anguish in this thought—this friend, after the absence of many years, had returned and claimed his friendship, and had received his confidences. To him he had poured out the grief of his heart—the confession of life-long sorrows which had been wrought by the very man to whom he told his tale. And this was the man who, under the plea of ancient friendship, had bought his son for gold ! Great Heaven ! the son of the woman whom he had ruined —and for gold ! He had drawn away his wife to ruin—he had come and drawn away his son— into what ? into a marriage with the daughter of his own mother's betrayer.

Such were the thoughts, mad, frenzied, that filled Lord Chetwynde's mind as he sat there stunned—paralyzed by this hideous accumulation of intolerable griefs. What was Zillah to him now ? The child of a foul traitor. The one to whom his noble son had been sold. That son had been, as he once said, the solace of his life. For his sake he had been content to live even under his load of shame and misery. For him he had labored ; for his happiness he had planned. And for what ? What ? That which was too hideous to think of—a living death—a union with one from whom he ought to stand apart for evermore.

Little did Zillah know what thoughts were sweeping and surging through the mind of Lord Chetwynde as she sat there watching him with her awful eyes. Little did she dream of the feelings with which, at that moment, he regarded her. Nothing of this kind came to her. One only thought was present—the anguish which he was enduring. The sight of that anguish was intolerable. She looked, and waited, and at last, unable to bear this any longer, she sprang forward, and tore his hands away from his face.

"It's not! It's not!" she gasped. "Say you do not believe it ! Oh, father ! It's impossible !"

The Earl withdrew his hands, and shrank away from her, regarding her with that blank gaze which shows that the mind sees not the material form toward which the eyes are turned, but is taken up with its own thoughts.

"Impossible ?" he repeated. "Yes. That is the word I spoke when I first heard that *she* had left me. Impossible? And why? Is a friend more true than a wife? After Lady Chetwynde failed me, why should I believe in Neville Pomeroy? And you—why did you not let me end my life in peace? Why did you bring to me this frightful—this damning evidence which destroys my faith not in man, but even in Heaven itself?"

"Father! Oh, father!" moaned Zillah. But the Earl turned away. She seized his hand again in both hers. Again he shrank away, and withdrew his hand from her touch. She was abhorrent to him then !

"HE SAT STARING BLANKLY AT VACANCY."

This was her thought. She stepped back, and at once a wild revulsion of feeling took place within her also. All the fierce pride of her hot, impassioned Southern nature rose up in rebellion against this sudden, this hasty change. Why should he so soon lose faith in her father? He guilty!—her father!—the noble—the gentle—the stainless—the true—he! the pure in heart—

the one who through all her life had stood before her as the ideal of manly honor and loyalty and truth? Never! If it came to a question between Lord Chetwynde and that idol of her young life, whose memory she adored, then Lord Chetwynde must go down. Who was he that dared to think evil for one moment of the noblest of men! Could he himself compare with the father whom she had lost, in all that is highest in manhood? No. The charge was foul and false. Lord Chetwynde was false for so doubting his friend.

All this flashed over Zillah's mind, and at that moment, in her revulsion of indignant pride, she forgot altogether all those doubts which, but a short time before, had been agitating her own soul—doubts, too, which were so strong that they had forced her to bring on this scene with the Earl. All this was forgotten. Her loyalty to her father triumphed over doubt, so soon as she saw another sharing that doubt.

But her thoughts were suddenly checked.

The Earl, who had but lately shrunk away from her, now turned toward her, and looked at her with a strange, dazed, blank expression of face, and wild vacant eyes. For a moment he sat turned toward her thus; and then, giving a deep groan, he fell forward out of his chair on the floor. With a piercing cry Zillah sprang toward him and tried to raise him up. Her cry aroused the household. Mrs. Hart was first among those who rushed to the room to help her. She flung her arms around the prostrate form, and lifted it upon the sofa. As he lay there a shudder passed through Zillah's frame at the sight which she beheld. For the Earl, in falling, had struck his head against the sharp corner of the table, and his white and venerable hairs were now all stained with blood, which trickled slowly over his wan pale face.

CHAPTER XIX.

A NEW PERPLEXITY.

At the sight of that venerable face, as white as marble, now set in the fixedness of death, whose white hair was all stained with the blood that oozed from the wound on his forehead, all Zillah's tenderness returned. Bitterly she reproached herself.

"I have killed him! It was all my fault!" she cried. "Oh, save him! Do something! Can you not save him?"

Mrs. Hart did not seem to hear her at all. She had carried the Earl to the sofa, and then she knelt by his side, with her arms flung around him. She seemed unconscious of the presence of Zillah. Her head lay on the Earl's breast. At last she pressed her lips to his forehead, where the blood flowed, with a quick, feverish kiss. Her white face, as it was set against the stony face of the Earl, startled Zillah. She stood mute.

The servants hurried in. Mrs. Hart roused herself, and had the Earl carried to his room. Zillah followed. The Earl was put to bed. A servant was sent off for a doctor. Mrs. Hart and Zillah watched anxiously till the doctor came. The doctor dressed the wound, and gave directions for the treatment of the patient. Quiet above all things was enjoined. Apoplexy was hinted at, but it was only a hint. The real conviction of the doctor seemed to be that it was mental trouble of some kind, and this conviction was shared by those who watched the Earl.

Zillah and Mrs. Hart both watched that night. They sat in an adjoining room. But little was said at first. Zillah was busied with her own

thoughts, and Mrs. Hart was preoccupied, and more distrait than usual.

Midnight came. For hours Zillah had brooded over her own sorrows. She longed for sympathy. Mrs. Hart seemed to her to be the one in whom she might best confide. The evident affection which Mrs. Hart felt for the Earl was of itself an inducement to confidence. Her own affection for the aged housekeeper also impelled her to tell her all that had happened. And so it was that, while they sat there together, Zillah gradually told her about her interview with the Earl.

But the story which Zillah told did not comprise the whole truth. She did not wish to go into details, and there were many circumstances which she did not feel inclined to tell to the housekeeper. There was no reason why she should tell about the secret cipher, and very many reasons why she should not. It was an affair which concerned her father and her family. That her own fears were well founded she dared not suppose, and therefore she would not even hint about such fears to another. Above all, she was unwilling to tell what effect the disclosure of that secret of hers had upon the Earl. Better far, it seemed to her, it would be to carry that secret to the grave than to disclose it in any confidence to any third person. Whatever the result might be, it would be better to hold it concealed between the Earl and herself.

What Zillah said was to the effect that she had been asking the Earl about Lady Chetwynde; that the mention of the subject had produced an extraordinary effect; that she wished to withdraw it, but the Earl insisted on knowing what she had to say.

"Oh," she cried, "how bitterly I lament that I said any thing about it! But I had seen something at home which excited my curiosity. It was about Lady Chetwynde. It stated that she eloped with a certain Redfield Lyttoun, and that the name was an assumed one; but what," cried Zillah, suddenly starting forward—"what is the matter?"

While Zillah was speaking Mrs. Hart's face—always pale—seemed to turn gray, and a shudder passed through her thin, emaciated frame. She pressed her hand on her heart, and suddenly sank back with a groan.

Zillah sprang toward her and raised her up. Mrs. Hart still kept her hand on her heart, and gave utterance to low moans of anguish. Zillah chafed her hands, and then hurried off and got some wine. At the taste of the stimulating liquor the poor creature revived. She then sat panting, with her eyes fixed on the floor. Zillah sat looking at her without saying a word, and afraid to touch again upon a subject which had produced so disastrous an effect. Yet why should it? Why should this woman show emotion equal to that of the Earl at the very mention of such a thing? There was surely some unfathomable mystery about it. The emotion of the Earl was intelligible—that of Mrs. Hart was not so. Such were the thoughts that passed through her mind as she sat there in silence watching her companion.

Hours passed without one word being spoken. Zillah frequently urged Mrs. Hart to go to bed, but Mrs. Hart refused. She could not sleep, she said, and she would rather be near the Earl.

At length Zillah, penetrated with pity for the poor suffering woman, insisted on her lying down on the sofa. Mrs. Hart had to yield. She lay down accordingly, but not to sleep. The sighs that escaped her from time to time showed that her secret sorrow kept her awake.

Suddenly, out of a deep silence, Mrs. Hart sprang up and turned her white face toward Zillah. Her large, weird eyes seemed to burn themselves into Zillah's brain. Her lips moved. It was but in a whisper that she spoke:

"Never—never—never—mention it again—either to him or to me. It is hell to both of us!"

She fell back again, moaning.

Zillah sat transfixed, awe-struck and wondering.

CHAPTER XX.

A MODEL NURSE, AND FRIEND IN NEED.

Zillah did not tell Hilda about the particular cause of the Earl's sickness for some time, but Hilda was sufficiently acute to conjecture what it might be. She was too wary to press-matters, and although she longed to know all, yet she refrained from asking. She knew enough of Zillah's frank and confiding nature to feel sure that the confidence would come of itself some day unasked. Zillah was one of those who can not keep a secret. Warm-hearted, open, and impulsive, she was ever on the watch for sympathy, and no sooner did she have a secret than she longed to share it with some one. She had divulged her secret to the Earl, with results that were lamentable. She had partially disclosed it to Mrs. Hart, with results equally lamentable. The sickness of the Earl and of Mrs. Hart was now added to her troubles; and the time would soon come when, from the necessities of her nature, she would be compelled to pour out her soul to Hilda. So Hilda waited.

Mrs. Hart seemed to be completely broken down. She made a feeble attempt to take part in nursing the Earl, but fainted away in his room. Hilda was obliged to tell her that she would be of more use by staying away altogether, and Mrs. Hart had to obey. She tottered about, frequently haunting that portion of the house where the Earl lay, and asking questions about his health. Zillah and Hilda were the chief nurses, and took turns at watching. But Zillah was inexperienced, and rather noisy. In spite of her affectionate solicitude she could not create new qualities within herself, and in one moment make herself a good nurse. Hilda, on the contrary, seemed formed by nature for the sick-room. Stealthy, quiet, noiseless, she moved about as silently as a spirit. Every thing was in its place. The medicines were always arranged in the best order. The pillows were always comfortable. The doctor looked at her out of his professional eyes, with cordial approval, and when he visited he gave his directions always to her, as though she alone could be considered a responsible being. Zillah saw this, but felt no jealousy. She humbly acquiesced in the doctor's decision; meekly felt that she had none of the qualities of a nurse; and admired Hilda's genius for that office with all her heart. Added to this conviction of her own inability, there was the consciousness that she had brought all this upon the Earl—a consciousness which brought on self-reproach and perpetual remorse. The very affection which she felt for Lord Chetwynde of itself incapacitated her. A good nurse should be cool. Like a good doctor or a good surgeon, his affections should not be too largely interested. It is a mistake to suppose that one's dear friends make one's best nurses. They are very well to look at, but not to administer medicine or smooth the pillow. Zillah's face of agony was not so conducive to recovery as the calm smile of Hilda. The Earl did not need kisses or hot tears upon his face. What he did need was quiet, and a regular administration of medicines presented by a cool, steady hand.

The Earl was very low. He was weak, yet conscious of all that was going on. Zillah's heart was gladdened to hear once more words of love from him. The temporary hardness of heart which had appalled her had all passed away, and the old affection had returned. In a few feeble words he begged her not to let Guy know that he was sick, for he would soon recover, and it would only worry his son. Most of the words which he spoke were about that son. Zillah would have given any thing if she could have brought Guy to that bedside. But that was impossible, and she could only wait and hope.

Weeks passed away, and in the interviews which she had with Hilda Zillah gradually let her know all that had happened. She told her about the discovery of the papers, and the effect which they had upon the Earl. At last, one evening, she gave the papers to Hilda. It was when Zillah came to sit up with the Earl. Hilda took the papers solemnly, and said that she would look over them. She reproached Zillah for not giving her her confidence before, and said that she had a claim before any one, and if she had only told her all about it at Pomeroy Court, this might not have happened. All this Zillah felt keenly, and began to think that the grand mistake which she had made was in not taking Hilda into her confidence at the very outset.

"I do not know what these papers may mean," said Hilda; "but I tell you candidly that if they contain what I suspect, I would have advised you never to mention it to Lord Chetwynde. It was an awful thing to bring it all up to him."

"Then you know all about it?" asked Zillah, wonderingly.

"Of course. Every body knows the sorrow of his life. It has been public for the last twenty years. I heard all about it when I was a little girl from one of the servants. I could have advised you to good purpose, and saved you from sorrow, if you had only confided in me."

Such were Hilda's words, and Zillah felt new self-reproach to think that she had not confided in her friend.

"I hope another time you will not be so wanting in confidence," said Hilda, as she retired. "Do I not deserve it?"

"You do, you do, my dearest!" said Zillah, affectionately. "I have always said that you were like a sister—and after this I will tell you every thing."

Hilda kissed her, and departed.

Zillah waited impatiently to see Hilda again. She was anxious to know what effect these papers would produce on her. Would she scout them as absurd, or believe the statement? When Hilda appeared again to relieve her, all Zillah's curiosity was expressed in her face. But Hilda said nothing about the papers. She urged Zillah to go and sleep.

"I know what you want to say," said she, "but I will not talk about it now. Go off to bed, darling, and get some rest. You need it."

So Zillah had to go, and defer the conversation till some other time. She went away to bed, and slept but little. Before her hour she was up and hastened back.

"Why, Zillah," said Hilda, "you are half an hour before your time. You are wearing yourself out."

"Did you read the papers?" asked Zillah, as she kissed her.

"Yes," said Hilda, seriously.

"And what do you think?" asked Zillah, with a frightened face.

"My darling," said Hilda, "how excited you are! How you tremble! Poor dear! What is the matter?"

"That awful confession!" gasped Zillah, in a scarce audible voice.

"My darling," said Hilda, passing her arm about Zillah's neck, "why should you take it so to heart? You have no concern with it. You are Guy Molyneux's wife. This paper has now no concern with you."

Zillah started back as though she had been stung. Nothing could have been more abhorrent to her, in such a connection, than the suggestion of her marriage.

"You believe it, then?"

"Believe it! Why, don't you?" said Hilda, in wondering tones. "You do, or you would not feel so. Why did you ask the Earl? Why

did you give it to me? Is it not your father's own confession?"

Zillah shuddered, and burst into tears.

"No," she cried at last; "I do not believe it. I will never believe it. Why did I ask the Earl! Because I believed that he would dispel my anxiety. That is all."

"Ah, poor child!" said Hilda, fondly. "You are too young to have trouble. Think no more of this."

"Think of it! I tell you I think of it all the time—night and day," cried Zillah, impetuously. "Think of it! Why, what else can I do than think of it?"

"But you do not believe it?"

"No. Never will I believe it."

"Then why trouble yourself about it?"

"Because it is a stain on my dear papa's memory. It is undeserved—it is inexplicable; but it is a stain. And how can I, his daughter, not think of it?"

"A stain!" said Hilda, after a thoughtful pause. "If there were a stain on such a name, I can well imagine that you would feel anguish. But there is none. How can there be? Think of his noble life spent in honor in the service of his country! Can you associate any stain with such a life?"

"He was the noblest of men!" interrupted Zillah, vehemently.

"Then do not talk of a stain," said Hilda, calmly. "As to Lord Chetwynde, he, at least, has nothing to say. To him General Pomeroy was such a friend as he could never have hoped for. He saved Lord Chetwynde from beggary and ruin. When General Pomeroy first came back to England he found Lord Chetwynde at the last extremity, and advanced sixty thousand pounds to help him. Think of that! And it's true. I was informed of it on good authority. Besides, General Pomeroy did more; for he intrusted his only daughter to Lord Chetwynde—"

"My God!" cried Zillah; "what are you saying? Do you not know, Hilda, that every word that you speak is a stab? What do you mean? Do you dare to talk as if my papa has shut the mouth of an injured friend by a payment of money? Do you mean me to think that, after dishonoring his friend, he has sought to efface the dishonor by gold? My God! you will drive me mad. You make my papa, and Lord Chetwynde also, sink down into fathomless depths of infamy."

"You torture my words into a meaning different from what I intended," said Hilda, quietly. "I merely meant to show you that Lord Chetwynde's obligations to General Pomeroy were so vast that he ought not even to suspect him, no matter how strong the proof."

Zillah waved her hands with a gesture of despair.

"No matter how strong the proof!" she repeated. "Ah! There it is again. You quietly assume my papa's guilt in every word. You have read those papers, and have believed every word."

"You are very unkind, Zillah. I was doing my best to comfort you."

"Comfort!" cried Zillah, in indescribable tones.

"Ah, my darling, do not be cross," said Hilda, twining her arms around Zillah's neck. "You know I loved your papa only less than you did. He was a father to me. What can I say? You yourself were troubled by those papers. So was I. And that is all I will say. I will not speak of them again."

And here Hilda stopped, and went about the room to attend to her duties as nurse. Zillah stood, with her mind full of strange, conflicting feelings. The hints which Hilda had given sank deep into her soul. What did they mean? Their frightful meaning stood revealed full before her in all its abhorrent reality.

Reviewing those papers by the light of Hilda's dark interpretation, she saw what they involved. This, then, was the cause of her marriage. Her father had tried to atone for the past. He had made Lord Chetwynde rich to pay for the dishonor that he had suffered. He had stolen away the wife, and given a daughter in her place. She, then, had been the medium of this frightful attempt at readjustment, this atonement for wrongs that could never be atoned for. Hilda's meaning made this the only conceivable cause for that premature engagement, that hurried marriage by the death-bed. And could there be any other reason? Did it not look like the act of a remorseful sinner, anxious to finish his expiation, and make amends for crime before meeting his Judge in the other world to which he was hastening? The General had offered up every thing to expiate his crime—he had given his fortune—he had sacrificed his daughter. What other cause could possibly have moved him to enforce the hideous mockery of that ghastly, that unparalleled marriage?

Beneath such intolerable thoughts as these, Zillah's brain whirled. She could not avoid them. Affection, loyalty, honor—all bade her trust in her father; the remembrance of his noble character, of his stainless life, his pure and gentle nature, all recurred. In vain. Still the dark suspicion insidiously conveyed by Hilda would obtrude; and, indeed, under such circumstances, Zillah would have been more than human if they had not come forth before her. As it was, she was only human and young and inexperienced. Dark days and bitter nights were before her, but among all none were more dark and bitter than this.

CHAPTER XXI.

A DARK COMMISSION.

THESE amateur nurses who had gathered about the Earl differed very much, as may be supposed, in their individual capacities. As for Mrs. Hart, she was very quickly put out of the way. The stroke which had prostrated her, at the outset, did not seem to be one from which she could very readily recover. The only thing which she did was to totter to the room early in the morning, so as to find out how the Earl was, and then to totter back again until the next morning. Mrs. Hart thus was incapable; and Zillah was not very much better. Since her conversation with Hilda there were thoughts in her mind so new, so different from any which she had ever had before, and so frightful in their import, that they changed all her nature. She became melancholy, self-absorbed, and preoccu-

pied. Silent and distrait, she wandered about the Earl's room aimlessly, and did not seem able to give to him that close and undivided attention which he needed. Hilda found it necessary to reproach her several times in her usual affectionate way; and Zillah tried, after each reproach, to rouse herself from her melancholy, so as to do better the next time. Yet, the next time she did just as badly; and, on the whole, acquitted herself but poorly of her responsible task.

And thus it happened that Hilda was obliged to assume the supreme responsibility. The others had grown more than ever useless, and she, accordingly, grew more than ever necessary. To this task she devoted herself with that assiduity and patience for which she was distinguished. The constant loss of sleep, and the incessant and weary vigils which she was forced to maintain, seemed to have but little effect upon her elastic and energetic nature. Zillah, in spite of her preoccupation, could not help seeing that Hilda was doing nearly all the work, and remonstrated with her accordingly. But in her earnest remonstrances Hilda turned a deaf ear.

"You see, dear," said she, "there is no one but me. Mrs. Hart is herself in need of a nurse, and you are no better than a baby, so how can I help watching poor dear Lord Chetwynde?"

"But you will wear yourself out," persisted Zillah.

"Oh, we will wait till I begin to show signs of weariness," said Hilda, in a sprightly tone. "At present, I feel able to spend a great many days and nights here."

Indeed, to all her remonstrances Hilda was quite inaccessible, and it remained for Zillah to see her friend spend most of her time in that sick-room, the ruling spirit, while she was comparatively useless. She could only feel gratitude for so much kindness, and express that gratitude whenever any occasion arose. While Hilda was regardless of Zillah's remonstrances, she was equally so of the doctor's warnings. That functionary did not wish to see his best nurse wear herself out, and warned her frequently, but with no effect whatever. Hilda's self-sacrificing zeal was irrepressible and invincible.

While Hilda was thus devoting herself to the Earl with such tireless patience, and exciting the wonder and gratitude of all in that little household by her admirable self-devotion, there was another who watched the progress of events with perfect calmness, yet with deep anxiety. Gualtier was not able now to give his music lessons, yet, although he no longer could gain admission to the inmates of Castle Chetwynde, his anxiety about the Earl was a sufficient excuse for calling every day to inquire about his health. On those inquiries he not only heard about the Earl, but also about all the others, and more particularly about Hilda. He cultivated an acquaintance with the doctor, who, though generally disposed to stand on his dignity toward musicians, seemed to think that Gualtier had gained from the Earl's patronage a higher title to be noticed than any which his art could give. Besides, the good doctor knew that Gualtier was constantly at the Castle, and naturally wished to avail himself of so good an opportunity of finding out all about the internal life of this noble but secluded family. Gualtier humored him to the fullest extent, and with a great appearance of frankness told him as much as he thought proper, and no more; in return for which confidence he received the fullest information as to the present condition of the household. What surprised Gualtier most was Hilda's devotion. He had not anticipated it. It was real, yet what could be her motive? In his own language—What game was the little thing up to? This was the question which he incessantly asked himself, without being able to answer it. His respect for her genius was too great to allow him for one moment to suppose that it was possible for her to act without some deep motive. Her immolation of self, her assiduity, her tenderness, her skill, all seemed to this man so many elements in the game which she was playing. And for all these things he only admired her the more fervently. That she would succeed he never for a moment doubted; though what it was that she might be aiming at, and what it was that her success might involve, were inscrutable mysteries.

What game is the little thing up to? he asked himself, affectionately, and with tender emphasis. What game? And this became the one idea of his mind. Little else were his thoughts engaged in, except an attempt to fathom the depths of Hilda's design. But he was baffled. What that design involved could hardly have been discovered by him. Often and often he wished that he could look into that sick-chamber to see what the "little thing was up to." Yet, could he have looked into that chamber, he would have seen nothing that could have enlightened him. He would have seen a slender, graceful form, moving lightly about the room, now stooping over the form of the sick man to adjust or to smooth his pillow, now watchfully and warily administering the medicine which stood near the bed. Hilda was not one who would leave any thing to be discovered, even by those who might choose to lurk in ambush and spy at her through a keyhole.

But though Hilda's plans were for some time impenetrable, there came at last an opportunity when he was furnished with light sufficient to reveal them—a lurid light which made known to him possibilities in her which he had certainly not suspected before.

One day, on visiting Chetwynde Castle, he found her in the chief parlor. He thought that she had come there purposely in order to see him; and he was not disappointed. After a few questions as to the Earl's health, she excused herself, and said that she must hurry back to his room; but, as she turned to go, she slipped a piece of paper into his hand, as she had done once before. On it he saw the following words: "*Be in the West Avenue, at the former place, at three o'clock.*"

Gualtier wandered about in a state of feverish impatience till the appointed hour, marveling what the purpose might be which had induced Hilda to seek the interview. He felt that the purpose must be of far-reaching importance which would lead her to seek him at such a time; but what it was he tried in vain to conjecture.

At last the hour came, and Gualtier, who had been waiting so long, was rewarded by the sight of Hilda. She was as calm as usual, but greeted him with greater cordiality than she was in the habit of showing. She also evinced greater cau-

tion than even on the former occasion, and led the way to a more lonely spot, and looked all around most carefully, so as to guard against the possibility of discovery. When, at length, she spoke, it was in a low and guarded voice.

"I am so worn down by nursing," she said, "that I have had to come out for a little fresh air. But I would not leave the Earl till they absolutely forced me. Such is my devotion to him that there is an impression abroad through the Castle that I will not survive him."

"Survive him? You speak as though he were doomed," said Gualtier.

"He—is—very—low," said Hilda, in a solemn monotone.

Gualtier said nothing, but regarded her in silence for some time.

"What was the cause of his illness?" he asked at length. "The doctor thinks that his mind is affected."

"For once, something like the truth has penetrated that heavy brain."

"Do you know any thing that can have happened?" asked Gualtier, cautiously.

"Yes; a sudden shock. Strange to say, it was administered by Mrs. Molyneux."

"Mrs. Molyneux!"

"Yes."

"I am so completely out of your sphere that I know nothing whatever of what is going on. How Mrs. Molyneux can have given a shock to the Earl that could have reduced him to his present state, I can not imagine."

"Of course it was not intentional. She happened to ask the Earl about something which revived old memories and old sorrows in a very forcible manner. He grew excited—so much so, indeed, that he fainted, and, in falling, struck his head. That is the whole story."

"May I ask," said Gualtier, after a thoughtful pause, "if Mrs. Molyneux's ill-fated questions had any reference to those things about which we have spoken together, from time to time?"

"They had—and a very close one. In fact, they arose out of those very papers which we have had before us."

Gualtier looked at Hilda, as she said this, with the closest attention.

"It happened," said Hilda, "that Mrs. Molyneux, on her last visit to Pomeroy Court, was seized with a fancy to examine her father's desk. While doing so, she found a secret drawer, which, by some singular accident, had been left started. and a little loose—just enough to attract her attention. This she opened, and in it, strange to say, she found that very cipher which I have told you of. A key accompanied it, by which she was able to read as much as we have read; and there were also those letters with which you are familiar. She took them to her room, shut herself up, and studied them as eagerly as ever either you or I did. She then hurried back to Chetwynde Castle, and laid every thing before the Earl. Out of this arose his excitement and its very sad results."

"I did not know that there were sufficient materials for accomplishing so much," said Gualtier, cautiously.

"No; the materials were not abundant. There was the cipher, with which no one would have supposed that any thing could be done. Then there were those other letters which lay with it in the desk, which corroborated what the cipher seemed to say. Out of this has suddenly arisen ruin and anguish."

"There was also the key," said Gualtier, in a tone of delicate insinuation.

"True," said Hilda; "had the key not been inclosed with the papers, she could not have understood the cipher, or made any thing out of the letters."

"The Earl must have believed it all."

"He never doubted for an instant. By the merest chance, I happened to be in a place where I saw it all," said Hilda, with a peculiar emphasis. "I thought that he would reject it at first, and that the first impulse would be to scout such a charge. But mark this"—and her voice grew solemn—"there must have been some knowledge in his mind of things unknown to us, or else he could never have been so utterly and completely overwhelmed. It was a blow which literally crushed him—in mind and body."

There was a long silence.

"And you think he can not survive this?" asked Gualtier.

"No," said Hilda, in a very strange, slow voice, "I do not think—that—he—can—recover. He is old and feeble. The shock was great. His mind wanders, also. He is sinking slowly, but surely."

She paused, and looked earnestly at Gualtier, who returned her look with one of equal earnestness.

"I have yet to tell you what purpose induced me to appoint this meeting," said she, in so strange a voice that Gualtier started. But he said not a word.

Hilda, who was standing near to him, drew nearer still. She looked all around, with a strange light in her eyes. Then she turned to him again, and said, in a low whisper:

"I want you to get me something."

Gualtier looked at her inquiringly, but in silence. His eyes seemed to ask her, "What is it?" She put her mouth close to his ear, and whispered something, heard only by him. But that low whisper was never forgotten. His face turned deathly pale. He looked away, and said not a word.

"Good-by," said Hilda; "I am going now." She held out her hand. He grasped it. At that moment their eyes met, and a look of intelligence flashed between them.

CHAPTER XXII.

THE JUDAS KISS.

IT has already been said that when the Earl rallied a little so as to recognize Zillah, all his old affection was exhibited, and the temporary aversion which he had manifested during that eventful time when he had seen the cipher writing had passed off without leaving any trace of its existence. It is quite likely indeed that the whole circumstance had been utterly obliterated from his memory, and when his eyes caught sight of Zillah she was to him simply the one whom he loved next best to Guy. His brain was in such a state that his faculties seemed dulled, and his memory nearly gone. Had he remembered that scene he would either have

continued to regard Zillah with horror, or else, if affection had triumphed over a sense of injury, he would have done something or said something in his more lucid intervals to assure Zillah of his continued love. But nothing of the kind occurred. He clung to Zillah like a child, and the few faint words which he addressed to her simply recognized her as the object of an affection which had never met with an interruption. They also had reference to Guy, as to whether she had written to him yet, and whether any more letters had been received from him. A letter, which came during the illness, she tried to read, but the poor weary brain of the sick man could not follow her. She had to tell him in a few general terms its contents.

For some weeks she had hoped that the Earl would recover, and therefore delayed sending the sad news to Guy. But at length she could no longer conceal from herself the fact that the illness would be long, and she saw that it was too serious to allow Guy to remain in ignorance. She longed to address him words of condolence, and sympathized deeply with him in the anxiety which she knew would be felt by a heart so affectionate as his.

And now as she thought of writing to him there came to her, more bitterly than ever, the thought of her false position. She write! She could not. It was Hilda who would write. Hilda stood between her and the one whom she wished to soothe. In spite of her warm and sisterly affection for her friend, and her boundless trust in her, this thought now sent a thrill of vexation through her; and she bitterly lamented the chain of events by which she had been placed in such a position. It was humiliating and galling. But could she not yet escape? Might she not even now write in her own name explaining all? No. It could not be—not now, for what would be the reception of such explanations, coming as they would with the news of his father's illness! Would he treat them with any consideration whatever? Would not his anxiety about his father lead him to regard them with an impatient disdain? But perhaps, on the other hand, he might feel softened and accept her explanation readily, without giving any thought to the strange deceit which had been practiced for so long a time. This gave her a gleam of hope; but in her perplexity she could not decide, so she sought counsel from Hilda as usual. Had Mrs. Hart being in the possession of her usual faculties she might possibly have asked her advice also; but, as it was, Hilda was the only one to whom she could turn.

Hilda listened to her with that sweet smile, and that loving and patient consideration, which she always gave to Zillah's confidences and appeals.

"Darling," said she, after a long and thoughtful silence, "I understand fully the perplexity which you feel. In fact, this letter *ought* to come from you, and from you only. I'm extremely sorry that I ever began this. I'm sure I did it from the *very best* motives. Who could ever have dreamed that it would become so embarrassing? And now I don't know what to do—that is, not just now."

"Do you think he would be angry at the deceit?"

"Do you yourself think so?" asked Hilda in reply.

HILDA WRITES TO GUY MOLYNEUX.

"Why, that is what I am afraid of; but then —isn't it possible that he might be—softened, you know—by anxiety?"

"People don't get softened by anxiety. They get impatient, angry with the world and with Providence. But the best way to judge is to put yourself in his situation. Suppose you were in India, and a letter was written to you by your wife—or your husband, I suppose I should say— telling you that your father was extremely ill, and that he himself had been deceiving you for some years. The writing would be strange—quite un- familiar; the story would be almost incredible; you wouldn't know what to think. You'd be deeply anxious, and yet half believe that some one was practicing a cruel jest on you. For my part, if I had an explanation to make I would wait for a time of prosperity and happiness. Misfortune makes people so bitter."

"That is the very thing that I'm afraid of," said Zillah, despairingly. "And—oh dear, what shall I do?"

"You must do one thing certainly, and that is write him about his father. You yourself must do it, darling."

"Why, what do you mean? You were just now showing me that this was the very thing which I could not do."

"You misunderstand me," said Hilda, with a smile. "Why, do you really mean to say that you do not see how easy it is to get out of this difficulty?"

"Easy! It seems to me a terrible one."

"Why, my darling child, don't you see that after you write your letter I can copy it? You surely have nothing so very private to say that you will object to that. I suppose all that you want to do is to break the news to him as gently and tenderly as possible. You don't want to indulge in expressions of personal affection, of course."

"Oh, my dearest Hilda!" cried Zillah, over- joyed. "What an owl I am not to have thought of that! It meets the whole difficulty. I write —you copy it—and it will be my letter after all. How I could have been so stupid I do not see. But I'm always so. As to any private confi- dences, there is no danger of any thing of that kind taking place between people who are so very peculiarly situated as we are."

"I suppose not," said Hilda, with a smile.

"But it's such a bore to copy letters."

"My darling, can any thing be a trouble that I do for you? Besides, you know how very fast I write."

"You are always so kind," said Zillah, as she kissed her friend fondly and tenderly. "I wish I could do something for you; but—poor me!— I don't seem able to do any thing for any body— not even for the dear old Earl. What wouldn't I give to be like you!"

"You are far better as you are, darling," said Hilda, with perhaps a double meaning in her words. "But now go and write the letter, and bring it to me, and I will copy it as fast as I can, and send it to the post."

Under these circumstances that letter was written.

The Earl lingered on in a low stage, with scarcely any symptoms of improvement. At first, indeed, there was a time when he had seemed better, but that passed away. The re- lapse sorely puzzled the doctor. If he had not been in such good hands he might have suspected the nurse of neglect, but that was the last thing that he could have thought of Hilda. Indeed, Hilda had been so fearful of the Earl's being neglected that she had, for his sake, assumed these all-engrossing cares. Singularly enough, however, it was since her assumption of the chief duties of nursing him that the Earl had relapsed. The doctor felt that nothing better in the way of nursing him could be conceived of. Zillah thought that if it had not been for Hilda the Earl would scarcely have been alive. As for Hilda herself, she could only meekly deprecate the doctor's praises, and sigh to think that such care as hers should prove so unavailing.

The Earl's case was, indeed, a mysterious one. After making every allowance for the shock which he might have experienced, and after laying all possible stress upon that blow on his head which he had suffered when falling forward, it still was a subject of wonder to the doctor why he should not recover. Hilda had told him in general terms, and with her usual delicacy, of the cause of the Earl's illness, so that the doctor knew that it arose from mental trouble, and not from physical ailment. Yet, even under these circumstances, he was puzzled at the complete prostration of the Earl, and at the adverse symptoms which appeared as time passed on.

The Earl slept most of the time. He was in a kind of stupor. This puzzled the doctor extremely. The remedies which he administered seemed not to have their legitimate effect. In fact they seemed to have no effect, and the most powerful drugs proved useless in this mysterious case.

"It must be the mind," said the doctor to himself, as he rode home one day after finding the Earl in a lower state than usual. "It must be the mind; and may the devil take the mind, for hang me if I can ever make head or tail of it!"

Yet on the night when the doctor soliloquized in this fashion a change had come over the Earl which might have been supposed to be for the better. He was exceedingly weak, so weak, indeed, that it was only with a great effort that he could move his hand; but he seemed to be more sensible than usual. That "mind" which the doctor cursed seemed to have resumed something of its former functions. He asked various questions; and, among others, he wished to hear Guy's last letter. This Hilda promised he should hear on the morrow. Zillah was there at the time, and the Earl cast an appealing glance toward her; but such was her confidence in Hilda that she did not dream of doing any thing in opposition to her decision. So she shook her head, and bending over the Earl, she kissed him, and said, "To-morrow."

The Earl, by a great effort, reached up his thin, feeble hand and took hers.

"You will not leave me?" he murmured.

"Certainly not, if you want me to stay," said Zillah.

The Earl, by a still greater effort, dragged her down nearer to him.

"Don't leave me with her," he whispered.

Zillah started at the tone of his voice. It was a tone of fear.

"What is it that he says?" asked Hilda, in a sweet voice.

The Earl frowned. Zillah did not see it, however. She looked back to Hilda and whispered, "He wants me to stay with him."

"Poor dear!" said Hilda. "Well, tell him that you will. It is a whim. He loves you, you know. Tell him that you'll stay."

And Zillah stooped down and told the Earl that she would stay.

There was trouble in the Earl's face. He lay silent and motionless, with his eyes fixed upon Zillah. Something there was in his eyes which expressed such mute appeal that Zillah wondered what it might be. She went over to him and sat by his side. He feebly reached out his thin hand. Zillah took it and held it in both of hers, kissing him as she did so.

"You will not leave me?" he whispered.

"No, dear father."

A faint pressure of her hand was the Earl's response, and a faint smile of pleasure hovered over his thin lips.

"Have you written to Guy?" he asked again.

"Yes. I have written for him to come home," said Zillah, who meant that Hilda had written in her name; but, in her mind, it was all the same. The Earl drew a deep sigh. There was trouble in his face. Zillah marked it, but supposed that he was anxious about that son who was never absent from his thoughts. She did not attempt to soothe his mind in any way. He was not able to keep up a conversation. Nor did she notice that the pressure on her hand was stronger whenever Hilda, with her light, stealthy step, came near; nor did she see the fear that was in his face as his eyes rested upon her.

The Earl drew Zillah faintly toward him. She bent down over him.

"Send her away," said he, in a low whisper.

"Who? Hilda?" asked Zillah, in wonder.

"Yes. You nurse me—you stay with me."

Zillah at once arose. "Hilda," said she, "he wants me to stay with him to-night. I suppose he thinks I give up too much to you, and neglect him. Oh dear, I only wish I was such a nurse as you! But, since he wishes it, I will stay to-night; and if there is any trouble I will call you."

"But, my poor child," said Hilda, sweetly, "you have been here all day."

"Oh, well, it is his wish, and I will stay here all night."

Hilda remonstrated a little; but, finding that Zillah was determined, she retired, and Zillah passed all that night with the Earl. He was uneasy. A terror seemed to be over him. He insisted on holding Zillah's hand. At times he would start and look fearfully around. Was it Hilda whom he feared? Whatever his fear was, he said nothing; but after each start he would look eagerly up at Zillah, and press her hand faintly. And Zillah thought it was simply the disorder of his nervous system, or, perhaps, the effect of the medicines which he had taken. As to those medicines, she was most careful and most regular in administering them. Indeed, her very anxiety about these interfered with that watchfulness about the Earl himself which was the chief requisite. Fully conscious that she was painfully irregular and unmethodical, Zillah gave her chief thought to the passage of the hours, so that every medicine should be given at the right time.

It was a long night, but morning came at last, and with it came Hilda, calm, refreshed, affectionate, and sweet.

"How has he been, darling?" she asked.

"Quiet," said Zillah, wearily.

"That's right; and now, my dearest, go off and get some rest. You must be very tired."

"THE EARL GASPED—'JUDAS!'"

So Zillah went off, and Hilda remained with the Earl.

Day was just dawning when Zillah left the Earl's room. She stooped over him and kissed him. Overcome by fatigue, she did not think much of the earnest, wistful gaze which caught her eyes. Was it not the same look which he had fixed on her frequently before?

The Earl again drew her down as she clasped his hand. She stooped over him.

"I'm afraid of *her*," he said, in a low whisper.

"Send Mrs. Hart."

Mrs. Hart? The Earl did not seem to know that she was ill. No doubt his mind was wandering. So Zillah thought, and the idea was natural. She thought she would humor the delirious fancy. So she promised to send Mrs. Hart.

"What did he say?" asked Hilda, following Zillah out. Zillah told her according to her own idea.

"Oh, it's only his delirium," said Hilda, "He'll take me for you when I go back. Don't let it trouble you. You might send Mathilde if you feel afraid; but I hardly think that Mathilde would be so useful here as I."

"*I* afraid? My dear Hilda, can I take his poor delirious fancy in earnest? Send Mathilde? I should hardly expect to see him alive again."

"Alive again!" said Hilda, with a singular intonation.

"Yes; Mathilde is an excellent maid, but in a sick-room she is as helpless as a child. She is far worse than I am. Do we ever venture to leave him alone with her?"

"Never mind. Do you go to sleep, darling, and sweet dreams to you."

They kissed, and Zillah went to her chamber.

It was about dawn, and the morning twilight but dimly illumined the hall. The Earl's room was dark, and the faint night light made objects only indistinctly perceptible. The Earl's white face was turned toward the door as Hilda entered, with imploring, wistful expectancy upon it. As he caught sight of Hilda the expression turned to one of fear—that same fear which Zillah had seen upon it. What did he fear? What was it that was upon his mind? What fearful thought threw its shadow over his soul?

Hilda looked at him for a long time in silence, her face calm and impassive, her eyes intent upon him. The Earl looked back upon her with unchanged fear—looking back thus out of his weakness and helplessness, with a fear that seemed intensified by the consciousness of that weakness. But Hilda's face softened not; no gleam of tenderness mitigated the hard lustre of her eyes; her expression lessened not from its set purpose. The Earl said not one word. It was not to her that he would utter the fear that was in him. Zillah had promised to send Mrs. Hart. When would Mrs. Hart come? Would she ever come, or would she never come? He looked away from Hilda feverishly, anxiously, to the door; he strained his ears to listen for footsteps. But no footsteps broke the deep stillness that reigned through the vast house, where all slept except these two who faced each other in the sick-room.

There was a clock at the end of the corridor outside, whose ticking sounded dull and muffled from the distance, yet it penetrated, with clear, sharp vibrations, to the brain of the sick man, and seemed to him, in the gathering excitement of this fearful hour, to grow louder and louder, till each tick sounded to his sharpened sense like the vibrations of a bell, and seemed to be the funeral knell of his destiny; sounding thus to his ears, solemnly, fatefully, bodingly; pealing forth thus with every sound the announcement that second after second out of those few minutes of time which were still left him had passed away from him forever. Each one of those seconds was prolonged to his excited sense to the duration of an hour. After each stroke he listened for the next, dreading to hear it, yet awaiting it, and all the while feeling upon him the eyes of one of whom he was to be the helpless, voiceless victim.

There had been but a few minutes since Zillah left, but they seemed like long terms of duration to the man who watched and feared. Zillah had gone, and would not return. Would Mrs. Hart ever come? Oh, could Mrs. Hart have known that this man, of all living beings, was thus watching and hoping for her, and that to this man of all others her presence would have given a heavenly peace and calm! If she could but have known this as it was then it would have roused her even from the bed of death, and brought her to his side though it were but to die at the first sight of him. But Mrs. Hart came not. She knew nothing of any wish for her. In her own extreme prostration she had found, after a wakeful night, a little blessed sleep, and the watcher watched in vain.

The clock tolled on.

Hilda looked out through the door. She turned and went out into the hall. She came back and looked around the room. She went to the window and looked out. The twilight was fading. The gloom was lessening from around the dim groves and shadowy trees. Morning was coming. She went back into the room, and once more into the hall. There she stood and listened. The Earl followed her with his eyes—eyes that were full of awful expectation.

Hilda came back. The Earl summoned all his strength, and uttered a faint cry. Hilda walked up to him; she stooped down over him. The Earl uttered another cry.

Hilda paused. Then she stooped down and kissed his forehead.

The Earl gasped. One word came hissing forth—

"Judas!"

*   *   *   *   *   *

CHAPTER XXIII.

THE HOUSE OF MOURNING.

ZILLAH had scarcely fallen asleep when a shrill cry roused her. She started up. Hilda stood by her side with wild excitement in her usually impassive face. A cold thrill ran through Zillah's frame. To see Hilda in any excitement was an unknown thing to her; but now this excitement was not concealed.

"Oh, my darling! my darling!" she cried.

"What? what?" Zillah almost screamed. "What is it? What has happened?" Fear told her. She knew what had happened. One thing, and one only, could account for this.

"He's gone! It's over! He's gone! He's gone! Oh, darling! How can I tell it? And so sudden! Oh, calm yourself!" And Hilda flung her arms about Zillah, and groaned.

Zillah's heart seemed to stand still. She flung off Hilda's arms, she tore herself away, and rushed to the Earl's room. Such a sudden thing as this—could it be? Gone! And it was only a few moments since she had seen his last glance, and heard his last words.

Yes; it was indeed so. There, as she entered that room, where now the rays of morning entered, she saw the form of her friend—that friend whom she called father, and loved as such. But the white face was no longer turned to greet her; the eyes did not seek hers, nor could that cold hand ever again return the pressure of hers. White as marble was that face now, still and set in the fixedness of death; cold as marble was now that hand which hers clasped in that first frenzy of grief and horror; cold as marble and as lifeless. Never again—never again might she hold commune with the friend who now was numbered with the dead.

She sat in that room stricken into dumbness by the shock of this sudden calamity. Time passed. The awful news flashed through the house. The servants heard it, and came silent and awe-struck to the room; but when they saw the white face, and the mourner by the bedside, they stood still, nor did they dare to cross the threshold. Suddenly, while the little group of servants stood there in that doorway, with the reverence which is always felt for death and for sorrow, there came one who forced her way through them and passed into the room. This one bore on her face the expression of a mightier grief than that which could be felt by any others—a grief unspeakable—beyond words, and beyond thought. White-haired, and with a face which now seemed turned to stone in the fixedness of its great agony, this figure tottered rather than walked into the room. There was no longer any self-restraint in this woman, who for years had lived under a self-restraint that never relaxed; there was no thought as to those who might see or hear; there was nothing but the utter abandonment of perfect grief—of grief which had reached its height and could know nothing more; there was nothing less than despair itself—that despair which arises when all is lost—as this woman flung herself past Zillah, as though she had a grief superior to Zillah's, and a right to pass even her in the terrible precedence of sorrow. It was thus that Mrs. Hart came before the presence of the dead and flung herself upon the inanimate corse, and wound her thin arms around that clay from which the soul had departed, and pressed her wan lips upon the cold brow from which the immortal dweller had passed away to its immortality.

In the depths of her own grief Zillah was roused by a cry which expressed a deeper grief than hers—a cry of agony—a cry of despair:

"Oh, my God! Oh, God of mercy! Dead! What? dead! Dead—and no explanation—no forgiveness!"

And Mrs. Hart fell down lifeless over the form of the dead.

Zillah rose with a wonder in her soul which alleviated the sorrow of bereavement. What was this? What did it mean?

"Explanation!" "Forgiveness!" What words were these? His housekeeper!—could she be any thing else? What had she done which required this lamentation? What was the Earl to her, that his death should cause such despair?

But amidst such thoughts Zillah was still considerate about this stricken one, and she called the servants, and they bore her away to her own room. This grief, from whatever cause it may have arisen, was too much for Mrs. Hart. Before this she had been prostrated. She now lost all consciousness, and lay in a stupor from which she could not be aroused.

The wondering questions which had arisen in Zillah's mind troubled her and puzzled her at first; but gradually she thought that she could answer them. Mrs. Hart, she thought, was wonderfully attached to the Earl. She had committed some imaginary delinquency in her management of the household, which, in her weak and semi-delirious state, was weighing upon her spirits. When she found that he was dead, the shock was great to one in her weak state, and she had only thought of some confession which she had wished to make to him.

When the doctor came that day he found Zillah still sitting there, holding the hand of the dead. Hilda came to tell all that she knew.

"About half an hour after Zillah left," she said, "I was sitting by the window, looking out to see the rising sun. Suddenly the Earl gave a sudden start, and sat upright in bed. I rushed over to him. He fell back. I chafed his hands and feet. I could not think, at first, that it was any thing more than a fainting fit. The truth gradually came to me. He was dead. An awful horror rushed over me. I fled from the room to Mrs. Molyneux, and roused her from sleep. She sprang up and hurried to the Earl. She knows the rest."

Such was Hilda's account.

As for the doctor, he could easily account for the sudden death. It was mind. His heart had been affected, and he had died from a sudden spasm. It was only through the care of Miss Krieff that the Earl had lived so long.

But so great was Hilda's distress that Zillah had to devote herself to the task of soothing her.

CHAPTER XXIV.

A LETTER AND ITS CONSEQUENCES.

SOME weeks passed, and Zillah's grief gradually became lessened. She was far better able to bear this blow at this time than that first

crushing blow which a few years before had descended so suddenly upon her young life. She began to rally and to look forward to the future. Guy had been written to, not by her, but, as usual, by Hilda, in her name. The news of her father's death had been broken to him as delicately as possible. Hilda read it to Zillah, who, after a few changes of expression, approved of it. This letter had the effect of impressing upon Zillah's mind the fact that Guy must soon come home. The absence must cease. In any case it could not last much longer. Either she would have had to join him, or he come back to her. The prospect of his arrival now stood before her, and the question arose how to meet it. Was it welcome or unpleasant? After all, was he not a noble character, and a valiant soldier—the son of a dear friend? Zillah's woman's heart judged him not harshly, and much of her thought was taken up with conjectures as to the probable results of that return. She began at length to look forward to it with hope; and to think that she might be happy with such a man for her husband. The only thing that troubled her was the idea that any man, however noble, should have the right of claiming her as his without the preliminary wooing. To a delicate nature this was intolerable, and she could only trust that he would be acceptable to her on his first appearance.

In the midst of these thoughts a letter arrived from Guy, addressed to that one who was now beyond its reach. Zillah opened this without hesitation, for Lord Chetwynde had always been in the habit of handing them to her directly he had read them.

Few things connected with those whom we have loved and lost are more painful, where all is so exquisitely painful, than the reading of letters by them or to them. The most trivial commonplaces—the lightest expressions of regard—are all invested with the tenderest pathos, and from our hearts there seems rung out at every line the despairing refrain of "nevermore—nevermore." It was thus, and with blending tears, that Zillah read the first part of Guy's letter, which was full of tender love and thoughtful consideration. Soon, however, this sadness was dispelled; her attention was arrested; and every other feeling was banished in her absorbing interest in what she read. After some preliminary paragraphs the letter went on thus:

"You will be astonished, my dear father, and, I hope, pleased, to learn that I have made up my mind to return to England as soon as possible. As you may imagine, this resolve is a sudden one, and I should be false to that perfect confidence which has always existed between us, if I did not frankly acquaint you with the circumstances which have led to my decision. I have often mentioned to you my friend Captain Cameron of the Royal Engineers, who is superintending the erection of some fortifications overlooking the mountain pass. Isolated as we are from all European society, we have naturally been thrown much together, and a firm friendship has grown up between us. We constituted him a member of our little mess, consisting of my two subalterns and myself, so that he has been virtually living with us ever since our arrival here.

"Not very long ago our little circle received a very important addition. This was Captain

Cameron's sister; who, having been left an orphan in England, and having no near relatives there, had come out to her brother. She was a charming girl. I had seen nothing of English ladies for a long time, and so it did not need much persuasion to induce me to go to Cameron's house after Miss Cameron had arrived. Circumstances, rather than any deliberate design on my part, drew me there more and more, till at length all my evenings were spent there, and, in fact, all my leisure time. I always used to join Miss Cameron and her brother on their morning rides and evening walks; and very often, if duty prevented him from accompanying her, she would ask me to take his place as her escort. She was also as fond of music as I am; and, in the evening, we generally spent most of the time in playing or singing together. She played accompaniments to my songs, and I to hers. We performed duets together; and thus, whether in the house or out of it, were thrown into the closest possible intercourse. All this came about so naturally that several months had passed away in this familiar association before I began even to suspect danger, either for myself or for her. Suddenly, however, I awakened to the consciousness of the fact as it was. All my life was filled by Inez Cameron—all my life seemed to centre around her—all my future seemed as black as midnight apart from her. Never before had I felt even a passing interest in any woman. Bound as I had been all my life, in boyhood by honor, and in early manhood by legal ties, I had never allowed myself to think of any other woman; and I had always been on my guard so as not to drift into any of those flirtations with which men in general, and especially we officers, contrive to fritter away the freshness of affection. Inexperience, combined with the influence of circumstances, caused me to drift into this position; and the situation became one from which it was hard indeed to extricate myself. I had, however, been on my guard after a fashion. I had from the first scrupulously avoided those *galanteries* and *façons de parler* which are more usual in Indian society than elsewhere. Besides, I had long before made Cameron acquainted with my marriage, and had taken it for granted that Inez knew it also. I thought, even after I had found out that I loved her, that there was no danger for her—and that she had always merely regarded me as a married man and a friend. But one day an accident revealed to me that she knew nothing about my marriage, and had taken my attentions too favorably for her own peace of mind. Ah, dear 'father, such a discovery was bitter indeed in many ways. I had to crush out my love for my sake and for hers. One way only was possible, and that was to leave her forever. I at once saw Cameron, and told him frankly the state of the case, so far as I was concerned. Like a good fellow, as he was, he blamed himself altogether. 'You see, Molyneux,' he said, 'a fellow is very apt to overlook the possible attractiveness of his own sister.' He made no effort to prevent me from going, but evidently thought it my only course. I accordingly applied at once for leave, and to-night I am about to start for Calcutta, where I will wait till I gain a formal permit, and I will never see Inez again. I have seen her for the last time. Oh, father! those words of warning

which you once spoke to me have become fatally true. Chetwynde has been too dearly bought. At this moment the weight of my chains is too heavy to be borne. If I could feel myself free once more, how gladly would I give up all my ancestral estates! What is Chetwynde to me? What happiness can I ever have in it now, or what happiness can there possibly be to me without Inez? Besides, I turn from the thought of her, with her refined beauty, her delicate nature, her innumerable accomplishments, her true and tender heart, and think of that other one, with her ungovernable passions, her unreasoning temper, and her fierce intractability, where I can see nothing but the soul of a savage, unredeemed by any womanly softness or feminine grace. Oh, father! was it well to bind me to a Hindu? You will say, perhaps, that I should not judge of the woman by the girl. But, father, when I saw her first at ten, I found her impish, and at fifteen, when I married her, she was no less so, only perhaps more intensified. Fierce words of insult were flung at me by that creature. My God! it is too bitter to think of. Her face is before me now, scowling and malignant, while behind it, mournful and pitying, yet loving, is the pale sweet face of Inez.

"But I dare not trust myself further. Never before have I spoken to you about the horror which I feel for that Hindu. I did not wish to pain you. I fear I am selfish in doing so now. But, after all, it is better for you to know it once for all. Otherwise the discovery of it would be all the worse. Besides, this is wrung out from me in spite of myself by the anguish of my heart.

"Let me do justice to the Hindu. You have spoken of her sometimes—not often, however, and I thank you for it—as a loving daughter to you. I thank her for that, I am sure. Small comfort, however, is this to me. If she were now an angel from heaven, she could not fill the place of Inez.

"Forgive me, dear father. This shall be the last of complaints. Henceforth I am ready to bear my griefs. I am ready for the sacrifice. I can not see *her* yet, but when I reach England I must see you somehow. If you can not meet me, you must manage to send her off to Pomeroy, so that I may see you in peace. With you, I will forget my sorrows, and will be again a light-hearted boy.

"Let me assure you that I mean to keep my promise made years ago when I was a boy. It shall be the effort of my life to make my wife happy. Whether I succeed or not will be another thing. But I must have time.

"No more now. I have written about this for the first and the last time. Give my warmest and fondest love to nurse. I hope to see you soon, and remain, dear father,

"Your affectionate son,
"GUY MOLYNEUX."

For some time after reading this letter Zillah sat as if stunned. At first she seemed scarcely able to take in its full meaning. Gradually, however, it dawned upon her to its widest extent. This, then, was the future that lay before her, and this was the man for whose arrival she had been looking with such mingled feelings. Little need was there now for mingled feelings. She knew well with what feeling to expect him. She had at times within the depths of her heart formed an idea that her life would not be loveless; but now—but now— This man who was her husband, and the only one to whom she could look for love—this man turned from her in horror; he hated her, he loathed her—worse, he looked upon her as a Hindu—worse still, if any thing could be worse, his hate and his loathing were made eternal; for he loved another with the ardor of a first fresh love, and his wife seemed to him a demon full of malignity, who stood between him and the angel of his heart and the heaven of his desires. His words of despair rang within her ears. The opprobrious epithets which he applied to her stung her to the quick. Passionate and hot-hearted, all her woman's nature rose up in arms at this horrible, this unlooked-for assault. All her pride surged up within her in deep and bitter resentment. Whatever she might once have been, she felt that she was different now, and deserved not this. At this moment she would have given worlds to be able to say to him, "You are free. Go, marry the woman whom you love." But it was too late.

Not the least did she feel Guy's declaration that he would try to make her happy. Her proud spirit chafed most at this. He was going to treat her with patient forbearance, and try to conceal his abhorrence. Could she endure this? Up and down the room she paced, with angry vehemence, asking herself this question.

She who had all her life been surrounded by idolizing love was now tied for life to a man whose highest desire with regard to her was that he might be able to endure her. In an agony of grief, she threw herself upon the floor. Was there no escape? she thought. None? none? Oh, for one friend to advise her!

The longer Zillah thought of her position the worse it seemed to her. Hours passed away, and she kept herself shut up in her room, refusing to admit any one, but considering what was best to do. One thing only appeared as possible under these circumstances, and that was to leave Chetwynde. She felt that it was simply impossible for her to remain there. And where could she go? To Pomeroy Court? But that had been handed over to him as part of the payment to him for taking her. She could not go back to a place which was now the property of this man. Nor was it necessary. She had money of her own, which would enable her to live as well as she wished. Thirty thousand pounds would give her an income sufficient for her wants; and she might find some place where she could live in seclusion. Her first wild thoughts were a desire for death; but since death would not come, she could at least so arrange matters as to be dead to this man. Such was her final resolve.

It was with this in her mind that she went out to Hilda's room. Hilda was writing as she entered, but on seeing her she hastily shut her desk, and sprang forward to greet her friend.

"My darling!" said she. "How I rejoice to see you! Is it some new grief? Will you never trust me? You are so reticent with me that it breaks my heart."

"Hilda," said she, "I have just been reading a letter from Lord Chetwynde to his father. He is about to return home."

Zillah's voice, as she spoke, was hard and metallic, and Hilda saw that something was wrong. She noticed that Zillah used the words Lord Chetwynde with stern emphasis, instead of the name Guy, by which she, like the rest, had always spoken of him.

"I am glad to hear it, dear," said Hilda, quietly, and in a cordial tone; "for, although you no doubt dread the first meeting, especially under such painful circumstances, yet it will be for your happiness."

"Hilda," said Zillah, with increased sternness, "Lord Chetwynde and I will never meet again."

Hilda started back with unutterable astonishment on her face.

"Never meet again!" she repeated—"not meet Lord Chetwynde—your husband? What do you mean?"

"I am going to leave Chetwynde as soon as possible, and shall never again cross its threshold."

Hilda went over to Zillah and put her arms around her.

"Darling," said she, in her most caressing tones, "you are agitated. What is it? You are in trouble. What new grief can have come to you? Will you not tell me? Is there any one living who can sympathize with you as I can?"

At these accents of kindness Zillah's fortitude gave way. She put her head on her friend's shoulder and sobbed convulsively. The tears relieved her. For a long time she wept in silence.

"I have no one now in the world but you, dearest Hilda. And you will not forsake me, will you?"

"Forsake you, my darling, my sister? forsake you? Never while I live! But why do you speak of flight and of being forsaken? What mad fancies have come over you?"

Zillah drew from her pocket the letter which she had read.

"Here," she said, "read this, and you will know all."

Hilda took the letter and read it in silence, all through, and then commencing it again, she once more read it through to the end.

Then she flung her arms around Zillah, impulsively, and strained her to her heart.

"You understand all now?"

"All," said Hilda.

"And what do you think?"

"Think! It is horrible!"

"What would you do?"

"I?" cried Hilda, starting up. "I would kill myself."

Zillah shook her head.

"I am not quite capable of that—not yet—though it may be in me to do it—some time. But now I can not. My idea is the same as yours, though. I will go into seclusion, and be dead to him, at any rate."

Hilda was silent for a few moments. Then she read the letter again.

"Zillah," said she, with a deep sigh, "it is very well to talk of killing one's self, as I did just now, or of running away; but, after all, other things must be considered. I spoke hastily; but I am calmer than you, and I ought to advise you calmly. After all, it is a very serious thing that you speak of; and, indeed, are you capable of such a thing? Whatever I may individually think of your resolve, I know that you are doing what the world will consider madness; and it is my duty to put the case plainly before you. In the first place, then, your husband does not love you, and he loves another—very hard to bear, I allow; but men are fickle, and perhaps ere many months have elapsed he may forget the cold English beauty as he gazes on your Southern face. You are very beautiful, Zillah; and when he sees you he will change his tone. He may love you at first sight."

"Then I should despise him," said Zillah, hotly. "What kind of love is that which changes at the sight of every new face? Besides, you forget how he despises me. I am a Hindu in his eyes. Can contempt ever change into love? If such a miracle could take place, I should never believe in it. Those bitter words in that letter would always rankle in my heart."

"That is true," said Hilda, sorrowfully. "Then we will put that supposition from us. But, allowing you never gain your husband's love, remember how much there is left you. His position, his rank, are yours by right—you are Lady Chetwynde, and the mistress of Chetwynde Castle. You can fill the place with guests, among whom you will be queen. You may go to London during the season, take the position to which you are entitled there as wife of a peer, and, in the best society which the world affords, you will receive all the admiration and homage which you deserve. Beauty like yours, combined with rank and wealth, may make you a queen of society. Have you strength to forego all this, Zillah?"

"You have left one thing out in your brilliant picture," replied Zillah. "All this may, indeed, be mine—but—mine on sufferance. If I can only get this as Lord Chetwynde's wife, I beg leave to decline it. Besides, I have no ambition to shine in society. Had you urged me to remember all that the Earl has done for me, and try to endure the son for the sake of the father, that might possibly have had weight. Had you shown me that my marriage was irrevocable, and that the best thing was to accept the situation, and try to be a dutiful wife to the son of the man whom I called father, you might perhaps for a moment have shaken my pride. I might have stifled the promptings of those womanly instincts which have been so frightfully outraged, and consented to remain passively in a situation where I was placed by those two friends who loved me best. But when you speak to me of the dazzling future which may lie before me as Lord Chetwynde's wife, you remind me how little he is dependent for happiness upon any thing that I can give him; of the brilliant career in society or in politics which is open to him, and which will render domestic life superfluous. I have thought over all this most fully; but what you have just said has thrown a new light upon it. In the quiet seclusion in which I have hitherto lived I had almost forgotten that there was an outside world, where men seek their happiness. Can you think that I am able to enter that world, and strive to be a queen of society, with no protecting love around me to warn me against its perils or to shield me from them? No! I see it all. Under no circumstances can I live with this man who abhors me. No toleration can be possible on either side. The best

F

thing for me to do is to die. But since I can not die, the next best thing is to sink out of his view into nothingness. So, Hilda, I shall leave Chetwynde, and it is useless to attempt to dissuade me."

Zillah had spoken in low, measured tones, in words which were so formal that they sounded like a school-girl's recitation—a long, dull monotone—the monotony of despair. Her face drooped—her eyes were fixed on the floor—her white hands clasped each other, and she sat thus —an image of woe. Hilda looked at her steadily. For a moment there flashed over her lips the faintest shadow of a smile—the lips curled cruelly, the eyes gleamed coldly—but it was for a moment. Instantly it had passed, and as Zillah ceased, Hilda leaned toward her and drew her head down upon her breast.

"Ah, my poor, sweet darling! my friend! my sister! my noble Zillah!" she murmured. "I will say no more. I see you are fixed in your purpose. I only wished you to act with your eyes open. But of what avail is it? Could you live to be scorned—live on sufferance? Never! . I would die first. What compensation could it be to be rich, or famous, when you were the property of a man who loathed you? Ah, my dear one! what am I saying? But you are right. Yes, sooner than live with that man I would kill myself."

A long silence followed.

"I suppose you have not yet made any plans, darling," said Hilda at last.

"Yes I have. A thousand plans at once came sweeping through my mind, and I have some general idea of what I am to do," said Zillah. "I think there will be no difficulty about the details. You remember, when I wished to run away, after dear papa's death—ah, how glad I am that I did not—how many happy years I should have lost—the question of money was the insuperable obstacle; but that is effectually removed now. You know my money is so settled that it is payable to my own checks at my bankers', who are not even the Chetwyndes' bankers; for the Earl thought it better to leave it with papa's men of business."

"You must be very careful," said Hilda, "to leave no trace by which Lord Chetwynde can find you out. You know that he will move heaven and earth to find you. His character and his strict ideas of honor would insure that. The mere fact that you bore his name, would make it gall and wormwood to him to be ignorant of your doings. Besides, he lays great stress on his promise to your father."

"He need not fear," said Zillah. "The dear old name, which I love almost as proudly as he does, shall never gain the lightest stain from me. Of course I shall cease to use it now. It would be easy to trace Lady Chetwynde to any place. My idea is, of course, to take an assumed name. You and I can live quietly and raise no suspicions that we are other than we seem. But, Hilda, are you sure that you are willing to go into exile with me? Can you endure it? Can you live with me, and share my monotonous life?"

Hilda looked steadily at Zillah, holding her hand the while.

"Zillah," said she, in a solemn voice, "whither thou goest, I will go; and where thou lodgest,

"WHITHER THOU GOEST, I WILL GO."

I will lodge. Thy people shall be my people, and thy God my God!"

A deep silence followed. Zillah pressed Hilda's hand and stifled a half sob.

"At any rate," said Hilda, "whoever else may fail, you—you have, at least, one faithful heart—one friend on whom you can always rely. No, you need not thank me," said she, as Zillah fondly kissed her and was about to speak; "I am but a poor, selfish creature, after all. You know I could never be happy away from you. You know that there is no one in the world whom I love but you; and there is no other who loves me. Do I not owe every thing to General Pomeroy and to you, my darling?"

"Not more than I owe to you, dear Hilda. I feel ashamed when I think of how much I made you endure for years, through my selfish exactions and my ungovernable temper. But I have changed a little I think. The Earl's influence over me was for good, I hope. Dear Hilda, we have none but one another, and must cling together."

Silence then followed, and they sat for a long time, each wrapped up in plans for the future.

* * *

CHAPTER XXV.

CUTTING THE LAST TIE.

FEARFUL that her courage might fail if she gave herself any more time to reflect on what she was doing, Zillah announced to the household, before the close of that day, that the shock of Lord Chetwynde's death rendered a change necessary for her, and that she should leave home necessary for her, and that she should leave home

as soon as she could conveniently do so. She also told them of their master's expected return, and that every thing must be in readiness for his reception, so that, on her return, she might have no trouble before her. She gave some faint hints that she might probably meet him at London, in order to disarm suspicion, and also to make it easier for Chetwynde himself to conceal the fact of her flight, if he wished to do so. She never ceased to be thoughtful about protecting his honor, as far as possible.

The few days before Zillah's departure were among the most wretched she had ever known. The home which she so dearly loved, and which she had thought was to be hers forever, had to be left, because she felt that she was not wanted there. She went about the grounds, visited every favorite haunt and nook—the spots endeared to her by the remembrance of many happy hours passed among them—and her tears flowed fast, and bitterly as she thought that she was now seeing them for the last time. The whole of the last day at Chetwynde she passed in the little church, under which every Molyneux had been buried for centuries back. It was full of their marble effigies. Often had she watched the sunlight flickering over their pale sculptured faces. One of these forms had been her especial delight; for she could trace in his features a strong family resemblance to Lord Chetwynde. This one's name was Guy. Formerly she used to see a likeness between him and the Guy who was now alive. He had died in the Holy Land; but his bones had been brought home, that they might rest in the family vault. She had been fond of weaving romances as to his probable history and fate; but no thought of him was in her mind to-day, as she wept over the resting-place of one who had filled a father's place to her, or as she knelt and prayed in her desolation to Him who has promised to be a father to the fatherless. Earnestly did she entreat that His presence might be with her, His providence direct her lonely way. Poor child! In the wild impulsiveness of her nature she thought that the sacrifice which she was making of herself and her hopes must be acceptable to Him, and pleasing in His sight. She did not know that she was merely following her own will, and turning her back upon the path of duty. That duty lay in simple acceptance of the fate which seemed ordained for her, whether for good or evil. Happy marriages were never promised by Him; and, in flying from one which seemed to promise unhappiness, she forgot that "obedience is better than sacrifice," even though the sacrifice be that of one's self.

Twilight was fast closing in before she reached the castle, exhausted from the violence of her emotion, and faint and weak from her long fasting. Hilda expressed alarm at her protracted absence, and said that she was just about going in search of her. "My darling," said she, "you will wear away your strength. You are too weak now to leave. Let me urge you, for the last time, to stay; give up your mad resolution."

"No," said Zillah. "You know you yourself said that I was right."

"I did not say that you were right, darling. I said what I would do in your place; but I did not at all say, or even hint, that it would be right."

"Never mind," said Zillah, wearily; "I have nerved myself to go through with it, and I can do it. The worst bitterness is over now. There is but one thing more for me to do, and then the ties between me and Chetwynde are severed forever."

At Hilda's earnest entreaty she took some refreshment, and then lay down to rest; but, feeling too excited to sleep, she got up to accomplish the task she had before her. This was to write a letter to her husband, telling him of her departure, and her reason for doing so. She wished to do this in as few words as possible, to show no signs of bitterness toward him, or of her own suffering. So she wrote as follows:

"CHETWYNDE CASTLE, *March* 20, 1859.

"MY LORD,—Your last letter did not reach Chetwynde Castle until after your dear father had been taken from us. It was therefore opened and read by me. I need not describe what my feelings were on reading it; but will only say, that if it were possible for me to free you from the galling chains that bind you to me, I would gladly do so. But, though it be impossible for me to render you free to marry her whom you love, I can at least rid you of my hated presence. I can not die; but I can be as good as dead to you. To-morrow I shall leave Chetwynde forever, and you will never see my face again. Search for me, were you inclined to make it, will be useless. I shall probably depart from England, and leave no trace of my whereabouts. I shall live under an assumed name, so as not to let the noble name of Chetwynde suffer any dishonor from *me*. If I *die*, I will take care to have the news sent to you.

"Do not think that I blame you. A man's love is not under his own control. Had I remained, I know that, as your wife, I should have experienced the utmost kindness and consideration. Such kindness, however, to a nature like mine would have been only galling. Something more than cold civility is necessary in order to render endurable the daily intercourse of husband and wife. Therefore I do not choose to subject myself to such a life.

"In this, the last communication between us, I must say to you what I intended to reserve until I could say it in person. It needed but a few weeks' intimate association with your dear father, whom I loved as my father, and whom I called by that name, to prove how utterly I had been mistaken as to the motives and circumstances that led to our marriage. I had his full and free forgiveness for having doubted him; and I now, as a woman, beg to apologize to you for all that I might have said as a passionate girl.

"Let me also assure you, my lord, of my deep sympathy for you in the trial which awaits you on your return, when you will find Chetwynde Castle deprived of the presence of that father whom you love. I feel for you and with you. My loss is only second to yours; for, in your father, I lost the only friend whom I possessed.

"Yours, very respectfully,
"ZILLAH."

Hilda of course had to copy this, for the objection to Zillah's writing was as strong as before, and an explanation was now more difficult to make than ever. Zillah, however, read it in Hilda's handwriting, and then Hilda took it, as she always did, to inclose it for the mail.

She took it to her own room, drew from her desk a letter which was addressed to Guy, and this was the one which she posted. Zillah's letter was carefully destroyed. Yet Zillah went with Hilda to the post-office, so anxious was she about her last letter, and saw it dropped in the box, as she supposed.

Then she felt that she had cut the last tie.

CHAPTER XXVI.
FLIGHT AND REFUGE.

ABOUT a fortnight after the events narrated in our last chapter a carriage stopped before the door of a small cottage situated in the village of Tenby on the coast of Pembrokeshire. Two ladies in deep mourning got out of it, and entered the gate of the garden which lay between them and the house; while a maid descended from the rumble, and in voluble French, alternating with broken English, besought the coachman's tender consideration for the boxes which he was handing down in a manner expressive of energy and expedition, rather than any regard for their contents. A resounding "thump" on the ground, caused by the sudden descent of one of her precious charges, elicited a cry of agony from the Frenchwoman, accompanied by the pathetic appeal:

"Oh, mon Dieu!· Qu'est ce que vous faites la? Prenez garde donc!"

This outbreak attracted the attention of the ladies, who turned round to witness the scene. On seeing distress depicted on every lineament of her faithful Abigail's face, the younger of the two said, with a faint smile:

"Poor Mathilde! That man's rough handling will break the boxes and her heart at the same time. But after all it will only anticipate the unhappy end, for I am sure that she will die of grief and ennui when she sees the place we have brought her to. She thought it dreadful at Chetwynde that there were so few to see and to appreciate the results of her skill, yet even there a few could occasionally be found to dress me for. But when she finds that I utterly repudiate French toilettes for sitting upon the rocks, and that the neighboring fishermen are not as a rule judges of the latest coiffure, I am afraid to think of the consequences. Will it be any thing less than a suicide, do you think, Hilda?"

"Well, Zillah," said Hilda, "I advised you not to bring her. A secret intrusted to many ceases to be a secret. It would have been better to leave behind you all who had been connected with Chetwynde, but especially Mathilde, who is both silly and talkative."

"I know that her coming is sorely against your judgment, Hilda; but I do not think that I run any risk. I know you despise me for my weakness, but I really like Mathilde, and could not give her up and take a new maid, unless I had to.' She is very fond of me, and would rather be with me, even in this outlandish place, than in London, even, with any one else. You know I am the only person she has lived with in England. She has no friends in the country, so her being French is in her favor. She has not the least idea in what county 'ce cher mais triste Shateveen' is situated; so she could not do much harm even if she would, especially as her pronunciation of the name is more likely to bewilder than to instruct her hearers."

By this time they had entered the house, and Zillah, putting her arm in Hilda's, proceeded to inspect the mansion. It was a very tiny one; the whole house could conveniently have stood in the Chetwynde drawing-room; but Zillah declared that she delighted in its snugness. Every thing was exquisitely neat, both within and without. The place had been obtained by Hilda's diligent search. It had belonged to a coast-guard officer who had recently died, and Hilda, by means of Gualtier, obtained possession of the whole place, furniture and all, by paying a high rent to the widow. A housekeeper and servants were included in the arrangements. Zillah was in ecstasies with her drawing-room, which extended the whole length of the house, having at the front an alcove window looking upon the balcony and thence upon the sea, and commanding at the back a beautiful view of the mountains beyond. The views from all the windows were charming, and from garret to cellar the house was nicely furnished and well appointed, so that after hunting into every nook and corner the two friends expressed themselves delighted with their new home.

The account which they gave of themselves to those with whom they were brought in contact was a very simple one, and not likely to excite suspicion. They were sisters—the Misses Lorton—the death of their father not long before had rendered them orphans. They had no near relations, but were perfectly independent as to means. They had come to Tenby for the benefit of the sea air, and wished to lead as quiet and retired a life as possible for the next two years. They had brought no letters, and they wished for no society.

They soon settled down into their new life, and their days passed happily and quietly. Neither of them had ever lived near the sea before, so that it was now a constant delight to them. Zillah would sit for hours on the shore, watching the breakers dashing over the rocks beyond, and tumbling at her feet; or she would play like a child with the rising tide, trying how far she could run out with the receding wave before the next white-crested billow should come seething and foaming after her, as if to punish her for her temerity in venturing within the precincts of the mighty ocean. Hilda always accompanied her, but her amusements took a much more ambitious turn. She had formed a passion for collecting marine curiosities; and while Zillah sat dreamily watching the waves, she would clamber over the rocks in search of sea-weeds, limpets, anemones, and other things of the kind, shouting out gladly whenever she had found any thing new. Gradually she extended her rambles, and explored all the coast within easy walking distance, and became familiar with every bay and outlet within the circuit of several miles. Zillah's strength had not yet fully returned, so that she was unable to go on these long rambles.

One day Zillah announced an intention of taking a drive inland, and urged Hilda to come with her.

"Well, dear, I would rather not unless you really want me to. I want very much to go on the shore to-day. I found some beautiful specimens on the cliffs last night; but it was growing too late for me to secure them, so I determined to do so as early as possible this afternoon."

"Oh," said Zillah, with a laugh, "I should not dream of putting in a rivalry with your new passion. I should not stand a chance against a shrimp; but I hope your new aquarium will soon make its appearance, or else some of your pets will come to an untimely end, I fear. I heard the house-maid this morning vowing vengeance against 'them nasty smellin' things as Miss Lorton were always a-litterin' the house with.'"

"She will soon get rid of them, then. The man has promised me the aquarium in two or three days, and it will be the glory of the whole establishment. But now—good-by, darling—I must be off at once, so as to have as much daylight as possible."

"You will be back before me, I suppose."

"Very likely; but if I am not, do not be anxious. I shall stay on the cliffs as late as I can."

"Oh, Hilda! I do not like your going alone. Won't you take John with you? I can easily drive by myself."

"Any fate rather than that," said Hilda, laughing. "What could I do with John?"

"Take Mathilde, then, or one of the maids."

"Mathilde! My dear girl, what are you thinking of? You know she has never ventured outside of the garden gate since we have been here. She shudders whenever she looks at 'cette vilaine mer,' and no earthly consideration could induce her to put her foot on the shore. But what has put it in your head that I should want any one with me to-day, when I have gone so often without a protector?"

"I don't know," said Zillah. "You spoke about not being home till late, and I felt nervous."

"You need not be uneasy then, darling, on that account. I shall leave the cliffs early. I only want to be untrammeled, so as to ramble about at random. At any rate I shall be home in good time for dinner, and will be as hungry as a hunter, I promise you. I only want you not to fret your foolish little head if I am not here at the very moment I expect."

"Very well," said Zillah, "I will not, and I must not keep you talking any longer."

"Au revoir," said Hilda, kissing her. "Au revoir," she repeated, gayly.

Zillah smiled, and as she rose to go and dress for the drive Hilda took her path to the cliffs.

It was seven o'clock when Zillah returned. "Is Miss Lorton in?" she asked, as she entered.

"No, miss," answered the maid.

"I will wait dinner then," said Zillah; and after changing her things she went out on the balcony to wait for Hilda's return.

Half an hour passed, and Hilda did not come. Zillah grew anxious, and looked incessantly at her watch. Eight o'clock came—a quarter after eight.

Zillah could stand it no longer. She sent for John.

"John," said she, "I am getting uneasy about Miss Lorton. I wish you would walk along the beach and meet her. It is too late for her to be out alone."

John departed on his errand, and Zillah felt a sense of relief at having done something, but this gave way to renewed anxiety as time passed, and they did not appear. At length, after what seemed an age to the suffering girl, John returned, but alone.

"Have you not found her?" Zillah almost shrieked.

"No, miss," said the man, in a pitying tone.

"Then why did you come back?" she cried.

"Did I not tell you to go on till you met her?"

"I went as far as I could, miss."

"What do you mean?" she asked, in a voice pitched high with terror.

The man came close up to her, sympathy and sorrow in his face.

"Don't take on so, miss," said he; "and don't be downhearted. I dare say she has took the road, and will be home shortly; that way is longer, you know."

"No; she said she would come by the shore. Why did you not go on till you met her?"

"Well, miss, I went as far as Lovers' Bay; but the tide was in, and I could go no farther."

Zillah, at this, turned deadly white, and would have fallen if John had not caught her. He placed her on the sofa and called Mathilde.

Zillah's terror was not without cause. Lovers' Bay was a narrow inlet of the sea, formed by two projecting promontories. At low tide a person could walk beyond these promontories along the shore; but at high tide the water ran up within; and there was no standing room any where within the inclosure of the precipitous cliff. At half tide, when the tide was falling, one might enter here; but if the tide was rising, it was of course not to be attempted. Several times strangers had been entrapped here, sometimes with fatal results. The place owed its name to the tragical end which was met with here by a lover who was eloping with his lady. They fled by the shore, and came to the bay, but found that the rising tide had made the passage of the further ledge impossible. In despair the lover seized the lady, and tried to swim with her around this obstacle, but the waves proved stronger than love; the currents bore them out to sea; and the next morning their bodies were found floating on the water, with their arms still clasped around one another in a death embrace. Such was the origin of the name; and the place had always been looked upon by the people here with a superstitious awe, as a place of danger and death.

The time, however, was one which demanded action; and Zillah, hastily gulping down some restoratives which Mathilde had brought, began to take measures for a search.

"John," said she, "you must get a boat, and go at once in search of Miss Lorton. Is there nowhere any standing room in the bay—no crevice in the rocks where one may find a foothold?"

"Not with these spring-tides, miss," said John. "A man might cling a little while to the rocks; but a weak lady—" John hesitated. .

"Oh, my God!" cried Zillah, in an agony; "she may be clinging there now, with every moment lessening her chance! Fly to the nearest fishermen, John! Ten pounds apiece if you get to the bay within half an hour! And any thing you like if you only bring her back safe!"

Away flew John, descending the rocks to the nearest cottage. There he breathlessly stated his errand; and the sturdy fisherman and his son were immediately prepared to start. The boat was launched, and they set out. It was slightly cloudy, and there seemed some prospect of a storm. Filled with anxiety at such an idea, and also inspired with enthusiasm by the large reward, they put forth their utmost efforts; and the boat shot through the water at a most unwonted pace. Twenty minutes after the boat had left the strand it had reached the bay. All thought of mere reward faded out soon from the minds of these honest men. They only thought of the young lady whom they had often seen along the shore, who might even now be in the jaws of death. Not a word was spoken. The sound of the waves, as they dashed on the rocks, alone broke the stillness. Trembling with excitement, they swept the boat close around the rocky promontory. John, standing up in the bow, held aloft a lantern, so that every cranny of the rocks might be brought out into full relief. At length an exclamation burst from him.

"Oh, Heavens! she's been here!" he groaned.

The men turned and saw in his hand the covered basket which Hilda always took with her on her expeditions to bring home her specimens. It seemed full of them now.

"Where did you find it?" they asked.

"Just on this here ledge of rock."

"She has put it down to free her hands. She may be clinging yet," said the old fisherman. "Let us call."

A loud cry, "Miss Lorton!" rang through the bay. The echo sent it reverberating back; but no human voice mingled with the sound.

Despondingly and fearfully they continued the search, still calling at times, until at last, as they reached the outer point, the last hope died, and they ceased calling.

"I'm afeard she's gone," said John.

The men shook their heads. John but expressed the general opinion.

"God help that poor young thing at the cottage!" said the elder fisherman. "She'll be mighty cut up, I take it, now." .

"They was all in all to each other," said John, with a sigh.

By this time they had rounded the point. Suddenly John, who had sat down again, called out:

"Stop! I see something on the water yonder!"

"SHE CLUTCHED HIS ARM IN A CONVULSIVE GRASP."

The men looked in the direction where he pointed, and a small object was visible on the surface of the water. They quickly rowed toward it. It was a lady's hat, which John instantly recognized as Hilda's. The long crape veil seemed to have caught in a stake which arose from the sandy beach above the water, placed there to mark some water level, and the hat floated there. Reverently, as though they were touching the dead, did those rough men disentangle the folds, and lay the hat on the basket.

"There is no hope now," said the younger fisherman, after a solemn silence. "May our dear Lord and our Blessed Lady," he added, crossing himself as he spoke, "have mercy on her soul!"

"Amen!" repeated the others, gently.

"However shall I tell my poor little missis," said John, wiping his eyes.

The others made no response. Soon they reached the shore again. The old man whispered a few words to his son, and then turned to John:

"I say, comrade," said he; "don't let her—" a jerk of his head in the direction of the cottage indicated to whom the pronoun referred—"don't let her give us that. We've done naught but what we'd have done for any poor creature among these rocks. We couldn't take pay for this night's job—my son nor me. And all we wish is, that it had been for some good; but it wasn't the Lord's will; and it ain't for us to say nothin' agin that; only you'll tell your missis, whose she be's a bit better, that we made bold to send her our respectful sympathy."

John gave this promise to the honest fellows, and then went slowly and sadly back to make his mournful report.

During John's absence Zillah had been waiting in an agony of suspense, in which Mathilde made feeble efforts to console her.. Wringing her hands, she walked up and down in front of the house; and at length, when she heard footsteps coming along the road, she rushed in that direction.

She recognized John. So great was her excitement that she could not utter one word. She clutched his arm in a convulsive grasp. John said nothing. It was easier for him to be silent. In fact he had something which was more eloquent than words. He mournfully held out the basket and the hat.

In an instant Zillah recognized them. She shrieked, and fell speechless and senseless on the hard ground.

CHAPTER XXVII.

AN ASTOUNDING LETTER.

IT needed but this new calamity to complete the sum of Zillah's griefs. She had supposed that she had already suffered as much as she could. The loss of her father, the loss of the Earl, the separation from Mrs. Hart, were each successive stages in the descending scale of her calamities. Nor was the least of these that Indian letter which had sent her into voluntary banishment from her home. It was not till all was over that she learned how completely her thoughts had associated themselves with the plans of the Earl, and how insensibly her whole future had become penetrated with plans about Guy. The overthrow of all this was bitter; but this, and all other griefs, were forgotten in the force of this new sorrow, which, while it was the last, was in reality the greatest. Now, for the first time, she felt how dear Hilda had been to her. She had been more than a friend — she had been an elder sister. Now, to Zillah's affectionate heart, there came the recollection of all the patient love, the kind forbearance, and the wise counsel of this matchless friend. Since childhood they had been inseparable. Hilda had rivaled even her doting father in perfect submission to all her caprices, and indulgence of all her whims. Zillah had matured so rapidly, and had changed so completely, that she now looked upon her former willful and passionate childhood with impatience, and could estimate at its full value that wonderful meekness with which Hilda had endured her wayward and imperious nature. Not one recollection of Hilda came to her but was full of incidents of a love and devotion passing the love of a sister.

It was now, since she had lost her, that she learned to estimate her, as she thought, at her full value. That loss seemed to her the greatest of all; worse than that of the Earl; worse even than that of her father. Never more should she experience that tender love, that wise patience, that unruffled serenity, which she had always known from Hilda. Never more should she possess one devoted friend — the true and tried friend of a life — to whom she might go in any sorrow, and know and feel that she would receive the sympathy of love and the counsel of wisdom. Nevermore — no, nevermore! Such was the refrain that seemed constantly to ring in her ears, and she found herself murmuring those despairing lines of Poe, where the solitary word of the Raven seems

"Caught from some unhappy master whom unmerciful Disaster
Followed fast and followed faster till his songs one burden bore—
Till the dirges of his Hope that melancholy burden bore
Of 'Never—nevermore!'"

It was awful to her to be, for the first time in her life, alone in the world. Hitherto, amidst her bitterest afflictions, she had always had some one whom she loved. After her father's death she had Lord Chetwynde and Mrs. Hart; and with these she always had Hilda. But now all were gone, and Hilda was gone. To a passionate and intense nature like hers, sorrow was capable of giving pangs which are unknown to colder hearts, and so she suffered to a degree which was commensurate with her ardent temperament.

Weeks passed on. Recovering from the first shock, she sank into a state of dreamy listlessness, which, however, was at times interrupted by some wild hopes which would intrude in spite of herself. These hopes were that Hilda, after all, might not be lost. She might have been found by some one and carried off somewhere. Wild enough were these hopes, and Zillah saw this plainly, yet still they would intrude. Yet, far from proving a solace, they only made her situation worse, since they kept her in a state of constant suspense—a suspense, too, which had no shadow of a foundation in reason. So, alone, and struggling with the darkest despair, Zillah passed the time, without having sufficient energy of mind left to think about her future, or the state of her affairs.

As to her affairs—she was nothing better than a child. She had a vague idea that she was rich; but she had no idea of where her money might be. She knew the names of her London agents; but whether they held any funds of hers or not, she could not tell. She took it for granted that they did. Child as she was, she did not know even the common mode of drawing a check. Hilda had done that for her since her flight from Chetwynde.

The news of the unhappy fate of the elder Miss Lorton had sent a shock through the quiet village of Tenby, and everywhere might be heard expressions of the deepest sympathy with the younger sister, who seemed so gentle, so innocent, so inexperienced, and so affectionate. All had heard of the anguish into which she had been thrown by the news of the fearful calamity, and a respectful commiseration for grief so great was exhibited by all. The honest fishermen who had gone first on the search on that eventful night had not been satisfied, but early on the following morning had roused all the fishing population, and fifty or sixty boats started off before dawn to scour the coast, and to examine the sea bottom. This they kept up for two or three days; but without success. Then, at last, they gave up the search. Nothing of this, however, was known to Zillah, who, at that particular time, was in the first anguish of her grief, and lay prostrated in mind and body. Even the chattering Mathilde was awed by the solemnity of woe.

The people of Tenby were nearly all of the humbler class. The widow who owned the house had moved away, and there were none with whom Zillah could associate, except the rector and his wife. They were old people, and had no children. The Rev. Mr. Harvey had lived there all his life, and was now well advanced in years. At the first tidings of the mournful event he had gone to Zillah's house to see if he could be of any assistance; but finding that she was ill in bed, he had sent his wife to offer her services. Mrs. Harvey had watched over poor Zillah in her grief, and had soothed her too. Mathilde would have been but a poor nurse for one in such a situation, and Mrs. Harvey's motherly care and sweet words of consolation had something, at least, to do with Zillah's recovery.

When she was better, Mrs. Harvey urged her to come and stay with them for a time. It would give her a change of scene, she said, and that was all-important. Zillah was deeply touched by her affectionate solicitude, but declined to leave her house. She felt, she said, as though solitude would be best for her under such circumstances.

"My dear child," said Mrs. Harvey, who had formed almost a maternal affection for Zillah, and had come to address her always in that way—"my dear child, you should not try to deepen your grief by staying here and brooding over it. Every thing here only makes it worse. You must really come with me, if for only a few days, and see if your distress will not be lightened somewhat."

But Zillah said that she could not bear to leave, that the house seemed to be filled with Hilda's presence, and that as long as she was there there was something to remind her of the one she had lost. If she went away she should only long to go back.

"But, my child, would it not be better for you to go to your friends?" said Mrs. Harvey, as delicately as possible.

"I have no friends," said Zillah, in a faltering voice. "They are all gone."

Zillah burst into tears; and Mrs. Harvey, after weeping with her, took her departure, with her heart full of fresh sympathy for one so sweet, and so unhappy.

Time passed on, and Zillah's grief had settled down into a quiet melancholy. The rector and his wife were faithful friends to this friendless girl, and, by a thousand little acts of sympathy, strove to alleviate the distress of her lonely situation. For all this Zillah felt deeply grateful, but nothing that they might do could raise her mind from the depths of grief into which it had fallen. But at length there came a day which was to change all this.

That day she was sitting by the front window in the alcove, looking out to where the sea was rolling in its waves upon the shore. Suddenly, to her surprise, she saw the village postman, who had been passing along the road, open her gate, and come up the path. Her first thought was that her concealment had been discovered, and that Guy had written to her. Then a wild thought followed that it was somehow connected with Hilda. But soon these thoughts were banished by the supposition that it was simply a note for one of the servants. After this she fell into her former melancholy, when suddenly she was roused by the entrance of John, who had a letter in his hand.

"A letter for you, miss," said John, who had no idea that Zillah was of a dignity which deserved the title of "my lady."

Zillah said not a word. With a trembling hand she took the letter and looked at it.

It was covered with foreign post-marks, but this she did not notice. It was the handwriting which excited her attention.

"Hilda!" she cried, and sank back breathless in her chair. Her heart throbbed as though it would burst. For a moment she could not move; but then, with a violent effort, she tore open the letter, and, in a wild fever of excited feeling, read the following:

"NAPLES, June 1, 1859.

"MY OWN DEAREST DARLING,—What you must have suffered in the way of wonder about my sudden disappearance, and also in anxiety about your poor Hilda, I can not imagine. I know that you love me dearly, and for me to vanish from your sight so suddenly and so strangely must have caused you at least some sorrow. If you have been sorrowing for me, my sweetest, do not do so any more. I am safe and almost well, though I have had a strange experience.

"When I left you on that ill-fated evening, I expected to be back as I said. I walked up the beach thoughtlessly, and did not notice the tide or any thing about it. I walked a long distance, and at last felt tired, for I had done a great deal that day. I happened to see a boat drawn up on the shore, and it seemed to be a good place to sit down and rest. I jumped in and sat down on one of the seats. I took off my hat and scarf, and luxuriated in the fresh sea breeze that was blowing over the water. I do not know how long I sat there—I did not think of it at that time, but at last I was roused from my pleasant occupation very suddenly and painfully. All at once I made the discovery that the boat was moving under me. I looked around in a panic. To my horror, I found that I was at a long distance from the shore. In an instant the truth flashed upon me. The tide had risen, the boat had floated off, and I had not noticed it. I was fully a mile away when I made this discovery, and, cool as I am (according to you), I assure you I nearly died of terror when the full reality of my situation occurred to me. I looked all around, but saw no chance of help. Far away on the horizon I saw numerous sails, and nearer to me I saw a steamer, but all were too distant to be of any service. On the shore I could not see a living soul.

"After a time I rallied from my panic, and began to try to get the boat back. But there were no oars, although, if there had been, I do not see how I could have used them. In my desperate efforts I tried to paddle with my hands, but, of course, it was utterly useless. In spite of all my efforts I drifted away further and further, and after a very long time, I do not know how long, I found that I was at an immense distance from the shore. Weakened by anxiety and fear, and worn out by my long-continued efforts, I gave up, and, sitting down again, I burst into a passion of tears. The day was passing on. Looking at the sun I saw that it was the time when you would be expecting me back. I thought of you, my darling, waiting for me—expecting me—wondering at my delay. How I cursed my folly and thoughtlessness in ever venturing into such danger! I thought of your increasing anxiety as you waited, while still I did not come. I thought, Oh, if she only knew where her poor Hilda is—what agony it would give her! But such thoughts were heart-breaking, and at last I dared not entertain them, and so I tried to turn my attention to the misery of my situation. Ah, my dearest, think—only think of me, your poor Hilda, in that boat, drifting helplessly along over the sea out into the ocean!

"With each moment my anguish grew greater. I saw no prospect of escape or of help. No ships came near; no boats of any kind were visible. I strained my eyes till they ached, but could see nothing that gave me hope. Oh, my darling, how can I tell you the miseries of that fearful time! Worse than all, do what I might,

DRIFTING OUT TO SEA.

I still could not keep away from me the thoughts of you, my sweetest. Still they would come—and never could I shake off the thought of your face, pale with loving anxiety, as you waited for that friend of yours who would never appear. Oh, had you seen me as I was—had you but imagined, even in the faintest way, the horrors that surrounded me, what would have been your feelings! But you could never have conceived it. No. Had you conceived it you would have sent every one forth in search of me.

"To add to my grief, night was coming on. I saw the sun go down, and still there was no prospect of escape. I was cold and wretched, and my physical sufferings were added to those of my mind. Somehow I had lost my hat and scarf overboard. I had to endure the chill wind that swept over me, the damp piercing blast that came over the waters, without any possibility of shelter. At last I grew so cold and benumbed that I lay down in the bottom of the boat, with the hope of getting out of the way of the wind. It was indeed somewhat more sheltered, but the shelter at best was but slight. I had nothing to cover myself with, and my misery was extreme.

"The twilight increased, and the wind grew stronger and colder. Worst of all, as I lay down and looked up, I could see that the clouds were gathering, and knew that there would be a storm. How far I was out on the sea I scarcely dared conjecture. Indeed, I gave myself up for lost, and had scarcely any hope. The little hope that was left was gradually driven away by the gathering darkness, and at length all around me was black. It was night. I raised myself up, and looked feebly out upon the waves. They were all hidden from my sight. I fell back, and lay there for a long time, enduring horrors, which,

in my wildest dreams, I had never imagined as liable to fall to the lot of any miserable human being.

"I know nothing more of that night, or of several nights afterward. When I came back to consciousness I found myself in a ship's cabin, and was completely bewildered. Gradually, however, I found out all. This ship, which was an Italian vessel belonging to Naples, and was called the *Vittoria*, had picked me up on the morning after I had drifted away. I was unconscious and delirious. They took me on board, and treated me with the greatest kindness. For the tender care which was shown me by these rough but kindly hearts Heaven only can repay them; I can not. But when I had recovered consciousness several days had elapsed, the ship was on her way to Naples, and we were already off the coast of Portugal. I was overwhelmed with astonishment and grief. Then the question arose, What was I to do? The captain, who seemed touched to the heart by my sorrow, offered to take the ship out of her course and land me at Lisbon, if I liked; or he would put me ashore at Gibraltar. Miserable me! What good would it do for me to be landed at Lisbon or at Gibraltar? Wide seas would still intervene between me and my darling. I could not ask them to land me at either of those places. Besides, the ship was going to Naples, and that seemed quite as near as Lisbon, if not more so. It seemed to me to be more accessible—more in the line of travel—and therefore I thought that by going on to Naples I would really be more within your reach than if I landed at any intervening point. So I decided to go on.

"Poor me! Imagine me on board a ship, with no change of clothing, no comforts or delicacies of any kind, and at the same time prostrated by sickness arising from my first misery. It was a kind of low fever, combined with delirium, that affected me. Most fortunately for me, the captain's wife sailed with him, and to her I believe my recovery is due. Poor dear Margarita! Her devotion to me saved me from death. I gave her that gold necklace that I have worn from childhood. In no other way could I fittingly show my gratitude. Ah, my darling! the world is not all bad. It is full of honest, kindly hearts, and of them all none is more noble or more pure than my generous friend the simple wife of Captain Gaddagli. May Heaven bless her for her kindness to the poor lost stranger who fell in her way!

"My sweet Zillah, how does all this read to you? Is it not wildly improbable? Can you imagine your Hilda floating out to sea, senseless, picked up by strangers, carried off to foreign countries? Do you not rejoice that it was so, and that you do not have to mourn my death? My darling, I need not ask. Alas! what would I not give to be sitting with your arms around me, supporting my aching head, while I told you of all my suffering?

"But I must go on. My exposure during that dreadful night had told fearfully upon me. During the voyage I could scarcely move. Toward its close, however, I was able to go on deck, and the balmy air of the Mediterranean revived me. At length we reached Naples Bay. As we sailed up to the city, the sight of all the glorious scenery on every side seemed to fill me with new life and strength. The cities along the shore, the islands, the headlands, the mountains, Vesuvius, with its canopy of smoke, the intensely blue sky, the clear transparent air, all made me feel as though I had been transported to a new world.

"I went at once to the Hôtel de l'Europe, on the Strada Toledo. It is the best hotel here, and is very comfortable. Here I must stay for a time, for, my darling, I am by no means well. The doctor thinks that my lungs are affected. I have a very bad cough. He says that even if I were able to travel, I must not think of going home yet, the air of Naples is my only hope, and he tells me to send to England for my friends. My friends! What friends have I? None. But, darling, I know that I have a friend—one who would go a long distance for her poor suffering Hilda. And now, darling, I want you to come on. I have no hesitation in asking this, for I know that you do not feel particularly happy where you are, and you would rather be with me than be alone. Besides, my dearest, it is to Naples that I invite you—to Naples, the fairest, loveliest place in all the world! a heaven upon earth! where the air is balm, and every scene is perfect beauty! You must come on, for your own sake as well as mine. You will be able to rouse yourself from your melancholy. We will go together to visit the sweet scenes that lie all around here; and when I am again by your side, with your hand in mine, I will forget that I have ever suffered.

"Do not be alarmed at the journey. I have thought out all for you. I have written to Mr. Gualtier, in London, and asked him to bring you on here. He will be only too glad to do us this service. He is a simple-minded and kind-hearted man. I have asked him to call on you

immediately to offer his services. You will see him, no doubt, very soon after you get this letter. Do not be afraid of troubling him. We can compensate him fully for the loss of his time. "And now, darling, good-by. I have written a very long letter, and feel very tired. Come on soon, and do not delay. I shall count the days and the hours till you join me. Come on soon, and do not disappoint your loving

"HILDA.

"P.S. — When you come, will you please bring on my turquoise brooch and my green bracelet. The little writing-desk, too, I should like, if not too much trouble. Of course you need not trouble about the house. It will be quite safe as it stands, under the care of your housekeeper and servants, till we get back again to England. Once more, darling, good-by.

"H."

This astonishing letter was read by Zillah with a tumult of emotions that may be imagined but not described. As she finished it the reaction in her feelings was too much to be borne. A weight was taken off her soul. In the first rush of her joy and thankfulness she burst into tears, and then once more read the letter, though she scarce could distinguish the words for the tears of joy that blinded her eyes.

To go to Naples—and to Hilda! what greater happiness could be conceived of? And that thoughtful Hilda had actually written to Gualtier! And she was alive! And she was in Naples! What a wonder to have her thus come back to her from the dead!

With such a torrent of confused thoughts Zillah's mind was filled, until at length, in her deep gratitude to Heaven, she flung herself upon her knees and poured forth her soul in prayer.

CHAPTER XXVIII.

BETRAYED.

ZILLAH's excitement was so great that, for all that night, she could not sleep. There were many things for her to think about. The idea that Hilda had been so marvelously rescued, and was still alive and waiting for her, filled her mind. But it did not prevent her from dwelling in thought upon the frightful scenes through which she had passed. The thought of her dear friend's lonely voyage, drifting over the seas in an open boat, unprotected from the storm, and suffering from cold, from hunger, and from sorrow till sense left her, was a painful one to her loving heart. Yet the joy that arose from the consciousness of Hilda's safety was of itself sufficient to counterbalance all else. Her safety was so unexpected, and the one fact was so overwhelming, that the happiness which it caused was sufficient to overmaster any sorrowful sympathy which she might feel for Hilda's misfortunes. So, if her night was sleepless, it was not sad. Rather it was joyful; and often and often, as the hours passed, she repeated that prayer of thankfulness which the first perusal of the letter had caused.

Besides this, the thought of going on to join Hilda was a pleasant one. Her friend had been so thoughtful that she had arranged all for her.

No companion could be more appropriate or more reliable than Mr. Gualtier, and he would certainly make his appearance shortly. She thought also of the pleasure of living in Naples, and recalled all that she had ever heard about the charms of that place. Amidst such thoughts as these morning came, and it was not until after the sun had risen that Zillah fell asleep.

Two days after the receipt of that letter by Zillah, Gualtier arrived. Although he had been only a music-teacher, yet he had been associated in the memory of Zillah with many happy hours at Chetwynde; and his instructions at Pomeroy Court, though at the time irksome to her, were now remembered pleasantly, since they were connected with the memories of her father; and on this occasion he had the additional advantage of being specially sent by Hilda. He seemed thus in her mind to be in some sort connected with Hilda. She had not seen him since the Earl's illness, and had understood from Hilda that he had gone to London to practice his profession.

As Gualtier entered, Zillah greeted him with a warmth which was unusual from her to him, but which can readily be accounted for under the circumstances. He seemed surprised and pleased. His small gray eyes twinkled, and his sallow cheeks flushed with involuntary delight at such marks of condescension. Yet in his manner and address he was as humble and as servile as ever. His story was shortly told. He had received, he said, a short note from Miss Krieff, by which he learned that, owing to an act of thoughtlessness on her part, she had gone adrift in a boat, and had been picked up by a ship on its way to Naples, to which place she had been carried. He understood that she had written to Lady Chetwynde to come and join her. Gualtier hoped that Lady Chetwynde would feel the same confidence in him which Miss Krieff had expressed in making known to him that they had been living under an assumed name. Of course, unless this had been communicated to him it would have been impossible for him to find her. He assured her that with him her secret was perfectly inviolable, that he was perfectly reliable, and that the many favors which he had received from General Pomeroy, from the late Earl, and from herself, would of themselves be sufficient to make him guard her secret with watchful vigilance, and devote himself to her interests with the utmost zeal and fidelity.

To Zillah, however, the voluble assurances of Gualtier's vigilance, secrecy, and fidelity were quite unnecessary. It was enough that she had known him for so many years. Her father had first made him known to her. After him her second father, Earl Chetwynde, had made him her teacher. Last of all, at this great hour in her life, Hilda herself had sent him to accompany her. It would have been strange indeed if, under such circumstances, any doubt whatever with regard to him had for one moment entered her mind.

On the day after the receipt of Hilda's letter Zillah had gone for the first time to the rectory, and told the joyful news to her kind friends there. She read the letter to them, while they listened to every word with breathless interest, often interrupting her with exclamations of pity, of sympathy, or of wonder. Most of all were they affected by the change which had come over Zillah, who in one night had passed from dull despair to life and joy and hope. She seemed to them now a different being. Her face was flushed with excitement; her deep, dark eyes, no longer downcast, flashed with radiant joy; her voice was tremulous as she read the letter, or spoke of her hope of soon rejoining Hilda. These dear old people looked at her till their eyes filled with tears; tears which were half of joy over her happiness, and half of sadness at the thought that she was to leave them.

"Ah, my child," said Mrs. Harvey, in a tremulous voice, "how glad I am that your dear sister has been saved by our merciful God; but how sad I feel to think that I shall lose you now, when I have come to love you so!"

Her voice had such inexpressible sadness, and such deep and true affection in its tones, that Zillah was touched to the heart. She twined her arms fondly about the neck of the old lady, and kissed her tenderly.

"Ah, my dearest Mrs. Harvey," said she, "how can I ever repay you for all your loving care of me! Do not think that I did not see all and feel all that you did for me. But I was so sad."

"But, my poor child," said the rector, after a long conversation, in which they had exhausted all the possibilities of Hilda's "situation," "this is a long journey. Who is this Mr. Gualtier? Do you know him? Would it not be better for me to go with you?"

"Oh, my kind friend, how good you are!" said Zillah, again overwhelmed with gratitude. "But there is no necessity. I have known Mr. Gualtier for years. He was my music-teacher for a long time before my dear father left me. He is very good and very faithful."

So no more was said on that matter.

Before Gualtier came Zillah had arranged every thing for her journey. She decided to leave the house just as it was, under the care of the housekeeper, with the expectation of returning at no very distant date. The rector promised to exercise a general supervision over her affairs. She left with him money enough to pay the year's rent in advance, which he was to transmit to the owner. Such arrangements as these gave great comfort to these kindly souls, for in them they saw signs that Zillah would return; and they both hoped that the "sisters" would soon tire even of Italy, and in a fit of homesickness come back again. With this hope they bade her adieu.

On leaving Tenby, Zillah felt nothing but delight. As the coach drove her to the station, as the railway train hurried her to London, as the tidal train took her to Southampton, as the packet bore her across the Channel, every moment of the time was filled with joyous anticipations of her meeting Hilda. All her griefs over other losses and other calamities had in one instant faded away at the news that Hilda was safe. That one thing was enough to compensate for all else.

Arriving at Paris, she was compelled to wait for one day on account of some want of connection in the trains for Marseilles. Gualtier acted as cicerone, and accompanied her in a carriage through the chief streets, through the Place de la Concorde, the Champs Elysées, and the Bois de Boulogne. She was sufficiently herself to experience delight in spite of her impatience, and to feel the wonder and admiration which the first sight of that gay and splendid capital always excites. But she was not willing to linger here. Naples was the goal at which she wished to arrive, and as soon as possible she hurried onward.

On reaching Marseilles she found the city crowded. The great movements of the Italian war were going on, and every thing was affected by it. Marseilles was one of the grand centres of action, and one of the chief dépôts for military supplies. The city was filled with soldiers. The harbor was full of transports. The streets were thronged with representatives of all the different regiments of the French army, from the magnificent steel-clad Cuirassiers, and the dashing Chasseurs de Vincennes, to the insouciant Zouaves and the wild Turcos. In addition to the military, the city was filled with civil officials, connected with the dispatch of the army, who filled the city, and rendered it extremely difficult for a stranger to find lodgings. Zillah was taken to the Hôtel de France, but it was full. Gualtier went round to all the other hotels, but returned with the unpleasant intelligence that all were likewise filled. But this did not very greatly disturb Zillah, for she hoped to be on board the steamer soon, and whether she found lodgings or not was a matter of indifference to her in comparison with prosecuting her journey. After several hours Gualtier returned once more, with the information that he had succeeded in finding rooms for her in this hotel. He had made an earnest appeal, he said, to the gallantry of some French officers, and they had given up their rooms for the use of the fair Anglaise. It was thus that Zillah was able to secure accommodation for the night.

All that evening Gualtier spent in searching for the Naples steamer. When he made his appearance on the following morning it was with news that was very unpleasant to Zillah. He informed her that the regular steamers did not run, that they had been taken up by the French government as transports for the troops, and, as far as he could learn, there were no provisions whatever for carrying the mails. He could scarcely think it possible that such should be the case, but so it was.

At this intelligence Zillah was aghast.

"No mail steamers?" said she. "Impossible! Even if they had taken up all of them for transports, something would be put on the route."

"I can assure you, my lady, that it is as I said. I have searched every where, and can not find out any thing," said Gualtier.

"You need not address me by my title," said Zillah. "At present I do not choose to adopt it."

"Pardon me," said Gualtier, humbly. "It is taken for granted in France that every wealthy English lady is titled—every French hotel-keeper will call you 'miladi,' and why should not I? It is only a form."

"Well," said Zillah, "let it pass. But what am I to do here? I must go on. Can I not go by land?"

"You forget, my lady, the war in Lombardy."

"But I tell you, I *must* go on," said Zillah, impatiently. "Cost what it may—even if I have to buy a steamer."

Gualtier smiled faintly.

"Even if you wished to buy a steamer, my lady, you could not. The French government has taken up all for transports. Could you not make up your mind to wait for a few days?"

"A few days!" cried Zillah, in tones of despair—"a few days! What! after hurrying here through France so rapidly! A few days! No. I would rather go to Spain, and catch the steamer at Gibraltar that Miss Krieff spoke of."

Gualtier smiled.

"That would take much longer time," said he. "But, my lady, I will go out again, and see if I can not find some way more expeditious than that. Trust to me. It will be strange if I do not find some way. Would you be willing to go in a sailing vessel?"

"Of course," said Zillah, without hesitation. "If nothing else can be found I shall be only too happy."

Upon this, Gualtier departed with the intention of searching for a sailing vessel. Zillah herself would have been willing to go in any thing. Such was her anxiety to get to Hilda, that rather than stay in Marseilles she would have been willing to start for Naples in an open boat. But on mentioning her situation to Mathilde she encountered, to her surprise, a very energetic opposition. That important personage expressed a very strong repugnance to any thing of the kind. , First, she dreaded a sea voyage in a sailing vessel; and secondly, having got back to France, she did not wish to leave it. If the regular mail vessel had been going she might not have objected, but as it was she did not wish to go. Mathilde was very voluble, and very determined; but Zillah troubled herself very little about this. To get to Hilda was her one and only desire. If Mathilde stood in the way she would go on in spite of her. She was willing to let Mathilde go, and set out unattended. To get to Naples, to join Hilda, whether in a steamer or a sailing vessel—whether with a maid or without one—that was her only purpose.

On the following morning Gualtier made his appearance, with the announcement that he had found a vessel. It was a small schooner which had been a yacht belonging to an Englishman, who had sold it at Marseilles for some reason or other to a merchant of the city. This merchant was willing to sell it, and Gualtier had bought it in her name, as he could find no other way of going on. The price was large, but "my lady" had said that she was willing to buy a steamer, and to her it would be small. He had ventured, therefore, to conclude the bargain. He had done more, and had even engaged a crew, so that all was in readiness to start.

At this news Zillah was overjoyed. Her longing to be with Hilda was so great that even if she had been a miser she would have willingly paid the price demanded, and far more. The funds which she had brought with her, and which Gualtier had kindly taken charge of, amounted to a considerable sum, and afforded ample means for the purchase of the vessel. The vessel was therefore regularly purchased, and Zillah at last saw a way by which she could once more proceed on her journey. Gualtier informed her that the remainder of that day would be needed for the completion of the preparations, and that they would be ready to leave at an early hour on the following morning. So Zillah awaited with impatience the appointed time.

Zillah awaked early on the following morning, but Mathilde was not to be found. Instead of Mathilde, a letter was awaiting her, which stated, in very respectful language, that the dread which that personage felt at going in a sailing vessel was so strong, and her love for her own dear country so great, that she had decided to remain where she was. She therefore had come to the conclusion to leave "miladi" without giving warning, although she would thereby lose what was due her, and she hoped that "miladi" would forgive her, and bear her in affectionate remembrance. With wishes and prayers for "miladi's" future happiness, Mathilde begged leave to subscribe herself "miladi's" most devoted and grateful servant.

Such was the final message of Mathilde to her indulgent mistress. But, although at any other time Zillah would have been both wounded and indignant at such desertion of her at such a time, yet now, in the one engrossing thought that filled her mind, she thought but little of this incident. At Naples, she thought, she could very easily fill her place. Now she would have to be without a maid for two or three days, but after all it would make no very great difference. She could rely upon herself, and endure a few days' discomfort very readily for Hilda's sake. It was with such feelings as these that she awaited the arrival of Gualtier. When he came, and heard of the departure of Mathilde, he appeared to be filled with indignation, and urged Zillah to wait one day more till he could get another maid for her. But Zillah refused. She was determined to go on, and insisted on starting at once for the yacht. Finding his remonstrances unavailing, the faithful Gualtier conducted her to the schooner, and, as all things were in readiness, they put out to sea immediately.

The schooner was a very handsome one, and on looking over it Zillah felt delighted with Gualtier's good taste, or his good fortune, whichever it might have been. It was, as has been said, a yacht, which had been the property of an Englishman who had sold it at Marseilles. The cabin was fitted up in the most elegant style, and was much more roomy than was common in vessels of that size. There was an outer cabin with a table in the middle and sofas on either side, and an inner cabin with capacious berths. The watchful attention of Gualtier was visible all around. There were baskets of rare fruits, boxes of bonbons, and cake-baskets filled with delicate macaroons and ratafias. There were also several books—volumes of the works of Lamartine and Chateaubriand, together with two or three of the latest English novels. He certainly had been particular to the last degree in attending to all of her possible wants.

After inspecting the arrangements of the cabin, Zillah went out on deck and seated herself at the stern, from which she watched the city which they were fast leaving behind them. On casting a casual glance around, it struck her for a moment that the crew were a remarkably ill-looking set of men; but she was utterly inexperienced, and she concluded that they were like all sailors, and should not be judged by the same standard as landsmen. Besides, was not her faithful Gualtier there, whose delicate attention was so evident even in the most minute circumstance which she had noticed? If the thought of the evil looks of the crew came to her, it was but for a moment; and in a moment it was dismissed. She was herself too guileless to be suspicious, and was far more ready to cast from her all evil thoughts than to entertain them. In her innocence and inexperience she was bold, when one more brave but more experienced would have been fearful.

The wind was fair, and the yacht glided swiftly out of the harbor. The sea was smooth, and Zillah could look all around her upon the glorious scene. In a few hours they had left the land far behind them, and then the grander features of the distant coast became more plainly visible. The lofty heights rose up above the sea receding backward, but ever rising higher, till they reached the Alpine summits of the inland. All around was the blue Mediterranean, dotted with white sails. All that she saw was novel and striking; she had never sailed in a yacht before; the water was smooth enough to be pleasant, and she gave herself up to a childlike joy.

On rising on the following morning they were far out of sight of land. A delicious repast was placed before her for her breakfast. After partaking she sat on deck, looking out upon the glorious sea, with such a feeling of dreamy enjoyment as she had scarcely ever known before. Her one chief thought was that every hour was bringing her nearer to Hilda. When tired of the deck she went below, and lay down in her cabin and read. So the hours passed. On that day Gualtier surpassed himself in delicate attention to every possible wish of hers. She herself was surprised at the variety of the dishes which composed her dinner. She could not help expressing her thanks.

Gualtier smiled, and murmured some scarce audible words.

Two days passed, and they were now far on their way. Gualtier assured her respectfully that on the following morning they would see the Apennines on the Italian shore. The voyage had not been so rapid as it might have been, but it had been exceedingly pleasant weather, and their progress had been satisfactory. That evening Zillah watched the sun as it set in glory below the watery horizon, and retired for the night with the thought that in two days more she would be with Hilda.

She slept soundly that night.

Suddenly she waked with a strange sensation. Her dreams had been troubled. She thought that she was drowning. In an agony she started up. Water was all around her in the berth where she was lying. The dim light of dawn was struggling through the sky-light, and she looked around bewildered, not knowing at first where she was. Soon, however, she remembered, and then a great horror came over her. *The vessel was sinking!*

All was still. She gave a wild cry, and started up, wading through the water to the door. She cried again and again, till her cries became shrieks. In vain. No answer came. Flinging a shawl around her she went into the outer cabin, and thence ascended to the deck.

No one was there.

No man was at the wheel. No watchers were visible. The vessel was deserted!

"AN AWFUL FEAR CAME OVER HER."

Louder and louder she shrieked. Her voice, borne afar over the wide waste of waters, died out in the distance, but brought no response. She hurried to the forecastle. The door was open. She called over and over again. There was no reply. Looking down in the dim morning twilight she could see plainly that the water had penetrated there.

An awful fear came over her.

The sails were lowered. The boat was gone. No one was on board besides herself. The schooner was sinking. She had been deserted. She had been betrayed. She would never see Hilda. Who had betrayed her? Was Hilda really at Naples? Had she really written that letter and sent Gualtier to her? A thousand horrid suspicions rushed through her mind. One thought predominated—*she had been betrayed!*

But why?

CHAPTER XXIX.

TWO NEW CHARACTERS.

IN spite of Gualtier's assurances, a steamer was running regularly between Naples and Marseilles, and the war had made no disturbance in the promptitude and dispatch of its trips. It belonged to a line whose ships went on to Malta, touching at Italian ports, and finally connecting with the steamers of the Peninsular and Oriental Company. The day after Zillah had left Marseilles one of these left Naples on its way to the former port, having on board the usual number and variety of passengers.

On the stern of this vessel stood two men, looking out over the water to where the purple Apennines arose over the Italian coast, where the grand figure of Vesuvius towered conspicuous, its smoke cloud floating like a pennon in the air. One of these men was tall, broad-shouldered, sinewy, with strong square head, massive forehead, firm chin, and eyes which held in their expression at once gentleness and determination; no very rare compound in the opinion of some, for there are those who think that the strongest and boldest natures are frequently the tenderest. He was a man of about fifty, or perhaps even sixty, but his years sat lightly on him; and he looked like a man whom any one might reasonably dread to meet with in a personal encounter. The other was much younger. His face was bronzed by exposure to a southern sun; he wore a heavy beard and mustache, and he had the unmistakable aspect of an English gentleman, while the marked military air which was about him showed that he was without doubt a British officer. He was dressed, however, as a civilian. His hat showed that he was in mourning; and a general sadness of demeanor which he manifested was well in keeping with that sombre emblem.

"Well, Windham," said the former, after a long silence, "I never thought that there was a place on this green earth that could take hold of me like that Italian city. I don't believe that there is a city any where that comes up to Naples. Even New York is not its equal. I wouldn't leave it now—no, *Sir!*—ten team of horses couldn't drag me away, only my family are waiting for me at Marseilles, you see—and I must join them. However, I'll go back again as soon as I can; and if I don't stay in that there country till I've *exhausted* it—squeezed it, and pressed out of it all the useful and entertaining information that it can give—why, then, my name's not Obed Chute."

The one called Windham gave a short laugh.

"You'll have a little difficulty in Lombardy, I think," said he.

"Why?"

"The war."

"The war? My friend, are you not aware that the war need not be any obstacle to a free American?"

"Perhaps not; but you know that armies in the field are not very much inclined to be respecters of persons, and the freest of free Americans might find himself in an Austrian or a French prison as a spy."

"Even so; but he would soon get out, and have an interesting reminiscence. That is one of the things that he would have to be prepared for. At any rate, I have made up my mind to go to Lombardy, and I'll take my family with me. I should dearly like to get a Concord coach to do it in, but if I can't I'll get the nearest approach to it I can find, and calmly trot on in the rear of the army. Perhaps I'll have a chance to take part in some engagement. I should like to do so, for the honor of the flag if nothing else."

"You remind me of your celebrated country-man, who was, as he said, 'blue moulded for want of a fight.'"

"That man, Sir, was a true representative American, and a type of our ordinary, everyday, active, vi-vacious Western citizen—the class of men that fell the forests, people the prairies, fight the fever, reclaim the swamps, tunnel the mountains, send railroads over the plains, and dam all the rivers on the broad continent. It's a pity that these Italians hadn't an army of these Western American men to lead them in their struggle for liberty."

"Do you think they would be better than the French army?"

"The French army!" exclaimed Obed Chute, in indescribable accents. "Yes. It is generally conceded that the French army takes the lead in military matters. I say so, although I am a British officer."

"Have you ever traveled in the States?" said Obed Chute, quietly.

"No. I have not yet had that pleasure."

"You have never yet seen our Western population. You don't know it, and you can't conceive it. Can you imagine the original English Puritan turned into a wild Indian, with all his original honor, and morality, and civilization, combining itself with the intense animalism, the capacity for endurance, and the reckless valor of the savage? Surround all this with all that tenderness, domesticity, and pluck which are the ineradicable characteristics of the Saxon race, and then you have the Western American man —the product of the Saxon, developed by long struggles with savages and by the animating influences of a boundless continent."

"I suppose by this you mean that the English race in America is superior to the original stock."

"That can hardly be doubted," said Obed Chute, quite seriously. "The mother country is small and limited in its resources. America is not a country. It is a continent, over which our race has spread itself. The race in the mother country has reached its ultimate possibility. In America it is only beginning its new career. To compare America with England is not fair. You should compare New York, New England, Virginia, with England, not America. Already we show differences in the development of the same race which only a continent could cause. Maine is as different from South Carolina as England from Spain. But you Europeans never seem able to get over a fashion that you have of regarding our boundless continent as a small country. Why, I myself have been asked by Europeans about the health of friends of theirs who lived in California, and whom I knew no more about than I did of the Chinese. The fact is, however, that we are continental, and nature is developing the continental American man to an astonishing extent.

"Now as to this Lombard war," continued Obed Chute, as Windham stood listening in silence, and with a quiet smile that relieved but slightly the deep melancholy of his face—"as to this Lombard war; why, Sir, if it were possible to collect an army of Western Americans and put them into that there territory"—waving his hand grandly toward the Apennines—"the way they would walk the Austrians off to their own country would be a caution. For the Western American man, as an individual, is physically and spiritually a *gigantic* being, and an army of such would be irresistible. Two weeks would wind up the Lombard war. Our Americans, Sir, are the most military people in the wide universe."

"As yet, though, they haven't done much to show their capacity," said Windham. "You don't call the Revolutionary war and that of 1812 any greater than ordinary wars, do you?"

"No, Sir; not at all," said Obed Chute. "We are well aware that in actual wars we have as yet done but little in comparison with our possibilities and capabilities. In the Revolutionary war, Sir, we were crude and unformed—we were infants, Sir, and our efforts were infantile. The swaddling bands of the colonial system had all along restrained the free play of the national muscle; and throughout the war there was no time for full development. Still, Sir, from that point of view, as an infant nation, we did remarkable well—re-markable. In 1812 we did not have a fair chance. We had got out of infancy, it is true; but still not into our full manhood. Besides, the war was too short. Just as we began to get into condition—just as our fleets and armies were ready to *do* something—the war came to an end. Even then, however, we did re-markable well—re-markable. But, after all, neither of these exhibited the American man in his boundless possibility before the world."

"You think, I suppose, that if a war were to come now, you could do proportionally better."

"Think it!" said Obed; "I know it. The American people know it. And they want, above all things, to have a chance to show it. You spoke of that American who was blue-moulded for want of a fight. I said that man was a typical American. Sir, that saying is profoundly true. Sir, the whole American nation is blue-moulded, Sir. It is spilin for want of a fight—a big fight."

"Well, and what do you intend to do about it?"

"Time will show," said Obed, gravely. "Already, any one acquainted with the manners of our people and the conduct of our government will recognize the remarkable fact that our nation is the most wrathy, cantankerous, high-mettled community on this green earth. Why, Sir, there ain't a foreign nation that can keep on friendly terms with us. It ain't ugliness, either—it's only a friendly desire to have a fight with somebody—we only want an excuse to begin. The only trouble is, there ain't a nation that reciprocates our peculiar national feeling."

"What can you do, then?" asked Windham, who seemed to grow quite amused at this conversation.

"That's a thing I've often puzzled over," said Obed, thoughtfully; "and I can see only one remedy for us."

"And what is that?"

"Well, it's a hard one—but I suppose it's got to come. You see, the only foreign countries that are near enough to us to afford a satisfactory field of operations are Mexico and British America. The first we have already tried. It was poor work, though. Our armies marched through Mexico as though they were going on a picnic. As to British America, there is no chance. The population is too small. No, there is only one way to gratify the national craving for a fight."

"I don't see it."

"Why," said Obed, dryly, "to get up a big fight among ourselves."

"Among yourselves?"

"Yes—quite domestic—and all by ourselves."

"You seem to me to speak of a civil war."

"That's the identical circumstance, and nothing else. It is the only thing that is suited to the national feeling; and what's more—it's got to come. I see the pointings of the finger of Providence. It's got to come—there's no help for it —and, mark me, when it does come it 'll be the tallest kind of fightin' that this revolving orb has yet seen in all its revolutions."

"You speak very lightly about so terrible a thing as a civil war," said Windham. "But do you think it possible? In so peaceful and well-ordered a country what causes could there be?"

"When the whole nation is pining and craving and spilin for a fight," said Obed, "causes will not be wanting. I can enumerate half a dozen now. First, there is the slavery question; secondly, the tariff question; thirdly, the suffrage question; fourthly, the question of the naturalization of foreigners; fifthly, the bank question; sixthly, the question of denominational schools."

Windham gave a short laugh.

"You certainly seem to have causes enough for a war, although, to my contracted European mind, they would all seem insufficient. Which of these, do you think, is most likely to be the cause of that civil war which you anticipate?"

"One, pre-eminently and inevitably," said Obed, solemnly. "All others are idle beside this one." He dropped abruptly the half gasconading manner in which he had been indulging, and, in a low voice, added, "In real earnest, Windham, there is one thing in America which is, every year, every month, every day, forcing on a war from which there can be no escape; a war which will convulse the republic and endanger its existence; yes, Sir, a war which will deluge the land with blood from one end to the other."

His solemn tone, his change of manner, and his intense earnestness, impressed Windham most deeply. He felt that there was some deep meaning in the language of Obed Chute, and that under his careless words there was a gloomy foreboding of some future calamity to his loved country.

"This is a fearful prospect," said he, "to one who loves his country. What is it that you fear?"

"One thing," said Obed—"one thing, and one only—slavery! It is this that has divided the republic and made of our country two nations, which already stand apart, but are every day drawing nearer to that time when a frightful struggle for the mastery will be inevitable. The South and the North must end their differences by a fight; and that fight will be the greatest that has been seen for some generations. There is no help for it. It must come. There are many in our country who are trying to postpone the evil day, but it is to no purpose. The time will come when it can be postponed no longer. Then the war must come, and it will be the slave States against the free."

"I never before heard an American acknowledge the possibility of such a thing," said Windham, "though in Europe there are many who have anticipated this."

THE CRYPTOGRAM. 97

"Many Americans feel it and fear it," said Obed, with unchanged solemnity; "but they do not dare to put their feelings or their fears in words. One may fear that his father, his mother, his wife, or his child, may die; but to put such a fear in words is heart-breaking. So we, who have this fear, brood over it in secret, and in every shifting scene of our national life we look fearfully for those coming events which cast their shadows before. The events which we watch with the deepest anxiety are the Presidential elections. Every four years now brings a crisis; and in one of these the long antagonism between North and South will end in war. But I hate to speak of this. What were we talking of? Of Lombardy and the Italian war. What do you think," he added, abruptly changing the conversation, "of my plan to visit the seat of war?"

"I think," said Windham, "that if any man is able to do Lombardy at such a time, you are that person."

"Well, I intend to try," said Obed Chute, modestly. "I may fail, though I generally succeed in what I set my mind on. I'll go, I think, as a fighting neutral."

"Prepared to fight on either side, I suppose."

"Yes; as long as I don't have to fight against Garibaldi."

"But, wouldn't you find your family a little embarrassing in case of a fight?"

"Oh no! they would always be safely in the rear, at the base of my line of operations. There will be no difficulty about it whatever. Americans are welcome all over Italy, especially at this time, for these Italians think that America sympathizes with them, and will help them; and as to the French—why, Boney, though an emperor, is still a democrat to his heart's core, and, I have no doubt, would give a warm reception to a fighting volunteer."

"Have you any acquaintance with any of the French generals, or have you any plan for getting access to Napoleon?"

"Oh no! I trust merely to the reason and good feeling of the man. It seems to me that a request from a free American to take part in a fight could hardly meet with any thing else except the most cordial compliance."

"Well, all I can say is, that if I were Louis Napoleon, I would put you on my staff," said Windham.

The name of Obed Chute has already been brought forward. He had embarked at Bombay on board the same steamer with Windham, and they had formed a friendship which after circumstances had increased. At first Windham's reserve had repelled advances; his sadness and preoccupation had repelled any intimacy; but before many days an event happened which threw them into close association. When about half-way on her voyage the steamer was discovered to be on fire. Panic arose. The captain tried to keep order among the sailors. This he was very easily able to do. But with the passengers it was another thing. Confusion prevailed every where, and the sailors themselves were becoming demoralized by the terror which raged among the others. In that moment of danger two men stood forth from among the passengers, who, by the force of their own strong souls, brought order out of that chaos. One of

these was Obed Chute. With a revolver in his hand he went about laying hold of each man who seemed to be most agitated, swearing that he would blow his brains out if he didn't "stop his infernal noise." The other was Windham, who acted in a different manner. He collected pipes, pumps, and buckets, and induced a large number to take part in the work of extinguishing the flames. By the attitude of the two the rest were either calmed or cowed; and each one recognized in the other a kindred spirit.

After landing at Suez they were thrown more closely together; their intimacy deepened on the way to Alexandria; and when they embarked on the Mediterranean they had become stronger friends than ever. Windham had told the other that he had recently heard of the death of a friend, and was going home to settle his affairs. He hinted also that he was in some government employ in India; and Obed Chute did not seek to know more. Contrary to the generally received view of the Yankee character, he did not show any curiosity whatever, but received the slight information which was given with a delicacy which showed no desire to learn more than Windham himself might choose to tell.

But for his own part he was as frank and communicative as though Windham had been an old friend or a blood relation. He had been kept in New York too closely, he said, for the last twenty years, and now wished to have a little breathing space and elbow-room. So he had left New York for San Francisco, partly on pleasure, partly on business. He spent some months in California, and then crossed the Pacific to China, touching at Honolulu and Nangasaki. He had left directions for his family to be sent on to Europe, and meet him at a certain time at Marseilles. He was expecting to find them there. He himself had gone from China to India, where he had taken a small tour though the country, and then had embarked for Europe. Before going back to America he expected to spend some time with his family in Italy, France, and Germany.

There was a grandeur of view in this man's way of looking upon the world which surprised Windham, and, to some degree, amused him. For Obed Chute regarded the whole world exactly as another man might regard his native county or town; and spoke about going from San Francisco to Hong-Kong, touching at Nangasaki, just as another might speak of going from Liverpool to Glasgow, touching at Rothsay. He seemed, in fact, to regard our planet as rather a small affair, easily traversed, and a place with which he was thoroughly familiar. He had written from San Francisco for his family to meet him at Marseilles, and now approached that place with the fullest confidence that his family would be there according to appointment. This type of man is entirely and exclusively the product of America, the country of magnificent distances, and the place where Nature works on so grand a scale that human beings insensibly catch her style of expression. Obed Chute was a man who felt in every fibre the oppressive weight of his country's grandeur. Yet so generous was his nature that he forbore to overpower others by any allusions to that grandeur, except where it was absolutely impossible to avoid it.

These two had gradually come to form a strong regard for one another, and Obed Chute did

G

not hesitate to express his opinion about his friend.

"I do not generally take to Britishers," said he, once, "for they are too contracted, and never seem to me to have taken in a full breath of the free air of the universe. They seem usually to have been in the habit of inhaling an enervating moral and intellectual atmosphere. But you suit me, you do. Young man, your hand."

And grasping Windham's hand, Obed wrung it so heartily that he forced nearly all feeling out of it.

"I suppose living in India has enabled me to breathe a broader moral atmosphere," said Windham, with his usual melancholy smile.

"I suppose so," said Obed Chute. "Something has done it, any how. You showed it when the steamer was burning."

"How?"

"By your eye."

"Why, what effect can one's moral atmosphere have on one's eyes?"

"An enormous effect," said Obed Chute. "It's the same in morals as in nature. The Fellahs of the Nile, exposed as they are to the action of the hot rays of the sun, as they strike on the sand, are universally troubled with ophthalmia. In our Mammoth Cave, in Kentucky, there is a subterranean lake containing fishes which have no eyes at all. So it is in character and in morals. I will point you out men whose eyes are inflamed by the hot rays of passion; and others who show by their eyes that they have lived in moral darkness as dense as 'that of 'the Kentucky cave. Take a thief. Do you not know him by his eye? It takes an honest man to look you in the face."

"You have done a great many things," said Windham, at another time. "Have you ever preached in your country?"

"No," said Obed Chute, with a laugh; "but I've done better—I've been a stump orator; and stump oratory, as it is practiced in America, is a little the tallest kind of preaching that this green earth" (he was fond of that expression) "has ever listened to. Our orb, Sir, has seen strange experiences; but it is getting rayther astonished at the performances of the American man."

"Generally," said Windham, "I do not believe in preaching so much as in practice; but when I see a man who can do both, I'm willing to listen, even if it be a stump speech that I hear. Still, I think that you are decidedly greater with a revolver in the midst of a crowd than you could be on a stump with a crowd before you."

Obed Chute shook his head solemnly.

"There," said he, "is one of the pecooliarities of you Europeans. You don't understand our national ways and manners. We don't separate saying and doing. With us every man who pretends to speak must be able to act. No man is listened to unless he is known to be capable of knocking down any one who interrupts him. In a country like ours speaking and acting go together. The Stump and the Revolver are two great American forces—twin born—the animating power of the Great Republic. There's no help for it. It must be so. Why, if I give offense in a speech, I shall of course be called to account afterward; and if I can't take care of myself and settle the account—why—where am I? Don't you see? Ours, Sir, is a singular state of society; but it is the last development of the human race, and, of course, the best."

Conversations like these diverted Windham and roused him from his brooding melancholy. Obed Chute's fancies were certainly whimsical; he had an odd love for paradox and extravagance; he seized the idea that happened to suggest itself, and followed it out with a dry gravity and a solemn air of earnestness which made all that he said seem like his profound conviction. Thus in these conversations Windham never failed to receive entertainment, and to be roused from his preoccupying cares.

CHAPTER XXX.

PICKED UP ADRIFT.

Two days passed since the steamer left Naples, and they were now far on their way. On the morning of the third Windham came on deck at an early hour. No one was up. The man at the wheel was the only one visible. Windham looked around upon the glorious scene which the wide sea unfolds at such a time. The sun had not yet risen, but all the eastern sky was tinged with red; and the wide waste of waters between the ship and that eastern horizon was colored with the ruddy hues which the sky cast downward. But it was not this scene, magnificent though it was, which attracted the thoughts of Windham as he stood on the quarter-deck. His face was turned in that direction; but it was with an abstracted gaze which took in nothing of the glories of visible nature. That deep-seated melancholy of his, which was always visible in his face and manner, was never more visible than now. He stood by the taffrail in a dejected attitude and with a dejected face—brooding over his own secret cares, finding nothing in this but fresh anxieties, and yet unable to turn his thoughts to any thing else. The steamer sped through the waters, the rumble of her machinery was in the air, the early hour made the solitude more complete. This man, whoever he was, did not look as though he were going to England on any joyous errand, but rather like one who was going home to the performance of some mournful duty which was never absent from his thoughts.

Standing thus with his eyes wandering abstractedly over the water, he became aware of an object upon its surface, which attracted his attention and roused him from his meditations. It struck him as very singular. It was at some considerable distance off, and the steamer was rapidly passing it. It was not yet sufficiently light to distinguish it well, but he took the ship's glass and looked carefully at it. He could now distinguish it more plainly. It was a schooner with its sails down, which by its general position seemed to be drifting. It was very low in the water, as though it were either very heavily laden or else water-logged. But there was one thing there which drew all his thoughts. By the foremast, as he looked, he saw a figure standing, which was distinctly waving something as if to attract the attention of the passing steamer. The figure looked like a woman. A longer glance convinced him that it was so in very deed, and that this lonely figure was some woman in distress. It seemed to appeal to himself and to himself alone, with that mute yet eloquent signal, and those despairing gestures. A strange pang shot through his heart—a pang sharp and unaccountable—something more than that which might be caused by any common scene of misery; it was a pang of deep pity and profound sympathy with this lonely sufferer, from whom the steamer's course was turned away, and whom the steersman had not regarded. He only had seen the sight, and the woman seemed to call to him out of her despair. The deep sea lay between; her presence was a mystery; but there seemed a sort of connection between him and her as though invisible yet resistless Fate had shown them to one another, and brought him here to help and to save. It needed but an instant for all these thoughts to flash through his mind. In an instant he flew below and roused the captain, to whom in a few hurried words he explained what had occurred.

The captain, who was dressed, hurried up and looked for himself. But by this time the steamer had moved away much further, and the captain could not see very distinctly any thing more than the outline of a boat.

"Oh, it's only a fishing-boat," said he, with an air of indifference.

"Fishing-boat! I tell you it is an English yacht," said Windham, fiercely. "I saw it plainly. The sails were down. It was water-logged. A woman was standing by the foremast."

The captain looked annoyed.

"It looks to me," said he, "simply like some heavily laden schooner."

"But I tell you she is sinking, and there is a woman on board," said Windham, more vehemently than ever.

"Oh, it's only some Neapolitan fish-wife."

"You must turn the steamer, and save her," said Windham, with savage emphasis.

"I can not. We shall be behind time."

"Damn time!" roared Windham, thoroughly roused. "Do you talk of time in comparison with the life of a human being? If you don't turn the steamer's head, I will."

"You!" cried the captain, angrily. "Damn it! if it comes to that, I'd like to see you try it. It's mutiny."

Windham's face grew white with suppressed indignation.

"Turn the steamer's head," said he, in stern cold tones, from which every trace of passion had vanished. "If you don't, I'll do it myself. If you interfere, I'll blow your brains out. As it is, you'll rue the day you ever refused. Do you know who I am?"

He stepped forward, and whispered in the captain's ear some words which sent a look of awe or fear into the captain's face. Whether Windham was the president of the company, or some British embassador, or one of the Lords of the Admiralty, or any one else in high authority, need not be disclosed here. Enough to say that the captain hurried aft, and instantly the steamer's head was turned.

As for Windham, he took no further notice of the captain, but all his attention was absorbed by the boat. It seemed water-logged, yet still it was certainly not sinking, for as the steamer drew nearer, the light had increased, and he could see plainly through the glass that the boat was still about the same distance out of the water.

Meanwhile Obed Chute made his appearance, and Windham, catching sight of him, briefly explained every thing to him. At once all Obed's most generous sympathies were roused. He took the glass, and eagerly scrutinized the vessel. He recognized it at once, as Windham had, to be an English yacht; he saw also that it was water-logged, and he saw the figure at the mast. But the figure was no longer standing erect, or waving hands, or making despairing signals. It had fallen, and lay now crouched in a heap at the foot of the mast. This Windham also saw. He conjectured what the cause of this might be. He thought that this poor creature had kept up her signals while the steamer was passing, until at last it had gone beyond, and seemed to be leaving her. Then hope and strength failed, and she sank down senseless. It was easy to understand all this, and nothing could be conceived of more touching in its mute eloquence than this prostrate figure, whose distant attitudes had told so tragical a story. Now all this excited Windham still more, for he felt more than ever that he was the savior of this woman's life. Fate had sent her across his path—had given her life to him. He only had been the cause why she should not perish unseen and unknown. This part which he had been called on to play of savior and rescuer—this sudden vision of woe and despair appealing to his mercy for aid—had chased away all customary thoughts, so that now his one idea was to complete his work, and save this poor castaway.

But meanwhile he had not been idle. The captain, who had been so strangely changed by a few words, had called up the sailors, and in an instant the fact was known to the whole ship's company that they were going to save a woman in distress. The gallant fellows, like true sailors, entered into the spirit of the time with the greatest ardor. A boat was got ready to be lowered, Windham jumped in, Chute followed, and half a dozen sailors took the oars. In a short time the steamer had come up to the place. She stopped; the boat was lowered; down went the oars into the water; and away sped the boat toward the schooner. Obed Chute steered. Windham was in the bow, looking eagerly at the schooner, which lay there in the same condition as before. The sun was now just rising, and throwing its radiant beams over the sea. The prostrate figure lay at the foot of the mast.

Rapidly the distance between the boat and the schooner was lessened by the vigorous strokes of the seamen. They themselves felt an interest in the result only less than that of Windham. Nearer and nearer they came. At length the boat touched the schooner, and Windham, who was in the bow, leaped on board. He hurried to the prostrate figure. He stooped down, and with a strange unaccountable tenderness and reverence he took her in his arms and raised her up. Perhaps it was only the reverence which any great calamity may excite toward the one that experiences such calamity; perhaps it was something more profound, more inexplicable—the outgoing of the soul—which may sometimes have a forecast of more than may be indicated to the material senses. This may seem like mysticism, but it is not intended as such. It is merely a statement of the well-known fact that sometimes, under certain circumstances, there arise within us unaccountable presentiments and forebodings, which seem to anticipate the actual future.

Windham then stooped down, and thus tenderly and reverently raised up the figure of the woman. The sun was still rising and gleaming over the waters, and gleaming thus, it threw its full rays into the face of the one whom he held supported in his arms, whose head was thrown back as it lay on his breast, and was upturned so that he could see it plainly.

And never, in all his dreams, had any face appeared before him which bore so rare and radiant a beauty as this one of the mysterious stranger whom he had rescued. The complexion was of a rich olive, and still kept its hue where another would have been changed to the pallor of death; the closed eyes were fringed with long heavy lashes; the eyebrows were thin, and loftily arched; the hair was full of waves and undulations, black as night, gleaming with its jetty gloss in the sun's rays, and in its disorder falling in rich luxuriant masses over the arms and the shoulder of him who supported her. The features were exquisitely beautiful; her nose a slight departure from the Grecian; her lips small

and exquisitely shapen; her chin rounded faultlessly. The face was thinner than it might have been, like the face of youth and beauty in the midst of sorrow; but the thinness was not emaciation; it had but refined and spiritualized those matchless outlines, giving to them not the voluptuous beauty of the Greek ideal, but rather the angelic or saintly beauty of the medieval. She was young too, and the bloom and freshness of youth were there beneath all the sorrow and the grief. More than this, the refined grace of that face, the nobility of those features, the stamp of high breeding which was visible in every lineament, showed at once that she could be no common person. This was no fisherman's wife—no peasant girl, but some one of high rank and breeding—some one whose dress proclaimed her station, even if her features had told him nothing.

"My God!" exclaimed Windham, in bewilderment. "Who is she? How came she here? What is the meaning of it?"

But there was no time to be lost in wonder or in vague conjectures. The girl was senseless. It was necessary at once to put her under careful treatment. For a moment Windham lingered, gazing upon that sad and exquisite face; and then raising her in his arms, he went back to the boat. "Give way, lads!" he cried; and the sailors, who saw it all, pulled with a will. They were soon back again. The senseless one was lifted into the steamer. Windham carried her in his own arms to the cabin, and placed her tenderly in a berth, and committed her to the care of the stewardess. Then he waited impatiently for news of her recovery.

Obed Chute, however, insisted on going back to the schooner for the sake of making a general investigation of the vessel. On going on board he found that she was water-logged. She seemed to have been kept afloat either by her cargo, or else by some peculiarity in her construction, which rendered her incapable of sinking. He tore open the hatchway, and pushing an oar down, he saw that there was no cargo, so that it must have been the construction of the vessel which kept her afloat. What that was, he could not then find out. He was compelled, therefore, to leave the question unsettled for the present, and he took refuge in the thought that the one who was rescued might be able to solve the mystery. This allayed for a time his eager curiosity. But he determined to save the schooner, so as to examine it afterward at his leisure. A hasty survey of the cabins, into which he plunged, showed nothing whatever, and so he was compelled to postpone this for the present. But he had a line made fast between the steamer and the schooner, and the latter was thus towed all the way to Marseilles. It showed no signs of sinking, but kept afloat bravely, and reached the port of destination in about the same condition in which it had been first found.

The stewardess treated the stranger with the utmost kindness and the tenderest solicitude, and, at length, the one who had thus been so strangely rescued came out of that senselessness into which she had been thrown by the loss of the hope of rescue. On reviving she told a brief story. She said that she was English, that her name was Lorton, and that she had been traveling to Marseilles in her own yacht. That the day before, on awaking, she found the yacht full

WINDHAM TENDERLY AND REVERENTLY RAISED HER.

of water and abandoned. She had been a day and a night alone in the vessel, without either food or shelter. She had suffered much, and was in extreme prostration, both of mind and body. But her strongest desire was to get to Naples, for her sister was there in ill health, and she had been making the journey to visit her.

Windham and Obed Chute heard this very strange narrative from the stewardess, and talked it over between themselves, considering it in all its bearings. The opinion of each of them was that there had been foul play somewhere. But then the question arose: why should there have been foul play upon an innocent young girl like this? She was an English lady, evidently of the higher classes; her look was certainly foreign, but her English accent was perfect. In her simple story she seemed to have concealed nothing. The exquisite beauty of the young girl had filled the minds of both of these men with a strong desire to find out the cause of her wrongs, and to avenge her. But how to do so was the difficulty. Windham had important business in England which demanded immediate attention, and would hardly allow him to delay more than a few days. Obed Chute, on the contrary, had plenty of time, but did not feel like trying to intrude himself on her confidence. Yet her distress and desolation had an eloquence which swayed both of these men from their common purposes, and each determined to postpone other designs, and do all that was possible for her.

In spite of an hour's delay in rescuing Miss Lorton, the steamer arrived at Marseilles at nearly the usual time, and the question arose, what was to be done with the one that they had rescued? Windham could do nothing; but Obed Chute could do something, and did do it. The young lady was able now to sit up in the saloon, and here it was that Obed Chute waited upon her.

"Have you any friends in Marseilles?" he asked, in a voice full of kindly sympathy.

"No," said Zillah, in a mournful voice; "none nearer than Naples."

"I have my family here, ma'am," said Obed. "I am an American and a gentleman. If you have no friends, would you feel any objection to stay with us while you are here? My family consists of my sister, two children, and some servants. We are going to Italy as soon as possible, and if you have no objection we can take you there with us—to Naples—to your sister."

Zillah looked up at the large honest face, whose kindly eyes beamed down upon her with parental pity, and she read in that face the expression of a noble and loyal nature.

"You are very—very kind," said she, in a faltering voice. "You will lay me under very great obligations. Yes, Sir, I accept your kind offer. I shall be only too happy to put myself under your protection. I will go with you, and may Heaven bless you!"

She held out her hand toward him. Obed Chute took that little hand in his, but restrained his great strength, and only pressed it lightly.

Meanwhile Windham had come in to congratulate the beautiful girl, whose face had been haunting him ever since that time when the sun lighted it up, as it lay amidst its glory of ebon hair upon his breast. He heard these last words, and stood apart, modestly awaiting some chance to speak.

Zillah raised her face.

Their eyes met in a long earnest gaze.

Zillah was the first to speak.

"You saved me from a fearful fate," she said, in low and tremulous tones. "I heard all about it."

Windham said nothing, but bowed in silence.

Zillah rose from her chair, and advanced toward him, her face expressing strong emotion. Now he saw, for the first time, her wondrous eyes, in all their magnificence of beauty, with their deep unfathomable meaning, and their burning intens-

ity of gaze. On the schooner, while her head lay on his breast, those eyes were closed in senselessness—now they were fixed on his.

"Will you let me thank you, Sir," she said, in a voice which thrilled through him in musical vibrations, "for my life, which you snatched from a death of horror? To thank you, is but a cold act. Believe me, you have my everlasting gratitude."

She held out her hand to Windham. He took it in both of his, and reverentially raised it to his lips. A heavy sigh burst from him, and he let it fall.

"Miss Lorton," said he, in his deep musical voice, which now trembled with an agitation to which he was unused, "if I have been the means of saving you from any evil, my own joy is so great that no thanks are needed from you; or, rather, all thankfulness ought to belong to me."

A deep flush overspread Zillah's face. Her large dark eyes for a moment seemed to read his inmost soul. Then she looked down in silence.

As for Windham, he turned away with something like abruptness, and left her with Obed Chute.

CHAPTER XXXI.

THE PREFECT OF POLICE.

OBED CHUTE had requested his business agents, Messrs. Bourdonnais Frères, to obtain a suitable place for his family on their arrival. He went first to their office, and learned that the family were then in Marseilles, and received their address. He then went immediately for Zillah, and brought her with him. The family consisted of two small girls, aged respectively eight and ten, two maids, a nurse, and a valet or courier, or both combined. A sister of Obed's had the responsibility of the party.

Delight at getting among any friends would have made this party welcome to her; but Miss Chute's thorough respectability made her position entirely unobjectionable. Obed Chute's feelings were not of a demonstrative character. He kissed his sister, took each of his little girls up in his arms, and held them there for about an hour, occasionally walking up and down the room with them, and talking to them all the time. He had brought presents from all parts of the world for every member of his family, and when at length they were displayed, the children made the house ring with their rejoicings. Zillah was soon on a home footing with this little circle. Miss Chute, though rather sharp and very angular, was still thoroughly kind-hearted, and sympathized deeply with the poor waif whom Providence had thrown under her protection. Her kind care and unremitting attention had a favorable effect; and Zillah grew rapidly better, and regained something of that strength which she had lost during the terrors of her late adventure. She was most anxious to go to Naples; but Obed told her that she would have to wait for the next steamer, which would prolong her stay in Marseilles at least a fortnight.

As soon as Obed had seen Zillah fairly settled in the bosom of his family, he set out to give information to the police about the whole matter. His story was listened to with the deepest attention. Windham, who was present, corroborated it; and finally the thing was considered to be of such importance that the chief of police determined to pay Zillah a visit on the following day, for the sake of finding out the utmost about so mysterious an affair. This official spoke English very well indeed, and had spent all his life in the profession to which he belonged.

Both Obed Chute and Windham were present at the interview which the chief of police had with Zillah, and heard all that she had to say in answer to his many questions. The chief began by assuring her that the case was a grave one, both as affecting her, and also as affecting France, and more particularly Marseilles. He apologized for being forced to ask a great many questions, and hoped that she would understand his motives, and answer freely.

Zillah told her story in very much the same terms that she had told it on board the steamer. Her father had died some years ago, she said. She and her sister had been living together in various parts of England. Their last home was Tenby. She then gave a minute account of the accident which had happened to Hilda, and showed the letter which had been written from Naples. This the chief of police scanned very curiously and closely, examining the envelope, the post-marks, and the stamps.

Zillah then proceeded to give an account of her journey until the arrival at Marseilles. She told him of the confusion which had prevailed, and how the mail steamers had been taken off the route, how Gualtier had found a yacht and purchased it for her, and how Mathilde had deserted her. Then she recounted her voyage up to the time when she had seen the steamer, and had fallen prostrate at the foot of the mast.

"What was the date of your arrival at Marseilles?" asked the chief, after long thought.

Zillah informed him.

"Who is Gualtier?"

"He is a teacher of music and drawing."

"Where does he live?"

"In London."

"Do you know any thing about his antecedents?"

"No."

"Have you known him long?"

"Yes; for five years."

"Has he generally enjoyed your confidence?"

"I never thought much about him, one way or the other. My father found him in London, and brought him to instruct me. Afterward—"

Zillah hesitated. She was thinking of Chetwynde.

"Well—afterward—?"

"Afterward," said Zillah, "that is, after my father's death, he still continued his instructions."

"Did he teach your sister also?"

"Yes."

"Your sister seems to have had great confidence in him, judging from her letter?"

"Yes."

"Did she ever make use of his services before?"

"No."

"Might she not have done so?"

"I don't see how. No occasion ever arose."

"Why, then, did she think him so trustworthy, do you suppose?"

"Why, I suppose because he had been known to us so long, and had been apparently a humble, devoted, and industrious man. We were quite solitary always. We had no friends, and so I suppose she thought of him. It would have been quite as likely, if I were in her situation, that I would have done the same—that is, if I had her cleverness."

"Your sister is clever, then?"

"Very clever indeed. She has always watched over me like a—like a mother," said Zillah, while tears stood in her eyes.

"Ah!" said the chief; and for a time he lost himself in thought.

"How many years is it," he resumed, "since your father died?"

"About five years."

"How long was this Gualtier with you before his death?"

"About six months."

"Did your father ever show any particular confidence in him?"

"No. He merely thought him a good teacher, and conscientious in his work. He never took any particular notice of him."

"What was your father?"

"A landed gentleman."

"Where did he live?"

"Sometimes in Berks, sometimes in London," said Zillah, in general terms. But the chief did not know any thing about English geography, and did not pursue this question any further. It would have resulted in nothing if he had done so, for Zillah was determined, at all hazards, to guard her secret.

"Did you ever notice Gualtier's manner?" continued the chief, after another pause.

"No; I never paid any attention to him, nor ever took any particular notice of any thing about him. He always seemed a quiet and inoffensive kind of a man."

"What do you think of him now?"

"I can scarcely say what. He is a villain, of course; but why, or what he could gain by it, is a mystery."

"Do you remember any thing that you can now recall which in any way looks like villainy?"

"No, not one thing; and that is the trouble with me."

"Did he ever have any quarrel of any kind with any of you?"

"Never."

"Was any thing ever done which he could have taken as an insult or an injury?"

"He was never treated in any other way than with the most scrupulous politeness. My father, my sister, and myself were all incapable of treating him in any other way."

"What was your sister's usual manner toward him?"

"Her manner? Oh, the usual dignified courtesy of a lady to an inferior."

"Did he seem to be a gentleman?"

"A gentleman? Of course not."

"He could not have imagined himself slighted, then, by any humiliation?"

"Certainly not."

"Could Gualtier have had any knowledge of your pecuniary affairs?"

"Possibly—in a general way."

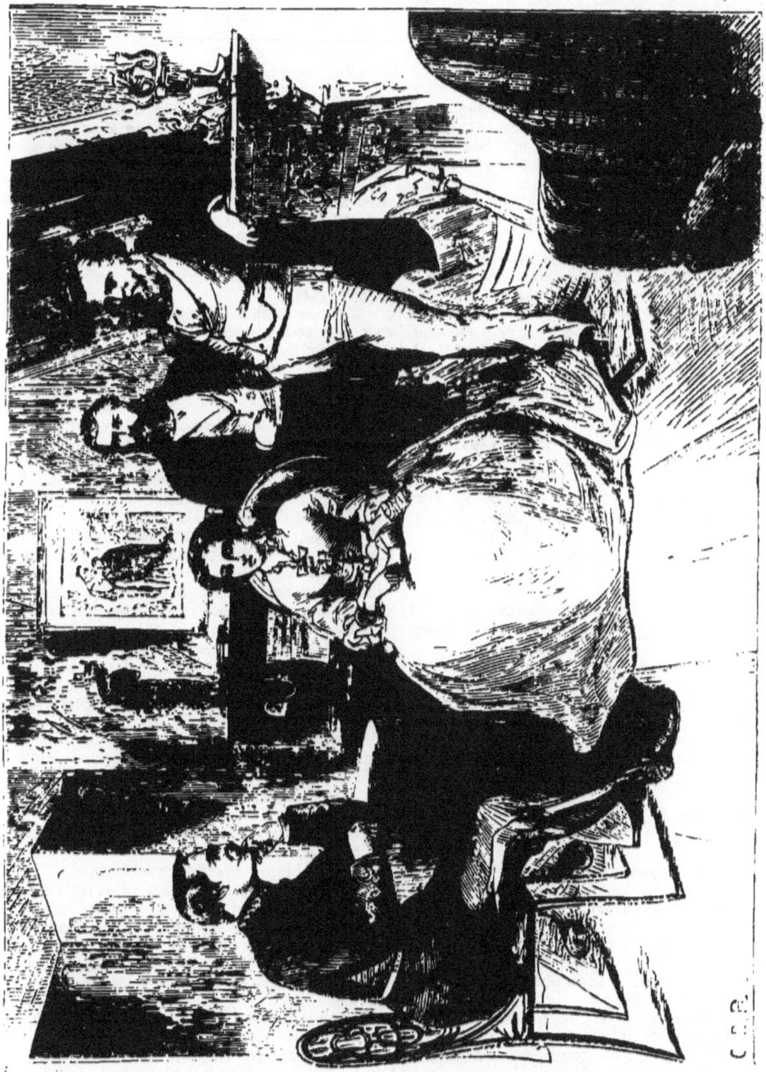

INTERVIEW BETWEEN THE CHIEF OF POLICE AND ZILLAH.

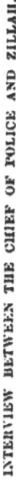

"You are rich, are you not?"

"Yes."

"Might he not have had some design on your money?"

"I have thought of that; but there are insuperable difficulties. There is, first, my sister: and, again, even if she had not escaped, how could he ever get possession of the property?"

The chief did not answer this. He went on to ask his own questions.

"Did you ever hear of the loss of any of your money in any way—by theft, or by forgery?"

"No."

"Did any thing of the kind take place in your father's lifetime?"

"Nothing of the kind whatever."

"Do you know any thing about the antecedents of your maid Mathilde?"

"No; nothing except what little information she may have volunteered. I never had any curiosity about the matter."

"What is her full name?"

"Mathilde Louise Grassier."

"Where does she belong?"

"She said once that she was born in Rouen; and I suppose she was brought up there, too, from her frequent references to that place. I believe she went from there to Paris, as lady's-maid in an English family, and from thence to London."

"How did you happen to get her?"

"My father obtained her for me in London."

"What is her character? Is she cunning?"

"Not as far as I have ever seen. She always struck me as being quite weak out of her own particular department. She was an excellent lady's-maid, but in other respects quite a child."

"Might she not have been very deep, nevertheless?"

"It is possible. I am not much of a judge of character; but, as far as I could see, she was simply a weak, good-natured creature. I don't think she would willingly do wrong; but I think she might be very easily terrified or persuaded. I think her flight from me was the work of Gualtier."

"Did she ever have any thing to do with him?"

"I never saw them together; in fact, whenever he was in the house she was always in my room. I don't see how it is possible that there could have been any understanding between them. For several years she was under my constant supervision, and if any thing of the kind had happened I would certainly recall it now, even if I had not noticed it at the time."

"Did you ever have any trouble with Mathilde?"

"None whatever."

"Weak natures are sometimes vengeful. Did Mathilde ever experience any treatment which might have excited vengeful feelings?"

"She never experienced any thing but kindness."

"Did your sister treat her with the same kindness?"

"Oh yes—quite so."

"When she lived in England did she ever speak about leaving you, and going back to France?"

"No, never."

"She seemed quite contented then?"

"Quite."

"But she left you very suddenly at last. How do you account for that?"

"On the simple grounds that she found herself in her own country, and did not wish to leave it; and then, also, her dread of a sea voyage. But, in addition to this, I think that Gualtier must have worked upon her in some way."

"How? By bribery?"

"I can scarcely think that, for she was better off with me. Her situation was very profitable."

"In what way, then, could he have worked upon her? By menaces?"

"Perhaps so."

"But how? Can you think of any thing in your situation which would, by any possibility, put any one who might be your maid in any danger, or in any fear of some imaginary danger?"

At this question Zillah thought immediately of her assumed name, and the possibility that Gualtier might have reminded Mathilde of this, and terrified her in some way. But she could not explain this; and so she said, unhesitatingly, "No."

The chief of police was now silent and meditative for some time.

"Your sister," said he at length—"how much older is she than you?"

"About four years."

"You have said that she is clever?"

"She is very clever."

"And that she manages the affairs?"

"Altogether. I know nothing about them. I do not even know the amount of my income. She keeps the accounts, and makes all the purchases and the payments—that is, of course, she used to."

"What is her character otherwise? Is she experienced at all in the world, or is she easily imposed upon?"

"She is very acute, very quick, and is thoroughly practical."

"Do you think she is one whom it would be easy to impose upon?"

"I know that such a thing would be extremely difficult. She is one of those persons who acquire the ascendency wherever she goes. She is far better educated, far more accomplished, and far more clever than I am, or can ever hope to be. She is clear-headed and clear-sighted, with a large store of common-sense. To impose upon her would be difficult, if not impossible. She is very quick to discern character."

"And yet she trusted this Gualtier?"

"She did; and that is a thing which is inexplicable to me. I can only account for it on the ground that she had known him so long, and had been so accustomed to his obsequiousness and apparent conscientiousness, that her usual penetration was at fault. I think she trusted him, as I would have done, partly because there was no other, and partly out of habit."

"What did you say was the name of the place where you were living when your sister met with her accident?"

"Tenby."

"Was Gualtier living in the place?"

"No."

"Where was he?"

"In London."

"How did your sister know that he was there?"

"I can not tell."

"Did you know where he was?"

"I knew nothing about him. But my sister managed our affairs; and when Gualtier left us I dare say he gave his address to my sister, in case of our wanting his services again."

"You dismissed Gualtier, I suppose, because you had no longer need for his services?"

"Yes."

"You say that she never treated him with any particular attention?"

"On the contrary, she never showed any thing but marked *hauteur* toward him. I was indifferent—she took trouble to be dignified."

"Have you any living relatives?"

"No—none."

"Neither on the father's side nor the mother's?"

"No."

"Have you no guardian?"

"At my father's death there was a guardian—a nominal one—but he left the country, and we have never seen him since."

"He is not now in England, then?"

"No."

The chief of police seemed now to have exhausted his questions. He rose, and, with renewed apologies for the trouble which he had given, left the room. Obed and Windham followed, and the former invited him to the library—a room which was called by that name from the fact that there was a book-shelf in it containing a few French novels. Here they sat in silence for a time, and at length the chief began to tell his conclusions.

"I generally keep my mind to myself," said he, "but it is very necessary for you to know what I conceive to be the present aspect of this very important case. Let us see, then, how I would analyze it.

"In the first place, remark the *position of the girls*.

"Two young, inexperienced girls, rich, alone in the world, without any relatives or any connections, managing their own affairs, living in different places—such is the condition of the principals in this matter. The guardian whom their father left has disappeared—gone perhaps to America, perhaps to India—no matter where. He is out of their reach.

"These are the ones with whom this Gualtier comes in contact. He is apparently a very ordinary man, perhaps somewhat cunning, and no doubt anxious to make his way in the world. He is one of those men who can be honest as long as he is forced to be; but who, the moment the pressure is taken off, can perpetrate crime for his own interests, without pity or remorse. I know the type well—cold-blooded, cunning, selfish, hypocritical, secretive, without much intellect, cowardly, but still, under certain circumstances, capable of great boldness. So Gualtier seems to me.

"He was in constant connection with these girls for five or six years. During that time he must have learned all about them and their affairs. He certainly must have learned how completely they were isolated, and how rich they were. Yet I do not believe that he ever had any thought during all that time of venturing upon any plot against them.

"It was Fate itself that threw into his hands an opportunity that could not be neglected. For, mark you, what an unparalleled opportunity it was. One of these sisters—the elder, the manager of affairs, and guardian of the other—meets with an accident so extraordinary that it would be incredible, were it not told in her own handwriting. She finds herself in Naples, ill, friendless, and but recently saved from death. She can not travel to join her sister, so she writes to her sister to come to her in Naples. But how can that young sister come? It is a long journey, and difficult for a friendless girl. She has no friends, so the elder Miss Lorton thinks very naturally of the faithful music-teacher, whom she has known so long, and who is now in London. She writes him, telling him the state of affairs, and no doubt offers him a sufficient sum of money to reward him for giving up his practice for a time. The same day that her sister received her letter, he also receives his.

"Can you not see what effect this startling situation would have on such a man? Here, in brief, he could see a chance for making his fortune, and getting possession of the wealth of these two. By making way with them, one after the other, it could easily be done. He had no pity in his nature, and no conscience in particular to trouble him. Nor were there any fears of future consequences to deter him. These friendless girls would never be missed. They could pass away from the scene, and no avenger could possibly rise up to demand an account of them at his hands. No doubt he was forming his plans from the day of the receipt of his letter all the way to Marseilles.

"Now, in the plot which he formed and carried out, I see several successive steps.

"The first step, of course, was to get rid of the maid Mathilde. Miss Lorton's description of her enables us to see how easily this could be accomplished. She was a timid creature, who does not seem to have been malicious, nor does she seem to have had any idea of fidelity. Gualtier may either have cajoled her, or terrified her. It is also possible that he may have bought her. This may afterward be known when we find the woman herself.

"The next step is evident. It was to get rid of the younger Miss Lorton, with whom he was traveling. It was easy to do this on account of her friendlessness and inexperience. How he succeeded in doing it we have heard from her own lips. He trumped up that story about the steamers not running, and obtained her consent to go in a yacht. This, of course, placed her alone in his power. He picked up a crew of scoundrels, set sail, and on the second night scuttled the vessel, and fled. Something prevented the vessel from sinking, and his intended victim was saved.

"Now what is his third step?

"Of course there can be only one thing, and that third step will be an attempt of a similar kind against the elder Miss Lorton. If it is not too late to guard against this we must do so at once. He is probably with her now. He can easily work upon her. He can represent to her that her sister is ill at Marseilles, and induce her to come here. He can not deceive her about the steamers, but he may happen to find her just after the departure of the steamer, and she, in her impatience, may consent to go in a sailing vessel, to meet the same fate which he designed for her sister.

"After this, to complete my analysis of this man's proceedings, there remains the fourth step.

"Having got rid of the sisters, the next purpose will be to obtain their property. Now if he is left to himself, he will find this very easy.

"I have no doubt that he has made himself fully acquainted with all their investments; or, if he has not, he will find enough among their papers, which will now be open to him. He can correspond with their agents, or forge drafts, or forge a power of attorney for himself, and thus secure gradually a control of all. There are many ways by which a man in his situation can obtain all that he wishes. Their bankers seem to be purely business agents, and they have apparently no one who takes a deeper interest in them.

"And now the thing to be done is to head him off. This may be done in various ways.

"First, to prevent the fulfillment of his design on the elder Miss Lorton, I can send off a message at once to the Neapolitan government, and obtain the agency of the Neapolitan police to secure his arrest. If he is very prompt he may have succeeded in leaving Naples with his victim before this; but there is a chance that he is resting on his oars, and, perhaps, deferring the immediate prosecution of the third step.

"Secondly, I must put my machinery to work to discover the maid Mathilde, and secure her arrest. She will be a most important witness in the case. If she is a partner in Gualtier's guilt, she can clear up the whole mystery.

"Thirdly, we must have information of all this sent to Miss Lorton's bankers in London, and her solicitors, so as to prevent Gualtier from accomplishing his fourth step, and also in order to secure their co-operation in laying a trap for him which will certainly insure his capture.

"As for the younger Miss Lorton, she had better remain in Marseilles for six or eight weeks, so that if the elder Miss Lorton should escape she may find her here. Meantime the Neapolitan police will take care of her, if she is in Naples, and communicate to her where her sister is, so that she can join her, or write her. At any rate, Miss Lorton must be persuaded to wait here till she hears from her sister, or of her."

Other things were yet to be done before the preliminary examinations could be completed. The first was the examination of the man who had disposed of the yacht to Gualtier. He was found without any difficulty, and brought before the chief. It seems he was a common broker, who had bought the vessel at auction, on speculation, because the price was so low. He knew nothing whatever about nautical matters, and hated the sea. He had hardly ever been on board of her, and had never examined her. He merely held her in his possession till he could find a chance of selling her. He had sold her for more than double the money that he had paid for her, and thought the speculation had turned out very good. Nothing had ever been told him as to any peculiarity in the construction of the yacht. As far as he knew, the existence of such could not have been found out.

On being asked whether the purchaser had assigned any reason for buying the vessel, he said no; and from that fact the chief seemed to form a more respectful opinion of Gualtier than he had hitherto appeared to entertain. Common cunning would have been profuse in stating motives, and have given utterance to any number of lies. But Gualtier took refuge in silence. He bought the vessel, and said nothing about motives or reasons. And, indeed, why should he have done so?

Obed and Windham visited the yacht, in company with the chief. She was in the dry dock, and the water had flowed out from her, leaving her open for inspection. Zillah's trunks were taken out and conveyed to her, though their contents were not in a condition which might make them of any future value. Still, all Zillah's jewelry was there, and all the little keepsakes which had accumulated during her past life. The recovery of her trunks gave her the greatest delight.

A very careful examination of the yacht was made by the chief of police and his two companions. In front was a roomy forecastle; in the stern was a spacious cabin, with an after-cabin adjoining; between the two was the hold. On close examination, however, an iron bulkhead was found, which ran the whole length of the yacht on each side. This had evidently been quite unknown to Gualtier. He and his crew had scuttled the vessel, leaving it, as they supposed, to sink; but she could not sink, for the air-tight compartments, like those of a life-boat, kept her afloat.

CHAPTER XXXII.

TOO MUCH TOGETHER.

WINDHAM had exhibited the deepest interest in all these investigations. On the day after Zillah's interview with the chief of police he called and informed them that his business in England, though important, was not pressing, and that he intended to remain in Marseilles for a few days, partly for the sake of seeing how the investigations of the police would turn out, and partly, as he said, for the sake of enjoying a little more of the society of his friend Chute. Thenceforth he spent very much of his time at Chute's hotel. and Zillah and he saw very much of one another. Perhaps it was the fact that he only was altogether of Zillah's own order; or it may have been the general charm of his manner, his noble presence, his elevated sentiments, his rich, full, ringing English voice. Whatever it may have been, however, she did not conceal the pleasure which his society afforded her. She was artless and open; her feelings expressed themselves readily, and were made manifest in her looks and gestures. Still, there was a melancholy behind all this which Windham could not but notice—a melancholy penetrating far beneath the surface talk in which they both indulged. He, on his part, revealed to Zillah un-mistakably the same profound melancholy which has already been mentioned. She tried to con-jecture what it was, and thought of no other thing than the bereavement which was indicated by the sombre emblem on his hat. Between these two there was never laughter, rarely levity; but their conversation, when it turned even on trifles, was earnest and sincere. Day after day passed, and each interview grew to be more pleasant than the preceding one. Often Obed Chute joined in the conversation; but their minds were of a totally different order from his; and never did they feel this so strongly as when some hard, dry, practical, and thoroughly sensi-ble remark broke in upon some little delicate flight of fancy in which they had been indulging.

One day Windham came to propose a ride. Zillah assented eagerly. Obed did not care to go, as he was anxious to call on the chief of po-lice. So Zillah and Windham rode out togeth-er into the country, and took the road by the sea coast, where it winds on, commanding magnifi-cent sea views or sublime prospects of distant mountains at almost every turning. Hitherto they had always avoided speaking of England. Each seemed instinctively to shun the mention of that name; nor did either ever seek to draw the other out on that subject. What might be the rank of either at home, or the associations or connections, neither ever ventured to inquire. Each usually spoke on any subject of a general nature which seemed to come nearest. On this occasion, however, Windham made a first at-tempt toward speaking about himself and his past. Something happened to suggest India. It was only with a mighty effort that Zillah kept down an impulse to rhapsodize about that glori-ous land, where all her childhood had been passed, and whose scenes were still impressed so vividly upon her memory. The effort at self-restraint was successful; nor did she by any word show how well known to her were those Indian scenes of which Windham went on to speak. He talked of tiger hunts; of long journeys through the hot plain or over the lofty mountain; of desperate fights with savage tribes. At length he spoke of the Indian mutiny. He had been at Delhi, and had taken part in the conflict and in the tri-umph. What particular part he had taken he did not say, but he seemed to have been in the thick of the fight wherever it raged. Carried away by the glorious recollections that crowded upon his memory, he rose to a higher eloquence than any which he had before attempted. The passion of the fight came back. He mentioned by name glorious companions in arms. He told of heroic exploits—dashing acts of almost superhuman valor, where human nature became ennobled and man learned the possibilities of man. The fer-vid excitement that burned in his soul was com-municated to the fiery nature of Zillah, who was always so quick to catch the contagion of any noble emotion; his admiration for all that was elevated and true and pure found an echo in the heart of her who was the daughter of General Pomeroy and the pupil of Lord Chetwynde. Having herself breathed all her life an atmos-phere of noble sentiments, her nature exulted in the words of this high-souled, this chivalric man, who himself, fresh from a scene which had tried men's souls as they had not been tried

for many an age, had shared the dangers and the triumphs of those who had fought and con-quered there. No, never before had Zillah known such hours as these, where she was brought face to face with a hero whose eye, whose voice, whose manner, made her whole being thrill, and whose sentiments found an echo in her inmost soul.

And did Windham perceive this? Could he help it? Could he avoid seeing the dark olive face which flushed deep at his words—the large, liquid, luminous eyes which, beneath those deep-fringed lids, lighted up with the glorious fires of that fervid soul—the delicate frame that quiv-ered in the strong excitement of impassioned feelings? Could he avoid seeing that this creat-ure of feeling and of passion thrilled or calmed, grew indignant or pitiful, became stern or tear-ful, just as he gave the word? Could he help seeing that it was in his power to strike the key-note to which all her sensitive nature would re-spond?

Yet in all Zillah's excitement of feeling she never asked any questions. No matter what might be the intensity of desire that filled her, she never forgot to restrain her curiosity. Had she not heard before of this regiment and that regiment from the letters of Guy? Windham seemed to have been in many of the places men-tioned in those letters. This was natural, as he belonged to the army which had taken Delhi. But in addition to this there was another won-der—there were those hill stations in which she had lived, of which Windham spoke so familiar-ly. Of course—she thought after due reflection —every British officer in the north of India must be familiar with places which are their common resort; but it affected her strangely at first; for hearing him speak of them was like hearing me speak of home.

Another theme of conversation was found in his eventful voyage from India. He told her about the outbreak of the flames, the alarm of the passengers, the coward mob of panic-strick-en wretches, who had lost all manliness and all human feeling in their abject fear. Then he de-scribed the tall form of Obed Chute as it towered above the crowd. Obed, according to Wind-ham's account, when he first saw him, had two men by their collars in one hand, while in the other he held his revolver. His voice with its shrill accent rang out like a trumpet peal as he threatened to blow out the brains of any man who dared to touch a boat, or to go off the quar-ter-deck. While he threatened he also taunted them. "*You* Britishers!" he cried. "If you are—which I doubt—then I'm ashamed of the mother country."

Now it happened that Obed Chute had al-ready given to Zillah a full description of his first view of Windham, on that same occasion. As he stood with his revolver, he saw Windham, he said—pale, stern, self-possessed, but active, with a line of passengers formed, who were busy passing buckets along, and he was just detail-ing half a dozen to relieve the sailors at the pumps. "That man," concluded Obed Chute, "had already got to work, while I was indulg-ing in a 'spread-eagle.'"

Windham, however, said nothing of himself, so that Zillah might have supposed, for all that he said, that he himself was one of that panic- •

stricken crowd whom Obed Chute had reviled and threatened.

Nor was this all. These rides were repeated every day. Obed Chute declared that this was the best thing for her in the world, and that she must go out as often as was possible. Zillah made no objection. So the pleasure was renewed from day to day. But Windham could speak of other things than battle, and murder, and sudden death. He was deeply read in literature. He loved poetry with passionate ardor. All English poetry was familiar to him. The early English metrical romance, Chaucer, Spenser, the Elizabethan dramatists, Waller, Marvell, and Cowley, Lovelace and Suckling, were all appreciated fully. He had admiration for the poets of the Restoration; he had no words to express the adoration which he felt for Milton; Gray and Collins he knew by heart; Thomson and Cowper he could mention with appreciation; while the great school of the Revolutionary poets rivaled all the rest in the admiration which they extorted from him. Tennyson and the Brownings were, however, most in his thoughts; and as these were equally dear to Zillah, they met on common ground. What struck Zillah most was the fact that occasional stray bits, which she had seen in magazines, and had treasured in her head, were equally known, and equally loved by this man, who would repeat them to her with his full melodious voice, giving thus a new emphasis and a new meaning to words whose meaning she thought she already felt to the full. In these was a deeper meaning, as Windham said them, than she had ever known before. He himself seemed to have felt the meaning of some of these. What else could have caused that tremulous tone which, in its deep musical vibrations, made these words ring deep within her heart? Was there not a profounder meaning in the mind of this man, whose dark eyes rested upon hers with such an unfathomable depth of tenderness and sympathy —those eyes which had in them such a magnetic power that even when her head was turned away she could *feel* them resting upon her, and knew that he was looking at her—with what deep reverence! with what unutterable longing! with what despair! Yes, despair. For on this man's face, with all the reverence and longing which it expressed, there was never any hope, there was never any look of inquiry after sympathy; it was reverence—silent adoration; the look that one may cast upon a divinity, content with the offer of adoration, but never dreaming of a return.

The days flew by like lightning. Zillah passed them in a kind of dream. She only seemed awake when Windham came. When he left, all was barrenness and desolation. Time passed, but she thought nothing of Naples. Obed had explained to her the necessity of waiting at Marseilles till fresh news should come from Hilda, and had been surprised at the ease with which she had been persuaded to stay. In fact, for a time Hilda seemed to have departed out of the sphere of her thoughts, into some distant realm where those thoughts never wandered. She was content to remain here—to postpone her departure, and wait for any thing at all. Sometimes she thought of the end of all this. For Windham must one day depart. This had to end.

It could not last. And what then? Then? Ah then! She would not think of it. Calamities had fallen to her lot before, and it now appeared to her that another calamity was to come —dark, indeed, and dreadful; worse, she feared, than others which she had braved in her young life.

For one thing she felt grateful. Windham never ventured beyond the limits of friendship. To this he had a right. Had he not saved her from death? But he never seemed to think of transgressing the strictest limits of conventional politeness. He never indulged at even the faintest attempt at a compliment. Had he even done this much it would have been a painful embarrassment. She would have been forced to shrink back into herself and her dreary life, and put an end to such interviews forever. But the trial did not come, and she had no cause to shrink back. So it was that the bright golden hours sped onward, bearing on the happy, happy days; and Windham lingered on, letting his English business go.

Another steamer had arrived from Naples, and yet another, but no word came from Hilda. Zillah had written to her address, explaining every thing, but no answer came. The chief of police had received an answer to his original message, stating that the authorities at Naples would do all in their power to fulfill his wishes; but since then nothing further had been communicated. His efforts to search after Gualtier and Mathilde, in France, were quite unsuccessful. He urged Obed Chute and Miss Lorton to wait still longer, until something definite might be found. Windham waited also. Whatever his English business was, he deferred it. He was anxious, he said, to see how these efforts would turn out, and he hoped to be of use himself.

Meanwhile Obed Chute had fitted up the yacht, and had obliterated every mark of the casualty with which she had met. In this the party sometimes sailed. Zillah might perhaps have objected to put her foot on board a vessel which was associated with the greatest calamity of her life; but the presence of Windham seemed to bring a counter-association which dispelled her mournful memories. She might not fear to trust herself in that vessel which had once almost been her grave, with the man who had saved her from that grave. Windham showed himself a first-rate sailor. Zillah wondered greatly how he could have added this to his other accomplishments, but did not venture to ask him. There was a great gulf between them; and to have asked any personal question, however slight, would have been an attempt to leap that gulf. She dared not ask any thing. She herself was in a false position. She was living under an assumed name, and constant watchfulness was necessary. The name "Lorton" had not yet become familiar to her ears. Often when addressed, she caught herself thinking that some one else was spoken to. But after all, as to the question of Windham's seamanship, that was a thing which was not at all wonderful, since every Englishman of any rank is supposed to own a yacht, and to know all about it.

Often Obed and his family went out with them; but often these two went out alone. Perhaps there was a conventional impropriety in this; but neither Obed nor his sister thought of it; Windham certainly was not the one to regard it; and Zillah was willing to shut her eyes to it. And so for many days they were thrown together. Cruising thus over the Mediterranean, that glory of seas—the blue, the dark, the deep—where the transparent water shows the sea depths far down, with all the wonders of the sea; where the bright atmosphere shows sharply defined the outlines of distant objects—cruising here on the Mediterranean, where France stretches out her hand to Italy; where on the horizon the purple hills arise, their tops covered with a diadem of snow; where the air breathes balm, and the tideless sea washes evermore the granite base of long mountain chains, evermore wearing away and scattering the débris along the sounding beach. Cruising over the Mediterranean—oh! what is there on earth equal to this? Here was a place, here was scenery, which might remain forever fixed in the memories of both of these, who now, day after day, under these cloudless skies, drifted along. Drifting? Yes, it was drifting. And where were they drifting to? Where? Neither of them asked. In fact, they were drifting nowhere; or, rather, they were drifting to that point where fate would interpose, and sever them, to send them onward upon their different courses. They might drift for a time; but, at last, they must separate, and then—what? Would they ever again reunite? Would they ever again meet? Who might say?

Drifting!

Well, if one drifts any where, the Mediterranean is surely the best place; or, at least, the most favorable, for there all things combine to favor, in the highest degree, that state of moral "drifting" into which people sometimes fall.

The time passed quickly. Weeks flew by. Nothing new had been discovered. No information had come from Naples. No letter had come from Hilda. While Zillah waited, Windham also waited, and thus passed six or seven weeks in Marseilles, which was rather a long time for one who was hurrying home on important business. But he was anxious, he said, to see the result of the investigations of the police. That result was, at length, made known. It was nothing; and the chief of police advised Obed Chute to go on without delay to Naples, and urge the authorities there to instant action. He seemed to think that they had neglected the business, or else attended to it in such a way that it had failed utterly. He assured Obed Chute that he would still exert all his power to track the villain Gualtier, and, if possible, bring him to justice. This, Obed believed that he would do; for the chief had come now to feel a personal as well as a professional interest in the affair, as though somehow his credit were at stake. Under these circumstances, Obed prepared to take his family and Miss Lorton to Naples, by the next steamer.

Windham said nothing. There was a pallor on the face of each of them as Obed told them his plan—telling it, too, with the air of one who is communicating the most joyful intelligence, and thinking nothing of the way in which such joyous news is received. Zillah made no observation. Involuntarily her eyes sought those of Windham. She read in his face a depth of despair which was without hope—profound—unalterable—unmovable.

That day they took their last ride. But few words passed between them. Windham was gloomy and taciturn. Zillah was silent and sad. At length, as they rode back, they came to a place on the shore a few miles away from the city. Here Windham reined in his horse, and, as Zillah stopped, he pointed out to the sea.

The sun was setting. Its rich red light fell full upon the face of Zillah, lighting it up with radiant glory as it did on that memorable morning when her beautiful face was upturned as her head lay upon his breast, and her gleaming ebon hair floated over his shoulders. He looked at her. Her eyes were not closed now, as they were then, but looked back into his, revealing in their unfathomable depths an abyss of melancholy, of sorrow, of longing, and of tenderness.

"Miss Lorton," said Windham, in a deep voice, which was shaken by an uncontrollable emotion, and whose tremulous tones thrilled through all Zillah's being, and often and often afterward recurred to her memory—"Miss Lorton, this is our last ride—our last interview. Here I will say my last farewell. To-morrow I will see you, but not alone. Oh, my friend, my friend, my sweet friend, whom I held in my arms once, as I saved you from death, we must now part forever! I go—I must go. My God! where? To a life of horror! to a living death! to a future without one ray of hope! Once it was dark enough, God knows; but now—but now it is intolerable; for since I have seen you I tremble at the thought of encountering that which awaits me in England!"

He held out his hand as he concluded. Zillah's eyes fell. His words had been poured forth with passionate fervor. She had nothing to say. Her despair was as deep as his. She held out her hand to meet his. It was as cold as ice. He seized it with a convulsive grasp, and his frame trembled as he held it.

Suddenly, as she looked down, overcome by her own agitation, a sob struck her ears. She looked up. He seemed to be devouring her with his eyes, as they were fixed on her wildly, hungrily, yet despairingly. And from those eyes, which had so often gazed steadily and proudly in the face of death, there now fell, drop by drop, tears which seemed wrung out from his very heart. It was but for a moment. As he caught her eyes he dropped her hand, and hastily brushed his tears away. Zillah's heart throbbed fast and furiously; it seemed ready to burst. Her breath failed; she reeled in her saddle. But the paroxysm passed, and she regained her self-command.

"Let us ride home," said Windham, in a stern voice.

They rode home without speaking another word.

The next day Windham saw them on board the steamer. He stood on the wharf and watched it till it was out of sight. Then he departed in the train for the north, and for England.

CHAPTER XXXIII.

THE AGENT'S REPORT.

On the south coast of Hampshire there is a little village which looks toward the Isle of Wight. It consists of a single street, and in

"THEY SAT DOWN ON SOME ROCKS THAT ROSE ABOVE THE SAND."

front is a spacious beach which extends for miles. It is a charming place for those who love seclusion to pass the summer months in, for the view is unsurpassed, and the chances for boating or yachting excellent. The village inn is comfortable, and has not yet been demoralized by the influx of wealthy strangers, while there are numerous houses where visitors may secure quiet accommodations and a large share of comfort.

It was about six weeks after the disappearance of Hilda, and about a fortnight after Zillah's departure in search of her, that a man drove into this village from Southampton, up to a house which was at the extreme eastern end, and inquired for Miss Davis. He was asked to come in; and after waiting for a few minutes in the snug parlor, a lady entered. The slender and elegant figure, the beautiful features, and well-bred air of this lady, need not be again described to those who have already become acquainted with Miss Krieff. Nor need Gualtier's personal appearance be recounted once more to those who have already a sufficient acquaintance with his physiognomy.

She shook hands with him in silence, and then, taking a chair and motioning him to another, she sat for some time looking at him. At length she uttered one single word:

"Well?"

"It's done," said Gualtier, solemnly. "It's all over."

Hilda caught her breath—giving utterance to what seemed something between a sob and a sigh, but she soon recovered herself.

Gualtier was sitting near to her. He leaned forward as Hilda sat in silence, apparently overcome by his intelligence, and in a low whisper he said:

"Do you not feel inclined to take a walk somewhere?"

Hilda said nothing, but, rising, she went up stairs, and in a few minutes returned dressed for a walk. The two then set out, and Hilda led the way to the beach. Along the beach they walked for a long distance, until at length they came to a place which was remote from any human habitation. Behind was the open country, before them the sea, whose surf came rolling in in long, low swells, and on either side lay the beach. Here they sat down on some rocks that rose above the sand, and for some time said nothing. Hilda was the first to speak. Before saying any thing, however, she looked all around, as though to assure herself that they were out of the reach of all listeners. Then she spoke, in a slow, measured voice:

"Is she gone, then?"

"She is," said Gualtier.

There was another long silence. What Hilda's feelings were could not be told by her face. To outward appearance she was calm and unmoved, and perhaps she felt so in her heart. It was possible that the thought of Zillah's death did not make her heart beat faster by one throb, or give her one single approach to a pang of remorse. Her silence might have been merely the meditation of one who, having completed one part of a plan, was busy thinking about the completion of the remainder. And yet, on the other hand, it may have been something more than this. Zillah in life was hateful, but Zillah dead was another thing; and if she had any softness, or any capacity for remorse, it might well have made itself manifest at such a time. Gualtier sat looking at her in silence, waiting for her to speak again, attending on her wishes as usual; for this man, who could be so merciless to others, in her presence resigned all his will to hers, and seemed to be only anxious to do her pleasure, whatever it might be.

"Tell me about it," said Hilda at length, without moving, and still keeping her eyes fixed abstractedly on the sea.

Gualtier then began with his visit to Zillah at Tenby. He spoke of Zillah's joy at getting the letter, and her eager desire to be once more with her friend, and so went on till the time of their arrival at Marseilles. He told how Zillah all the way could talk of nothing else than Hilda; of her feverish anxiety to travel as fast as possible; of her fearful anticipations that Hilda might have a relapse, and that after all she might be too late; how excited she grew, and how despairing, when she was told that the steamers had stopped running, and how eagerly she accepted his proposal to go on in a yacht. The story of such affectionate devotion might have moved even the hardest heart, but Hilda gave no sign of any feeling whatever. She sat motionless—listening, but saying nothing. Whether Gualtier himself was trying to test her feelings by telling so piteous a story, or whether some remorse of his own, and some compassion for so loving a heart, still lingering within him, forced him to tell his story in this way, can not be known. Whatever his motives were, no effect was produced on the listener, as far as outward signs were concerned.

"With Mathilde," said he, "I had some difficulty. She was very unwilling to leave her mistress at such a time to make a voyage alone, but she was a timid creature, and I was able to work upon her fears. I told her that her mistress had committed a crime against the English laws in running away and living under an assumed name; that her husband was now in England, and would certainly pursue his wife, have her arrested, and punish severely all who had aided or abetted her. This terrified the silly creature greatly; and then, by the offer of a handsome sum and the promise of getting her a good situation, I soothed her fears and gained her consent to desert her mistress. She is now in London, and has already gained a new situation."

"Where?" said Hilda, abruptly.

"In Highgate Seminary, the place that I was connected with formerly. She is teacher of French, on a good salary."

"Is that safe?" said Hilda, after some thought.

"Why not?"

"She might give trouble."

"Oh no. Her situation is a good one, and she need never leave it."

"I can scarcely see how she can retain it long; she may be turned out, and then—we may see something of her."

"You forget that I am aware of her movements, and can easily put a stop to any efforts of that kind."

"Still I should be better satisfied if she were in France—or somewhere."

"Should you? Then I can get her a place in France, where you will never hear of her again."

Hilda was silent.

"My plan about the yacht," said Gualtier, "was made before I left London. I said nothing to you about it, for I thought it might not succeed. The chief difficulty was to obtain men devoted to my interests. I made a journey to Marseilles first, and found out that there were several vessels of different sizes for sale. The yacht was the best and most suitable for our purposes, and, fortunately, it remained unsold till I had reached Marseilles again with her. I obtained the men in London. It was with some difficulty, for it was not merely common ruffians that I wanted, but seamen who could sail a vessel, and at the same time be willing to take part in the act which I contemplated. I told them that all which was required of them was to sail for two days or so, and then leave the vessel. I think they imagined it was a plan to make money by insuring the vessel and then deserting her. Such things are often done. I had to pay the rascals heavily; but I was not particular, and, fortunately, they all turned out to be of the right sort, except one—but no matter about him."

"Except one!" said Hilda. "What do you mean by that?"

"I will explain after a while," said Gualtier.

"If she had not been so innocent," said Gualtier, "I do not see how my plan could have succeeded. But she knew nothing. She didn't even know enough to make inquiries herself. She accepted all that I said with the most implicit trust, and believed it all as though it were Gospel. It was, therefore, the easiest thing in the world to manage her. Her only idea was to get to you."

Gualtier paused for a moment.

"Go on," said Hilda, coldly.

"Well, all the preparations were made, and the day came. Mathilde had left. She did not seem to feel the desertion much. She said nothing at all to me about the loss of her maid, although after three or four years of service it must have been galling to her to lose her maid so abruptly, and to get such a letter as that silly thing wrote at my dictation. She came on board, and seemed very much satisfied with all the arrangements. I had done every thing that I could think of to make it pleasant for her—on the same principle, I suppose," he added, dryly, "that they have in jails—where they are sure to give a good breakfast to a poor devil on the morning of his execution."

"You may as well omit allusions of that sort," said Hilda, sternly.

Gualtier made no observation, but proceeded with his narrative.

"We sailed for two days, and, at length, came to within about fifty miles of Leghorn. During all that time she had been cheerful, and was much on deck. She tried to read, but did not seem able to do so. She seemed to be involved in thought, as a general thing; and, by the occasional questions which she asked, I saw that all her thoughts were about you and Naples. So passed the two days, and the second night came."

Gualtier paused.

Hilda sat motionless, without saying a word. Gualtier himself seemed reluctant to go on; but he had to conclude his narrative, and so he forced himself to proceed.

"It was midnight"—he went on, in a very low voice—"it was exceedingly dark. The day had been fine, but the sky was now all overclouded. The sea, however, was comparatively smooth, and every thing was favorable to the undertaking. The boat was all ready. It was a good-sized boat, which we had towed behind us. I had prepared a mast and a sail, and had put some provisions in the locker. The men were all expecting—"

"Never mind your preparations," exclaimed Hilda, fiercely. "Omit all that—go on, and don't kill me with your long preliminaries."

"If you had such a story to tell," said Gualtier, humbly, "you would be glad to take refuge for a little while in preliminaries."

Hilda said nothing.

"It was midnight," said Gualtier, resuming his story once more, and speaking with perceptible agitation in the tones of his voice—"it was midnight, and intensely dark. The men were at the bow, waiting. All was ready. In the cabin all had been still for some time. Her lights had been put out an hour previously."

"Well?" said Hilda, with feverish impatience, as he again hesitated.

"Well," said Gualtier, rousing himself with a start from a momentary abstraction into which he had fallen—"the first thing I did was to go down into the hold with some augers, and bore holes through the vessel's bottom."

Another silence followed.

"Some augers," said Hilda, after a time. "Did you need more than one?"

"One might break."

"Did any one go with you?" she persisted.

"Yes—one of the men—the greatest ruffian of the lot. 'Black Bill,' he was called. I've got something to tell you about him. I took him down to help me, for I was afraid that I might not make a sure thing of it. Between us we did the job. The water began to rush in through half a dozen holes, which we succeeded in making, and we got out on deck as the yacht was rapidly filling."

Again Gualtier paused for some time.

"Why do you hesitate so?" asked Hilda, quite calmly.

Gualtier looked at her for a moment, with something like surprise in his face; but without making any reply, he went on:

"I hurried into the cabin and listened. There was no sound. I put my ear close to the inner door. All was utterly and perfectly still. She was evidently sleeping. I then hurried out and ordered the men into the boat. Before embarking myself I went back to the hold, and reached my hands down. I felt the water. It was within less than three feet of the deck. It had filled very rapidly. I then went on board the boat, unfastened the line, and we pulled away, steering east, as nearly as possible toward Leghorn. We had rowed for about half an hour, when I recollected that I ought to have locked the cabin door. But it was too late to return. We could never have found the schooner if we had tried. The night was intensely dark. Besides, by that time the schooner—was at the bottom of the sea!"

A long silence followed. Hilda looked steadily out on the water, and Gualtier watched her with hungry eyes. At last, as though she felt his eyes upon her, she turned and looked at him. A great change had come over her face. It was fixed and rigid and haggard—her eyes had something in them that was awful. Her lips were white—her face was ashen. She tried to speak, but at first no sound escaped. At last she spoke in a hoarse voice utterly unlike her own.

"She is gone, then."

"For evermore!" said Gualtier.

Hilda turned her stony face once more toward the sea, while Gualtier looked all around, and then turned his gaze back to this woman for whom he had done so much.

"After a while"—he began once more, in a slow, dull voice—"the wind came up, and we

II

"BLACK BILL HAS KEPT ON MY TRACK."

hoisted sail. We went on our way rapidly, and by the middle of the following day we arrived at Leghorn. I paid the men off and dismissed them. I myself came back to London immediately, over the Alps, through Germany. I thought it best to avoid Marseilles. I do not know what the men did with themselves; but I think that they would have made some trouble for me if I had not hurried away. Black Bill said as much when I was paying them. He said that when he made the bargain he thought it was only some 'bloody insurance business,' and, if he had known what it was to have been, he would have made a different bargain. As it was, he swore I ought to double the amount I had promised. I refused, and we parted with some high words—he vowing vengeance, and I saying nothing."

"Ah!" said Hilda, who had succeeded in recovering something of her ordinary calm, "that was foolish in you—you ought to have satisfied their demands."

"I have thought so since."

"They may create trouble. You should have stopped their mouths."

"That is the very thing I wished to do; but I was afraid of being too lavish, for fear that they would suspect the importance of the thing.

I thought if I appeared mean and stingy and poor they might conclude that I was some very ordinary person, and that the affair was of a very ordinary kind—concerning very common people. If they suspected the true nature of the case they would be sure to inform the police. As it is, they will hold their tongues; or, at the worst, they will try and track me."

"Track you?" said Hilda, who was struck by something in Gualtier's tone.

"Yes; the fact is—I suppose I ought to tell you—I have been tracked all the way from Leghorn."

"By whom?"

"Black Bill—I don't know how he managed it, but he has certainly kept on my track. I saw him at Brieg, in Switzerland, first; next I saw him in the railway station at Strasbourg; and yesterday I saw him in London, standing opposite the door of my lodgings, as I was leaving for this place."

"That looks bad," said Hilda, seriously.

"He is determined to find out what this business is, and so he watches me. He doesn't threaten, he doesn't demand money—he is simply watching. His game is a deep one."

"Do you suppose that the others are with him?"

"Not at all. I think he is trying to work this up for himself."

"It is bad," said Hilda. "How do you know that he is not in this village?"

"As to that, it is quite impossible—and I never expect to see him again, in fact."

"Why not?"

"Because I have thrown him off the track completely. While I was going straight to London it was easy for him to follow—especially as I did not care to dodge him on the continent; but now, if he ever catches sight of me again he is much deeper than I take him to be."

"But perhaps he has followed you here."

"That is impossible," said Gualtier, confidently. "My mode of getting away from London was peculiar. As soon as I saw him opposite my lodgings my mind was made up; so I took the train for Bristol, and went about forty miles, when I got out and came back; then I drove to the Great Northern Station immediately, went north about twenty miles, and came back; after this I took the Southampton train, and came down last night. It would be rather difficult for one man to follow another on such a journey. As to my lodgings, I do not intend to go back. He will probably inquire, and find that I have left all my things there, and I dare say he will watch that place for the next six months at least, waiting for my return. And so I think he may be considered as finally disposed of."

"You do not intend to send for your things, then?"

"No. There are articles there of considerable value; but I will let them all go—it will be taken as a proof that I am dead. My friend Black Bill will hear of this, and fall in with that opinion. I may also arrange a 'distressing casualty' paragraph to insert in the papers for his benefit."

Hilda now relapsed into silence once more, and seemed to lose herself in a fit of abstraction so profound that she was conscious of nothing around her. Gualtier sat regarding her silently, and wondering whither her thoughts were tending. A long time passed. The surf was rolling on the shore, the wind was blowing lightly and gently over the sea; afar the blue water was dotted with innumerable sails; there were ships passing in all directions, and steamers of all sizes leaving behind them great trails of smoke. Over two hours had passed since they first sat down here, and now, at length, the tide, which had all the while been rising, began to approach them, until at last the first advance waves came within a few inches of Hilda's feet. She did not notice it; but this occurrence gave Gualtier a chance to interrupt her meditations.

"The tide is rising," said he, abruptly; "the next wave will be up to us. We had better move."

It was with a start that Hilda roused herself. Then she rose slowly, and walked up the beach with Gualtier.

"I should like very much to know," said he, at length, in an insinuating voice, "if there is any thing more that I can do just now."

"I have been thinking," said Hilda, without hesitation, "of my next course of action, and I have decided to go back to Chetwynde at once."

"To Chetwynde!"

"Yes, and to-morrow morning."

"To-morrow!"

"There is no cause for delay," said Hilda. "The time has at last come when I can act."

"To Chetwynde!" repeated Gualtier. "I can scarcely understand your purpose."

"Perhaps not," said Hilda, dryly; "it is one that need not be explained, for it will not fail to reveal itself in the course of time under any circumstances."

"But you have some ostensible purpose for going there. You can not go there merely to take up your abode on the old footing."

"I do not intend to do that," was the cool response. "You may be sure that I have a purpose. I am going to make certain very necessary arrangements for the advent of Lady Chetwynde."

"Lady Chetwynde!" repeated Gualtier, with a kind of gasp.

"Yes," said Hilda, who by this time had recovered all her usual self-control, and exhibited all her old force of character, her daring, and her coolness, which had long ago given her such an ascendency over Gualtier. "Yes," she repeated, quietly returning the other's look of amazement, "and why should I not? Lady Chetwynde has been absent for her health. Is it not natural that she should send me to make preparations for her return to her own home? She prefers it to Pomeroy."

"Good God!" said Gualtier, quite forgetting himself, as a thought struck him which filled him with bewilderment. Could he fathom her purpose? Was the idea that occurred to him in very deed the one which was in her mind? Could it be? And was it for this that he had labored?

"Is Lord Chetwynde coming home?" he asked at length, as Hilda looked at him with a strange expression.

"Lord Chetwynde?" I should say, most certainly not."

"Do you know for certain?"

"No. I have narrowly watched the papers, but have found out nothing, nor have any letters come which could tell me; but I have reasons for supposing that the very last thing that Lord Chetwynde would think of doing would be to come home."

"Why do you suppose that? Is there not his rank, his position, and his wealth?"

"Yes; but the correspondence between him and Lady Chetwynde has for years been of so very peculiar a character—that is, at least, on Lady Chetwynde's part—that the very fact of her being in England would; to a man of his character, be sufficient, I should think, to keep him away forever. And therefore I think that Lord Chetwynde will endure his grief about his father, and perhaps overcome it, in the Indian residency. to which he was lately appointed. Perhaps he may end his days there—who can tell? If he should, it would be too much to expect that Lady Chetwynde would take it very much to heart."

"But it seems to me, in spite of all that you have said, that nine men out of ten would come home. They could be much happier in England, and the things of which you have spoken would not necessarily give trouble."

"That is very true; but, at the same time, Lord Chetwynde, in my opinion, happens to be that tenth man who would not come home; for, if he did, it would be Lady Chetwynde's money that he would enjoy, and to a man of his nature this would be intolerable—especially as she has been diligently taunting him with the fact that he has cheated her for the last five years."

Gualtier heard this with fresh surprise.

"I did not know before that there had been so very peculiar a correspondence," said he.

"I think that it will decide him to stay in India."

"But suppose, in spite of all this, that he should come home."

"That is a fact which should never be lost sight of," said Hilda, very gravely—"nor is it ever lost sight of; one must be prepared to encounter such a thing as that."

"But how?"

"Oh, there are various ways," said Hilda. "He can be avoided, shunned, fled from," said Gualtier, "but how can he be encountered?"

"If he does come," said Hilda, "he will be neither avoided nor shunned. He will be most assuredly encountered—and that, too, *face to face!*"

Gualtier looked at her in fresh perplexity. Not yet had he fathomed the full depth of Hilda's deep design.

CHAPTER XXXIV.

REMODELING THE HOUSEHOLD.

Two or three days afterward, Hilda, attended by Gualtier, drove up to the inn of the little village near Chetwynde Castle. Gualtier stopped here, and Hilda drove on to the Castle itself. Her luggage was with her, but it was small, consisting of only a small trunk, which looked as though it were her intention to make but a short stay. On her arrival the servants all greeted her respectfully, and asked eagerly after Lady Chetwynde. Her ladyship, Hilda informed them, was still too unwell to travel, but was much better than when she left. She had sent her to make certain arrangements for the reception of Lord Chetwynde, who was expected from India at no very distant date. She did not as yet know the time of his probable arrival; but when she had learned it she herself would come to Chetwynde Castle to receive him; but until that time she would stay away. The place where she was staying just at present was particularly healthy. It was a small village on the coast of Brittany, and Lady Chetwynde was anxious to defer her return to the latest possible moment. Such was the information which Hilda condescended to give to the servants, who received the news with unfeigned delight, for they all dearly loved that gentle girl, whose presence at Chetwynde had formerly brightened the whole house, and with whose deep grief over her last bereavement they had all most sincerely sympathized.

Hilda had many things to do. Her first duty was to call on Mrs. Hart. The poor old housekeeper still continued in a miserable condition, hovering, apparently, between life and death, and only conscious at intervals of what was going on around her. That consciousness was not strong enough to make her miss the presence of Zillah, nor did her faculties, even in her most lucid intervals, seem to be fully at work. Her memory did not appear to suggest at any time those sad events which had brought her down to this. It was only at times that she exhibited any recollection of the past, and that was confined altogether to "Guy;" to him whom in whispered words she called "her boy.". Mrs. Hart was not at all neglected. Susan, who had once been the upper house-maid, had of late filled the place of housekeeper, which she could easily do, as the family was away, and the duties were light. She also, with her sister Mary, who was the under house-maid, was assiduous in watching at the bedside of the poor old creature, who lay there hovering between life and death. Nothing, indeed, could exceed the kindness and tenderness of these two humble but noble-hearted girls; and even if Zillah herself could have been brought to that bedside the poor sufferer could not have met with more compassionate affection, and certainly could not have found such careful nursing.

Hilda visited Mrs. Hart, and exhibited such tenderness of feeling that both Susan and Mary were touched by it. They knew that Mrs. Hart had never loved her, but it seemed now as if Hilda had forgotten all that former coldness, and was herself inspired by nothing but the tenderest concern. But Hilda had much to attend to, and after about half an hour she left the room to look after those more important matters for which she had come.

What her errand was the servants soon found out. It was nothing less than a complete change in the household. That household had never been large, for the late Earl had been forced by his circumstances to be economical. He never entertained company, and was satisfied with keeping the place, inside and outside, in an ordinary state of neatness.

The servants who now remained may easily be mentioned. Mathilde had gone away. Mrs. Hart lay on a sick-bed. There was Susan, the upper house-maid, and Mary, her sister, the under house-maid. There was Roberts, who had been the late Earl's valet, a smart, active young man, who was well known to have a weakness for Susan; there was the cook, Martha, a formidable personage, who considered herself the most

important member of that household; and besides these there were the coachman and the groom. These composed the entire establishment. It was for the sake of getting rid of these, in as quiet and inoffensive a way as possible, that Hilda had now come; and toward evening she began her work by sending for Roberts.

"Roberts," said she, with dignity, as that very respectable person made his appearance, carrying in his face the consciousness of one who had possessed the late Earl's confidence, "I am intrusted with a commission from her ladyship to you. Lord Chetwynde is coming home, and great changes are going to be made here. But her ladyship can not forget the old household; and she told me to mention to you how grateful she felt to you for all your unwearied care and assiduity in your attendance upon your late master, especially through his long and painful illness; and she is most anxious to know in what way she can be of service to you. Her ladyship has heard Mathilde speak of an understanding which exists between you and Susan, the upper house-maid; and she is in hopes that she may be able to further your views in the way of settling yourself; and so she wished me to find out whether you had formed any plans, and what they were."

"It's like her ladyship's thoughtfulness and consideration," said Roberts, gratefully, "to think of the likes of me. I'm sure I did nothing for my lord beyond what it were my bounden dooty to do; and a pleasanter and affabler spoken gentleman than his lordship were nobody need ever want to see. I never expect to meet with such another. As to Susan and me," continued Roberts, looking sheepish, "we was a-thinkin' of a public, when so be as we could see our way to it."

"Where were you thinking of taking one?"

"Well, miss, you see I'm a Westmorelandshire man; and somehow I've a hankerin' after the old place."

"And you're quite right, Roberts," said Hilda, in an encouraging tone. "A man is always happier in his native place among his own people. Have you heard of an opening there?"

Roberts, at this, looked more sheepish still, and did not answer until Hilda had repeated her question.

"Well, to be plain with you, miss," said he, "I had a letter this very week from my brother, telling me of a public in Keswick as was for sale —good-will, stock, and all, and a capital situation for business—towerists the whole summer through, and a little somethin' a-doin' in winter. Susan and me was a-regrettin' the limitation of our means, miss."

"That seems a capital opening, Roberts," said Hilda, very graciously. "It would be a pity to lose it. What is the price?"

"Well, miss, it's a pretty penny, but it's the stand makes it, miss—right on the shores of the lake—boats to let at all hours, inquire within. They are a-askin' five hundred pound, miss."

"Is that unreasonable?"

"Situation considered, on the contrary, miss; and Susan and me has two hundred pound between us in the savings-bank. My lord was a generous master. Now if her ladyship would lend me the extry money I'd pay her back as fast as I made it."

"There is no necessity for that," said Hilda.

"Three hundred pounds happens to be the very sum which her ladyship mentioned to me. So now I commission you in her name to make all the necessary arrangements with your brother; or, better still, go at once yourself—a man can always arrange these matters more satisfactorily himself—and I will let you have the money in three days, with Lady Chetwynde's best wishes for the success of your undertaking; and we will see," she added, with a smile, "if we can not get pretty Susan a wedding-dress, and any thing else she may need. Before a week is over you shall be mine host of the Keswick Inn. And now," she concluded, gayly, "go and make your arrangements with Susan, and don't let any foolish bashfulness on her part prevent you from hastening matters. It would not do for you to let this chance slip through your fingers. I will see that she is ready. Her ladyship has something for her too, and will not let her go to you empty-handed."

"I never, never can thank her ladyship nor you enough," said Roberts, "for what you have done for me this day. Might I make so bold as to write a letter to her ladyship, to offer her my respectful dooty?"

"Yes, Roberts—do so, and give me the letter. I shall be writing to-night, and will inclose it. By-the-by, are not Mary and Susan sisters?"

"They be, miss—sisters and orphelins."

"Well, then," said she, "see that you do not take more than you are entitled to; for though her ladyship lets you carry Susan off, you must not cast covetous eyes on Mary too; for though I allow she would make a very pretty little bar-maid, she is a particularly good house-maid, and we can't spare her."

Roberts grinned from ear to ear.

"I can't pretend to manage the women, miss," said he; "you must speak to Mary;" and then, with a low bow, Roberts withdrew.

Hilda gave a sigh of relief. "There are three disposed of," she murmured. "This is a fair beginning."

On the following day she gave Roberts a check for the money, drawn by *Zillah Chetwynde*. Waving off his thanks, she dismissed him, and sent for the cook. That functionary quickly appeared. She was short of stature, large of bulk, red of face, fluent of speech, hasty of temper—*au reste*, she was a good cook and faithful servant. She bobbed to Hilda on entering, and, closing the door, stood with folded arms and belligerent aspect, like a porcupine armed for defense on the slightest appearance of hostilities.

"Good-morning, Martha," said Hilda, with great suavity. "I hope your rheumatism has not been troubling you since the warm weather set in?"

Martha bobbed with a more mollified air.

"Which, exceptin' the elber jints, where it's settled, likewise the knee jints—savin' of your presence, miss—it's the same; for to go down on my bended knees, miss, it's what I couldn't do, not if you was to give me a thousand-pun note in my blessed hand, and my Easter dooty not bein' able to perform, miss, which it be the first time it ever wor the case; an' it owing to the rheumatiz; otherwise I am better, miss, and thank you kindly."

"Her ladyship is very sorry," continued Hilda. "She is unable to return herself just yet, but she has asked me to attend to several mat-

ters for her, and one of them is connected with you, Martha. She has received a letter from his lordship stating that he was bringing with him a staff of servants, and among them a French cook."

Here Martha assumed the porcupine again, with every quill on end; but she said nothing, though Hilda paused for an instant. Martha wished to commit Miss Krieff to a proposition, that she might have the glory of rejecting it with scorn. So Hilda went on:

"Your mistress was afraid that you might not care about taking the place of under-cook where you have been head, and as she was anxious to avoid hurting your feelings in any way, she wished me to tell you of this beforehand."

Another moment and the apoplexy which had been threatening since the moment when "under-cook" had been mentioned would have been a fact, but luckily for Martha her overcharged feelings here broke forth with accents of bitterest scorn:

"Which she's *very* kind. Hunder-cook, indeed! which it's what I never abore yet, and never will abear. I've lived at Chetwyn this twenty year, gurl and woman, and hopes as I 'ave done my dooty, and giv satisfaction, which my lord were a gentleman, an' found no fault with his wittles, but ate them like a Christian and a nobleman, a-thankin' the Lord, and a-sayin', 'I never asks to see a tidier or a 'olesomer dinner than Martha sends, which she's to be depended on as never bein' raw nor yet done to rags;' an' now when, as you may say, gettin' on in years, though not that old neither as to be de-. pendent or wantin' in sperrit, to have a French cook set over me a talkin' furrin languidgis and a cookin' up goodness ony knows what messes as 'ud pison a Christian stomach to as much as look at, and a horderin' about Marthar here and Marthar there, it's what I can't consent to put up with, and nobody as wasn't a mean spereted creetur could expect it of me, which it's not as I wish to speak disrespectful of her ladyship, which I considers a lady and as allers treated me as sich, only expectin' to hend my days in Chetwyn it's come sudden like; but thanks to the blessed saints, which I 'ave put by as will keep me from the wukkus and a charge on nobody; and I'd like to give warnin', if you please, miss, and if so be as I could leave before monseer arrive."

Here Martha paused, not from lack of material, but from sheer want of breath. She would have been invincible in conversation but for that fatal constitutional infirmity—shortness of breath. This brought her to a pause in the full flow of her eloquence.

Hilda took advantage of the lull.

"Your mistress," said she, "feared that you would feel as you do on the subject, and her instructions to me were these: 'Try and keep Martha if you possibly can—we shall not easily replace her; but if she seems to fear that this new French cook may be domineering'" (fresh and alarming symptoms of apoplexy), "' and may make it uncomfortable for her, we must think of her instead of ourselves. She has been too faithful a servant to allow her to be trampled upon now; and if you find that she will not really consent to stop, you must get her a good place—'"

"Which, if you please, mum," said Martha, interrupting her excitedly, "we won't talk about a place—it is utter-ly useless, and I might be for-gettin' myself; but I never thought," she continued, brushing away a hasty tear, "as it was Master Guy, meaning my lord, as would send old Martha away."

"Oh, I am sure he did not mean to do that," said Hilda, kindly; "but gentlemen have not much consideration, you know, and he is accustomed to French cookery." The softer mood vanished at the hated name.

"And he'll never grow to be the man his father were," said she, excitedly, "on them furrin gimcracks and kickshaws as wouldn't nourish a babby, let alone a full-growed man, and 'e a Henglishman. But it's furrin parts as does it. I never approved of the harmy."

"Her ladyship told me," said Hilda, with her usual placidity, and without taking any notice of the excited feeling of the other, "that if you insisted on going I was to give you twenty pounds, with her kind regards, to buy some remembrance."

"Which she's very kind," rejoined Martha, rather quickly, and with some degree of asperity; "and if you'll give her my grateful dooty, I'd like to leave as soon as may be."

"Well, if you are anxious to do so, I suppose you can. What kitchen-maids are there?"

"Well, miss," said Martha, with dignity, yet severity, "sich drabs of girls as I 'ave 'nd would 'ave prevoked a saint, and mayhap I was a little hasty; but takin' up a sauce-pan, and findin' it that dirty as were scandlus to be'old, I throwed the water as were bin it over 'er, and the sauce-pan with it, an' she declared she'd go, which as the 'ousekeeper bein' in bed, as you know, miss, an' there likely to remain for hevermore, she did, an' good riddance to her, say I—ungrateful hussy as had jist got her wages the day before, and 'ad a comfortable 'ome."

"It does not matter. I suppose the French cook will bring his own subordinates."

"Wery like, miss," said Martha, sharply. "I leave this very day. Good-mornin', miss."

"Oh no; don't be in such a hurry," said Hilda. "You have a week before you. Let me see you before evening, so that I may give you what your mistress has sent."

Martha sullenly assented, and withdrew.

The most difficult part of Hilda's business had thus been quietly accomplished. Nothing now remained but to see the coachman and groom, each of whom she graciously dismissed with a handsome present. She told them, however, to remain for about a week, until their successors might arrive. The large present which the liberality of Lady Chetwynde had given them enabled them to bear their lot with patience, and even pleasure.

After about a week Gualtier came up to Chetwynde Castle. He had been away to London, and brought word to Hilda that some of the new servants were expected in a few days. It was soon known to Roberts, Susan, and Mary that Gualtier had been made steward by Lady Chetwynde. He took possession of one of the rooms, and at once entered upon the duties of this office. On the day of his arrival Hilda left, saying to the remaining servants that she would never come back again, as she intended to live in the south of France. She shook hands with each of them very graciously, making each one a present in her own name, and accompanying it with

a neat little speech. She had never been popular among them; but now the thought that they would never see her again, together, perhaps, with the very handsome presents which she had made, and her very kind words, affected them deeply, and they showed some considerable feeling.

Under such circumstances Hilda took her departure from Chetwynde Castle, leaving Gualtier in charge. In a few days the new servants arrived, and those of the old ones who had thus far remained now took their departure. The household was entirely remodeled. The new ones took up their places; and there was not one single person there who knew any thing whatever about the late Earl, or Hilda, or Gualtier. The old ones were scattered abroad, and it was not within the bounds of ordinary possibility that any of them would ever come near the place.

In thus remodeling the household it was somewhat enlarged. There was the new housekeeper, a staid, matronly, respectable-looking woman; three house-maids, who had formerly lived in the north of England; a coachman, who had never before been out of Kent; a butler, who had formerly served in a Scotch family; two footmen, one of whom had served in Yorkshire, and the other in Cornwall; two grooms, who had been bred in Yorkshire; a cook, who had hitherto passed all her life in London; and three kitchen-maids, who also had served in that city. Thus the household was altogether new, and had been carefully collected by Gualtier with a view rather to the place from which they had come than to any great excellence on the part of any of them. For so large a place it was but a small number, but it was larger than the household which had been dismissed, and they soon settled down into their places.

One only was left of the old number. This was Mrs. Hart. But she lay on her sick-bed, and Hilda looked upon her as one whose life was doomed. Had any thought of her possible recovery entered her mind, she would have contrived in some way to get rid of her. In spite of her illness, she did not lack attention; for the new housekeeper attached herself to her, and gave her the kindliest care and warmest sympathy.

Last of all, so complete had been Hilda's precautions in view of possible future difficulties, that when Gualtier came as the new steward, he came under a new name, and was known to the household as Mr. M'Kenzie.

CHAPTER XXXV.

THE LADY OF THE CASTLE.

THE new household had been led to expect the arrival of Lady Chetwynde at any moment. They understood that the old household had not given satisfaction, that after the death of the late Earl Lady Chetwynde had gone away to recruit her health, and, now that she was better, she had determined to make a complete change. When she herself arrived other changes would be made. This much Gualtier managed to communicate to them, so as to give them some tangible idea of the affairs of the family and prevent idle conjecture. He let them know, also, that Lord Chetwynde was in India, and might come home at any moment, though his engagements there were so important that it might be impossible for him to leave.

After a few days Lady Chetwynde arrived at the Castle, and was greeted with respectful curiosity by all within the house. Her cold and aristocratic bearing half repelled them, half excited their admiration. She was very beautiful, and her high breeding was evident in her manner; but there was about her such frigidity and such loftiness of demeanor that it repelled those who would have been willing to give her their love. She brought a maid with her who had only been engaged a short time previously; and it was soon known that the maid stood in great awe of her mistress, who was haughty and exacting, and who shut herself off altogether from any of those attempts at respectful sympathy which some kind-hearted lady's-maids might be inclined to show. 'The whole household soon shared in this feeling; for the lady of the Castle showed herself rigid in her requirements of duty and strict in her rule, while, at the same time, she made her appearance but seldom. She never visited Mrs. Hart, but once or twice made some cold inquiries about her of the housekeeper. She also gave out that she would not receive any visitors—a precautionary measure that was not greatly needed; for Chetwynde Castle was remote from the seats of the county families, and any changes there would not be known among them for some time.

The lady of the Castle spent the greater part of her time in her boudoir, alone, never tolerating the presence of even her maid except when it was absolutely necessary, but requiring her to be always near in case of any need for her presence arising. The maid attributed this strange seclusion to the effects of grief over her recent bereavement, or perhaps anxiety about her husband; while the other servants soon began to conjecture that her husband's absence arose from some quarrel with a wife whose haughty and imperious demeanor they all had occasion to feel.

It was thus, then, that Hilda had entered upon her new and perilous position, to attain to which she had plotted so deeply and dared so much. Now that she had attained it, there was not an hour, not a moment of the day, in which she did not pay some penalty for the past by a thousand anxieties. To look forward to such a thing as this was one thing; but to be here, where she had so often longed to be, was quite another thing. It was the hackneyed fable of Damocles with the sword over his head over again. She was standing on treacherous ground, which at any moment might give way beneath her feet and plunge her in an abyss of ruin. To live .thus face to face with possible destruction, to stare death in the face every day, was not a thing conducive either to mildness or to tenderness in any nature, much less in one like hers.

In that boudoir where she spent so much of her time, while her maid wondered how she employed herself, her occupation consisted of but one thing. It was the examination of papers, followed by deep thought over the result of that examination. Every mail brought to her address newspapers both from home and abroad. Among the latter were a number of Indian papers, published in various places, including some that were printed in remote towns in the north.

There were the Delhi *Gazette*, the Allahabad *News*, and the Lahore *Journal*, all of which were most diligently scanned by her. Next to these were the *Times* and the *Army and Navy Gazette*. No other papers or books, or prints of any kind, had any interest in her eyes.

It was natural that her thoughts should thus refer to India. All her plans had succeeded, as far as she could know, and. finally, she had remodeled the household at Chetwynde in such a way that not one remained who could by any possibility know about the previous inmates. She was here as Lady Chetwynde, the lady of Chetwynde Castle, ruler over a great estate, mistress of a place that might have excited the envy of any one in England, looked up to with awful reverence by her dependents, and in the possession of every luxury that wealth could supply. But still the sword was suspended over her head, and by a single hair—a sword that at any moment might fall. What could she know about the intentions of Lord Chetwynde all this time? What were his plans or purposes? Was it not possible, in spite of her firmly expressed convictions to the contrary, that he might come back again to England? And then what? Then—ah! that was the thing beyond which it was difficult for her imagination to go—the crisis beyond which it was impossible to tell what the future might unfold. It was a moment which she was ever forced to anticipate in her thoughts, against which she had always to arm herself, so as to be not taken at unawares.

She had thrown herself thus boldly into Chetwynde Castle, into the very centre of that possible danger which lay before her. But was it necessary to run so great a risk? Could she not at least have gone to Pomeroy Court, and taken up her abode there? Would not this also have been a very natural thing for the daughter of General Pomeroy? It would, indeed, be natural, and it might give many advantages. In the first place, there would be no possibility that Lord Chetwynde, even if he did return from India, would ever seek her out there. She might communicate with him by means of those letters which for years he had received. She might receive his answers, and make known to him whatever she chose, without being compelled to see him face to face. By such a course she might gain what she wished without endangering her safety.

All this had occurred to her long before, and she had regarded it in all its bearings. Nevertheless, she had decided against it, and had chosen rather to encounter the risk of her present action. It was from a certain profound insight into the future. She thought that it was best for Lady Chetwynde to go to Chetwynde Castle, not to Pomeroy Court. By such an act scandal would be avoided. If Lord Chetwynde did not come, well and good; if he did, why then he must be met face to face; and in such an event she trusted to her own genius to bring her out of so frightful a crisis. That meeting would bring with it much risk and many dangers; but it would also bring its own peculiar benefits. If it were once successfully encountered her position would be insured, and the fear of future danger would vanish. For that reason, if for no other, she determined to go to Chetwynde Castle, run every risk, and meet her fate.

While Hilda was thus haughty and repellent to her servants, there was one to whom she was accessible; and this was the new steward, Gualtier, with whom she had frequent communications about the business of the estate. Their interviews generally took place in that morning-room which has already been described, and which was so peculiarly situated that no prying servants could easily watch them or overhear their conversation, if they were careful.

One day, after she had dined, she went to this room, and ordered her maid to tell the steward that she would like to see him. She had that day received a number of Indian papers, over which she had passed many hours; for there was something in one of them which seemed to excite her interest, and certainly gave occupation to all her mind.

Gualtier was prompt to obey the mandate. In a few minutes after Hilda had entered the room he made his appearance, and bowed in silence. Hilda motioned him to a chair, in which he seated himself. The intercourse of these two had now become remarkable for this, that their attitude toward one another had undergone a change corresponding to their apparent positions. Hilda was Lady Chetwynde, and seemed in reality, even in her inmost soul, to feel herself to be so. She had insensibly caught that grand air which so lofty a position might be supposed to give; and it was quite as much her own feeling as any power of consummate acting which made her carry out her part so well. A lofty and dignified demeanor toward the rest of the household might have been but the ordinary act of one who was playing a part; but in Hilda this demeanor extended itself even to Gualtier, toward whom she exhibited the same air of conscious social superiority which she might have shown had she been in reality all that she pretended to be. Gualtier, on his part, was equally singular. He seemed quietly to accept her position as a true and valid one, and that, too, not only before the servants, when it would have been very natural for him to do so, but even when they were alone. This, however, was not so difficult for him, as he had always been in the habit of regarding her as his social superior; yet still, considering the confidences which existed between this extraordinary pair, it was certainly strange that he should have preserved with such constancy his attitude of meek subservience. Here, at Chetwynde, he addressed her as the steward of the estates should have done; and even when discussing the most delicate matters his tone and demeanor corresponded with his office.

On this occasion he began with some intelligence about the state of the north wall, which bounded the park. Hilda listened wearily till he had finished. Then she abruptly brought forward all that was in her thoughts. Before doing so, however, she went to the door to see that no one was present and listening there, as she had herself once listened. To those who were at all on their guard there was no danger. The morning-room was only approached by a long, narrow hall, in which no one could come without being detected, if any one in the room chose to watch. Hilda now took her seat on a chair from which she could look up the hall, and thus, feeling secure from observation or from listeners, she began, in a low voice:

"I received the Indian papers to-day."

"I was aware of that, my lady," said Gualtier, respectfully. "Did you see any thing in them of importance?"

"Nothing certain, but something sufficient to excite concern."

"About Lord Chetwynde?"

"Yes."

"He can not be coming home, surely?" said Gualtier, interrogatively.

"I'm afraid that he is."

Gualtier looked serious.

"I thought," said he, "my lady, that you had nearly given up all expectation of seeing him for some time to come."

"I have never yet given up those expectations. I have all along thought it possible, though not probable; and so I have always watched all the papers to see if he had left his station."

"I suppose he would not write about his intentions."

"To whom could he think of writing?" asked Hilda, with a half sneer.

"I thought that perhaps he might write to Lady Chetwynde."

"Lady Chetwynde's letters to him have been of such a character that it is not very likely that he will ever write to her again, except under the pressure of urgent necessity."

"Have you seen any thing in particular in any of the papers about him?" asked Gualtier, after some silence.

"Yes. In one. It is the Allahabad News. The paragraph happened to catch my eye by the merest accident, I think. There is nothing about it in any of the other Indian papers. See; I will show it to you."

And Hilda, drawing a newspaper from her pocket, unfolded it, and pointing to a place in one of the inside columns, she handed it to Gualtier. He took it with a bow, and read the following:

"PERSONAL.—We regret to learn that Lord Chetwynde has recently resigned his position as Resident at Lahore. The recent death of his father, the late Earl of Chetwynde, and the large interests which demand his personal attention, are assigned as the causes for this step. His departure for England will leave a vacancy in our Anglo-Indian service which will not easily be filled. Lord Chetwynde's career in this important part of the empire has been so brilliant, that it is a matter for sincere regret that he is prevented, by any cause, from remaining here. In the late war he made his name conspicuous by his valor and consummate military genius. In the siege of Delhi he won laurels which will place his name high on the roll of those whom England loves to honor. Afterward, in the operations against Tantia Topee, his bold exploits will not soon be forgotten. His appointment to the Residency at Lahore was made only a few months since; yet in that short time he has shown an administrative talent which, without any reflection on our other able officials, we may safely pronounce to be very rare in the departments of our civil service. He is but a young man yet; but seldom has it happened that one so young has exhibited such mature intellectual powers, and such firm decision in the management of the most delicate cases. A gallant soldier, a wise ruler, and a genial friend, Lord Chetwynde will be missed in all those departments of public and private life of which he has been so conspicuous an ornament. As journalists, we wish to record this estimate of his virtues and his genius, and we feel sure that it will be shared by all who have been in any way familiar with the career of this distinguished gentleman. For the rest, we wish him most cordially a prosperous voyage home; and we anticipate for him in the mother country a career corresponding with his illustrious rank, and commensurate with the brilliant opening which he made in this country during those recent 'times which tried men's souls.'"

Gualtier read this paragraph over twice, and

then sat for some time in thought. At last he looked up at Hilda, who had all this time been intently watching him.

"That's bad," exclaimed he, and said no more.

"It seems that, after all, he is coming," said Hilda.

"Have you seen his name in any of the lists of passengers?"

"No."

"Then he has not left yet."

"Perhaps not; but still I can not trust to that altogether. His name may be omitted."

"Would such a name as his be likely to be omitted?"

"I suppose not; and so he can not have left India as yet—unless, indeed, he has come under an assumed name."

"An assumed name! Would he be capable of that? And if he were, what motive could he have?"

"Ah! there I am unable to find an answer. I'm afraid I have been judging of Lord Chetwynde by that." And Hilda pointed to the portrait of the young officer, Guy Molyneux, over the fire-place. "Years have changed him, and I have not made allowance for the years. I think now that this Lord Chetwynde must be very different from that Guy Molyneux. This hero of Delhi; this assailant of Tantia Toupi; this dashing officer, who is at once brilliant in the field and in the social circle; this man who, in addition to all this, has proved himself to be a wise ruler, with a 'genius for administration,' is a man who, I confess, dawns upon me so suddenly that it gives me a shock. I have been thinking of an innocent boy. I find that this boy has grown to be a great, brave, wise, strong man! There, I think, is the first mistake that I have made."

Hilda's words were full of truth and meaning. Gualtier felt that meaning.

"You have an alternative still," said he.

"What is that?"

"You need not stay here."

"What! Run away from him—in fear?" said Hilda, scornfully. "Run away from this place before I even know for certain that he is coming? That, at least, I will not do."

"There is Pomeroy Court," hinted Gualtier.

"No. Chetwynde Castle is my only home. I live here, or—nowhere. If I have to encounter him, it shall be face to face, and here in this house—perhaps in this room. Had I seen this a month ago my decision might have been different, though I don't know even that; but now, under any circumstances, it is too late to go back, or to swerve by one hair's breadth from the path which I have laid down for myself. It is well that I have seen all this"—and she pointed to the newspaper—"for it has given me a new view of the man. I shall not be so likely to underrate him now; and being forewarned I will be forearmed."

"There is still the probability," said Gualtier, thoughtfully, "that he may not come to England."

"There is a possibility," said Hilda, "certainly; but it is not probable, after so decided an act performed by one in so important a position, that he will remain in India. For why should he remain there? What could possibly cause him to resign, except the fixed intention of coming home? No; there can not be the slight-est doubt that his coming home is as certain as the dawn of to-morrow. What I wonder at, however, is, that he should delay; I should have expected to hear of his arrival in London. Yet that can not be, for his name is not down at all; and if he had come, surely a name like his could not by any possibility be omitted. No, he can not have come just yet. But he will, no doubt, come in the next steamer."

"There is yet another chance," said Gualtier.

"What is that?"

"He may come to England, and yet not come here to Chetwynde."

"I have thought of that too," said Hilda, "and used to think of it as very probable indeed; but now a ray of light has been let into my mind, and I see what manner of man he is. That boy"—and she again pointed to the portrait—"was the one who misled me. Such a one as he might have been so animated by hate that he might keep away so as not to be forced to see his detested wife. But this man is different. This soldier, this ruler, this mature man—who or what is his wife, hated though she be, or what is she to him in any way, that she should prove the slightest obstacle in the path of one like him? He would meet her as her lord and master, and brush her away as he would a moth."

"You draw this absent man in grand colors," said Gualtier. "Perhaps, my lady, your imagination is carrying you away. But if he is all this that you say, how can you venture to meet him? Will you risk being thus 'brushed away,' as you say, 'like a moth?'"

Hilda's eyes lighted up.

"I am not one who can be brushed away," said she, calmly; "and, therefore, whatever he is, and whenever he comes, I will be prepared to meet him."

Hilda's tone was so firm and decided that it left no room for further argument or remonstrance. Nor did Gualtier attempt any. Some conversation followed, and he soon took his departure.

CHAPTER XXXVI.

FACE TO FACE.

SOME time passed away after the conversation related in the last chapter, and one evening Hilda was in her boudoir alone, as usual. She was somewhat paler, more nervous, and less calm than she had been a few months previously. Her usual stealthy air had now developed into one of wary watchfulness, and the quiet noiselessness of her actions, her manner, and her movements had become intensified into a habit of motionless repose, accompanied by frequent fits of deep abstraction. On the present occasion she was reclining on her couch, with her hand shading her eyes. She had been lying thus for some time, lost in thought, and occasionally rousing herself sharply from her meditations to look around her with her watchful and suspicious eyes. In this attitude she remained till evening came, and then, with the twilight, she sank into a deep abstraction, one so deep that she could not readily rouse herself.

It was with a great start, therefore, that she rose to her feet as a sudden noise struck her ears. It was the noise of a carriage moving rapidly up through the avenue toward the house. For a carriage to come to Chetwynde Castle at any time was a most unusual thing; but for one to come after dark was a thing unheard of. At once there came to Hilda a thought like lightning as to who it might be that thus drove up; the thought was momentous and overwhelming; it might have been sufficient to have destroyed all courage and all presence of mind had her nerves been, by the slightest degree, less strong. But as it was, her nerve sustained her, and her courage did not falter for one single instant. With a calm face and firm step she advanced to the window. With a steady hand she drew the curtains aside and looked out. Little could he seen amidst the gloom at first; but at length, as she gazed, she was able to distinguish the dim outline of a carriage, as it emerged from the shadows of the avenue and drove up to the chief door.

Then she stepped back toward the door of her boudoir, and listened, but nothing could be heard. She then lighted two lamps, and, turning to a cheval-glass at one end of her room, she put one lamp on each side, so that the light might strike on her to the best advantage, and then scrutinized herself with a steady and critical glance. Thus she stood for a long time, watchful and motionless, actuated by a motive far different from any thing like vanity; and if she received gratification from a survey of herself, it was any thing but gratified pride. It was a deeper motive than girlish curiosity that inspired such stern self-inspection; and it was a stronger feeling than vanity that resulted from it. It was something more than things like these which made her, at so dread a moment, look so anxiously at her image in the glass.

As she stood there a tap came at the door.

"Come in," said Hilda, in her usual calm tone, turning as she spoke to face the door.

It was the maid.

"My lady," said she, "his lordship has just arrived."

To her, at that moment, such intelligence could have been nothing less than tremendous. It told her that the crisis of her life had come; and to meet it was inevitable, whatever the result might be. He had come. He, the one whom she must face; not the crude boy, but the man, tried in battle and in danger and in judgment, in the camp and in the court; the man who she now knew well was not surpassed by many men among that haughty race to which he belonged. This man was accustomed to face guilt and fear; he had learned to read the soul; he had become familiar with all that the face may make known of the secret terrors of conscience. And how could she meet the calm eyes of one who found her here in such a relation toward him? Yet all this she had weighed before in her mind; she was not unprepared. The hour and the man had come. She was found ready.

She regarded the maid for a few moments in silence. At last she spoke.

"Very well," she said, coldly, and without any perceptible emotion of any kind. "I will go down to meet his lordship."

His lordship has just arrived! The words had been spoken, and the speaker had departed, but the words still echoed and re-echoed through the soul of the hearer. What might this involve? and what would be the end of this arrival?

Suddenly she stepped to the door and called the maid.

"Has any one accompanied his lordship?"

"No, my lady."

"He came alone?"

"Yes, my lady."

"Did Mr. M'Kenzie see him?"

"No, my lady. He is not in the house."

Hilda closed the door, went back, and again stood before the mirror. Some time elapsed as she stood there regarding herself, with strange thoughts passing through her mind. She did not find it necessary, however, to make any alterations in her appearance. She did not change one fold in her attire, or vary one hair of her head from its place. It was as though this present dress and this present appearance had been long ago decided upon by her for just such a meeting as this. Whether she had anticipated such a meeting so suddenly—whether she was amazed or not—whether she was at all taken by surprise or not, could not appear in any way from her action or her demeanor. In the face of so terrible a crisis, whose full meaning and import she must have felt profoundly, she stood there, calm and self-contained, with the self-poise of one who has been long prepared, and who, when the hour big with fate at last may come, is not overwhelmed, but rises with the occasion, goes forth to the encounter, and prepares to contend with destiny.

It was, perhaps, about half an hour before Hilda went down. She went with a steady step and a calm face down the long corridor, down the great stairway, through the chief hall, and at length entered the drawing-room.

On entering she saw a tall man standing there, with his back turned toward the door, looking up at a portrait of the late Earl. So intently was he occupied that he did not hear her entering; but a slight noise, made by a chair as she passed it, startled him, and he turned and looked at her, disclosing to her curious yet apprehensive gaze the full features and figure of the new Lord Chetwynde. On that instant, as he turned and faced her, she took in his whole face and mien and stature. She saw a broad, intellectual brow, covered with dark clustering hair; a face bronzed by the suns of India and the exposure of the campaign, the lower part of which was hidden by a heavy beard and mustache; and a tall, erect, stalwart frame, with the unmistakable air of a soldier in every outline. His mien had in it a certain indescribable grace of high breeding, and the commanding air of one accustomed to be the ruler of men. His eyes were dark, and full of quiet but resistless power; and they beamed upon her lustrously, yet gloomily, and with a piercing glance of scrutiny from under his dark brows. His face bore the impress of a sadness deeper than that which is usually seen—sadness that had reigned there long—a sadness, too, which had given to that face a more sombre cast than common, from some grief which had been added to former ones. It was but for a moment that he looked at her, and then he bowed with grave courtesy. Hilda also bowed without a word, and then waited for Lord Chetwynde to speak.

But Lord Chetwynde did not speak for some time. His earnest eyes were still fixed upon the one before him, and though it might have been rudeness, yet it was excusable, from the weight which lay on his soul.

"HILDA STOOD THERE, CALM, WATCHFUL, AND EXPECTANT."

Hilda, for her part, stood there, calm, watchful, and expectant. That slender and graceful figure, with its simple and elegant dress, which set off to the utmost the perfection of her form, looked certainly unlike the ungrown girl whom Lord Chetwynde had seen years before. Still more unlike was the face. Pale, with delicate, transparent skin, it was not so dark as that face which had dwelt in his memory. Her eyes did not seem so wild and staring as those of the imp whom he had married; but deep, dark, and strong in their gaze, as they looked back steadily into his. The hair was now no longer disordered, but enfolded in its dark, voluminous masses, so as to set off to the best advantage the well-shaped head, and slender, beautifully rounded neck. The one whom he remembered had been hideous; this one was beautiful. But the beauty that he saw was, nevertheless, hard, cold, and repellent. For Hilda, in her beauty and grace and intellectual subtilty, stood there watchful and vigilant, like a keen fencer on guard, waiting to see what the first spoken word might disclose; waiting to see what that grand lordly face, with its air of command, its repressed grief, its deep piercing eyes, might shadow forth.

A singular meeting; but Lord Chetwynde seemed to think it natural enough, and after a few moments he remarked, in a quiet voice:

"Lady Chetwynde, the morning-room will be more suitable for the interview which I wish, and, if you have no objection, we will go there."

At the sound of these words a great revulsion took place in Hilda's feelings, and a sense of triumph succeeded to that intense anxiety which for so long a time had consumed her. The sound of that name by which he had addressed her had shown her at once that the worst part of this crisis had passed away. He had seen her. He had scrutinized her with those eyes which seemed to read her soul, and the end was that he had taken her for what she professed to be. He had called her "Lady Chetwynde!" After this what more was there which could excite fear? Was not her whole future now secured by the utterance of those two words? Yet Hilda's self-control was so perfect, and her vigilance so consummate, that no change whatever expressed in her face the immense revolution of feeling within her. Her eyes fell—that was all; and as she bowed her head silently, by that simple gesture which was at once natural and courteous, she effectually concealed her face; so that, even if there had been a change in its expression, it could not have been seen. Yet, after all, the triumph was but instantaneous. It passed away, and soon there came another feeling, vague, indefinable—a premonition of the future—a presentiment of gloom; and though the intensity of the suspense had passed, there still remained a dark anxiety and a fear which were unaccountable.

Lord Chetwynde led the way to the morning-room, and on arriving there he motioned her to a seat. Hilda sat down. He sat opposite in another chair, not far off. On the wall, where each could see it, hung his portrait—the figure of that beardless, boyish, dashing young officer—very different from this matured, strong-souled man; so different, indeed, that it seemed hardly possible that they could be the same.

Lord Chetwynde soon began.

"Lady Chetwynde," said he, again addressing her by that name, and speaking in a firm yet melancholy voice, "it is not often that a husband and a wife meet as you and I do now; but then it is not often that two people become husband and wife as you and I have. I have come from India for the sake of having a full understanding with you. I had, until lately, an idea of coming here under an assumed name, with the wish of sparing you the embarrassment which I supposed that the presence of Lord Chetwynde himself might possibly cause you. In fact, I traveled most of the way home from India under an assumed name with that intent. But before

I reached England I concluded that there was no necessity for trying to guard against any embarrassment on your part, and that it would be infinitely better to see you in my own person and talk to you without disguise."

He paused for a moment.

"Had you chosen to come all the way in your own name, my lord," said Hilda, speaking now for the first time, "I should have seen your name in the list of passengers, and should have been better prepared for the honor of your visit."

"Concealment would have been impossible," continued Lord Chetwynde, gloomily, half to himself, and without appearing to have heard Hilda's words, "here, in my home. Though all the old servants are gone, still the old scenes remain; and if I had come here as a stranger I should have shown so deep an interest in my home that I might have excited suspicion. But the whole plan was impossible, and, after all, there was no necessity for it, as I do not see that your feelings have been excited to madness by my appearance. So far, then, all is well. And now to come to the point; and you, I am sure, will be the first to excuse my abruptness in doing so. The unfortunate bond that binds us is painful enough to you. It is enough for me to say that I have come home for two reasons: first, to see my home, possibly for the last time; and secondly, to announce to you the decision at which I have arrived with regard to the position which we shall hereafter occupy toward one another."

Hilda said nothing. Awe was a feeling which was almost unknown to her; but something of that had come over her as, sitting in the presence of this man, she heard him say these words; for he spoke without any particular reference to her, and said them with a grand, authoritative air, with the tone of one accustomed to rule and to dispense justice. In uttering these concluding words it seemed to be his will, his decision, that he was announcing to some inferior being.

"First," he went on to say, "let me remind you of our unhappy betrothal. You were a child, a boy. Our parents are responsible for that. They meant well. Let us not blame them.

"Then came our marriage by the death-bed of your father. You were excited, and very naturally so. You used bitter words to me then which I have never forgotten. Every taunt and insult which you then uttered has lived in my memory. Why? Not because I am inclined to treasure up wrong. No. Rather because you have taken such extreme pains to keep alive the memory of that event. You will remember that in every one of those letters which you have written to me since I left England there has not been one which has not been filled with innuendoes of the most cutting kind, and insults of the most galling nature. My father loved you. I did not. But could you not, for his sake, have refrained from insult? Why was it necessary to turn what at first was merely coolness into hate and indignation?

"I speak bitterly about those letters of yours. It was those which kept me so long in India. I could not come to see my father because you were here, and I should have to come and see you. I could not give him trouble by letting him know the truth, because he loved you. Thus you kept me away from him and from my home at a time when I was longing to be here; and, finally, to crown your cruelty, you sedulously concealed from me the news of my father's illness till it was too late. He died; and then—then you wrote that hideous letter, that abomination of insult and vindictiveness, that cruel and cowardly stab, which you aimed at a heart already wrung by the grief of bereavement! In the very letter which you wrote to tell me of that sudden and almost intolerable calamity you dared to say that my father—that gentle and noble soul, who so loved you and trusted you—that he, the stainless gentleman, the soul of honor—*he* had cheated *you*, and that his death was the punishment inflicted by Providence for his sin; that he had made a cunning and dishonest plan to get you for the sake of your fortune; that *I* had been his accomplice; and that by his death the vengeance of Divine justice was manifested on both of us!"

Deep and low grew the tones of Lord Chetwynde's voice as he spoke these words—deep and low, yet restrained with that restraint which is put over the feelings by a strong nature, and yet can not hide that consuming passion which underlies all the words, and makes them burn with intensest heat. Here the hot fire of his indignation seemed to be expressed in a blighting and withering power; and Hilda shrank within herself involuntarily in fear, trembling at this terrific denunciation.

Lord Chetwynde made a slight gesture.

"Calm yourself," said he; "you can not help your nature. Do you suppose for one moment that I, by any possibility, can expect an explanation? Not at all. I have mentioned this for the first and for the last time. Even while your letters were lying before me I did not deign to breathe one word about them to my father, from whom I kept no other secret, even though I knew that, while he loved you and trusted you, both his love and his trust were thrown away. I would not add to his troubles by showing him the true character of the woman to whom he had sold me and bound me fast, and whom he looked on with affection. That sorrow I determined to spare him, and so I kept silent. So it was that I always spoke of you with the formulas of respect, knowing well all the time that you yourself did not deserve even that much. But *he* deserved it, and I quenched my own indignation for his sake. But now there is no longer any reason why I should play the hypocrite, and so I speak of these things. I say this simply to let you know how your conduct and character are estimated by one whose opinion is valued by many honorable gentlemen.

"Even after his death," continued Lord Chetwynde, "I might possibly have had some consideration for you, and, perhaps, would not have used such plain language as I now do. But one who could take advantage of the death of my father to give vent to spleen, and to offer insult to one who had never offended her, deserves no consideration. Such conduct as yours, Lady Chetwynde, toward me, has been too atrocious to be ever forgiven or forgotten. To this you will no doubt say, with your usual sneer, that my forgiveness is not desired. I am glad if it is not.

"To your father, Lady Chetwynde, I once made a vow that I would always be careful about your happiness. I made it thoughtlessly, not

knowing what I was promising, not in any way understanding its full import. I made it when full of gratitude for an act of his which I regarded only by itself, without thinking of all that was required of me. I made it as a thoughtless boy. But that vow I intend now, as a mature man, to fulfill, most sacredly and solemnly. For I intend to care for your happiness, and that, too, in a way which will be most agreeable to you. I shall thus be able to keep that rash and hasty vow, which I once thought I would never be able to keep. The way in which I intend to keep it is one, Lady Chetwynde, which will insure perfect happiness to one like you; and as you are, no doubt, anxious to know how it is possible for me to do such a thing, I will hasten to inform you.

"The way in which I intend, Lady Chetwynde, to fulfill my vow and secure your perfect happiness is, first of all, by separating myself from you forever. This is the first thing. It is not such an accomplishment of that vow as either your father or mine anticipated; but in your eyes and mine it will be a perfect fulfillment. Fortunate it is for me that the thing which you desire most is also the very thing which I most desire. Your last letter settled a problem which has been troubling me for years.

"This, however, is only part of my decision. I will let you know the rest as briefly as possible. When your father came from India, and made that memorable visit to my father, which has cost us both so dear, Chetwynde was covered with mortgages to the extent of sixty thousand pounds. Your father made an unholy bargain with mine, and in order to secure a protector for you, he gave to my father the money which was needed to disencumber the estate. It was, in fact, your dowry, advanced beforehand.

"The principals in that ill-omened arrangement are both dead. I am no longer a boy, but a man; the last of my line, with no one to consider but myself. An atrocious wrong has been done, unintentionally, to me, and also to you. That wrong I intend to undo, as far as possible. I have long ago decided upon the way. I intend to give back to you this dowry money; and to do so I will break the entail, sell Chetwynde, and let it go to the hands of strangers. My ancient line ends in me. Be it so. I have borne so many bitter griefs that I can bear this with resignation. Never again shall you, Lady Chetwynde, have the power of flinging at me that taunt which you have so often flung. You shall have your money back, to the last farthing, and with interest for the whole time since its advance. In this way I can also best keep my vow to General Pomeroy; for the only mode by which I can secure your happiness is to yield the care of it into your own hands.

"For the present you will have Chetwynde Castle to live in until its sale. Every thing here seems quite adapted to make you happy. You seem to have appropriated it quite to yourself. I can not find one of those faithful old domestics with whom my boyhood was passed. You have surrounded yourself with your own servants. Until your money is paid you will be quite at liberty to live here, or at Pomeroy Court, whichever you prefer. Both are yours now, the Castle as much as Pomeroy Court, as you remarked, with your usual delicacy, in your last letter, since they both represent your own money.

"And now," said Lord Chetwynde, in conclusion, "we understand one another. The time for taunts and sneers, for you, is over. Any letters hereafter that may come to me in your handwriting will be returned unopened. The one aim of my life hereafter shall be to undo, as far as possible, the wrong done to us both by our parents. That can never be all undone; but, at any rate, you may be absolutely certain that you will get back every penny of the money which is so precious to you, with interest. As to my visit here, do not let it disturb you for one moment. I have no intention of making a scene for the benefit of your gaping servants. My business now is solely to see about my father's papers, to examine them, and take away with me those that are of immediate use. While I am here we will meet at the same table, and will be bound by the laws of ordinary courtesy. At all other times we need not be conscious of one another's existence. I trust that you will see the necessity of avoiding any open demonstrations of hatred, or even dislike. Let your feelings be confined to yourself, Lady Chetwynde; and do not make them known to the servants, if you can possibly help it."

Lord Chetwynde seemed to have ended; for he arose and sauntered up to the portrait, which he regarded for some time with fixed attention, and appeared to lose himself in his thoughts. During the remarks which he had been making Hilda had sat looking at the floor. Unable to encounter the stern gaze of the man whom she felt to be her master, she had listened in silence, with downcast eyes. There was nothing for her to say. She therefore did the very best thing that she could do under the circumstances—she said nothing. Nor did she say any thing when he had ended. She saw him absorb himself in regarding his own portrait, and apparently lose himself in his recollections of the past. Of her he seemed to have now no consciousness. She sat looking at him, as his side face was turned toward her, and his eyes fixed on the picture. The noble profile, with its clear-cut features, showed much of the expression of the face—an expression which was stern, yet sad and softened—that face which, just before, had been before her eyes frowning, wrathful, clothed with consuming terrors—a face upon which she could not look, but which now was all mournful and sorrowful. And now, as she gazed, the hard rigidity of her beautiful features relaxed, the sharp glitter of her dark eyes died out, their stony lustre gave place to a soft light, which beamed upon him with wonder, with timid awe—with something which, in any other woman, would have looked like tenderness. She had not been prepared for one like this. In her former ideas of him he had been this boy of the portrait, with his boyish enthusiasm, and his warm, innocent temperament. This idea she had relinquished, and had known that he had changed during the years into the heroic soldier and the calm judge. She had tried to familiarize herself with this new idea, and had succeeded in doing so to a certain extent. But, after all, the reality had been too much for her. She had not been prepared for one like this, nor for such an effect as the sight of him had produced. At this first interview he had overpowered her utterly, and she had sat dumb and motionless before him. All the sneering speeches which she had prepared in anticipation of the meeting were useless. She found no place for them. But there was one result to this interview which affected her still more deeply than this discovery of his moral superiority. The one great danger which she had always feared had passed away. She no longer had that dread fear of discovery which hitherto had harassed her; but in the place of this there suddenly arose another fear—a fear which seemed as terrible as the other, which darkened over her during the course of that scene till its close, and afterward—such an evil as she never before could have thought herself capable of dreading, yet one which she had brought upon herself.

What was that?

His contempt—his hate—his abhorrence—this was the thing which now seemed so terrible to her.

For in the course of that interview a sudden change had come over all her feelings. In spite of her later judgment about him, which she had expressed to Gualtier, there had been in her mind a half contempt for the man whom she had once judged of by his picture only, and whom she recollected as the weak agent in a forced marriage. That paragraph in the Indian paper had certainly caused a great change to take place in her estimate of his character; but, in spite of this, the old contempt still remained, and she had reckoned upon finding beneath the mature man, brave though he was, and even wise though he might be, much of that boy whom she had despised. But all this passed away as a dream, out of which she had a rude awakening. She awoke suddenly to the full reality, to find him a strong, stern, proud man, to whom her own strength was as weakness. While he uttered his grand maledictions against her he seemed to her like a god. He was a mighty being, to whom she looked up from the depths of her soul, half in fear, half in adoration. In her weakness she admired his strength; and in her wily and tortuous subtlety she worshiped this straightforward and upright gentleman, who scorned craft and cunning, and who had sat in stern judgment upon her, to make known to her his will.

For some time she sat looking at him as he stood, with her whole nature shaken by these new, these unparalleled emotions, till, finally, with a start, she came to herself, and, rising slowly, she glided out of the room.

CHAPTER XXXVII.

AN EFFORT AT CONCILIATION.

LORD CHETWYNDE's occupations kept him for the greater part of his time in his father's library, where he busied himself in examining papers. Many of these he read and restored to their places, but some he put aside, in order to take them with him. Of the new steward he took no notice whatever. He considered the dismissal of the old one and the appointment of Gualtier one of those abominable acts which were consistent with all the other acts of that woman whom he supposed to be his wife. Besides, the papers which he sought had reference to the past, and

"HE SOUGHT OUT HIS FATHER'S GRAVE, AND STOOD MUSING THERE."

had no connection with the affairs of the present. In the intervals of his occupation he used to go about the grounds, visiting every one of those well-known places which were associated with his childhood and boyhood. He sought out his father's grave, and stood musing there with feelings which were made up of sadness, mingled with something like reproach for the fearful mistake which his father had made in the allotment of the son's destiny. True, he had been one of the consenting parties; but when he first gave that consent he was little more than a boy, and not at all capable of comprehending the full meaning of such an engagement. His father had ever since solemnly held him to it, and had appealed to his sense of honor in order to make him faithful. But now the father was dead, the son was a mature man, tried in a thousand scenes of difficulty and danger—one who had learned to think for himself, who had gained his manhood by a life of storms, in which of late there had been crowded countless events, each of which had had their weight in the development of his character. They had left him a calm, strong, resolute man—a man of thought and of action—a graduate of the school of Indian affairs—a school which, in times that tried men's souls, never failed to supply men who were equal to every emergency.

At the very outset he had found out the condition of Mrs. Hart. The sight of his loved nurse, thus prostrated, filled him with grief. The housekeeper who now attended her knew nothing whatever of the cause of her prostration. Lord Chetwynde did not deign to ask any questions of Hilda; but in his anxiety to learn about Mrs. Hart, he sought out the doctor who had attended his father, and from him he learned that Mrs. Hart's illness had been caused by her anxiety about the Earl. The knowledge of this increased, if possible, his own care. He made the closest inquiry as to the way in which she was treated, engaged the doctor to visit her, and doubled the housekeeper's salary on condition that she would be attentive to his beloved nurse. These measures were attended with good results, for under this increased care Mrs. Hart began to show signs of improvement. Whether she would ever again be conscious was yet a question. The doctor considered her mind to be irretrievably affected. '

Meanwhile, throughout all these days, Hilda's mind was engrossed with the change which had come over her—a change so startling and so unexpected that it found her totally unprepared to deal with it. They met every day at the dinner-table, and at no other times. Here Lord Chetwynde treated her with scrupulous courtesy; yet beyond the extreme limits of that courtesy she found it impossible to advance. Hilda's manner was most humble and conciliatory. She who all her life had felt defiant of others, or worse, now found herself enthralled and subdued by the spell of this man's presence. Her wiliness, her stealthiness, her constant self-control, were all lost and forgotten. She had now to struggle incessantly against that new tenderness which had sprung up unbidden within her. She caught herself looking forward wistfully every day to the time when she could meet him at the table and hear his voice, which, even in its cold, constrained tones, was enough for her happiness. It was in vain that she reproached and even cursed herself for her weakness. The weakness none the less existed; and all her life seemed now to centre around this man, who hated her. Into a position like this she had never imagined that she could possibly be brought. All her cunning and all her resources were useless here. This man seemed so completely beyond her control that any effort to win him to her seemed useless. He believed her to be his wife, he believed himself bound by honor to secure her happiness, and yet his abhorrence of her was so strong that he never made any effort to gain her for himself. Now Hilda saw with bitterness that she had gone too far, and that her plans and her plots were recoiling upon her own head. They had been too successful. The sin of Lord Chetwynde's wife had in his eyes proved unpardonable.

Hilda's whole life now became a series of alternate struggles against her own heart, and longings after another who was worse than indifferent to her. Her own miserable weakness, so unexpected, and yet so complete and hopeless, filled her at once with anger and dismay. To find all her thoughts both by day and night filled with this one image was at once mortifying and terrible. The very intensity of her feelings, which would not stop short at death itself to gain their object, now made her own sufferings

all the greater. Every thing else was forgotten except this one absorbing desire; and her complicated schemes and far-reaching plans were thrust away. They had lost their interest. Henceforth all were reduced to one thought—how to gain Lord Chetwynde to herself.

As long as she staid, something like hope remained; but when he would leave, what hope could there be? Would he not leave her forever? Was not this the strongest desire of his heart? Had he not said so? Every day she watched, with a certain chilling fear at her heart, to see if there were signs of his departure. As day succeeded to day, however, and she found him still remaining, she began to hope that he might possibly have relented somewhat, and that the sentence which he had spoken to her might have become modified by time and further observation of her.

So at the dinner-table she used to sit, looking at him, when his eyes were turned away, with her earnest, devouring gaze, which, as soon as he would look at her again, was turned quickly away with the timidity of a young bashful child. Such is the tenderness of love that Hilda, who formerly shrank at nothing, now shrank away from the gaze of this man. Once, by a great effort, as he entered the dining-room she held out her hand to greet him. Lord Chetwynde, however, did not seem to see it, for he greeted her with his usual distant civility, and treated her as before. Once more she tried this, and yet once again, but with the same result; and it was then that she knew that Lord Chetwynde *refused* to take her hand. It was not oversight—it was a deliberate purpose. At another time it would have seemed an insult which would have filled her with rage; now it seemed a slight which filled her with grief. So humiliated had she become, and so completely subdued by this man, that even this slight was not enough, but she still planned vague ways of winning his attention to her, and of gaining from him something more than a remark about the weather or about the dishes.

At length one day she formed a resolution, which, after much hesitation, she carried out. She was determined to make one bold effort, whatever the result might be. It was at their usual place of meeting—the dinner-table.

"My lord," said she, with a tremulous voice, "I wish to have an interview with you. Can you spare me the time this evening?"

She looked at him earnestly, with mute inquiry. Lord Chetwynde regarded her in some surprise. He saw her eyes fixed upon him with a timid entreaty, while her face grew pale with suspense. Her breathing was rapid from the agitation that overcame her.

"I had some business this evening," said Lord Chetwynde, coldly, "but as you wish an interview, I am at your service."

"At what time, my lord?"

"At nine," said Lord Chetwynde.

Nine o'clock came, and Hilda was in the morning-room, which she had mentioned as the place of meeting, and Lord Chetwynde came there punctually. She was sitting near the window. Her pale face, her rich black locks arranged in voluminous masses about her head, her dark penetrating eyes, her slender and graceful figure, all conspired to make Hilda beautiful and attractive in a rare degree. Added to this there was a certain entreaty on her face as it was turned toward him, and a soft, timid lustre in her eyes which might have affected any other man. She rose as Lord Chetwynde entered, and bowed her beautiful head, while her graceful arms, and small, delicately shaped hands hung down at her side.

Lord Chetwynde bowed in silence.

"My lord," said Hilda, in a voice which was tremulous from an uncontrollable emotion, "I wished to see you here. We met here once before; you said what you wished; I made no reply; I had nothing to say; I felt your reproaches; they were in some degree just and well-merited; but I might have said something—only I was timid and nervous, and you frightened me."

Here Hilda paused, and drew a long breath. Her emotion nearly choked her, but the sound of her own voice sustained her, and, making an effort, she went on:

"I have nothing to say in defense of my conduct. It has made you hate me. Your hate is too evident. My thoughtless spite has turned back upon myself. I would willingly humiliate myself now if I thought that it would affect you or conciliate you. I would acknowledge any folly of mine if I thought that you could be brought to look upon me with leniency. What I did was the act of a thoughtless girl, angry at finding herself chained up for life, spiteful she knew not why. I had only seen you for a moment, and did not know you. I was mad. I was guilty; but still it is a thing that may be considered as not altogether unnatural under the circumstances. And, after all, it was not sincere—it was pique, it was thoughtlessness—it was not that deep-seated malice which you have laid to my charge. Can you not think of this? Can you not imagine what may have been the feelings of a wild, spoiled, untutored girl, one who was little better than a child, one who found herself shackled she knew not how, and who chafed at all restraint? Can you not understand, or at least imagine, such a case as this, and believe that the one who once sinned has now repented, and asks with tears for your forgiveness?"

Tears? Yes, tears were in the eyes of this singular girl, this girl whose nature was so made up of strength and weakness. Her eyes were suffused with tears as she looked at Lord Chetwynde, and finally, as she ceased, she buried her face in her hands and sobbed aloud.

Now, nothing in nature so moves a man as a woman's tears. If the woman be beautiful, and if she loves the man to whom she speaks, they are irresistible. And here the woman was beautiful, and her love for the man whom she was addressing was evident in her face and in the tones of her voice. Yet Lord Chetwynde sat unmoved. Nothing in his face or in his eyes gave indications of any response on his part. Nothing whatever showed that any thing like soft pity or tender consideration had modified the severity of his purpose or the sternness of his fixed resolve. Yet Lord Chetwynde by nature was not hard-hearted, and Hilda well knew this. In the years which she had spent at the Castle she had heard from every quarter—from the Earl, from Mrs. Hart, and from the servants—tales without number about his generosity, his self-denial, his kindliness, and tender consideration for

the feelings of others. Besides this, he had received from his father along with that chivalrous nature the lofty sentiments of a knight-errant, and in his boyish days had always been ready to espouse the cause of any one in distress with the warmest enthusiasm. In Hilda's present attitude, in her appearance, in her words, and above all in her tears, there was every thing that would move such a nature to its inmost depths. Had he ever seen any one at once so beautiful and so despairing; and one, too, whose whole despair arose from her feelings for him? Even his recollections of former disdain might lose their bitterness in the presence of such utter humiliation, such total self-immolation as this. His nature could not have changed, for the Indian paper alluded to his "genial" character, and his "heroic qualities." He must be still the same. What, then, could there be which would be powerful enough to harden his feelings and steel his heart against such a woeful and piteous sight as that which was now exhibited to him? All these things Hilda thought as she made her appeal, and broke down so completely at its close; these things, too, she thought as the tears streamed from her eyes, and as her frame was shaken by emotion.

Lord Chetwynde sat looking at her in silence for a long time. No trace whatever of commiseration appeared upon his face; but he continued as stern, as cold, and as unmoved, as in that first interview when he had told her how he hated her. Bitter indeed must that hate have been which should so crush out all those natural impulses of generosity which belonged to him; bitter must the hate have been; and bitter too must have been the whole of his past experience in connection with this woman, which could end in such pitiless relentlessness.

At length he answered her. His tone was calm, cool, and impassive, like his face; showing not a trace of any change from that tone in which he always addressed her; and making known to her, as she sat with her face buried in her hands, that whatever hopes she had indulged in during his silence, those hopes were altogether vain.

"Lady Chetwynde," he began, "all that you have just said I have thought over long ago, from beginning to end. It has all been in my mind for years. In India there were always hours when the day's duties were over, and the mind would turn to its own private and secret thoughts. From the very first, you, Lady Chetwynde, were naturally the subject of those thoughts to a great degree. That marriage scene was too memorable to be soon forgotten, and the revelation of your character, which I then had, was the first thing which showed me the full weight of the obligation which I had so thoughtlessly accepted. Most bitterly I lamented, on my voyage out, that I had not contrived some plan to evade so hasty a fulfillment of my boyish promise, and that I had not satisfied the General in some way which would not have involved such a scene. But I could not recall the past, and I felt bound by my father's engagement. As to yourself, I assure you that in spite of your malice and your insults I felt most considerately toward you. I pitied you for being, like myself, the unwilling victim of a father's promise and of a sick man's whim, and learned to make allowance for every word

I

and action of yours at that time. Not one of those words or actions had the smallest effect in imbittering my mind toward you. Not one of those words which you have just uttered has suggested an idea which I have not long ago considered, and pondered over in secret, in silence, and in sorrow. I made a large allowance also for that hate which you must have felt toward one who came to you as I did, in so odious a character, to violate, as I did, the sanctities of death by the mockery of a hideous marriage. All this—all this has been in my mind, and nothing that you can say is able in any way to bring any new idea to me. There are other things far deeper and far more lasting than this, which can not be answered, or excused, or explained away—the long persistent expressions of unchanging hate."

Lord Chetwynde was silent. Hilda had heard all this without moving or raising her head. Every word was ruin to her hopes. But she still hoped against hope, and now, since she had an opportunity to speak, she still tried to move this obdurate heart.

"Hate!" she exclaimed, catching at his last word—"hate! what is that? the fitful, spiteful feeling arising out of the recollection of one miserable scene—or perhaps out of the madness of anger at a forced marriage. What is it? One kind word can dispel it."

As she said this she did not look up. Her face was buried in her hands. Her tone was half despairing, half imploring, and broken by emotion.

"True," said Lord Chetwynde. "All that I have thought of, and I used to console myself with that. I used to say to myself, 'When we meet again it will be different. When she knows me she can not hate me.'"

"You were right," faltered Hilda, with a sob which was almost a groan. "And what then? Say—was it a wonder that I should have felt hate? Was there ever any one so tried as I was? My father was my only friend. He was father and mother and all the world to me. He was brought home one day suddenly, injured by a frightful accident, and dying. At that unparalleled moment I was ordered to prepare for marriage. Half crazed with anxiety and sorrow, and anticipating the very worst—at such a time death itself would have been preferable to that ceremony. But all my feelings were outraged, and I was dragged down to that horrible scene. Can you not see what effect the recollection of this might afterward have? Can you not once again make allowances, and think those thoughts which you used to think? Can you not still see that you were right in supposing that when we might meet all would be different, and that she who might once have known you could not hate you?"

"No," said Lord Chetwynde, coldly and severely.

Hilda raised her head, and looked at him with mute inquiry.

"I will explain," said Lord Chetwynde. "I have already said all that I ought to say; but you force me to say more, though I am unwilling. Your letters, Lady Chetwynde, were the things which quelled and finally killed all kindly feelings."

"Letters!" burst in Hilda, with eager vehe-

mence. "They were the letters of a hot-tempered girl, blinded by pique and self-conceit, and carelessly indulging in a foolish spite which in her heart she did not seriously feel."

"Pardon me," said Lord Chetwynde, with cold politeness, "I think you are forgetting the circumstances under which they were written—for this must be considered as well as the nature of the compositions themselves. They were the letters of one whom my father loved, and of whom he always spoke in the tenderest language, but who yet was so faithless to him that she never ceased to taunt me with what she called our baseness. She never spared the old man who loved her. For months and for years these letters came. It was something more than pique, something more than self-conceit or spite, which lay at the bottom of such long-continued insults. The worst feature about them was their cold-blooded cruelty. Nothing in my circumstances or condition could prevent this—not even that long agony before Delhi"—added Lord Chetwynde, in tones filled with a deeper indignation—"when I, lost behind the smoke and cloud and darkness of the great struggle, was unable to write for a long time; and, finally, was able to give my account of the assault and the triumph. Not even that could change the course of the insults which were so freely heaped upon me. And yet it would have been easy to avoid all this. Why write at all? There was no heavy necessity laid upon you. That was the question which I used to put to myself. But you persisted in writing, and in sending to me over the seas, with diabolical pertinacity, those hideous letters in which every word was a stab."

While Lord Chetwynde had been speaking Hilda sat looking at him, and meeting his stern glance with a look which would have softened any one less bitter. Paler and paler grew her face, and her hands clutched one another in tremulous agitation, which showed her strong emotion.

"Oh, my lord!" she cried, as he ceased, "can you not have mercy? Think of that black cloud that came down over my young life, filling it with gloom and horror. I confess that you and your father appeared the chief agents; but I learned to love *him*, and then all my bitterness turned on *you*—you, who seemed to be so prosperous, so brave, and so honored. It was you who seemed to have blighted my life, and so I was animated by a desire to make you feel something of what I had felt. My disposition is fiery and impetuous; my father's training made it worse. I did not know you; I only felt spite against you, and thus I wrote those fatal letters. I thought that you could have prevented that marriage if you had wished, and therefore could never feel any thing but animosity. But now the sorrows through which I have passed have changed me, and you yourself have made me see how mad was my action. But oh, my lord, believe me, it was not deliberate, it was hasty passion! and now I would be willing to wipe out every word in those hateful letters with my heart's blood!"

Hilda's voice was low but impassioned, with a certain burning fervor of entreaty; her words had become words almost of prayer, so deep was her humiliation. Her face was turned toward him with an imploring expression, and her eyes were fixed on his in what seemed an agony of suspense. But not even that white face, with its ashen lips and its anguish, nor those eyes with their overflowing tears, nor that voice with its touching pathos of woe, availed in any way to call up any response of pity and sympathy in the breast of Lord Chetwynde.

"You use strong language, Lady Chetwynde," said he, in his usual tone. "You forget that it is you yourself who have transformed all my former kindliness, in spite of myself, into bitterness and gall. You forget, above all, that last letter of yours. You seem to show an emotion which I once would have taken as real. Pardon me if I now say that I consider it nothing more than consummate acting. You speak of consideration. You hint at mercy. Listen, Lady Chetwynde"—and here Lord Chetwynde raised his right hand with solemn emphasis. "You turned away from the death-bed of my father, the man who loved you like a daughter, to write to me that hideous letter which you wrote—that letter, every word of which is still in my memory, and rises up between us to sunder us for evermore. You went beyond yourself. To have spared the living was not needed; but it was the misfortune of your nature that you could not spare the dead. While he was, perhaps, yet lying cold in death near you, you had the heart to write to me bitter sneers against him. Even without that you had done enough to turn me from you always. But when I read that, I then knew most thoroughly that the one who was capable, under such circumstances, of writing thus could only have a mind and heart irretrievably bad—bad and corrupt and base. Never, never, never, while I live, can I forget the utter horror with which that letter filled me!"

"Oh, my God!" said Hilda, with a groan.

Lord Chetwynde sat stern and silent.

"You are inflexible in your cruelty," said Hilda at length, as she made one last and almost hopeless effort. "I have done. But will you not ask me something? Have you nothing to ask about your father? He loved me as a daughter. I was the one who nursed him in his last illness, and heard his last words. His dying eyes were fixed on me!"

As Hilda said this a sharp shudder passed through her.

"No," said Lord Chetwynde, "I have nothing to ask—nothing from you! Your last letter has quelled all desire. I would rather remain in ignorance, and know nothing of the last words of him whom I so loved than ask of you."

"He called me his daughter. He loved me," said Hilda, in a broken voice.

"And yet you were capable of turning away from his death-bed and writing that letter to his son. You did it coolly and remorselessly."

"It was the anguish of bereavement and despair."

"No; it was the malignancy of the Evil One. Nothing else could have prompted those hideous sneers. In real sorrow sneering is the last thing that one thinks of. But enough. I do not wish to speak in this way to a lady. Yet to you I can speak in no other way. I will therefore retire."

And, with a bow, Lord Chetwynde withdrew.

Hilda looked after him, as he left, with staring eyes, and with a face as pallid as that of a corpse.

She rose to her feet. Her hands were clenched tight.

"He loves another," she groaned; "otherwise he never, never, never could have been so pitiless!"

CHAPTER XXXVIII.

SETTING THE DOG ON THE LION'S TRACK.

AFTER this failure in the effort to come to an understanding with Lord Chetwynde, Hilda sank into despondency. She scarcely knew what there was to be done when such an appeal as this had failed. She had humbled herself in the dust before him—she had manifested unmistakably her love, yet he had disregarded all. After this what remained? It was difficult to say. Yet, for herself, she still looked forward to the daily meeting with him: glad of this, since fate would give her nothing better. The change which had come over her was not one which could be noticed by the servants, so that there was no chance of her secret being discovered by them; but there was another at Chetwynde Castle who very quickly discovered all, one who was led to this perhaps by the sympathy of his own feelings. There was that secret within his own heart which made him watchful and attentive and observant. No change in her face and manner, however slight, could fail to be noticed by this man, who treasured up every varying expression of hers within his heart. And this change which had come over her was one which affected him by much more than the mere variation of features. It entered into his daily life and disarranged all his plans.

Before the arrival of Lord Chetwynde, Gualtier, in his capacity of steward, had been accustomed to have frequent interviews with Hilda. Now they were all over. Since that arrival he had not spoken to her once, nor had he once got so much as a glance of her eye. At first he accounted for it from very natural causes. He attributed it to the anxiety which she felt at the presence of Lord Chetwynde, and at the desperate part which she had to play. For some time this seemed sufficient to account for every thing. But afterward he learned enough to make him think it possible that there were other causes. He heard the gossip of the servants' hall, and from that he learned that it was the common opinion of the servants that Lady Chetwynde was very fond of Lord Chetwynde, but that the latter was very distant and reserved in his manner toward her. This started him on a new track for conjecture, and he soon learned and saw enough to get some general idea of the truth. Yet, after all, it was not the actual truth which he conjectured. His conclusion was that Hilda was playing a deep game in order to win Lord Chetwynde's affection to herself. The possibility of her actually loving him did not then suggest itself. He looked upon it as one of those profound pieces of policy for which he was always on the look-out from her. The discovery of this disturbed him. The arrival of Lord Chetwynde had troubled him; but this new plan of Hilda's troubled him still more, and all the more because he was now shut out from her confidence.

"The little game is up to a new game; and she'll beat," he said to himself; "she'll beat, for she always beats. She's got a long head, and I can only guess what it is that she is up to. She'll never tell me." And he thought, with some pensiveness, upon the sadness of that one fact, that she would never tell him. Meanwhile he contented himself with watching until something more definite could be known.

Lord Chetwynde had much to occupy him in his father's papers. He spent the greater part of his time in the library, and though weeks passed he did not seem to be near the end of them. At other times he rode about the grounds or sauntered through the groves. The seclusion in which the Castle had always been kept was not disturbed. The county families were too remote for ordinary calling, or else they did not know of his arrival. Certain it is that no one entered these solitary precincts except the doctor. The state of things here was puzzling to him. He saw Lord Chetwynde whenever he came, but he never saw Lady Chetwynde. On his asking anxiously about her he was told that she was well. It was surprising to him that she never showed herself, but he attributed it to her grief for the dead. He did not know what had become of Miss Krieff, whose zeal in the sick-room had won his admiration. Lord Chetwynde was too haughty for him to question, and the servants were all new faces. It was therefore with much pleasure that he one day saw Gualtier. Him he accosted, shaking hands with him earnestly, and with a familiarity which he had never cared to bestow in former days. But curiosity was stronger than his sense of personal dignity. Gualtier allowed himself to be questioned, and gave the doctor that information which he judged best for the benefit of the world without. Lady Chetwynde, he told him, was still mourning over the loss of her best friend, and even the return of her husband had not been sufficient to fill the vacant place. Miss Krieff, he said, had gone to join her friends in North Britain, and he, Gualtier, had been appointed steward in place of the former one, who had gone away to London. This information was received by the doctor with great satisfaction, since it set his mind at rest completely about certain things which had puzzled him.

That evening one of the servants informed Gualtier that Lady Chetwynde wished to see him in the library. His pale face flushed up, and his eyes lightened as he walked there. She was alone. He bowed reverentially, yet not before he had cast toward her a look full of unutterable devotion. She was paler than before. There was sadness on her face. She had thrown herself carelessly in an arm-chair, and her hands were nervously clutching one another. Never before had he seen any thing approaching to emotion in this singular being. Her present agitation surprised him, for he had not suspected the possibility of any thing like this.

She returned his greeting with a slight bow, and then fell for a time into a fit of abstraction, during which she did not take any further notice of him. Gualtier was more impressed by this than by any other thing. Always before she had been self-possessed, with all her faculties alive and in full activity. Now she seemed so dull and so changed that he did not know what to think. He began to fear the approach of some calamity by which all his plans would be ruined.

"Mr. M'Kenzie," said Hilda, rousing herself at length, and speaking in a harsh, constrained voice, which yet was low and not audible except to one who was near her, "have you seen Lord Chetwynde since his arrival?"

"No, my lady," said Gualtier, respectfully, yet wondering at the abruptness with which she introduced the subject. For it had always hitherto been her fashion to lead the conversation on by gradual approaches toward the particular thing about which she might wish to make inquiries.

"I thought," she continued, in the same tone, "that he might have called you up to gain information about the condition of the estate."

"No, my lady, he has never shown any such desire. In fact, he does not seem to be conscious that there is such a person as myself in existence."

"Since he came," said Hilda, dreamily, "he has been altogether absorbed in the investigation of papers relating to his father's business affairs; and as he has not been here for many years, during which great changes must have taken place in the condition of things, I did not know but that he might have sought to gain information from you."

"No, my lady," said Gualtier once more, still preserving that unfaltering respect with which he always addressed her, and wondering whither these inquiries might be tending, or what they might mean. That she should ask him any thing about Lord Chetwynde filled him with a vague alarm, and seemed to show that the state of things was unsatisfactory, if not critical. He was longing to ask about that first meeting of hers with Lord Chetwynde, and also about the position which they at present occupied toward one another—a position most perplexing to him, and utterly inexplicable. Yet on such subjects as these he did not dare to speak. He could only hope that she herself would speak of them to him, and that she had chosen this occasion to make a fresh confidence to him.

After his last answer Hilda did not say any thing for some time. Her nervousness seemed to increase. Her hands still clutched one another; and her bosom heaved and fell in quick, rapid breathings which showed the agitation that existed within her.

"Lord Chetwynde," said Hilda at last, rousing herself with a visible effort, and looking round with something of her old stealthy watchfulness—"Lord Chetwynde is a man who keeps his own counsel, and does not choose to give even so much as a hint about the nature of his occupations. He has now some purpose on his mind which he does not choose to confide to me, and I do not know how it is possible for me to find it out. Yet it is a thing which must be of importance, for he is not a man who would stay here so long and labor so hard on a mere trifle. His ostensible occupation is the business of the estate, and certain plans arising in connection with this; but beneath this ostensible occupation there is some purpose which it is impossible for me to fathom. Yet I must find it out, whatever it is, and I have invited you here to see if I could not get your assistance. You once went to work keenly and indefatigably to investigate something for me; and here is an occasion on which, if you feel inclined, you can again exercise your talents. It may result in something of the greatest importance."

Hilda had spoken in low tones, and as she concluded she looked at Gualtier with a penetrating glance. Such a request showed him that he was once more indispensable. His heart beat fast, and his face lighted up with joy.

"My lady," said he, in a low, earnest voice, "it surely can not be necessary for me to tell you that I am always ready to do your bidding, whatever it may be. There is no necessity to remind me of the past. When shall I begin this? At once? Have you formed any plan of action which you would like me to follow?"

"Only in a general way," said Hilda. "It is not at Chetwynde that I want you to work, but elsewhere. You can do nothing here. I myself have already done all that you could possibly do, and more too, in the way of investigation in this house. But in spite of all my efforts I have found nothing, and so I see plainly that the search must be carried on in another place."

"And where may that be?" asked Gualtier.

"He has some purpose in his mind," Hilda went on to say—"some one engrossing object, I know not what, which is far more important than any thing relating to business, and which is his one great aim in life at present. This is what I wish to find out. It may threaten danger, and if so I wish to guard against it."

"Is there any danger?" asked Gualtier, cautiously.

"Not as yet—that is, so far as I can see."

"Does he suspect any thing?" said Gualtier, in a whisper.

"Nothing."

"You seem agitated."

"Never mind what I seem," said Hilda, coldly; "my health is not good. As to Lord Chetwynde, he is going away in a short time, and the place to which he goes will afford the best opportunity for finding out what his purpose is. I wish to know if it is possible for you in any way to follow him so as to watch him. You did something once before that was not more difficult."

Gualtier smiled.

"I think I can promise, my lady," said he, "that I will do all that you desire. I only wish that it was something more difficult, so that I could do the more for you."

"You may get your wish," said Hilda, gloomily, and in a tone that penetrated to the inmost soul of Gualtier. "You may get your wish, and that, too, before long. But at present I only wish you to do this. It is a simple task of watchfulness and patient observation."

"I will do it as no man ever did it before," said Gualtier. "You shall know the events of every hour of his life till he comes back again."

"That will do, then. Be ready to leave whenever he does. Choose your own way of observing him, either openly or secretly; you yourself know best."

Hilda spoke very wearily, and rose to withdraw. As she passed, Gualtier stood looking at her with an imploring face. She carelessly held out her hand. He snatched it in both of his and pressed it to his lips.

"My God!" he cried, "it's like ice! What is the matter?"

Hilda did not seem to hear him, but walked slowly out of the room.

About a week after this Lord Chetwynde took his departure.

CHAPTER XXXIX.

OBED STANDS AT BAY.

On leaving Marseilles all Zillah's troubles seemed to return to her once more. The presence of Windham had dispelled them for a time; now that he was present no longer there was nothing to weigh down any one, and among all her sorrows her latest grief stood pre-eminent. The death of the Earl, the cruel discovery of those papers in her father's drawer by which there seemed to be a stain on her father's memory, the intolerable insult which she had endured in that letter from Guy to his father, the desperate resolution to fly, the anguish which she had endured on Hilda's account, and, finally, the agony of that lone voyage in the drifting schooner —all these now came back to her with fresher violence, recurring again with overpowering force from the fact that they had been kept off so long. Yet there was not one memory among all these which so subdued her as the memory of the parting scene with Windham. This was the great sorrow of her life. Would she ever meet him again? Perhaps not. Or why should she? Of what avail would it be?

Passing over the seas she gave herself up to her recollections, and to the mournful thoughts that crowded in upon her. Among other things, she could not help thinking and wondering about Windham's despair. What was the reason that he had always kept such a close watch over himself? What was the reason why he never ventured to utter in words that which had so often been expressed in his eloquent face? Above all, what was the cause of that despairing cry which had escaped him when they exchanged their last farewell? It was the recognition on his part of some insuperable obstacle that lay between them. That was certain. Yet what could the obstacle be? Clearly, it could not have been the knowledge of her own position. It was perfectly evident that Windham knew nothing whatever about her, and could have not even the faintest idea of the truth. It must therefore be, as she saw it, that this obstacle could only be one which was in connection with himself. And what could that be? Was he a priest under vows of celibacy? She smiled at the preposterous idea. Was he engaged to be married in England, and was he now on the way to his bride? Could this be it? and was his anguish the result of the conflict between love and honor in his breast? This may have been the case. Finally, was he married already? She could not tell. She rather fancied that it was an engagement, not a marriage; and it was in this that she thought she could find the meaning of his passionate and despairing words.

Passing over those waters where once she had known what it was to be betrayed, and had tasted of the bitterness of death, she did not find that they had power to renew the despair which they once had caused. Behind the black memory of that hour of anguish rose up another memory which engrossed all her thoughts. If she had tears, it was for this. It was Windham, whose image filled all her soul, and whose last words echoed through her heart. For as she gazed on these waters it was not of the drifting schooner that she thought, not of the hours of intense watchfulness, not of the hope deferred that gradually turned into despair; it was rather of the man who, as she had often heard since, was the one who first recognized her, and came to her in her senselessness, and bore her in his arms back to life. Had he done well in rescuing her? Had he not saved her for a greater sorrow? Whether he had or not mattered not. He had saved her, and her life was his. That strange rescue constituted a bond between them which could not be dissolved. Their lives might run henceforth in lines which should never meet, but still they belonged henceforth to one another, though they might never possess one another. Out from among these waters there came also sweeter memories—the memories of voyages over calm seas, under the shadow of the hoary Alps, where they passed away those golden hours, knowing that the end must come, yet resolved to enjoy to the full the rapture of the present. These were the thoughts that sustained her. No grief could rob her of these; but in cherishing them her soul found peace.

Those into whose society she had been thrown respected her grief and her reticence. For the first day she had shut herself up in her room; but the confinement became intolerable, and she was forced to go out on deck. She somewhat dreaded lest Obed Chute, out of the very kindness of his heart, would come and try to entertain her. She did not feel in the mood for talking. Any attempt at entertaining her she felt would be unendurable. But she did not know the perfect refinement of sentiment that dwelt beneath the rough exterior of Obed. He seemed at once to divine her state of mind. With the utmost delicacy he found a place for her to sit, but said little or nothing to her, and for all the remainder of the voyage treated her with a silent deference of attention which was most grateful. She knew that he was not neglectful. She saw a hundred times a day that Obed's mind was filled with anxiety about her, and that to minister to her comfort was his one idea. But it was not in words that this was expressed. It was in helping her up and down from the cabin to the deck, in fetching wraps, in speaking a cheerful word from time to time, and, above all, in keeping his family away from her, that he showed his watchful attention. Thus the time passed, and Zillah was left to brood over her griefs, and to conjecture hopelessly and at random about the future. What would that future bring forth? Would the presence of Hilda console her in any way? She did not see how it could. After the first joy of meeting, she felt that she would relapse into her usual sadness. Time only could relieve her, and her only hope was reunion.

At last they landed at Naples. Obed took the party to a handsome house on the Strada Nuova, where he had lodged when he was in Naples before, and where he obtained a suite of apartments in front, which commanded a magnificent view of the bay, with all its unrivaled scenery, together with the tumultuous life of the street below. Here he left them, and departed himself almost immediately to begin his search after Hilda. Her letter mentioned that she was stopping at the "Hôtel de l'Europe," in the Strada Toledo; and to this place he first directed his way.

On arriving here he found a waiter who could speak English, which was a fortunate thing, in his opinion, as he could not speak a word of any other language. He at once asked if a lady by the name of Miss Lorton was stopping here. The waiter looked at him with a peculiar glance, and surveyed him from head to foot. There was something in the expression of his face which appeared very singular to Obed—a mixture of eager curiosity and surprise, which to him, to say the least, seemed uncalled for under the circumstances. He felt indignant at such treatment from a waiter.

"If you will be kind enough to stare less and answer my question," said he, "I will feel obliged; but perhaps you don't understand English."

"I beg pardon," said the other, in very good English; "but what was the name of the lady?"

"Miss Lorton," said Obed.

The waiter looked at him again with the same peculiar glance, and then replied:

"I don't know, but I will ask. Wait here a moment."

Saying this, he departed, and Obed saw him speaking to some half a dozen persons in the hall very earnestly and hurriedly; then he went off, and in about five minutes returned in company with the master of the hotel.

"Were you asking after a lady?" said he, in very fair English, and bowing courteously to Obed.

"I was," said Obed, who noticed at the same time that this man was regarding him with the same expression of eager and scrutinizing curiosity which he had seen on the face of the other.

"And what was the name?"

"Miss Lorton."

"Miss Lorton?" repeated the other; "yes, she is here. Will you be kind enough to follow me to the parlor until I see whether she is at home or not, and make her acquainted with your arrival?"

At this information, which was communicated with extreme politeness, Obed felt such immense relief that he forgot altogether about the very peculiar manner in which he had been scrutinized. A great weight seemed suddenly to have been lifted off his soul. For the first time in many weeks he began to breathe freely. He thought of the joy which he would bring to that poor young girl who had been thrown so strangely under his protection, and who was so sad. For a moment he hesitated whether to wait any longer or not. His first impulse was to hurry away and bring her here; but then in a moment he thought it would be far better to wait, and to take back Miss Lorton with him in triumph to her sister.

The others watched his momentary hesitation with some apparent anxiety; but at length it was dispelled by Obed's reply:

"Thank you. I think I had better wait and see her. I hope I won't be detained long."

"Oh no. She is doubtless in her room. You will only have to wait a few minutes."

Saying this, they led the way to a pleasant

apartment looking out on the Strada Toledo, and here Obed took a seat, and lost himself in speculations as to the appearance of the elder Miss Lorton. In about five minutes the door was opened, and the master of the hotel made his appearance again.

"I find," said he, politely, "that Miss Lorton is not in. She went out only a few minutes before you came. She left word with her maid, however, that she was going to a shop up the Strada Toledo to buy some jewelry. I am going to send a messenger to hasten her return. Shall I send your name by him?"

"Well," said Obed, "I don't know as it's necessary. Better wait till I see her myself."

The landlord said nothing, but looked at him with strange earnestness.

"By-the-way," said Obed, "how is she?"

"She?"

"Yes; Miss Lorton."

"Oh," said the landlord, "very well."

"She recovered from her illness then?"

"Oh yes."

"Is she in good spirits?"

"Good spirits?"

"Yes; is she happy?"

"Oh yes."

"I am glad to hear it. I was afraid she might be melancholy."

"Oh no," said the landlord, with some appearance of confusion; "oh no. She's very well. Oh yes."

His singular behavior again struck Obed rather oddly, and he stared at him for a moment. But he at last thought that the landlord might not know much about the health or the happiness of his guest, and was answering from general impressions.

"I will hasten then, Sir," said the landlord, advancing to the door, "to send the messenger; and if you will be kind enough to wait, she will be here soon."

He bowed, and going out, he shut the door behind him. Obed, who had watched his embarrassment, thought that he heard the key turn. The thing seemed very odd, and he stepped up to the door to try it. It was locked!

"Well, I'll be darned!" cried Obed, standing before the door and regarding it with astonishment. "I've seen some curious foreign fashions, but this here Italian fashion of locking a man in is a little the curiousest. And what in thunder is the meaning of it?"

He looked at the door with a frown, while there was that on his face which showed that he might be deliberating whether to kick through the panels or not. But his momentary indignation soon subsided, and, with a short laugh, he turned away and strolled up to the window with an indifferent expression. There he drew up an arm-chair, and seating himself in this, he looked out into the street. For some time his attention and his thoughts were all engaged by the busy scene; but at length he came to himself, and began to think that it was about time for the return of Miss Lorton. He paced up and down the room impatiently, till growing tired of this rather monotonous employment, he sought the window again. Half an hour had now passed, and Obed's patience was fast failing. Still he waited on, and another half hour passed. Then he deliberated whether it would not be better to go back to his rooms, and bring the younger Miss Lorton here to see her sister. But this thought he soon dismissed. Having waited so long for the sake of carrying out his first plan, it seemed weak to give it up on account of a little impatience. He determined, however, to question the landlord again; so he pulled at the bell.

No answer came.

He pulled again and again for some minutes. Still there was no answer.

He now began to feel indignant, and determined to resort to extreme measures. So going to the door, he rapped upon it with his stick several times, each time waiting for an answer. But no answer came. Then he bent incessantly against the door, keeping up a long, rolling, rattling volley of knocks without stopping, and making noise enough to rouse the whole house, even if every body in the house should happen to be in the deepest of slumbers. Yet even now for some time there was no response; and Obed at length was beginning to think of his first purpose, and preparing to kick through the panels, when his attention was aroused by the sound of heavy footsteps in the hall. They came nearer and nearer as he stood waiting, and at length stopped in front of the door. His only thought was that this was the lady whom he sought; so he stepped back, and hastily composed his face to a pleasant smile of welcome. With this pleasant smile he awaited the opening of the door.

But as the door opened his eyes were greeted by a sight very different from what he anticipated. No graceful lady-like form was there—no elder and maturer likeness of that Miss Lorton whose face was now so familiar to him, and so dear—but a dozen or so gens d'armes, headed by the landlord. The latter entered the room, while the others stood outside in the hall.

"Well," said Obed, angrily. "What is the meaning of this parade? Where is Miss Lorton?"

"These gentlemen," said the landlord, with much politeness, "will convey you to the residence of that charming lady."

"It seems to me," said Obed, sternly, "that you have been humbugging me. Give me a civil answer, or I swear I'll wring your neck. Is Miss Lorton here or not?"

The landlord stepped back hastily a pace or two, and made a motion to the gens d'armes. A half dozen of these filed into the room, and arranged themselves by the windows. The rest remained in the hall.

"What is the meaning of this?" said Obed. "Are you crazy?"

"The meaning is this," said the other, sharply and fiercely. "I am not the landlord of the Hôtel de l'Europe, but sub-agent of the Neapolitan police. And I arrest you in the name of the king."

"Arrest me!" cried Obed. "What the deuce do you mean?"

"It means, Monsieur, that you are trapped at last. I have watched for you for seven weeks, and have got you now. You need not try to resist. That is impossible."

Obed looked round in amazement. What was the meaning of it all? There were the gens d'armes—six in the hall, and six in the room. All were armed. All looked prepared to fall on him at the slightest signal.

"Are you a born fool?" he cried at last, turn-

ing to the "agent." "Do you know what you are doing? I am an American, a native of the great republic, a free man, and a gentleman. What do you mean by this insult, and these beggarly policemen?"

"I mean this," said the other, "that you are my prisoner."

"I am, am I?" said Obed, with a grim smile. "A prisoner! My friend, that is a difficult thing to come to pass without my consent."

And saying this, he quietly drew a revolver from his breast pocket.

"Now," said he, "my good friend, look here. I have this little instrument, and I'm a dead shot. I don't intend to be humbugged. If any one of you dare to make a movement I'll put a bullet through you. And you, you scoundrel, stand where you are, or you'll get the first bullet. You've got hold of the wrong man this time, but I'm going to get satisfaction for this out of your infernal beggarly government. As to you, answer my questions. First, who the deuce do you take me to be? You've made some infernal mistake or other."

The agent cowered beneath the stern eye of Obed. He felt himself covered by his pistol, and did not dare to move. The gens d'armes looked disturbed, but made no effort to interfere. They felt that they had to do with a desperate man, and waited for orders.

"Don't you hear my question?" thundered Obed. "What the deuce is the meaning of this, and who the deuce do you take me for? Don't move," he cried, seeing a faint movement of the agent's hand; "or I'll blow your brains out; I will, by the Eternal!"

"Beware," faltered the agent; "I belong to the police. I am doing my duty."

"Pooh! What is your beggarly police to me, or your beggarly king either, and all his court? There are a couple of Yankee frigates out there that could bring down the whole concern in a half hour's bombardment. You've made a mistake, you poor, pitiful concern; but I'm in search of information, and I'm bound to get it. Answer me now without any more humbugging. What's the meaning of this?"

"I was ordered to watch for any one who might come here and ask for '*Miss Lorton*,'" said the agent, who spoke like a criminal to a judge. "I have watched here for seven weeks. You came to-day, and you are under arrest."

"Ah?" said Obed, as a light began to flash upon him. "Who ordered you to watch?"

"The prefect."

"Do you know any thing about the person whom you were to arrest?"

"No."

"Don't you know his crime?"

"No. It had something to do with the French police."

"Do you know his name?"

"Yes."

"What was it?"

"*Gualtier*," said the agent.

"And you think I am Gualtier?"

"Yes."

"And so there is no such person as Miss Lorton here?"

"No."

"Hasn't she been here at all?"

"No; no such person has ever been here."

"That 'll do," said Obed, gravely, and with some sadness in his face. As he spoke, he put back his revolver into his pocket. "My good friend," said he, "you've made a mistake, and put me to some annoyance, but you've only done your duty. I forgive you. I am not this man Gualtier whom you are after, but I am the man that is after him. Perhaps it would have been better for me to have gone straight to the police when I first came, but I thought I'd find her here. However, I can go there now. I have a message and a letter of introduction to the prefect of police here from the prefect at Marseilles, which I am anxious now to deliver as soon as possible. So, my young friend, I'll go with you after all, and you needn't be in the least afraid of me."

The agent still looked dubious; but Obed, who was in a hurry now, and had got over his indignation, took from his pocket-book some official documents bearing the marks of the French prefecture, and addressed to that of Naples. This satisfied the agent, and, with many apologies, he walked off with Obed down to the door, and there entering a cab, they drove to the prefecture.

CHAPTER XL.

GLIMPSES OF THE TRUTH.

MEANWHILE, during Obed's absence, Zillah remained in the Strada Nuova. The windows looked out upon the street and upon the bay, commanding a view of the most glorious scenery on earth, and also of the most exciting street spectacles which any city can offer. Full of impatience though she was, she could not remain unaffected by that first glimpse of Naples, which she then obtained from those windows by which she was sitting. For what city is like Naples? Beauty, life, laughter, gayety, all have their home here. The air itself is intoxication. The giddy crowds that whirl along in every direction seem to belong to a different and a more joyous race than sorrowing humanity. For ages Naples has been "the captivating," and still she possesses the same charm, and she will possess it for ages yet to come.

The scene upon which Zillah gazed was one which might have brought distraction and alleviation to cares and griefs even heavier than hers. Never had she seen such a sight as this which she now beheld. There before her spread away the deep blue waters of Naples Bay, dotted by the snow-white sails of countless vessels, from the small fishing-boat up to the giant ship of war. On that sparkling bosom of the deep was represented almost every thing that floats, from the light, swift, and curiously rigged lateen sloop, to the modern mail-packet. Turning from the sea the eye might rest upon the surrounding shores, and find there material of even deeper interest. On the right, close by, was the projecting castle, and sweeping beyond this the long curving beach, above which, far away, rose the green trees of the gardens of the Villa Reale. Farther away rose the hills on whose slope stands what is claimed to be the grave of Virgil, whose picturesque monument, whether it be really his or not, suggests his well-known epitaph:

"I sing flocks, tillage, heroes. Mantua gave
Me life; Brundusium death; Naples a grave."

Through those hills runs the Titanic grotto of Posilippo, which leads to that historic land beyond—the land of the Cumæans and Oscans; or, still more, the land of the luxurious Romans of the empire; where Sylla lived, and Cicero loved to retire; which Julius loved, and Horace, and every Roman of taste or refinement. There spread away the lake Lucrine, bordered by the Elysian Fields; there was the long grotto through which Æneas passed; where once the Cumæan Sibyl dwelt and delivered her oracles. There was Misenum, where once the Roman navy rode at anchor; Baiæ, where once all Roman luxury loved to pass the summer season; Puteoli, where St. Paul landed when on his way to Cæsar's throne. There were the waters in which Nero thought to drown Agrippina, and over which another Roman emperor built that colossal bridge which set at defiance the prohibition of nature. There was the rock of Ischia, terminating the line of coast; and out at sea, immediately in front, the isle of Capri, forever associated with the memory of Tiberius, with his deep wiles, his treachery, and his remorseless cruelty. There, too, on the left and nearest Capri, were the shores of Sorrento, that earthly paradise whose trees are always green, whose fruits always ripe; there the cave of Polyphemus penetrates the lofty mountains, and brings back that song of Homer by which it is immortalized. Coming nearer, the eye rested on the winding shores of Castellamare, on vineyards and meadows and orchards, which fill all this glorious land. Nearer yet the scene was dominated by the stupendous form of Vesuvius, at once the glory and the terror of all this scene, from whose summit there never ceases to come that thin line of smoke, the symbol of possible ruin to all who dwell within sight of it. Round it lie the buried cities, whose charred remains have been exhumed to tell what may yet be the fate of those other younger cities which have arisen on their ashes.

While the scene beyond was so enthralling, there was one nearer by which was no less so. This was the street itself, with that wild, never-ending rush of riotous, volatile, multitudinous life, which can be equaled by no other city. There the crowd swept along on horseback, on wheels, on foot; gentlemen riding for pleasure, or dragoons on duty; parties driving into the country; tourists on their way to the environs; market farmers with their rude carts; wine-sellers; fig-dealers; peddlers of oranges, of dates, of anisette, of water, of macaroni. Through the throng innumerable calashes dashed to and fro, crowded down, in true Neapolitan fashion, with inconceivable numbers; for in Naples the calash is not full unless a score or so are in some way clinging to it—above, below, before, behind. There, too, most marked of all, were the lazaroni, whose very existence in Naples is a sign of the ease with which life is sustained in so fair a spot, who are born no one knows where, who live no one knows how, but who secure as much of the joy of life as any other human beings; the strange result of that endless combination of races which have come together in Naples—the Greek, the Italian, the Norman, the Saracen, and Heaven only knows what else.

Such scenes as these, such crowds, such life, such universal movement, for a long time attracted Zillah's attention; and she watched them with childish eagerness. At last, however, the novelty was over, and she began to wonder why Obed Chute had not returned. Looking at her watch, she found, to her amazement, that two hours had passed since his departure. He had left at ten; it was then mid-day. What was keeping him? She had expected him back before half an hour, but he had not yet returned. She had thought that it needed but a journey to the Hôtel de l'Europe to find Hilda, and bring

her here. Anxiety now began to arise in her mind, and the scenes outside lost all charm for her. Her impatience increased till it became intolerable. Miss Chute saw her agitation, and made some attempt to soothe her, but in vain. In fact, by one o'clock, Zillah had given herself up to all sorts of fears. Sometimes she thought that Hilda had grown tired of waiting, and had gone back to England, and was now searching through France and Italy for her; again she thought that perhaps she had experienced a relapse and had died here in Naples, far away from all friends, while she herself was loitering in Marseilles; at another time her fears took a more awful turn—her thoughts turned on Gualtier—and she imagined that he had, perhaps, come on to Naples to deal to Hilda that fate which he had tried to deal to her. These thoughts were all maddening, and filled her with uncontrollable agitation. She felt sure at last that some dread thing had happened, which Obed Chute had discovered, and which he feared to reveal to her. Therefore he kept away; and on no other grounds could she account for his long-continued absence.

Two o'clock passed—and three, and four, and five. The suspense was fearful to Zillah, so fearful, indeed, that at last she felt that it would be a relief to hear any news—even the worst.

At length her suspense was ended. About half past five Obed returned. Anxiety was on his face, and he looked at Zillah with an expression of the deepest pity and commiseration. She on her part advanced to meet him with white lips and trembling frame, and laid on his hand her own, which was like ice.

"You have not found her?" she faltered, in a scarce audible voice.

Obed shook his head.

"She is dead, then!" cried Zillah; "she is dead! She died here—among strangers—in Naples, and I—I delayed in Marseilles!"

A deep groan burst from her, and all the anguish of self-reproach and keen remorse swept over her soul.

Obed Chute looked at her earnestly and mournfully.

"My child," said he, taking her little hand tenderly in both of his—"my poor child—you need not be afraid that your sister is dead. She is alive—as much as you are."

"Alive!" cried Zillah, rousing herself from her despair. "Alive! God be thanked! Have you found out that? But where is she?"

"Whether God is to be thanked or not I do not know," said Obed; "but it's my solemn belief that she is as much alive as she ever was."

"But where is she?" cried Zillah, eagerly. "Have you found out that?"

"It would take a man with a head as long as a horse to tell that," said Obed, sententiously.

"What do you mean? Have you not found out that? How do you know that she is alive? You only hope so—as I do. You do not know so. Oh, do not, do not keep me in suspense."

"I mean," said Obed, slowly and solemnly. "that this sister of yours has never been in Naples; that there is no such steamer in existence as that which she mentions in her letter which you showed me; that there is no such ship, and no such captain, and no such captain's wife, as those which she writes about; that no such person was ever picked up adrift in that way, and brought here, except your own poor innocent, trustful, loving self—you, my poor dear child, who have been betrayed by miserable assassins. And by the Eternal!" cried Obed, with a deeper solemnity in his voice, raising up at the same time his colossal arm and his clenched fist to heaven—"by the Eternal! I swear I'll trace all this out yet, and pay it out in full to these infernal devils!"

"Oh, my God!" cried Zillah. "What do you mean? Do you mean that Hilda has not been here at all?"

"No such person has ever been in Naples."

"Why, was she not picked up adrift? and where could they have taken her?"

"She never was picked up. Rely upon that. No such ship as the one she mentions has ever been here."

"Then she has written down 'Naples' in mistake," cried Zillah, while a shudder passed through her at Obed's frightful insinuation.

"No," said Obed. "She wrote it down deliberately, and wrote it several times. Her repetition of that name, her description of the charms of Naples, show that she did this intentionally. Besides, your envelope has the Naples postage stamps and the Naples post-marks. It was mailed here, whether it was written here or not. It was sent from here to fetch you to this place, on this journey, which resulted as you remember."

"Oh, my God!" cried Zillah, as the full horror of Obed's meaning began to dawn upon her. "What do you mean? What do you mean? Do you wish to drive me to utter despair? Tell me where you have been and what you have done. Oh, my God! Is any new grief coming?"

"My child, the Lord on high knows," said Obed Chute, with solemn emphasis, "that I would cut off my right hand with my own bowie-knife, rather than bring back to you the news I do. But what can be done? It is best for you to know the whole truth, bitter as it is."

"Go on," said Zillah, with an effort to be calm.

"Come," said Obed, and he led her to a seat. "Calm yourself, and prepare for the worst. For at the outset, and by way of preparation and warning, I will say that yours is a little the darkest case that I ever got acquainted with. The worst of it is that there is ever so much behind it all which I don't know any thing about."

Zillah leaned her head upon her hand and looked at him with awful forebodings.

"When I left you," said Obed Chute, "I went at once to the Hôtel de l'Europe, expecting to find her there, or at least to hear of her. I will not relate the particulars of my inquiry there. I will only say that no such person as Miss Lorton had been there. I found, however, that the police had been watching there for seven weeks for Gualtier. I went with them to the Prefecture of Police. I gave my letter of introduction from the prefect of Marseilles, and was treated with the utmost attention. The prefect himself informed me that they had been searching into the whole case for weeks. They had examined all the vessels that had arrived, and had inspected all their logs. They had searched through foreign papers. They had visited every house in the city to which a stranger might go.

The prefect showed me his voluminous reports, and went with me to the Harbor Bureau to show me the names of ships which arrived here and were owned here. Never could there be a more searching investigation than this had been. What was the result?

"Listen," said Obed, with impressive emphasis, yet compassionately, as Zillah hung upon his words. "I will tell you all in brief. First, no such person as Miss Lorton ever came to the Hôtel de l'Europe. Secondly, no such person ever came to Naples at all. Thirdly, no ship arrived here at the date mentioned by your sister. Fourthly, no ship of that name ever came here at all. Fifthly, no ship arrived here at any time this year that had picked up any one at sea. The whole thing is untrue. It is a base fiction made up for some purpose."

"A fiction!" cried Zillah. "Never—never—she could not so deceive me."

"Can the writing be forged?"

"I don't see how it can," said Zillah, piteously. "I know her writing so well," and she drew the letter from her pocket. "See—it is a very peculiar hand—and then, how could any one speak as she does about those things of hers which she wished me to bring? No—it can not be a forgery."

"It is not," said Obed Chute. "It is worse."

"Worse?"

"Yes, worse. If it had been a forgery she would not have been implicated in this. But now she does stand implicated in this horrible betrayal of you."

"Heavens! how terrible! It must be impossible. Oh, Sir! we have lived together and loved one another from childhood. She knows all my heart, as I know hers. How can it be? Perhaps in her confusion she has imagined herself in Naples."

"No," said Obed, sternly. "I have told you about the post-marks."

"Oh, Sir! perhaps her mind was wandering after the suffering of that sea voyage."

"But she never had any voyage," said Obed Chute, grimly. "This letter was written by her somewhere with the intention of making you believe that she was in Naples. It was mailed here. If she had landed in Palermo or any other place you would have had some sign of it. But see—there is not a sign. Nothing but 'Naples' is here, inside and out—nothing but 'Naples;' and she never came to Naples! She wrote this to bring you here."

"Oh, my God! how severely you judge her! You will drive me mad by insinuating such frightful suspicions. How is it possible that one whom I know so well and love so dearly could be such a demon as this? It can not be."

"Listen, my child," said Obed Chute, tenderly. "Strengthen yourself. You have had much to bear in your young life, but this is easier to bear than that was which you must have suffered that morning when you first woke and found the water in your cabin. Tell me—in that hour when you rushed up on deck and saw that you were betrayed—in that hour—did no thought come to your mind that there was some other than Gualtier who brought this upon you?"

Zillah looked at him with a frightened face, and said not a word.

"Better to face the worst. Let the truth be known, and face it, whatever it is. Look, now. She wrote this letter which brought you here—this letter — every word of which is a lie; she it was who sent Gualtier to you to bring you here; she it was who recommended to you that miscreant who betrayed you, on whose tracks the police of France and Italy are already set. How do you suppose she will appear in the eyes of the French police? Guilty, or not guilty?"

Zillah muttered some inarticulate words, and then suddenly gasped out, "But the hat and the basket found by the fishermen?"

"Decoys—common tricks," said Obed Chute, scornfully. "Clumsy enough, but in this case successful."

Zillah groaned, and buried her face in her hands.

A long silence followed.

"My poor child," said Obed Chute at last, "I have been all the day making inquiries every where, and have already engaged the police to search out this mystery. There is one thing yet, however, which I wish to know, and you only can tell it. I am sorry to have to talk in this way, and give you any new troubles, but it is for your sake only, and for your sake there is nothing which I would not do. Will you answer me one question?"

Zillah looked up. Her face had now grown calm. The agitation had passed. The first shock was over, but this calm which followed was the calm of fixed grief—a grief too deep for tears.

"My question is this, and it is a very important one: Do you know, or can you conceive of any motive which could have actuated this person to plot against you in this way?"

"I do not."

"Think."

Zillah thought earnestly. She recalled the past, in which Hilda had always been so devoted; she thought of the dying Earl by whose bedside she had stood so faithfully; she thought of her deep sympathy with her when the writings were found in her father's desk; she thought of that deeper sympathy which she had manifested when Guy's letter was opened; she thought of her noble devotion in giving up all for her and following her into seclusion; she thought of their happy life in that quiet little sea-side cottage. As all these memories rose before her the idea of Hilda being a traitor seemed more impossible than ever. But she no longer uttered any indignant remonstrance.

"I am bewildered," she said. "I can think of nothing but love and fidelity in connection with her. All our lives she has lived with me and loved me. I can not think of any imaginable motive. I can imagine that she, like myself, is the victim of some one else, but not that she can do any thing else than love me."

"Yet she wrote that letter which is the cause of all your grief. Tell me," said he, after a pause, "has she money of her own?"

"Yes—enough for her support."

"Is she your sister?"

Zillah seemed startled.

"I do not wish to intrude into your confidence —I only ask this to gain some light while I am groping in the dark."

"She is not. She is no relation. But she has lived with me all my life, and is the same as a sister."

"Does she treat you as her equal?"

"Yes," said Zillah, with some hesitation, "that is—of late."

"But you have been her superior until of late?"

"Yes."

"Would you have any objection to tell her name?"

"Yes," said Zillah; "I can not tell it. I will tell this much : Lorton is an assumed name. It belongs neither to her nor to me. My name is not Lorton."

"I knew that," said Obed Chute. "I hope you will forgive me. It was not curiosity. I wished to investigate this to the bottom; but I am satisfied—I respect your secret. Will you forgive me for the pain I have caused you?"

Zillah placed her cold hand in his, and said:

"My friend, do not speak so. It hurts me to have you ask my forgiveness."

Obed Chute's face beamed with pleasure.

"My poor child," he said, "you must go and rest yourself. Go and sleep; perhaps you will be better for it."

And Zillah dragged herself out of the room.

CHAPTER XLI.

OBED ON THE RAMPAGE.

A LONG illness was the immediate result of so much excitement, suffering, and grief. Gradually, however, Zillah struggled through it; and at last, under the genial sky of Southern Italy, she began to regain her usual health. The kindness of her friends was unfaltering and incessant. Through this she was saved, and it was Obed's sister who brought her back from the clutches of fever and the jaws of death. She had as tender a heart as her brother, and had come to love as a sister or a daughter this poor, friendless, childlike girl, who had been thrown upon their hands in so extraordinary a manner. Brought up in that puritanical school which is perpetually on the look-out for "special providences," she regarded Zillah's arrival among them as the most marked special providence which she had ever known, and never ceased to affirm that something wonderful was destined to come of all this. Around this faithful, noble-hearted, puritanical dame, Zillah's affections twined themselves with something like filial tenderness, and she learned in the course of her illness to love that simple, straightforward, but high-souled woman, whose love she had already won. Hitherto she had associated the practice of chivalrous principles and the grand code of honor exclusively with lofty gentlemen like the Earl and her father, or with titled dames; now, however, she learned that here, in Obed Chute, there was as fine an instinct of honor, as delicate a sentiment of loyalty to friendship, as refined a spirit of knight-errantry, as strong a zeal to succor the weak and to become the champion of the oppressed, and as profound a loathing for all that is base and mean, as in either of those grand old gentlemen by whom her character had been moulded. Had Obed Chute been born an English lord his manners might have had a finer polish, but no training known among the sons of men could have given him a truer appreciation of all that is noble and honorable and chivalrous. This man, whose life had been passed in what Zillah considered as "vulgar trade," seemed to her to have a nature as pure and as elevated as that of the Chevalier Bayard, that hero *sans peur et sans reproche.*

Obed, as has already been seen, had a weakness for Neapolitan life, and felt in his inmost soul that strange fascination which this city possesses. He had traversed every nook and corner of Naples, and had visited, with a strange mixture of enthusiasm and practical observation, all its environs. In the course of his wanderings he had fallen in with a party of his countrymen, all of whom were kindred spirits, and who hailed his advent among them with universal appreciation. Without in any way neglecting Zillah, he joined himself to these new friends, and accompanied them in many an excursion into the country about Naples—to Capua, to Cumæ, to Pæstum, and to many other places. To some of these places it was dangerous to go in these unsettled times; but this party laughed at dangers. They had acquired a good-natured contempt for Italians and Italian courage; and as each man, in spite of the Neapolitan laws, carried his revolver, they were accustomed to venture any where with the most careless ease, and the most profound indifference to any possible danger. In fact, any approach to danger they would have hailed with joy, and to their adventurous temper the appearance of a gang of bandits would have been the greatest blessing which this land could afford.

The whole country was in a most disturbed condition. The Lombard war had diffused a deep excitement among all classes. Every day new rumors arose, and throughout the Neapolitan dominions the population were filled with strange vague desires. The government itself was demoralized—one day exerting its utmost power in the most repressive measures, and on the next recalling its own acts, and retreating in fear from the position which it had taken up. The troops were as agitated as the people. It was felt that in case of an attempt at revolution they could not be relied upon. In the midst of all other fears one was predominant, and was all comprised in one magic word—the name of that one man who alone, in our age, has shown himself able to draw nations after him, and by the spell of his presence to paralyze the efforts of kings. That one word was "Garibaldi."

What he was, or what he was to do, were things which were but little known to these ignorant Neapolitans. They simply accepted the name as the symbol of some great change by which all were to be benefited. He was, in their thoughts, half hero, half Messiah, before whom all opposing armies should melt away, and by whom all wrongs should be redressed. Through the heart of this agitated mass there penetrated the innumerable ramifications of secret societies, whose agents guided, directed, and intensified the prevalent excitement. These were the men who originated those daily rumors which threw both government and people into a fever of agitation; who taught new hopes and new desires to the most degraded population of Christendom, and inspired even the lazzaroni with wild ideas of human rights—of liberty, fraternity, and equal-

ity. These agents had a far-reaching purpose, and to accomplish this they worked steadily, in all parts and among all classes, until at last the whole state was ripe for some vast revolution. Such was the condition of the people among whom Obed and his friends pursued their pleasures.

The party with which Obed had connected himself was a varied one. There were two officers from those "Yankee frigates" which he had hurled in the teeth of the police agent at the Hôtel de l'Europe; two young fellows fresh from Harvard, and on their way to Heidelberg, who had come direct from New York to Naples, and were in no hurry to leave; a Southerner, fresh from a South Carolina plantation, making his first tour in Europe; a Cincinnati lawyer; and a Boston clergyman traveling for his health, to recruit which he had been sent away by his loving congregation. With all these Obed at once fraternized, and soon became the acknowledged leader, though, as he could not speak Italian, he was compelled to delegate all quarrels with the natives to the two Heidelbergians, who had studied Italian on their way out, and had aired it very extensively since their arrival.

Having exhausted the land excursions, the party obtained a yacht, in which they intended to make the circuit of the bay. On their first voyage they went around its whole extent, and then, rounding the island of Capri, they sailed along the coast to the southeast without any very definite purpose.

The party presented a singular appearance. All were dressed in the most careless manner, consulting convenience without any regard to fashion. The Heidelbergians had made their appearance in red flannel shirts and broad-brimmed felt hats, which excited such admiration that the others at once determined to equal them. Obed, the officers, and the South Carolinian went off, and soon returned with red flannel shirts and wide-awake hats of their own, for which they soon exchanged their more correct costume. The lawyer and the clergyman compromised the matter by donning reefing jackets; and thus the whole party finally set out, and in this attire they made their cruise, with many loud laughs at the strange transformation which a change of dress had made in each other's appearance.

In this way they made the circuit of the bay, and proceeded along the coast until they came opposite to Salerno. It was already four o'clock, and as they could not get back to Naples that day they decided to land at this historic town, with the hope that they might be rewarded by some adventure. The yacht, therefore, was headed toward the town, and flew rapidly over the waves to her destination.

On rounding a headland which lay between them and the town their progress was slow. As they moved toward the harbor they sat lazily watching the white houses as they stretched along the winding beach, and the Boston clergyman, who seemed to be well up in his medieval history, gave them an account of the former glories of this place, when its university was the chief medical school of Europe, and Arabian and Jewish professors taught to Christian students the mysteries of science. With their attention thus divided between the learned dissertation of the clergyman and the charms of the town, they approached their destination.

It was not until they had come quite near that they noticed an unusual crowd along the shore. When they did notice it they at first supposed that it might be one of those innumerable saints' days which are so common in Italy. Now, as they drew nearer, they noticed that the attention of the crowd was turned to themselves. This excited their wonder at first, but after a time they thought that in so dull a place as Salernô the arrival of a yacht was sufficient to excite curiosity, and with this idea many jokes were bandied about. At length they approached the principal wharf of the place, and directed the yacht toward it. As they did so they noticed a universal movement on the part of the crowd, who made a rush toward the wharf, and in a short time filled it completely. Not even the most extravagant ideas of Italian laziness and curiosity could account for this intense interest in the movements of an ordinary yacht; and so our Americans soon found themselves lost in an abyss of wonder.

Why should they be so stared at? Why should the whole population of Salerno thus turn out, and make a wild rush to the wharf at which they were to land? It was strange; it was inexplicable; it was also embarrassing. Not even the strongest curiosity could account for such excitement as this.

"What 'n thunder does it all mean?" said Obed, after a long silence.

"There's something up," said the Cincinnati lawyer, sententiously.

"Perhaps it is a repetition of the landing at Naples on a grander scale," said the clergyman. "I remember when I landed there at least fifty lazaroni followed me to carry my carpet-bag."

"Fifty?" cried one of the Heidelbergians. "Why, there are five hundred after us!"

"But these are not lazaroni," said Obed. "Look at that crowd! Did you ever see a more respectable one?"

In truth, the crowd was in the highest degree respectable. There were some workmen, and some lazaroni. But the greater number consisted of well-dressed people, among whom were intermingled priests and soldiers, and even women. All these, whatever their rank, bore in their faces an expression of the intensest curiosity and interest. The expression was unmistakable, and as the yacht came nearer, those on board were able to see that they were the objects of no common attention. If they had doubted this, this doubt was soon dispelled; for as the yacht grazed the wharf a movement took place among the crowd, and a confused cry of applause arose.

For such a welcome as this the yachting party were certainly not prepared. All looked up in amazement, with the exception of Obed. He alone was found equal to the occasion. Without stopping to consider what the cause of such a reception might be, he was simply conscious of an act of public good-will, and prepared to respond in a fitting manner. He was standing on the prow at the time, and drawing his tall form to its full height, he regarded the crowd for a moment with a benignant smile; after which he removed his hat and bowed with great *empressement*.

At this there arose another shout of applause from the whole crowd, which completed the amazement of the tourists. Meanwhile the yacht swung up close to the wharf, and as there was nothing else to be done they prepared to land, leaving her in charge of her crew, which consisted of several sailors from one of the American frigates. The blue shirts of these fellows formed a pleasing contrast to the red shirts and reefing jackets of the others, and the crowd on the wharf seemed to feel an indiscriminate admiration for the crew as well as for the masters. Such attentions were certainly somewhat embarrassing, and presented to these adventurous spirits a novel kind of difficulty; but whether novel or not, there was now no honorable escape from it, and they had to encounter it boldly by plunging into the midst of the crowd. So they landed—eight as singular figures as ever disturbed the repose of this peaceful town of Salerno. Obed headed the procession, dressed in a red shirt with black trowsers, and a scarf tied round his waist, while a broad-brimmed felt hat shaded his expansive forehead. His tall form, his broad shoulders, his sinewy frame, made him by far the most conspicuous member of this company, and attracted to him the chief admiration of the spectators. Low, murmured words arose as he passed amidst them, expressive of the profound impression which had been produced by the sight of his magnificent physique. After him came the others in Indian file; for the crowd was dense, and only parted sufficiently to allow of the progress of one man at a time. The Southerner came next to Obed, then the Heidelbergians, then the naval officers, while the clergyman and the Cincinnati lawyer, in their picturesque pea-jackets, brought up the rear. Even in a wide-awake American town such a company would have attracted attention; how much more so in this sleepy, secluded, quiet, Italian town! especially at such a time, when all men everywhere were on the look-out for great enterprises.

Obed marched on with his friends till they left the wharf and were able to walk on together more closely. The crowd followed. The Americans took the middle of the street, and walked up into the town through what seemed the principal thoroughfare. The crowd pressed after them, showing no decrease whatever in their ardent curiosity, yet without making any noisy demonstrations. They seemed like men who were possessed by some conviction as to the character of these strangers, and were in full sympathy with them, but were waiting to see what they might *do*. The Americans, on their side, were more and more surprised at every step, and could not imagine any cause whatever for so very singular a reception. They did not even know whether to view it as a hostile demonstration, or as a sort of triumphant reception. They could not imagine what they had done which might merit either the one or the other. All that was left for them to do, therefore, they did; and that means, they accepted the situation, and walked along intent only upon the most prosaic of purposes—the discovery of a hotel. At length, after a few minutes' walk, they found the object of their search in a large stucco edifice which bore the proud title of "Hôtel de l'Univers" in French. Into this they turned, seeking refuge and refreshment. The crowd without respected their seclusion. They did not pour into the hotel and fill it to overflowing from top to bottom, but simply stood outside, in front, in a densely packed mass, from which arose constantly the deep hum of earnest, animated, and eager conversation.

On entering they were accosted by the landlord, who received them with the utmost obsequiousness, and a devotion which was absolute. He informed them that the whole hotel was at their disposal, and wished to know at what time their excellencies would be pleased to dine. Their excellencies informed him, through the medium of the Heidelbergians, that they would be pleased to dine as soon as possible; whereupon the landlord led them to a large upper room and bowed himself out.

Their room looked out upon the street. · There was a balcony in front of the windows; and, as they sat there waiting, they could see the dense crowd as it stood in front of the hotel— quiet, orderly, waiting patiently; yet waiting for what? That was the problem. It was so knotty a problem that it engaged all their thoughts and discussions while they were waiting · for dinner, and while they were eating their dinner. At last that solemn meal was over, and they arose refreshed; but the peaceful satisfaction that generally ensues after such an important meal was now very seriously disturbed, in their case, by the singular nature of their situation. There was the crowd outside still, though it was already dusk.

"I think," said Obed, "that I'll step out and see what is going on. I'll just look around, you know."

Saying this, Obed passed through the open window, and went out on the balcony. His appearance was the cause of an immense sensation. For a moment the crowd was hushed, and a thousand eyes were fixed in awe and admiration upon his colossal form. Then the silence was suddenly broken by loud, long, and wild acclamations, "Viva la Liberta!" "Viva la Republica!" "Viva l'Italia!" "Viva Vittore Emmanuele!" "Viva Garibaldi!"

This last word was caught up with a kind of mad enthusiasm, and passed from mouth to mouth till it drowned all other cries.

"What 'n thunder's all this?" cried Obed, putting his head into the room, and looking at the Heidelbergians. "See here—come out here," he continued, "and find out what in the name of goodness it all means, for I'll be durned if I can make head or tail of it."

At this appeal the Heidelbergians stepped out, and after them came the naval officers, while the rest followed, till the whole eight stood on the balcony.

Their appearance was greeted with a thunder of applause.

Obed knew not what it all meant, nor did any of the others; but as he was the acknowledged leader he felt upon him the responsibility of his situation, and so, with this feeling animating him, he responded to the salutation of the crowd by a low bow.

It was now dusk, and the twilight of this southern climate was rapidly deepening, when suddenly the Americans were aware of a sound in the distance like the galloping of horses. The sound seemed to strike the crowd below at the same moment. Cries arose, and they fell back quickly on either side of the road, leaving a broad path in their midst. The Americans did not have a long time left to them for conjecture or for wonder. The sounds drew nearer and nearer, until at last, through the gloom, a body of dragoons were plainly seen galloping down the street. They dashed through the crowd, they reined in their horses in front of the hotel, and, at the sharp word of command from their leader, a number of them dismounted, and followed him inside, while the rest remained without.

The crowd stood breathless and mute. The Americans saw in this a very singular variation to the events of the evening, and, as they could no more account for this than for those which had preceded it, they waited to see the end. They did not have to wait long.

A noise in the room which they had left roused them. Looking in they saw about a dozen dragoons with the captain and the landlord. The dragoons had arranged themselves in line at the word of command, and the landlord stood with a terror-stricken face beside the captain.

"Ah!" said Obed, who had looked through the window into the room, "this looks serious. There's some absurd mistake somewhere, but just now it does seem as though they want us, so I move that we go in and show ourselves."

Saying this he entered the room, followed by the others, and the eight Americans ranged themselves quietly opposite the dragoons. The sight of these red-shirted strangers produced a very peculiar effect on the soldiers, as was evident by their faces and their looks; and the captain, as he regarded the formidable proportions of Obed, seemed somewhat overawed. But he soon overcame his emotion, and, stepping forward, he exclaimed:

"Siete nostri prigionieri. Rendetevi."

"What's that he says?" asked Obed.

"He says we're his prisoners," said one of the Heidelbergians, "and calls on us to surrender."

"Tell him," said Obed, unconsciously parodying Leonidas—"Tell him to come on and take us."

The Heidelbergian translated this verbatim. The captain looked puzzled.

"Boys," said Obed, "you may as well get your revolvers ready."

At this quiet hint every one of the Americans, including even the Boston clergyman, drew forth his revolver, holding it carelessly, yet in such a very handy fashion that the captain of the dragoons looked aghast.

"I will have no resistance," said he. "Surrender, or you will be shot down."

"Ha, ha!" said the Heidelbergian. "Do you see our revolvers? Do you think that we are the men to surrender?"

"I have fifty dragoons outside," said the officer.

"Very well, we have forty-eight shots to your fifty," said the Heidelbergian, whose Italian, on this occasion, "came out uncommonly strong," as Obed afterward said when the conversation was narrated to him.

"I am commanded to arrest you," said the officer.

"Well, go back and say that you tried, and couldn't do it," said the Heidelbergian.

"Your blood will be on your own heads."

"Pardon me; some of it will be on yours, and some of your own blood also," retorted the Heidelbergian, mildly.

"Advance!" cried the officer to his soldiers. "Arrest these men."

The soldiers looked at their captain, then at the Americans, then at their captain again, then at the Americans, and the end of it was that they did not move.

"Arrest them!" roared the officer.

The Americans stood opposite with their revolvers leveled. The soldiers stood still. They would not obey.

"My friend," said the Heidelbergian, "if your men advance, you yourself will be the first to fall, for I happen to have you covered by my pistol. I may as well tell you that it has six shots, and if the first fails, the second will not."

The officer turned pale. He ordered his men to remain, and went out. After a few moments he returned with twelve more dragoons. The Americans still stood watchful, with their revolvers ready, taking aim.

"You see," cried the officer, excitedly, "that you are overpowered. There are as many men outside. For the last time I call on you to surrender. If you do not I will give no quarter. You need not try to resist."

"What is it that he says?" asked Obed.

The Heidelbergian told him.

Obed laughed.

"Ask him why he does not come and take us," said he, grimly. "We have already given him leave to do so."

The Heidelbergian repeated these words. The captain, in a fury, ordered his men to advance. The Americans fully expected an attack, and stood ready to pour in a volley at the first movement on the part of the enemy. But the enemy did not move. The soldiers stood motionless. They did not seem afraid. They seemed rather as if they were animated by some totally different feeling. It had been whispered already that the Neapolitan army was unreliable. This certainly looked like it.

"Cowards!" cried the captain, who seemed to think that their inaction arose from fear. "You will suffer for this, you scoundrels! Then, if you are afraid to advance, make ready! present! fire!"

His command might as well have been addressed to the winds. The guns of the soldiers stood by their sides. Not one of them raised his piece. The captain was thunder-struck; yet his surprise was not greater than that of the Americans when this was hastily explained to them by the Heidelbergians. Evidently there was disaffection among the soldiers of his Majesty of Naples when brought into the presence of Red Shirts.

The captain was so overwhelmed by this discovery that he stood like one paralyzed, not knowing what to do. This passive disobedience on the part of his men was a thing so unexpected that he was left helpless, without resources.

Meanwhile the crowd outside had been intensely excited. They had witnessed the arrival of the dragoons. They had seen them dismount and enter the hotel after the captain. They had seen the captain come down after another detachment. They had known nothing of what was going on inside, but conjectured that a desperate struggle was inevitable between the Red Shirts and the dragoons. As an unarmed crowd they could offer no active intervention, so they held their peace for a time, waiting in breathless suspense for the result. The result seemed long delayed. The troopers did not seem to gain that immediate victory over the Red Shirts which had been fearfully anticipated. Every moment seemed to postpone such a victory, and render it impossible. Every moment restored the courage of the crowd, which at first had been panic-stricken. Low murmurs passed among them, which deepened into words of remonstrance, and strengthened into cries of sympathy for the Red Shirts; until, at last, these cries arose to shouts, and the shouts arose wild and high, penetrating to that upper room where the assailants confronted their cool antagonists.

The cries had an ominous sound.

"Viva la Liberta!" "Viva la Republica!" "Viva Garibaldi!"

At the name Garibaldi, a wild yell of applause resounded wide and high—a long, shrill yell, and the name was taken up in a kind of mad fervor till the shout rose to a frenzy, and nothing was heard but the confused outcries of a thousand discordant voices, all uttering that one grand name, "Garibaldi!" "Garibaldi!" "Garibaldi!"

The Americans heard it. What connection there was between themselves and Garibaldi they did not then see, but they saw that somehow the people of Salerno had associated them with the hero of Italy, and were sympathizing with them. Obed Chute himself saw this, and understood this, as that cry came thundering to his ears. He turned to his friends.

"Boys," said he, "we came here for a dinner and a night's rest. We've got the dinner, but the night's rest seems to be a little remote. There's such an infernal row going on all around that, if we want to sleep this blessed night, we'll have to take to the yacht again, and turn in there, sailor fashion. So I move that we adjourn to that place, and put out to sea."

His proposal was at once accepted without hesitation.

"Very well," said Obed. "Now follow me. March!"

With his revolver in his extended hand, Obed strode toward the door, followed by the others. The dragoons drew back and allowed them to pass out without resistance. They descended the stairs into the hall. As they appeared at the doorway they were recognized by the crowd, and a wild shout of triumph arose, in which nothing was conspicuous but the name of Garibaldi. The mounted dragoons outside did not attempt to resist them. They looked away, and did not seem to see them at all. The crowd had it all their own way.

Through the crowd Obed advanced, followed by his friends, and led the way toward the yacht. The crowd followed. They cheered; they shouted; they yelled out defiance at the king; they threw aside all restraint, and sang the Italian version of the "Marseillaise." A wild enthusiasm pervaded all, as though some great victory had been won, or some signal triumph achieved. But amidst all their shouts and cries and applause and songs one word was pre-eminent, and that one word was the name of "*Garibaldi!*"

But the Americans made no response. They marched on quietly to their yacht, and pushed off from the wharf. A loud, long cheer followed them from the crowd, which stood there watching their departure; and, as the yacht moved away, cheer after cheer arose, which gradually died away in the distance.

They passed that night on the sea instead of at the hotel at Salerno. But they did not have much sleep. Their wonderful adventure formed the theme of discussion all night long. And at last the only conclusion which they could come to was this, that the red-shirted strangers had been mistaken for Garibaldini; that Obed Chute had been accepted as Garibaldi himself; and, finally, that the subjects of the king of Naples, and his soldiers also, were in a fearful state of disaffection.

Not long after, when Garibaldi himself passed through this very town, the result confirmed the conjectures of these Americans.

CHAPTER XLII.

ANOTHER REVELATION.

TIME passed on, and Zillah once more regained something like her old spring and elasticity; yet the sadness of her situation was noway relaxed. In addition to the griefs of the past, there now arose the problem of the future. What was she to do? Was she to go on thus forever with these kind friends? or was she to leave them? The subject was a painful and a perplexing one, and always brought before her the utter loneliness of her position with the most distressing distinctness. Generally she fought against such feelings, and tried to dismiss such thoughts, but it was difficult to drive them from her mind.

At length it happened that all her funds were exhausted, and she felt the need of a fresh supply. So she conferred with Obed Chute, and told him the name of her London bankers, after which he drew out a check for her for a hundred pounds, which she signed. The draft was then forwarded.

A fortnight passed away. It was during this interval that Obed had his famous Salerno expedition, which he narrated to Zillah on his return, to her immense delight. Never in his life had Obed taken such pleasure in telling a story as on this occasion. Zillah's eager interest, her animated face, her sparkling eyes, all encouraged him to hope that there was yet some spirit left in her in spite of her sorrows; and at length, at the narration of the reception of the Neapolitan's order to surrender, Zillah burst into a fit of laughter that was childish in its *abandon* and heartiness.

About a week or ten days after this, Obed came home one day with a very serious face. Zillah noticed it at once, and asked him anxiously if any thing had happened.

"My poor child," said he, "I'm afraid that there is more trouble in store for you. I feared

as much some time ago, but I had to wait to see if my fears were true."

Zillah regarded him fearfully, not knowing what to think of such an ominous beginning. Her heart told her that it had some reference to Hilda. Had he found out any thing about her? Was she ill? Was she dying? These were her thoughts, but she dared not put them into words.

"I've kept this matter to myself till now," continued Obed; "but I do not intend to keep it from you any longer. I've spoken to sister about it, and she thinks that you'd better know it. At any rate," he added, "it isn't as bad as some things you've borne; only it comes on top of the rest, and seems to make them worse."

Zillah said not a word, but stood awaiting in fear this new blow.

"Your draft," said Obed, "has been returned."

"My draft returned?" said Zillah, in astonishment. "What do you mean?"

"I will tell you all I know," said Obed. "There is villainy at the bottom of this, as you will see. Your draft came back about ten days ago. I said nothing to you about it, but took it upon myself to write for explanations. Last evening I received this"—and he drew a letter from his pocket. "I've meditated over it, and shown it to my sister, and we both think that there are depths to this dark plot against you which none of us as yet have even begun to fathom. I've also forwarded an account of this and a copy of this letter to the police at Marseilles, and to the police here, to assist them in their investigations. I'm afraid the police here won't do much, they're so upset by their panic about Garibaldi."

As Obed ended he handed the letter to Zillah, who opened it without a word, and read as follows:

"LONDON, *September* 10, 1859.

"SIR,—In answer to your favor of 7th instant, we beg leave to state that up to the 15th of June last we held stock and deposits from Miss Ella Lorton—*i. e.*, consols, thirty thousand pounds (£30,000); also cash, twelve hundred and seventy-five pounds.ten shillings (£1275 10s.). On the 15th of June last the above-mentioned Miss Ella Lorton appeared in person, and, with her own check, drew out the cash balance. On the 17th June she came in person and withdrew the stock, in consols, which she had deposited with us, amounting to thirty thousand pounds (£30,000) as aforesaid. That it was Miss Ella Lorton herself there is no doubt; for it was the same lady who deposited the funds, and who has sent checks to us from time to time. The party you speak of, who sent the check from Naples, must be an impostor, and we recommend you to hand her over to the police.

"We have the honor to be, Sir, your most obedient servants, TILTON AND BROWNE.

"OBED CHUTE, Esq."

On reading this Zillah fell back into a chair as though she had been shot, and sat looking at this fatal sheet with wild eyes and haggard face. Obed made an effort to cry for help, but it sounded like a groan. His sister came running in, and seeing Zillah's condition, she took her in her arms.

"Poor child! poor sweet child!" she cried.

"HIS SISTER, SEEING ZILLAH'S CONDITION, TOOK HER IN HER ARMS."

"It's too much! It's too much! She will die if this goes on."

But Zillah rapidly roused herself. It was no soft mood that was over her now; it was not a broken heart that was now threatening her. This letter seemed to throw a flood of light over her dark and mysterious persecution, which in an instant put an end to all those tender longings after her loved Hilda which had consumed her. Now her eyes flashed, and the color which had left her cheeks flushed back again, mounting high with the full sweep of her indignant passion. She started to her feet, her hands clenched, and her brows frowning darkly.

"You are right," she said to Obed, in a low, stern voice. "I am betrayed—and she—*she* *alone* has been my betrayer. She! my sister! the one who lived on my father's bounty; who was my companion in childhood; who shared my bed; who had all my love and trust—she has betrayed me! Ah, well," she added, with a long sigh; "since it is so, it is best for me to know it. Do not be grieved, dear friends. Do not look so sadly and so tenderly at me. I know your loving hearts. You, at least, do not look us though you believed me to be an impostor."

And she held out her hands to the brother and sister. Obed took that little hand which she extended, and pressed it reverently to his lips.

"Sit down, my poor child," said Miss Chute, tenderly. "You are excited. Try to be calm, if you can."

"I am calm, and I will be calm," said Zillah, faintly.

"Come," said Obed. "We will talk no more about it now. To-morrow, or next day, or next week, we will talk about it. You must rest. You must drive out, or sail out, or do something. I'll tell you what I'll do. I'll order the yacht and take you to Salerno."

Zillah looked at him with a faint smile, appreciating his well-meant reference to that famous town, and Obed left her with his sister.

A week passed, and Zillah was not allowed to speak of this subject. But all the time she was oppressed by a sense of her utterly desperate situation. As long as she had believed herself rich she had not felt altogether helpless; but now!—now she found herself a pauper, alone in the wide world, a dependent on the kindness of these noble-hearted friends. What could she do? This could not go on forever. What could she do—she, a girl without resources? How could she ever support herself? What would become of her?

Could she go back to that home from which she had fled? Never! That thought came once, and was instantly scouted as impossible. Sooner than do that she would die of starvation. What, then, could she do? Live on as a burden to these kind friends? Alas! how could she? She thought wildly of being a governess; but what could she tench?—she, who had idled away nearly all her life. Then she thought of trying to get back her money from those who had robbed her. But how could this be done? For, to do this, it would be necessary to obtain the help of Obed Chute; and, in that case, she would have to tell him all. And could she do this? Could she reveal to another the secret sorrow of her life? Could she tell him about their fatal marriage; about the Earl; about Guy's letter, and her flight from home? No; these things were too sacred to be divulged to any one, and the very idea of making them known was intolerable. But if she began to seek after Hilda it would be necessary to tell her true name, at least to Obed Chute, and all about her, a thing which would involve the disclosure of all her secret. It could not be done. Hilda had betrayed her, sought out her life, and robbed her—of this there no longer remained any doubt; and she was helpless; she could neither seek after her rights, nor endeavor to obtain redress for her wrongs.

At length she had a conversation with Obed

Chute about her draft. She told him that when she first went to Tenby her sister had persuaded her to withdraw all her money from her former bankers and deposit it with Messrs. Tilton and Browne. Hilda herself had gone to London to have it done. She told Obed that they were living in seclusion, that Hilda had charge of the finances, and drew all the checks. Of course Messrs. Tilton and Browne had been led to believe that she was the Ella Lorton who had deposited the money. In this way it was easy for her, after getting her sister out of the way, to obtain the money herself.

After Obed Chute heard this he remained silent for a long time.

"My poor child," said he at last, in tones full of pity, "you could not imagine once what motive this Hilda could have for betraying you. Here you have motive enough. It is a very coarse one; but yet men have been betraying one another for less than this since the world began. There was once a certain Judas who carried out a plan of betrayal for a far smaller figure. But tell me. Have you never associated Gualtier and Hilda in your thoughts as partners in this devilish plot?"

"I see now that they must have been," said Zillah. "I can believe nothing else."

"You have said that Gualtier was in attendance on you for years?"

"Yes."

"Did you ever notice any thing like friendship between these two?"

"She always seemed to hold herself so far above him that I do not see how they could have had any understanding."

"Did he seem to speak to her more than to you?"

"Not at all. I never noticed it. He accompanied her to London, though, when she went about the money."

"That looks like confidence. And then she sent him to take you to Naples to put you out of the way?"

Zillah sighed.

"Tell me. Do you think she could have loved Gualtier?"

"It seems absurd. Any thing like love between those two is impossible."

"It's my full and firm conviction," said Obed Chute, after deep thought, "that this Gualtier gained your friend's affections, and he has been the prime mover in this. Both of them must be deep ones, though. Yet I calculate she is only a tool in his hands. Women will do any thing for love. She has sacrificed you to him. It isn't so bad a case as it first looked."

"Not so bad!" said Zillah, in wonder. "What is worse than to betray a friend?"

"When a woman betrays a friend for the sake of a lover she only does what women have been engaged in doing ever since the world began. This Gualtier has betrayed you both—first by winning your friend's love, and then by using her against you. And that is the smart game which he has played so well as to net the handsome figure of £30,000 sterling—one hundred and fifty thousand dollars—besides that balance of £1200 and upward—six thousand dollars more."

Such was Obed Chute's idea, and Zillah accepted it as the only true solution. Any other solution would force her to believe that Hilda had been a hypocrite all her life—that her devotion was a sham, and her love a mockery. Such a thing seemed incredible, and it seemed far more natural to her that Hilda had acted from some mad impulse of love in obedience to the strong temptation held out by a lover. Yes, she thought, she had placed herself in his power, and did whatever he told her, without thinking of the consequences. The plot, then, must be all Gualtier's. Hilda herself never, never, never could have formed such a plan against one who loved her. She could not have known what she was doing. She could not have deliberately sold her life and robbed her. So Zillah tried to think ; but, amidst these thoughts, there arose the memory of that letter from Naples—that picture of the voyage, every word of which showed such devillish ingenuity, and such remorseless pertinacity in deceiving. Love may do much, and tempt to much, she thought ; but, after all, could such a letter have emanated from any one whose heart was not utterly and wholly bad and corrupt? All this was terrible to Zillah.

"If I could but redress your wrongs," said Obed, one day—"if you would only give me permission, I would start to-morrow for England, and I would track this pair of villains till I compelled them to disgorge their plunder, and one of them, at least, should make acquaintance with the prison hulks of Botany Bay. But you will not let me," he added, reproachfully.

Zillah looked at him imploringly.

"I have a secret," said she, "a secret which I dare not divulge. It involves others. I have sacrificed every thing for this. I can not mention it even to you. And now all is lost, and I have nothing. There is no help for it, none." She seemed to be speaking to herself. "For then," she continued, "if they were hunted down, names would come out, and then all would be known. And rather than have all known"—her voice grew higher and sterner as she spoke, expressing a desperate resolve—"rather than have all known, I would die—yes, by a death as terrible as that which stared me in the face when I was drifting in the schooner!"

Obed Chute looked at her. Pity was on his face. He held out his hand and took hers.

"It shall not be known," said he. "Keep your secret. The time will come some day when you will be righted. Trust in God, my child."

The time passed on, but Zillah was now a prey to this new trouble. How could she live? She was penniless. Could she consent to remain thus a burden on kind friends like these? These thoughts agitated her incessantly, preying upon her mind, and never leaving her by night or by day. She was helpless. How could she live? By what means could she hope to get a living?

Her friends saw her melancholy, but attributed it all to the greater sorrows through which she had passed. Obed Chute thought that the best cure was perpetual distraction. So he busied himself with arranging a never-ending series of expeditions to all the charming environs of Naples. Pompeii and Herculaneum opened before them the wonders of the ancient world. Vesuvius was scaled, and its crater revealed its awful depths. Baiæ, Misenum, and Puzzuoli were explored. Pæstum showed them its eternal temples. They lingered on the beach at Salerno. They stood where never-ending spring abides, and never-withering flowers, in the vale of Sorrento—the fairest spot on earth ; best representative of a lost Paradise. They sailed over every part of that glorious bay, where earth and air and sea all combine to bring into one spot all that this world contains of beauty and sublimity, of joyousness and loveliness, of radiance and of delight. Yet still, in spite of all this, the dull weight of melancholy could not be removed, but never ceased to weigh her down.

At length Zillah could control her feelings no longer. One day, softened by the tender sympathy and watchful anxiety of these loving friends, she yielded to the generous promptings of her heart and told them her trouble.

"I am penniless," she said, as she concluded her confession. "You are too generous, and it is your very generosity that makes it bitter for me to be a mere dependent. You are so generous that I will ask you to get me something to do: I know you will. There, I have told you all, and I feel happier already."

As she ended a smile passed over the face of Obed Chute and his sister. The relief which they felt was infinite. And this was all !

"My child," said Obed Chute, tenderly, "there are twenty different things that I can say, each of which would put you perfectly at ease. I will content myself, however, with merely one or two brief remarks. In the first place allow me to state that you are not penniless. Do you think that you are going to lose all your property? No—by the Eternal! no! I, Obed Chute, do declare that I will get it back some day. So dismiss your fears, and dry your tears, as the hymn-book says. Moreover, in the second place, you speak of being a dependent and a burden. I can hardly trust myself to speak in reply to that. I will leave that to sister. For my own part, I will merely say that you are our sunshine—you make our family circle bright as gold. To lose you, my child, would be—well, I won't say what, only when you leave us you may leave an order at the nearest stone-cutter's for a tombstone for Obed Chute."

He smiled as he spoke—his great rugged features all irradiated by a glow of enthusiasm and of happiness.

"But I feel so dependent—such a burden," pleaded Zillah.

"If that is the case," said Obed Chute, "then your feelings shall be consulted. I will employ you. You shall have an honorable position. Among us the best ladies in the land become teachers. President Fillmore's daughter taught a school in New England. It is my purpose now to engage you as governess."

"As governess ?"

"Yes, for my children."

"But I don't know any thing."

"I don't care—I'm going to engage you as governess all the same. Sister teaches them the rudiments. What I want you to teach them is music."

"Music ? I'm such a wretched player."

"You play well enough for me—well enough to teach them ; and the beauty of it is, even if you don't play well now, you soon will. Doesn't Franklin or somebody say that one learns by teaching ?"

Zillah's face spoke unutterable gratitude.

"This," said Obed Chute, "is purely a business transaction. I'll only give you the usual payment—say five hundred dollars a year, and found."

"And—what?"

"Found—that is, board, you know, and clothing, of course, also. Is it a bargain?"

"Oh, my best friend! how can I thank you? What can I say?"

"Say! why, call me again your 'best friend;' that is all the thanks I want."

So the engagement was made, and Zillah became a music-teacher.

CHAPTER XLIII.

THE REPORT.

DURING Lord Chetwynde's absence Hilda received constant communications from Gualtier. He had not very much to tell her, though his watchfulness was incessant. He had contrived to follow Lord Chetwynde to London, under different disguises, and with infinite difficulty; and also to put up at the same house. Lord Chetwynde had not the remotest idea that he was watched, and took no pains to conceal any of his motions. Indeed, to a mind like his, the idea of keeping any thing secret, or of going out of his way to avoid notice, never suggested itself. He was perfectly open and free from disguise. He stopped at the Hastings House, an elegant and quiet hotel, avoided the clubs, and devoted himself altogether to business. At this house Gualtier stopped also, but could find out nothing about Lord Chetwynde's business. He could only learn this much, that Lord Chetwynde went every day, at eleven o'clock, to the office of his solicitors, Messrs. Pendergrast Brothers, with whom he was closeted for an hour or more. Evidently there was some very important business between them; but what that business was, or to whom it might have reference, was a perfect mystery to Gualtier. This was about the sum and substance of the information which his letters conveyed to the anxious Hilda.

For her part, every thing which Gualtier mentioned about Lord Chetwynde was read by her with eager curiosity. She found herself admiring the grand calm of this man whom she loved, this splendid carelessness, this frank and open demeanor. That she herself was cunning and wily, formed no obstacle to her appreciation of frankness in others; perhaps, indeed, the absence of those qualities in herself made her admire them in others, since they were qualities which she could never hope to gain. Whatever his motive or purpose might be, he was now seeking to carry it out in the most open manner, never thinking of concealment. She was working in the dark; he was acting in the broad light of day. Her path, as she looked back upon it, wound on tortuously amidst basenesses and treacheries and crimes; his was straight and clear, like the path of the just man's—not dark, but rather a shining light, where all was open to the gaze of the world. And what communion could there be between one like him and one like her? Could any cunning on her part impose upon him? Could she ever conceal from him

her wily and tortuous nature? Could he not easily discover it? Would not his clear, open, honest eyes see through and through the mask of deceit with which she concealed her true nature? There was something in his gaze which she never could face—something which had a fearful significance to her—something which told her that she was known to him, and that all her character lay open before him, with all its cunning, its craft, its baseness, and its wickedness. No arts or wiles of hers could avail to blind him to these things. This she knew and felt, but still she hoped against hope, and entertained vague expectations of some final understanding between them.

But what was the business on which he was engaged? What was it that thus led him so constantly to his solicitors? This was the problem that puzzled her. Various solutions suggested themselves. One was that he was merely anxious to see about breaking the entail so as to pay her back the money which General Pomeroy had advanced. This he had solemnly promised. Perhaps his long search through his father's papers had reference to this, and his business with his solicitors concerned this, and this only. This seemed natural. But there was also another solution to the problem. It was within the bounds of possibility that he was taking measures for a divorce. How he could obtain one she did not see, but he might be trying to do so. She knew nothing of the divorce law, but had a general idea that nothing except crime or cruelty could avail to break the bonds of marriage. That Lord Chetwynde was fixed in his resolve to break all ties between them was painfully evident to her; and whatever his immediate purpose might now be, she saw plainly that it could only have reference to this separation. It meant that, and nothing else. He abhorred her, and was determined to get rid of her at all hazards. This she plainly saw.

At length, after a few weeks' absence, Gualtier returned. Hilda, full of impatience, sent for him to the morning-room almost as soon as he had arrived, and went there to wait for his appearance. She did not have to wait long. In a few minutes Gualtier made his appearance, obsequious and deferential as usual.

"You are back alone," said she, as she greeted him.

"Yes; Lord Chetwynde is coming back to-morrow or next day, and I thought it better for me to come back first so as to see you before he came."

"Have you found out any thing more?"

"No, my lady. In my letters I explained the nature of the case. I made all the efforts I could to get at the bottom of this business, and to find out what you called the purpose of his life. But you see what insuperable obstacles were in the way. It was absolutely impossible for me to find out any thing in particular about his affairs. I could not possibly gain access to his papers. I tried to gain information from one of the clerks of Pendergrast—formed an acquaintance with him, gave him a dinner, and succeeded in getting him drunk; but even that was of no avail. The fellow was communicative enough, but the trouble was he didn't know any thing himself about this thing, and had no more knowledge of Lord Chetwynde's business or purposes than I myself had. I have done all that was possible for a man in my situation, and grieve deeply that I have nothing more definite to communicate."

"You have done admirably," said Hilda; "nothing more was possible. I only wished you to watch, and you have watched to good purpose. This much is evident, from your reports, that Lord Chetwynde has some all-engrossing purpose. What it is can not be known now, but must be known some day. At present I must be content with the knowledge that this purpose exists."

"I have formed some conjectures," said Gualtier.

"On what grounds? On any other than those which you have made known to me?"

"No. You know all."

"Never mind, then. I also have formed conjectures, and have a larger and broader ground on which to build them. What I want is not conjectures of any kind, but facts. If you have any more facts to communicate, I should like very much to hear them."

"Alas, my lady, I have already communicated to you all the facts that I know."

Hilda was silent for some time.

"You never spoke to Lord Chetwynde, I suppose?" said she at length.

"Oh no, my lady; I did not venture to come into communication with him at all."

"Did he ever see you?"

"He certainly cast his eyes on me, once or twice, but without any recognition in them. I really don't think that he is conscious of the existence of a person like me."

"Don't be too sure of that. Lord Chetwynde is one who can see every thing without appearing to see it. His eye can take in at one glance the minutest details. He is a man who is quite capable of making the discovery that you were the steward of Chetwynde. What measure did you take to avoid discovery?"

Gualtier smiled.

"The measures which I took were such that it would have puzzled Fouché himself to penetrate my disguise. I rode in the same compartment with him, all the way to London, dressed as an elderly widow."

"A widow?"

"Yes; with a thick black veil, and a very large umbrella. It is simply impossible that he could penetrate my disguise, for the veil was too thick to show my features."

"But the hotel?"

"At the hotel I was a Catholic priest, from Novara, on my way to America. I wore spectacles, with dark glasses. No friend could have recognized me, much less a stranger."

"But if you went with the clerks of Pendergrast, that was an odd disguise."

"Oh, when I went with them, I dropped that. I became an American naval officer, belonging to the ship *Niagara*, which was then in London. I wore a heavy beard and mustache, and talked through my nose. Besides, I would drink nothing but whisky and sherry cobblers. My American trip proved highly advantageous."

"And do you feel confident that he has not recognized you?"

"Confident! Recognition was utterly impossible. It would have required my nearest friend

or relative to have recognized me, through such disguises. Besides, my face is one which can very easily be disguised. I have not strongly marked features. My face can easily serve for an Italian priest, or an American naval officer. I am always careful to choose only such parts as nature has adapted me for."

"And Lord Chetwynde is coming back?"

"Yes."

"When?"

"To-morrow, or next day."

"I wonder how long he will stay?"

"That is a thing which no one can find out so well as yourself."

Hilda was silent.

"My lady," said Gualtier, after a long pause.

"Well?"

"You know how ready I am to serve you."

"Yes," said Hilda, dreamily.

"If this man is in your way he can be removed, as others have been removed," said Gualtier, in a low voice. "Some of them have been removed by means of my assistance. Is this man in your way? Is he? Shall I help you? For when he goes away again I can become his valet. I can engage myself, bring good recommendations, and find employment from him, which will bring me into close contact. Then, if you find him in your way, I can remove the obstacle."

Hilda's eyes blazed with a lurid light. She looked at Gualtier like a wrathful demon. The words which she spoke came hissing out, hot and fierce:

"Curse you! You do not know what you are saying. I would rather lose a thousand such as you than lose *him*! I would rather die myself than have one hair of his head injured!"

Gualtier looked at her, transfixed with amazement. Then his head sank down. These words crushed him.

"Can I ever hope for forgiveness?" he faltered at last. "I misunderstood you. I am your slave. I—I only wished to serve you."

Hilda waved her hand.

"You do not understand," said she, as she rose. "Some day you will understand all."

"Then I will wait," said Gualtier, humbly. "I have waited for years. I can still wait. I only live for you. Forgive me."

Hilda looked away, and Gualtier sat, looking thoughtfully and sadly at her.

"There is one thing," said he, "which you were fortunate to think of. You guarded against a danger which I did not anticipate."

"Ah!" said Hilda, roused by the mention of danger. "What is that?"

"The discovery of so humble a person as myself. Thanks to you, my assumed name has saved me. But at the same time it led to an embarrassing position, from which I only escaped by my own wit."

"What do you allude to?" asked Hilda, with languid curiosity.

"Oh, it's the doctor. You know he has been attending Mrs. Hart. Well, some time ago, before I left for London, he met me, and talked about things in general. Whenever he meets me he likes to get up a conversation, and I generally avoid him; but this time I couldn't. After a time, with a great appearance of concern, he said:

"I RODE WITH HIM ALL THE WAY TO LONDON, DRESSED AS AN ELDERLY WIDOW."

" 'I am sorry to hear, Mr. Gualtier, that you are about to be superseded.'

" 'Superseded!' said I. 'What do you mean?'

" 'I hear from some gossip of the servants that there is a new steward.'

" 'A new steward! This is the first that I have heard of it,' said I. 'I am the only steward here.'

" 'This one,' said he, 'is—a—Mr. M'Kenzie.'

" 'M'Kenzie!' said I, instantaneously—

'M'Kenzie!' And I laughed. 'Why, I am Mr. M'Kenzie.'

"'You!' said he, in utter amazement. 'Isn't your name Gualtier?'

"'Oh no,' said I; 'that is a name which I adopted, when a music-teacher, for professional purposes. Foreign names are always liked better than native ones. My real name is M'Kenzie. The late Earl knew all about it, and so does Lady Chetwynde.'

"The doctor looked a little puzzled, but at last accepted my explanation and went off. Still I don't like the look of the thing."

"No," said Hilda, who had listened with no great interest, "it's not pleasant. But, after all, there was no danger even if he had thought you an impostor."

"Pardon me, my lady; but doctors are great gossips, and can send a story like this flying through the county. He may do so yet."

At another time Hilda would have taken more interest in this narration, but now she seemed so preoccupied that her usual vigilance had left her. Gualtier noticed this, but was scarcely surprised. It was only a fresh proof of her infatuation.

So after a few moments of silent thoughtfulness he left the room.

CHAPTER XLIV.

A STRANGE ENCOUNTER.

On the day after Gualtier's interview with Hilda, Lord Chetwynde was still in London, occupied with the business which had brought him there. It was between ten and eleven in the morning, and he was walking down Piccadilly on his way to the City, where he had an appointment with his solicitors. He was very much preoccupied, and scarcely noticed any thing around him. Walking on in this mood he felt his arm seized by some one who had come up behind him, and a voice exclaimed:

"Windham! by all that's great! How are you, old fellow?" and before he had time to recover from his surprise, his hand was seized, appropriated, and nearly wrung off by Obed Chute.

To meet Obed Chute thus in London was certainly strange, yet not so very much so, after all. London is vast, multitudinous, enormous—a nation rather than a city, as De Quincey well remarks—a place where one may hide and never be discovered; yet after all there are certain streets where strangers are most frequent, and that two strangers should meet one another here in one of these few thoroughfares is more common than one would suppose. After the first surprise at such a sudden greeting Windham felt it to be a very natural thing for Obed Chute to be in London, and evinced as much pleasure at meeting him as was shown by the other.

"Have you been here ever since your return to England?" he asked.

"Oh no," said Windham, "I've only been here a short time, and I have to leave this afternoon."

"I'm sorry for that; I should like to see you —but I suppose it can't be helped; and then I must go back immediately."

"Ah! You are on your way to America, then?"

"America! Oh no. I mean—go back to Italy."

"Italy?"

"Yes; we're all there yet."

"I hope Miss Chute and your family are all well?" said Lord Chetwynde, politely.

"Never better," said Obed.

"Where are you staying now?"

"In Naples."

"It's a very pleasant place."

"Too pleasant to leave."

"By-the-way," said Lord Chetwynde, after a pause, and speaking with assumed indifference, "were you ever able to find out any thing about —Miss Lorton?"

His indifference was but poorly carried out. At the mention of that name he stammered, and then stopped short.

But Obed did not notice any peculiarity. He answered, quickly and earnestly:

"It's that very thing, Windham, that has brought me here. I've left her in Naples."

"What?" cried Lord Chetwynde, eagerly; "she is with you yet, then?"

"Yes."

"In Naples?"

"Yes—with my family. Poor little thing! Windham, I have a story to tell about her that will make your heart bleed, if you have the heart of a man."

"My God!" cried Lord Chetwynde, in deep emotion; "what is it? Has any thing new happened?"

"Yes, something new—something worse than before."

"But she—she is alive—is she not—she is well—she—"

"Thank God, yes," said Obed, not noticing the intense emotion of the other; "yes—she has suffered, poor little girl, but she is getting over it—and one day I hope she may find some kind of comfort. But at present, and for some time to come, I'm afraid that any thing like happiness or peace or comfort will be impossible for her."

"Is she very sad?" asked Lord Chetwynde, in a voice which was tremulous from suppressed agitation.

"The poor child bears up wonderfully, and struggles hard to make us think that she is cheerful; but any one who watches her can easily see that she has some deep-seated grief, which, in spite of all our care, may even yet wear away her young life. Windham, I've heard of cases of a broken heart. I think I once in my life saw a case of that kind, and I'm afraid that this case will—will come at last to be classed in that list."

Lord Chetwynde said nothing. He had nothing to say—he had nothing to do. His face in the few moments of this conversation had grown ghastly white, his eyes were fixed on vacancy, and an expression of intense pain spread over his features. He walked along by Obed Chute's side with the uncertain step of one who walks in a dream.

Obed said nothing for some time. His own thoughts were reverting to that young girl whom he had left in Naples buried under a mountain of woe. Could he ever draw her forth from that overwhelming grief which pressed her down?

They went on together through several streets without any particular intention, each one occupied with his own thoughts, until at last they found themselves at St. James's Park. Here they entered, and walked along one of the chief avenues.

"You remember, Windham," said Obed at last—"of course you have not forgotten the story which Miss Lorton told about her betrayal."

Lord Chetwynde bowed, without trusting himself to speak.

"And you remember the villain's name, too, of course."

"Yes—Gualtier," said Lord Chetwynde.

"I put the case in the hands of the Marseilles police, and you know that up to the time when we left nothing had been done. Nothing has been done since of any consequence. On my way here I stopped at Marseilles, and found that the police had been completely baffled, and had found no trace whatever either of Gualtier or of the maid Mathilde. When I arrived at Marseilles I found that the police there had been on the look-out for that man for seven weeks, but in spite of the most minute inquiry, and the most vigilant watchfulness, they had seen no sign of any such person. The conclusion that I have come to is that he never went to Naples—at least not after his crime. Nor, on the other hand, is it likely that he remained in France. The only thing that I can think of is that both he and the maid Mathilde went back to England."

"There is Germany," said Lord Chetwynde, who had not lost a word, "or the other states of Italy. Florence is a pleasant place to go to. Above all, there is America—the common land of refuge to all who have to fly from the Old World."

"Yes, all that is true—very true. It may be so; but I have an idea that the man may still be in England, and I have some hope of getting on his track now. But this is not the immediate purpose of my coming. That was caused by a discovery of new features in this dark case, which show a deliberate plan on the part of Gualtier and others to destroy Miss Lorton so as to get her money."

"Have you found out any thing else? Has any fresh calamity fallen upon that innocent head?" asked Lord Chetwynde, in breathless anxiety. "At any rate, it can not be so bad as what she has already suffered."

"In one sense it is not so bad, but in another sense it is worse."

"How?"

"Why, it is not so bad, for it only concerns the loss of money; but then, again, it is far worse, for"—and Obed's voice dropped low—"for it shows her that there is an accomplice of Gualtier's, who has joined with him in this crime, and been a principal in it, and this accomplice is—her sister!"

"Great God!" cried Lord Chetwynde, aghast. "Her sister?"

"Her sister," said Obed, who did not, as yet, think it necessary to tell what Zillah had revealed to him in confidence about their not being sisters.

Lord Chetwynde seemed overwhelmed.

Obed then began and detailed to him every circumstance of the affair of the draft, to all of which the other listened with rapt attention. A long discussion followed this revelation. Lord Chetwynde could not help seeing that Miss Lorton had been betrayed by her sister as well as by Gualtier, and felt painfully affected by the cold-blooded cruelty with which the abstraction of the money was managed. To him this "Ella Lorton" seemed wronged as no one had ever been wronged before, and his heart burned to assist Obed Chute in his work of vengeance.

He said as much. "But I fear," he added, "that there is not much chance. At any rate, it will be a work of years; and long before then, in fact, before many weeks, I expect to be on my way back to India. As to this wretched, this guilty pair, it is my opinion that they have fled to America. Hilda Lorton can not be old in crime, and her first instinct would be to fly from England. If you ever find those wretches, it will be there."

"I dare say you are right," said Obed. "But," he added, in tones of grim determination, "if it takes years to find this out, I am ready. I am willing to spend years in the search. The police of Italy and of France are already on the track of this affair. It is my intention to direct the London police to the same game, and on my way back I'll give notice at Berlin and Vienna, so as to set the Prussian and Austrian authorities to work. If all these combined can't do any thing, then I'll begin to think that these devils are not in Europe. If they are in America, I know a dozen New York detectives that can do something in the way of finding out even more artful scoundrels than these. For my own part, if, after ten years of incessant labor, any light is thrown on this, I shall be fully rewarded. I'd spend twice the time if I had it for her, the poor little thing!"

Obed spoke like a tender, pitying father, and his tones vibrated to the heart of Lord Chetwynde.

For a time he was the subject of a mighty struggle. The deepest feelings of his nature were all concerned here. Might he not now make this the object of his life—to give up every thing, and search out these infernal criminals, and avenge that fair girl whose image had been fixed so deeply on his heart? But, then, he feared this task. Already she had chained him to Marseilles, and still he looked back with anguish upon the horror of that last parting with her. All his nature yearned and longed to feel once more the sunshine of her presence; but, on account of the very intensity of that longing, the dictates of honor and duty bade him resist the impulse. The very tenderness of his love—its all-consuming ardor—those very things which impelled him to espouse her cause and fight her battles and win her gratitude, at the very same time held him back and bade him avoid her, and tear her image from his heart. For who was he, and what was he, that he should yield to this overmastering spell which had been thrown over him by the witchery of this young girl? *Had he not his wife?* Was she not at Chetwynde Castle? That odious wife, forced on him in his boyhood, long since grown abhorrent, and now standing up, an impassable barrier between him and the dearest longings of his heart. So he crushed down desire; and, while assenting to Obed's plans, made no proposal to assist him in any way in their accomplishment.

At the end of about two hours Obed announced his intentions at present. He had come first and more especially to see Messrs. Tilton and Browne, with a hope that he might be able to trace the affair back far enough to reach Hilda Lorton; and secondly, to set the London police to work.

"Will you make any stay?" asked Lord Chetwynde.

"No, not more than I can help. I can find out soon whether my designs are practicable or not. If they can not be immediately followed out, I will leave it to the police, who can do far better than me, and go back to Naples. Miss Lorton is better there, and I feel like traveling about Italy till she has recovered. I see that the country is better for her than all the doctors and medicines in the world. A sail round Naples Bay may rouse her from the deepest melancholy. She has set her heart on visiting Rome and Florence. So I must go back to my little girl, you see."

"Those names," said Lord Chetwynde, calmly, and without exhibiting any signs of the emotion which the allusion to that "little girl" caused in his heart—"those names ought certainly to be traceable—'Hilda Lorton,' 'Ella Lorton.' The names are neither vulgar nor common. A properly organized effort ought to result in some discovery. 'Hilda Lorton,' 'Ella Lorton,'" he repeated, "'Hilda,' 'Ella'—not very common names—'Hilda,' 'Ella.'"

He repeated these names thus over and over, but the names gave no hint to the speaker of the dark, deep mystery which lay beneath. As for Obed, he knew that Hilda was not Hilda Lorton, and that a search after any one by that name would be useless. Zillah had told him that she was not her sister. At length the two friends separated, Lord Chetwynde saying that he would remain in London till the following day, and call on Obed at his hotel that evening to learn the result of his labors. With this each went about his own business; but into the mind of Lord Chetwynde there came a fresh anxiety, which made him have vague desires of flying away forever—off to India, to Australia—any where from the power of his overmastering, his hopeless love. And amidst all this there came a deep longing to go to Italy—to Naples, to give up every thing—to go back with Obed Chute. It needed all the strength of his nature to resist this impulse, and even when it was overcome it was only for a time. His business that day was neglected, and he waited impatiently for the evening.

Evening came at last, and Lord Chetwynde went to Obed's hotel. He found his friend there, looking somewhat dejected.

"I suppose you have accomplished nothing," he said. "I see it in your face."

"You're about right," said Obed. "I'm going back to Naples to-morrow."

"You've failed utterly, then?"

"Yes, in all that I hoped. But still I have done what I could to put things on the right track."

"What have you done?"

"Well, I went first to Tilton and Browne. One of my own London agents accompanied me there, and introduced me. They were at once very eager to do all that they could for me. But I soon found out that nothing could be done. That girl—Windham—that girl," repeated Obed, with solemn emphasis, "is a little the deepest party that it's ever been my lot to come across. How any one brought up with my little girl" (this was the name that Obed loved to give to Zillah) "could develop such superhuman villainy, and such cool, calculating, far-reaching craft, is more than I can understand. She knocks me, I confess. But, then, the plan may all be the work of Gualtier."

"Why, what new thing have you found out?"

"Oh, nothing exactly new; only this, that the deposit of Miss Lorton's funds and the withdrawal, which were all done by her in Miss Lorton's name and person, were managed so cleverly that there is not the slightest ghost of a clew by which either she or the money can be traced. She drew the funds from one banker and deposited them with another. I thought I should be able to find out the banker from whom they were drawn, but it is impossible. Before I came here I had written to Tilton and Browne, and they had made inquiries from all the London bankers, but not one of them had any acquaintance whatever with that name. It must have been some provincial bank, but which one can not be known. The funds which she deposited were in Bank of England notes, and these, as well as the consols, gave no indication of their last place of deposit. It was cleverly managed, and I think the actors in this affair understand too well their business to leave a single mark on their trail. The account had only been with Tilton and Browne for a short time, and they could not give me the slightest assistance. And so I failed there completely.

"I then went to the police, and stated my case. The prefect at Marseilles had already been in communication with them about it. They had made inquiries at all the schools and seminaries, had searched the directories, and every thing else of that kind, but could find no music-teacher mentioned by the name of Gualtier. They took it for granted that the name was an assumed one. They had also investigated the name 'Lorton,' and had found one or two old county families; but these knew nothing of the young ladies in question. They promised to continue their search, and communicate to me any thing that might be discovered. There the matter rests now, and there I suppose it must rest until something is done by somebody. When I have started the Austrian and Prussian police on the same scent I will feel that nothing more can be done in Europe. I suppose it is no use to go to Spain or Russia or Turkey. By-the-way, there is Belgium. I mustn't forget that."

It was only by the strongest effort that Lord Chetwynde was able to conceal the intensity of his interest in Obed's revelations. All that day his own business had been utterly forgotten, and all his thoughts had been occupied with Zillah and her mysterious sorrows. When he left Marseilles he had sought to throw away all concern for her affairs, and devote himself to the Chetwynde business. But Obed's appearance had brought back before him in fresh strength all his memories of Zillah, and the darker color which her tragedy assumed excited the deepest feelings of his nature. He struggled against this in vain, and his future plans took a coloring from this, which afterward resulted in very important events.

The two friends talked over this matter, in which both were so deeply interested, far into the hours of the morning, and at length they bade each other good-by. On the following day Obed was to go to Naples, and Lord Chetwynde back to the Castle.

CHAPTER XLV.

ANOTHER EFFORT.

THE words of Hilda produced a deeper effect upon Gualtier than she could have imagined. Accustomed to rule him and to have her words received and her commands obeyed without remonstrance, she had grown to think that those words of hers were all-sufficient by themselves, and needed no explanation. She did not make allowance for the feelings, the thoughts, and, above all, for the passions of one like Gualtier. She was taken up with her own plans, her cares, her desires, and her purposes. He, on his part, was absorbed in one desire, and all that desire was centered upon the one who held herself so grandly aloof from him, using him as her tool, but never deigning to grant him any thing more than some slight word or act of kindness. Her last words had sunk deep into his soul. They revealed to him the true condition of things. He learned now, for the first time, that she loved Lord Chetwynde, and was anxious to gain his love in return. Lord Chetwynde, he saw, was not an obstacle to be removed from her path, but rather an object of yearning desire, which was to be won for herself. He saw that she wished to be in reality that which she was now only in name, and that falsely — namely, Lady Chetwynde. To a mind like his such a discovery was bitter indeed. All the vengeful feelings that lay dormant within him were aroused, and henceforth all the hate which he was capable of feeling was turned toward this man, who had so easily gained for himself that love for which he had labored so long, so arduously, and yet so vainly. Had he not devoted years to the task of acquiring that love? Had he not labored with patience and unfaltering devotion? Had he not endured slights and insults without number? Had he not crossed the ocean in her service in search of information which she wished to gain? And for all this what reward had he received? Nothing more than a cold smile. But here came this man who was at once a stranger and an enemy—a man who abhorred her, a man whom she ought to hate, on whom she had wrought fearful injuries; and lo, instead of hating, she loved him in a moment! Bitter indeed were the thoughts of Gualtier as these things came to his mind. Scorn for himself, or slights, or indifference, he might have borne in patient waiting; but when the one who showed this indifference and this scorn proved eager to sacrifice him, herself, and every thing else to the man whom she ought to hate, then his position became intolerable—unendurable. The dislike which he had felt toward Lord Chetwynde soon grew to bitter hate, and the hate rapidly became so strong that nothing but implacable vengeance would appease it.

Two or three days after Gualtier's arrival Lord Chetwynde returned. His return was quiet and undemonstrative. The servants greeted their master with the usual respectful welcome, but he took no notice of them. He went to the library, to which his portmanteau was carried, and after remaining there a few moments he went to Mrs. Hart's room. The housekeeper was there.

"How has she been ?" he asked.

"Very much better."

"Is she conscious ?"

"Not yet, altogether, but she is beginning to be."

"What does the doctor say ?"

"He has great hopes, he says; and he tells me that unremitting care may yet bring her around. He seems to be very hopeful."

"You have attended her, I hope, as I directed."

"Yes, my lord. I have devoted most of my time to her. I have neglected the house for her sake. I told Lady Chetwynde that Mrs. Hart depended upon me, and that I would nurse her."

"That was not necessary. She might be displeased if the house were neglected."

"Oh no, my lord. She showed the strongest interest in Mrs. Hart, and I have to bring her reports of the doctor's opinions every day."

"Ah! well. I am glad that you have been so attentive. You must continue to do so. Devote yourself chiefly to her. It is my will. If you get into any trouble while I am away, let me know, will you ? I have given you my address, and any letter from you will reach me there."

"Yes, my lord."

Lord Chetwynde then returned to the library, and to his business.

Yes. It was true that Mrs. Hart was recovering. She had come out of that deep stupor in which she had lain so long. The assiduous attentions which she had received were chiefly the cause of this. Hilda had heard of this, and was greatly troubled. In Mrs. Hart's recovery she saw one great danger, yet it was a danger which she felt herself powerless to avert. The housekeeper had been engaged now in this new duty directly by Lord Chetwynde, and in her present position she did not dare to remonstrate. She thought that Lord Chetwynde either understood her, or at least suspected her; and believed that any act of hers which might lead to the delay of Mrs. Hart's recovery would be punished by him with implacable vengeance. In this delicate position, therefore, she found that the only possible course open to her was to wait patiently on her opportunities. If the worst came to the worst, and Mrs. Hart recovered, her only resource would be to leave Chetwynde for a time at least. For such a step she had prepared herself, and for it she had every excuse. Lord Chetwynde, at least, could neither blame her nor suspect her if she did so. She could retire quietly to Pomeroy Court, and there await the issue of events. Such a step in itself was not unpleasant, and she would have carried it into execution long ago had it not been for the power which Lord Chetwynde exerted over her. It was this, and this only, which forced her to stay.

Gualtier also was not unmindful of this. On the day of his arrival he had learned that Mrs. Hart was recovering and might soon be well. He understood perfectly all that was involved in her recovery, and the danger that might attend upon it. For Mrs. Hart would at once recognize Hilda, and ask after Zillah. There was now no chance to do any thing. Lord Chetwynde watched over her as a son might watch over a mother. These two thus stood before him as a standing menace, an ever-threatening danger in that path from which other dangers had been removed at such a hazard and at such a cost. What could he do? Nothing. It was for Hilda to act in this emergency. He himself was powerless. He feared also that Hilda herself did not realize the full extent of her danger. He saw how abstracted she had become, and how she was engrossed by this new and unlooked-for feeling which had taken full possession of her heart. One thing alone was possible to him, and that was to warn Hilda. Perhaps she knew the danger, and was indifferent to it; perhaps she was not at all aware of it; in any case, a timely warning could not possibly do any harm, and might do a great deal of good. Under these circumstances he wrote a few words, which he contrived to place in her hands on the morning when Lord Chetwynde arrived. The words were these:

"*Mrs. Hart is recovering, and the doctor hopes that she will soon be entirely well.*"

Hilda read these words gloomily, but nothing could be done except what she had already decided to do. She burned the note, and returned to her usual meditations. The arrival of Lord Chetwynde soon drove every thing else out of her mind, and she waited eagerly for the time for dinner, when she might see him, hear his voice, and feast her eyes upon his face.

On descending into the dining-room she found Lord Chetwynde already there. Without a thought of former slights, but following only the instincts of her own heart, which in its ardent passion was now filled with joy at the sight of him, she advanced toward him with extended hand. She did not say a word. She could not speak. Her emotion overpowered her. She could only extend her hand and look up into his face imploringly.

Lord Chetwynde stood before her, cold, reserved, with a lofty hauteur on his brow, and a coldness in his face which might have repelled any one less impassioned. But Hilda was desperate. She had resolved to make this last trial, and stake every thing upon this. Regardless, therefore, of the repellent expression of his face, and the coldness which was manifested in every lineament, she determined to force a greeting from him. It was with this resolve that she held out her hand and advanced toward him.

But Lord Chetwynde stood unmoved. His hands hung down. He looked at her calmly, yet coldly, without anger, yet without feeling of any kind. As she approached he bowed.

"You will not even shake hands with me?" faltered Hilda, in a stammering voice.

"Of what avail would that be?" said Lord Chetwynde. "You and I are forever separate. We must stand apart forever. Why pretend to a friendship which does not exist? I am not your friend, Lady Chetwynde."

Hilda was silent. Her hand fell by her side. She shrank back into herself. Her disappointment deepened into sadness unutterable, a sadness that was too profound for anger, a sadness beyond words. So the dinner passed on. Lord Chetwynde was calm, stern, fixed in his feelings and in his purpose. Hilda was despairing, and voiceless in that despair. For the first time she began to feel that all was lost.

───────

CHAPTER XLVI.

THE TABLES TURNED.

LORD CHETWYNDE had the satisfaction of seeing that Mrs. Hart recovered steadily. Day after day she improved, and at length became conscious of surrounding objects. After having gained consciousness her recovery became more rapid, and she was at length strong enough for him to visit her. The housekeeper prepared her for the visit, so that the shock might not be too great. To her surprise she found that the idea of his presence in the same house had a better effect on her than all the medicines which she had taken, and all the care which she had received. She said not a word, but lay quiet with a smile upon her face, as one who is awaiting the arrival of some sure and certain bliss. It was this expression which was on her face when Lord Chetwynde entered. She lay back with her face turned toward the door, and with all that wistful yet happy expectancy which has been mentioned. He walked up to her, took her thin, emaciated hands in his, and kissed her pale forehead.

"My own dear old nurse," he said, "how glad I am to find you so much better!"

Tears came to Mrs. Hart's eyes. "My boy!" she cried—"my dearest boy, the sight of you gives me life!" Sobs choked her utterance. She lay there clasping his hand in both of hers, and wept.

Mrs. Hart had already learned from the housekeeper that she had been ill for many months, and her own memory, as it gradually rallied from the shock and collected its scattered energies, brought back before her the cause of her illness. Had her recovery taken place at any other time, her grief might have caused a relapse; but now she learned that Lord Chetwynde was here watching over her—"her boy," "her darling," "her Guy"—and this was enough to counterbalance the grief which she might have felt. So now she lay holding his hand in hers, gazing up into his face with an expression of blissful contentment and of perfect peace; feeding all her soul in that gaze, drawing from him new strength at every glance, and murmuring words of fondest love and endearment. As he sat there the sternness of Lord Chetwynde's features relaxed, the eyes softened into love and pity, the hard lines about the mouth died away. He seemed to feel himself a boy again, as he once more held that hand which had guided his boyhood's years.

He staid there for hours. Mrs. Hart would not let him go, and he did not care to do violence to her affections by tearing himself away. She seemed to cling to him as though he were the only living being on whom her affections were fixed. He took to himself all the love of this poor, weak, fond creature, and felt a strange pleasure in it. She on her part seemed to acquire new strength from his presence.

"I'm afraid, my dear nurse," said he, "that I am fatiguing you. I will leave you now and come back again."

"No, no," said Mrs. Hart, earnestly; "do not leave me. You will leave me soon enough. Do not desert me now, my own boy—my sweet child—stay by me."

"But all this fatigues you."

"No, my dearest—it gives me new strength—such strength as I have not known for a long time. If you leave me I shall sink back again into weakness. Do not forsake me."

So Lord Chetwynde staid, and Mrs. Hart made him tell her all about what he had been doing during the years of his absence. Hours passed away in this conversation. And he saw, and wondered as he saw it, that Mrs. Hart grew stronger every moment. It seemed as if his presence brought to her life and joy and strength. He laughingly mentioned this.

"Yes, my dearest," said Mrs. Hart, "you are right. You bring me new-life. You come to me like some strong angel, and bid me live. I dare say I have something to live for, though what it is I can not tell. Since he has gone I do not see what there is for me to do, or why it should be that I should linger on in life, unless it may be for you."

"For me—yes, my dear nurse," said Lord Chetwynde, fondly kissing her pale brow—"yes, it must be for me. Live, then, for me."

"You have others who love you and live for you," said Mrs. Hart, mournfully. "You don't need your poor old nurse now." ·

Lord Chetwynde shook his head.

"No others can supply your place," said he. "You will always be my own dear old nurse."

Mrs. Hart looked up with a smile of ecstasy.

"I am going away," said Lord Chetwynde, after some further conversation, "in a few days, and I do not know when I will be back, but I want you, for my sake, to try and be cheerful, so as to get well as soon as possible."

"Going away!" gasped Mrs. Hart, in strong surprise. "Where to?"

"To Italy. To Florence," said Lord Chetwynde.

"To Florence?" .

"Yes." ›

"Why do you leave Chetwynde?"

"I have some business," said he, "of a most important kind; so important that I must leave every thing and go away."

"Is your wife going with you?"

"No—she will remain here," said Lord Chetwynde, dryly.

Mrs. Hart could not help noticing the very peculiar tone in which he spoke of his wife.

"She will be lonely without you," said she.

"Well—business must be attended to, and this is of vital importance," was Lord Chetwynde's answer.

Mrs. Hart was silent for a long time.

"Do you expect ever to come back?" she asked at last.

"I hope so."

"But you do not know so?"

"I should be sorry to give up Chetwynde forever," said he.

"Is there any danger of that?"

"Yes. I am thinking of it. The affairs of the estate are of such a nature that I may be compelled to sacrifice even Chetwynde. You know that for three generations this prospect has been before us."

"But I thought that danger was averted by your marriage?" said Mrs. Hart, in a low voice.

"It was averted for my father's lifetime, but now it remains for me to do justice to those who were wronged by that arrangement; and justice shall be done, even if Chetwynde has to be sacrificed."

"I understand," said Mrs. Hart, in a quiet, thoughtful tone—"and you are going to Florence?"

"Yes, in a few days. But you will be left in the care of those who love you."

"Lady Chetwynde used to love me," said Mrs. Hart; "and I loved her."

"I am glad to know that—more so than I can say."

"She was always tender and loving and true. Your father loved her like a daughter."

"So I have understood."

"You speak coldly."

"Do I? I was not aware of it. No doubt her care will be as much at your service as ever, and when I come back again I shall find you in a green old age—won't I? Say I shall, my dear old nurse."

Tears stood in Mrs. Hart's eyes. She gazed wistfully at him, but said nothing.

A few more interviews took place between these two, and in a short time Lord Chetwynde bade her an affectionate farewell, and left the place once more.

On the morning after his departure Hilda was in the morning-room waiting for Gualtier, whom she had summoned. Although she knew that Lord Chetwynde was going away, yet his departure seemed sudden, and took her by surprise. He went away without any notice, just as he had done before, but somehow she had expected some formal announcement of his intention, and, because he had gone away without a word, she began to feel aggrieved and injured. Out of this there grew before her the memory of all Lord Chetwynde's coolness toward her, of the slights and insults to which he had subjected her, of the abhorrence which he had manifested toward her. She felt that she was despised. It was as though she had been foully wronged. To all these this last act was added. He had gone away without a word or a sign—where, she knew not—why, she could not tell. It was his abhorrence for her that had driven him away—this was evident.

"Hell hath no fury like a woman scorned." And this woman, who found herself doubly and trebly scorned, lashed herself into a fury of indignation. In this new-found fury she found the first relief which she had known from the torments of unrequited passion, from the longing and the craving and the yearning of her hot and fervid nature. Into this new fit of indignation she flung herself with complete abandonment. Since he scorned her, he should suffer—this was her feeling. Since he refused her love, he should feel her vengeance. He should know that she might be hated, but she was not one who could be despised. For every slight which he had heaped upon her he should pay with his heart's blood. Under the pangs of this new disappointment she writhed and groaned in her anguish, and all the tumults of feeling which she had endured ever since she saw him now seemed to congregate and gather themselves up into one outburst of furious and implacable vengefulness. Her heart beat hot and fast in her fierce excitement. Her face was pale, but the hectic flush on either cheek told of the fires within; and the nervous agitation of her manner, her clenched hands, and heaving breast, showed that the last remnant of self-control was forgotten and swept away in this furious rush of passion. It was in such a mood as this that Gualtier found her as he entered the morning-room to which she had summoned him.

Hilda at first did not seem to see him, or at any rate did not notice him. She was sitting as before in a deep arm-chair, in the depths of which her slender figure seemed lost. Her hands were clutched together. Her face was turned toward that portrait over the fire-place, which represented Lord Chetwynde in his early youth. Upon that face, usually so like a mask, so impassive, and so unapt to express the feelings that existed within, there was now visibly expressed an array of contending emotions. She had thrown away or lost her self-restraint; those feelings raged and expressed themselves uncontrolled, and Gualtier for the first time saw her off her guard. He entered with his usual stealthy tread, and watched her for some time as she sat looking at the picture. He read in her face the emotions which were expressed there. He saw disappointment, rage, fury, love, vengeance, pride, and desire all contending together. He learned for the first time that this woman whom he had believed to be cold as an icicle was as hot-hearted as a volcano; that she was fervid, impulsive, vehement, passionate, intense in love and in hate. As he learned this he felt his soul sink within him as he thought that it was not reserved for him, but for another, to call forth all the fiery vehemence of that stormy nature.

She saw him at last, as with a passionate gesture she tore her eyes away from the portrait, which seemed to fascinate her. The sight of Gualtier at once restored her outward calm. She was herself once more. She waved her hand loftily to a seat, and the very fact that she had made this exhibition of feeling before him seemed to harden that proud manner which she usually displayed toward him.

"I have sent for you," said she, in calm, measured tones, "for an important purpose. You remember the last journey on which I sent you?"

"Yes, my lady."

"You did that well. I have another one on which I wish you to go. It refers to the same person."

"Lord Chetwynde?"

Hilda bowed.

"I am ready," said Gualtier.

"He left this morning, and I don't know where he has gone, but I wish you to go after him."

"I know where he intended to go."

"How? Where?"

"Some of the servants overheard him speaking to Mrs. Hart about going to Italy."

"Italy!"

"Yes. I can come up with him somewhere, if you wish it, and get on his track. But what is it that you wish me to do?"

"In the first place, to follow him up."

"How—at a distance—or near him? That is to say, shall I travel in disguise, or shall I get employ near his person? I can be a valet, or a courier, or any thing else."

"Any thing. This must be left to you. I care not for details. The grand result is what I look to."

"And what is the grand result?"

"Something which you yourself once proposed," said Hilda, in low, stern tones, and with deep meaning.

Gualtier's face flushed. He understood her.

"I know," said he. "He is an obstacle, and you wish this obstacle removed."

"Yes."

"You understand me exactly, my lady, do you?" asked Gualtier, earnestly. "You wish it removed—*just as other obstacles have been removed*. You wish never to see him again. You wish to be your own mistress henceforth—and always."

"You have stated exactly what I mean," said Hilda, in icy tones.

Gualtier was silent for some time.

"Lady Chetwynde," said he at length, in a tone which was strikingly different from that with which for years he had addressed her— "Lady Chetwynde, I wish you to observe that this task upon which you now send me is far different from any of the former ones which I have undertaken at your bidding. I have always set out without a word—like one of those Haschishim of whom you have read, when he received the mandate of the Sheik of the mountains. But the nature of this errand is such that I may never see you again. The task is a perilous one. The man against whom I am sent is a man of singular acuteness, profound judgment, dauntless courage, and remorseless in his vengeance. His acuteness may possibly enable him to see through me, and frustrate my plan before it is fairly begun. What then? For me, at least, there will be nothing but destruction. It is, therefore, as if I now were standing face to face with death, and so I crave the liberty of saying something to you this time, and not departing in silence."

Gualtier spoke with earnestness, with dignity, yet with perfect respect. There was that in his tone and manner which gave indications of a far higher nature than any for which Hilda had ever yet given him credit. His words struck her strangely. They were not insubordinate, for he announced his intention to obey her; they were not disrespectful, for his manner was full of his old reverence; but they seemed like an assertion of something like manhood, and like a blow against that undisputed ascendency which she had so long maintained over him. In spite of her preoccupation, and her tempestuous passion, she was forced to listen, and she listened with a vague surprise, looking at him with a cold stare.

"You seem to me," said she, "to speak as though you were unwilling to go—or afraid."

"Pardon me, Lady Chetwynde," said Gualtier, "you can not think that. I have said that I would go, but that, as I may never see you again, I wish to say something. I wish, in fact, now, after all these years, to have a final understanding with you."

"Well?" said Hilda.

"I need not remind you of the past," said Gualtier, "or of my blind obedience to all your mandates. Two events at least stand out conspicuously. I have assisted you to the best of my power. Why I did so must be evident to you. You know very well that it was no sordid motive on my part, no hate toward others, no desire for vengeance, but something far different —something which has animated me for years, so that it was enough that you gave a command for me to obey. For years I have been thus at your call like a slave, and now, after all these years— now, that I depart on my last and most perilous mission, and am speaking to you words which may possibly be the last that you will ever hear from me—I wish to implore you, to beseech you, to promise me that reward which you must know I have always looked forward to, and which can be the only possible recompense to one like me for services like mine."

He stopped and looked imploringly at her.

"And what is that?" asked Hilda, mechanically, as though she did not fully understand him.

"Yourself," said Gualtier, in a low, earnest voice, with all his soul in the glance which he threw upon her.

The moment that he said the word Hilda started back with a gesture of impatience and contempt, and regarded him with an expression of anger and indignation, and with a frown so black that it seemed as if she would have blasted him with her look had she been able. Gualtier, however, did not shrink from her fierce glance. His eyes were no longer lowered before hers. He regarded her fixedly, calmly, yet respectfully, with his head erect, and no trace of his old unreasoning submission in his face and manner. Surprised as Hilda had evidently been at his words, she seemed no less surprised at his changed demeanor. It was the first time in her life that she had seen in him any revelation of manhood; and that view opened up to her very unpleasant possibilities.

"This is not a time," she said at length, in a sharp voice, "for such nonsense as this."

"I beg your pardon, Lady Chetwynde," said Gualtier, firmly, "I think that this and no other is the time. Whether it be 'nonsense' or not need not be debated. It is any thing but nonsense to me. All my past life seems to sweep up to this moment, and now is the crisis of my fate. All my future depends upon it, whether for weal or woe. Lady Chetwynde, do not call it nonsense—do not underrate its importance. Do not, I implore you, underrate me. Thus far you have tacitly assumed that I am a feeble and almost imbecile character. It is true that my abject devotion to you has forced me to give a blind obedience to all your wishes. But mark this well, Lady Chetwynde, such obedience itself involved some of the highest qualities of manhood. Something like courage and fortitude and daring was necessary to carry out those plans of yours which I so willingly undertook. I do not wish to speak of myself, however. I only wish to show you that I am in earnest, and that though you may treat this occasion with levity, I can not. All my life, Lady Chetwynde, hangs on your answer to my question."

Gualtier's manner was most vehement, and indicative of the strongest emotion, but the tones of his voice were low and only audible to Hilda. Low as the voice was, however, it still none the less exhibited the intensity of the passion that was in his soul.

Hilda, on the contrary, evinced a stronger rage at every word which he uttered. The baleful light of her dark eyes grew more fiery in its concentrated anger and scorn.

"It seems to me," said she, in her most contemptuous tone, "that you engage to do my will only on certain conditions; and that you are taking advantage of my necessities in order to drive a bargain."

"You are right, Lady Chetwynde," said Gualtier, calmly. "I am trying to drive a bargain; but remember it is not for money—it is for yourself."

"And I," said Hilda, with unchanged scorn, "will never submit to such coercion. When you dare to dictate to me, you mistake my character utterly. What I have to give I will give freely. My gifts shall never be extorted from me, even though my life should depend upon my compliance or refusal. The tone which you have chosen to adopt toward me is scarcely one that will make me swerve from my purpose, or alter any decision which I may have made. You have deceived yourself. You seem to suppose that you are indispensable to me, and that this is the time when you can force upon me any conditions you choose. As far as that is concerned, let me tell you plainly that you may do what you choose, and either go on this errand or stay. In any case, by no possibility, will I make any promise whatever."

This Hilda said quickly, and in her usual scorn. She thought that such indifference might bring Gualtier to terms, and make him decide to obey her without extorting this promise. For a moment she thought that she had succeeded. At her words a change came over Gualtier's face. He looked humbled and sad. As she ceased, he turned his eyes imploringly to her, and said:

"Lady Chetwynde, do not say that. I entreat you to give me this promise."

"I will not!" said Hilda, sharply.

"Once more I entreat you," said Gualtier, more earnestly.

"Once more I refuse," said Hilda. "Go and do this thing first, and then come and ask me."

"Will you then promise me?"

"I will tell you nothing now."

"Lady Chetwynde, for the last time I implore you to give me some ground for hope at least. Tell me—if this thing be accomplished, will you give me what I want?"

"I will make no engagement whatever," said Hilda, coldly.

Gualtier at this seemed to raise himself at once above his dejection, his humility, and his prayerful attitude, to a new and stronger assertion of himself.

"Very well," said he, gravely and sternly. "Now listen to me, Lady Chetwynde. I will no longer entreat—I insist that you give me this promise."

"Insist!"

Nothing can describe the scorn and contempt of Hilda's tone as she uttered this word.

"I repeat it," said Gualtier, calmly, and with deeper emphasis. "*I insist* that you give me your promise."

"My friend," said Hilda, contemptuously, "you do not seem to understand our positions. This seems to me like impertinence, and, unless you make an apology, I shall be under the very unpleasant necessity of obtaining a new steward."

As Hilda said this she turned paler than ever with suppressed rage.

Gualtier smiled scornfully.

"It seems to me," said he, "that you are the one who does not, or will not, understand our respective positions. You will *not* dismiss *me* from the stewardship, Lady Chetwynde, for you will be too sensible for that. You will retain me in that dignified office, for you know that I am indispensable to you, though you seemed to deny it a moment since. You have not forgotten the relations which we bear to one another. There are certain memories which rise between us two which will never escape the recollection of either of us till the latest moment of our lives ; some of these are associated with the General, some with the Earl, and some—with *Zillah !*"

He stopped, as though the mention of that last name had overpowered him. As for Hilda, the pallor of her face grew deeper, and she trembled with mingled agitation and rage.

"Go!" said she. "Go! and let me never see your face again!"

"No," said Gualtier, "I will not go till I choose. As to seeing my face again, the wish is easier said than gained. No, Lady Chetwynde. *You are in my power !* You know it. I tell it to you here, and nothing can save you from me if I turn against you. You have never understood me, for you have never taken the trouble to do so. You have shown but little mercy toward me. When I have come home from serving you—*you know how*—hungering and thirsting for some slight act of appreciation, some token of thankfulness, you have always repelled me, and denied what I dared not request. Had you but given me the kind attention which a master gives to a dog, I would have followed you like a dog to the world's end, and died for you —like a dog, too," he added, in an under-tone. "But you have used me as a stepping-stone; thinking that, like such, I could be spurned aside when you were done with me. You have not thought that I am not a stone or a block, but a man, with a man's heart within me. And it is now as a man that I speak to you, because you force me to it. I tell you this, that you are in my power, and you must be mine!"

"Are you a madman?" cried Hilda, overwhelmed with amazement at this outburst. "Have you lost your senses? Fool! If you mean what you say, I defy you! Go, and use your power! *I* in the power of such as you?— Never!"

Her brows contracted as she spoke, and from beneath her black eyes seemed to shoot baleful fires of hate and rage unutterable. The full intensity of her nature was aroused, and the expression of her face was terrible in its fury and malignancy. But Gualtier did not recoil. On the contrary, he feasted his eyes on her, and a smile came to his features.

"You are beautiful!" said he. "You have a demon beauty that is overpowering. Oh, beautiful fiend! You can not resist. You must be mine—and you shall! I never saw you so lovely. I love you best in your fits of rage."

"Fool!" cried Hilda. "This is enough. You are mad, or else drunk ; in either case you shall not stay another day in Chetwynde Castle. Go! or I will order the servants to put you out."

"There will be no occasion for that," said Gualtier, coolly. "I am going to leave you this very night to join Lord Chetwynde."

"It is too late now; your valuable services are no longer needed," said Hilda, with a sneer. "You may spare yourself the trouble of such a journey. Let me know what is due you, and I will pay it."

"You will pay me only one thing, and that is *yourself*," said Gualtier. "If you do not choose to pay *that* price you must take the consequences. I am going to join Lord Chetwynde, whether you wish me to or not. But, remember this!"—and Gualtier's voice grew menacing in its intonations—"remember this; it depends upon you in what capacity I am to join him. You are the one who must say whether I shall go to him as his enemy or his friend. If I go as his enemy, you know what will happen; if I go as his friend, it is you who must fall. Now, Lady Chetwynde, do you understand me?"

As Gualtier said this there was a deep meaning in his words which Hilda could not fail to understand, and there was at the same time such firmness and solemn decision that she felt that he would certainly do as he said. She saw at once the peril that lay before her. An alternative was offered : the one was, to come to terms with him ; the other, to accept utter and hopeless ruin. That ruin, too, which he menaced was no common one. It was one which placed her under the grasp of the law, and from which no foreign land could shelter her. All her prospects, her plans, her hopes, were in that instant dashed away from before her; and she realized now, to the fullest extent, the frightful truth that she was indeed completely in the power of this man. The discovery of this acted on her like a shock, which sobered her and drove away her passion.

She said nothing in reply, but sat down in silence, and remained a long time without speaking. Gualtier, on his part, saw the effect of his last words, but he made no effort to interrupt her thoughts. He could not yet tell what she in her desperation might decide ; he could only wait for her answer. He stood waiting patiently.

At last Hilda spoke :

"You've told me bitter truths—but they are truths. Unfortunately, I am in your power. If you choose to coerce me I must yield, for I am not yet ready to accept ruin."

"You promise then?"

"Since I must—I do."

"Thank you," said Gualtier; "and now you will not see me again till all is over either with *him* or with *me*."

He bowed respectfully and departed. After he had left, Hilda sat looking at the door with a face of rage and malignant fury. At length, starting to her feet, she hurried up to her room.

CHAPTER XLVII.

HILDA SEES A GULF BENEATH HER FEET.

THE astonishing change in Gualtier was an overwhelming shock to Hilda. She had committed the fatal mistake of underrating him, and of putting herself completely in his power. She had counted on his being always humble and docile, always subservient and blindly obedient. She had put from her all thoughts of a possible day of reckoning. She had fostered his devotion to her so as to be used for her own ends, and now found that she had raised up a power which might sweep her away. In the first assertion of that power she had been vanquished, and compelled to make a promise which she had at first refused with the haughtiest contempt. She could only take refuge in vague plans of evading her promise, and in punishing Gualtier for what seemed to her his unparalleled audacity.

Yet, after all, bitter as the humiliation had been, it did not lessen her fervid passion for Lord Chetwynde, and the hate and the vengeance that had arisen when that passion had been contemned. After the first shock of the affair with Gualtier had passed, her madness and fury against him passed also, and her wild spirit was once again filled with the all-engrossing thought of Lord Chetwynde. Gualtier had gone off, as he said, and she was to see him no more for some time—perhaps never. He had his own plans and purposes, of the details of which Hilda knew nothing, but could only conjecture. She felt that failure on his part was not probable, and gradually, so confident was she that he would succeed, Lord Chetwynde began to seem to her not merely a doomed man, but a man who had already undergone his doom. And now another change came over her—that change which Death can make in the heart of the most implacable of men when his enemy has left life forever. From the pangs of wounded love she had sought refuge in vengeance—but the prospect of a gratified vengeance was but a poor compensation for the loss of the hope of a requited love. The tenderness of love still remained, and it struggled with the ferocity of vengeance. That love pleaded powerfully for Lord Chetwynde's life. Hope came also, to lend its assistance to the arguments of love. Would it not be better to wait—even for years—and then perhaps the fierceness of Lord Chetwynde's repugnance might be allayed? Why destroy him, and her hope, and her love, forever, and so hastily? After such thoughts as these, however, the remembrance of Lord Chetwynde's contempt was sure to return and intensify her vengeance.

Under such circumstances, when distracted by so many cares, it is not surprising that she forgot all about Mrs. Hart. She had understood the full meaning of Gualtier's warning about her prospective recovery, but the danger passed from her mind. Gualtier had gone on his errand, and she was sure he would not falter. Shut up in her own chamber, she awaited in deep agitation the first tidings which he might send. Day succeeded to day; no tidings came; and at last she began to hope that he had failed—and the pleasantest sight which she could have seen at that time would have been Gualtier returning disappointed and baffled.

Meanwhile, Mrs. Hart, left to herself, steadily and rapidly recovered. Ever since her first recognition of Lord Chetwynde her improvement had been marked. New ideas seemed to have come to her; new motives for life; and with these the desire of life; and at the promptings of that desire health came back. This poor creature, even in the best days of her life at Chetwynde Castle, had not known any health beyond that of a moderate kind; and so a moderate recovery would suffice to give her what strength she had lost. To be able to wander about the house once more was all that she needed, and this was not long denied her.

In a few days after Gualtier's departure she was able to go about. She walked through the old familiar scenes, traversed the well-known halls, and surveyed the well-remembered apartments. One journey was enough for the first day. The next day she went about the grounds, and visited the chapel, where she sat for hours on the Earl's tomb, wrapped in an absorbing meditation. Two or three days passed on, and she walked about as she used to. And now a strong desire seized her to see that wife of Lord Chetwynde whom she so dearly loved and so fondly remembered. She wondered that Lady Chetwynde had not come to see her. She was informed that Lady Chetwynde was ill. A deep sympathy then arose in her heart for the poor friendless lady—the fair girl whom she remembered—and whom she now pictured to herself as bereaved of her father, and scorned by her husband. For Mrs. Hart rightly divined the meaning of Lord Chetwynde's words. She thought long over this, and at last there arose within her a deep yearning to go and see this poor friendless orphaned girl, whose life had been so sad, and was still so mournful.

So one day, full of such tender feelings as these, and carrying in her mind the image of that beautiful young girl who once had been so dear to her, she went up herself to the room where Hilda staid, and asked the maid for Lady Chetwynde.

"She is ill," said the maid.

Mrs. Hart waved her aside with serene dignity and entered. The maid stood awe-struck. For Mrs. Hart had the air and the tone of a lady, and now when her will was aroused she very well knew how to put down an unruly servant. So she walked grandly past the maid, who looked in awe upon her stately figure, her white face, with its refined features, and her venerable hair, and passed through the half-opened door into Hilda's room.

Hilda had been sitting on the sofa, which was near the window. She was looking out abstractedly, thinking upon the great problem which lay before her, upon the solution of which she could not decide, when suddenly she became aware of some one in the room. She looked up. It was Mrs. Hart!

At the sight her blood chilled within her. Her face was overspread with an expression of utter horror. The shock was tremendous. She had forgotten all about the woman. Mrs. Hart had been to her like the dead, and now to see her thus suddenly was like the sight of the dead. Had the dead Earl come into her room and stood before her in the cerements of the grave she would not have been one whit more horrified, more bewildered.

L.

But soon in that strong mind of hers reason regained its place. She saw how it had been, and though she still wondered how Mrs. Hart had come into her room, yet she prepared as best she might to deal with this new and unexpected danger. She arose, carefully closed the door, and then turning to Mrs. Hart she took her hand, and said, simply,

"I'm so glad to see you about again."

"Where is Lady Chetwynde?"

This was all that Mrs. Hart said, as she withdrew her hand and looked all about the room. Like lightning Hilda's plan was decided upon.

"Wait a moment," said she; and, going into the ante-room, she sent her maid away upon some errand that would detain her for some time. Then she came back and motioned Mrs. Hart to a chair, while she took another.

"Did not Lord Chetwynde tell you about Lady Chetwynde?" she asked, very cautiously. She was anxious, first of all, to see how much Mrs. Hart knew.

"No," said Mrs. Hart, "he scarcely mentioned her name." She looked suspiciously at Hilda while she spoke.

"That is strange," said Hilda. "Had you any conversations with him?"

"Yes, several."

"And he did not tell you?"

"He told me nothing about her," said Mrs. Hart, dryly.

Hilda drew a long breath of relief.

"It's a secret in this house," said she, "but you must know it. I will tell you all about it. After the Earl's death Lady Chetwynde happened to come across some letters written by his son, in which the utmost abhorrence was expressed for the girl whom he had married. I dare say the letters are among the papers yet, and you can see them. One in particular was fearful in its denunciations of her. He reviled her, called her by opprobrious epithets, and told his father that he would never consent to see her. Lady Chetwynde saw all these. You know how high-spirited she was. She at once took fire at these insults, and declared that she would never consent to see Lord Chetwynde. She wrote him to that effect, and then departed from Chetwynde Castle forever."

Mrs. Hart listened with a stern, sad face, and said not a word.

"I went with her to a place where she is now living in seclusion. I don't think that Lord Chetwynde would have come home if he had not known that she had left. Hearing this, however, he at once came here."

"And you?" said Mrs. Hart, "what are you doing here? Are you the Lady Chetwynde of whom the servants speak?"

"I am, temporarily," said Hilda, with a sad smile. "It was Zillah's wish. She wanted to avoid a scandal. She sent off all the old servants, hired new ones, and persuaded me to stay here for a time as Lady Chetwynde. She found a dear old creature to nurse you, and never ceases to write about you and ask how you are."

"And you live here as Lady Chetwynde?" asked Mrs. Hart, sternly.

"Temporarily," said Hilda—"that was the arrangement between us. Zillah did not want to have the name of Chetwynde dishonored by

stories that his wife had run away from him. She wrote Lord Chetwynde to that effect. When Lord Chetwynde arrived I saw him in the library, and he requested me to stay here for some months until he had arranged his plans for the future. It was very considerate in Zillah, but at the same time it is very embarrassing to me, and I am looking eagerly forward to the time when this deceit can be over, and I can rejoin my friend once more. I am so glad, my dear Mrs. Hart, that you came in. It is such a relief to have some one to whom I can unburden myself. I am very miserable, and I imagine all the time that the servants suspect me. You will, of course, keep this a profound secret, will you not, my dear Mrs. Hart? and help me to play this wretched part, which my love for Zillah has led me to undertake?"

Hilda's tone was that of an innocent and simple girl who found herself in a false position. Mrs. Hart listened earnestly without a word, except occasionally. The severe rigidity of her features never relaxed. What effect this story, so well told, produced upon her, Hilda could not know. At length, however, she had finished, and Mrs. Hart arose.

"You will keep Zillah's secret?" said Hilda, earnestly. "It is for the sake of Lord Chetwynde."

"You will never find me capable of doing any thing that is against his interests," said Mrs. Hart, solemnly; and without a bow, or an adieu, she retired. She went back to her own room to ponder over this astonishing story.

Meanwhile, Hilda, left alone to herself, was not altogether satisfied with the impression which had been made on Mrs. Hart. She herself had played her part admirably—her story, long prepared in case of some sudden need like this, was coherent and natural. It was spoken fluently and unhesitatingly; nothing could have been better in its way, or more convincing; yet she was not satisfied with Mrs. Hart's demeanor. Her face was too stern, her manner too frigid; the questions which she had asked spoke of suspicion. All these were unpleasant, and calculated to awaken her fears. Her position had always been one of extreme peril, and she had dreaded some visitor who might remember her face. She had feared the doctor most, and had carefully kept out of his way. She had not thought until lately of the possibility of Mrs. Hart's recovery. This came upon her with a suddenness that was bewildering, and the consequences she could not foretell.

And now another fear suggested itself. Might not Lord Chetwynde himself have some suspicions? Would not such suspicions account for his coldness and severity? Perhaps he suspected the truth, and was preparing some way in which she could be entrapped and punished. Perhaps his mysterious business in London related to this alone. The thought filled her with alarm, and now she rejoiced that Gualtier was on his track. She began to believe that she could never be safe until Lord Chetwynde was "removed." And if Lord Chetwynde, then others. Who was this Mrs. Hart that she should have any power of troubling her? Measures might easily be taken for silencing her forever, and for "removing" such a feeble old obstacle as this. Hilda knew means by which this could be effected. She

"SHE STOOD FOR A LITTLE WHILE AND LISTENED."

knew the way by which the deed could be done, and she had nerve enough to do it.

The appearance of this new danger in Chetwynde Castle itself gave a new direction to her troubles. It was as though a gulf had suddenly yawned beneath her feet. All that night she lay deliberating as to what was best to do under the circumstances. Mrs. Hart was safe enough for a day or two, but what might she not do hereafter in the way of mischief? She could not be got rid of, either, in an ordinary way. She had been so long in Chetwynde Castle that it seemed morally impossible to dislodge her. Certainly she was not one who could be paid and packed off to some distant place like the other servants. There was only one way to get rid of her, and to this one way Hilda's thoughts turned gloomily.

Over this thought she brooded through all the following day. Evening came, and twilight deepened into darkness. At about ten o'clock Hilda left her room and quietly descended the great staircase, and went over toward the chamber occupied by Mrs. Hart. Arriving at the door she stood without for a little while and listened. There was no noise. She gave a turn to the knob and found that the door was open. The room was dark. She has gone to bed, she thought. She went back to her own room again, and in about half an hour she returned. The door of Mrs. Hart's room remained ajar as she had left it. She pushed it farther open, and put her head in. All was still. There were no sounds of breathing there. Slowly and cautiously she advanced into the room. She drew nearer to the bed. There was no light whatever, and in the intense darkness no outline revealed the form of the bed to her. Nearer and nearer she drew to the bed, until at last she touched it. Gently, yet swiftly, her hands passed over its surface, along the quilts, up to the pillows. An involuntary cry burst from her—

The bed was empty!

CHAPTER XLVIII..

FROM LOVE TO VENGEANCE, AND FROM VENGEANCE TO LOVE.

On the night of this last event, before she retired to bed, Hilda learned more. Leaving Mrs. Hart's room, she called at the housekeeper's chambers to see if the missing woman might be there. The housekeeper informed her that she had left at an early hour that morning, without saying a word to any one, and that she herself had taken it for granted that her ladyship knew all about it. Hilda heard this without any comment; and then walked thoughtfully to her own room.

She certainly had enough care on her mind to occupy all her thoughts. The declaration of Gualtier was of itself an ill-omened event, and she no longer had that trust in his fidelity which she once had, even though he now might work in the hope of a reward. It seemed to her that with the loss of her old ascendency over him she would lose altogether his devotion; nor could the remembrance of his former services banish that deep distrust of him which, along with her bitter resentment of his rebellion, had arisen in her mind. The affair of Mrs. Hart seemed worse yet. Her sudden appearance, her sharp questionings, her cold incredulity, terminated at last by her prompt flight, were all circumstances which filled her with the most gloomy forebodings. Her troubles seemed now to increase every day, each one coming with startling suddenness, and each one being of that sort against which no precautions had been taken, or even thought of.

She passed an anxious day and a sleepless night. On the following morning a letter was brought to her. It had a foreign post-mark, and the address showed the handwriting of Gualtier. This at once brought back the old feelings about Lord Chetwynde, and she tore it open with feverish impatience, eager to know what the contents might be, yet half fearful of their import. It was written in that tone of respect which Gualtier had never lost but once, and which he had now resumed. He informed her that on leaving Chetwynde he had gone at once up to London, and found that Lord Chetwynde was stopping at the same hotel where he had put up last. He formed a bold design, which he put in execution, trusting to the fact that Lord Chetwynde had never seen him more than twice at the Castle, and on both occasions had seemed not even to have looked at him. He therefore got himself up very carefully in a foreign fashion, and, as he spoke French perfectly, he went to Lord Chetwynde and offered himself as a valet or courier. It happened that Lord Chetwynde actually needed a man to serve him in this capacity, a fact which Gualtier had found out in the hotel, and so the advent of the valet was quite welcome. After a brief conversation, and an inquiry into his knowledge of the languages and the routes of travel on the Continent, Lord Chetwynde examined his letters of recommendation, and, finding them very satisfactory, he took him into his employ. They remained two days longer in London, during which Gualtier made such good use of his time and opportunities that he managed to gain access to Lord Chetwynde's papers, but found among them nothing of any importance whatever, from which he concluded that all his papers of any consequence must have been deposited with his solicitors. At any rate it was impossible for him to find out any thing from this source.

Leaving London they went to Paris, where they passed a few days, but soon grew weary of the place; and Lord Chetwynde, feeling a kind of languor, which seemed to him like a premonition of disease, he decided to go to Germany. His first idea was to go to Baden, although it was not the season; but on his arrival at Frankfort he was so overcome by the fatigue of traveling that he determined to remain for a time in that city. His increasing languor, however, had alarmed him, and he had called in the most eminent physicians of the place, who, at the time the letter was written, were prescribing for him. The writer said that they did not seem to think that this illness had any thing very serious in it, and simply recommended certain changes of diet and various kinds of gentle exercise, but he added that in his opinion *there was something in it, and that this illness was more serious than was supposed.* As for the sick man himself, he was much discouraged. He had grown tired of his physicians and of Frankfort, and wished to go on to Baden, thinking that the change might do him good. He seemed anxious for constant change, and spoke as though he might leave Baden for some other German city, or perhaps go on to Italy, to which place his thoughts, for some reason or other, seemed always turning with eager impatience.

As Hilda read this letter, and took in the whole of its dark and hidden meaning, all her former agitation returned. Once more the question arose which had before so greatly harassed her. The disappearance of Mrs. Hart, and the increasing dangers which had been gathering around her head, had for a time taken up her thoughts, but now her great, preoccupying care came back with fresh vehemence, and resumed more than its former sway. Mrs. Hart was forgotten as completely as though she had never existed. Gualtier's possible infidelity to her suggested itself no more; it was Lord Chetwynde and Lord Chetwynde only, his sickness, his peril, his doom, which came to her mind. On one side stood Love, pleading for his life; on the other Vengeance, demanding its sacrifice.

Shall he live, or shall he die?
This was the question which ever and ever rang in her soul. "Shall he live, or die? Shall he go down to death, doomed by me, and thus end all my hope, or shall he live to scorn me?" In his death there was the satisfaction of vengeance, but there was also the death of hope. In his death there was fresh security for herself; but in his death her own life would lie dead. On each side there were motives most powerful over a mind like hers, yet so evenly balanced that she knew not which way to turn, or in which way to incline. Death or life?—life or death? Thus the question came.

And the hours passed on; and every hour, she well knew, was freighted with calamity; every hour was dragging Lord Chetwynde on to that point at which the power to decide upon his fate would be hers no longer.

Why hesitate?
This was the form which the question took at last, and under which it forced itself more and more upon her. Why hesitate? To hesitate was of itself to doom him to death. If he was to be saved, there was no time for delay. He must be saved at once. If he was to be saved, she must act herself, and that, too, promptly and energetically. Her part could not be performed by merely writing a letter, for the letter might be delayed, or it might be miscarried, or it might be neglected and disobeyed. She could not trust the fulfillment of a command of mercy to Gualtier. She herself could alone fulfill such a purpose. She herself must act by herself.

As she thought of this her decision was taken. Yes, she would do it. She herself would arrest his fate, for a time at least. Yes—he should live, and she herself would fly to his aid, and stand by his side, and be the one who would snatch him from his doom.

Now, no sooner was this decision made than there came over her a strange thrill of joy and exultation. He should live! he should live! this was the refrain which rang in her thoughts. He should live; and she would be the life-giver. At last he would be forced to look upon her with eyes of gratitude at least, if not of affection. It should no longer be in his power to scorn her, or to turn away coldly and cruelly from her proffered hand. He should yet learn to look upon her as his best friend. He should learn to call her by tender names; and speak to her words of fondness, of endearment, and of love. Now, as deep as her despondency had been, so high rose her joy at this new prospect; and her hope, which rose out of this resolution, was bright to a degree which was commensurate with the darkness of her previous despair. He

shall live; and he shall be mine—these were the words upon which her heart fed itself, which carried to that heart a wild and feverish joy, and drove away those sharp pangs which she had felt. And now the love which burned within her diffused through all her being those softer qualities which are born of love; and the hate and the vengeance upon which she had of late sustained her soul were forgotten. Into her heart there came a tenderness all feminine, and a thing unknown to her before that fateful day on which she had first seen Lord Chetwynde; a tenderness which filled her with a yearning desire to fly to the rescue of this man, whom she had but lately handed over to the assassin. She hungered and thirsted to be near him, to stand by his side, to see his face, to touch his hand, to hear his voice, to give to him that which should save him from the fate which she herself had dealt out to him by the hands of her own agent. It was thus that her love at last triumphed over her vengeance, and, sweeping onward, drove away all other thoughts and feelings. Hers was the love of the tigress; but even the love of the tigress is yet love; and such love has its own profound depths of tenderness, its capacity of intense desire, its power of complete self-abnegation or of self-immolation—feelings which, in the tigress kind of love, are as deep as in any other, and perhaps even deeper.

But from her in that dire emergency the one thing that was required above all else was haste. That she well knew. There was no time for delay. There was one at the side of Lord Chetwynde whose heart knew neither pity nor remorse, whose hand never faltered in dealing its blow, and who watched every failing moment of his life with unshaken determination. To him her cruel and bloody behests had been committed in her mad hour of vengeance; those behests he was now carrying out as much for his own sake as for hers; accomplishing the fulfillment of his own purposes under the cloak of obedience to her orders. He was the destroying angel, and his mission was death. He could not know of the change which had come over her; nor could he dream of the possibility of a change. She alone could bring a reprieve from that death, and stay his hand.

Haste, then—she murmured to herself—oh, haste, or it will soon be too late! Fly! Leave every thing and fly! Every hour brings him nearer to death until that hour comes when you may save him from death. Haste, or it may be too late—and the mercy and the pity and the tenderness of love may be all unavailing!

It was with the frantic haste which was born of this new-found pity that Hilda prepared for her journey. Her preparations were not extensive. A little luggage sufficed. She did not wish a maid. She had all her life relied upon herself, and now set forth upon this fateful journey alone and unattended, with her heart filled with one feeling only, and only one hope. It needed but a short time to complete her preparations, and to announce to the astonished domestics her intention of going to the Continent. Without noticing their amazement, or caring for it, she ordered the carriage for the nearest station, and in a short time after her first decision she was seated in the cars and hurrying onward to London.

Arriving there, she made a short stay. She had some things to procure which were to her of infinite importance. Leaving the hotel, she went down Oxford Street till she came to a druggist's shop, which she entered, and, going up to the clerk, she handed him a paper, which looked like a doctor's prescription. The clerk took it, and, after looking at it, carried it to an inner office. After a time the proprietor appeared. He scanned Hilda narrowly, while she returned his glance with her usual haughtiness. The druggist appeared satisfied with his inspection.

"Madame," said he, politely, "the ingredients of this prescription are of such a nature that the law requires me to know the name and address of the purchaser, so as to enter them on the purchase book."

"My address," said Hilda, quietly, "is Mrs. Henderson, 51 Euston Square."

The druggist bowed, and entered the name carefully on his book, after which he himself prepared the prescription and handed it to Hilda. She asked the price, and, on hearing it, flung down a sovereign, after which she was on the point of leaving without waiting for the change, when the druggist called her back.

"Madame," said he, "you are leaving without your change."

Hilda started, and then turning back she took the change and thanked him.

"I thought you said it was twenty shillings," she remarked, quietly, seeing that the druggist was looking at her with a strange expression.

"Oh no, madame; I said ten shillings."

"Ah! I misunderstood you," and with these words Hilda took her departure, carrying with her the precious medicine.

That evening she left London, and took the steamer for Ostend. Before leaving she had sent a telegraphic message to Gualtier at Frankfort, announcing the fact that she was coming on, and asking him, if he left Frankfort before her arrival, to leave a letter for her at the hotel, letting her know where they might go. This she did for a twofold motive: first, to let Gualtier know that she was coming; and secondly, to secure a means of tracking them if they went to another place. But the dispatch of this message filled her with fresh anxiety. She feared first that the message might not reach its destination in time; and then that Gualtier might utterly misunderstand her motive—a thing which, under the circumstances, he was certain to do—and, under this misapprehension, hurry up his work, so as to have it completed by the time of her arrival. These thoughts, with many others, agitated her so much that she gradually worked herself into an agony of fear; and the swiftest speed of steamboat or express train seemed slow to the desire of that stormy spirit, which would have forced its way onward, far beyond the speed which human contrivances may create, to the side of the man whom she longed to see and to save. The fever of her fierce anxiety, the vehemence of her desire, the intensity of her anguish, all worked upon her delicate organization with direful effect. Her brain became confused, and thoughts became dreams. For hours she lost all consciousness of surrounding objects. Yet amidst all this confusion of a diseased and overworked brain, and amidst this delirium of wild thought, there was ever prominent her one idea—her one purpose. How she passed that journey she could not afterward remember, but it was at length passed, and, following the guidance of that strong purpose, which kept its place in her mind when other things were lost, she at last stood in the station-house at Frankfort.

"Drive to the Hôtel Rothschild," she cried to the cabman whom she had engaged. "Quick! for your life!"

The cabman marked her agitation and frenzy. He whipped up his horses, the cab dashed through the streets, and reached the hotel. Hilda hurried out and went up the steps. Tottering rather than walking, she advanced to a man who had come to meet her. He seemed to be the proprietor.

"Lord Chetwynde!" she gasped. "Is he here?" She spoke in German.

The proprietor shook his head.

"He left the day before yesterday."

Hilda staggered back with a low moan. She did not really think that he could be here yet, but she had hoped that he might be, and the disappointment was great.

"Is there a letter here," she asked, in a faint voice, "for Lady Chetwynde?"

"I think so. I'll see."

Hurrying away he soon returned with a letter in his hand.

"Are you the one to whom it is addressed?" he asked, with deep respect.

"I am Lady Chetwynde," said Hilda, and at the same time eagerly snatched the letter from his hand. On the outside she at once recognized the writing of Gualtier. She saw the address, "Lady Chetwynde." In an instant she tore it open, and read the contents.

The letter contained only the following words:

"FRANKFORT, HÔTEL ROTHSCHILD,
October 30, 1859.

"We leave for Baden to-day. Our business is progressing very favorably. We go to the Hôtel Français at Baden. If you come on you must follow us there. If we go away before your arrival I will leave a note for you."

The letter was as short as a telegram, and as unsatisfactory to a mind in such a state as hers. It had no signature, but the handwriting was Gualtier's.

Hilda's hand trembled so that she could scarcely hold it. She read it over and over again. Then she turned to the landlord.

"What time does the next train leave for Baden?" she asked.

"To-morrow morning at 5 A.M., miladi."

"Is there no train before?"

"No, miladi."

"Is there no steamer?"

"No, miladi—not before to-morrow morning. The five o'clock train is the first and the quickest way to go to Baden."

"I am in a great hurry," said Hilda, faintly. "I must be called in time for the five o'clock train."

"You shall be, miladi."

"Send a maid—and let me have my room now—as soon as possible—for I am worn out."

As she said this she tottered, and would have fallen, but the landlord supported her, and called for the maids. They hurried forward, and Hilda was carried up to her room and tenderly put to bed. The landlord was an honest, tender-hearted German. Lord Chetwynde had been a guest of sufficient distinction to be well remembered by a landlord, and his ill health had made him more conspicuous. The arrival of this devoted wife, who herself seemed as ill as her husband, but who yet, in spite of weakness, was hastening to him with such a consuming desire to get to him, affected most profoundly this honest landlord, and all others in the hotel. That evening, then, Hilda's faith and love and constancy formed the chief theme of conversation; the visitors of the hotel heard the sad story from the landlord, and deep was the pity, and profound the sympathy, which were expressed by all. To the ordinary pathos of this affecting example of conjugal love some additional power was lent by the extreme beauty, the excessive prostration and grief, and, above all, the illustrious rank of this devoted woman.

Hilda was put to bed, but there was no sleep for her. The fever of her anxiety, the shock of her disappointment, the tumult of her hopes and fears, all made themselves felt in her overworked brain. She did not take the five o'clock train on the following day. The maid came to call her, but found her in a high fever, eager to start, but quite unable to move. Before noon she was delirious.

In that delirium her thoughts wandered over those scenes which for the past few months had been uppermost in her mind. Now she was shut up in her chamber at Chetwynde Castle reading the Indian papers; she heard the roll of carriage wheels; she prepared to meet the new-comer face to face. She followed him to the morning-room, and there listened to his fierce maledictions. On the occasion itself she had been dumb before him, but in her delirium she had words of remonstrance. These words were expressed in every varying shade of entreaty, deprecation, conciliation, and prayer. Again she watched a stern, forbidding face over the dinner-table, and sought to appease by kind words the just wrath of the man she loved. Again she held out her hand, only to have her humble advances repelled in coldest scorn. Again she saw him leave her forever without a word of farewell—without even a notice of his departure, and she remained to give herself up to vengeance.

That delirium carried her through many past events. Gualtier again stood up before her in rebellion, proud, defiant, merciless, asserting himself, and enforcing her submission to his will. Again there came into her room, suddenly, and like a spectre, the awful presence of Mrs. Hart, with her white face, her stern looks, her sharp inquiries, and her ominous words. Again she pursued this woman to her own room, in the dark, and ran her hands over the bed, and found that bed empty.

But Lord Chetwynde was the central object of her delirious fancies. It was to him that her thoughts reverted from brief wanderings over reminiscences of Gualtier and Mrs. Hart. Whatever thoughts she might have about these, those thoughts would always at last revert to him. And with him it was not so much the past that suggested itself to her diseased imagination as the future. That future was sufficiently dark and terrible to be portrayed in fearful colors by

her incoherent ravings. There were whispered words—words of frightful meaning, words which expressed those thoughts which in her sober senses she would have died rather than reveal. Had any one been standing by her bedside who knew English, he might have learned from her words a story of fearful import—a tale which would have chilled his blood, and which would have shown him how far different this sick woman was from the fond, self-sacrificing wife, who had excited the sympathy of all in the hotel. But there was none who could understand her. The doctor knew no language beside his own, except a little French; the maids knew nothing but German. And so it was that while Hilda unconsciously revealed the whole of those frightful secrets which she carried shut up within her breast, that revelation was not intelligible to any of those who were in contact with her. Well was it for her at that time that she had chosen to come away without her maid; for had that maid been with her then she would have learned enough of her mistress to send her flying back to England in horror, and to publish abroad the awful intelligence.

Thus a week passed—a week of delirium, of ravings, of incoherent speeches, unintelligible to all those by whom she was surrounded. At length her strong constitution triumphed over the assaults of disease. The fever was allayed, and sense returned; and with returning sense there came the full consciousness of her position. The one purpose of her life rose again within her mind, and even while she was too weak to move she was eager to be up and away.

"How long will it be," she asked of the doctor, "before I can go on my journey?"

"If every thing is favorable, miladi," answered the doctor, "as I hope it will be, you may be able to go in about a week. It will be a risk, but you are so excited that I would rather have you go than stay."

"A week! A week!" exclaimed Hilda, despairingly. "I can not wait so long as that. No. I will go before then—or else I will die."

"If you go before a week," said the doctor, warningly, and with evident anxiety, "you will risk your life."

"Very well then, I will risk my life," said Hilda. "What is life worth now?" she murmured, with a moan of anguish. "I must and will go on, if I die for it—and in three days."

The doctor made no reply. He saw her desperation, and perceived that any remonstrance would be worse than useless. To keep such a resolute and determined spirit chained here in a sick-chamber would be impossible. She would chafe at the confinement so fiercely that a renewal of the fever would be inevitable. She would have to be allowed her own way. Most deeply did he commiserate this devoted wife, and much did he wonder how it had happened that her husband had gone off from her thus, at a time when he himself was threatened with illness. And now, as before, those kindly German hearts in the hotel, on learning this new outburst of conjugal love, felt a sympathy which was beyond all expression. To none of them had there ever before been known any thing approaching to so piteous a case as this.

The days passed. Hilda was avaricious about every new sign of increasing strength. Her strong determination, her intense desire, and her powerful will, at last triumphed over bodily pain and weakness. It was as she said, and on the third day she managed to drag herself from her bed and prepare for a fresh journey. In preparation for this, however, she was compelled to have a maid to accompany her, and she selected one of those who had been her attendants, an honest, simple-hearted, affectionate German girl —Gretchen by name, one who was just suited to her in her present situation.

She made the journey without any misfortune. On reaching Baden she had to be lifted into the cab. Driving to the Hôtel Français, she reached it in a state of extreme prostration, and had to be carried to her rooms. She asked for a letter. There was one for her. Gualtier had not been neglectful, but had left a message. It was very much like the last.

"BADEN, HÔTEL FRANÇAIS, *November* 2, 1859.
"We leave for Munich to-day, and will stop at the Hôtel des Etrangers. Business progressing most favorably. If we go away from Munich I will leave a note for you."

The letter was dated November 2, but it was now the 10th of that month, and Hilda was far behind time. She had nerved herself up to this effort, and the hope of finding the object of her search at Baden had sustained her. But her new-found strength was now utterly exhausted by the fatigue of travel, and the new disappointment which she had experienced created discouragement and despondency. This told still more upon her strength, and she was compelled to wait here for two days, chafing and fretting against her weakness.

Nothing could exceed the faithful attention of Gretchen. She had heard at Frankfort, from the gossip of the servants, the story of her mistress, and all her German sentiment was roused in behalf of one so sorrowful and so beautiful. Her natural kindness of heart also led to the utmost devotion to Hilda, and, so far as careful and incessant attention could accomplish any thing, all was done that was possible. By the 13th of November Hilda was ready to start once more, and on that morning she left for Munich. This journey was more fatiguing than the last. In her weak state she was almost overcome. Twice she fainted away in the cars, and all of Gretchen's anxious care was required to bring her to her destination. The German maid implored her with tears to get out at some of the towns on the way. But Hilda resolutely refused. She hoped to find rest at Munich, and to stop short of that place seemed to her to endanger her prospect of success. Again, as before, the strong soul triumphed over the infirmity of the body, and the place of her destination was at last attained.

She reached it more dead than alive. Gretchen lifted her into a cab. She was taken to the Hôtel des Etrangers. At the very first moment of her entrance into the hall she had asked a breathless question of the servant who appeared:

"Is Lord Chetwynde here?"
"Lord Chetwynde? No. He has gone."
"Gone!" said Hilda, in a voice which was like a groan of despair. "Gone! When?"
"Nearly a week ago," said the servant.

At this Hilda's strength again left her utterly, and she fell back almost senseless. She was car-

ried to her room. Then she rallied by a mighty effort, and sent Gretchen to see if there was a letter for her. In a short time the maid reappeared, bringing another of those welcome yet tantalizing notes, which always seemed ready to mock her, and to lure her on to fresh disappointment. Yet her impatience to read its contents had in no way diminished, and it was with the same impetuous fever of curiosity as before that she tore open the envelope and devoured the contents. This note was much like the others, but somewhat more ominous.

It read as follows:

"MUNICH, HÔTEL DES ETRANGERS,
November 9, 1859.
"We leave for Lausanne to-day. We intend to stop at the Hôtel Gibbon. It is not probable that any further journey will be made. Business most favorable, and prospects are that every thing will soon be brought to a successful issue."

CHAPTER XLIX.

THE ANGUISH OF THE HEART.

As Hilda read these ominous words a chill like that of death seemed to strike to her inmost soul. Her disappointment on her arrival here had already been bitter enough. She had looked upon Munich as the place where she would surely find the end of her journey, and obtain the reward of her labors. But now the object of her search was once more removed, and a new journey more fatiguing than the others was set before her. Could she bear it?—she who even now felt the old weakness, and something even worse, coming back irresistibly upon her. Could she, indeed, bear another journey? This question she put to herself half hopelessly; but almost immediately her resolute soul asserted itself, and proudly answered it. Bear such a journey? Ay, this journey she could bear, and not only this, but many more. Even though her old weakness was coming back over her frail form, still she rose superior to that weakness, and persisted in her determination to go on, and still on, without giving up her purpose, till she reached Lord Chetwynde, even though it should only be at the moment of her arrival to drop dead at his feet.

There was more now to stimulate her than the determination of a resolute and invincible will. The words of that last note had a dark and ominous meaning, which affected her more strongly by far than any of the others. The messages which they bore had not been of so fearful an import as this.

The first said that the "business" was progressing *very favorably.*

The second, that it was progressing *most favorably.*

This last one told her that the business *would soon be brought to a successful issue.*

Well she knew the meaning of these words. In these different messages she saw so many successive stages of the terrific work which was going on, and to avert which she had endured so much, at the cost of such suffering to herself. She saw the form of Lord Chetwynde failing more and more every day, and still, while he struggled against the approach of insidious disease, yielding, in spite of himself, to its resistless progress. She saw him going from place to place, summoning the physicians of each town where he stopped, and giving up both town and physicians in despair. She saw, also, how all the time there stood by his side one who was filled with one dark purpose, in the accomplishment of which he was perseveringly cruel and untiringly patient—one who watched the growing weakness of his victim with cold-blooded interest, noting every decrease of strength, and every sign which might give token of the end—one, too, who thought that she was hastening after him to join in his work, and was only delaying in order to join him when all was over, so as to give him her congratulations, and bestow upon him the reward which he had made her promise that she would grant.

Thoughts like these filled her with madness. Wretched and almost hopeless, prostrated by her weakness, yet consumed by an ardent desire to rush onward and save the dying man from the grasp of the destroyer, her soul became a prey to a thousand contending emotions, and endured the extreme of the anguish of suspense. Such a struggle as this proved too much for her. One night was enough to prostrate her once more to that stage of utter weakness which made all hope of travel impossible. In that state of prostration her mind still continued active, and the thoughts that never ceased to come were those which prevented her from rallying readily. For the one idea that was ever present was this, that while she was thus helpless, *her work was still going on*—that work which she had ordered and directed. That emissary whom she had sent out was now, as she well knew, fulfilling her mandate but too zealously. The power was now all in his own hands. And she herself—what could she do? He had already defied her authority—would he now give up his purpose, even if she wished? She might have telegraphed from London a command to him to stop all further proceedings till she came; but, even if she had done so, was it at all probable that he, after what had happened, would have obeyed? She had not done so, because she did not feel in a position to issue commands any longer in her old style. The servant had assumed the air and manner of a master, and the message which she had sent had been non-committal. She had relied upon the prospect of her own speedy arrival upon the scene, and upon her own power of confronting him, and reducing him to obedience in case of his refusal to fall in with her wishes.

But now it had fallen out far differently from what she had expected, and the collapse of her own strength had ruined all. Now every day and every hour was taking hope away from her, and giving it to that man who, from being her tool, had risen to the assertion of mastership over her. Now every moment was dragging away from her the man whom she sought so eagerly—dragging him away from her love to the darkness of that place to which her love and her longing might never penetrate.

Now, also, there arose within her the agonies of remorse. Never before had she understood the fearful meaning of this word. Such a feeling had never stirred her heart when she handed over to the betrayer her life-long friend, her almost sister, the one who so loved her, the trustful, the innocent, the affectionate Zillah; such a

feeling had not interfered with her purpose when Gualtier returned to tell of his success, and to mingle with his story the recital of Zillah's love and longing after her. But now it was different. Now she had handed over to that same betrayer one who had become dearer to her than life itself —one, too, who had grown dearer still ever since that moment when she had first resolved to save him. If she had never arrived at such a resolution—if she had borne with the struggles of her heart, and the tortures of her suspense—if she had fought out the battle in solitude and by herself, alone at Chetwynde, her sufferings would have been great, it is true, but they would never have arisen to the proportions which they now assumed. They would never have reduced her to this anguish of soul which, in its reaction upon the body, thus deprived her of all strength and hope. That moment when she had decided against vengeance, and in favor of pity, had borne for her a fearful fruit. It was the point at which all her love was let loose suddenly from that repression which she had striven to maintain over it, and rose up to gigantic proportions, filling all her thoughts, and overshadowing all other feelings. That love now pervaded all her being, occupied all her thoughts, and absorbed all her spirit. Once it was love; now it had grown to something more, it had become a frenzy; and the more she yielded to its overmastering power, the more did that power enchain her.

Tormented and tortured by such feelings as these, her weary, overworn frame sank once more, and the sufferings of Frankfort were renewed at Munich. On the next day after her arrival she was unable to leave. For day after day she lay prostrate, and all her impatient eagerness to go onward, and all her resolution, profited nothing when the poor frail flesh was so weak. Yet, in spite of all this, her soul was strong; and that soul, by its indomitable purpose, roused up once more the shattered forces of the body. A week passed away, but at the end of that week she arose to stagger forward.

Her journey to Lausanne was made somehow— she knew not how—partly by the help of Gretchen, who watched over her incessantly with inexhaustible devotion—partly through the strength of her own forceful will, which kept before her the great end which was to crown so much endeavor. She was a shattered invalid on this journey. She felt that another such a journey would be impossible. She hoped that this one would end her severe trials. And so, amidst hope and fear, her soul sustained her, and she went on. Such a journey as this to one less exhausted would have been one memorable on account of its physical and mental anguish, but to Hilda, in that extreme of suffering, it was not memorable at all. It was less than a dream. It was a blank. How it passed she knew not. Afterward she only could remember that in some way it did pass.

On the twenty-second day of November she reached Lausanne. Gretchen lifted her out of the coach, and supported her as she tottered into the Hôtel Gibbon. A man was standing in the doorway. At first he did not notice the two women, but something in Hilda's appearance struck him, and he looked earnestly at her.

An exclamation burst from him.

"My God!" he groaned.

HILDA'S ARRIVAL AT THE HOTEL GIBBON.

For a moment he stood staring at them, and then advanced with a rapid pace.

It was Gualtier.

Hilda recognized him, but said nothing. She could not speak a word. She wished to ask for something, but dreaded to ask that question, for she feared the reply.

In that interval of fear and hesitation Gualtier had leisure to see, in one brief glance, all the change that had come over her who had once been so strong, so calm, so self-reliant, so unmoved by the passions, the feelings, and the weaknesses of ordinary humanity. He saw and shuddered. Thin and pale and wan, she now stood before him, tottering feebly with unsteady step, and staying herself on the arm of her maid. Her cheeks, which, when he last saw them, were full and rounded with the outlines of youth and health, were now hollow and sunken. Around her eyes were those dark clouded marks which are the sure signs of weakness and disease. Her hands, as they grasped the arms of the maid, were thin and white and emaciated. Her lips were bloodless. It was the face of Hilda, indeed, but Hilda in sorrow, in suffering, and in grief—such a face as he had never imagined. But there were some things in that face which belonged to the Hilda of old, and had not changed. The eyes still flashed dark and piercing; they at least had not failed; and still their penetrating gaze rested upon him with no diminution in their power. Still the rich masses of ebon hair wreathed themselves in voluminous folds, and from out the luxuriant black masses of that hair the white face looked forth with its pallor rendered more awful from the contrast. Yet now that white face was a face of agony, and the eyes which, in their mute entreaty, were turned toward him, were fixed and staring. As he came up to her she grasped his arm; her lips moved; but for a time no audible sound escaped. At length she spoke, but it was in a whisper:

"Is he alive?"

And that was all that she said. She stood there panting, and gasping for breath, awaiting his reply with a certain awful suspense.

"Yes, my lady," said Gualtier, in a kind of bewilderment, as though he had not yet got over the shock of such an apparition. "He is alive yet."

"God be thanked!" moaned Hilda, in a low voice. "I have arrived in time—at last. He must be saved—and he shall be saved. Come."

She spoke this last word to Gualtier. By her

words, as well as by her face and manner, he saw that some great change had come over her, but why it was, he knew not yet. He plainly perceived, however, that she had turned from her purpose, and now no longer desired the death of the man whom she had commissioned him to destroy. In that moment of hurried thought he wondered much, but, from his knowledge of the recent past, he made a conjecture which was not far from the truth.

"Come," said Hilda. "I have something to say to you. I wish to see you alone. Come." And he followed her into the hotel.

CHAPTER L.

BLACK BILL.

ON the day after his meeting with Lord Chetwynde Obed had intended to start for Naples. Lord Chetwynde had not chosen to tell Obed his real name; but this maintenance of his incognito was not at all owing to any love of mystery, or any desire to keep a secret. He chose to be "Windham" because Obed thought him so, and he had no reason for being otherwise with him. He thought, also, that to tell his real name might involve a troublesome explanation, which was not desirable, especially since there was no need for it. Had that explanation been made, had the true name been made known at this interview, a flood of light would have poured down upon this dark matter, and Obed would have had at last the key to every thing. But this revelation was not made, and Windham took his departure from his friend.

On the following morning, while Obed was dressing, a note was brought to his room. It was from the police, and requested a visit from him, as matters of importance had been found out with reference to the case which he had intrusted to them. At this unexpected message Obed's start for Naples was postponed, and he hurried off as rapidly as possible to the office.

On arriving there he soon learned the cause of the note. An event had occurred which was in the highest degree unexpected, and had not arisen out of the ordinary inquiries of the detectives at all. It seems that on the evening of the previous day a man had come voluntarily to lodge information against this same Gualtier for the purpose of having a search made after him. He was one of the worst characters in London, well known to the police, and recognized by them, and by his own ruffian companions, under the name of "Black Bill." In order that Obed might himself hear what he had to say, they had detained the informer, and sent for him.

Obed was soon brought face to face with this new actor in the great tragedy of Zillah's life. He was a short, stout, thick-set man, with bull neck, broad shoulders, deep chest, low brow, flat nose, square chin, and small black eyes, in which there lay a mingled expression of ferocity and cunning. His very swarthy complexion, heavy black beard, and thick, matted, coal-black hair, together with his black eyes, were sufficiently marked to make him worthy of the name of "Black Bill." Altogether, he looked like a perfect type of perfect ruffianism; and Obed involuntarily felt a cold shudder pass over him as he

thought of Zillah falling into the hands of any set of villains of which this man was one.

On entering the room Black Bill was informed that Obed was largely interested in the affair which he had made known, and was bidden to tell his story once more. Thereupon Black Bill took a long and very comprehensive stare at Obed from head to foot, after which he went on to narrate his story.

He had been engaged in the month of June, he said, by a man who gave his name as Richards. He understood that he was to take part in an enterprise which was illegal, but attended with no risk whatever. It was simply to assist in sinking a vessel at sea. Black Bill remarked, with much naïveté, that he always was scrupulous in obeying the laws; but just at that time he was out of tin, and yielded to the temptation. He thought it was a case where the vessel was to be sunk for the sake of the insurance. Such things were very common, and friends of his had assisted before in similar enterprises. The price offered for his services was not large—only fifty pounds—and this also made him think it was only some common case.

He found that three other men had also been engaged. They were ordered to go to Marseilles, and wait till they were wanted. Money was given them for the journey, and a certain house was mentioned as the place where they should stay.

They did not have long to wait. In a short time the man who had employed them called on them, and took them down to the harbor, where they found a very handsome yacht. In about an hour afterward he returned, accompanied this time by a young and beautiful lady. Black Bill and all the men were very much struck by her appearance. They saw very well that she belonged to the upper classes. They saw also that their employer treated her with the deepest respect, and seemed almost like her servant. They heard her once call him "Mr. Gualtier," and knew by this that the name "Richards" was an assumed one. They all wondered greatly at her appearance, and could not understand what was to be her part in the adventure. Judging from what they heard of the few words she addressed to this Gualtier, they saw that she was expecting to sail to Naples, and was very eager to arrive there.

At last the second night came. Gualtier summoned Black Bill at midnight, and they both went into the hold, where they bored holes. The other men had meanwhile got the boat in readiness, and had put some provisions and water in her. At last the holes were bored, and the vessel began to fill rapidly. Black Bill was ordered into the boat, Gualtier saying that he was going to fetch the young lady. The men all thought then that she had been brought on board merely to be forced into taking part in the sinking of the vessel. None of them understood the idea of the thing at all.

They waited for a time, according to Black Bill. The night was intensely dark, and they could hear nothing, when suddenly Gualtier came to the boat and got in.

"Where's the girl?" said Black Bill.

"She won't come," said Gualtier, who at the same time unloosed the boat. "She won't come," he repeated. "Give way, lads."

The "lads" refused, and a great outcry arose. They swore that they would not leave the vessel without the girl, and that if he did not go back instantly and get her, they would pitch him overboard and save her themselves. Black Bill told him they thought it was only an insurance business, and nothing like this.

Gualtier remained quite calm during this outcry. As soon as he could make himself heard he told them, in a cool voice, that he was armed with a revolver, and would shoot them all down if they did not obey him. He had hired them for this, he said, and they were in for it. If they obeyed him, he would pay them when they got ashore; if not, he would blow their brains out. Black Bill said that at this threat he drew his own pistol and snapped it at Gualtier. It would not go off. Gualtier then laughed, and said that pistols which had a needle run down the nipple did not generally explode—by which Black Bill saw that his pistol had been tampered with.

There was a long altercation, but the end of it was that Gualtier gave them a certain time to decide, after which he swore that he would shoot them down. He was armed, he was determined; they were unarmed, and at his mercy; and the end of it was, they yielded to him and rowed away. One thing which materially influenced them was, that they had drifted away from the schooner, and she had been lost in the deep darkness of the night. Besides, before their altercation was over, they all felt sure that the vessel had sunk. So they rowed on sullenly all that night and all the next day, with only short intervals of rest, guarded all the time by Gualtier, who, pistol in hand, kept them to their work.

They reached the coast at a point not far from Leghorn. It was a wild spot, with wooded shores. Here Gualtier stepped out, paid them, and ordered them to go to Leghorn. As for himself, he swore they should never see him again. They took the money, and rowed off for a little distance along the shore, when Black Bill made them put him ashore. They did so, and rowed on. He plunged into the woods, and walked back till he got on Gualtier's trail, which he followed up. Black Bill here remarked, with a mixture of triumph and mock contrition, that an accident in his early life had sent him to Australia, in which country he had learned how to notice the track of animals or of man in any place, however wild. Here Gualtier had been careless, and his track was plain. Black Bill thus followed him from place to place, and after Gualtier reached the nearest railway station was easily able to keep him in sight.

In this way he had kept him in sight through North Italy, over the Alps, through Germany, and, finally, to London, where he followed him to the door of his lodgings. Here he had made inquiries, and had learned that Gualtier was living there under the name of Mr. Brown; that he had only been there a few weeks, but seemed inclined to stay permanently, as he had brought there his clothes, some furniture, and all his papers, together with pictures and other valuables. Black Bill then devoted himself to the task of watching him, which he kept up for some time, till one day Gualtier left by rail for the west, and never returned. Black Bill had watched ever since, but had seen nothing of him. He thought he must have gone to America.

Here Black Bill paused for a while, and Obed asked him one or two questions.

"What is the reason," he asked, "that you did not give information to the police at first, instead of waiting till now?"

"A question like that there," said Black Bill, "is easy enough to answer. You see I wanted for to play my hown little game. I wanted fur to find out who the gal was. If so be as I'd found out that, I'd have had somethin' to work on. That's fust an' foremost. An' next, you understand, I was anxious to git a hold of him, so as to be able to pay off that oncommon black score as I had agin him. Arter humbuggin' me, hocusin' my pistol, an' threat'nin' murder to me, an' makin' me work wuss than a galley-slave in that thar boat, I felt petiklar anxious to pay him off in the same coin. That's the reason why I sot up a watch on him on my own account, instead of telling the beaks."

"Do you know," asked Obed again, "what has become of the others that were with you in the boat?"

"Never have laid eyes on 'em since that blessed arternoon when I stepped ashore to follow Gualtier. P'r'aps they've been nabbed—p'r'aps they're sarvin' their time out in the galleys—p'r'aps they've jined the Italian army—p'r'aps they've got back here again. Wot's become of them his Honor here knows better'n me."

After this Black Bill went on, and told all the rest that he had to say. He declared that he had watched Gualtier's lodgings for more than three months, expecting that he would return. At last he disguised himself and went there to make inquiries. The keeper of the house told him that nothing had been heard from "Mr. Brown" since he left, and he had packed away all his things in hope of his return. But a Liverpool paper had recently been sent to him with a marked paragraph, giving an account of the recovery of the body of a man who had been drowned, and who in all respects seemed to resemble his late lodger. Why it had been sent to him he did not know; but he thought that perhaps some paper had been found in the pockets of the deceased, and the authorities had sent this journal to the address, thinking that the notice might thus reach his friends.

After this Black Bill began to lose hope of success. He did not believe that Gualtier had perished, but that it was a common trick to give rise to a belief in the mind of his lodging-house keeper that he had met with his death. In this belief he waited for a short time to see if any fresh intelligence turned up; but at length, as Gualtier made no sign, and Black Bill's own resources were exhausted, he had concluded that it would be best to make known the whole circumstance to the police.

Such was the substance of his narrative. It was interrupted by frequent questions; but Black Bill told a coherent tale, and did not contradict himself. There was not the slightest doubt in the minds of his hearers that he was one of the greatest scoundrels that ever lived, but at the same time there was not the slightest doubt that on this occasion he had not taken part willingly against the life of the young girl. He and his associates, it was felt, had been tricked and overreached by the superior cunning of Gualtier. They saw also, by Black Bill's account, that this

Gualtier was bold and courageous to a high degree, with a cool calculation and a daring that were not common among men. He had drawn these men into the commission of what they expected would be some slight offense, and then forced them to be his unwilling allies in a foul murder. He had paid them a small price for the commission of a great crime. He had bullied them, threatened them, and made them his slaves by his own clever management and the force of his own nature, and that, too, although these very men were, all of them, blood-stained ruffians, the most reckless among the dregs of society. From Black Bill's story Obed gained a new view of Gualtier.

After Black Bill had been dismissed, the lodging-house keeper, who had been sent for, made his appearance. His account was quite in accordance with what had been said. This man, whom he called *Brown*, had taken lodgings with him in May last, and had staid a few weeks. He then had been absent for a fortnight or so. On his return he passed a few days in the house, and then left, since which time he had not been heard of. The Liverpool paper which had been sent him gave the only hint at the possible cause of his absence. In reply to an inquiry from Obed, the landlord stated that Mr. Brown's effects seemed to be very valuable. There was a fine piano, a dozen handsome oil-paintings, a private desk, an iron box, a jewel box, and a trunk, which, from its weight, was filled with something perhaps of value. On the whole, he could not think that such things would be left by any one without some effort to regain possession of them. If they were sold at a sacrifice, they would bring a very large sum.

The lodging-house keeper was then allowed to take his departure, after which Obed and the magistrate discussed for some time the new appearance which had been given to this affair. Their conclusions were similar, in most respects.

It seemed to them, first, that this Gualtier, whose names were so numerous, had planned his crime with a far-reaching ingenuity not often to be met with, and that after the accomplishment of his crime he was still as ingenious in his efforts after perfect concealment. He had baffled the police of France, of Italy, and of England thus far. He had also baffled completely that one enemy who had so long a time followed on his track. His last act in leaving his lodgings was well done—though putting the notice in the Liverpool paper, and sending it to the landlord, seemed more clumsy than his usual proceedings. It was readily concluded that the notice in that paper was only a ruse, in order to secure more perfect concealment, or, perhaps, elude pursuit more effectually.

It seemed also most likely, under the circumstances, that he had actually gone as far as Liverpool, and from that port to America. If that were the case it would be difficult, if not impossible, ever to get on his track or discover him. The only chance appeared to be in the probability that he would send, in some way or other, for those things which he had left in the lodging-house. Judging by the enumeration which the landlord had given, they were too valuable to be lost, and in most cases the owner would make some effort to recover them. The magistrate said that he would direct the landlord to keep the

things carefully, and, if any inquiry ever came after them, to give immediate information to the police. This was evidently the only way of ever catching Gualtier.

The motive for this crime appeared quite plain to these inquirers. Judging by the facts, it seemed as though Gualtier and Hilda had been lovers, and had planned this so as to secure all the property of the younger sister. To Obed the motive was still more plain, though he did not tell what he knew—namely, the important fact that Hilda was not the sister at all of her victim, and that her own property was small in comparison with that of the one at whose life she aimed. He thought that to tell this even to the police would be a violation of sacred confidence. After the commission of the crime it seemed plain that these criminals had taken to flight together, most probably to America. This they could easily do, as their funds were all portable.

A careful look-out at the lodging-house was evidently the only means by which the track of the fugitives could be discovered. Even this would take a long time, but it was the only thing that could be done.

After this a careful examination was made of the things which Gualtier had left behind at the lodging-house. The pictures were found to be very valuable ; the piano, also, was new—one of Collard's—and estimated to be worth one hundred and fifty pounds. The jewel box was found to contain articles of great value, some diamond rings, and turquoise and pearl. Many of the things looked like keepsakes, some of them having inscriptions, such as "To M.—from G.," "To M.—from L.," "From Mother." These seemed like things which no living man could willingly give up. How could it be known that Gualtier had indeed given up such sacred possessions as these?

On opening the trunks, one was found to contain books, chiefly French novels, and the other clothes. None of these gave any fresh clew to the home or the friends of the fugitive.

Last of all was the writing-desk. This was opened with intense curiosity. It was hoped that here something might be discovered.

It was well filled with papers. But a short examination served to show that, in the first place, the papers were evidently considered very valuable by the owner ; and, in the second place, that they were of no earthly value to any one else. They were, in short, three different manuscript novels, whose soiled and faded appearance seemed to speak of frequent offerings to different publishers, and as frequent refusals. There they lay, still cherished by the author, inclosed in his desk, lying there to be claimed perhaps at some future time. There were, in addition to these, a number of receipted bills, and some season tickets for railways and concerts—and that was all.

Nothing, therefore, was discovered from this examination. Yet the result gave hope. It seemed as if no man would leave things like these —this piano, these pictures, these keepsakes— and never seek to get them again. Those very manuscript novels, rejected as they had been, were still things which the author would not willingly give up. The chances, therefore, were very great that at some time, in some way, some application would be made for this property. And on this the magistrate relied confidently.

Obed spent another day in London, and had another interview with the magistrate. He found, however, that nothing more could be done by him, or by any one else, at present, and so he returned to Naples *via* Marseilles. He called on the prefect of police at the latter city to acquaint him with the latest intelligence of this affair; heard that nothing more had been discovered about Mathilde, and then went on his way, arriving in due time at his destination. He told his sister the result of his journey, but to Zillah he told nothing at all about it. Having done all that man could do, Obed now settled himself down once more in Naples, beguiling his time between the excitement of excursions with his friends, and the calm of domestic life with his family. Naples, on the whole, seemed to him the pleasantest spot to stay in that he had seen for a long time, and he enjoyed his life there so much that he was in no hurry to leave it.

CHAPTER LL.

A STARTLING PROPOSAL.

OBED and his family thus remained in Naples, and Zillah at last had an occupation. The new duties which she had undertaken gave her just enough of employment to fill the day and occupy her thoughts. It was a double blessing. In the first place it gave her a feeling of independence; and again, and especially, it occupied her thoughts, and thus prevented her mind from preying upon itself. Then she was able to gain alleviation for the troubles that had so long oppressed her. She felt most profoundly the change from the feeling of poverty and dependence to one of independence, when she was actually "getting her own living." She knew that her independence was owing to the delicate generosity of Obed Chute, and that under any other circumstances she would probably have had no refuge from starvation; but her gratitude to her friends did not lessen at all her own self-complacency. There was a childish delight in Zillah over her new position, which was due, perhaps, to the fact that she had always looked upon herself as hopelessly and incurably dull; but now the discovery that she could actually fill the position of music-teacher brought her a strange triumph, which brightened many a dark hour.

Zillah already had understood and appreciated the delicate feeling and high-toned generosity of Obed Chute and his sister. Nothing could increase the deep admiration which she felt for those simple, upright, honest souls, whose pure affection for her had proved such a blessing. If there had been nothing else, her very gratitude to them would have been a stimulus such as the ordinary governess never has. Under such a stimulus the last vestige of Zillah's old willfulness died out. She was now a woman, tried in the crucible of sorrow, and in that fiery trial the dross had been removed, and only the pure gold remained. The wayward, impetuous girl had reached her last and fullest development, and she now stood forth in adversity and affliction, right noble in her character—an earnest woman, devoted, tender, enthusiastic, generous.

The fondness and admiration of her friends increased every day. The little children, whose musical education she had now begun, had already learned to love her; and when she was transformed from a friend to a teacher they loved her none the less. Zillah's capacity for teaching was so remarkable that it surprised herself, and she began to think that she had not been understood in the old days. But then, in the old days, she was a petted and spoiled child, and would never try to work until the last year of her life with the Earl, after he had extorted from her a promise to do differently.

Obed Chute saw her success in her new position with undisguised satisfaction. But now that she had become a governess he was not at all inclined to relax his exertions in her behalf. She was of too much importance, he said, to waste her life and injure her health in constant drudgery, and so he determined that she should not suffer for want of recreation. In Naples there need never be any lack of that. The city itself, with its noisy, laughing, jovial population, seems to the English eye as though it was keeping one perpetual holiday. The Strada Toledo looks to the sober northerner as though a constant carnival were going on. Naples has itself to offer to the visitor, with its never-ending gayety and its many-sided life—its brilliant cafés, its lively theatres, its gay pantomimes, its buffooneries, its macaroni, its lazaroni, and its innumerable festivities. Naples has also a cluster of attractions all around it, which keep their freshness longer than those of any other city. Among these Obed Chute continued to take Zillah. To him it was the best happiness that he could desire when he had succeeded in making the time pass pleasantly for her. To see her face flush up with that innocent girlish enthusiasm, and to hear her merry laugh, which was still childlike in its freshness and abandon, was something so pleasant that he would chuckle over it to himself all the evening afterward.

So, as before, they drove about the environs or sailed over the bay. Very little did Obed Chute know about that historic past which lived and breathed amidst all these scenes through which he wandered. No student of history was he. To him the cave of Polyphemus brought no recollections; the isle of Capri was a simple isle of the sea, and nothing more; Misenum could not give to his imagination the vanished Roman navies; Puzzuoli could not show the traces of Saint Paul; and there was nothing which could make known to him the mighty footprints of the heroes of the past, from the time of the men of Osca, and Cumæ, and the builders of Pæstum's Titan temples, down through all the periods of Roman luxury, and through all gradations of men from Cicero to Nero, and down farther to the last, and not the least of all, Belisarius. The past was shut out, but it did not interfere with his simple-hearted enjoyment. The present was sufficient for him. He had no conception of art; and the proudest cathedrals of Naples, or the noblest sculptures of her museums, or the most radiant pictures, never awakened any emotion within him. Art was dumb to him; but then there remained something greater than art, and that was nature. Nature showed him here her rarest and divinest beauty; and if in the presence of such beauty as that—beauty which glowed in immortal lineaments wherever he turned his eyes —if before this he slighted the lesser beauties of

"ZILLAH'S CAPACITY FOR TEACHING SURPRISED HERSELF."

art, he might be sneered at by the mere dilettante, but the emotions of his own soul were none the less true and noble.

One day they had arranged for a sail to Capri. Miss Chute could not go, and Zillah went with Obed Chute alone. She had frequently done so before. It was a glorious day. Most days in Naples are glorious. The Neapolitan boatmen sang songs all the way—songs older, perhaps, than the time of Massaniello—songs which may have come down from Norman, or even from Roman days. There was one lively air which amused Zillah—

> "How happy is the fisher's life,
>   Eccomi Eccola,
> The fisher and his faithful wife,
>   Eccola!"

It was a lively, ringing refrain, and the words had in them that sentiment of domestic life which is not usually found in Continental songs. The sea glittered around them. The boat danced lightly over the waves. The gleaming atmosphere showed all the scenery with startling distinctness. (Where is there an atmosphere like that of Naples?) The sky was of an intense blue, and the deep azure of the sea rivaled the color of the sky that bent above it. The breeze that swept over the sea brought on its wings life and health and joy. All around there flashed before them the white sails of countless boats that sped in every direction over the surface of the waters.

They landed in Capri, and walked about the island. They visited the cave, and strolled along the shore. At length they sat down on a rock, and looked over the waters toward the city. Before them spread out the sea, bounded by the white gleaming outline of Naples, which extended far along the shore; on the left was Ischia; and on the right Vesuvius towered on high, with its smoke cloud hovering over it, and streaming far along through the air. Never before had the Bay of Naples seemed so lovely. Zillah lost herself in her deep admiration. Obed Chute also sat in profound silence. Usually he talked; now, however, he said nothing. Zillah thought that he, like herself, was lost in the beauty of this matchless scene.

At length the long silence was broken by Obed Chute.

"My child," said he, "for the last few weeks I have been thinking much of you. You have wound yourself around my heart. I want to say something to you now which will surprise you, perhaps—and, indeed, I do not know how you will take it. But in whatever way you take it, do not be afraid to tell me exactly how you feel. Whatever you may say, I insist on being your friend. You once called me your 'best friend.' I will never do any thing to lose that title."

Zillah looked up in wonder. She was bewildered. Her brain whirled, and all presence of mind left her. She suspected what was coming, but it seemed too extraordinary, and she could scarcely believe it. She looked at him thus bewildered and confused, and Obed went calmly on.

"My child," said he, "you are so noble and so tender that it is not surprising that you have fixed yourself fast in my old heart. You are very dear and very precious to me. I do not know how I could bear to have you leave me. I hope to have you near me while I live, in some way or other. How shall it be? Will you be a daughter to me—or will you be a wife?"

Obed Chute paused. He did not look at her as he said this. He did not see the crimson flush that shot like lightning over that white and beau-.tiful face. He looked away over the sea.

But a deep groan from Zillah aroused him. He started and turned.

Her face was upturned to his with an expression of agony. She clasped his arms with a convulsive grasp, and seemed to gasp for breath.

"Oh God!" she cried. "Is this so? I must tell you this much, then—I will divulge my secret. Oh, my friend—I am married!"

CHAPTER LII.

A BETTER UNDERSTANDING.

For a long time not a word was spoken. Obed sat thunder-struck by this intelligence. He looked at her in wonder, as her fair girlish face was turned toward him, not knowing how to receive this unparalleled communication.

"Oh, my friend," said Zillah, "have I ever in any way shown that I could have expected this? Yes, I am married—and it is about my marriage that the secret of my life has grown. Forgive me if I can not tell you more."

"Forgive you? What are you saying, my child?" said Obed Chute, tenderly. "I am the one who must be forgiven. I have disturbed and troubled you, when I was only seeking to secure your happiness."

By this time Obed had recovered from his surprise, and began to contemplate the present state of affairs in their new aspect. It certainly was strange that this young girl should be a married woman, but so it was; and what then? "What then?" was the question which suggested itself to Zillah also. Would it make any difference—or rather would it not make all the difference in the world? Hitherto she had felt unembarrassed in his society, but hereafter all would be different. Never again could she feel the same degree of ease as before in his presence. Would he not hereafter seem to her and to himself as a rejected lover?

But these thoughts soon were diverted into another channel by Obed Chute himself.

"So you are married?" said he, solemnly.

"Yes," faltered Zillah.

"Well, my child," said Obed, with that same tenderness in his voice, which was now so fa-

miliar to her, "whether it is for good or evil I do not seek to know. I only say this, that if there is any thing which I could do to secure your happiness, you could not find any one who would do more for you than Obed Chute."

"Oh, my friend!"

"Just now," said Obed Chute, "I asked you to be my wife. Do not avoid the subject, my child. I am not ashamed of having made that proposal. It was for your happiness, as I thought, as well as for my own. I loved you; and I thought that, perhaps, if you were my wife, I could make you happier than you now are. But since it is not to be, what then? Why, I love you none the less; and if you can not be my wife, you shall be my daughter. Do not look upon me as a passionate youth. My love is deep and tender and self-sacrificing. I think, perhaps, it is much more the love of a father than that of a husband, and that it is just as well that there are obstacles in the way of my proposal. Do not look so sad, my little child," continued Obed Chute, with increased tenderness. "Why should you? I am your friend, and you must love me as much as you can—like a daughter. Will you be a daughter to me? Will you trust me, my child, and brighten my life as you have been doing?"

He held out his hand.

Zillah took it, and burst into tears. A thousand contending emotions were in her heart and agitating her.

"Oh, my friend and benefactor!" said she; "how can I help giving you my love and my gratitude? You have been to me a father and a friend—"

"Say no more," said Obed, interrupting her. "It is enough. We will forget that this conversation has taken place. And as for myself, I will cherish your secret, my child. It is as safe with me as it would be with yourself only."

Now as he spoke, with his frank, generous face turned toward her, and the glow of affection in his eyes, Zillah felt as though it would be better to give him her full confidence and tell him all. In telling him that she was married she had made a beginning. Why should she not tell every thing, and make known the secret of her life? It would be safe with him. It would be a fair return for his generous affection. Above all, it would be frank and honest. He would then know all about her, and there would be nothing more to conceal.

Thus she thought; but still she shrank from such a confession and such a confidence. It would involve a disclosure of all the most solemn and sacred memories of her life. It would do violence to her most delicate instincts. Could she do this? It was impossible. Not unless Obed Chute insisted on knowing every thing could she venture to lay bare her past life, and make known the secrets of her heart. And she well knew that such a thing would never be required of her, at least by this generous friend. Indeed, she knew well that he would be most likely to refuse her confidence, even if she were to offer it on such an occasion as this.

"I feel," said Zillah at length, as these thoughts oppressed her, "that I am in a false position. You have been so generous to me that you have a right to know all about me. I ought to let you know my true name, and make you acquainted with the story of my life."

" You ought to do nothing of the sort," said Obed Chute. " There are some things which can not be breathed to any human being. Do you form so low an estimate of me, my dear child, as to think that I would wish to have your confidence unless it was absolutely necessary, and for your own good ? No. · You do not understand me. The affection which I have for you, which you call generosity, gives me no such claim, and it gives me no desire to tear open those wounds which your poor heart must feel so keenly. Nothing can prevent my loving you. I tell you you are my daughter. I accept you as you are. I wish to know nothing. I know enough of you from my knowledge of your character. I only know this, that you have suffered ; and I should like very much to be able to console you or make you happier."

" You have done very much for me," said Zillah, looking at him with deep emotion.

" Nothing, as far as I am concerned ; but it is pleasant to me to know that any thing which I have done is grateful to you," said Obed, calmly and benignantly. " Keep your secret to yourself, my dear child. You came to me from the sea ; and I only hope that you will continue with me as long as you can to brighten my life, and let me hear your voice and see your face. And that is a simple wish. Is it not, my child ?"

" You are overwhelming me with your goodness," said Zillah, with another grateful glance.

She was most grateful for the way in which Obed had given up his idea of matrimony. Had he shown the excitement of a disappointed lover, then there would have been a dark future before her. She would have had to leave his family, among whom she had found a home. But Obed showed nothing of this kind. He himself said that, if he could not have her as a wife, he would be satisfied to have her as a daughter. And when he learned that she was married, he at once took up the paternal attitude, and the affection which he expressed was that tender yet calm feeling which might become a father. At the expression of such a feeling as this Zillah's generous and loving heart responded, and all her nature warmed beneath its genial influence. Yes, she would be to him as a daughter ; she would show him all the gratitude and devotion of which she was capable. Under such circumstances as these her life could go on as it had before, and the interview of to-day would not cast the slightest shadow over the sunshine of the future. So she felt, and so she said.

Obed took pains to assure her over and over again how entirely he had sunk all considerations of himself in his regard for her, and that the idea of making her his wife was not more precious than that of making her his daughter.

" It was to have you near me," said he, " to make you happy, to give you a home which should be all yours ; but this can be done in another and a better way, my child ; so I am content, if you are."

Before they left the place Zillah gave him, in general terms, an outline of her secret, without mentioning names and places. She said that she was married when very young, that her father had died, that the man to whom she had been married disliked her, and she had not seen him for years ; that once she had seen a letter which he had written to a friend, in which

M

he alluded to her in such insulting language, and with such expressions of abhorrence, that she had gone into seclusion, and had determined to preserve that seclusion till she died. Hilda, she said, had accompanied her, and she had believed her to be faithful until the recent discovery of her treachery.

This much Zillah felt herself bound to tell Obed Chute. From this he could at once understand her situation, while at the same time it would be impossible for him to know who she was or who her friends were. That she would not tell to any human being.

All the sympathies of Obed Chute's nature were aroused as he listened to what Zillah told him. He was indignant that she should have been led through any motive into such a marriage. In his heart he blamed her friends, whoever they were, and especially her father. But most of all he blamed this unknown husband of hers, who, after consenting to a marriage, had chosen to insult and revile her. What he thought he did not choose to say, but to himself he registered a vow that, if he could ever find out this villain, he would avenge all Zillah's wrongs in his heart's blood, which vow brought to his heart a great peace and calm.

This day was an eventful one for Zillah, but the result was not what might at one time have been feared. After such an interchange of confidence there was an understanding between her and her friend, which deepened the true and sincere friendship that existed between them. Zillah's manner toward him became more confiding, more trustful—in short, more filial. He, too, insensibly took up the part of a parent or guardian ; yet he was as solicitous about her welfare and happiness as in the days when he had thought of making her his wife.

CHAPTER LIII.

" COME !"

This was the word which Hilda had addressed to Gualtier in front of the Hôtel Gibbon at Lausanne, and, saying this, she tottered toward the door, supported by Gretchen. That stout German maid upheld her in her strong arms, as a mother might hold up a child as it learns to walk, ere yet its unsteady feet have found out the way to plant themselves. Gualtier had not yet got over the shock of such a surprise, but he saw her weakness, and was sufficiently himself to offer his arm to assist his mistress. But Hilda did not seem to see it. At any rate she did not accept the offer. Her only aim was to get into the hotel, and the assistance of Gretchen was quite enough for her.

Although Gretchen thus supported her, still even the slight exertion which she made, even the motion of her limbs which was required of her, though they scarcely felt her weight, was too much for her in her weakness and prostration. She panted for breath in her utter exhaustion, and at length, on reaching the hall, she stood for a few moments at the foot of the stairway, as though struggling to regain her breath, and then suddenly fainted away in the arms of Gretchen.

At this the stout maid took her in her arms,

and carried her up stairs, while Gualtier led the way to the suite of apartments occupied by Lord Chetwynde. Here Hilda was placed on a sofa, and after a time came to herself.

She then told Gretchen to retire. The maid obeyed, and Hilda and Gualtier were left alone. The latter stood regarding her, with his pale face full of deep anxiety and apprehension, dreading he knew not what, and seeing in her something which seemed to take her beyond the reach of that coercion which he had once successfully applied to her.

"Tell me," cried Hilda, the instant that Gretchen had closed the door after her, looking around at the same time with something of her old sharp vigilance—"tell me, it is not too late yet to save him?"

"To save him!" repeated Gualtier.

"Yes. That is what brought me here."

Gualtier looked at her with eager scrutiny, seeking to fathom her full meaning. Suspecting the truth, he was yet unwilling to believe it. His answer was given in slow, deliberate tones.

"No," said he, "it is—not—yet—too—late—to—save him—if that is really what you wish."

"That is what I have come for," said Hilda; "I am going to take my place at his bedside, to undo the past, and bring him back to life. That is my purpose. Do you hear?" she said, while her white lips quivered with excitement, and her shattered frame trembled with the intensity of her emotion.

"I hear, my lady," said Gualtier, with his old respect, but with a dull light in his gray eyes, and a cold and stern intonation which told of the anger which was rising within him.

Once he had shaken off her authority, and had spoken to her with the tone of a master. It was not probable that he would recede now from the stand which he had then taken. But, on the other hand, Hilda did not now seem like one over whom his old menaces would have any effect. There was in her, besides her suffering, an air of reckless self-sacrifice, which made it seem as if no threats of his could again affect her.

"You hear?" said she, with feverish impatience. "Have you nothing more to say?"

"No, nothing. It is for you to speak," said Gualtier, gruffly. "You began."

"He must be saved," said Hilda; "and I must save him; and you must help me."

Gualtier turned away his head, while a dark frown came over his face. The gesture excited Hilda still more.

"What!" she hissed, springing to her feet, and grasping his arm, "do you hesitate? Do you refuse to assist me?"

"Our relations are changed," said Gualtier, slowly, turning round as he spoke. "This thing I will not do. I have begun my work."

As he turned he encountered the eyes of Hilda, which were fixed on him—stern, wrathful, menacing.

"You have begun it!" she repeated. "It was my work—not yours. I order you to desist, and you must obey. You can not do any thing else. To go on is impossible, if I stand between you and him. Only one thing is left for you, and that is to obey me, and assist me as before."

"Obey you!" said Gualtier, with a cold and almost ferocious glance. "The time for obedience I think is past. That much you ought to

know. And what is it that you ask? What? To thrust from me the dearest hope of my life, and just as it was reaching fruition."

Hilda's eyes were fastened on Gualtier as he said these words. The scorn with which he disowned any obedience, the confidence with which he spoke of that renunciation of his former subordination, were but ill in accordance with those words with which he expressed his "dearest hope."

"Dearest hope!" said Hilda—"fruition! If you knew any thing, you would know that the time for that is rapidly passing, and only your prompt obedience and assistance will benefit you now."

"Pardon me," said Gualtier, hastily; "I forgot myself in my excitement. But you ask impossible things. I can not help you here. The obstacle between you and me was nearly removed—and you ask me to replace it."

"Obstacle!" said Hilda, in scorn. "Is it thus that you mention him?" In her weakness her wrath and indignation burst forth. "That man whom you call an obstacle is one for whose sake I have dragged myself over hundreds of miles; for whom I am now ready to lay down my life. Do not wonder. Do not question me. Call it passion—madness—any thing—but do not attempt to thwart me. Speak now. Will you help me or not?"

"Help you!" cried Gualtier, bitterly, "help you! to what? to do that which will destroy my last hope—and after I have extorted from you your promise! Ask me any thing else."

"I want nothing else."

"You may yet want my aid."

"If you do not help me now, I shall never want you."

"You have needed me before, and will need me again."

"If he dies, I shall never need you again."

"If he dies, that is the very time when you will need me."

"No, I shall not—for if he dies I will die myself!" cried Hilda, in a burst of uncontrollable passion.

Gualtier started, and his heart sank within him. Long and earnestly he looked at her, but he saw that this was more than a fitful outburst of passion. Looking on her face with its stern and fixed resolve, with its intense meaning, he knew that what she had said was none other than her calm, set purpose. He saw it in every one of those faded lineaments, upon which such a change had been wrought in so short a time. He read it in the hollows round her eyes, in her sunken cheeks, in her white, bloodless lips, her thin, emaciated hands, which were now clenched in desperate resolve. From this he saw that there was no appeal. He learned how strong that passion must be which had thus overmastered her, and was consuming all the energies of her powerful nature. To this she was sacrificing the labor of years, and all the prospects which now lay before her; to this she gave up all her future life, with all its possibilities of wealth and honor and station. A coronet, a castle, a princely revenue, rank, wealth, and title, all lay before her within her grasp; yet now she turned her back upon them, and came to the bedside of the man whose death was necessary to her success, to save him from death. She trampled her own interests in the dust; she threw to the winds the hard-won results of treachery and crime, and only that she might be near him who abhorred her, and whose first word on coming back to consciousness might be an imprecation. Beside this man who hated her, he who adored her was as nothing, and all his devotion and all his adoration were in one moment forgotten.

All these thoughts flashed through the mind of Gualtier as at that instant he comprehended the situation. And what was he to do? Could he associate himself with her in this new purpose? He could not. He might have refrained from the work of death at the outset, if she had bid him refrain, but now that he had begun it, it was not easy to give it up. She had set him to the task. It had been doubly sweet to him. First, it was a delight to his own vindictive nature; and secondly, he had flattered himself that this would be an offering well pleasing to the woman whom he adored. She had set him to this task, and when it was fully completed he might hope for an adequate reward. From the death of this man he had accustomed himself to look forward in anticipation of the highest happiness for himself. All his future grew bright from the darkness of this deed.

Now in one instant his dream was dispelled. The very one who had commanded him to do this now came in a kind of frenzy, with a face like that of death, bidding him to stay his hand. Deep, dark, and bitter was that disappointment, and all the more so from its utter suddenness. And because he could read in her face and in her words not only the change that had taken place, but also the cause of that change, the revulsion of feeling within himself became the more intolerable. His nature rose up in rebellion against this capricious being. How could he yield to her wishes here? He could not sway with every varying feeling of hers. He could not thus retire from his unfinished work, and give up his vengeance.

Indignant as he was, there was yet something in Hilda's countenance which stirred to its depths the deep passion of his nature. Her face had the expression of one who had made up her mind to die. To such a one what words could he say—what arguments could he use? For a time pity overmastered anger, and his answer was mild.

"You ask impossibilities," said he. "In no case can I help you. I will not even let you do what you propose."

Hilda looked at him with a cold glance of scorn. She seated herself once more.

"You will not let me!" she repeated.

"Certainly not. I shall go on with the work which I have begun. But I will see that you receive the best attention. You are excited now. Shall I tell the maid to come to you? You had better put an end to this interview; it is too much for you. You need rest."

Gualtier spoke quietly, and seemed really to feel some anxiety about her excitement. But he miscalculated utterly the nature of Hilda, and relied too much on the fact that he had once terrified her. These cool words threw into Hilda a vivid excitement of feeling, which for a time turned all her thoughts upon this man, who under such circumstances dared to resume that

tone of impudent superiority which once before he had ventured to adopt. Her strength revived under such a stimulus, and for a time her bitter contempt and indignation stilled the deep sorrow and anxiety for her heart.

The voice with which she answered was no longer agitated or excited. It was cool, firm, and penetrating—a tone which reminded him of her old domineering manner.

"You are not asked to give up your work," said she. "It is done. You are dismissed."

"Dismissed!" said Gualtier, with a sneer. "You ought to know that I am not one who can be dismissed."

"I know that you can be, and that you are," said Hilda. "If you were capable of understanding me you would know this. But you, base and low-born hireling that you are, what can there be in common between one like you and one like me?"

"One thing," said Gualtier. "Crime!"

Hilda changed not a feature.

"What care I for that? It is over. I have passed into another life. Your coarse and vulgar threats avail nothing. This moment ends all communication between us forever. You may do what you like. All your threats are useless. Finally, you must go away at once."

"Go away?"

"Yes—at once—and forever. These rooms shall never see you again. I am here, and will stay here."

"You?"

"I!"

"You have no right here."

"I have."

"What right?"

"The right of love," said Hilda. "I come to save him!"

"You tried to kill him."

"That is passed. I will save him now."

"You are mad. You know that this is idle. You know that I am a determined and desperate man."

"Pooh! What is the determination or the desperation of one like you? I know well what you think. Once you were able to move me by your threats. That is passed. My resolve and my despair have placed me beyond your reach forever. Go—go away. Begone! Take your threats with you, and do your worst."

"You are mad—you are utterly mad," said Gualtier, confounded at the desperation of one whom he felt was so utterly in his power; one, too, who herself must have known this. "You have forgotten your past. Will you force me to remind you of it?"

"I have forgotten nothing," said Hilda; "but I care nothing for it."

"You must care for it. You will be forced to. Your future happens to depend on it."

"My future happens to be equally indifferent to me," said Hilda. "I have given up all my plans and hopes. I am beyond your reach, at any rate. You are powerless against me now."

Gualtier smiled.

"You speak lightly," said he, "of the past and the future. You are excited. If you think calmly about your position, you will see that you are now more in my power than ever; and you will see, also, that I am willing to use that power. Do not drive me to extremes."

"These are your old threats," said Hilda, with bitter contempt. "They are stale now."

"Stale!" repeated Gualtier. "There are things which can never be stale, and in such things you and I have been partners. Must I remind you of them?"

"It's not at all necessary. You had much better leave, and go back to England, or any where else."

These words stung Gualtier.

"I will recall them," he cried, in a low, fierce voice. "You have a convenient memory, and may succeed for a time in banishing your thoughts, but you have that on your soul which no efforts of yours can banish—things which must haunt you, cold-blooded as you are, even as they have haunted me—my God!—and haunt me yet."

"The state of your mind is of no concern to me. You had better obey my order, and go, so as not to add any more to your present apparent troubles."

"Your taunts are foolish," said Gualtier, savagely. "You are in my power. What if I use it?"

"Use it, then."

Gualtier made a gesture of despair.

"Do you know what it means?" he exclaimed.

"I suppose so."

"You do not—you can not. It means the downfall of all your hopes, your desires, your plans."

"I tell you I no longer care for things like those."

"You do not mean it—you can not. What! can you come down from being Lady Chetwynde to plain Hilda Krieff?"

"I have implied that, I believe," said Hilda, in the same tone. "Now you understand me. Go and pull me down as fast as you like."

"But," said Gualtier, more excitedly, "you do not know what you are saying. There is something more in store for you than mere humiliation—something worse than a change in station—something more terrible than ruin itself. You are a criminal. You know it. It is for this that you must give your account. And, remember, such crimes as yours are not common ones. Such victims as the Earl of Chetwynde and Zillah are not those whom one can sacrifice with impunity. It is such as these that will be traced back to you, and woe be to you when their blood is required at your hands! Can you face this prospect? Is this future so very indifferent to you? If you have nothing like remorse, are you also utterly destitute of fear?"

"Yes," said Hilda.

"I don't believe it," said Gualtier, rudely.

"That is because you think I have no alternative," said Hilda; "it is a mistake into which a base and cowardly nature might naturally fall."

"You have no alternative," said Gualtier. "It's impossible."

"I have," said Hilda, calmly.

"What?"

She whispered one word. It struck upon Gualtier's ear with fearful emphasis. It was the same word which she had once whispered to him in the park at Chetwynde. He recoiled with horror. A shudder passed through him. Hilda looked at him with calm and unchanged contempt.

"You dare not," he cried.

"Dare not?" she repeated. "What I dare administer to others I dare administer to myself. Go and perform your threats! Go with your information—go and let loose the authorities upon me! Go! Haste! Go—and see—see how quickly and how completely I will elude your grasp! As for you—your power is gone. You made one effort to exert it, and succeeded for the moment. But that has passed away. Never—never more can any threats of yours move me in the slightest. You know that I am resolute. Whether you believe that I am resolute about this matter or not makes no difference—whatever to me. You are to go from this place at once—away from this place, and this town. That is my mandate. I am going to stay; and, since you have refused your assistance, I will do without it henceforth."

At these words Gualtier's face grew pale with rage and despair. He knew well Hilda's resolute character. That her last determination would be carried out he could scarcely doubt. Yet still his rage and his pride burst forth.

"Hilda Krieff," said he, for the first time discarding the pretense of respect and the false title by which he had so long addressed her, "do you not know who you are? What right have you to order me away, and stay here yourself—you with the Earl of Chetwynde—you, an unmarried girl? Answer me that, Hilda Krieff."

"What right?" said Hilda, as loftily as before, utterly unmoved by this utterance of her true name. "What right? The right of one who comes in love to save the object of her love. That is all. By that right I dismiss you. I drive you away, and stand myself by his bedside."

"You are very bold and very reckless," said he, with his white face turned toward her, half in rage, half in despair. "You are flinging yourself into a position which it will be impossible for you to hold, and you are insulting and defying one who can at any moment have you thrust from the place. I, if I chose, could now, at this instant, have you arrested, and in this very room."

"You!" said Hilda, with a sneer.

"Yes, I," said Gualtier, emphatically. "I have but to lodge my information with the authorities against you, and before ten minutes you would be carried away from this place, and separated from that man forever. Yes, Hilda Krieff, I can do that, and you know it; and yet you dare to taunt me and insult me, and drive me on to do things of which I might afterward repent. God knows I do not wish to do any thing but what is in accordance with your will. At this moment I would still obey any of your commands but this one; yet you try me more than mortal nature can endure, and I warn you that I will not bear it."

Hilda laughed.

Since this interview had commenced, instead of growing weaker, she had seemed rather to grow stronger. It was as though the excitement had been a stimulus, and had roused her to a new life. It had torn her thoughts suddenly and violently away from the things over which she had long brooded. Pride had been stirred up, and had repaired the ravages of love. At this last threat of Gualtier's she laughed.

"Poor creature!" she said. "And do you really think you can do any thing here? Your only place where you have any chance is in England, and then only by long and careful preparation. What could you do here in Lausanne?"

"I could have you flung in prison, and separated from him forever," said Gualtier, fiercely.

"You! you! And pray do you know who you are? Lord Chetwynde's valet! And who would take your word against Lord Chetwynde's wife?"

"That you are not."

"I am," said Hilda, firmly.

"My God! what do you mean?"

"I mean that I will stand up for my rights, and crush you into dust if you dare to enter into any frantic attempt against me here. You! why, what are you? You are Lord Chetwynde's scoundrel valet, who plotted against his master. Here in these rooms are the witnesses and the proofs of your crimes. You would bring an accusation against me, would you? You would inform the magistrates, perhaps, that I am not Lady Chetwynde—that I am an impostor—that my true name is Hilda Krieff—that I sent you on an errand to destroy your master? And pray have you thought how you could prove so wild and so improbable a fiction? Is there one thing that you could bring forward? Is there one living being who would sustain the charge? You know that there is nothing. Your vile slander would only recoil on your own head; and even if I did nothing—even if I treated you and your charge with silent contempt, you yourself would suffer, for the charge would excite such suspicion against you that you would undoubtedly be arrested.

"But, unfortunately for you, I would not be silent. I would come forward and tell the magistrates the whole truth. And I think, without self-conceit, there is enough in my appearance to win for me belief against the wild and frenzied fancies of a vulgar valet like you. Who would believe you when Lady Chetwynde came forward to tell her story, and to testify against you?

"I will tell you what Lady Chetwynde would have to say. She would tell how she once employed you in England; how you suffered some slight from her; how you were dismissed from her service. That then you went to London, and engaged yourself as valet to Lord Chetwynde, by whom you were not known; that, out of vengeance, you determined to ruin him. That Lady Chetwynde was anxious about her husband, and, hearing of his illness, followed him from place to place; that, owing to her intense anxiety, she broke down and nearly died; that she finally reached this place to find her villainous servant—the one whom she had dismissed—acting as her husband's valet. That she turned him off on the spot, whereupon he went to the authorities, and lodged some malicious and insane charges against her. But Lady Chetwynde would have more than this to say. She could show certain vials, which are no doubt in these rooms, to a doctor; and he could analyze their contents; and he could tell to the court what it was that had caused this mysterious disease to one who had always before been so healthy. And where do you think your charge would be in the face of Lady Chetwynde's story; in the face of the evidence of the vials and the doctor's analysis?"

Hilda paused and regarded Gualtier with cold contempt. Gualtier felt the terrible truth of all that she had said. He saw that here in Lausanne he had no chance. If he wished for vengeance he would have to delay it. And yet he did not wish for any vengeance on her. She had for the present eluded his grasp. In spite of his assertion of power over her—in spite of the coercion by which he had once extorted a promise from her—he was, after all, full of that same all-absorbing love and idolizing affection for her which had made him for so many years her willing slave and her blind tool. Now this sudden reassertion of her old supremacy, while it roused all his pride and stimulated his anger, excited also at the same time his admiration.

He spoke at length, and his tone was one of sadness.

"There is one other thing which is against me," said he; "my own heart. I can not do any thing against you."

"Your heart," said Hilda, "is very ready to hold you back when you see danger ahead."

Gualtier's pale face flushed.

"That's false," said he, "and you know it. Did my heart quail on that midnight sea when I was face to face with four ruffians and quelled their mutiny? You have already told me that it was a bold act."

"Well, at least you were armed, and they were not," said Hilda, with unchanged scorn.

"Enough," cried Gualtier, flushing a deeper and an angrier red. "I will argue with you no more. I will yield to you this time. I will leave the hotel and Lausanne. I will go to England. He shall be under your care, and you may do what you choose.

"But remember this," he continued, warningly, "I have your promise, given to me solemnly, and that promise I will yet claim. This man may recover; but, if he does, it will only be to despise you. His abhorrence will be the only reward that you can expect for your passion and your mad self-sacrifice. But even if it were possible for him to love you—yes, to love you as you love him—even then you could not have him. For I live; and while I live you could never be his. No, never. I have your promise, and I will come between you and him to sunder you forever and to cast you down. That much, at least, I can do, and you know it.

"And now farewell for the present. In any event you will need me again. I shall go to Chetwynde Castle, and wait there till I am wanted. The time will yet come, and that soon, when you will again wish my help. I will give you six months to try to carry out this wild plan of yours. At the end of that time I shall have something to do and to say; but I expect to be needed before then. If I am needed, you may rely upon me as before. I will forget every injury and be as devoted as ever."

With these ominous words Gualtier withdrew.

Hilda sank back in her chair exhausted, and sat for some time pressing her hand on her heart.

At length she summoned her strength, and, rising to her feet, she walked feebly through several rooms. Finally she reached one which was darkened. A bed was there, on which lay a figure. The figure was quite motionless; but her heart told her who this might be.

CHAPTER LIV.

NURSING THE SICK.

THE figure that lay upon the bed as Hilda entered the room sent a shock to her heart at the first glance. Very different was this one from that tall, strong man who but lately, in all the pride of manly beauty and matured strength, overawed her by his presence. What was he now? Where now was all that virile force, and strong, resistless nature, whose overmastering power she had experienced? Alas! but little of it could be seen in this wasted and emaciated figure that now lay before her, seemingly at the last verge of life. His features had grown thin and attenuated, his lips were drawn tight over his teeth, his face had the stamp of something like death upon it. He was sleeping fitfully, but his eyes were only half closed. His thin, bony hands moved restlessly about, and his lips muttered inarticulate words from time to time. Hilda placed her hand on his forehead. It was cold and damp. The cold sent a chill through every nerve. She bent down low over him. She devoured him with her eyes. That face, worn away by the progress of disease, that now lay unconscious, and without a ray of intelligence beneath her, was yet to her the best thing in all the world, and the one for which she would willingly give up the world. She stooped low down. She pressed her lips to his cold forehead. An instant she hesitated, and then she pressed her lips this time to the white lips that were before her. The long, passionate kiss did not wake the slumberer. He knew not that over him was bending one who had once sent him to death, but who now would give her own life to bring him back from that death to which she had sent him.

Such is the change which can be worked in the basest nature by the power of almighty love. Here it was made manifest. These lips had once given the kiss of Judas. On this face of hers the Earl of Chetwynde had gazed in horror; and these hands of hers, that now touched tremblingly the brow of the sick man, had once wrought out on him that which would never be made known. But the lips which once gave the kiss of Judas now gave that kiss which was the outpouring of the devotion of all her soul, and these hands were ready to deal death to herself to rescue him from evil. She twined her arms around his neck, and gazed at him as though her longing eyes would devour every lineament of his features. Again and again she pressed her lips to his, as though she would thus force upon him life and health and strength. But the sick man lay unconscious in her arms, all unheeding that full tide of passionate love which was surging and swelling within her bosom.

At last footsteps aroused her. A woman entered. She walked to the bedside and looked with tender sympathy at Hilda. She had heard from Gretchen that this was Lady Chetwynde, who had come to nurse her husband.

"Are you the nurse?" asked Hilda, who divined at one glance the character of the new-comer.

"Yes, my lady."

"Well, I am to be the nurse after this, but I should like you to remain. You can wait in one of the ante-rooms."

"Forgive me, my lady, if I say that you yourself are in need of a nurse. You will not be able to endure this fatigue. You look overworn now. Will you not take some rest?"

"No," said Hilda, sharply and decisively.

"My lady," said the nurse, "I will watch while you are resting."

"I shall not leave the room."

"Then, my lady, I will spread a mattress on the sofa, and you may lie down."

"No, I am best here by his side. Here I can get the only rest and the only strength that I want. I must be near enough to touch his hand and to see his face. Here I will stay."

"But, my lady, you will break down utterly."

"No, I shall not break down. I shall be strong enough to watch him until he is either better or worse. If he gets better, he will bring me back to health; if he gets worse, I will accompany him to the tomb."

Hilda spoke desperately. Her old self-control, her reticence, and calm had departed. The nurse looked at her with a face full of sympathy, and said not a word. The sight of this young and beautiful wife, herself so weak, so wan, and yet so devoted, so young and beautiful, yet so wasted and emaciated, whose only desire was to live or die by the side of her husband, roused all the feelings of her heart. To some Hilda's conduct would have been unintelligible; but this honest Swiss nurse was kind-hearted and sentimental, and the fervid devotion and utter self-abnegation of Hilda brought tears to her eyes.

"Ah, my lady," said she, "I see I shall soon have two to nurse."

"Well, if you have, it will not be for long," said Hilda.

The nurse sighed and was silent.

"May I remain, my lady, or shall I go?" she asked.

"You may go just now. See how my maid is doing, and if she wants any directions."

The nurse retired, and Hilda was alone with the sick man. She sat on the bedside leaning over him, and twined her arms about him. There, as he lay, in his weakness and senselessness, she saw her own work. It was she, and no other, who had doomed him to this. Too well had her agent carried out the fatal commission which she had given. As his valet he had had constant access to the person of Lord Chetwynde, and had used his opportunities well. She understood perfectly how it was that such a thing as this had been brought about. She knew every part of the dread process, and had read enough to know the inevitable results.

And now—would he live or die? Life was low. Would it ever rally again? Had she come in time to save him, or was it all too late? The reproaches which she hurled against herself were now overwhelming her, and these reproaches alternated with feelings of intense tenderness. She was weak from her own recent illness, from the unwonted fatigue which she had endured, and from the excitement of that recent interview with Gualtier. Thus torn and tossed and distracted by a thousand contending emotions, Hilda sat there until at length weakness and fatigue overpowered her. It seemed to her that a change was coming over the face of the sick man. Suddenly he moved, and in such a way that his face was turned full toward her as she lay on his side.

"NO; I AM BEST HERE BY HIS SIDE."

At that moment it seemed to her that the worst had come—that at last death himself had placed his stamp there, and that there was now no more hope. The horror of this fancy altogether overcame her. She fell forward and sank down.

When at length the nurse returned she found Hilda senseless, lying on the bed, with her arm still under the head of Lord Chetwynde. She called Gretchen, and the two made a bed on the sofa, where they lifted Hilda with tenderest care. She lay long unconscious, but at last she recovered. Her first thoughts were full of bewilderment, but finally she comprehended the whole situation.

Now at length she found that she had been wasting precious moments upon useless reflections and idle self-reproaches. If she had come to save, that safety ought not to be delayed. She hurriedly drew from her pocket a vial and opened it. It was the same which she had obtained from the London druggist. She smelled it, and then tasted it. After this she rose up, in spite of the solicitations of the nurse and Gretchen, and tottered toward the bed with unsteady steps, supported by her attendants. Then she seated herself on the bedside, and, asking for a spoon, she tried with a trembling hand to pour out some of the mixture from the vial. Her hands shook so that she could not. In despair she allowed the nurse to administer it, while Gretchen supported her, seating herself behind her in such a way that Hilda could lean against her, and still see the face of the sick man. In this position she watched while the nurse put the liquid into Lord Chetwynde's mouth, and saw him swallow it.

"My lady, you must lie down, or you will never get over this," said the nurse, earnestly, and passing her arms around Hilda, she gently drew her back to the sofa, assisted by Gretchen. Hilda allowed herself to be moved back without a word. For the remainder of that day she watched, lying on her sofa, and gave directions about the regular administration of the medicine. At her request they drew the sofa close up to the bedside of Lord Chetwynde, and propped her up high with pillows. There she lay weakly, with her face turned toward him, and her hand clasping his.

Night came, and Hilda still watched. Fatigue and weakness were fast overpowering her. Against these she struggled bravely, and lay with her eyes fixed on Lord Chetwynde. In that sharp exercise of her senses, which were all aroused in his behalf, she became at last aware of the fact that they were getting beyond her control. Before her eyes, as she gazed upon this man, there came other and different visions. She saw another sick-bed, in a different room from this, with another form stretched upon it—a form like this, yet unlike, for it was older—a form with venerable gray hairs, with white, emaciated face, and with eyes full of fear and entreaty. At that sight horror came over her. She tried to rouse herself from the fearful state into which she was drifting. She summoned up all that remained of her physical and mental energy. The struggle was severe. All things round her seemed to change incessantly into the semblances of other things; the phantoms of a dead past—a dead but not a forgotten past—crowded around her, and all the force of her will was unavailing to repel them. She shuddered as she discovered the full extent of her own weakness, and saw where she was drifting. For she was drifting helplessly into the realm of shadowy memories; into the place where the past holds its empire; surrounded by all those forms which time and circumstance have rendered dreadful; forms from which memory shrinks, at whose aspect the soul loses all its strength. Here they were before her; kept back so long, they now crowded upon her; they asserted themselves, they forced themselves before her in her weakness. Her brain reeled; the strong, active intellect, which in health had been so powerful, now, in her hour of weakness, failed her. She struggled against these horrors, but the struggle was unavailing, and at last she yielded—she failed—she sank down headlong and helplessly into the abyss of forgotten things, into the thick throng of forms and images from which for so long a time she had kept herself apart.

Now they came before her.

The room changed to the old room at Chetwynde Castle. There was the window looking out upon the park. There was the door opening into the hall. Zillah stood there, pale and fearful, bidding her good-night. There was the bed upon which lay the form of a venerable man, whose face was ever turned toward her with its expression of fear, and of piteous entreaty. "Don't leave me," he murmured to the phantom form of Zillah. "Don't leave me with her," and his thin finger pointed to herself. But Zillah, ignorant of all danger, promised to send Mrs. Hart. And Zillah walked out, standing at the door for a time to give her last look—the look which the phantom of this vision now had. Then, with a momentary glance, the phantom figure of Zillah faded away, and only the prostrate figure of the Earl appeared before her, with the white face, and the venerable hair, and the imploring eyes.

Then she walked to the window and looked out; then she walked to the door and looked down the hall. Silence was every where. All were asleep. No eye beheld her. Then she returned. She saw the white face of the sick man, and the imploring eyes encountered hers. Again she walked to the window; then she went to his bedside.

She stooped down. His white face was beneath her, with the imploring eyes. She kissed him.

"Judas!"

That was the sound that she heard—the last sound—for soon in that abhorrent vision the form of the dead lay before her, and around it the household gathered; and Zillah sat there, with a face of agony, looking up to her and saying:

"I am the next victim!"

Then all things were forgotten, and innumerable forms and phantoms came confusedly together.

She was in delirium.

CHAPTER LV.

SETTING A TRAP.

GUALTIER was true to his word. On the evening of the day when he had that interview with Hilda he left the hotel, and Lausanne also, and set out for England. On the way he had much to think of, and his thoughts were not at all pleasant. This frenzy of Hilda's had taken him by complete surprise, and her utter recklessness of life, or all the things most desirable in life, were things on which he had never counted. Her dark resolve also which she had announced to him, the coolness with which she listened to his menaces, and the stern way in which she turned on him with menaces of her own, showed him plainly that, for the present at least, she was beyond his reach, and nothing which he might do could in any way affect her. Only one thing gave him hope, and that was the utter madness and impossibility of her design. He did not know what might have passed between her and Lord Chetwynde before, but he conjectured that she had been treated with insult great enough to inspire her with a thirst for vengeance. He now hoped that Lord Chetwynde, if he did recover, would regard her as before. He was not a man to change; his mind had been deeply imbittered against the woman whom he believed his wife, and recovery of sense would not lessen that bitterness. So Gualtier thought, and tried to believe, yet in his thoughts he also considered the possibility of a reconciliation. And, if such a thing could take place, then his mind was fully made up what to do. He would trample out all feelings of tenderness, and sacrifice love to full and complete vengeance. That reconciliation should be made short-lived, and should end in utter ruin to Hilda, even if he himself descended into the same abyss with her.

Thoughts like these occupied his mind until he reached London. Then he drove to the Strand Hotel, and took two front-rooms on the second story looking out upon the street, commanding a view of the dense crowd that always went thronging by.

Here, on the evening of his arrival, his thoughts turned to his old lodging-house, and to those numerous articles of value which he had left there. He had once made up his mind to let them go, and never seek to regain possession of them. He was conscious that to do so would be to endanger his safety, and perhaps to put a watchful pursuer once more on his track. Yet there was something in the thought which was attractive. Those articles were of great intrinsic value, and some of them were precious souvenirs, of little worth to any one else, yet to him beyond price. Would it not be worth while to make an effort at least to regain possession of them? If it could be done, it would represent so much money at the least, and that was a thing which it was needful for him to consider. And, in any case, those mementoes of the past were sufficiently valuable to call for some effort and some risk. The more he thought of this, the more resistless became the temptation to make this effort and run this risk.

And what danger was there? What was the risk, and what was there to fear? Only one person was in existence from whom any danger could possibly be apprehended. That one was Black Bill, who had tracked him to London, and afterward watched at his lodgings, and whom he had feared so much that for his sake, and for his alone, he had given up every thing. And now the question that arose was this, did Black Bill really require so much precaution, and so great a sacrifice? It was not likely that Black Bill could have given any information to the police; that would have been too dangerous to himself. Besides, if the police had heard of such a story, they would have given some sign. In England every thing is known, and the police are forced to work openly. Their detective system is a clumsy one compared with the vast system of secrecy carried on on the Continent. Had they found out any thing whatever about so important a case as this, some kind of notice or other would have appeared in the papers. Gaultier had never ceased to watch for some such notice, but had never found one. So, with such opinions about the English police, he naturally concluded that they knew nothing about him.

It was therefore Black Bill, and Black Bill only, against whom he had to guard. As for him it was indeed possible, he thought, that he was still watching, but hardly probable. He was not in a position to spend so many months in idle watching, nor was he able to employ a confederate. Still less was it possible for such a man to win the landlord over to his side, and thus get his assistance. The more he thought of these things the more useless did it seem to entertain any further fear, and the more irresistible did his desire become to regain possession of those articles, which to him were of so much value. Under such circumstances, he finally resolved to make an effort.

Yet, so cautious was he by nature, so wary and vigilant, and so accustomed to be on his guard, that in this case he determined to run no risk by any exposure of his person to observation. He therefore deliberated carefully about various modes by which he could apply to the landlord. At first he thought of a disguise; but finally rejected this idea, thinking that, if Black Bill were really watching, he would expect some kind of a disguise. At last he decided that it would be safest to find some kind of a messenger, and send him, after instructing him what to ask for and what to say.

With this resolve he took a walk out on the Strand on the following morning, looking carefully at the faces of the great multitude which thronged the street, and trying to find some one who might be suited to his purpose. In that crowd there were many who would have gladly undertaken his business if he had asked them, but Gaultier had made up his mind as to the

kind of messenger which would be best suited to him, and was unwilling to take any other.

Among the multitude which London holds almost any type of man can be found, if one looks long enough. The one which Gaultier wished is a common kind there, and he did not have a long search. A street boy, sharp, quick-witted, nimble, cunning—that was what he wanted, and that was what he found, after regarding many different specimens of that tribe and rejecting them. The boy whom he selected was somewhat less ragged than his companions, with a demure face, which, however, to his scrutinizing eyes, did not conceal the precocious maturity of mind and fertility of resource which lay beneath. A few words sufficed to explain his wish, and the boy eagerly accepted the task. Gaultier then took him to a cheap clothing store, and had him dressed in clothes which gave him the appearance of being the son of some small tradesman. After this he took him to his room in the hotel, and carefully instructed him in the part that he was to perform. The boy's wits were quickened by London life; the promise of a handsome reward quickened them still more, and at length, after a final questioning, in which he did his part to satisfaction, Gaultier gave him the address of the lodging-house.

"I am going west," said he; "I will be back before eight o'clock. You must come at eight exactly."

"Yes 'r," said the boy.

"Very well. Now go." And the boy, with a bob of his head, took his departure.

The boy went off, and at length reached the place which Gaultier had indicated. He rang at the door.

A servant came.

"Is this Mr. Gillis's?"

"Yes."

"Is he in?"

"Do you want to see him?"

"Yes."

"What for?"

"Particular business."

"Come in," said the servant; and the boy entered the hall and waited. In a few moments Mr. Gillis made his appearance. He regarded the boy carefully from head to foot.

"Come into the parlor," said he, leading the way into a room on the right. The boy followed, and Mr. Gillis shut the door.

"Well," said he, seating himself, "what is it that you want of me?"

"My father," said the boy, "is a grocer in Blackwall. He got a letter this morning from a friend of his who stopped here some time back. He had to go to America of a sudden and left his things, and wants to get 'em."

"Ah!" said Mr. Gillis. "What is the name of the lodger?"

"Mr. Brown," said the boy.

"Brown?" said Mr. Gillis. "Yes, there was such a lodger, I think; but I don't know about his things. You wait here a moment till I go and ask Mrs. Gillis."

Saying this Mr. Gillis left the room. After about fifteen or twenty minutes he returned.

"Well, my boy," said he, "there are some things of Mr. Brown's here yet, I believe; and you have come for them? Have you a wagon?"

"HE CAREFULLY INSTRUCTED HIM IN THE PART HE WAS TO PERFORM."

"No. I only come to see if they were here, and to get your bill."

"And your father is Mr. Brown's friend?"

"Yes 'r."

"And Mr. Brown wrote to him?"

"Yes 'r."

"Well, you know I wouldn't like to give up the things on an uncertainty. They are very valuable. I would require some order from your father."

"Yes 'r."

Mr. Gillis asked a number of questions of the boy, to which he responded without hesitation, and then left the room again, saying that he would go and make out Mr. Brown's bill.

He was gone a long time. The boy amused himself by staring at the things in the room, at the ornaments, and pictures, and began to think that Mr. Gillis was never coming back, when at last footsteps were heard in the hall, the door opened, and Mr. Gillis entered, followed by two other men. One of these men had the face of a prize-fighter, or a ticket-of-leave man, with abundance of black hair and beard; his eyes were black and piercing, and his face was the same which has already been described as the face of Black Bill. But he was respectably dressed in black, he wore a beaver hat, and had lost something of his desperate air. The fact is, the police had taken Black Bill into their employ, and he was doing very well in his new occupation. The other was a sharp, wiry man, with a cunning face and a restless, fidgety manner. Both he and Black Bill looked carefully at the boy, and at length the sharp man spoke:

"You young rascal, do you know who I am?"

The boy started and looked aghast, terrified by such an address.

"No, Sir," he whimpered.

"Well, I'm Thomas S. Davis, detective. Do you understand what that means?"

"Yes 'r," said the boy, whose self-possession completely vanished at so formidable an announcement.

"Come now, young fellow," said Davis, "you've got to own up. Who are you?"

"I'm the son of Mr. B. F. Baker, grocer, Blackwall," said the boy, in a quick monotone.

"What street?"

"Queen Street, No. 17," said the boy.

"There ain't no such street."

"There is, 'cos he lives there."

"You young rascal, don't you suppose I know?"

"Well, I oughter know the place where I was bred and bornd," said the boy.

"You're a young scamp. You needn't try to come it over me, you know. Why, I know Blackwall by heart. There isn't such a street there. Who sent you here?"

"Father."

"What for?"

"He got a letter from a man as used to stop here, askin' of him to get his things away."

"What is the name of the man?"

"Mr. Brown."

"Brown?"

"Yes 'r."

"Where is this Mr. Brown now?"

"In Liverpool."

"How did he get there?"

"He's just come back from America."

"See here, boy, you've got to own up," said Davis, suddenly. "I'm a detective. We belong to the police. So make a clean breast of it."

"Oh, Sir!" said the boy, in terror.

"Never mind 'Oh, Sir!' but own up," said Davis. "You've got to do it."

"I ain't got nothin' to own up. I'm sure I don't see why you're so hard on a poor cove as never did you no harm, nor nobody else."

And saying this the boy sniveled violently.

"I s'pose your dear mamma dressed you up in your Sunday clothes to come here?" said the detective, sneeringly.

"No, Sir," said the boy, "she didn't, 'cos she's dead, she is."

"Why didn't your father come himself?"

"'Cos he's too busy in his shop."

"Did you ever hear the name of this Brown before to-day?"

"No, Sir, never as I knows on."

"But you said he is a friend of your father's."

"So he is, Sir."

"And you never heard his name before?"

"Never, Sir, in my life, Sir—not this Brown."

"Is your father a religious man?"

"A what, Sir?"

"A religious man."

"I dunno, Sir."

"Does he go to church?"

"Oh, yes 'r, to meetin' on Sundays."

"What meeting?"

"Methodist, Sir."

"Where?"

"At No. 13 King Street," said the boy, without a moment's hesitation.

"You young jackass," said Davis. "No. 13 King Street, and all the numbers near it in Blackwall, are warehouses—what's the use of trying to humbug me?"

"Who's a-tryin' to humbug you?" whimpered the boy: "I don't remember the numbers. It's somewhere in King Street. I never go myself."

"You don't, don't you?"

"No, Sir."

"Now, see here, my boy," said Davis, sternly, "I know you. You can't come it over me. You've got into a nice mess, you have. You've got mixed in with a conspiracy, and the law's goin' to take hold of you at once unless you make a clean breast of it."

"Oh Lord!" cried the boy. "Stop that. What am I a-doin' of?"

"Nonsense, you young rascal! Listen to me

now, and answer me. Do you know any thing about this Brown?"

"No, Sir. Father sent me."

"Well, then, let me tell you the police are after him. He's afraid to come here, and sent you. Don't you go and get mixed up with him. If you do, it 'll be worse for you. This Brown is the biggest villain in the kingdom, and any man that catches him 'll make his blessed fortune. We're on his tracks, and we're bound to follow him up. So tell me the truth—where is he now?"

"In Liverpool, Sir."

"You lie, you young devil! But, if you don't own up, it 'll be worse for you."

"How's a poor cove like me to know?" cried the boy. "I'm the son of a honest man, and I don't know any thing about your police."

"You'll know a blessed sight more about it before you're two hours older, if you go on humbuggin' us this fashion," said Davis, sternly.

"I ain't a-humbuggin'."

"You are—and I won't stand it. Come now. Brown is a murderer, do you hear? There's a reward offered for him. He's got to be caught. You've gone and mixed yourself up with this business, and you'll never get out of the scrape till you make a clean breast of it. That's all bosh about your father, you know."

"It ain't," said the boy, obstinately.

"Very well, then," said Davis, rising. "You've got to go with us. We'll go first to Blackwall, and, by the Lord, if we can't find your father, we'll take it out of you. You'll be put in the jug for ten years, and you'll have to tell after all. Come along now."

Davis grasped the boy's hand tightly and took him out of the room. A cab was at the door. Davis, Black Bill, and the boy got into it and drove along through the streets. The boy was silent and meditative. At last he spoke:

"It's no use goin' to Blackwall," said he, sulkily. "I ain't got no father."

"Didn't I know that?" said Davis. "You were lying, you know. Are you goin' to own up?"

"I s'pose I must."

"Of course you must."

"Well, will you let me go if I tell you all?"

"If you tell all we'll let you go sometime, but we will want you for a while yet."

"Well," said the boy, "I can't help it. I s'pose I've got to tell."

"Of course you have. And now, first, who sent you here?"

"Mr. Brown."

"Ah! Mr. Brown himself. Where did you see him?"

"In the Strand."

"Did you ever see him before?"

"No. He picked me up, and sent me here."

"Do you know where he is lodging?"

"Yes 'r."

"Where?"

"At the Strand Hotel. He took me into his room and told me what I was to do. I didn't know any thing about him or his business. I only went on an errand."

"Of course you did," said Davis, encouragingly. "And, if you tell the truth, you'll be all right; but if you try to humbug us," he added, sternly, "it 'll be the worse for you. Don't you go and mix yourself up in a murder case. I don't want any thing more of you than for you to take us to this man's room. You were to see him again to-day—of course."

"Yes 'r."

"At what time?"

"Eight o'clock."

"Well—it's now four. You take us to his room, and we'll wait there."

The boy assented, and the cab drove off for the Strand Hotel.

The crowd in front of the hotel was so dense that it was some time before the cab could approach the entrance. At last they reached it and got out, Black Bill first, and then Davis, who still held the hand of the boy in a tight grasp, for fear that he might try to escape. They then worked their way through the crowd and entered the hotel. Davis said something to the clerk, and then they went up stairs, guided by the boy to Gualtier's room.

On entering it no one was there. Davis went into the adjoining bedroom, but found it empty. A carpet-bag was lying on the floor open. On examining it Davis found only a shaving-case and some changes of linen.

"We'll wait here," said Davis to Black Bill, as he re-entered the sitting-room. "He's out now. He'll be back at eight to see the boy. We've got him at last."

And then Black Bill spoke for the first time since the boy had seen him. A grim smile spread over his hard features.

"Yes," said he, "we've got him at last!"

CHAPTER LVI.

MEANWHILE Hilda's position was a hard one. Days passed on. The one who came to act as a nurse was herself stricken down, as she had already been twice before. They carried her away to another room, and Gretchen devoted herself to her care. Delirium came on, and all the past lived again in the fever-tossed mind of the sufferer. Unconscious of the real world in which she lay, she wandered in a world of phantoms, where the well-remembered forms of her past life surrounded her. Some deliriums are pleasant. All depend upon the ruling feelings of the one upon whom it is fixed. But here the ruling feeling of Hilda was not of that kind which could bring happiness. Her distracted mind wandered again through those scenes through which she had passed. Her life at Chetwynde, with all its later horrors and anxieties, came back before her. Again and again the vision of the dying Earl tormented her. What she said these foreign nurses heard, but understood not. They soothed her as best they might, and stood aghast at her sufferings, but were not able to do any thing to alleviate them. Most of all, however, her mind turned to the occurrences of the last few days and weeks. Again she was flying to the bedside of Lord Chetwynde; again the anguish of suspense devoured her, as she struggled against weakness to reach him; and again she felt overwhelmed by the shock of the first sight of the sick man, on whom she thought that she saw the stamp of death.

Meanwhile, as Hilda lay senseless, Lord Chetwynde hovered between life and death. The physician who had attended him came in on the morning after Hilda's arrival, and learned from the nurse that Lady Chetwynde had come suddenly, more dead than alive, and was herself struck down by fever. She had watched him all night from her own couch, until at last she had lost consciousness; but all her soul seemed bent on one thing, and that was that a certain medicine should be administered regularly to Lord Chetwynde. The doctor asked to see it. He smelled it and tasted it. An expression of horror passed over his face.

"My God!" he murmured. "I did not dare to suspect it! It must be so!"

"Where is Lord Chetwynde's valet?" he asked at length, after a thoughtful pause.

"I don't know, Sir," said the nurse. "He always is here. I don't see him now."

"I haven't seen him since Lady Chetwynde's arrival."

"Did my lady see him?"

"I think she did, Sir."

"You don't know what passed?"

"No, Sir. Except this, that the valet hurried out, looking very pale, and has not been back since."

"Ah!" murmured the doctor to himself. "She has suspected something, and has come on. The valet has fled. Could this scoundrel have been the guilty one? Who else could it be? And he has fled. I never liked his looks. He had the face of a vampire."

The doctor took away some of the medicine with him, and at the same time he took with him one of the glasses which stood on a table near the bed. Some liquid remained in it. He took these away to subject them to chemical analysis. The result of that analysis served to confirm his suspicions. When he next came he directed the nurse to administer the antidote regularly, and left another mixture also.

Lord Chetwynde lay between life and death. At the last verge of mortal weakness, it would have needed but a slight thing to send him out of life forever. The only encouraging thing about him for many days was that he did not get worse. From this fact the doctor gained encouragement, though he still felt that the case was desperate. What suspicions he had formed he kept to himself.

Hilda, meanwhile, prostrated by this new attack, lay helpless, consumed by the fierce fever which rioted in all her veins. Fiercer and fiercer it grew, until she reached a critical point, where her condition was more perilous than that of Lord Chetwynde himself. But, in spite of all that she had suffered, her constitution was strong. Tender hands were at her service, kindly hearts sympathized with her, and the doctor, whose nature was stirred to its depths by pity and compassion for this beautiful stranger, who had thus fallen under the power of so mysterious a calamity, was unremitting in his attentions. The crisis of the fever came, and all that night, while it lasted, he staid with her, listening to her disconnected ravings, and understanding enough of them to perceive that her fancy was bringing back before her that journey from England to Lausanne, whose fatigues and anxieties had reduced her to this.

"My God!" cried the doctor, as some sharper lamentation burst from Hilda; "it would be better for Lord Chetwynde to die than to survive a wife like this!"

With the morning the crisis had passed, and, thanks to the doctor's care, the result was favorable. Hilda fell into a profound sleep, but the fever had left her, and the change was for the better.

When the doctor returned once more he found her awake, without fever, yet very feeble.

"My lady," said he, "you must be more careful of yourself for the sake of others. Lord Chetwynde is weak yet, and though his symptoms are favorable, yet he requires the greatest care."

"And do you have hope of him?" asked Hilda, eagerly. This was the one thought of her mind.

"I do have hope," said the doctor.

Hilda looked at him gratefully.

"At present," said the doctor, "you must not think or talk about any thing. Above all, you must restrain your feelings. It is your anxiety about Lord Chetwynde that is killing you. Save yourself for his sake."

"But may I not be carried into his room?" pleaded Hilda, in imploring tones.

"No; not to-day. Leave it to me. Believe me, my lady, I am anxious for his recovery and for yours. His recovery depends most of all upon you."

"Yes," said Hilda, in a faint voice; "far more than you know. There is a medicine which he must have."

"He has been taking it through all his sickness. I have not allowed that to be neglected," said the doctor.

"You have administered that?"

"Most certainly. It is his only hope."

"And do you understand what it is?"

"Of course. More—I understand what it involves. But do not fear. The danger has passed now. Do not let the anguish of such a discovery torment you. The danger has passed. He is weak now, and it is only his weakness that I have to contend with."

"You understand all, then?" repeated Hilda.

"Yes, all. But you must not speak about it now. Have confidence in me. The fact that I understand the disease will show you that I know how to deal with it. It baffled me before; but, as soon as I saw the medicine that you gave, I suspected and understood."

Hilda looked at him with awful inquiry.

"Be calm, my lady," said the doctor, in a sympathetic voice. "The worst is over. You have saved him."

"Say that again," said Hilda. "Have I, indeed, done any thing? Have I, indeed, saved him?"

"Most undoubtedly. Had it not been for you he would by this time have been in the other world," said the doctor, solemnly.

Hilda drew a deep sigh.

"That is some consolation," she said, in a mournful voice.

"You are too weak now to talk about this. Let me assure you again that you have every reason for hope. In a few days you may be removed to his apartment, where your love and devotion will soon meet with their reward."

"Tell me one thing," asked Hilda, earnestly. "Is Lord Chetwynde still delirious?"

"Yes—but only slightly so. It is more like a quiet sleep than any thing else; and, while he sleeps, the medicines are performing their appropriate effect upon him. Every thing is progressing favorably, and when he regains his senses he will be changed very much for the better. But now, my lady, you must think no more about it. Try and get some sleep. Be as calm in your mind as you can until to-morrow."

And with these words the doctor left.

On the following day he came again, but refused to speak on the subject of Lord Chetwynde's illness; he merely assured Hilda that he was still in an encouraging condition, and told her that she herself must keep calm, so that her recovery might be more rapid. For several days he forbade a renewal of the subject of conversation, with the intention, as he said, of sparing her every thing which might agitate her. Whether his precautions were wise or not may be doubted. Hilda sometimes troubled herself with fancies that the doctor might, perhaps, suspect all the truth; and though she succeeded in dismissing the idea as absurd, yet the trouble which she experienced from it was sufficient to agitate her in many ways. That fever-haunted land of delirium, out of which she had of late emerged, was still near enough to throw over her soul its dark and terrific shadows. It needed but a slight word from the doctor, or from any one else, to revive the accursed memories of an accursed past.

Several days passed away, and, in spite of her anxieties, she grew stronger. The longing which she felt to see Lord Chetwynde gave strength to her resolution to grow stronger; and, as once before, her ardent will seemed to sway the functions of the body. The doctor noticed this steady increase of strength one day, and promised her that on the following day she should be removed to Lord Chetwynde's room. She received this intelligence with the deepest gratitude.

"Lord Chetwynde's symptoms," continued the doctor, "are still favorable. He is no longer in delirium, but in a kind of gentle sleep, which is not so well defined as to be a stupor, but is yet stronger than an ordinary sleep. The medicine which is being administered has this effect. Perhaps you are aware of this?"

Hilda bowed.

"I was told so."

"Will you allow me to ask how it was that you obtained that particular medicine?" he asked. "Do you know what it involves?"

"Yes," said Hilda; "it is only too well known to me. The horror of this well-nigh killed me."

"How did you discover it—or how did you suspect it?"

Hilda answered, without a moment's hesitation:

"The suddenness of Lord Chetwynde's disease alarmed me. His valet wrote about his symptoms, and these terrified me still more. I hurried up to London and showed his report to a leading London physician. He looked shocked, asked me much about Lord Chetwynde's health, and gave me this medicine. I suspected from his manner what he feared, though he did not express his fear in words. In short, it seemed to me, from what he said, that this medicine was the *antidote to some poison*."

"You are right," said the doctor, solemnly; and then he remained silent for a long time.

"Do you suspect any one?" he asked at last. Hilda sighed, and slowly said:

"Yes—I do."

"Who is the one?"

She paused. In that moment there were struggling within her thoughts which the doctor did not imagine. Should she be so base as to say what was in her mind, or should she not? That was the question. But rapidly she pushed aside all scruples, and in a low, stern voice she said:

"I suspect his valet."

"I thought so," said the doctor. "It could have been no other. But he must have had a motive. Can you imagine what motive there could have been?"

"I know it only too well," said Hilda, "though I did not think of this till it was too late. He was injured, or fancied himself injured, by Lord Chetwynde, and his motive was vengeance."

"And where is he now?" asked the doctor.

"He was thunder-struck by my appearance. He saw me nearly dead. He helped me up to his master's room. I charged him with his crime. He tried to falter out a denial. In vain. He was crushed beneath the overwhelming surprise. He hurried out abruptly, and has fled, I suppose forever, to some distant country. As for me, I forgot all about him, and fainted away by the bedside of my husband."

The doctor sighed heavily, and wiped a tear from his eye.

He had never known so sad a case as this.

* * *

CHAPTER LVII.

BACK TO LIFE.

On the next day, according to the doctor's promise, Hilda was taken into Lord Chetwynde's room. She was much stronger, and the new-found hope which she possessed of itself gave her increased vigor. She was carried in, and gently laid upon the sofa, which had been rolled up close by the bedside of Lord Chetwynde. Her first eager look showed her plainly that during the interval which had elapsed since she saw him last a great improvement had taken place. He was still unconscious, but his unconsciousness was that of a deep, sweet sleep, in which pleasant dreams had taken the place of delirious fancies. His face had lost its aspect of horror; there was no longer to be seen the stamp of death; the lips were full and red; the cheeks were no longer sunken; the dark circles had passed away from around the eyes; and the eyes themselves were now closed, as in sleep, instead of having that half-open appearance which before was so terrible and so deathlike. The chill damp had left his forehead. It was the face of one who is sleeping in pleasant slumber, instead of the face of one who was sinking rapidly into the realm where the sleep is eternal. All this Hilda saw at the first glance.

Her heart thrilled within her at the rapture of that discovery. The danger was over. The crisis had passed. Now, whether he lay there for a longer or a shorter period, his recovery at last was certain, as far as any thing human and mortal can be certain. Now her eyes, as they turned toward him, devoured him with all their old eagerness. Since she had seen him last she too had gone down to the gates of death, and she had come back again to take her place at his side. A strange joy and a peace that passed all understanding arose within her. She sent the nurse out of the room, and once more was alone with this man whom she loved. His face was turned toward her. She flung her arms about him in passionate eagerness, and, weak as she was, she bent down her lips to his. Unconscious he lay there, but the touch of his lips was now no longer like the touch of death.

She herself seemed to gain new strength from the sight of him as he thus lay in that manly beauty, which, banished for a time, had now returned again. She lay there on her sofa by his bedside, and held his hand in both of hers. She watched his face, and scanned every one of those noble lineaments, which now lay before her with something like their natural beauty. Hopes arose within her which brought new strength every moment. This was the life which she had saved. She forgot—did not choose to think—that she had doomed this life to death, and chose only to think that she had saved it from death. Thus she thought that, when Lord Chetwynde came forth out of his senselessness, she would be the first object that would meet his gaze, and he would know that he had been saved from death by her.

Here, then, she took up her place by his bedside, and saw how every day he grew better. Every day she herself regained her old strength, and could at length walk about the room, though she was still thin and feeble. So the time passed; and in this room the one who first escaped from the jaws of death devoted herself to the task of assisting the other.

At last, one morning as the sun rose, Lord Chetwynde waked. He looked around the room. He lifted himself up on his elbow, and saw Hilda asleep on the sofa near his bed. He felt bewildered at this strange and unexpected figure. How did she get here? A dim remembrance of his long sickness suggested itself, and he had a vague idea of this figure attending upon him. But the ideas and remembrances were too shadowy to be grasped. The room he remembered partially, for this was the room in which he had sunk down into this last sickness at Lausanne. But the sleeping form on the sofa puzzled him. He had seen her last at Chetwynde. What was she doing here? He scanned her narrowly, thinking that he might be mistaken from some chance resemblance. A further examination, however, showed that he was correct. Yes, this was "his wife," yet how changed! Pale as death was that face; those features were thin and attenuated; the eyes were closed; the hair hung in black masses round the marble brow; an expression of sadness dwelt there; and in her fitful, broken slumber she sighed heavily. He looked at her long and steadfastly, and then sank wearily down upon the pillows, but still kept his eyes fixed upon this woman whom he saw there. How did she get here? What was she doing? What did it all mean? His remembrance could not supply him with facts which might answer this question. He could not understand, and so he lay there in bewilderment, making feeble conjectures.

When Hilda opened her eyes the first thing that she saw was the face of Lord Chetwynde, whose eyes were fixed upon hers. She started and looked confused; but amidst her confusion an expression of joy darted across her face, which was evident and manifest to Lord Chetwynde. It was joy—eager, vivid, and intense; joy mingled with surprise; and her eyes at last rested on him with mute inquiry.

"Are you at last awake, my lord?" she murmured. "Are you out of your stupor?"

"I suppose so," said Lord Chetwynde. "But I do not understand this. I think I must be in Lausanne."

"Yes, you are in Lausanne, my lord, at the Hôtel Gibbon."

"The Hôtel Gibbon?" repeated Lord Chetwynde.

"Yes. Has your memory returned yet?"

"Only partially. I think I remember the journey here, but not very well. I hardly know where I came from. It must have been Baden." And he tried, but in vain, to recollect.

"You went from Frankfort to Baden, thence to Munich, and from Munich you came here."

"Yes," said Lord Chetwynde, slowly, as he began to recollect. "You are right. I begin to remember. But I have been ill, and I was ill at all these places. How long have I been here?"

"Five weeks."

"Good God!" cried Lord Chetwynde. "Is it possible? I must have been senseless all the time."

"Yes, this is the first time that you have come to your senses, my lord."

"I can scarcely remember any thing."

"Will you take your medicine now, my lord?"

"My medicine?"

"Yes," said Hilda, sitting up and taking a vial from the table; "the doctor ordered this to be given to you when you came out of your stupor."

"Where is my nurse?" asked Lord Chetwynde, abruptly, after a short but thoughtful silence.

"She is here, my lord. She wants to do your bidding. I am your nurse."

"You!"

"Yes, my lord. And now—do not speak, but take your medicine," said Hilda; and she poured out the mixture into a wine-glass and handed it to him.

He took it mechanically, and without a word, and then his head fell back, and he lay in silence for a long time, trying to recall his scattered thoughts. While he thus lay Hilda reclined on the sofa in perfect silence, motionless yet watchful, wondering what he was thinking about, and waiting for him to speak. She did not venture to interrupt him, although she perceived plainly that he was fully awake. She chose rather to leave him to his own thoughts, and to rest her fate upon the course which those thoughts might take. At last the silence was broken.

"I have been very ill?" he said at last, inquiringly.

"Yes, my lord, very ill. You have been down to the very borders of the grave."

"Yes, it must have been severe. I felt it coming on when I arrived in France," he murmured; "I remember now. But how did you hear about it?"

"Your valet telegraphed. He was frightened," said she, "and sent for me."

"Ah?" said Lord Chetwynde.

Hilda said nothing more on that subject. She would wait for another and a better time to tell him about that. The story of her devotion and of her suffering might yet be made known to him, but not now, when he had but partly recovered from his delirium.

Little more was said. In about an hour the nurse came in and sat near him. After some time the doctor came and congratulated him.

"Let me congratulate you, my lord," said he, "on your favorable condition. You owe your life to Lady Chetwynde, whose devotion has surpassed any thing that I have ever seen. She has done every thing—I have done nothing."

Lord Chetwynde made some commonplace compliment to his skill, and then asked him how long it would be before he might recover.

"That depends upon circumstances," said the doctor. "Rest and quiet are now the chief things which are needed. Do not be too impatient, my lord. Trust to these things, and rely upon the watchful care of Lady Chetwynde."

Lord Chetwynde said nothing. To Hilda, who had listened eagerly to this conversation, though she lay with closed eyes, his silence was perplexing. She could not tell whether he had softened toward her or not. A great fear arose within her that all her labor might have been in vain; but her matchless patience came to her rescue. She would wait—she would wait—she should at last gain the reward of her patient waiting.

The doctor, after fully attending to Lord Chetwynde, turned to her.

"You are weak, my lady," he said, with respectful sympathy, and full of pity for this devoted wife, who seemed to him only to live in her husband's presence. "You must take more care of yourself for his sake."

Hilda murmured some inarticulate words, and the doctor, after some further directions, withdrew.

Days passed on. Lord Chetwynde grew stronger every day. He saw Hilda as his chief attendant and most devoted nurse. He marked her pale face, her wan features, and the traces of suffering which still remained visible. He saw that all this had been done for his sake. Once, when she was absent taking some short rest, he had missed that instant attention which she had shown. With a sick man's impatience, he was troubled by the clumsiness of the hired nurse, and contrasted it with Hilda's instant readiness, and gentle touch, and soft voice of love.

At last, one day when Hilda was giving him some medicine, the vial dropped from her hands, and she sank down senseless by his bedside. She was carried away, and it was long before she came to herself.

"You must be careful of your lady, my lord," said the doctor, after he had seen her. "She has worn herself out for you, and will die some day by your bedside. Never have I seen such tenderness, and such fond devotion. She is the one who has saved you from death. She is now giving herself to death to insure your recovery. Watch over her. Do not let her sacrifice herself now. The time has come when she can spare herself. Surely now, at last, there ought to be some peace and rest for this noble-hearted, this gentle, this loving, this devoted lady!"

And as all Hilda's devotion came before the mind of this tender-hearted physician he had to wipe away his tears, and turn away his head to conceal his emotion.

But his words sank deep into Lord Chetwynde's soul.

CHAPTER LVIII.
AN EXPLANATION.

TIME passed away, and Lord Chetwynde steadily recovered. Hilda also grew stronger, and something like her former vigor began to come back. She was able, in spite of her own weakness, to keep up her position as nurse; and when the doctor remonstrated she declared, piteously, that Lord Chetwynde's bedside was the place where she could gain the most benefit, and that to banish her from it would be to doom her to death. Lord Chetwynde was perplexed by this devotion, yet he would not have been human if he had not been affected by it.

As he recovered, the one question before his mind was, what should he do? The business with reference to the payment of that money which General Pomeroy had advanced was arranged before he left England. It was this which had occupied so much of his thoughts. All was arranged with his solicitors, and nothing remained for him to do. He had come to the Continent without any well-defined plans, merely in search after relaxation and distraction of mind. His eventful illness had brought other things before him, the most prominent thing among which was the extraordinary devotion of this woman, from whom he had been planning an eternal separation. He could not now accuse her of baseness. Whatever she might once have done she had surely atoned for during those hours when she stood by his bedside till she herself fell senseless, as he had seen her fall. It would have been but a common generosity which would have attributed good motives to her; and he could not help regarding her as full of devotion to himself.

Under these circumstances it became a very troublesome question to know what he was to do. Where was he to go? Should he loiter about the Continent as he once proposed? But then, he was under obligations to this devoted woman, who had done so much for him. What was he to do with regard to her? Could he send her home coldly, without a word of gratitude, or without one sign expressive of that thankfulness which any human being would feel under such circumstances? He could not do that. He must do or say something expressive of his sense of obligation. To do otherwise—to leave her abruptly —would be brutal. What could he do? He could not go back and live with her at Chetwynde. There was another, whose image filled all his heart, and the memory of whose looks and words made all other things unattractive. Had it not been for this, he might have yielded to pity, if not to love. Had it not been for this, he would have spoken tender words to that slender, white-faced woman who, with her imploring eyes, hovered about him, finding her highest happiness

in being his slave, seeking her only recompense in some kindly look, or some encouraging word. All the circumstances of his present position perplexed him. He knew not what to do: and, in this perplexity, his mind at length settled upon India as the shortest way of solving all difficulties. He could go back there again, and resume his old duties. Time might alleviate his grief over his father, and perhaps it might even mitigate the fervor of that fatal passion which had arisen in his heart for another who could never be his. There, at any rate, he would have sufficient occupation to take up his thoughts, and break up that constant tendency which he now had toward memories of the one whom he had lost. Amidst all his perplexity, therefore, the only thing left for him seemed to be India. The time was approaching when he would be able to travel once more. Lausanne is the most beautiful place in the world, on the shore of the most beautiful of lakes, with the stupendous forms of the Jura Alps before it; but even so beautiful a place as this loses all its charms to the one who has been an invalid there, and the eye which has gazed upon the most sublime scenes in nature from a sick-bed loses all power of admiring their sublimity. And so Lord Chetwynde wearied of Lausanne, and the Lake of Geneva, and the Jura Alps, and, in his restlessness, he longed for other scenes which might be fresher, and not connected with such mournful associations. So he began to talk in a general way of going to Italy. This he mentioned to the doctor, who happened one day to ask him how he liked Lausanne. The question gave him an opportunity of saying that he looked upon it simply as a place where he had been ill, and that he was anxious to get off to Italy as soon as possible.

"Italy?" said the doctor.

"Yes."

"What part are you going to?"

"Oh, I don't know. Florence, I suppose— at first—and then other places. It don't much matter."

Hilda heard this in her vigilant watchfulness. It awakened fears within her that all her devotion had been in vain, and that he was planning to leave her. It seemed so. There was, therefore, no feeling of gratitude in his heart for all she had done. What she had done she now recalled in her bitterness—all the love, the devotion, the idolatry which she had lavished upon him would be as nothing. He had regained the control of his mind, and his first thought was to fly. The discovery of this indifference of his was terrible. She had trusted much to her devotion. She had thought that, in a nature like his, which was at once so pure, so high-minded, and so chivalrous, the spectacle of her noble self-sacrifice, combined with the discovery of her profound and all-absorbing love, would have awakened some response, if it were nothing stronger than mere gratitude. And why should it not be so? she thought. If she were ugly, or old, it would be different. But she was young; and, more than this, she was beautiful. True, her cheeks were not so rounded as they once were, her eyes were more hollow than they used to be, the pallor of her complexion was more intense than usual, and her lips were not so red; but what then? These were the signs and the marks which had been left upon her face by that deathless devotion which she had shown toward him. If there was any change in her, he alone was the cause, and she had offered herself up to him. That pallor, that delicacy, that weakness, and that emaciation of frame were all the visible signs and tokens of her self-sacrificing love for him. These things, instead of repelling him, ought to attract him. Moreover, in spite of all these things, even with her wasted form, she could see that she was yet beautiful. Her dark eyes beamed more darkly than before from their hollow orbs, against the pallor of her face the ebon hair shone more lustrously, as it hung in dark voluminous masses downward, and the white face itself showed features that were faultlessly beautiful. Why should he turn away from so beautiful a woman, who had so fully proved her love and her devotion? She felt that after this conspicuous example of her love he could never again bring forward against her those old charges of deceit which he had once uttered. These, at least, were dead forever. All the letters which she had written from the very first, on to that last letter of which he had spoken so bitterly—all were now amply atoned for by the devotion of the last few weeks—a devotion that shrank not from suffering, nor even from death itself. Why then did he not reciprocate? Why was it that he held himself aloof in such a manner from her caresses? Why was it that when her voice grew tremulous from the deep love of her heart she found no response, but only saw a certain embarrassment in his looks? There must be some cause for this. If he had been heart-whole, she thought, he must have yielded. There is something in the way. There is some other love. Yes, that is it, she concluded; it is what I saw before. He loves another!

At length, one day, Lord Chetwynde began to speak to her more directly about his plans. He had made up his mind to make them known to her, and so he availed himself of the first opportunity.

"I must soon take my departure, Lady Chetwynde," said he, as he plunged at once into the midst of affairs. "I·have made up my mind to go to Italy next week. As I intend to return to India I shall not go back to England again. All my business affairs are in the hands of my solicitors, and they will arrange all that I wish to be done."

By this Lord Chetwynde meant that his solicitors would arrange with Hilda those money-matters of which he had once spoken. He had too much consideration for her to make any direct allusion to them now, but wished, nevertheless, that she should understand his words in this way.

And in this way she did understand them. Her comprehension and apprehension were full and complete. By his tone and his look more than by his words she perceived that she had gained nothing by all her devotion. He had not meant to inflict actual suffering on her by these words. He had simply used them because he thought that it was best to acquaint her with his resolve in the most direct way, and, as he had tried for a long time to find some delicate way of doing this without success, he had at length, in desperation, adopted that which was most simple and plain. But to Hilda it was abrupt, and although she was not altogether unprepared, yet

it came like a thunder-clap, and for a moment she sank down into the depths of despair.

Then she rallied. In spite of the consciousness of the truth of her position—a truth which was unknown to Lord Chetwynde—she felt as though she were the victim of ingratitude and injustice. What she had done entitled her, she thought, to something more than a cold dismissal. All her pride and her dignity arose in arms at this slight. She regarded him calmly for a few moments as she listened to his words. Then all the pent-up feelings of her heart burst forth irrepressibly.

"Lord Chetwynde," said she, in a low and mournful voice, "I once would not have said to you what I am now going to say. I had not the right to say it, nor if I had would my pride have permitted me. But now I feel that I have earned the right to say it; and as to my pride, that has long since been buried in the dust. Besides, your words render it necessary that I should speak, and no longer keep silence. We had one interview, in which you did all the speaking and I kept silence. We had another interview in which I made a vain attempt at conciliation. I now wish to speak merely to explain things as they have been, and as they are, so that hereafter you may feel this, at least, that I have been frank and open at last.

"Lord Chetwynde, you remember that old bond that bound me to you. What was I? A girl of ten—a child. Afterward I was held to that bond under circumstances that have been impressed upon my memory indelibly. My father in the last hour of his life, when delirium was upon him, forced me to carry it out. You were older than I. You were a grown man. I was a child of fourteen. Could you not have found some way of saving me? I was a child. You were a man. Could you not have obtained some one who was not a priest, so that such a mockery of a marriage might have remained a mockery, and not have become a reality? It would have been easy to do that. My father's last hours would then have been lightened all the same, while you and I would not have been joined in that irrevocable vow. I tell you, Lord Chetwynde, that, in the years that followed, this thought was often in my mind, and thus it was that I learned to lay upon you the chief blame of the events that resulted.

"You have spoken to me, Lord Chetwynde, in very plain language about the letters that I wrote. You found in them taunts and sneers which you considered intolerable. Tell me, my lord, if you had been in my position, would you have been more generous? Think how galling it is to a proud and sensitive nature to discover that it is tied up and bound beyond the possibility of release. Now this is far worse for a woman than it is for a man. A woman, unless she is an Asiatic and a slave, does not wish to be given up unasked. I found myself the property of one who was not only indifferent to me, but, as I plainly saw, averse to me. It was but natural that I should meet scorn with scorn. In your letters I could read between the lines, and in your cold and constrained answers to your father's remarks about me I saw how strong was your aversion. In your letters to me this was still more evident. What then? I was proud and impetuous, and what you merely hinted at I expressed openly and unmistakably.

N

You found fault with this. You may be right, but my conduct was after all natural.

"It is this, Lord Chetwynde, which will account for my last letter to you. Crushed by the loss of my only friend, I reflected upon the difference between you and him, and the thought brought a bitterness which is indescribable. Therefore I wrote as I did. My sorrow, instead of softening, imbittered me, and I poured forth all my bitterness in that letter. It stung you. You were maddened by it and outraged. You saw in it only the symptoms and the proofs of what you chose to call a 'bad mind and heart.' If you reflect a little you will see that your conclusions were not so strictly just as they might have been. You yourself, you will see, were not the immaculate being which you suppose yourself to be.

"I say to you now, Lord Chetwynde, that all this time, instead of hating you, I felt very differently toward you. I had for you a feeling of regard which, at least, may be called sisterly. Associating with your father as I did, possessing his love, and enjoying his confidence, it would have been strange if I had not sympathized with him somewhat in his affections. Your name was always on his lips. You were the one of whom he was always speaking. When I wished to make him happy, and such a wish was always in my heart, I found no way so sure and certain as when I spoke in praise of you. During those years when I was writing those letters which you think showed a 'bad mind and heart,' I was incessantly engaged in sounding your praises to your father. What he thought of me you know. If I had a 'bad mind and heart,' he, at least, who knew me best, never discovered it. He gave me his confidence—more, he gave me his love.

"Lord Chetwynde, when you came home and crushed me with your cruel words I said nothing, for I was overcome by your cruelty. Then I thought that the best way for me to do was to show you by my life and by my acts, rather than by any words, how unjust you had been. How you treated my advances you well know. Without being guilty of any discourtesy, you contrived to make me feel that I was abhorrent. Still I did not despair of clearing my character in your sight. I asked an interview. I tried to explain, but, as you well remember, you coolly pushed all my explanations aside as so much hypocritical pretense. My lord, you were educated by your father in the school of honor and chivalry. I will not ask you now if your conduct was chivalrous. I only ask you, was it even just?

"And all this time, my lord, what were my feelings toward you? Let me tell you, and you yourself can judge. I will confess them, though nothing less than despair would ever have wrung such a confession out of me. Let me tell you then, my lord, what my feelings were. Not as expressed in empty words or in prolix letters, but as manifested by acts.

"Your valet wrote me that you were ill. I left immediately, filled with anxiety. Anxiety and fatigue both overpowered me. When I reached Frankfort I was struck down by fever. It was because I found that you had left that my fever was so severe. Scarce had I recovered than I hurried to Baden, finding out your address from the people of the Frankfort Hotel. You had gone to Munich. I followed you to Munich, so weak that I had to be carried into my cab at Baden, and out of it at Munich. At Munich another attack of fever prostrated me. I had missed you again, and my anxiety was intolerable. A thousand dreary fears oppressed me. I thought that you were dying—"

Here Hilda's voice faltered, and she stopped for a time, struggling with her emotion.

"I thought that you were dying," she repeated. "In my fever my situation was rendered infinitely worse by this fear. But at length I recovered, and went on. I reached Lausanne. I found you at the last point of life. I had time to give you your medicine and leave directions with your nurse, and then I fell down senseless by your side.

"My lord, while *you* were ill *I* was worse. My life was despaired of. Would to God that I had died then and there in the crisis of that fever! But I escaped it, and once more rose from my bed.

"I dragged myself back to your side, and staid there on my sofa, keeping watch over you, till once more I was struck down. Then I recovered once more, and gained health and strength again. Tell me, my lord," and Hilda's eyes seemed to penetrate to the soul of Lord Chetwynde as she spoke—"tell me, is this the sign of a 'bad mind and heart?'"

As Hilda had spoken she had evinced the strongest agitation. Her hands clutched one another, her voice was tremulous with emotion, her face was white, and a hectic flush on either cheek showed her excitement. Lord Chetwynde would have been either more or less than human if he had listened unmoved. As it was, he felt moved to the depths of his soul. Yet he could not say one word.

"I am alone in the world," said Hilda, mournfully. "You promised once to see about my happiness. That was a vow extorted from a boy, and it is nothing in itself. You said, not long ago, that you intended to keep your promise by separating yourself from me and giving me some money. Lord Chetwynde, look at me, think of what I have done, and answer. Is this the way to secure my happiness? What is money to me? Money! Do I care for money? What is it that I care for? I? I only wish to die! I have but a short time to live. I feel that I am doomed. Your money, Lord Chetwynde, will soon go back to you. Spare your solicitors the trouble to which you are putting them. If you can give me death, it will be the best thing that you can bestow. I gave you life. Can you not return the boon by giving me death, my lord?"

These last words Hilda wailed out in low tones of despair which vibrated in Lord Chetwynde's breast.

"At least," said she, "do not be in haste about leaving me. I will soon leave you forever. It is not much I ask. Let me only be near you for a short time, my lord. It is a small wish. Bear with me. You will see, before I die, that I have not altogether a 'bad mind and heart.'"

Her voice sank down into low tones of supplication; her head drooped forward; her intense feeling overcame her; tears burst from her eyes and flowed unchecked.

"Lady Chetwynde," said Lord Chetwynde, in deep emotion, "do as you wish. You have my gratitude for your noble devotion. I owe my life to you. If you really care about accompanying me I will not thwart your wishes. I can say no more. And let us never again speak of the past."

And this was all that Lord Chetwynde said.

CHAPTER LIX.

ON THE ROAD.

BEFORE Lord Chetwynde left Lausanne the doctor told him all about the poison and the antidote. He enlarged with great enthusiasm upon Lady Chetwynde's devotion and foresight; but his information caused Lord Chetwynde to meditate deeply upon this thing. Hilda found out that the doctor had said this, and gave her explanation. She said that the valet had described the symptoms; that she had asked a London doctor, who suspected poison, and gave her an antidote. She herself, she said, did not know what to think of it, but had naturally suspected the valet. She had charged him with it on her arrival. He had looked very much confused, and had immediately fled from the place. His guilt, in her opinion, had been confirmed by his flight. To her opinion Lord Chetwynde assented, and concluded that his valet wished to plunder him. He now recalled many suspicious circumstances about him, and remembered that he had taken the man without asking any one about him, satisfied with the letters of recommendation which he had brought, and which he had not taken the trouble to verify. He now believed that these letters were all no better than forgeries, and that he had well-nigh fallen a victim to one of the worst of villains. In his mind this revelation of the doctor only gave a new claim upon his gratitude toward the woman who had rescued him.

Shortly after he started for Italy. Hilda went with him. His position was embarrassing. Here was a woman to whom he lay under the deepest obligations, whose tender and devoted love was manifested in every word and action, and yet he was utterly incapable of reciprocating that love. She was beautiful, but her beauty did not affect him; she was, as he thought, his wife, yet he could never be a husband to her. Her piteous appeal had moved his heart, and forced him to take her with him, yet he was looking forward impatiently for some opportunity of leaving her. He could think of India only as the place which was likely to give him this opportunity, and concluded that after a short stay in Florence he would leave for the East, and resume his old duties. Before leaving Lausanne he wrote to the authorities in England, and applied to be reinstated in some position in the Indian service, which he had not yet quitted, or, if possible, to go back to his old place. A return to India was now his only hope, and the only way by which he could escape from the very peculiar difficulties of his situation.

It was a trying position, but he took refuge in a certain lofty courtesy which well became him, and which might pass very well for that warmer feeling of which he was destitute. His natural kindliness of disposition softened his manner toward Hilda, and his sense of obligation made him tenderly considerate. If Hilda could have been content with any thing except positive love, she would have found happiness in that gentle and kindly and chivalrous courtesy which she received at the hands of Lord Chetwynde. Content with this she was not. It was something different from this that she desired; yet, after all, it was an immense advance on the old state of things. It gave her the chance of making herself known to Lord Chetwynde, a chance which had been denied to her before. Conversation was no longer impossible. At Chetwynde Castle there had been nothing but the most formal remarks; now there were things which approximated almost to an interchange of confidence. By her devotion, and by her confession of her feelings, she had presented herself to him in a new light, and that memorable confession of hers could not be forgotten. It was while traveling together that the new state of things was most manifest to her. She sat next to him in the carriage; she touched him; her arm was close to his. That touch thrilled through her, even though she knew too well that he was cold and calm and indifferent. But this was, at least, a better thing than that abhorrence and repugnance which he had formerly manifested; and the friendly smile and the genial remark which he often directed to her were received by her with joy, and treasured up in the depths of her soul as something precious.

Traveling thus together through scenes of grandeur and of beauty, seated side by side, it was impossible to avoid a closer intimacy than common. In spite of Lord Chetwynde's coolness, the very fact that he was thus thrown into constant contact with a woman who was at once beautiful and clever, and who at the same time had made an open confession of her devotion to him, was of itself sufficient to inspire something like kindliness of sentiment at least in his heart, even though that heart were the coldest and the least susceptible that ever beat. The scenes through which they passed were of themselves calculated in the highest degree to excite a communion of soul. Hilda was clever and well-read, with a deep love for the beautiful, and a familiar acquaintance with all modern literature. There was not a beautiful spot on the road which had been sung by poets or celebrated in fiction of which she was ignorant. Ferney, sacred to Voltaire; Geneva, the birth-place of Rousseau; the Jura Alps, sung by Byron; the thousand places of lesser note embalmed by French or German writers in song and story, were all greeted by her with a delight that was girlish in its enthusiastic demonstrativeness. Lord Chetwynde, himself intellectual, recognized and respected the brilliant intellect of his companion. He saw that the woman who had saved his life at the risk of her own, who had dropped down senseless at his bedside, overworn with duties self-imposed through love for him—the woman who had overwhelmed him with obligations of gratitude—could also dazzle him with her intellectual brilliancy, and surpass him in familiarity with the greatest geniuses of modern times.

Another circumstance had contributed toward the formation of a closer association between these two. Hilda had no maid with her, but was traveling unattended. On leaving Lausanne she found that Gretchen was unwilling to go to Italy, and had, therefore, parted with her with many kind words, and the bestowal of presents sufficiently valuable to make the kind-hearted German maid keep in her memory for many years to come the recollection of that gentle suffering English lady, whose devotion to her husband had been shown so signally, and almost at the cost of her own life. Hilda took no maid with her. Either she could not obtain one in so small a place as Lausanne, or else she did not choose to employ one. Whatever the cause may have been, the result was to throw her more upon the care of Lord Chetwynde, who was forced, if not from gratitude at least from common politeness, to show her many of those little attentions which are demanded by a lady from a gentleman. Traveling together as they did, those attentions were required more frequently than under ordinary circumstances; and although they seemed to Lord Chetwynde the most ordinary commonplaces, yet to Hilda every separate act of attention or of common politeness carried with it a joy which was felt through all her being. If she had reasoned about that joy, she might perhaps have seen how unfounded it was. But she did not reason about it; it was enough to her that he was by her side, and that acts like these came from him to her. In her mind all the past and all the future were forgotten, and there was nothing but an enjoyment of the present.

Their journey lay through regions which presented every thing that could charm the taste or awaken admiration. At first there was the grandeur of Alpine scenery. From this they emerged into the softer beauty of the Italian clime. It was the Simplon Road which they traversed, that gigantic monument to the genius of Napoleon, which is more enduring than even the fame of Marengo or Austerlitz; and this road, with its alternating scenes of grandeur and of beauty, of glory and of gloom, had elicited the utmost admiration from each. At length, one day, as they were descending this road on the slope nearest Italy, on leaving Domo d'Ossola, they came to a place where the boundless plains of Lombardy lay stretched before them. There the verdurous fields stretched away beneath their eyes—an expanse of living green; seeming like the abode of perpetual summer to those who looked down from the habitation of winter. Far away spread the plains to the distant horizon, where the purple Apennines arose bounding the view. Nearer was the Lago Maggiore with its wondrous islands, the Isola Bella and the Isola Madre, covered with their hanging gardens, whose green foliage rose over the dark blue waters of the lake beneath; while beyond that lake lay towns and villages and hamlets, whose far white walls gleamed brightly amidst the vivid green of the surrounding plain; and vineyards also, and groves and orchards and forests of olive and chestnut trees. It was a scene which no other on earth can surpass, if it can equal, and one which, to travelers descending the Alps, has in every age brought a resistless charm.

This was the first time that Hilda had seen this glorious land. Lord Chetwynde had visited Naples, but to him the prospect that lay beneath was as striking as though he had never seen any of the beauties of Italy. Hilda, however, felt its power most. Both gazed long and with deep admiration upon this matchless scene without uttering one word to express their emotions; viewing it in silence, as though to break that si-

lence would break the spell which had been thrown over them by the first sight of this wondrous land. At last Hilda broke that spell. Carried away by the excitement of the moment she started to her feet, and stood erect in the carriage, and then burst forth into that noble paraphrase which Byron has made of the glorious sonnet of Filicaja:

"Italia! O Italia! thou who hast
    The fatal gift of beauty, which became
A funeral dower of present woes and past,
    On thy sweet brow is sorrow plowed by shame,
    And annals graven in characters of flame.
O God! that thou wert in thy nakedness
    Less lovely, or more powerful, and couldst claim
Thy right, and awe the robbers back, who press
To shed thy blood and drink the tears of thy distress."

She stood like a Sibyl, inspired by the scene before her. Pale, yet lovely, with all her intellectual beauty refined by the sorrows through which she had passed, she herself might have been taken for an image of that Italy which she thus invoked. Lord Chetwynde looked at her, and amidst his surprise at such an outburst of enthusiasm he had some such thoughts as these. But suddenly, from some unknown cause, Hilda sank back into her seat, and burst into tears. At the display of such emotion Lord Chetwynde looked on deeply disturbed. What possible connection there could be between these words and her agitation he could not see. But he was full of pity for her, and he did what was most natural. He took her hand, and spoke kind words to her, and tried to soothe her. At his touch her agitation subsided. She smiled through her tears, and looked at him with a glance that spoke unutterable things. It was the first time that Lord Chetwynde had shown toward her any thing approaching to tenderness.

On that same day another incident occurred. A few miles beyond Domo d'Ossola there was an inn where they had stopped to change horses. They waited here for a time till the horses were ready, and then resumed their journey. The road went on before them for miles, winding along gently in easy curves and with a gradual descent toward those smiling vales which lay beneath them. As they drove onward each turn in the road seemed to bring some new view before them, and to disclose some fresh glimpse to their eyes of that voluptuous Italian beauty which they were now beholding, and which appeared all the lovelier from the contrast which it presented to that sublime Alpine scenery—the gloom of awful gorges, the grandeur of snow-capped heights through which they had been journeying.

Inside the carriage were Lord Chetwynde and Hilda. Outside was the driver. Hilda was just pointing out to Lord Chetwynde some peculiar tint in the purple of the distant Apennines when suddenly the carriage gave a lurch, and, with a wild bound, the horses started off at full speed down the road. Something had happened. Either the harness had given way or the horses were frightened; at any rate, they were running away at a fearful pace, and the driver, erect on his seat, was striving with all his might to hold in the maddened animals. His efforts were all to no purpose. On they went, like the wind, and the carriage, tossed from side to side at their wild springs, seemed sometimes to leap into the air. The road before them wound on down a spur of the mountains, with deep ravines on

"HE LAID HER DOWN UPON THE GRASS."

one side—a place full of danger for such a race as this.

It was a fearful moment. For a time Hilda said not a word; she sat motionless, like one paralyzed by terror; and then, as the carriage gave a wilder lurch than usual, she gave utterance to a loud cry of fear, and flung her arms around Lord Chetwynde.

"Save me! oh, save me!" she exclaimed.

She clung to him desperately, as though in thus clinging to him she had some assurance of safety. Lord Chetwynde sat erect, looking out upon the road before him, down which they were dashing, and saying not a word. Mechanically he put his arm around this panic-stricken woman, who clung to him so tightly, as though by that silent gesture he meant to show that he would protect her as far as possible. But in so perilous a race all possibility of protection was out of the question.

At last the horses, in their onward career, came to a curve in the road, where, on one side, there was a hill, and on the other a declivity. It was a sharp turn. Their impetus was too swift to be readily stayed. Dashing onward, the carriage was whirled around after them, and was thrown off the road down the declivity. For a

few paces the horses dragged it onward as it lay on its side, and then the weight of the carriage was too much for them. They stopped, then staggered, then backed, and then, with a heavy plunge, both carriage and horses went down into the gully beneath.

It was not more than thirty feet of a descent, and the bottom was the dry bed of a mountain torrent. The horses struggled and strove to free themselves. The driver jumped off uninjured, and sprang at them to stop them. This he succeeded in doing, at the cost of some severe bruises.

Meanwhile the occupants of the carriage had felt the full consciousness of the danger. As the carriage went down Hilda clung more closely to Lord Chetwynde. He, on his part, said not a word, but braced himself for the fall. The carriage rolled over and over in its descent, and at last stopped. Lord Chetwynde, with Hilda in his arms, was thrown violently down. As soon as he could he raised himself and drew Hilda out from the wreck of the carriage.

She was senseless.

He laid her down upon the grass. Her eyes were closed, her hair was all disordered, her face was as white as the face of a corpse. A stream of blood trickled down over her marble forehead from a wound in her head. It was a piteous sight.

Lord Chetwynde took her in his arms and carried her off a little distance, to a place where there was some water in the bed of the brook. With this he sought to restore her to consciousness. For a long time his efforts were unavailing.

At last he called to the driver.

"Tie up one of the horses and get on the other," he said, "and ride for your life to the nearest house. Bring help. The lady is stunned, and must be taken away as soon as possible. Get them to knock up a litter, and bring a couple of stout fellows back to help us carry her. Make haste—for your life."

The driver at once comprehended the whole situation. He did as he was bid, and in a few minutes the sound of his horse's hoofs died away in the distance.

Lord Chetwynde was left alone with Hilda.

She lay in his arms, her beautiful face on his shoulder, tenderly supported ; that face white, and the lips bloodless, the eyes closed, and blood trickling from the wound on her head. It was not a sight upon which any one might look unmoved.

And Lord Chetwynde was moved to his inmost soul by that sight.

Who was this woman? His wife! the one who stood between him and his desires.

Ah, true! But she was something more.

And now, as he looked at her thus lying in his arms, there came to him the thought of all that she had been to him—the thought of her undying love—her matchless devotion. That pale face, those closed eyes, those mute lips, that beautiful head, stained with oozing blood, all spoke to him with an eloquence which awakened a response within him.

Was this the end of all that love and that devotion? Was this the fulfillment of his promise to General Pomeroy? Was he doing by this woman as she had done by him? Had she not made more than the fullest atonement for the offenses and follies of the past? Had she not followed him through Europe to seek him and to snatch him from the grasp of a villain? Had she not saved his life at the risk of her own? Had she not stood by his side till she fell lifeless at his feet in her unparalleled self-devotion?

These were the questions that came to him.

He loved her not ; but if he wished for love, could he ever find any equal to this? That poor, frail, slender frame pleaded piteously ; that white face, as it lay upturned, was itself a prayer.

Involuntarily he stooped down, and in his deep pity he pressed his lips to that icy brow. Then once more he looked at her. Once more he touched her, and this time his lips met hers.

"My God!" he groaned ; "what can I do? Why did I ever see—that other one?"

An hour passed, and the driver returned. Four men came with him, carrying a rude litter. On this Hilda's senseless form was placed. And thus they carried her to the nearest house, while Lord Chetwynde followed in silence and in deep thought.

CHAPTER LX.

THE CLAWS OF THE AMERICAN EAGLE.

At length Obed prepared to leave Naples and visit other places in Italy. He intended to go to Rome and Florence, after which he expected to go to Venice or Milan, and then across the Alps to Germany. Two vetturas held the family, and in due time they arrived at Terracina. Here they passed the night, and early on the following day they set out, expecting to traverse the Pontine Marshes and reach Albano by evening.

These famous marshes extend from Terracina to Nettuno. They are about forty-five miles in length and from four to twelve in breadth. Drained successively by Roman, by Goth, and by pope, they successively relapsed into their natural state, until the perseverance of Pius VI. completed the work. It is now largely cultivated, but the scenery is monotonous and the journey tedious. The few inhabitants found here got their living by hunting and by robbery, and are distinguished by their pale and sickly appearance. At this time the disturbed state of Italy, and particularly of the papal dominions, made traveling sometimes hazardous, and no place was more dangerous than this. Yet Obed gave this no thought, but started on the journey with as much cheerfulness as though he were making a railway trip from New York to Philadelphia.

About half-way there is a solitary inn, situated close by the road-side, with a forlorn and desolate air about it. It is two stories high, with small windows, and the whitewashed stone walls made it look more like a lazaretto than any thing else. Here they stopped two hours to feed the horses and to take their déjeuner. The place was at this time kept by a miserable old man and his wife, on whom the unhealthy atmosphere of the marshes seemed to have brought a premature decay. Obed could not speak Italian, so that he was debarred from the pleasure of talking with this man ; but he exhibited much sympathy toward him, and made him a present of a bundle of cigars — an act which the old man viewed, at first, with absolute incredulity, and at length with unutterable gratitude.

Leaving this place they drove on for about two miles, when suddenly the carriage in which Obed and the family were traveling fell forward with a crash, and the party were thrown pellmell together. The horses stopped. No injury was done to any one, and Obed got out to see what had taken place. The front axle was broken.

Here was a very awkward dilemma, and it was difficult to tell what ought to be done. There was the other carriage, but it was small, and could not contain the family. The two maids, also, would have to be left behind. Obed thought, at first, of sending on his family and waiting ; but he soon dismissed this idea. For the present, at least, he saw that they would have to drive back to the inn, and this they finally did. Here Obed exerted all his ingenuity and all his mechanical skill in a futile endeavor to repair the axle. But the rough patch which he succeeded at last in making was so inefficient that, on attempting to start once more, the carriage again broke down, and they were forced to give up this hope.

Three hours had now passed away, and it had already grown altogether too late to think of trying to finish the journey. Again the question arose, what was to be done? To go back was now as much out of the question as to go forward. One resource only seemed left them, and that was to stay here for the night, and send back to Terracina for a new carriage. This decision Obed finally arrived at, and he communicated it to his valet, and ordered him to see if they could have any accommodations for the night.

The valet seemed somewhat alarmed at this proposal.

"It's a dangerous place," said he. "The country swarms with brigands. We had better take the ladies back."

"Take the ladies back!" cried Obed. "How can we do that? We can't all cram into the small carriage. And, besides, as to danger—by this time it's as dangerous on the road as it is here."

"Oh no; travelers will be upon the road—"

"Pooh! there's no danger when one is inside of a stone house like this. Why, man, this house is a regular fort. Besides, who is there that would attack an inn?"

"The brigands," said the valet. "They're all around, prowling about, and will be likely to pay a visit here. This house, at the best of times, does not have a good name."

"Well," said Obed, "let them come on."

"You forget, Sir," said the valet, "that you are alone."

"Not a bit of it," said Obed; "I'm well aware that I'm alone."

"But you're worse than alone," remonstrated the valet, earnestly. "You have your family. That is the thing that makes the real danger; for, if any thing happens to you, what will become of them?"

"Pooh!" said Obed; "there are plenty of 'ifs' whenever any man is on the look-out for danger. Now, I ain't on the look-out. Why should I trouble myself? Whenever any enemy shows himself I'll be ready. If a man is always going to imagine danger, and borrow trouble, what will become of him? This place seems to me the best place for the family now—far better than the road, at any rate. I wouldn't have them dragged back to Terracina on any account. It 'll be dark long before we get there, and traveling by night on the Pontine Marshes ain't particularly healthy. There's less risk for them here than any where else; so, young man, you'd better look up the beds, and see what they can do for us."

The valet made some further remonstrances; he described the ruthless character of the Italian brigands, told Obed about the dangerous condition of the country, hinted that the old man and his wife were themselves possibly in alliance with the brigands, and again urged him to change his plans. But Obed was not moved in the slightest degree by these representations. He had considered it all, he said, and had made up his mind. As he saw it, all the risk, and all the fatigue too, which was quite as important a thing, were on the road, and whatever safety there was, whether from brigands or miasma, lay in the inn.

The valet then went to see about the accommodations for the party. They were rude, it is true, yet sufficient in such an emergency. The old man and his wife bestirred themselves to make every thing ready for the unexpected guests, and, with the assistance of the maids, their rooms were prepared.

After this the valet drove back with the vetturino, promising to come as early as possible on the following day.

During Obed's conversation with the valet the ladies had been in the hotel, and had therefore heard nothing of what had been said. They were quite ignorant of the existence of any danger, and Obed thought it the best plan to keep them in ignorance, unless actual danger should arise. For his own part, he had meant what he said. He was aware that there was danger; he knew that the country was in an unsettled and lawless condition, and that roving bands of robbers were scouring the papal territories. From the very consciousness that he had of this danger, he had decided in favor of stopping. He believed the road to be more dangerous than the inn. If there was to be any attack of brigands, he much preferred to receive it here; and he thought this a more unlikely place for such an attack than any other.

The warning of the valet made a sufficiently deep impression upon him to cause him to examine very carefully the position of his rooms, and the general appearance of the house. The house itself was as strong as a fortress, and a dozen men, well posted, could have defended it against a thousand. But Obed was alone, and had to consider the prospects of one man in a defense. The rooms which he occupied favored this. There were two. One was a large one at the end of the house, lighted by one small window. This his family and Zillah occupied; somewhat crowded, it is true, yet not at all uncomfortable. A wide hearth was there, and a blazing peat fire kept down the chill of the marshy exhalations. Outside of this was a smaller room, and this was Obed's. A fire was burning here also. A window lighted it, and a stout door opened into the hall. The bed was an old-fashioned four-posted structure of enormous weight.

All these things Obed took in with one rapid glance, and saw the advantages of his position. In these rooms, with his revolver and his ammunition, he felt quite at ease. He felt somewhat grieved at that moment that he did not know Italian, for he wished very much to ask some questions of the old inn-keeper; but this was a misfortune which he had to endure.

As long as the daylight lasted Obed wandered about outside. Then dinner came, and after that the time hung heavily on his hands. At last he went to his room; the family had retired some time before. There was a good supply of peat, and with this he replenished the fire. Then he drew the massive oaken bedstead in front of the door, and lounged upon it, smoking and meditating.

The warnings of the valet had produced this effect at least upon Obed, that he had concluded not to go to sleep. He determined to remain awake, and though such watchfulness might not be needed, yet he felt that for his family's sake it was wisest and best. To sit up one night, or rather to lounge on a bed smoking, was nothing, and there was plenty of occupation for his thoughts.

Time passed on. Midnight came, and nothing had occurred. Another hour passed; and then another. It was two o'clock.

About a quarter of an hour after this Obed was roused by a sudden knocking at the door of the inn. Shouts followed. He heard the old man descend the stairs. Then the door was opened, and loud noisy footsteps were heard entering the inn.

At this Obed began to feel that his watchfulness was not useless.

Some time now elapsed. Those who had come were sufficiently disorderly. Shouts and cries and yells arose. Obed imagined that they were refreshing themselves. He tried to guess at tho possible number, and thought that there could not be more than a dozen, if so many. Yet he had acquired such a contempt for Italians, and had such confidence in himself, that he felt very much the same, at the prospect of an encounter with them, as a grown man might feel at an encounter with as many boys.

During this time he made no change in his position. His revolver was in his breast pocket, and he had cartridges enough for a long siege. He smoked still, for this habit was a deeply confirmed one with Obed; and lolling at the foot of the bed, with his head against the wall, he awaited further developments.

At last there was a change in the noise. A silence followed; and then he heard footsteps moving toward the hall. He listened. The footsteps ascended the stairs!

They ascended the stairs, and came nearer and nearer. There did not seem to be so many as a dozen. Perhaps some remained below. Such were his thoughts.

They came toward his room.

At length he heard the knob of the door turning gently. Of course, as the door was locked, and as the bed was in front of it, this produced no effect. On Obed the only effect was that he sat upright and drew his revolver from his pocket, still smoking.

Then followed some conversation outside.

Then there came a knock.

"Who's there?" said Obed, mildly.

"Aperite!" was the answer, in a harsh voice.

"What?"

"Aperite. Siamo poveri. Date vostro argento."

"Me don't understand Italian," said Obed. "Me American. Speeky English, and go to blazes!"

At this there was a pause, and then a dull deep crash, as if the whole body outside had precipitated themselves against the door.

Obed held his pistol quickly toward the door opposite the thinnest panel, which had yielded slightly to that blow, and fired.

Once!

Twice!!

Thrice!!!

Three explosions burst forth.

And then came sharp and sudden deep groans of pain, intermingled with savage yells of rage. There was a sound as of bodies falling, and retreating footsteps, and curses low and deep.

Loud outcries came from the adjoining room. The noise had awakened the family.

Obed stepped to the door.

"Don't be afraid," said he, quietly. "It's

only some brigands. But keep cool. I'll take care of you. Perhaps you'd better get up and dress, though. At any rate, keep cool. You needn't bother as long as you've got me."

AFTER her accident Hilda was carried to the nearest house, and there she recovered, after some time, from her swoon. She knew nothing of what Lord Chetwynde had thought and done during that time when she lay in his arms, and he had bent over her so full of pity and sorrow. Some time elapsed before she saw him, for he had ridden off himself to the nearest town to get a conveyance. When he returned it was very late, and she had to go to bed through weakness. And thus they did not meet until the following morning.

When they did meet Lord Chetwynde asked kindly about her health, but evinced no stronger feeling than kindness—or pity. She was pale and sad; she was eager for some sign of tenderness, but the sign was not forthcoming. Lord Chetwynde was kind and sympathetic. He tried to cheer her; he exerted himself to please her and to soothe her, but that was all. That self-reproach which had thrilled him as she lay lifeless in his arms had passed as soon as she left those arms, and, in the presence of the one absorbing passion of his soul, Hilda was nothing.

When they resumed their journey it was as before. He was courteous to an extreme. He anticipated her wishes and saw after her comforts with the greatest solicitude, but never did he evince any desire to pass beyond the limits of conventional politeness. To him she was simply a lady traveling in his company, to whom he was under every obligation, as far as gratitude was concerned, or kindly and watchful attention, but toward whom no feeling of tenderness ever arose.

He certainly neglected none of those ordinary acts of courteous attention which are common between gentlemen and ladies. At Milan he took her around to see all the sights of that famous city. The Breda Palace, the Amphitheatre, above all, the Cathedral, were visited, and nothing was omitted which might give her pleasure. Yet all this was different from what it had been before. Since the accident Hilda had grown more sad, and lost her sprightliness and enthusiasm. On first recovering her senses she had learned about the events of that accident, and that Lord Chetwynde had tried to bring her to life again. She had hoped much from this, and had fully expected when she saw him again to find in him something softer than before. In this she had been utterly disappointed. Her heart now sank within her, and scarcely any hope was left. Languid and dull, she tried no longer to win Lord Chetwynde by brilliancy of conversation, or by enthusiastic interest in the beautiful of nature and of art. These had failed once; why should she try them again? And since he had been unmoved by the spectacle of her lifeless form—the narrow escape from death of one who he well knew would die to save him—what was there left for her to do?

At length they resumed their journey, and in due time reached Florence. Here new changes took place. Their arrival here terminated that close association enforced by their journey which had been so precious to Hilda. Here Lord Chetwynde of course drifted away, and she could not hope to see him except at certain stated intervals. Now more than ever she began to lose hope. The hopes that she had once formed seemed now to be baseless. And why, she asked herself bitterly—why was it so impossible for him to love her? Would not any other man have loved her under such circumstances?

At Florence Lord Chetwynde went his own way. He visited most of the places of interest in company with her, took her to the Duomo, the Church of Santa Croce, the Palazzi Vecchio and Pitti, walked with her through the picture-galleries, and drove out with her several times. After this there was nothing more to be done, and he was left to his own resources, and she, necessarily, to hers. She could not tell where he went, but merely conjectured that he was idling about without any particular purpose, in the character of a common sight-seer.

Hilda thus at length, left so much to herself, without the joy of his presence to soften her, grew gradually hopeless and desperate; and there began to rise within her bitter feelings, like those of former days. In the midst of these her darker nature made itself manifest, and there came the vengeful promptings of outraged love. With her vengeance meant something more than it did with common characters; and when that fit was on her there came regrets that she had ever left Chetwynde, and gloomy ideas about completing her interrupted work after all. But these feelings were fitful, for at times hope would return again, and tenderness take the place of vindictiveness. From hope she would again sink into despair, and sometimes meditate upon that dark resolve which she had once hinted to Gualtier at the Hôtel Gibbon.

Amidst all this her pride was roused. Why should she remain in this position—a hanger-on—forcing herself on an unwilling man who at best only tolerated her? The only soft feeling for her that had ever arisen in his heart was nothing more than pity. Could she hope that ever this pity would change to love, or that even the pity itself would last? Was he not even now longing to get rid of her, and impatiently awaiting tidings of his Indian appointment? To go to India, she saw plainly, simply meant to get rid of her. This, she saw, was his fixed determination. And for her—why should she thus remain, so deeply humiliated, when she was not wanted?

So she argued with herself, but still she staid on. For love makes the proudest a craven, and turns the strength of the strongest into weakness; and so, in spite of herself, she staid, because she could not go.

Meanwhile the state of Lord Chetwynde's mind was not by any means enviable. He found himself in a position which was at once unexpected and, to him, extremely embarrassing. Every feeling of gratitude, every prompting of common generosity, compelled him to exhibit toward Hilda a greater degree of kindness than existed in his heart. The association of a long journey had necessarily thrown him upon her society, and there had been times when he had found her agreeable; there had also been that memorable episode when her poor, pale face, with its stain of blood over the white forehead, had drawn forth his deepest pity, and roused him to some approach to tenderness. But with the occasion the feeling had passed; and the tenderness, born of so piteous a sight, returned no more. Her own dullness afterward deprived him even of the chance of finding her an agreeable companion. He saw that she was deeply melancholy. Yet what could he do? Even if he had wished it he could not have forced himself to love this woman, notwithstanding her devotion to himself. And this he did not even wish. Not all his sense of honor, not all his emotions of gratitude, not all his instincts of generosity, not even the remembrance of his solemn promise to General Pomeroy, could excite within him any desire that his heart might change from its affection and its longing for another, to yield that love to her.

True, once or twice his heart had smote him as he thought of his utter coldness and want of gratitude toward this woman who had done so much for him. This feeling was very painful on that day of the accident. Yet it passed. He could not force himself to muse over his own shortcomings. He could not bring himself to wish that he should be one whit more grateful to her or more tender. Any thought of her being ever more to him than she was now seemed repugnant. Any wish for it was out of the question. Indeed, he never thought of it as being within the bounds of possibility. For behind all these late events there lay certain things which made it impossible for him, under ordinary circumstances, ever to become fully reconciled to her.

For, after all, in his cooler moods he now felt how she was associated with the bitterest memories of his life. She it was who had been the cause, unwilling no doubt as he now thought, but still no less the cause of the blight that had descended upon his life. As that life had passed he could not help, cursing the day when first General Pomeroy proposed that unholy agreement. It was this that had exiled him from his native land and would keep him an exile forever. It was this which denied to him the joys of virtuous love, when his heart had been filled with one image—an image which now was never absent. Bound by the law to this woman, who was named his wife, he could never hope in any way to gain that other one on whom all his heart was fixed. Between him and those hopes that made life precious she stood and rendered those hopes impossible.

Then, too, he could not avoid recalling his life in India, which she had tried to make, as far as in her lay, one long misery, by those malevolent letters which she had never ceased to write. Above all, he could never forget the horror of indignation which had been awakened within him by that last letter, and the fierce vows which he had made to be avenged on her. All this was yet in his memory in spite of the events of later days. True, she had relented from her former savage spirit, and had changed from hate to love. She had traveled far to save him from death. She had watched by him day and night till her own life well-nigh gave way. She had repented, and had marked her repentance by a devotion which could not be surpassed. For all this he felt grateful. His gratitude, indeed, had been so profound and so sincere that it had risen up between him and his just hate, and had forced him to forgive her fully and freely, and to the uttermost, for all that she had done of her own accord, and also for all of which she had been the accidental cause. He had lost his repugnance to her. He could now talk to her, he could even take her hand, and could have transient emotions of tenderness toward her. But what then? What was the value of these feelings? He had forgiven her, but he had not forgotten the past. That was impossible. The memory of that past still remained, and its results were still before him. He felt those results every hour of his life. Above all, she still stood before him as the one thing, and the only thing, which formed an obstacle between him and his happiness. He might pity her, he might be grateful to her; but the intense fervor of one passion, and the longing desire to which it gave rise, made it impossible for her ever to seem to him any thing else than the curse of his life.

At Florence he was left more to himself. He was no longer forced to sit by her side. He gradually kept by himself; for, though he could tolerate her, he could not seek her. Indeed, his own feelings impelled him to avoid her. The image of that one who never left his memory had such an effect on him that he preferred solitude and his own thoughts. In this way he could best struggle with himself and arrange his lonely and desolate future. India now appeared the one hope that was left him. There he might find distraction from troublesome thoughts in his old occupations, and among his old associates. He had bidden farewell to Chetwynde forever. He had left the fate of Chetwynde in the hands of his solicitors; he had signed away all his rights; he had broken the entail; and had faced the prospect of the extinction of his ancient family. This resolution had cost him so much that it was impossible now to go back from it. The exhibition of Hilda's devotion never changed his resolution for an instant. The papers still remained with his solicitors, nor did he for one moment dream of countermanding the orders which he had once given.

What Lord Chetwynde most desired was solitude. Florence had been chosen by him as a resting-place where he might await letters from England about his Indian appointment, and for those letters he waited every day. Under these circumstances he avoided all society. He had taken unpretending lodgings, and in the Hôtel Meubles, overlooking the Ponta della Trinita, he was lost in the crowd of fellow-lodgers. His suite of apartments extended over the third story. Below him was a Russian Prince and a German Grand Duke, and above and all around was a crowd of travelers of all nations. He brought no letters. He desired no acquaintances. Florence, under the new régime, was too much agitated by recent changes for its noblesse to pay any attention to a stranger, however distinguished, unless he was forced upon them; and so Lord Chetwynde had the most complete isolation. If

Hilda had ever had any ideas of going with Lord Chetwynde into Florentine society she was soon undeceived, when, as the days passed, she found that Florentine society took no notice of her. Whatever disappointment she may have felt, Lord Chetwynde only received gratification from this, since it spared him every annoyance, and left him to himself, after the first week or so.

By himself he thus occupied his time. He rode sometimes through the beautiful country which surrounds Florence on every side. When weary of this he used to stroll about the city, along the Lungh' Arno, or through the Casino, or among the churches. But his favorite place of resort was the Boboli Gardens; for here there was sufficient life and movement to he found among the throng of visitors; or, if he wished seclusion, he could find solitude among the sequestered groves and romantic grottoes of this enchanting spot.

Here one day he wandered, and found a place among the trees which commanded a view of one of the principal avenues of the gardens. In the distance there opened a vista through which was revealed the fair outline of Florence, with its encircling hills, and its glorious Val d'Arno. There arose the stupendous outline of Il Duomo, the stately form of the Baptistery, the graceful shaft of the Campanile, the medieval grandeur of the Palazzo Vecchio; and the severe Etruscan massiveness of the Pitti Palace was just below. Far away the Arno wound on, through the verdurous plain, while on either side the hills arose dotted with white villas and deep green olive groves. Is there any view on earth which can surpass this one, where

"Arno wins us to the fair white walls,
    Where the Etrurian Athens claims and keeps
  A softer feeling for her fairy halls.
  Girt by her theatre of hills, she reaps
  Her corn and wine and oil, and Plenty leaps
To laughing life, with her redundant horn.
    Along the banks where smiling Arno sweeps
  Was modern Luxury of Commerce born,
And buried Learning rose, redeemed, to a now morn."

It was upon this scene that Lord Chetwynde was looking out, lost in thoughts which were sometimes taken up with the historic charms of this unrivaled valley, and sometimes with his own sombre future, when suddenly his attention was arrested by a figure passing along the pathway immediately beneath him. The new-comer was a tall, broad-shouldered, square-faced man; he wore a dress-coat and a felt hat; he had no gloves, but his thumbs were inserted in the armholes of his waistcoat; and as he sauntered along he looked around with a leisurely yet comprehensive stare. Lord Chetwynde was seated in a place which made him unseen to any in the path, while it afforded him the fullest opportunities of seeing others. This man, who thus walked on, turned his full face toward him and disclosed the well-known features of Obed Chute.

The sight of this man sent a strange thrill to the inmost heart of Lord Chetwynde. He here! In Florence! And his family, were they with him? And she—when he saw him in London he said that she was yet with him—was she with him now? Such were the thoughts which came to Lord Chetwynde at the sight of that face. The next instant he rose, hurried down to the path after Obed, who had strode onward and catching his arm, he said:

"Mr. Chute, you here! When did you arrive?"

Obed turned with a start and saw his friend.

"Windham again!" he exclaimed, "by all that's wonderful! But how did you get here?"

"I? Oh, I've been here two or three weeks. But it doesn't seem possible that it should really be you," he added, with greater warmth than was usual to him, as he wrung Obed's hand.

"It's possible," said Obed, with a characteristic squeeze of Lord Chetwynde's hand, which made it numb for half an hour afterward. "It's possible, my boy, for it's the actual fact. But still, I must say, you're about the last man I expected to see in these diggins. When I saw you in London you were up to your eyes in business, and were expectin' to start straight off and make a bee-line for India."

"Well, that is what I'm doing now; I'm on my way there."

"On your way there? You don't say so! But you'll stay here some time?"

"Oh yes; I've some little time to spare. The fact is I came here to pass my leisure time. I'm expecting a letter every day which may send me off. But it may not come for weeks."

"And you're going back to India?" said Obed.

"Yes."

"I should think you'd rather stay home—among your friends."

"Well—I don't know," said Lord Chetwynde, with assumed indifference. "The fact is, life in India unfits one for life in England. We get new tastes and acquire new habits. I never yet saw a returned Indian who could be content. For my part, I'm too young yet to go in for being a returned Indian; and so after I finished my business I applied for a reappointment."

"There's a good deal in what you say," remarked Obed. "Your British island is contracted. A man who has lived in a country like India feels this. We Americans, accustomed as we are to the unlimited atmosphere of a boundless continent, feel depressed in a country like England. There is in your country, Sir, a physical and also a moral constraint which, to a free, republican, continental American, is suffocating. And hence my dislike to the mother country."

They walked on together chatting about numerous things. Obed referred once more to India.

"It's queer," said he; "your British Empire is so tremendous that it seems to cover the earth. After I left the States it seemed to me that I couldn't go any where without seeing the British flag. There was Australia, a continent in itself; and Hong Kong; and India, another continent; and Aden, and Malta. You have a small country too, not much larger than New York State."

"Well," said Lord Chetwynde, with a smile, "we once owned a great deal more, you know. We had colonies that were worth all the rest. Unfortunately those colonies took it into their heads to set up for themselves, and started that independent nation of the Stars and Stripes that you belong to. If it hadn't been for that abominable Stamp Act, and other acts equally abominable, you and I might now be under the same flag, belonging to an empire which might set the whole united world at defiance. It's a pity it was not so. The only hope now left is that our countries may always be good friends, as they are now, as you and I are—as we always are, whenever we meet under such circumstances as those which occurred when you and I became acquainted. 'Blood is thicker than water,' said old Tatnall, when he sent his Yankee sailors to help Admiral Hope; and the same sentiment is still in the mind of every true Englishman whenever he sees an American of the right sort."

"Them's my sentiments," said Obed, heartily. "And although I don't generally hanker after Britishers, yet I have a kind of respect for the old country, in spite of its narrowness and contraction, and all the more when I see that it can turn out men like you."

After a short stroll the two seated themselves in a quiet sequestered place, and had a long conversation. Obed informed him of the many events which had occurred since their last meeting. The news about Black Bill was received by Lord Chetwynde with deep surprise, and he had a strong hope that this might lead to the capture of Gualtier. Little did he suspect the close connection which he had had with the principals in this crime.

He then questioned Obed, with deep interest, about his life in Naples, about his journey to Florence, and many other things, with the purpose of drawing him on to speak about one whom he could not name without emotion, but about whom he longed to hear. Obed said nothing about her; but, in the course of the conversation, he told all about that affair in the Pontine Marshes, in which he recently vanished from view at a very critical moment.

Obed's account was given with his usual modesty; for this man, who was often so grandiloquent on the subject of his country, was very meek on the subject of himself. To give his own words would be to assign a very unimportant part to the chief actor in a very remarkable affair, so that the facts themselves may be more appropriately stated. These facts Lord Chetwynde gathered from Obed's narrative in spite of his extreme modesty.

After Obed's shot, then, there had been silence for a time, or rather inaction among the assailants. The agitation of his family excited his sympathy, and once more he reassured them, telling them that the affair was not worth thinking about, and urging them to be calm. His words inspired courage among them, and they all arose and dressed. Their room was at the end of the building, as has been said. Obed's room adjoined it, and the only entrance into their room was through his. A narrow passage ran from the central hall as far as the wall of their room, and on the side of the passage was the door which led into Obed's.

After putting some more peat on the fire, he called to his sister to watch at the window of her room, and then replenishing his pipe, and loading the discharged chambers of his revolver, he awaited the renewal of hostilities. The long silence that followed showed him that his fire had been very serious, and he began to think that they would not return. So the time passed until five o'clock came. The women in the adjoining room were perfectly silent, but watchful, and apparently calm. Below there were occasional sounds of footsteps, which showed that the assailants were still in the place. The excitement

"TO SPRING FORWARD WITH LEVELED PISTOL UPON HIS ASSAILANTS WAS THE WORK
OF A MOMENT."

of the occasion was rather agreeable to Obed than otherwise. He felt that he had the advantage in every respect, and was certain that there could not be very many assailants below. Their long delay in resuming the assault showed that they were cowed.

At last, however, to his intense gratification, he heard footsteps on the stairs. He knew by the sound that there could not be more than four, or perhaps six. When near his door the footsteps stopped. There was a momentary silence, and then suddenly a tremendous blow, and a panel of the door crashed in at the stroke of an axe, the head of which followed it. Quick as lightning Obed took aim. He saw how the axe had fallen, and judged exactly the position of the man that dealt the blow. He fired. A shriek followed. That shot had told. Wild curses arose. There was a mad rush at the door, and again the axe fell.

Once more Obed watched the fall of the axe and fired. Again that shot told. There were groans and shrieks of rage, and deep, savage curses.

And now at last Obed rose to the level of the occasion. He rapidly reloaded the emptied chambers of his revolver. Stepping to the door of the inner room he spoke some soothing words, and then hurrying back, he drew the ponderous bedstead away. Outside he heard shuffling, as of footsteps, and thought they might be dragging away those who had been wounded last. All this had been done in a moment. To unlock the door, to spring forward with leveled pistol upon his assailants, was but the work of another moment.

It was now dim morning twilight. The scene outside was plainly revealed. There were three men dragging away two—those two who had been wounded by the last shots. On these Obed sprang. One went down before his shot. The others, with a cry of terror, ran down the stairs, and out of the house. Obed pursued. They ran wildly up the road. Again Obed fired, and one wretch fell. Then he put the revolver in his pocket, and chased the other man. The distance between them lessened rapidly. At last Obed came up. He reached out his arm and caught him by the collar. With a shriek of terror the scoundrel stopped, and fell on his knees, uttering frantic prayers for mercy, of which Obed understood not one word. He dragged him back to the house, found a rope in the stable, bound him securely, and put him in the dining-room. Then he went about to seek the landlord. He could not be found. Both he and his wife had apparently fled. But Obed found something else.

In a lower room that opened into the dining-room were three men on two beds, wounded, faint, and shivering with terror. These were the men that had been wounded at the first attack. In the anguish of their pain they made gestures of entreaty, of which Obed took no notice. Up stairs in the hall were those two whom he had struck with his last shots. There were no others to be seen.

After finishing his search, Obed went up the road, and carried back the man whom he had shot. He then informed his family of the result. In the midst of their horror at this tragedy, and their joy at escaping from a terrible fate, they felt a certain pity for these sufferers, wretches though they were. Obed shared this feeling. His anger had all departed with the end of the fight. He lifted one by one the wounded wretches, putting them on the beds in the rooms which he had hired. Then he and his sister dressed their wounds. Thus the night ended, and the sun at last arose.

About two hours after sunrise it happened that a troop of papal gendarmerie came along. Obed stopped them, and calmly handed over the prisoners to their care. They seemed bewildered, but took charge of them, evidently not at all comprehending the situation. An hour or so afterward the valet arrived with a fresh carriage, and after hearing Obed's story with wonder he was able to explain it to the soldiers.

Obed then set out for Rome, and, after some stay, came on to Florence.

Such was the substance of his story.

CHAPTER LXII.

THE VILLA.

THERE were many things in Obed Chute's narration which affected Lord Chetwynde profoundly. The story of that adventure in the Pontine Marshes had an interest for him which was greater than any that might be created by the magnificent prowess and indomitable pluck that had been exhibited on that occasion by the modest narrator. Beneath the careless and off-hand recital of Obed Lord Chetwynde was able to perceive the full extent of the danger to which he had been exposed, and from which his own cool courage had saved him. An ordinary man, under such circumstances, would have basely yielded; or, if the presence of his family had inspired him with unusual courage, the courage would have been at best a sort of frenzy, at the impulse of which he might have devoted his own life to the love which he had for his family, and thrown that life away without saving them. But in Obed's quiet and unpretending narrative he recognized the presence of an heroic soul; one which in the midst of the most chivalrous, the most absolute, and the most perfect devotion—in the midst of the most utter abnegation of self—could still maintain the serenest calm and the most complete presence of mind in the face of awful danger. Every point in that story pro-

duced an effect on the mind of the listener, and roused his fullest sympathy. He had before his eyes that memorable scene: Obed watching and smoking on his bed by the side of the door—the family sleeping peacefully in the adjoining room —the sound of footsteps, of violent knockings, of furious entrance, of wild and lawless mirth. He imagined the flight of the old man and his wife, who in terror, or perhaps through cunning and treachery, gave up their hotel and their guests to the fury of the brigands. He brought before his mind that long time of watchful waiting when Obed lay quietly yet vigilantly reclining on the bed, with his pipe in his mouth and his pistol in his pocket, listening to the sounds below, to see what they might foreshadow; whether they told of peace or of war, whether they announced the calm of a quiet night or the terrors of an assault made by fiends—by those Italian brigands whose name has become a horror, whose tenderest mercies are pitiless cruelty, and to fall into the hands of whom is the direst fate that man or woman may know.

One thought gave a horror to this narrative. Among the women in that room was the one who to him was infinitely dearer than any other upon earth. And this danger had threatened her—a danger too horrible to think of—one which made his very life-blood freeze in the course of this calm narration. This was the one thing on which his thoughts turned most; that horrible, that appalling danger. So fearful was it to him that he envied Obed the privilege of having saved her. He longed to have been there in Obed's place, so as to have done this thing for her. He himself had once saved her from death, and that scene could never depart from his memory; but now it seemed to him, as though the fate from which he had saved her was as nothing when compared to the terror of that danger from which she had been snatched by Obed.

Yet, during Obed's narrative, although these feelings were within his heart, he said little or nothing. He listened with apparent calmness, offering no remark, though at that time the thoughts of his heart were so intense. In fact, it was through the very intensity of his feelings that he forced himself to keep silence. For if he had spoken he would have revealed all. If he had spoken he would have made known, even to the most careless or the most preoccupied listener, all the depth of that love which filled his whole being. Her very name to him was something which he could not mention without visible emotion. And she, in fearful peril, in terrific danger, in a situation so horrible, could not be spoken of by one to whom she was so dear and so precious.

And so he listened in silence, with only a casual interjection, until Obed had finished his story. Then he made some appropriate remarks, very coolly, complimentary to the heroism of his friend; which remarks were at once quietly scouted by Obed as altogether inappropriate.

"Pooh!" said he; "what was it, after all? These Italians are rubbish, at the best. They are about equal to Mexicans. You've read about our Mexican war, of course. To gain a victory over such rubbish is almost a disgrace."

So Obed spoke about it, though whether he felt his exploit to be a disgrace or not may very reasonably be doubted.

Yet, in spite of Lord Chetwynde's interest in the affair of the Pontine Marshes, there was another story of Obed's which produced a deeper effect on his mind. This was his account of his interview with Black Bill, to which he had been summoned in London. The story of Black Bill which Obed gave was one which was full of awful horror. It showed the unrelenting and pitiless cruelty of those who had made themselves her enemies; their profound genius for plotting, and their far-reaching cunning. He saw that these enemies must be full of boldness and craft far beyond what is ordinarily met with. Black Bill's account of Gualtier's behavior on the boat when the men tried to mutiny impressed him deeply. The man that could commit such a deed as he had done, and then turn upon a desperate crew as he did, to baffle them, to subdue them, and to bring them into submission to his will, seemed to him to be no common man. His flight afterward, and the easy and yet complete way in which he had eluded all his pursuers, confirmed this view of his genius. Obed himself, who had labored so long, and yet so unsuccessfully, coincided in this opinion.

The chief subject of interest in these affairs to both of these men was Zillah; yet, though the conversation revolved around her as a centre, no direct allusion was for some time made to her present situation. Yet all the while Lord Chetwynde was filled with a feverish curiosity to know where she was, whether she was still with Obed's family, or had left them; whether she was far away from him, or here in Florence. Such an immensity of happiness or of misery seemed to him at that time to depend on this thing that he did not dare to ask the question. He waited to see whether Obed himself might not put an end to this suspense. But Obed's thoughts were all absorbed by the knotty question which had been raised by the appearance of Black Bill with his story. From the London police he had received no fresh intelligence since his departure, though every day he expected to hear something. From the Marseilles authorities he had heard nothing since his last visit to that city, and a letter which he had recently dispatched to the prefect at Naples had not yet been answered. As far as his knowledge just yet was concerned, the whole thing had gone into a more impenetrable mystery than ever, and the principals in this case, after committing atrocious crimes, after baffling the police of different nations, seemed to have vanished into the profoundest obscurity. But on this occasion he reiterated that determination which he had made before of never losing sight of this purpose, but keeping at it, if need were, for years. He would write to the police, he said, perpetually, and would give information to the authorities of every country in Europe. On his return to America he would have an extensive and comprehensive search instituted. He would engage detectives himself in addition to any which the police might send forth. Above all, he intended to make free use of the newspapers. He had, he said—and in this he was a true American—great faith in advertising. He had drawn up in his mind already the formulas of various kinds of notices which he intended to have inserted in the principal papers, by which he hoped to get on the track of the criminals. Once on their track, he felt assured of success.

The unexpected addition of Black Bill to the number of actors in this important case was rightly considered by Obed as of great moment. He had some idea of seeking him out on his return to London, and of employing him in this search. Black Bill would be stimulated to such a search by something far more powerful than any mere professional instinct or any hope of reward. The vengeance which he cherished would make him go on this errand with an ardor which no other could feel. He had his own personal grievance against Gualtier. He had shown this by his long and persistent watch, and by the malignancy of his tone when speaking of his enemy. Besides this, he had more than passion or malignancy to recommend him; he had that qualification for the purpose which gave aim and certainty to all his vengeful desires. He had shown himself to have the instinct of a bloodhound, and the stealthy cunning of an Indian in following on the trail of his foe. True he had been once outwitted, but that arose from the fact that he was forced to watch, and was not ready to strike. The next time he would be ready to deal the blow, and if he were once put on the trail, and caught up with the fugitive, the blow would fall swiftly and relentlessly.

Debate about such things as these took up two or three hours, during which time Lord Chetwynde endured his suspense. At length they rose to leave the gardens, and then, as they were walking along, he said, in as indifferent a tone as he could assume:

. "Oh—by-the-way—Miss Lorton is here with your family, I suppose?"

"Yes," said Obed; "she is with us still."

At this simple answer Lord Chetwynde's heart gave a great bound, and then seemed to stop beating for some seconds. He said nothing.

"She is here now in Florence with us," continued Obed. "She is quite one of the family. We all call her Ella now; she insisted on it. I have taken a villa a few miles away. Ella prefers the country. We often drive into the city. It's a wonder to me that we never met before."

"Yes; it is odd."

"She came in with us this morning with a watch, which she left at Penafrio's to be mended. It will be done this evening. She could not wait for it, so I staid, so as to take it out to her to-night. I strolled about the town, and finally wandered here, which I think the prettiest place in Florence. I'd been walking through the gardens for an hour before you saw me."

"How has she been of late?"

"Very well indeed—better, in fact, than she has ever been since I first saw her. She was not very well at Naples. The journey here did her much good, and the affair of the Pontine Marshes roused her up instead of agitating her. She behaved like a trump—she was as cool as a clock; but it was a coolness that arose from an excitement which was absolutely red-hot, Sir. She seemed strung up to a pitch ten notes higher than usual, and once or twice as I caught her eyes they seemed to me to have a deep fire in them that was stunning! I never, in all my born days, saw the equal of that little thing," exclaimed Obed, tenderly.

"It's having an occupation," he continued, "as I believe, that's done her this good. She was afraid she would be a dependent, and the fear arose out of a noble feeling. Now she finds her position an honorable one. It gives her a fine feeling of pride. The poor little thing seems to have been brought up to do nothing at all; but now the discovery that she can do something actually intoxicates her. And the beauty of it is, she does it well. Yes, Sir. My children have been pushed along at a tre-mendous pace, and they love Ella better than me or sister ten times. But you'll see for yourself, for you've got to come right straight out with me, my boy. You, Wind-ham, are the one that Ella would rather see than any other. You're the man that saved her from death, and gave her to me."

At this Lord Chetwynde's stout heart, that had never quailed in the face of death, throbbed fever-ishly in his intense joy, and his whole frame thrilled at the thought that arose in his mind. Going to her was easy enough, through Obed's warm friendship. And he was going to her! This was the only thought of which he was con-scious.

The carriage was waiting in front of the watch-maker's shop, and the watch was ready; so they drove out without delay. It seemed to Lord Chetwynde like a dream. He was lost in an-ticipations of the coming meeting—that meeting which he had never dared to hope for, but which was now before him.

Obed Chute, on coming to Florence, had rent-ed a villa on the slopes of the hills overlooking Val d'Arno. It was about twelve or fifteen miles away. The road ran through the plain, and then ascended the hills gently, in a winding direction, till it reached the place. The villa was surrounded by beautiful grounds, wherein trim gardens were seen, and fair winding walks, in-terspersed with fountains and statuary and pavil-ions. Besides these there were extensive forests of thick-growing trees, whose dense branches, in-terlacing overhead, threw down heavy shadows. Through these dim woods many pathways pene-trated, leading to sequestered nooks and roman-tic grottoes. Here there wandered several little brooklets, and in the midst of the forest there was a lake, or rather a pond, from the middle of which rose a marble Triton, which perpetually spouted forth water from his shell. The villa it-self was of generous dimensions, in that style which is so familiar to us in this country, with broad piazzas and wide porticoes, and no lack of statuary. Here Obed Chute had made him-self quite at home, and confided to Lord Chet-wynde the fact that he would prefer this to his house on the Hudson River if he could only see the Stars and Stripes floating from the Campa-nile at Florence. As this was not likely to hap-pen, he was forced to look upon himself as mere-ly a pilgrim and a sojourner.

Lord Chetwynde entered the villa. Obed re-mained behind for a few moments to give some directions to the servants. A lofty hall ran through the villa, with statues on each side, and a fountain at the farthest end. On either side there were doors opening into spacious apart-ments. Lord Chetwynde turned to the right, and entered a magnificent room, which extend-ed the whole length of the house. He looked around, and his attention was at once arrested by a figure at the farthest end. It was a lady, whose youthful face and slender figure made his

heart beat fast and furiously; for, though he could not distinguish her features, which were partly turned away, yet the shape was familiar, and was associated with the sweetest memories of his life. The lady was sitting in a half-re-clining position on an Egyptian couch, her head was thrown back, a book hung listlessly in one hand, and she seemed lost in thought. So deep was her abstraction that the noise of Lord Chet-wynde's steps on the marble floor did not arouse her. When he saw her he paused involuntarily, and stood for a few moments in silence.

Yes, it was she! One look told him this. It was the one who for so long a time had been in all his thoughts, who in his illness had been ever present to his delirious dreams. It was the one to whom his heart had never ceased to turn since that first day when that head had lain for a moment on his breast, and that rich, luxuriant hair had flowed in a sea of glory over his arms, burnished by the red rays of the rising sun. He walked softly forward and drew near. Then the noise of his footsteps roused her. She turned.

There came over her face the sudden light of joyous and rapturous wonder. In that sudden rapture she seemed to lose breath and sense. She started forward to her feet, and the book fell from her hand. For an instant she pressed her hand to her heart, and then, with both hands outstretched, and with her beautiful face all aglow with joy and delight that she could not conceal, she stepped forward. But suddenly, as though some other thought occurred, she stopped, and a crimson glow came over her pale face. She cast down her eyes and stood waiting.

Lord Chetwynde caught her outstretched hand, which still was timidly held toward him, in both of his, and said not one word. For a time nei-ther of them spoke, but he held her hand, and she did not withdraw it.

"Oh!" he cried, suddenly, as though the words were torn from him, "how I have longed for this moment!"

She looked at him hastily and confusedly, and then withdrew her hand, while another flush swept over her face.

"Mr. Windham," she faltered, in low tones, "what an unexpected pleasure! I—I thought you were in England."

"And so I was," said Lord Chetwynde, as he devoured her with the ardent gaze of his eyes; "but my business was finished, and I left—"

"How did you find us out?" she asked, smil-ingly, as, once more resuming her self-possession, she sat down again upon the Egyptian sofa and picked up her book. "Have you been in corre-spondence with Mr. Chute?"

"No," laughed Lord Chetwynde. "It was fate that threw him into my way at the Boboli Gardens this morning. I have been here for-well, for a small eternity—and was thinking of going away when he came up, and now I am reconciled to all my past."

A silence followed, and each seemed to take a hasty glance at the other. On Zillah's face there were the traces of sorrow; its lines had grown finer, and its air more delicate and spiritual. Lord Chetwynde's face, on the other hand, showed still the marks of that disease which had brought him to death's door, and no longer had that glow of manly health which had been its characteristic at Marseilles.

"SHE SEEMED LOST IN THOUGHT."

"You have been ill," said Zillah, suddenly, and with some alarm in her voice.

"Yes," said Lord Chetwynde, sadly; "I have been as near death as it is possible for one to be and live."

"In England?"

"No; in Switzerland."

"Switzerland?"

"Yes."

"I thought that perhaps some private troubles in England had caused it," said Zillah, with tones of deep sympathy, for she recollected his last words to her, which expressed such fearful anticipations of the future.

"No; I bore all that. It was an unexpected circumstance," he said, in a cautious tone, "that caused my illness. But the Italian air has been beneficial. But you—how have you been? I fear that you yourself have been ill."

"I have had some troubles," Zillah replied.

Lord Chetwynde forbore to question her about those troubles. He went on to speak about the air of Val d'Arno being the best thing in the world for all illness, and congratulated her on having so beautiful a spot in which to live. Zillah grew enthusiastic in her praises of Florence and all the surrounding scenery; and as each learned how long the other had been here they wondered why they had not met.

"But I," said Zillah, "have not gone often to the city since the first week. It is so beautiful here."

"And I," said Lord Chetwynde, "have ridden all about the environs, but have never been near here before. And even if I had, I should have gone by it without knowing or suspecting that you were here."

Obed Chute had much to see about, and these two remained long together. They talked over many things. Sometimes there were long pauses, which yet were free from embarrassment. The flush on Zillah's cheek, and the kindling light of her eye, showed a pleasure which she could not conceal. Happiness was so strange to her that she welcomed eagerly this present hour, which was so bright to her poor sorrow-laden heart. Lord Chetwynde forgot his troubles, he banished the future, and, as before, he seized the present, and enjoyed it to the full.

Obed returned at last and joined them. The time fled by rapidly. Lord Chetwynde made a move to return at about eleven o'clock, but Obed would not allow him. He made him stay that night at the villa.

CHAPTER LXIII.

A CHANGE.

ALTHOUGH Lord Chetwynde was always out by day, yet he had always returned to his rooms at night, and therefore it was a matter of surprise to Hilda, on this eventful night, that twelve o'clock came without any signs of his return. In her wild and ungovernable passion her whole life had now grown to be one long internal struggle, in which it was with difficulty that she kept down the stormy feelings within her. This night she had grown more nervous than usual. It was as though she had attained to the culmination of the long excitements through which she had passed. His absence filled her with a thousand fears. The longing of her heart grew intolerable as the hours passed by without any signs of his return. Weary of calling to her servant to ask if he had come back, she at last dismissed the servant to bed, and sat herself at the door of her room, listening for the sound of footsteps. In that watchful attitude she sat, dumb and motionless; but the hours passed by her as she sat there, and still he came not. Through those hours her mind was filled with a thousand fears and fancies. Sometimes she thought that he had been assassinated. At other times she fancied that Gualtier might have broken his promise, and come back from London, full of vengeance, to track the man whom he hated. These ideas, however, at length left her, and another took possession of her, which was far more natural and probable, and which finally became a deep and immovable conviction. She thought that Lord Chetwynde had at last yielded to his aversion; and unwilling, from motives of gratitude, to have any formal farewell, he had concluded to leave her abruptly.

"Yes," she said to herself, as this thought first came to her, "that is it. He wearies of my perpetual presence. He does not wish to subject himself to my mean entreaties. He has cut the connection abruptly, and is this night on his way to Leghorn to take the steamer. He has gone to India, and left me forever. To-morrow, no doubt, I shall get a letter acquainting me with the irrevocable step, and bidding me an eternal farewell."

The more she thought of this the more intense her conviction became, until at last, from the force of her own fancies, she became as certain of this as though some one had actually told her of his departure. Then there came over her a mighty sense of desolation. What should she do now? Life seemed in that instant to have lost all its sweetness and its meaning. Again there came to her that thought which many times during the last few weeks had occurred, and now had grown familiar—the awful thought of suicide. The life she lived had already grown almost intolerable from its unfulfilled wishes, and its longings against hope; but now the last hope had departed, and life itself was nothing but a burden. Should she not lay it down?

So the night passed, and the morning came, but through all that night sleep came not. And the dawn came, and the hours of the day passed by, but she sat motionless. The servants came, but were sent away; and this woman of feeling

O

and of passion, who once had risen superior to all feeling, now lay a prey to an agony of soul that threatened reason and life itself.

But suddenly all this was brought to an end. At about mid-day Lord Chetwynde returned. Hilda heard his footstep and his voice. A great joy darted through her, and her first impulse was to fling herself upon him, and weep tears of happiness upon his breast. But that was a thing which was denied her—a privilege which might never be hers. After the first wild impulse and the first rush of joy she restrained herself, and, locking the door of her room, she sat listening with quick and heavy breathing. She heard him speak a few careless words to the servant. She heard him go to his room, where he staid for about an hour. She watched and waited, but restrained every impulse to go out. "I have tormented him too much," she said to herself. "I have forced myself upon him; I have made myself common. A greater delicacy and a more retiring habit will be more agreeable to him. Let me not destroy my present happiness. It is joy enough that my fears are dispersed, and that he has not yet left me." So she restrained herself—though that self-restraint was the mightiest task which she had ever undertaken—and sat passively listening, when every feeling prompted her to rush forth eagerly to greet him.

He went away that day, and came back by midnight. Hilda did not trouble him, and they met on the following morning.

Now, at the first glance which she stole at him, she noted in him a wonderful change. His face had lost its gloom; there was an expression of peace and blissful tranquillity which she had never observed before, and which she had never thought possible to one who had appeared to her as he always had. She sat wondering as they waited for breakfast to be served—a meal which they generally took together—and baffled herself in vain conjectures. A great change had certainly come over him. He greeted her with a bright and genial smile. He had shaken her hand with the warm pressure of a good-hearted friend. He was sprightly even with the servants. He noticed the exquisite beauty of the day. He had something to say about many little trifles. Even in his best moods, during the journey, he had never been like this. Then he had never been otherwise than reserved and self-contained: his face had never altogether lost its cloud of care. Now there was not a vestige of care to be seen; he was joyous; he was even hilarious; and seemed at peace with himself and all the world.

What had happened?

This was the question which Hilda incessantly asked herself. It needed something unusual to change so completely this strong nature, and transform the sadness which had filled it into peace and joy. What had happened? What thing, of what kind, would be necessary to effect such a change? Could it be gratified vengeance? No; the feeling was too light for that. Was it the news of some sudden fortune? She did not believe that if Lord Chetwynde heard that he had inherited millions it would give such joy as this, which would make itself manifest in all his looks and words and acts and tones. What would be needed to produce such a change in herself? Would vengeance, or riches, or honor be sufficient? No. One thing alone could do this. Were she, by any possibility, ever to gain Lord Chetwynde to herself, then she felt that she would know the same sweet peace and calm joy as that which she now read in his face. In that event she thought that she could look upon her worst enemy with a smile. But in him what could it mean? Could it be possible that he had any one whose smile would bring him such peace as this? Once before she suspected that he loved another. Could it be within the bounds of possibility that the one whom he loved lived in Florence?

This thought filled her with dismay. And yet, why not? Had he not set out from England for Italy? Had he not dragged himself out of his sick-room, almost before he could walk, to pursue his journey? Had he not broken off almost all intercourse with herself after the first week of their arrival? Had he not been occupied with some engrossing business all the time since then? What business could have at once so occupied him and so changed him, if it were not something of this kind? There was one thing which could at once account for his coolness to her and his inaccessibility to her advances, for his journey to Florence, for his occupation all the time, and now for this strange mood of happiness which had come so suddenly yet so gently over him. And that one thing, which alone, to her mind, could at once account for all these things, was Love.

The time passed, and Lord Chetwynde's new mood seemed lasting. Never had he been so considerate, so gentle, and so kind to Hilda. At any other time, or under any other circumstances, this change would have stimulated her mind to the wildest hopes; but now it prompted fears which filled her with despair. So, as the days passed, the struggle raged within her breast. Meanwhile Lord Chetwynde was a constant visitor at the villa of Obed Chute, and a welcome guest to all. As the days passed the constant association which he had with Zillah made each better known to the other than ever before. The tenderness that existed between them was repressed in the presence of the others; but on the frequent occasions when they were left alone together it found expression by acts if not by words, by looks if not by acts. Lord Chetwynde could not forget that first look of all-absorbing and overwhelming joy with which Zillah had greeted him on his sudden appearance. A master, to a certain extent, over himself, he coerced himself so far as not to alarm Zillah by any tender words or by any acts which told too much; yet in his face and in his eyes he could read, if she chose, all his devotion. As for Zillah, the change which she had felt from the dull monotony of her past to the vivid joy of the present was so great and so powerful that its effects were too manifest to be concealed. She could not conceal the glow of health that sprang to her cheek, the light that kindled in her eye, the resonant tone that was added to her voice, and the spring that came to her step: Nor could she, in her girlish innocence, conceal altogether how completely she now rested all her hopes and all her happiness upon Lord Chetwynde; the flush of joy that arose at his arrival, the sadness that oversprend her at his departure. But Obed Chute and his sister were not observant; and

these things, which would have been so manifest to others, were never noticed by them. It seemed to both of them as though Zillah merely shared the pleasure which they felt in the society of this Windham, whom Obed loved and admired, and they thought that Zillah's feelings were merely of the same character as their own.

Neither Lord Chetwynde nor Zillah cared to disclose the true state of the case. Lord Chetwynde wished to see her every day, but did not wish them to know that he came every day. That might seem strange to them. In point of fact, they would have thought nothing of it, but would have welcomed him as warmly as ever; but Lord Chetwynde could not feel sure of this. And if he visited her every day, he did not wish to let the world know it. How it happened can not be told; by what mysterious process it occurred can scarcely be related; such a process is too indefinable for description; but certain it is that a mysterious understanding sprang up between him and Zillah, so that on every alternate day when he rode toward the villa he would leave his horse at a house about a quarter of a mile away, and walk to the nearest part of the park, where there was a small gate among the trees. Here he usually entered, and soon reached a small kiosk near that pond among the woods which has already been spoken of. The household was so small and so quiet, and the woods were so unfrequented and so shadowy, that there was scarcely any possibility of interruption. Even if they had been discovered there by Obed himself, Lord Chetwynde's presence of mind could have readily furnished a satisfactory story to account for it. He had already arranged that in his mind. He would have "happened to meet" Zillah on the road near the gate, and come in here with her. By this it will be seen, on the strength of this mysterious understanding, that Zillah was not averse to this clandestine meeting. In fact, she always was there. Many times they met there in the weeks which Lord Chetwynde passed in Florence, and never once did she fail to be there first to await him.

Perhaps it was because each had a secret belief that this was all temporary—a happiness, a bliss, in fact, in this part of their mortal lives, but a bliss too great to last. Perhaps it was this that gave Zillah the courage and spirit to be at the trysting-place to receive this man who adored her, and never to fail to be there first—to think that not to be there first would be almost a sin—and so to receive his deep and fervent expressions of gratitude for her kindness, which were reiterated at every meeting. At any rate, Zillah was always there on the days when Lord Chetwynde wished her to be there; and on the occasions when he visited the villa she was not there, but was seated in the drawing-room to receive him. Obed Chute thought that Lord Chetwynde came three times a week. Zillah knew that he came seven times a week.

For some time this state of things had continued. Windham was the chosen friend of Obed, and the favored guest at Obed's villa. Zillah knew that this could not last, and used to try to check her happiness, and reason it down. But as the hour of the tryst approached all attempts of this kind were forgotten, and she was there watching and waiting.

To her, one day thus waiting, Lord Chetwynde

came with a sad smile on his face, and something in his eyes which threw a chill over Zillah's heart. They talked a little while, but Lord Chetwynde was melancholy and preoccupied.

"You do not look well to-day," said Zillah, wonderingly, and in tones which were full of sympathy. "I hope nothing has happened?"

Lord Chetwynde looked earnestly at her and sighed heavily.

"Miss Lorton," said he, sadly, "something has happened which has thrown the deepest gloom over me. Shall I tell you? Will you sympathize with my gloom? I will tell you. I have this day received a letter giving me my appointment to a post in India, for which I have been waiting for a long time."

"India!"

Zillah gasped this out with white lips, while her face assumed the ashen hue of despair.

"India!" she repeated, as her great eyes were fixed in agony upon him; and then she stopped, pressing her hand to her heart.

The anguish of that look was so intense that Lord Chetwynde was shaken to the soul. He caught her hand in his, scarce knowing what he did.

"Oh, Miss Lorton," he cried, "do not look so at me. I am in despair; I am heart-broken; I dare not look at the future; but the future is not immediate; I can yet wait a few weeks; and you will still come here, will you not—to see me?"

Zillah caught her hand away, and her eyes fell. Tears dropped from beneath her heavy lashes. But she said not a word.

"At any rate, tell me this," cried Lord Chetwynde, "when I am gone, Miss Lorton, you will not forget me? Tell me this."

Zillah looked at him with her large, spiritual eyes, whose fire seemed now to burn into his soul, and her lips moved:

"Never!"

That was the only word that she said.

CHAPTER LXIV.

THE MASQUERADE.

OBED CHUTE came home one day full of news, and particularly dilated upon the grandeur of a masquerade ball which was to take place at the Villa Rinalci. He wished to go, and to take Zillah. The idea filled all his mind, and his excitement was speedily communicated to Zillah, and to Lord Chetwynde, who happened to be there at the time. Obed had learned that it was to be conducted with the highest degree of magnificence. He had talked about it with some Americans with whom he had met in the café, and, as he had never seen one, he was eager to go. Lord Chetwynde expressed the same desire, and Zillah at once showed a girlish enthusiasm that was most gratifying to Obed. It was soon decided that they all should go. A long conversation followed about the dresses, and each one selected what commended itself as the most agreeable or becoming. Obed intended to dress as a Western trapper, Zillah as an Athenian maid of the classic days, while Lord Chetwynde decided upon the costume of the Cavaliers. A merry evening was spent in settling upon these

details, for the costume of each one was subjected to the criticism of the others, and much laughter arose over the various suggestions that were made from time to time about the best costume.

For some days Lord Chetwynde busied himself about his costume. He had to have it made especially for the occasion, and tailors had to be seen, and measurements had to be taken. Of course this did not interfere in the smallest degree with his constant attendance upon Zillah, for every day he was punctual at the trysting-place or in the villa.

Meanwhile Hilda's intolerable anxiety had taken another and a very natural turn. She began to feel intensely curious about the object of Lord Chetwynde's daily occupations. Having once come to the conclusion that there was a woman in the case, every hour only strengthened this conviction, until at length it was as firmly fixed in her mind as the belief in her own existence. The pangs of jealousy which she suffered from this cause were as extreme as those which she had suffered before from fear, or anxiety, or suspense, both when hurrying on to save Lord Chetwynde, and when watching at his bedside. In her wild, ungovernable passion and her uncontrollable love she felt the same vehement jealousy which a betrothed mistress might feel, and the same unreasoning indignation which a true and lawful wife might have when suspecting a husband's perfidy. Such feelings filled her with an insatiable desire to learn what might be his secret, and to find out at all costs who this one might be of whose existence she now felt confident. Behind this desire there lay an implacable resolve to take vengeance in some way upon her, and the discovery of her in Hilda's mind was only synonymous with the deadly vengeance which she would wreak upon this destroyer of her peace.

It was difficult, however, to accomplish such a desire. Little or nothing could be found out from the servants, nor was there any one whom she could employ to observe her "husband's" actions. Now she began to feel the need of that deep devotion and matchless fidelity which she had once received from Gualtier. But he was far away. Could she not send for him? She thought of this often, but still delayed to do so. She felt sure that the moment she gave the command he would leave every thing and come to do her bidding. But she hesitated. Even in her unscrupulous mind there was a perception of the fitness of things, and she was slow to call to her assistance the aid of the man who so deeply loved her, when her purpose was to remove or to punish her rival in the affections of another man, or rather an obstacle in the way of securing his affections. Deprived thus of all aid, it was difficult for her to find out any thing.

At length Lord Chetwynde became interested in the affair of the masquerade. The state of mind into which he had fallen ever since the discovery of Zillah had deprived him of that constant reticence which used to be his characteristic. He was now pleasant and genial and talkative. This change had inspired alarm in Hilda rather than joy, and she had considered this the chief reason for believing that love was the animating motive with him now. After the masquerade had been mentioned he himself spoke about it. In the fullness of his joy it slipped from him incidentally in the course of conversation, and Hilda, after wondering why he should mention such a thing, began to wonder what interest the thing might have to him. No doubt he was going. Of that she felt assured. If so, the mysterious being to whom she believed he was devoted would necessarily be there too. She believed that the expectation of being there with her had so intoxicated him that this masquerade was the chief thing in his thoughts, and therefore he had made mention of it. So she watched to find out the meaning of this.

One day a parcel came for Lord Chetwynde. The servants were out of sight, and she opened it. It was a suit of clothes in the Cavalier fashion, with every accessory necessary to make up the costume. The meaning of this was at once evident to her. He was going to this masquerade as a Cavalier. What then? This discovery at once made plain before her all that she might do. Under these circumstances it would be possible for her to follow and to track him. Perhaps her own good fortune and cleverness might enable her to discover the one to whom he was devoted. But a complete disguise was necessary for herself. She was not long in choosing such a disguise. She decided upon the costume of the *Compagnia della Misericordia*—one which was eminently Florentine, and, at the same time, better adapted for purposes of concealment than any other could possibly be. It consists of a black robe with a girdle, and a hood thrown over the head in such a way as to show only the eyes. It would be as suitable a disguise for a woman as for a man, and would give no possible chance of recognition. At the same time, belonging as it did to that famous Florentine society, it would be recognized by all, and while insuring a complete disguise, would excite no comment.

Lord Chetwynde left early on the morning of the fête, taking his costume with him, showing Hilda that he was evidently going in company with others. It was with great impatience that she waited the progress of the hours; and when, at length, the time came, and she was deposited at the gate of the Villa Rinalci, her agitation was excessive. Entering here, she found the grounds illuminated.

They were extensive, and filled with groves and spacious avenues and dashing fountains and beautiful sculptures. Already a large crowd had assembled, and Hilda walked among them, watching on every side for the man whom she sought. In so large a place as this, where the grounds were so extensive, it was difficult indeed to find any particular person, and two hours passed away in a vain search. But she was patient and determined, and there was but one idea in her mind. The music and the gayety of the assembled throng did not for one moment divert her, though this was the first scene of the kind that she had ever beheld, and its novelty might well have attracted her attention. The lights which flashed out so brightly through the gloom of night—the noisy crowds which thronged every where—the foaming spray that danced upward from the fountains, gleaming in the light of the lamps—the thousand scenes of mirth and revelry that arose on every side—all these had no attraction for this woman, who had come here for one purpose only, and who carried this purpose deep in her heart. The company wore every imaginable attire. Most of them were in masks, but some of them had none;

while Hilda, in her mournful robe, that spoke to all of death and funereal rites, was alone in the singularity of her costume.

She wandered throughout all the grounds, and through the villa itself, in search of one thing, but that one thing she could not find. At length her weary feet refused to support her any longer in what seemed a hopeless search, and she sat down near one of the fountains in the central avenue, and gave herself up to despondent thoughts.

About half an hour passed, when suddenly two figures approached that riveted her attention. They were a man and a woman. Her heart beat fast. There was no mistake about the man. His dress was the dress which she herself had seen and examined. He wore a domino, but beneath it could be seen his whiskers, cut after the English fashion, and long and pendent. But Hilda knew that face so familiarly that there was no doubt in her mind, although the only saw the lower portion. And a woman was with him, resting on his arm. They passed by her in silence. Hilda waited till they had gone by, and then arose and followed stealthily. Now had come the time for discovery, perhaps for vengeance. In her wild impulse she had brought a dagger with her, which she had secreted in her breast. As she followed her hand played mechanically with the hilt of this dagger. It was on this that she had instinctively placed her ultimate resolve. They walked on swiftly, but neither of them turned to see whether they were followed or not. The idea of such a thing never seemed to have entered into the mind of either of them. After a time they left the avenue, and turned into a side-path; and, following its course, they went onward to the more remote parts of the grounds. Here there were but few people, and these grew fewer as they went on. At length they came to the end of this path, and turned to the right. Hilda hurried onward stealthily, and, turning, saw an arbor embowered among the trees. Near by was a light, which hung from the branch of a tree on one side. She heard low voices, and knew that they had gone into the arbor. She crept up behind it, and got close to it—so close, indeed, that they, while sitting at the back, had but a few inches between themselves and this listener. The rays of the lantern shone in, so that Hilda could see, as they sat between her and the light, the outlines of their forms. But that light was obstructed by the leaves that clung to the arbor, and in the shadow their features were invisible. Two dark figures were before her, and that was all.

"We can stay here alone for some time," said Lord Chetwynde, after a long silence. He spoke in a whisper, which, however, was perfectly audible to Hilda.

"Yes," said the other, speaking in the same whisper. "He is amusing himself in the Grand Avenue."

"And we have an hour, at least, to ourselves. We are to meet him at the Grand Fountain. He will wait for us."

There was another silence.

Hilda heard this with strange feelings. Who was this *he* of whom they spoke? Was he the husband of this woman? Of course. There was no other explanation. They could not be so cautious and so regardful about any other. Nor, indeed, did the thought of any other come into her mind in that hour of excitement. She thought that she could understand it all. Could she but find out this woman's name, then it would be possible to take vengeance in a better and less dangerous way than by using the dagger. She could find out this injured husband, and use him as an instrument for vengeance. And, as this thought came to her, she sheathed her dagger.

The conversation began again. As before, it was in a whisper.

"We are secluded here. No one can see us. It is as quiet as our kiosk at the villa."

"Heavens!" thought Hilda. "A trysting-place!"

A sigh escaped the other.

"You are sighing," said Lord Chetwynde. "Are you unhappy?"

"I'm only too happy; but I—I—I'm thinking of the future."

"Don't think of the future. The present is our only concern. When I think of the future, I feel as though I should go mad. The future! My God! Let me banish it from my thoughts. Help me to forget it. You alone can!"

And even in that whisper, which reached Hilda's ears, there was an impassioned and infinite tenderness which pierced her heart.

"Oh God!" she thought, "how he loves her! And I—what hope have I?"

"What blessed fortune was it," resumed Lord Chetwynde, "that led me to you here in Florence—that brought us both here to this one place, and threw us again into one another's society? When I left you at Marseilles I thought that I had lost you forever!"

The lady said nothing.

But Hilda had already learned this much—first, that both were English. The lady, even in her whisper, showed this. Again, she learned that they had met before, and had enjoyed one another's society in this way. Where? At Marseilles. Her vivid imagination at once brought before her a way in which this might have been done. She was traveling with her husband, and Lord Chetwynde had met her. Probably they had sailed in the same steamer. Possibly they had come all the way from India together. This now became her conviction.

"Have you forgotten Marseilles?" continued Lord Chetwynde. "Do you remember our last sail? do you remember our last ride?"

"Yes," sighed the lady.

"And do you remember what I said?"

"I have not forgotten."

There was a long silence.

"This can not last much longer," said Lord Chetwynde. "I must go to India."

He stopped.

The lady's head sank forward. Hilda could see this through the shadows of the foliage.

"It can not last much longer," said Lord Chetwynde, in a louder voice, and a groan escaped him as he spoke. "I must leave you; I must leave you forever!"

He paused, and folding his arms, leaned back, while Hilda saw that his frame was shaken with extraordinary excitement. At length he leaned forward again. He caught her hand and held it. The lady sat motionless, nor did she attempt to withdraw her hand. They sat in perfect silence for a long time, but the deep breathing of

each, which seemed like long-drawn sighs, was audible to Hilda, as she listened there; and it told how strong was the emotion within them. But the one who listened was the prey of an emotion as mighty as theirs.

Neither of these three was conscious of time. Wrapped up in their own feelings, they were overwhelmed by a tide of passion that made them oblivious of all things else. There were the lovers, and there was the vigilant watcher; but which of these three was a prey to the strongest emotion it would be difficult to tell. On the one side was the mighty power of love; on the other the dread force of hate. Tenderness dwelt here; vengeance waited there. Close together were these three, but while Hilda heard even the very breathing of the lovers, they were unconscious of her presence, and heard not the beating of that baleful heart, which now, filled with quenchless hate, throbbed vehemently and rapidly in the fury of the hour.

Unconscious of all else, and oblivious of the outer world—and why? They loved. Enough. Each knew the love of the other, though no words had spoken it.

"Oh, my friend!" suddenly exclaimed Lord Chetwynde, in a voice which was low and deep and full of passion—a voice which was his own, and no longer a whisper—"Oh, my friend! my beloved! forgive my words; forgive my wildness, my passion; forgive my love. It is agony to me when I know that I must lose you. Soon we must part; I must go, my beloved! my own! I must go to the other end of the earth, and never, never, never more can we hope to meet again. How can I give you up? There is a gulf between us that divides you from me. How can I live without you?"

These words poured forth from him in passionate impetuosity—burning words they were, and the lady whose hand he clasped seemed to quiver and tremble in sympathy with their meaning. He clung to her hand. Every moment deprived him more and more of that self-restraint and that profound consideration for her which he had so long maintained. Never before had he so forgotten himself as to speak words like these. But now separation was near, and she was alone with him, and the hour and the opportunity were his.

"I can not give you up. My life without you is intolerable," he groaned. "God knows how I have struggled against this. You know how faithfully I have kept a guard over my words and acts. But now my longing overmasters me. My future is like hell without you. Oh, love! oh, Ella! listen to me! Can you give me up? Will you be willing to do wrong for my sake? *Will you come with me?*"

A deep silence followed, broken by a sob from the lady.

"You are mine! you are mine!" he cried. "Do not let me go away into desolation and despair. Come with me. We will fly to India. We will be happy there through life. We will forget all the miseries that we have known in the great joy that we will have in one another's presence. Say that you will. See! I give up every thing; I throw all considerations to the winds. I trample even on *honor* and *duty* for your sake. Come with me!"

He paused, breathless from the terrible emotion that had now overpowered him. The lady trembled. She tried to withdraw her hand, but he clung to it. She staggered to her feet, and stood trembling.

"Oh!" she faltered, "do not tempt me! I am weak. I am nothing. Do not; do not!"

"Tempt you?' No, no!" cried Lord Chetwynde, feverishly. "Do not say so. I ask you only to save me from despair."

He rose to his feet as he said this, and stood by her, still holding that hand which he would not relinquish. And the one who watched them in her agony saw an anguish as intense as hers in that quivering frame which half shrank away from Lord Chetwynde, and half advanced toward him; in those hands, one of which was held in his, while the other was clasped to her heart; and in Lord Chetwynde himself, who, though he stood there before her, yet stood trembling from head to foot in the frightful agitation of the hour. All this Hilda saw, and as she saw it she learned this—that all the hopes which she had ever formed of winning this man to herself were futile and baseless and impossible. In that moment they faded away; and what was left? What? Vengeance!

Suddenly Lord Chetwynde roused himself from the struggle that raged within him. It was as though he had resolved to put an end to all these conflicts with himself. He dragged Zillah toward him. Wildly and madly he seized her. He flung his arms about her, and pressed her to his heart.

"My love! my darling!" he exclaimed, in low tones that were broken, and scarce audible in the intensity of his emotion, "you can not—you will not—you dare not refuse me!"

Zillah at first was overwhelmed by this sudden outburst. But soon, by a mighty effort, she seemed to gain control over herself. She tore herself away, and staggered back a few paces.

"Spare me!" she gasped. "Have pity! have mercy! If you love me, I implore you by your love to be merciful! I am so weak. As you hope for heaven, spare me!"

She was trembling violently, and her words were scarcely coherent. At the deep and piteous entreaty of her voice Lord Chetwynde's heart was touched. With a violent effort he seemed to regain his self-control. A moment before he had been possessed of a wild, ungovernable passion, which swept all things away. But now this was succeeded by a calm, and he stood for a time silent.

"You will forgive me," he said at last, sadly. "You are more noble than I am. You do right to refuse me. My request seems to you like madness. Yes, you are right to refuse, even though I go into despair. But listen, and you will see how it is. I love you, but can never win you, for there is a gulf between us. You may have suspected—I am married already! Between us there stands one who keeps us forever asunder; and — that — one — I — hate — worse — than — death!"

He spoke these last words slowly, and with a savage emphasis, into which all the intensity of his love had sent an indescribable bitterness.

And there was one who heard those words, in whose ears they rang like a death-knell; one crouched behind among the shrubbery, whose hands clung to the lattice of the arbor; who, though secure in her concealment, could scarcely hide the anguish which raged within her. At these words the anguish burst forth. A groan escaped her, and all her senses seemed to fail in that moment of agony.

Zillah gave a cry.

"What was that? Did you hear it?" she exclaimed, catching Lord Chetwynde's arm.

Lord Chetwynde had heard it also.

"It's nothing," said he, after listening for a moment. "Perhaps it's one of the deer."

"I'm afraid," said Zillah.

"Afraid! Am not I with you?"

"Let us go," murmured Zillah. "The place is dreadful; I can scarcely breathe."

"Take off your mask," said Lord Chetwynde; and with trembling hands he assisted her to remove it. His tone and manner reassured her. She began to think that the sound was nothing after all. Lord Chetwynde himself thought but little of it. His own excitement had been so intense that every thing else was disregarded. He saw that she was alarmed, but attributed this to the excitement which she had undergone. He now did his best to soothe her, and in his new-found calm he threw away that impetuosity which had so overpowered her. At last she regained something like her former self-possession.

"We must go back," said he at length. "Wait here a few moments, and I will go up the path a short distance to see if the way is clear."

He went out, and went, as he said, a little distance up the path.

Scarcely had his footsteps died out in the distance when Zillah heard a noise directly behind her. She started. In her agitated state she was a prey to any feeling, and a terror crept over her. She hastened out with the intention of following Lord Chetwynde.

The figure, crouching low behind the arbor, had seen Lord Chetwynde's departure. Now her time had come—the time for vengeance! His bitter words had destroyed all hope, and all of that patient cunning which she might otherwise have observed. Blind with rage and passion, there was only one thought in her mind, and that was instant and immediate vengeance. She caught her dagger in her hand, and strode out upon her victim.

The light which hung from the branch of the tree shone upon the arbor. The back-ground was gloomy in the dense shadow, while the intervening space was illumined. Hilda took a few quick paces, clutching her dagger, and in a moment she reached the place. But in that instant she beheld a sight which sent through her a pang of sudden horror—so sharp, so intense, and accompanied by so dread a fear, that she seemed to turn to stone as she gazed.

It was a slender figure, clothed in white, with a white mantle gathered close about the throat, and flowing down. The face was white, and in this dim light, defined against the dark back-ground of trees, it seemed like the face of the dead. The eyes—large, lustrous, burning—were fixed on her, and seemed filled with consuming fire as they fastened themselves on her. The dark hair hung down in vast voluminous folds, and by its contrast added to the marble whiteness of that face. And that face! It was a face which was never absent from her thoughts,

"SHE BEHELD A SIGHT WHICH SENT THROUGH HER A PANG OF HORROR."

a face which haunted her dreams—the face of her victim—the face of Zillah!

Hilda had only one thought, and that was this, that the sea had given up its dead, and that her victim had come to confront her now; in the hour of vengeance to stand between her and an-

other victim. It was but for an instant that she stood, yet in that instant a thousand thoughts swept through her mind. But for an instant; and then, with a loud, piercing shriek, she leaped back, and with a thrill of mortal terror plunged into the thick wood and fled afar—fled with the feeling that the avenger was following fast after her.

The shriek roused Lord Chetwynde. He rushed back. Zillah had fainted, and was lying senseless on the grass. He raised her in his arms, and held her pressed convulsively to his heart, looking with unutterable longing upon her pale face, and pressing his burning lips to her cold brow. There was a great terror in his heart, for he could not think what it might be that had happened, and he feared that some sudden alarm had done this. Bitterly he reproached himself for so agitating her. He had excited her with his despair; and she, in her agitation, had become an easy prey to any sudden fear. Something had happened, he could not tell what, but he feared that he had been to some extent the cause, by the agitation which he had excited within her. All these thoughts and fears were in his mind as he held her upraised in his arms, and looked wildly around for some means of restoring her. A fountain was playing not far away, under the trees, and the babble of running water came to his ears amidst the deep stillness. There he carried his precious burden, and dashed water in her face, and chafed her hands, and murmured all the time a thousand words of love and tenderness. To him, in his intense anxiety, the moments seemed hours, and the passage of every moment threw him into despair. But at last she revived, and finally opened her eyes to see the face of Lord Chetwynde bending over her.

"Thank God!" he murmured, as her opening eyes met his.

"Do not leave me!" moaned Zillah. "It may come again, and if it does I shall die!"

"Leave you!" said Lord Chetwynde; and then he said nothing more, but pressed her hand in silence.

After a few moments she arose, and leaning heavily on his arm she walked with him up the path toward the fountain. On the way, with many starts and shudders of sudden fear, she told him what had happened. She had heard a noise among the trees, and had hurried out, when suddenly a figure rushed up to her—an awful figure! It wore a black robe, and over its head was a cowl with two holes for the eyes. This figure waved its arms wildly, and finally gave a long, wild yell, which pierced to her heart. She fell senseless. Never while life lasts, she said, would she be able to forget that abhorrent cry.

Lord Chetwynde listened eagerly.

"That dress," he said, "is the costume of a Florentine society that devotes itself to the burial of the dead. Some one has worn it here. I'm afraid we have been watched. It looks like it."

"Watched! who could think of such a thing?"

"I don't know," said Lord Chetwynde, thoughtfully. "It may have been accidental. Some masker has watched us, and has tried to frighten you. That is all. If I thought that we could have any enemy, I would say that it was his work. But that is impossible. We are unknown here. At any rate, you must not think that there has been any thing supernatural about it. It seems to me," he concluded, "that we have been mistaken for some others."

This way of accounting for it served to quiet Zillah's fears, and by the time that they reached the fountain she was more calm. Obed Chute was waiting there, and as she pleaded fatigue, he at once had the carriage ordered.

CHAPTER LXV.

HILDA'S DECISION.

HILDA fled, and continued long in that frantic flight through the thick woods. As the branches of the underbrush crackled behind her, it seemed to her that it was the noise of pursuit, and the horror of that unexpected vision was before her, for to face it again seemed to her worse than death. She was strong of soul naturally; her nerves were not such as give way beneath the pressure of imagination; she was not a woman who was in any degree liable to the ordinary weaknesses of a woman's nature; but the last few months had opened new feelings within her, and under the assault of those fierce, resistless feelings the strength of her nature had given way. Even had she possessed all her old strength, the sight of this unparalleled apparition might have overwhelmed her, but as it was, it seemed to make her insane. Already shaken to her inmost soul by long suffering and wild alternations of feeling, she had that night attained the depths of despair in those words which she had overheard. Immediately upon that there came the direful phantom, which she felt that she could not look upon and live. That face seemed to burn itself into her mind. It was before her as she fled, and a great horror thrilled through her, driving her onward blindly and wildly, until at last nature itself gave way, and she fell shrieking with terror.

Then sense left her.

How long she lay she knew not. There was no one near to bring back the lost sense. She awaked shuddering. She had never fainted thus before, and it seemed to her now as though she had died and risen again to the sadness of life. Around her were the solemn forest trees. The wind sighed through their branches. The sun was almost at the meridian. It was not midnight when she fainted. It was mid-day almost when she recovered. There was a sore pain at her heart; all her limbs seemed full of bruises; but she dragged herself to a little opening in the trees where the rays of the sun came down, and there the sun's rays warmed her once more into life. There, as she sat, she recalled the events of the night. The horror had passed, and she no longer had that awful sense of a pursuing phantom; but there remained the belief, fixed within her soul, that she had seen the form of the dead. She was not superstitious, but in this instance the sight, and the effects of that sight, had been so tremendous that she could not reason them away.

She tried to dismiss these thoughts. What was she to do? She knew not. And now as she thought there came back to her the remembrance of Lord Chetwynde's words, and the utterance of his hate. This recollection rose up above the remembrance of her terrors, and gave her something else for thought. What should she do? Should she give up her purpose and return to England? This seemed to her intolerable. Chetwynde Castle had no attractions;

and even if she were now assured beyond all doubt that she should be for all the rest of her life the acknowledged mistress of Chetwynde—even if the coronet were fixed on her brow beyond the chance of removal—even if the court and the aristocracy of England were eager to, receive her into their midst—yet even then she found in these things nothing which could alleviate her grief, and nothing which could afford any attraction. Her life was now penetrated with one idea, and that idea was all set upon Lord Chetwynde. If he was lost to her, then there was only one of two alternatives—death to herself, or vengeance. Could she die? Not yet. From that she turned, not in fear, but rather from a feeling that something yet remained to be done. And now, out of all her thoughts and feelings, the idea of vengeance rose up fiercely and irresistibly. It returned with something of that vehemence which had marked its presence on the previous night, when she rushed forth to satisfy it, but was so fearfully arrested. But how could she now act? She felt as though the effort after vengeance would draw her once more to confront the thing of horror which she had already met with. Could she face it again?

Amidst all these thoughts there came to her the memory of Gualtier. He was yet faithful, she believed, and ready to act for her in any way, even if it required the sacrifice of his own life. To him she could now turn. He could now do what she could not. If she had him once more to act as her right hand, she might use him as a means for observation and for vengeance. She felt now most keenly her own weakness, and longed with a weary sense of desolation for some one who might assist her, and do this work which lay before her.

At last she rose to go. The warmth of the sun had restored something of her strength. The new resolutions which she had formed had given energy to her soul. She wandered about through the wood, and at length reached a stonewall. It looked like the boundary of the villa. She followed this for some distance, expecting to reach the gate, and at length came to a place where a rock arose by the side of the wall. Going up to the top of this, she looked over the wall, and saw the public road on the other side, with Florence in the distance. She saw pretty nearly where she was, and knew that this was the nearest point to her lodgings. To go back to the chief entrance would require a long detour. It would also excite surprise. One in her peculiar costume, on going out of the grounds, might be questioned; she thought it better to avoid this. She looked up and down the road, and seeing no one coming, she stepped to the top of the wall and let herself down on the opposite side. In a few moments she was on the road, on her way back to Florence. Reaching the city, she at once went to the hotel, and arrived at her rooms without observation.

That same day she sent off an urgent letter to Gualtier, asking him to come to Florence at once. After this excitement she kept her bed for a few days. Lord Chetwynde heard that she was ill without expressing any emotion. When at length he saw her he spoke in his usual courteous manner, and expressed his pleasure at seeing her again. But these empty words, which used to excite so much hope within her, now fell indifferently on her ears. She had made up her mind now. She knew that there was no hope. She had called to her side the minister of her vengeance. Lord Chetwynde saw her pale face and downcast eyes, but did not trouble himself to search into the cause of this new change in her. She seemed to be growing indifferent to him, he thought; but the change concerned him little. There was another in his heart, and all his thoughts were centered on that other.

After the masquerade Lord Chetwynde had hurried out to the villa, on the following day, to make inquiries about her health. He found Zillah still much shaken, and exhibiting sufficient weakness to excite his anxiety. Which of the many causes that she had for agitation and trouble might now be disturbing her he could not tell, but he sought to alleviate her troubles as much as possible. His departure for India had to be postponed, for how could he leave her in such a state? Indeed, as long as Obed Chute remained in Florence he did not see how he could leave for India at all.

CHAPTER LXVI.

FAITHFUL STILL.

WHEN Hilda sent off her note to Gualtier she felt certain that he would come to her aid. All that had passed between them had not shaken the confidence which she felt in his willingness to assist her in a thing like this. She understood his feelings so perfectly that she saw in this purpose which she offered him something which would be more agreeable to him than any other, and all that he had ever expressed to her of his feelings strengthened this view. Even his attempts to gain the mastery over her, his coercion by which he forced from her that memorable promise, his rage and his menaces at Lausanne, were so many proofs of his love for her and his malignant hate to Lord Chetwynde. The love which she had once despised while she made use of it she now called to her aid, so as to make use of it again, not thinking of what the reward would be which he would claim, not caring what his hope might be, indifferent to whatever the future might now reveal, and intent only upon securing in the best and quickest way the accomplishment of her own vengeful desires.

This confidence which she felt in Gualtier was not unfounded, nor was her hope disappointed. In about a week after she had sent her letter she received an answer. It was dated Florence. It showed that he had arrived in the city, and informed her that he would call upon her as soon as he could do so with safety. There was no signature, but his handwriting was well known to her, and told her who the writer was.

About an hour after her receipt of the letter Gualtier himself was standing in her presence. He had not changed in appearance since she last saw him, but had the same aspect. Like all pale and cadaverous men, or men of consumptive look, there could be scarcely any change in him which would be for the worse. In Hilda, however, there was a very marked change, which was at once manifest to the searching gaze of his small, keen eyes as they rested upon her. She was not, indeed, so wretched in her appearance as on that eventful day when she had astonished him by her arrival at Lausanne. Her face was not emaciated, nor were her eyes set in dark cavernous hollows as then, nor was there on her brow the stamp of mortal weakness. What Gualtier saw in her now had reference to other things. He had seen in her nervousness and agitation before, but now he marked in her a loss of all her old self-control, a certain feverish impatience, a wild and unreasoning eagerness—all of which seemed to rise out of recklessness and desperation. Her gestures were vehement, her words careless and impassioned in tone. It was in all this that he marked the greatness of the change in her. The feverish warmth with which she greeted him was of itself totally different from her old manner, and from its being so different it seemed to him unnatural. On the whole, this change struck him painfully, and she seemed to him rather like one in a kind of delirium than one in her sober senses.

"When I last bade you good-by," said she, alluding in this very delicate way to their parting at the hotel in Lausanne, "you assured me that I would one day want your services. You were right. I was mad. I have overcome my madness. I do want you, my friend—more than ever in my life before. You are the only one who can assist me in this emergency. You gave me six months, you remember, but they are not nearly up. You understood my position better than I did."

She spoke in a series of rapid phrases, holding his hand the while, and looking at him with burning intensity of gaze—a gaze which Gualtier felt in his inmost soul, and which made his whole being thrill. Yet that clasp of his hand and that gaze and those words did not inspire him with any pleasant hope. They hardly seemed like the acts or words of Hilda, they were all so unlike herself. Far different from this was the Hilda whom he had known and loved so long. That one was ever present in his mind, and had been for years—her image was never absent. Through the years he had feasted his soul in meditations upon her grand calm, her sublime self-poise, her statuesque beauty, her superiority to all human weakness, whether of love or of remorse. Even in those collisions into which she had come with him she had risen in his estimation. At Chetwynde she had shown some weakness, but in her attitude to him he had discovered and had adored her demoniac beauty. At Lausanne she had been even grander, for then she had defied his worst menaces, and driven him utterly discomfited from her presence. Such was the Hilda of his thoughts. He found her now changed from this, her lofty calm transformed to feverish impatience, her domineering manner changed to one of obsequiousness and flattery. The qualities which had once excited his admiration appeared now to have given way to others altogether commonplace. He had parted with her thinking of her as a powerful demon, he came back to her finding her a weak woman. But nothing in his manner showed his thoughts. Beneath all these lay his love, and the old devotion manifested itself in his reply.

"You know that always and under all circumstances, my lady, you can command my services. Only one exceptional case has ever arisen, and that you yourself can understand and excuse."

Hilda sat down, motioning him also to a seat, and for a moment remained silent, leaning her head on her hand in deep thought. Gualtier waited for her next words.

"You must not expose yourself to danger," said she at length.

"What danger?"

"*He* will recognize you if he sees you here."

"I know that, and have guarded against it. He is not at home now, is he?"

"No."

"I knew that very well, and waited for his departure before venturing here. I know very well that if he were to catch even the faintest glimpse of me he would recognize me, and it would be somewhat difficult for me to escape. But to-day I happened to see him go out of the Porta Livorna, and I know he is far off by this time. So, you see, I am as cautious as ever. On the whole, and as a general thing, I intend to be guided by circumstances. Perhaps a disguise may be necessary, but that depends upon many different things. I will have, first of all, to learn from you what it is that you want me to do, and then I can arrange my plan of action. But before you begin I think I ought to tell you a very remarkable incident which happened in London not long ago—and one, too, which came very near bringing my career, and yours also, my lady, to a very sudden and a very unpleasant termination."

At this Hilda gave a start.

"What do you mean?" she asked, hurriedly.

"Oh, only this, that a very nice little trap was laid for me in London, and if I had not been unusually cautious I would have fallen into it. Had that been the case all would have been up with me; though as to you, I don't see how your position would have been affected. For," he added, with deep and uncontrollable emotion, "whatever may happen to me, you must know enough of me by this time, in spite of my occasional rebellions, to be as sure of my loyalty to you as of your own existence, and to know that there could be no possibility of my revealing any thing about you; no," he added, as his clenched fist fell upon the table, and his face flushed up deeply at his rising feeling—"no, not even if it were still the fashion to employ torture; not even the rack could extort from me one syllable that could implicate you. After all that I have said, I swear that by all that is most holy!"

He did not look at Hilda as he said this, but his eyes were cast on the floor, and he seemed rather like a man who was uttering a resolution to himself than like one who was making a statement to another. But Hilda showed no emotion that corresponded with his. Any danger to Gualtier, even though she herself were implicated, had no terrors for her, and could not make her heart throb faster by one single pulsation. She had other things on her mind, which to her far outweighed any considerations of personal danger. Personal danger, indeed, instead of being dreaded, would now, in her present mood, have been almost welcomed, so as to afford some distraction from the torture of her thoughts. In the secret of her heart she more than once wished and longed for some appalling calamity—something which might have power to engage all her thoughts and all her mind. The anguish of her heart, arising out of her love for

Lord Chetwynde, had grown so intolerable that any thing, even danger, even discovery, even death itself, seemed welcome now.

It was this feeling which filled her as she went on to ask Gualtier about the nature of the danger which he had escaped, wishing to know what it might be, yet indifferent to it except so far as it might prove to be a distraction to her cares.

When Gualtier last vanished from the scene he had sent the boy to his lodging-house, with the agreement that he should meet him at eight o'clock. The boy's visit and its results have already been narrated.

As for Gualtier, he was profoundly conscious all the while of the possibility that a trap might be laid for him, and that, if this were the case, the advent of his messenger would be seized upon by those who might be in pursuit of him, so as to get on his track. The very cautiousness which had caused him to seek out so carefully a proper messenger, and instruct him in the part which he was to play, kept him on the anxious look-out for the progress of events. From the time that the boy left he stationed himself at the window of his room, which commanded a view of the main entrance, and watched with the closest scrutiny every one who came into the hotel. After a time he thought that the supposed pursuers might come in by some other entrance. With this fear he retreated into his bedroom, which also looked out in front, and locked the door. He found another door here which led into an adjoining room, which was occupied. The key of the door between the bedroom and the sitting-room fitted this other door, so that he was able to open it. The occupant was not in. Through this door he designed to retreat in case of a surprise. But he still thought it most likely that any pursuers would come in by the main door of the hotel, relying upon his information to the boy that he was to be absent. So with this view he stationed himself at the bedroom window, he had at first stationed himself at the sitting-room window, and watched the main entrance. It was a task which needed the utmost vigilance. A great crowd was thronging there and sweeping by; and among the multitudes that filled the sidewalk it was impossible to distinguish any particular forms or faces except among those who passed up the steps into the hotel. Any one who had less at stake would have wearied of such a task, self-imposed as it was; but Gualtier had too much at stake to allow of weariness, and therefore he kept all his senses wide awake, looking with his eyes at the main entrance, and with his ears listening to the footsteps that came along the hall, to discover any signs of danger to himself.

At last a cab drove up and stopped in front of the door. Gualtier, who had been watching every thing, noticed this also. A man got out. The sight of that man sent a shock to Gualtier's heart. He knew that face and that figure in spite of the changed dress. It was Black Bill. A second look to confirm that first impression was enough. Like lightning there came to his mind the thought that Black Bill had been watching for him ever since with inexhaustible patience, had encountered the boy, perhaps with the co-operation of the landlord, and had now come to arrest him. One moment sufficed to bring to his mind the thought, and the fear which was born of the thought. Without waiting to take another glance, or to see who else might be in the cab, he hastily unlocked the doors of the bedroom, glided into the hall, passed down a back stairway, and left the hotel by a side entrance far removed from the front-door. Then darting swiftly forward he mingled with the crowd in the Strand, and was soon lost to the pursuit of any followers.

Such was Gualtier's story. To all this strange account Hilda listened attentively.

"It seems," said she at length, "as though Black Bill has been more persevering than we supposed."

"Far more so than I supposed," said Gualtier. "I thought that he would have given up his watch long ago; or that, whether he wished or not, he had been forced to do so from want of resources. But, after all, he certainly has managed to hold on in some way. I suppose he has secured the co-operation of the landlord, and has got up some business at no great distance from the place, so that on the appearance of my messenger he was sent for at once."

"Did you see the others in the cab?"

"No; Black Bill was enough for me. I suppose the boy was there with him."

"Don't you think it likely that Black Bill may have had some communication with the police?"

"I have thought over that question, and it does not seem probable. You see Black Bill is a man who has every reason to keep clear of the police, and the very information which he would give against me would be equally against himself. Such information would first of all lead to his own arrest. He would know that, and would keep clear of them altogether. Besides, he is an old offender, and beyond a doubt very well known to them. His past career has, no doubt, been marked by them; and this information which he would give would be to them merely a confession of fresh crime. Finding themselves unable to catch me, they would satisfy themselves by detaining him. Oh no; Black Bill is altogether too cunning to have any thing to do with the police."

"All that you have been saying," remarked Hilda, "is very well in its way, but unfortunately it is based on the supposition that Black Bill would tell the truth to the police. But, on the contrary, it is highly probable that he would do nothing of the kind. He has ingenuity enough, no doubt, to make up a story to suit his particular case, and to give it such a coloring as to keep himself free from every charge."

"I don't see how he could do that very well. After all, what would be the essence of his story? Simply this: that a crime had been committed, and that he, with some others, had participated in it. The other offenders would be out of reach. What then? What? Why, Black Bill, from the fact of his own acknowledgment, would be taken in charge."

"I don't see that. As I see it, there are various ways by which a man with any cunning could throw all the guilt on another. He might deny that he knew any one was on board, but only suspected it. He might swear that he and the rest were forced into the boat by you, he and they being unarmed, and you well armed. There are other suppositions also by which he would be able to present himself in the light of an innocent seaman, who, forced to witness the commission of a crime, had lost no time to communicate to the authorities the knowledge of that crime."

"There is something in what you say. But in that case it would have been necessary for him to inform the police months ago."

"Very well; and why may he not?"

"He may have; but it strikes me that he would be more inclined to work the thing up himself; for in that case, if he succeeded, the prize would be all his own."

Some further discussion followed, and then Hilda asked:

"I suppose, by the way you speak, that you saw nothing more of them?"

"No."

"You were not tracked?"

"No."

"Where did you go after leaving the hotel?"

"I left London that evening for Southampton, and then I went west to Bristol; after that to Chetwynde. I staid at Chetwynde till I got your note."

"Did you not see any thing in any of the papers which might lead to the suspicion that you were sought after, or that any thing was being done?"

"No, nothing whatever."

"If any thing is going on, then, it must be in secret."

"Yes; and then, you know, in a country like England it is impossible for the police to work so comprehensively or so efficiently as they do on the Continent—in France, for instance."

"I wonder if the French police are at work?"

"How could they be?"

"I hardly know, unless Black Bill has really informed the London police, and they have communicated to the authorities in France. Of course it all depends on him. The others can have done nothing. He alone is the man from whom any danger could possibly arise. His steady perseverance has a dangerous look, and it is difficult to tell what may come of it yet."

After some further conversation Hilda proceeded to give Gualtier a general idea of the circumstances which had taken place since they parted at Lausanne. Her account was brief and meagre, since she did not wish to say more than was absolutely necessary. From what she said Gualtier gathered this, however—that Lord Chetwynde had continued to be indifferent to Hilda, and he conjectured that his indifference had grown into something like hostility. He learned, moreover, most plainly that Hilda suspected him of an intrigue with another woman, of whom she was bitterly jealous, and it was on this rival whom she hated that she desired that vengeance for which she had summoned him. This much he heard with nothing but gratification, since he looked upon her jealousy as the beginning of hate; and the vengeance which she once more desired could hardly be thwarted a second time.

When she came to describe the affair of the masquerade, however, her tone changed, and she became much more explicit. She went into all the details of that adventure with the utmost minuteness, describing all the particulars of every scene, the dresses which were worn both by Lord Chetwynde and herself, and the general appearance of the grounds. On these she lingered long, describing little incidents in her search, as though unwilling to come to the dénouement. When she reached this point of her story she became deeply agitated, and as she described the memorable events of that meeting with the fearful figure of the dead the horror that filled her soul was manifest in her looks and in her words, and communicated itself to Gualtier so strongly that an involuntary shudder passed through him.

After she had ended he was silent for a long time.

"You do not say any thing?" said she.

"I hardly know what to say on the instant," was the reply.

"But are you not yourself overawed when you think of my attempt at vengeance being foiled in so terrible a manner? What would you think if yours were to be baffled in the same way? What would you say, what would you do, if there should come to you this awful phantom? Oh, my God!" she cried, with a groan of horror, "shall I ever forget the agony of that moment when that shape stood before me, and all life seemed on the instant to die out into nothingness!"

Gualtier was silent for a long time, and profoundly thoughtful.

"What are you thinking about?" asked Hilda at last, with some impatience.

"I am thinking that this event may be accounted for on natural grounds," said he.

"No," said Hilda, warmly; "nothing in nature can account for it. When the dead come back to life, reason falters."

She shuddered as she spoke.

"Yes, my lady," said Gualtier, "but the dead do *not* come back to life. You have seen an apparition, I doubt not; but that is a very different thing from the actual manifestation of the dead. What you saw was but the emanation of your own brain. It was your own fancies which thus became visible, and the image which became apparent to your eye was precisely the same as those which come in delirium. A glass of brandy or so may serve to bring up before the eyes a thousand abhorrent spectres. You have been ill, you have been excited, you have been taking drugs; add to this that on that occasion you were in a state of almost frenzy, and you can at once account for the whole thing on the grounds of a stimulated imagination and weak or diseased optic nerves. I can bring forward from various treatises on the optic nerves hundreds of cases as singular as yours, and apparently as unaccountable. Indeed, if I find that this matter continues to affect you so deeply," he continued, with a faint smile, "my first duty will be to read up exclusively on the subject, and have a number of books sent here to you, so as to let you see and judge for yourself."

CHAPTER LXVII.

A SHOCK.

GUALTIER made still further explanations on this point, and mentioned several special cases of apparitions and phantom illusions of which he had read. He showed how in the lives of many great men such things had taken place. The case of Brutus was one, that of Constantine another. Mohammed, he maintained, saw real apparitions of this sort, and was thus prepared, as he thought, for the prophetic office. The anchorites and saints of the Middle Ages had the same experience. Jeanne d'Arc was a most conspicuous instance. Above all these stood forth two men of a later day, the representatives of two opposite principles, of two systems which were in eternal antagonism, yet these two were alike in their intense natures, their vivid imaginations, and the force of their phantom illusions. Luther threw his ink-bottle at the head of the devil, and Loyola had many a midnight struggle with the same grim personage.

To all this Hilda listened attentively, understanding fully his theory, and fully appreciating the examples which he cited in order to illustrate that theory, whether the examples were those well-known ones which belong to general history, or special instances which had come under his own personal observation. Yet all his arguments and examples failed to have any effect upon her whatever. After all there remained fixed in her mind, and immovable, the idea that she had seen the dead, and in very deed; and that Zillah herself had risen up before her eyes to confound her at the moment of the execution of her vengeance. Such a conviction was too strong to be removed by any arguments or illustrations. That conviction, moreover, had been deepened and intensified by the horror which had followed when she had fled in mad fear, feeling herself pursued by that abhorrent shape, till she had fallen senseless. Nothing of this could be argued away. Nor did she choose to argue about it. While she listened carefully and attentively to Gualtier's words, she scarcely attempted any rejoinder, but contented herself with a quiet reiteration of her former belief.

So this was dismissed. One thing remained, however, and that was the conclusion that Lord Chetwynde was carrying on a desperate intrigue with some English married lady, though whether the husband of this lady was himself English or Italian could not be told. It was evident that Lord Chetwynde's case was not that of the conventional cicisbeo. There was too much desperation in his love. This explained the course which would be easiest to them. To track Lord Chetwynde, and find out who this woman was, should be the first thing. On learning this he was to leave the rest to Hilda. Hilda's work of vengeance would begin with a revelation of the whole case to the supposed husband, and after this they could be guided by circumstances.

With such an understanding as this Gualtier withdrew to begin his work at once. Lord Chetwynde's visits to the villa continued as before, and under the same highly romantic circumstances. Going to India seemed removed from his thoughts further and further every day. He did not feel capable of rousing himself to such an effort. As long as he had the presence and the society of "Miss Lorton," so long he would stay, and as there was no immediate prospect of Obed Chute's leaving Florence, he had dismissed all ideas of any very immediate departure on his part. As for Zillah she soon recovered her health and spirits, and censed to think about the fearful figure in the summer-

house of the fête champêtre. Lord Chetwynde also resumed that strong control over himself which he had formerly maintained, and guarded very carefully against any new outbreak like that of the Villa Rinalci. Yet though he could control his acts, he could not control his looks; and there were times in these sweet, stolen interviews of theirs when his eyes would rest on her with an expression which told more plainly than words the story of his all-absorbing love and tenderness.

But while Lord Chetwynde was thus continuing his secret visits, there was one on his track whom he little suspected. Looking upon his late valet as a vulgar villain, whom his own carelessness had allowed to get into his employ, he had let him go, and had never made any effort to follow him or punish him. As for Hilda, if he ever gave her a thought, it was one of vexation at finding her so fond of him that she would still stay with him rather than leave. "Why can't she go quietly back to Chetwynde?" he thought; and then his more generous nature interposed to quell the thought. He could not forget her devotion in saving his life; though there were times when he felt that the prolongation of that life was not a thing to be thankful for.

As for the family, every thing went on pleasantly and smoothly. Obed was always delighted to see Windham, and would have felt disappointed if he had missed coming every alternate day. Miss Chute shared her brother's appreciation of the visitor. Zillah herself showed no signs which they were able to perceive of the depth of her feelings. Filled, as she was, with one strong passion, it did not interfere with the performance of her duties; nor, if it had done so, would her friends have noticed it. She had the morning hours for the children, and the afternoon for Lord Chetwynde.

In setting about this new task Gualtier felt the need of caution. It was far more perilous than any which he had yet undertaken. Once he relied upon Lord Chetwynde's ignorance of his face, or his contemptuous indifference to his existence. On the strength of this he had been able to come to him undiscovered and to obtain employment. But now all was changed. Lord Chetwynde was keen and observant. When he had once chosen to take notice of a face he would not readily forget it; and to venture into his presence now would be to insure discovery. To guard against that was his first aim, and so he determined to adopt some sort of a disguise. Even with a disguise he saw that it would be perilous to let Lord Chetwynde see him. Hilda had told him enough to make known to him that his late master was fully conscious now of the cause of his disease, and suspected his valet only, so that the watch of the pursuer must now be maintained without his ever exposing himself to the view of this man.

After a long and careful deliberation he chose for a disguise the costume of a Tuscan peasant. Although he had once told Hilda that he never adopted any disguises but such as were suited to his character, yet on this occasion his judgment was certainly at fault, since such a disguise was not the one most appropriate to a man of his appearance and nature. His figure had none of the litheness and grace of movement which is so common among that class, and his sallow skin

"HE FOLLOWED WATCHFULLY AND STEALTHILY."

had nothing in common with the rich olive complexion of the Tuscan face. But it is just possible that Gualtier may have had some little personal vanity which blinded him to his shortcomings in this respect. The pallor of his face was, however, to some extent corrected by a red kerchief which he bound around his head, and the effect of this was increased by a dark wig and mustache. Trusting to this disguise, he prepared for his undertaking.

The next day after his interview with Hilda he obtained a horse, and waited at a spot near Lord Chetwynde's lodgings, wearing a voluminous cloak, one corner of which was flung over his left shoulder in the Italian fashion. A horse was brought up to the door of the hotel; Lord Chetwynde came out, mounted him, and rode off. Gualtier followed at a respectful distance, and kept up his watch for about ten miles. He was not noticed at all. At length he saw Lord Chetwynde ride into the gateway of a villa and disappear. He did not care about following any further, and was very well satisfied with having found out this much so easily.

Leaving his horse in a safe place, Gualtier then posted himself amidst a clump of trees, and kept up his watch for hours. He had to wait almost until midnight; then, at last, his patience was rewarded. It was about half past eleven when he saw Lord Chetwynde come out and pass down the road. He himself followed, but did not go back to town. He found an inn on the road, and put up here for the night.

On the following day he passed the morning in strolling along the road, and had sufficient acquaintance with Italian to inquire from the people about the villa where Lord Chetwynde had gone. He learned that it belonged to a rich Milor Inglese, whose name no one knew, but who was quite popular with the neighboring peasantry. They spoke of ladies in the villa; one old one, and another who was young and very beautiful. There were also children. All this was very gratifying to Gualtier, who, in his own mind, at once settled the relationship of all these. The old woman was the mother, he thought, or perhaps the sister of the Milor Inglese; the young lady was his wife, and they had children. He learned that the Milor Inglese was over fifty years old, and the children were ten and twelve; a circumstance which seemed to show that the younger lady must at least be thirty. He would have liked to ask more, but was afraid to be too inquisitive, for fear of exciting suspicion. On the whole, he was very well satisfied with the information which he had gained; yet there still remained far more to be done, and there was the necessity of continued watching in person. To this necessity he devoted himself with untiring and zealous patience.

For several days longer he watched thus, and learned that on alternate days Lord Chetwynde was accustomed to ride in at the chief gate, while on the other days he would leave his horse behind and walk in at a little private gate at the nearer end of the park, and some considerable distance from the main entrance. This at once excited his strongest suspicions, and his imagination suggested many different motives for so very clandestine yet so very methodical a system of visiting. Of course he thought that it had reference to a lady, and to nothing else. Then the question arose once more—what to do. It was difficult to tell; but at length his decision was made. He saw that the only way to get at the bottom of this mystery would be to enter the grounds and follow Lord Chetwynde. Such an enterprise was manifestly full of danger, but there was positively no help for it. He could not think of going back to Hilda until he had gained some definite and important information; and all that he had thus far discovered, though very useful as far as it went, was still nothing more than preliminary. The mystery had not yet been solved. He had only arrived at the beginning of it. The thought of this necessity, which was laid upon him, determined him to make the bold resolution of running all risks, and of tracking Lord Chetwynde through the smaller gate.

So on one of those days when he supposed that Lord Chetwynde would be coming there he entered the little gate and concealed himself in the woods, in a place from which he could see any one who might enter while he himself would be free from observation.

He was right in his conjectures. In about half an hour the man whom he was expecting came along, and entering the gate, passed close beside him. Gualtier waited for a time, so as to put a respectful distance between himself and the other. Then he followed watchfully and stealthily, keeping always at the same distance behind. For a hundred yards or so the path wound on so that it was quite easy to follow without being perceived. The path was broad, smooth, well-kept, with dark trees overhanging, and thus shrouding it in gloom. At last Lord Chetwynde suddenly turned to the left into a narrow, rough pathway that scarce deserved the name, for it was little better than a track. Gualtier followed. This path wound so much, and put so many intervening obstacles between him and the other, that he was forced to hurry up so as to keep nearer. In doing so he stepped suddenly on a twig which lay across the track. It broke with a loud snap. At that moment Lord Chetwynde was but a few yards away. He turned, and just as Gualtier had poised himself so as to dart back, he caught the eyes of his enemy fixed upon him. There was no time to wait. The danger of discovery was too great. In an instant he plunged into the thick, dense underbrush, and ran for a long distance in a winding direction. At first he heard Lord Chetwynde's voice shouting to him to stop, then steps

as if in pursuit; but finally the sounds of pursuit ceased, and Gualtier, discovering this, stopped to rest. The fact of the case was, that Lord Chetwynde's engagement was of too great importance to allow him to be diverted from it—to run the risk of being late at the tryst for the sake of any vagabond who might be strolling about. He had made but a short chase, and then turned back for a better purpose.

Gualtier, while he rested, soon discovered that he had not the remotest idea of his position. He was in the middle of a dense forest. The underbrush was thick. He could see nothing which might give him any clew to his whereabouts. After again assuring himself that all was quiet, he began to move, trying to do so in as straight a line as possible, and thinking that he must certainly come out somewhere.

He was quite right; for after about half an hour's rough and difficult journeying he came to a path. Whether to turn up or down, to the right or the left, was a question which required some time to decide; but at length he turned to the right, and walked onward. Along this he went for nearly a mile. It then grew wider, and finally became a broad way with thick, well-cut hedges on either side. It seemed to him that he was approaching the central part of these extensive grounds, and perhaps the house itself. This belief was confirmed soon by the appearance of a number of statues and vases which ornamented the pathway. The fear of approaching the house and of being seen made him hesitate for some time; yet his curiosity was strong, and his eagerness to investigate irrepressible. He felt that this opportunity was too good a one to lose, and so he walked on rapidly yet watchfully. At length the path made a sudden sweep, and he saw a sight before him which arrested his steps. He saw a broad avenue, into which his path led not many paces before him. And at no great distance off, toward the right, appeared the top of the villa emerging from among trees. Yet these things did not attract his attention, which centered itself wholly on a man whom he saw in the avenue.

This man was tall, broad-shouldered, with rugged features and wide, square brow. He wore a dress-coat and a broad-brimmed hat of Tuscan straw. In an instant, and with a surprise that was only equaled by his fear, Gualtier recognized the form and features of Obed Chute, which had, in one interview in New York, been very vividly impressed on his memory. Almost at the same time Obed happened to see him, so that retreat was impossible. He looked at him carelessly and then turned away; but a sudden thought seemed to strike him; he turned once more, regarded the intruder intently, and then walked straight up to him.

CHAPTER LXVIII.

THE VISION OF THE DEAD.

GUALTIER stood rooted to the spot, astounded at such a discovery. His first impulse was flight. But that was impossible. The hedgeway on either side was high and thick, preventing any escape. The flight would have to be made along the open path, and in a chase he did not feel confident that he could escape. Besides, he felt more like relying on his own resources. He had a hope that his disguise might conceal him. Other thoughts also passed through his mind at that moment. How did this Obed Chute come here? Was *he* the Milor Inglese? How did he come into connection with Lord Chetwynde, of all others? Were they working together on some dark plot against Hilda? That seemed the most natural thing to believe.

But he had no time for thought, for even while these were passing through his mind Obed was advancing toward him, until finally he stood before him, confronting him with a dark frown. There was something in his face which showed Gualtier that he was recognized.

"Yon!" cried Obed; "you! I thought so, and it is so, by the Lord! I never forget a face. You scoundrel! what do you want? What are you doing here? What are you following me for? Are you on that business again? Didn't I give you warning in New York?"

There was something so menacing in his look, and in his wrathful frown, that Gualtier started back a pace, and put his hand to his breast-pocket to seize his revolver.

"No you don't!" exclaimed Obed, and quick as lightning he seized Gualtier's hand, while he held his clenched fist in his face.

"I'm up to all those tricks," he continued, "and you can't come it over me, you scoundrel! Here—off with all that trash."

And knocking off Gualtier's hat, as he held his hand in a grasp from which the unhappy prisoner could not release himself, he tore off his wig and his mustache.

Gualtier was not exactly a coward, for he had done things which required great boldness and presence of mind, and Obed himself had said this much in his criticisms upon Black Bill's story; but at the present moment there was something in the tremendous figure of Obed, and also in the fear which he had that all was discovered, which made him cower into nothingness before his antagonist. Yet he said not a word.

"And now," said Obed, grimly, "perhaps you'll have the kindness to inform me what you are doing here—you, of all men in the world—dodging about in disguise, and tracking my footsteps. What the devil do you mean by sneaking after me again? You saw me once, and that ought to have been enough. What do you want? Is it something more about General Pomeroy? And what do you mean by trying to draw a pistol on me on my own premises? Tell me the truth, you mean, sallow-faced rascal, or I'll shake the bones out of your body!"

In an ordinary case of sudden seizure Gualtier might have contrived to get out of the difficulty by his cunning and presence of mind. But this was by no means an ordinary case. This giant who thus seemed to come down upon him as suddenly as though he had dropped from the skies, and who thundered forth these fierce, imperative questions in his ear, did not allow him much space in which to collect his thoughts, or time to put them into execution. There began to come over him a terror of this man, whom he fancied to be intimately acquainted with his whole career. "Thus conscience does make cowards of us all," and Gualtier, who was generally not a coward, felt very much like one on

this occasion. Morally, as well as physically, he felt himself crushed by his opponent. It was, therefore, with utter helplessness, and the loss of all his usual strength of mind and self-control, that he stammered forth his answer:

"I—I came here—to—to get some information."

"You came to get information, did you? Of course you did. Spies generally do."

"I came to see you."

"To see *me*, hey? Then why didn't you come like a man? What's the meaning of this disguise?"

"Because you refused information once, and I thought that if I came in another character, with a different story, I might have a better chance."

"Pooh! don't I see that you're lying? Why didn't you come up through the avenue like a man, instead of sneaking along the paths? Answer me that."

"I wasn't sneaking. I was merely taking a little stroll in your beautiful grounds."

"Wasn't sneaking?" repeated Obed; "then I'd like very much to know what sneaking is, for my own private information. If any man ever looked like a sneak, you did when I first caught your eye."

"I wasn't sneaking," reiterated Gualtier; "I was simply strolling about. I found a gate at the lower end of the park, and walked up quietly. I was anxious to see you."

"Anxious to see me?" said Obed, with a peculiar intonation.

"Yes."

"Why, then, did you look scared out of your life when you did see me? Answer me that."

"My answer is," said Gualtier, with an effort at calmness, "that I neither looked scared nor felt scared. I dare say I may have put myself on my guard, when you rushed at me."

"I didn't rush at you."

"It seemed to me so, and I fell back a step, and prepared for the shock."

"Fell back a step!" sneered Obed; "you looked around to see if you had any ghost of a chance to run for it, and saw you had none. That's about it."

"You are very much mistaken," said Gualtier.

"Young man," replied Obed, severely, "I'm *never* mistaken! So dry up."

"Well, since I've found you," said Gualtier, "will you allow me to ask you a question?"

"What's that?—*you* found *me*? Why, you villain! I found *you*. You are a cool case, too. Answer *you* a question? Not a bit of it. But I'll tell you what I will do. I intend to teach you a lesson that you won't forget."

"Beware," said Gualtier, understanding the other's threat—"beware how you offer violence to me."

"Oh, don't trouble yourself at all. I intend to beware. My first idea was to kick you all the way out; but you're such a poor, pale, pitiful concern that I'll be satisfied with only one parting kick. So off with you!"

At this Obed released his grasp, and keeping Gualtier before him he forced him along the avenue toward the gate.

"You needn't look round," said Obed, grimly, as he noticed a furtive glance of Gualtier's. "And you needn't try to get at your revolver. Tain't any manner of use, for I've got one, and can use it better than you, being an American born. You needn't try to walk faster either," he continued, "for you can't escape. I can run faster than you, my legs being longer. You don't know the grounds, either, half so well as I do, although I dare say you've been sneaking about here ever since I came. But let me tell you this, my friend, for your information. You can't come it over me, nohow; for I'm a free American, and I always carry a revolver. Take warning by that one fact, and bear this in mind too—that if I ever see your villainous face about here again, or if I find you prowling about after me any where, I swear I'll blow your bloody brains out as sure as my name's Obed Chute. I'll do it. I will, by the Eternal!"

With such cheerful remarks as these Obed entertained his companion, or prisoner, whichever he was, until they reached the gate. The porter opened it for them, and Gualtier made a wild bound forward. But he was not quick enough; for Obed, true to his promise, was intent on giving him that last kick of which he had spoken. He saw Gualtier's start, and he himself sprang after him with fearful force. Coming up to him, he administered to him one single blow with his foot, so tremendous that it was like the stroke of a catapult, and sent the unhappy wretch headlong to the ground.

After doing this Obed calmly went back, and thought for some time on this singular adventure. He had his own ideas as to the pertinacity of this man, and attributed it to some desire on his part to investigate the old affair of the Chetwynde elopement. What his particular personal interest might be he could not tell, nor did he care much. In fact, at this time the question of his visitor's motives hardly occupied his mind at all, so greatly were his thoughts occupied with pleasurable reminiscences of his own parting salute.

As for Gualtier, it was different; and if his thoughts were also on that parting salute, it was for some time. The blow had been a terrible one; and as he staggered to his feet he found that he could not walk without difficulty. He dragged himself along, overcome by pain and bitter mortification, cursing at every step Obed Chute and all belonging to him, and thus slowly and sullenly went down the road. But the blow of the catapult had been too severe to admit of an easy recovery. Every step was misery and pain; and so, in spite of himself, he was forced to stop. But he dared not rest in any place along the road-side; for the terror of Obed Chute was still strong upon him, and he did not know but that this monster might still take it into his head to pursue him, so as to exact a larger vengeance. So he clambered up a bank on the road-side, where some trees were, and among these he lay down, concealing himself from view.

Pain and terror and dark apprehensions of further danger affected his brain. Concealed among these trees, he lay motionless, hardly daring to breathe, and scarcely able to move. Amidst his pain there still came to him a vague wonder at the presence of Obed Chute here in such close friendship with Lord Chetwynde. How had such a friendship arisen? How was it possible that these two had ever become acquainted? Lord Chetwynde, who had passed his later life in India, could scarcely ever have

P

heard of this man; and even if he had heard of this man, his connection with the Chetwynde family had been of such a nature that an intimate friendship like this was the last thing which might be expected. Such a friendship, unaccountable as it might be, between these two, certainly existed, for he had seen sufficient proofs of it: yet what Lord Chetwynde's aims were he could not tell. It seemed as though, by some singular freak of fortune, he had fallen in love with Obed Chute's wife, and was having clandestine meetings with her somewhere. If so, Obed Chute was the very man to whom Hilda might reveal her knowledge, with the assurance that the most ample vengeance would be exacted by him on the destroyer of his peace and the violator of his friendship.

Amidst his pain, and in spite of it, these thoughts came, and others also. He could not help wondering whether in this close association of these two they had not some one common purpose. Was it possible that they could know any thing about Hilda? This was his first thought; and nothing could show more plainly the unselfish nature of the love of this base man than that at a time like this he should think of her rather than himself. Yet so it was. His thought was, Do they suspect her? Has Lord Chetwynde some dark design against her, and are they working in unison? As far as he could see there was no possibility of any such design. Hilda's account of Lord Chetwynde's behavior toward her showed him simply a kind of tolerance of her, as though he deemed her a necessary evil; but none of that aversion which he would have shown had he felt the faintest suspicion of the truth. That truth would have been too terrific to have been borne thus by any one. No. He must believe that Hilda was really his wife, or he could not be able to treat her with that courtesy which he always showed—which, cold though it might be in her eyes, was still none the less the courtesy which a gentleman shows to a lady who is his equal. But had he suspected the truth she would have been a criminal of the basest kind, and courtesy from him to her would have been impossible. He saw plainly, therefore, that the truth with regard to Hilda could not be in any way even suspected, and that thus far she was safe.

Another thing showed that there could be no connection between these two arising out of their family affairs. Certainly Lord Chetwynde, with his family pride, was not the man who could ally himself to one who was familiar with the family shame; and, moreover, Hilda had assured him, from her own knowledge, that Lord Chetwynde had never learned any thing of that shame. He had never known it at home, he could not have found it out very easily in India, and in whatever way he had become acquainted with this American, it was scarcely probable that he could have found it out from him. Obed Chute was evidently his friend; but for that very reason, and from the very nature of the case, he could not possibly be known to Lord Chetwynde as the sole living contemporary witness of his mother's dishonor. Obed Chute himself was certainly the last man in the world, as Gualtier thought, who would have been capable of volunteering such information as that. These conclusions to which he came were natural, and were based on self-evident truths. Yet still the question remained: How was it that these two men, who more than all others were connected with those affairs which most deeply affected himself and Hilda, and from whom he had the chief if not the only reason to fear danger, could now be joined in such intimate friendship? And this was a question which was unanswerable.

As Hilda's position seemed safe, he thought of his own, and wondered whether there could be danger to himself from this. Singularly enough, on that eventful day he had been seen by both Lord Chetwynde and Obed Chute. Lord Chetwynde, he believed, could not have recognized him, or he would not have given up the pursuit so readily. Obed Chute had not only recognized him, but also captured him, and not only captured him, but very severely punished him; yet the very fact that Obed Chute had suffered him to go showed how complete his ignorance must be of the true state of the case. If he had but known even a portion of the truth he would never have allowed him to go; if he and Lord Chetwynde were really allied in an enterprise such as he at first feared when he discovered that alliance, then he himself would have been detained. True, Obed Chute knew no more of him than this, that he had once made inquiries about the Chetwynde family affairs; yet, in case of any serious alliance on their part, this of itself would have been sufficient cause for his detention. Yet Obed Chute had sent him off. What did that show? This, above all, that he could not have any great purpose in connection with his friend.

Amidst all these thoughts his sufferings were extreme. He lay there fearful of pursuit, yet unable to move, distracted by pain both of body and mind. Time passed on, but his fears continued unabated. He was excited and nervous. The pain had brought on a deep physical prostration, which deprived him of his usual self-possession. Every moment he expected to see a gigantic figure in a dress-coat and a broad-brimmed hat of Tuscan straw, with stern, relentless face and gleaming eyes, striding along the road toward him, to seize him in a resistless grasp, and send him to some awful fate; or, if not that, at any rate to administer to him some tremendous blow, like that catapultian kick, which would hurl him in an instant into oblivion.

The time passed by. He lay there in pain and in fear. Excitement and suffering had disordered his brain. The constant apprehension of danger made him watchful, and his distempered imagination made him fancy that every sound was the footstep of his enemy. Watchful against this, he held his pistol in his nerveless grasp, feeling conscious at the same time how ineffectively he would use it if the need for its use should arise. The road before him wound round the hill up which he had clambered in such a way that but a small·part of it was visible from where he sat. Behind him rose the wall of the park, and all around the trees grew thickly and sheltered him.

Suddenly, as he looked there with ceaseless vigilance, he became aware of a figure that was moving up the road. It was a woman's form. The figure was dressed in white, the face was white, and round that face there were gathered great masses of dark hair. To his disordered senses it seemed at that moment as if this figure glided along the ground.

Filled with a kind of horror, he raised himself up, one hand still grasping the pistol, while the other clutched a tree in front of him with a convulsive grasp, his eyes fixed on this figure. Something in its outline served to create all this new fear that had arisen, and fascinated his gaze. To his excited sensibility, now rendered morbid by the terrors of the last few hours, this figure, with its white robes, seemed like something supernatural sent across his path. It was dim twilight, and the object was a little indistinct; yet he could see it sufficiently well. There was that about it which sent an awful suspicion over him. All that Hilda had told him recurred to his mind.

And now, just as the figure was passing, and while his eyes were riveted on it, the face slowly and solemnly turned toward him.

At the sight of the face which was thus presented there passed through him a sudden pang of unendurable anguish—a spasm of terror so intolerable that it might make one die on the spot. For a moment only he saw that face. The next moment it had turned away. The figure passed on. Yet in that moment he had seen the face fully and perfectly. He had recognized it! He knew it as the face of one who now lay far down beneath the depths of the sea—of one whom he had betrayed—whom he had done to death! This was the face which now, in all the pallor of the grave, was turned toward him, and seemed to change him to stone as he gazed.

The figure passed on—the figure of Zillah—to this conscience-stricken wretch a phantom of the dead; and he, overwhelmed by this new horror, sank back into insensibility.

CHAPTER LXIX.

THE VISION OF THE LOST.

IT was twilight when Gualtier sank back senseless. When he at last came to himself it was night. The moon was shining brightly, and the wind was sighing through the pines solemnly and sadly. It was some time before he could recall his scattered senses so as to understand where he was. At last he remembered, and the gloom around him gave additional force to the thrill of superstitious horror which was excited by that remembrance. He roused himself with a wild effort, and hunted in the grass for his pistol, which now was his only reliance. Finding this, he hurried down toward the road. Every limb now ached, and his brain still felt the stupefying effects of his late swoon. It was only with extreme difficulty that he could drag himself along; yet such was the horror on his mind that he despised the pain, and hurried down the road rapidly, seeking only to escape as soon as possible out from among the shadows of these dark and terrible woods, and into the open plain. His hasty, hurried steps were attended with the severest pain, yet he sped onward, and, at last, after what seemed to him an interminable time, he emerged out of the shadows of the forest into the broad, bright moonlight of the meadows which skirt the Arno. Hurrying along for a few hundred yards, he sank down at last by the road-side, completely exhausted. In about an hour he resumed his journey, and then sank exhausted once more, after traversing a few miles. It was sunrise before he reached the inn where he stopped. All that day and the next night he lay in bed. On the following day he went to Florence; and, taking the hour when he knew that Lord Chetwynde was out, he called on Hilda.

He had not been there or seen her since that visit which he had paid on his first arrival at Florence from England. He had firmly resolved not to see her until he had done something of some consequence, and by this resolution he intended that he should go to her as the triumphant discoverer of the mystery which she sought to unravel. Something had, indeed, been done, but the dark mystery lay still unrevealed; and what he had discovered was certainly important, yet not of such a kind as could excite any thing like a feeling of triumph. He went to her now because he could not help it, and went in bitterness and humiliation. That he should go at all under such circumstances only showed how complete and utter had been his discomfiture. But yet, in spite of this, there had been no cowardice of which he could accuse himself, and he had shrunk from no danger. He had dared Lord Chetwynde almost face to face. Flying from him, he had encountered one whom he might never have anticipated meeting. Last of all, he had been overpowered by the phantom of the dead. All these were sufficient causes for an interview with Hilda, if it were only for the sake of letting her know the fearful obstacles that were accumulating before her, the alliance of her worst enemies, and the reappearance of the spectre.

As Hilda entered the room and looked at him, she was startled at the change in him. The hue of his face had changed from its ordinary sallow complexion to a kind of grizzly pallor. His hands shook with nervous tremulousness, his brow was contracted through pain, his eyes had a wistful eagerness, and he seemed twenty years older.

"You do not look like a bearer of good news," said she, after shaking hands with him in silence.

Gualtier shook his head mournfully.

"Have you found out nothing?"

He sighed.

"I'm afraid I've found out too much by far."

"What do you mean?"

"I hardly know. I only know this, that my searches have shown me that the mystery is deeper than ever."

"You seem to me to be very quickly discouraged," said Hilda, in a disappointed tone.

"That which I have found out and seen," said Gualtier, solemnly, "is something which might discourage the most persevering, and appall the boldest. My lady," he added, mournfully, "there is a power at work which stands between you and the accomplishment of your purpose, and dashes us back when that purpose seems nearest to its attainment."

"I do not understand you," said Hilda, slowly, while a dark foreboding arose in her mind, and a fearful suspicion of Gualtier's meaning. "Tell me what you mean, and what you have been doing since I saw you last. You certainly must have had a very unusual experience."

It was with an evident effort that Gualtier was able to speak. His words came painfully and slowly, and in this way he told his story.

He began by narrating the steps which he had taken to secure himself from discovery by the use of a disguise, and his first tracking of Lord Chetwynde to the gates of the villa. He described the situation to her very clearly, and told her all that he had learned from the peasants. He then told her how, by long watching, he had discovered Lord Chetwynde's periodical visits, alternately made at the great and the small gate, and had resolved to find out the reason of such very singular journeys.

To all this Hilda listened with breathless interest and intense emotion, which increased, if possible, up to that time when he was noticed and pursued by Lord Chetwynde. Then followed the story of his journey through the woods and the paths till he found himself face to face with Obed Chute.

At the mention of this name she interrupted him with an exclamation of wonder and despair, followed by many questions. She herself felt all that perplexity at this discovery of his friendship with Lord Chetwynde which Gualtier had felt, and all the thoughts which then had occurred to him now came to her, to be poured forth in innumerable questions. Such questions he was, of course, unable to answer. The appearance of this man upon the scene was a circumstance which excited in Hilda's mind vague apprehensions of some unknown danger; yet his connection with Lord Chetwynde was so inexplicable that it was impossible to know what to think or to fear.

The discussion of this new turn in the progress of things took up some time. Exciting as this intelligence had been to Hilda, the conclusion of Gualtier's narrative was far more so. This was the climax, and Gualtier, who had been weak and languid in speaking about the other things, here rose into unusual excitement, enlarging upon every particular in that occurrence, and introducing all those details which his own vivid imagination had in that moment of half delirium thrown around the figure which he had seen.

"It floated before me," said he, with a shudder; "its robes were white, and hung down as though still dripping with the water of the sea. It moved noiselessly until it came opposite to me, and then turned its full face toward me. The eyes were bright and luminous, and seemed to burn into my soul. They are before me yet. Never shall I forget the horror of that moment. When the figure passed on I fell down senseless."

"In the name of God!" burst forth Hilda, whose eyes dilated with the terror of that tale, while she trembled from head to foot in fearful sympathy, "is this true? Can it be? Did you, too, see her?"

"Herself, and no other!" answered Gualtier, in a scarce audible voice.

"Once before," said Hilda, "that apparition came. It was to me. You know what the effect was. I told you. You were then very cool and philosophical. You found it very easy to account for it on scientific principles. You spoke of excitement, imagination, and diseased optic nerves. Now, in your own case, have you been able to account for this in the same way?"

"I have not," said Gualtier. "Such arguments to me now seem to be nothing but words

—empty words, satisfactory enough, no doubt, to those who have never had this revelation of another world, but idle and meaningless to those who have seen what I have seen. Why, do I not know that she is beneath the Mediterranean, and yet did I not see her myself? You were right, though I did not understand your feelings, when you found all my theories vain. Now, since I have had your experience, I, too, find them vain. It's the old story—the old, old hackneyed saying," he continued, wearily—

"'There are more things in heaven and earth, Horatio, Than are dreamt of in your philosophy.'"

A long silence followed.

"We have been warned," said Hilda at length. "The dead arise before us," she continued, solemnly, "to thwart our plans and our purposes. The dead wife of Lord Chetwynde comes back from beneath the sea to prevent our undertakings, and to protect him from us."

Gualtier said nothing. In his own soul he felt the deep truth of this remark. Both sat now for some time in silence and in solemn meditation, while a deep gloom settled down upon them.

At last Gualtier spoke.

"It would have been far better," said he, "if you had allowed me to complete that business. It was nearly done. The worst was over. You should not have interfered."

Hilda made no reply. In her own heart there were now wild desires, and already she herself had become familiar with this thought.

"It can yet be done," said Gualtier.

"But how can you do it again—after this?" said Hilda.

"You are now the one," replied Gualtier. "You have the power and the opportunity. As for me, you know that I could not become his valet again. The chance was once all my own, but you destroyed it. I dare not venture before him again. It would be ruin to both of us. He would recognize me under any disguise, and have me at once arrested. But if you know any way in which I can be of use, or in which I can have access to his presence, tell me, and I will gladly risk my life to please you."

But Hilda knew of none, and had nothing to say.

"You, and you alone, have the power now," said Gualtier; "this work must be done by you alone."

"Yes," said Hilda, after a pause. "It is true, I have the power—I have the power," she repeated, in a tone of gloomy resolve, "and the power shall be exercised, either on him, or on myself."

"On yourself!"

"Yes."

"Are you still thinking of such a thing as that?" asked Gualtier, with a shudder.

"That thought," said Hilda, calmly, "has been familiar to me before, as you very well know. It is still a familiar one, and it may be acted upon at any moment."

"Would you dare to do it?"

"Dare to do it!" repeated Hilda. "Do you ask me that question of me after what I told you at Lausanne? Did I not tell you there that what I dared to administer to another, I dared also to administer to myself? You surely must remember how weak all those menaces of yours proved

when you tried to coerce me again as you had done once before. You must know the reason why they were so powerless. It was because to me all life, and all the honors and pleasures of life, had grown to be nothing without that one aim after which I was seeking. Do you not understand yet?"

"My God!" was Gualtier's reply, "how you love that man!" These words burst forth involuntarily, as he looked at her in the anguish of his despair.

Hilda's eyes fastened themselves on his, and looked at him out of the depths of a despair which was deeper than his own—a despair which had now made life valueless.

"You can not—you will not," exclaimed Gualtier, passionately.

"I can," said Hilda, "and it is very possible that I will."

"You do not know what it is that you speak about."

"I am not afraid of death," said Hilda, coldly, "if that is what you mean. It can not be worse than this life of mine."

"But you do not understand what it means," said Gualtier. "I am not speaking of the mere act itself, but of its consequences. Picture to yourself Lord Chetwynde exulting over this, and seeing that hated obstacle removed which kept him from his perfect happiness. You die, and you leave him to pursue uninterrupted the joy that he has with his paramour. Can you face such a thought as that? Would not this woman rejoice at hearing of such a thing? Do you wish to add to their happiness? Are you so sublimely self-sacrificing that you will die to make Lord Chetwynde happy in his love?"

"How can he be happy in his love?" said Hilda. "She is married."

"She may not be. You only conjecture that. It may be her father whom she guards against, or her guardian. Obed Chute is no doubt the man—either her father or guardian, and Lord Chetwynde has to guard against suspicion. But what then? If you die, can he not find some other, and solace himself in her smiles, and in the wealth that will now be all his own?"

These words stung Hilda to the quick, and she sat silent and thoughtful. To die so as to get rid of trouble was one thing, but a death which should have such consequences as these was a very different thing. Singularly enough, she had never thought of this before. And now, when the thought came, it was intolerable. It produced within her a new revolution of feeling, and turned her thoughts away from that gloomy idea which had so often haunted her.

"He is the only one against whom you can work," continued Gualtier; "and you alone have the power of doing it."

Hilda said nothing. If this work must be done by her, there were many things to be considered, and these required time.

"But you will not desert me," said she, suddenly; for she fancied from Gualtier's manner that he had given up all further idea of helping her.

His face flushed.

"Is it possible that you can still find any way to employ me? This is more than I hoped for. I feared that your indignation at my failure would cause you to dismiss me as useless. If

"THE DEAD AND THE LOST ALL COME TO ME."

you can find any thing for me to do, I can assure you that the only happiness that I can have will be in doing that thing."

"Your failure," said Hilda, "was not your fault. You have done well, and suffered much. I am not ungrateful. You will be rewarded yet. I shall yet have something for you to do. I will send for you when the time comes."

She rose as she said this, and held out her hand to Gualtier. He took it respectfully, and with an earnest look at her, full of gratitude and devotion, he withdrew.

Hilda sat for a long time involved in deep thought. What should be her next plan of action? Many different things suggested themselves, but all seemed equally impracticable, or at least objectionable. Nor was she as yet prepared to begin with her own hands, and by herself, that part which Gualtier had suggested. Not yet were her nerves steady enough. But the hint which Gualtier had thrown out about the probable results of her own death upon Lord Chetwynde did more to reconcile her to life than any thing that could have happened short of actually gaining him for herself.

Wearied at last of fruitless plans and resultless thoughts, she went out for a walk. She dressed herself in black, and wore a heavy black crape veil which entirely concealed the features. She knew no one in Florence from whom she needed to disguise herself, but her nature was of itself secretive, and even in a thing like this she chose concealment rather than openness. Besides, she had some vague hopes that she might encounter Lord Chetwynde somewhere, perhaps with this woman, and could watch him while unobserved herself.

She walked as far as the church of Santa Croce. She walked up the steps with a vague idea of going in.

As she walked up there came a woman down the steps dressed in as deep mourning as Hilda herself. She was old, she was slender, her veil was thrown back, and the white face was plainly visible to Hilda as she passed. Hilda stood rooted to the spot, though the other woman did not notice her emotion, nor could she have seen her face through the veil. She stood paralyzed, and looking after the retreating figure as it moved away.

"The dead and the lost," she murmured, as she stood there with clasped hands—"the dead and the lost all come to me! Mrs. Hart! About her face there can be no mistake. What is she doing here—in the same town with Lord Chetwynde? Am I ruined yet or not? I'm afraid I have not much time left me to run my course."

In deep despondency she retraced her steps, and went back to her room.

CHAPTER LXX.

NEW PROJECTS.

THE unexpected appearance of Mrs. Hart was in many respects, and for many reasons, an awful shock to Hilda. It was a new danger, less terrible than that which had arisen from the phantom which had twice appeared, yet perhaps in reality more perilous. It filled her with apprehensions of the worst. All that night she lay awake thinking over it. How had Mrs. Hart come to Florence, and why, and what was she doing here? Such were her thoughts. Was she also in connection with Lord Chetwynde and with this Obed Chute? It seemed probable. If so, then it seemed equally probable that there was some design on foot against her. At first the thought of this inspired in her a great fear, and a desire to fly from the impending danger. For a moment she almost decided to give up her present purpose forever, collect as much money as she could, and fly to some distant place, where she might get rid of all her danger and forget all her troubles. But this thought was only momentary, for higher than her desire for comfort or peace of mind rose her thirst for vengeance. It would not satisfy her that she alone should suffer. Lord Chetwynde also should have his own share, and she would begin by unmasking him and revealing his intrigue to her supposed husband.

On the following day Gualtier called, and in a few words she told him what had taken place.

"Are you really confident that it was Mrs. Hart?" he asked, with some anxiety.

"As confident as I am of my own existence. Indeed, no mistake was possible."

Gualtier looked deeply troubled.

"It looks bad," said he; "but, after all, there are ways of accounting for it. She may have heard that Lord Chetwynde intended to go to Italy and to Florence—for it was quite possible that he mentioned it to her at the Castle—and when she went away she may have intended to come here in search of him. I dare say she went to London first, and found out from his solicitors where he had gone. There isn't the slightest probability, at any rate, that he can have met with her. If he had met with her, you would have known it yourself soon enough. She would have been here to see his wife, with the same affectionate solicitude which she showed once before—which you told me of. No. Rest assured Lord Chetwynde knows nothing of her presence here. There are others who take up all his thoughts. It seems probable, also, that she has just arrived, and there is no doubt that she is on the look-out for him. At any rate, there is one comfort. You are sure, you say, that she did not recognize you?"

"No; that was impossible; for I wore a thick veil. No one could possibly distinguish my features."

"And she can not, of course, suspect that you are here?"

"She can not have any such suspicion, unless we have been ourselves living in the dark all this time—unless she is really in league with Lord Chetwynde. And who can tell? Perhaps all this time this Chute and Mrs. Hart and Lord Chetwynde have their own designs, and are quietly weaving a net around me from which I can not escape. Who can tell? Ah! how easily I could escape—if it were not for one thing!"

"Oh, as to that, you may dismiss the idea," said Gualtier, confidently; "and as for Lord Chetwynde, you may rest assured that he does not think enough about you to take the smallest trouble one way or another."

Hilda's eyes blazed.

"He shall have cause enough to think about me yet," she cried. "I have made up my mind what I am to do next."

"What is that?"

"I intend to go myself to Obed Chute's villa."

"The villa! Yourself!"

"Yes."

"You!"

"I—myself. You can not go."

"No. But how can you go?"

"Easily enough. I have nothing to fear."

"But this man is a perfect demon. How will you be able to encounter him? He would treat you as brutally as a savage. I know him well. I have reason to. You are not the one to go there."

"Oh yes, I am," said Hilda, carelessly. "You forget what a difference there is between a visit from you and a visit from me."

"There is a difference, it is true; but I doubt whether Obed Chute is the man to see it. At any rate, you can not think of going without some pretext. And what one can you possibly have that will be at all plausible?"

"Pretext! I have the best in the world. It is hardly a pretext either. I intend to go openly, in my own proper person—as Lady Chetwynde."

"As Lady Chetwynde!" repeated Gualtier, in amazement. "What do you mean? Would it be too much to ask you what your plan may be, or what it is that you may have in view?"

"It's simple enough," said Hilda. "It is this. You will understand it readily enough, I think. You see, I have discovered by accident some mysterious writing in cipher, which by another accident I have been enabled to unravel. Now you understand that this writing makes very serious charges indeed against my father, the late General Pomeroy. He is dead; but I, as an affectionate daughter, am most anxious to understand the meaning of this fearful accusation thus made against the best of men. I have seen the name of this Obed Chute mentioned in some of the papers connected with the secret writing, and have found certain letters from him referring to the case. Having heard very unexpectedly that he is in Florence, I intend to call on him to implore him to explain to me all this mystery."

"That is admirable," said Gualtier.

"Of course it is," said Hilda; "nothing, indeed, could be better. This will give me admission to the villa. Once in there, I shall have to rely upon circumstances. Whatever those circumstances may be, I shall, at least, be confronted with Lord Chetwynde, and find out who this woman is. I hope to win the friendship and the confidence of these people. They will pity me, sympathize with me, and invite me there. If Lord Chetwynde is such a friend, they can hardly overlook his wife. The woman, whoever she may be, even if she hates me, as she must, will yet see that it is her best policy to be at least civil to me. And that will open a way to final and complete vengeance."

To this plan Gualtier listened in unfeigned admiration.

"You have solved the mystery!" said he, excitedly. "You will—you must succeed, where I have failed so miserably."

"No," said Hilda, "you have not failed. Had it not been for you I could never have had this chance. It is by your discovery of Obed Chute that you have made my present course possible. You have suffered for my cause, but your sufferings will make that cause at last triumphant."

"For such a result as that I would suffer ten thousand times more," said Gualtier, in impassioned tones.

"You will not be exposed to any further sufferings, my friend," said Hilda. "I only want your assistance now."

"It is yours already. Whatever you ask I am ready to do."

"What I ask is not much," said Hilda. "I merely want you to be near the spot, so as to be in readiness to assist me."

"On the spot! Do you mean at the villa?"

"No, not at the villa, but near it, somewhere along the road. I wish you to see who goes and comes. Go out there to-day, and watch. You need not go within a mile of the villa itself; that will be enough. You will then know when Lord Chetwynde comes. You can watch from behind some hedge, I suppose. Can you do that?"

"That?—that is but a slight thing. Most willingly will I do this, and far more, no matter what, even if I have to face a second time that phantom."

"I will go out to-morrow, or on the following day. I want you to be on the watch, and see who may go to the villa, so that when I come you may let me know. I do not want to call unless I positively know that Lord Chetwynde will be there, and the family also. They may possibly go out for a drive, or something may happen, and this is what I want you to be on the look-out for. If Lord Chetwynde is there, and that woman, there will probably be a scene," continued Hilda, gloomily; "but it will be a scene in which, from the very nature of the case, I ought to be triumphant. I've been suffering too much of late. It is now about time for a change, and it seems to me that it is now my turn to have good fortune. Indeed, I can not conceive how there can be any failure. The only possible awkwardness would be the presence of Mrs. Hart. If she should be there, then—why, then, I'm afraid all would be over. That is a risk, however, and I must run it."

"That need not be regarded," said Gualtier. "If Mrs. Hart had found Lord Chetwynde, you would have known it before this."

"That is my chief reliance."

"Have you those papers?"

"Papers?"

"Yes; the cipher and the letters."

"Oh yes. Did I not say that I had them all?"

"No. I thought that you had given them all to—to her," said Gualtier.

"So I did; but I got them back, and have kept them, I don't know why. I suppose it was from an instinct of forecast. Whatever was the reason, however, they are now of priceless value. For they enable me now to go as the daughter of one who has been charged in these papers with the commission of the most atrocious crimes. This must all be explained to me, and by this Obed Chute, who is the only living person who can do it."

"I am glad that what I have done will be useful to you," said Gualtier. "You may trust to me now to do all that man can do. I will go and watch and wait till you come."

Hilda thereupon expressed the deepest gratitude to him, and she did this in language far more earnest than any which she had ever before used to him. It may have been the consciousness that this would be the last service which he was to perform for her; it may have been an intentional recognition of his past acts of love and devotion; it may have been a tardy act of recognition of all his fidelity and constancy; but, whatever it was, her words sank deep into his soul.

"Those words," said he, "are a reward for all the past. May I not yet hope for a future reward?"

"You may, my friend. Did I not give you my promise?"

"Hilda!"

This word burst from him. It was the first time that he had so addressed her. Not even in the hour of his triumph and coercion had he ventured upon this. But now her kindness had emboldened him. He took her hand, and pressed it to his lips.

"I have a presentiment of evil," said he. "We may never meet again. But you will not forget me?"

Hilda gave a long sigh.

"If we meet again," said she, "we shall see enough of one another. If not"—and she paused for a moment—"if not, then"—and a solemn cadence came to her voice—"then you will be the one who will remember, and I shall be the one to be remembered. Farewell, my friend!"

She held out her hand.

Once more Gualtier pressed it to his lips. Then he took his departure.

CHAPTER LXXI.

A RACE FOR LIFE.

ON leaving Hilda Gualtier went out to the villa. Before his departure he furnished himself with a new disguise, different from his former one, and one, too, which he thought would be better adapted to his purposes of concealment. A gray wig, a slouched hat, and the dress of a peasant, served to give him the appearance of an aged countryman, while a staff which he held in his hand, and a stoop in his shoulders, heightened the disguise. He got a lift on a wine-cart for some miles, and at length reached a place not far away from the villa.

The villa itself, as it rose up from among surrounding trees, on a spur of the Apennines, was in sight. On either side of the valley rose the mountains. The Arno, as it wound along, approached the place on this side of the valley, and the mountains were not more than half a mile distant, though on the other the plain was several miles in width. The place which Gualtier had chosen seemed to him to be quite near enough to the villa for observation, and far enough distant for safety. The thought of a possible encounter with Obed Chute was ever present in his mind, and this time he determined to guard against all surprise, and, if an encounter should be inevitable, to use his revolver before his enemy could prevent him. His pride and his manhood both urged him to gain some satisfaction for that shame on both which he had experienced.

After watching one afternoon he obtained lodging at a humble farm-house, and when the next morning came he rose refreshed by sleep, and encouraged by the result of his meditations. He began to be hopeful about final success. The scheme which Hilda had formed seemed to be one which could not fail by any possibility. Whatever Hilda's own purposes might be, to him they meant one thing plainly, and that was a complete and irreparable breach between herself and Lord Chetwynde. To him this was the first desire of his heart, since that removed the one great obstacle that lay between him and her. If he could only see her love for Lord Chetwynde transformed to vengeance, and find them changed from their present attitude of friendship to one of open and implacable enmity, then his own hopes and prospects would be secured, as he thought. Already he saw the beginning of this. In Hilda's manner, in her tone, in her looks, he marked the fierce anger and vengeful feeling which had now taken possession of her. He had witnessed also a greater consideration for himself, arising this time not out of coercion, but from free-will. All this was in his favor. Whether she could ever fully succeed in her thirst for vengeance did not much matter. Indeed, it was better for him that the desire should not be carried out, but that she should remain unsatisfied, for then Lord Chetwynde would only become all the more hateful to her every day, and that hate would serve to give to him fresh opportunities of binding her to himself.

All these thoughts encouraged him. A hope began to rise within his heart brighter than any which he had ever dared to entertain before. He found himself now so completely identified with Hilda's dearest plans and purposes, and so much deeper an understanding between them, that it was impossible for him to refrain from encouraging his hopes to the utmost.

Now, as he sat there watching, his fears of danger grew weaker, and he felt emboldened to venture nearer, so as to fulfill to the utmost the wishes of Hilda. Her image drove out from his thoughts the frowning face of Obed Chute, and the white form of that phantom whose aspect had once crushed him into lifelessness. He thought that it was but a feeble devotion to wait in ambush at such a distance when, by venturing nearer, he might learn much more. Hours passed, and there was no sign of any one belonging to the villa either going or coming, and at length the thought that was in his mind grew

too strong to be resisted. He determined to venture nearer—how near he did not know; at any rate, he could safely venture much nearer than this. Had he not his disguise, and was he not armed? And when he met Hilda would it not be shame to him if he could only tell her that he had staid so far away, and had feared to venture nearer?

He started off. His bowed form, white face, peasant garb, and the staff which supported his unsteady steps, he thought would be surely an impenetrable disguise. True, once before the keen glance of Obed Chute had penetrated his disguise, but then the circumstances under which they met were suspicious. Now, even if he should chance to meet him, he could not be suspected. Who would suspect an aged peasant toiling along the public highway?

He gained fresh courage at every step. As he drew nearer and still nearer to the villa he began to think of venturing into the grounds once more. He thought that if he did so he could be more guarded, and steal along through the trees, beside the paths, and not on them. The thought became a stronger temptation to him every moment, and at length, as he advanced nearer, he had almost decided to venture into that little gate, which was now full in view. He sat down by the road-side and looked at it. At length he rose and walked on, having made up his mind to pass through, at any rate, and be guided by circumstances. It would be something to his credit, he thought, if he could only tell Hilda that he had been in those grounds again.

But as he advanced he heard the sound of approaching wheels. Some carriage was coming rapidly down the road toward him, and he paused for a moment, as the idea struck him that possibly the tremendous Obed Chute might be in it. He walked on very slowly, looking keenly ahead.

Soon the carriage came into view from behind a bend in the road. A thrill passed through Gualtier in spite of himself. He grasped his staff in his right hand, and plunging his left into his breast-pocket, he grasped his pistol. Nearer and nearer the carriage came, and he could easily recognize the square face, broad shoulders, and stalwart frame of Obed Chute. With him there was a lady, whose face he could not as yet recognize. And now there arose within him an intense desire to see the face of this lady. She was beyond a doubt the very one of whom Lord Chetwynde was so eager and so constant in his pursuit. Could he but see her face once it would be a great gain, for he could recognize her elsewhere, and thus do something of importance in assisting Hilda. With this determination in his mind he went on, and bowing down his head like a decrepit old man, he hobbled along, leaning on his staff, but at the same time keeping his eyes upturned and fixed on the lady.

The carriage came nearer and nearer. A strange feeling came over Gualtier—something like an anguish of fear and of wonder. At last the lady's face became plainly discernible. That face! White it was, and the whiteness was intensified by the deep blackness of the hair, while the eyes were large and lustrous, and rested full upon him in something like pity. That face! Was this another vision?

Great God!

"'STOP!' SHE CRIED, TEARING WITH ONE HAND AT THE REINS."

A groan burst from him as this face thus revealed itself. What was this? What did it mean? Was this, too, a phantom? Was it a deceit and mockery of his senses? Was it an eidolon from the realms of death, or could it be an actual material object—a living being? Here was one whom he *knew* to be dead. How came she here? Or by what marvel could any one else so resemble her? Yet it was not a resemblance. It was *herself!*

His brain whirled. All thoughts of all things else faded away in that horror and in that surprise. Spell-bound he stood, while his face was upturned and his eyes were fixed on the lady.

And thus, as he stood rooted to the spot, motionless and staring, the carriage came whirling up and flashed past him. That singular figure, in the peasant garb, with rigid face, and with horror in his eyes, which stared like the eyes of a maniac, attracted the look of the lady. At first she had a vague idea that it was a beggar, but on coming closer she recognized all. As the carriage dashed by she sprang suddenly to her feet with a piercing scream. She snatched the reins convulsively and tore at them in a sort of frenzy.

"It is *he!* It is *he!* Stop!" she cried, tearing with one hand at the reins and with the other gesticulating vehemently in some uncontrollable passion. "It is he—it is Gualtier! Stop! Quick! Seize him, or it. will be too late!"

That scream and those words roused Obed. He, too, had noticed the figure by the roadside, but he had only thrown a careless glance. The words of Zillah, however, thrilled through him. He pulled in the horses savagely. They were foaming and plunging.

As he did this Zillah dropped the reins, and with trembling frame, and eyes flashing with excitement, stood staring back.

"There! there!" she cried—"there, I tell you, is Gualtier, my assassin! He is disguised! I know him! It is Gualtier! He is tracking me now! Stop him! Seize him! Don't let him escape! Make haste!"

These words burst from her like a torrent, and these, with her wild gesticulations, showed the intensity of her excitement. In an instant Obed had divined the whole meaning of this. A man in disguise had already penetrated even into his grounds. This he thought was the same man, in another disguise, still haunting the place and prowling about with his sinister motive. By

Zillah's words he saw that she had recognized this man as that very Gualtier after whom he had been searching so long, and whose name had been so constantly in his mind. And now, in the same instant, he saw that the man who had once sought him in America, and who had recently ventured into his park, was the very one who had betrayed Miss Lorton—the man on whose track he had been setting the police of England, France, and Italy.

It was but for an instant that this thought filled his mind. In another instant Obed had flung down the reins and sprung into the road.

Meanwhile Gualtier had stood motionless, horror-stricken, and paralyzed. But the scream of Zillah and her frantic words had shown him beyond the possibility of a doubt that she was at any rate *alive*, and more than this, that she had recognized him. How she had thus come to life he could not know, nor was there time to conjecture. For now another danger was impending, and, in the person of Obed Chute, was rushing down swiftly upon him. At the sight of this new peril he hesitated not a moment, but snatched his pistol, took aim, and fired shot after shot. But in his haste and agitation a correct aim was impossible. He fired wildly. Four bullets, one after the other, whistled through the air past Obed's head, yet he still came on. The vision of that awful face rushing down upon him thus through the smoke-clouds, with vengeance gleaming from the eyes, and the resolute mouth close shut in implacable sternness, was sufficient to show Gualtier that his career was nearly run. He had a sudden feeling that all was lost. With a wild leap he bounded over the ditch by the road-side, and tore over the fields with the frantic speed of one flying from death.

But the avenger was at his heels.

To fly from vengeance and from death is a thing that brings a strong motive to exertion, but there are other things sometimes which may give an equal impulse. Gualtier was lithe, sinewy, and agile, nimble of foot too, and inspired by the consciousness of danger; but the man who pursued him was one whose mighty thews and sinews had been formed under the shadows of the Alleghanies, and trained by years of early experience to every exercise of strength. This man also was inspired by a feeling which could contribute a motive for exertion as powerful as the fear which filled the heart of Gualtier, and his own pride, his honor, and his affection for Zillah, all urged him on. He followed fast, and followed faster. Gualtier had a long start, but Obed steadily gained, until at last the fugitive could hear the footsteps of his pursuer.

Between the skirts of the hills and the Arno there was a plain about two miles in width. On the other side of the river the fields spread away again for a wider extent, interspersed with groves and vineyards. The Arno was full, and flowing rapidly. Here, then, seemed to be to the fugitive the last chance for escape—here, in that swift-flowing river. Gualtier could swim admirably. Toward this river he turned his flying steps, thinking that his pursuer might not be able to follow, and hoping for safety here. Yet all the time he expected to hear a pistol-shot, for Obed had already told him, in that memorable meeting in the park, that he carried a revolver. That he did not use it now seemed to Gualtier to show plainly that he must have left it behind. As for Obed, he neither fired a pistol-shot nor threatened to fire one. He did not even draw his revolver from his pocket. He simply ran as fast as he could after the fugitive.

That fugitive, in order to gain the river, was compelled to run obliquely, and thus he gave an additional advantage to his pursuer, who tried to head him off, and thus was able to gain on him by some additional paces. But to Gualtier that river-bank was now the place of salvation, and that was at any rate a last resort. Besides this, his pistol still was in his hand, and in it there still remained two shots, which might yet avail him at the last moment. Onward, then, he bounded with frantic exertions while these thoughts sped through his mind. But, mingled with these, there came strange floating thoughts of that figure in the carriage—that one who had met with a wondrous resurrection from the death to which he had sent her, and who was now looking on at his flight, and the pursuit of her avenger. All these various thoughts swept confusedly through his brain in the madness of that hour; for thus it is that often, when death seems to impend, the mind becomes endowed with colossal powers, and all the events of a stormy and agitated life can be crowded into one moment. Now, as Gualtier fled, and as he contrived his plan of escape by the river, there were in his mind, parallel with these thoughts, others of equal power—thoughts of that fair young girl whom he had cast adrift in a sinking ship on the wide midnight sea. Saved she had been, beyond a doubt, for there she was, with her eyes fixed on him in his agony. Avenged she would be also, unless he could escape that terrible pursuer who now every moment came faster and faster behind.

Avenged? No, not yet. Still there was a chance. The river flowed near with its full stream. The opposite shores seemed to invite him; the trees and groves and vineyards there seemed to beckon him onward. At last his feet were on the bank. One plunge, he thought, and he would be safe. But for one instant he delayed that plunge. There were other desires in his heart than that of safety—there was the desire for vengeance. Still there was a chance left. His pistol was in his hand—it yet held two shots. In these he might find both safety and vengeance.

Suddenly he turned as he reached the bank, and instantaneously he discharged the last shots of the pistol at his pursuer. Then he plunged headlong into the river.

Another pursuer, even if he had not fallen, might have faltered at all these pistol-shots. Not so Obed. To him the revolver was a familiar thing—a toy, in fact, the sport of all his life. Often before had pistol-shots whistled about his head, and under circumstances far more dangerous than this. Obed's life had been a varied one, and he could tell many strange tales of adventures in the western parts of America—that country where civilized man has encountered, and can still encounter, those tribes which are his most formidable foes. If at that moment Obed could have bared his mighty body to plunge into the Arno, he could have exhibited a vast number of old scars from wounds which had been received in Kansas, in

California, and in Mexico. But Obed had not time to bare his mighty body. As those last pistol-shots flashed before him he had not time even to wink his eyes, but rushing on with unabated vigor, he reached the river's bank, and in a moment had plunged in after Gualtier.

The fugitive heard that plunge. He heard behind him the quick strokes of a strong swimmer, and then he knew and felt that all was lost. Upon that last chance he had staked everything, and that last chance had failed utterly. This man who had insulted him, bullied him, and overpowered him—this man who had been impervious to his shots on the road and on the river-bank—this man who had gained on him steadily in that desperate race for life which he had run—this demon of a man was now gaining on him in the water also! If his pursuer had stood on the bank and had shot him, he might have received the wound and sank to death without a murmur. But to be followed so, to be caught, to be dragged back—this was the terror and the shame. This stimulated him to fiercer exertions. Despair itself gave a kind of madness to his efforts. But terror and shame and despair itself could not snatch him from the grasp of his remorseless pursuer. Nearer and nearer that pursuer came; more and more desperate grew Gualtier's efforts. In vain. As he struck out with almost superhuman exertions he suddenly felt his foot grasped by a resistless hand. All was over. That despair which a moment before had intensified his efforts now relaxed his strength. He felt himself dragged back to the shore from which he had been flying. He was lost! He struggled no longer to escape, but only to keep his head above water, from an instinct of self-preservation. And in that anguish of fear and despair that now settled upon his soul he had a vague terror that on the moment of landing he would be annihilated.

But, instead of that, he felt himself raised to his feet, and the strong grasp relaxed its hold. He looked up at his captor, and saw him standing before him regarding him with a grim smile.

"So you're the Gualtier, are you," said Obed, "of whose exploits I have heard so much? You're rather a small parcel, I should say, but you've done con-siderable mischief, somehow."

Gualtier did not know what to make of this, but thought it only a little preliminary play, after which he would be flung headlong into the river by some catapultian kick.

"See here," said Obed; "a fellow that pretends to carry a revolver ought to be ashamed of himself for firing such shots as you did. You infernal fool, you! you've gone and lost six of the best chances any man ever had, and not one of them 'll ever come again. What is worse, you've gone and disgraced America in the person of her great national and original weapon—the everlasting revolver. Don't you feel like a fool? You know you do!"

At this extraordinary address Gualtier was, if possible, still more bewildered.

"You deserved to be caught," continued Obed, "for you tempted Providence. Providence gave you the most glorious chance I ever saw in all my born days. After using up your chance with the revolver you had this here boundless plain to run upon. Why, I've dodged a hundred Indians in my day with less of a chance, and all the odds against me, for they were firing at me. But you couldn't be shot down, for I didn't happen to feel inclined to use my revolver. It didn't seem fair." And saying this, Obed tenderly drew out his revolver from his breast-pocket, and exhibited it in a loving way to the astounded Gualtier.

"I saw," he continued, "that it would be a most unscientific waste of lead. The very first shot you fired showed that you were utterly unacquainted with our American invention, and the next was as bad. Why, out of the whole six only one hit me. See here."

And Obed held up his left hand. The last joint of the middle finger had been shot off, and blood was still flowing.

Gualtier looked at this with fresh amazement.

"Why," said Obed, "if I'd had one-tenth part of your chances, and had been in your place, I'd have got off. With such a start I'd engage to escape from a dozen men. I'd drop six with the pistol, and dodge the other six. See here. Do you see that bit of woods?" And taking Gualtier's arm, he pointed to a clump of trees that rose like an island from the plain. "Do you see that?"

Gualtier said nothing.

"Well, I'll tell you what you'd ought to do. You'd ought to have made straight for that in a bee-line; then dodged behind it. Perhaps I'd have followed; but then you could have crossed to the other side, got out of sight, and while I was looking for you, off you'd get to the river. If I'd have gone on the opposite side you could have cut off among the mountains. A man," concluded Obed, in a tone of intense solemnity—"a man that could throw away such a chance as that has tempted Providence, and don't deserve any thing. Young man, you're a gone sucker!"

Gualtier heard all this, and understood this eccentric but grim address. He felt that it was all over with him. He had one desperate thought of snatching at the revolver, which Obed still held in his hand with apparent carelessness; but he saw that such an attempt would be madness. The very instant that he had looked Obed had noticed it, and understood it.

He gave a low laugh.

"You'd better not," said he, and then motioned him toward the carriage. Gualtier walked on in silence. Obed did not deign to touch his prisoner, nor did Gualtier dare to make any effort to escape. There was no chance now, since that other chance had failed; and, besides, the sight of Obed's revolver was itself sufficient to prevent such an attempt.

"You've showed considerable sense in walking quietly along," said Obed, as they came near to the carriage. "If you'd tried to run it would have been worse for you. You'd have lost a limb, sure."

Then Obed stopped, and forced him to look at the ground which they had gone over, and showed what excellent chances he had thrown away.

On reaching the carriage Zillah was calmer, though still greatly excited. She said nothing to Gualtier, nor did the latter venture to look at her. In the flight his wig and hat had fallen off, so that now his hated face was distinctly visible.

Obed put his hand for a moment on Gualtier's shoulder.

"Is this the man?" he asked.

Zillah bowed.

On this Obed made his prisoner get on the front seat of the carriage, and drove rapidly back to the villa.

CHAPTER LXXII.

IN PRISON.

GUALTIER was driven back to the villa, quite in ignorance as to his final destination. He was on the front seat, not bound at all, and there was one moment when there seemed a last chance of escape. It was at a time when Zillah had noticed Obed's wound, and began to question him about it with eager sympathy, while Obed tried to assure her that it was nothing. But Zillah would not be satisfied. She insisted on binding it up. She took her handkerchief, and, though she knew no more about such things than a child, prepared to do what she could. Obed soon saw her ignorance, and proceeded to give her directions. At last he took her handkerchief and tore it into several strips, with a laughing promise to tear his up some day for her. At this moment he was quite intent on Zillah, and she was absorbed in her work. It seemed to Gualtier that he was forgotten. The carriage, also, was ascending the hill. On each side were lofty trees overshadowing it, while beyond them lay a deep forest. All this Gualtier saw. Here was a last chance. Now or never might he escape. He watched for an instant. Obed was showing Zillah how to make the knot, when suddenly, with a quick leap, Gualtier sprang from the carriage seat out into the road. He stumbled and fell forward as his feet touched the road, but in an instant he recovered himself. The road-side was a steep bank, which ascended before him, covered with forests. Beyond this were the wild woods, with rocks and underbrush. If he could but get there he might find a refuge. Thither he fled with frantic haste. He rushed up the steep ascent, and in among the trees. For some distance the wood was open, and the trees rose on high at wide distances with no underbrush. Beyond that there was a denser growth. Through this he ran, stimulated by this new chance for life, and wishing that he had once again that revolver whose shots he had wasted.

As he leaped from the carriage Zillah had given a loud cry, and in another moment Obed had divined the cause and had sprung out in pursuit. Gualtier's start did not amount to more than a dozen paces. Obed also was armed. His chance of escape was therefore small indeed. Small as it was, however, it was enough to stimulate him, and he hurried onward, hearing at every pace the step of his pursuer. At length he reached the thicker part of the wood. He turned and doubled here like a fox. He did not know where to go, but sought to gain some slight advantage. He thought that he might find some place where for a few moments he might baffle his pursuer. This was the hope that now remained. Turning and doubling, therefore, and winding, he continued his flight; but the pursuer still maintained his pursuit, and as yet Gualtier had gained no advantage. In fact, he had lost ground gradually, and the underbrush had not delayed the progress of Obed. Gualtier felt this, but still strove to attain his purpose.

At last he saw a place where there was a steep precipice, thickly wooded up to its very margin and then descending abruptly. Toward this he fled, thinking that some place might show itself where he might descend, and where his pursuer might fear to follow. He bounded along in a winding direction, trying to conceal his purpose. At length he reached the edge of the precipice. At the point to which he had come the descent was abrupt, but ledges jutted out from the side of the cliff, and seemed to afford a chance for a descent to one who was bold enough to venture. There was no time for examination or for hesitation. Swiftly Gualtier ran on till he reached what seemed a favorable place, and then, throwing himself over, his feet caught a projecting ledge, and he reached down his hand to secure a grasp of a rock, so as to let himself down further. He looked down hurriedly so as to see the rock which he wished to grasp, when at that very instant his arm was seized, and a low, stern voice said:

"No go! Up with you, you scoundrel! and thank the Lord I don't blow your brains out."

He was dragged up, flung on the ground, and his hands bound tightly behind him with Obed's handkerchief. After this he was dragged back to the carriage.

So failed his last hope.

"You couldn't have done it," said Obed. "I saw it all the time. I could have shot you fifty times, but, as I knew I was going to catch you, I didn't touch my pistol. I don't blame you for making the trial. I'd have done the same. But you see now that you have got your hands tied up by way of punishment. You can't say but that I've treated you on the square, any how."

Gualtier said nothing, but was taken back and put in the carriage once more. Zillah saw that his hands were tied, and felt more secure as to the result of this second capture.

The carriage now soon reached the villa. Here Obed handed out Zillah, and gave orders to the servants to make ready the brougham. He informed Zillah that he himself intended to take Gualtier to the city and hand him over to the authorities; and that she might make her mind easy as to his capture this time, for he would not allow even an attempt at an escape again.

During these preparations Obed stood waiting near the carriage, while Gualtier sat there with his hands bound. Gladly would he have availed himself of any other chance, however desperate, but there was none. His hands were bound, his enemy was watchful and armed. Under such circumstances there remained no hope. His last attempt had been made boldly and vigorously, but it had failed. So he gave himself up to despair.

The brougham was soon ready. Obed put Gualtier inside and got in himself after him. Then they drove away. Lord Chetwynde was expected that afternoon, and he might meet him on the road. He had made up his mind, however, not to recognize him, but to let him learn the great event from Zillah herself. After giving information to his sister as to the time at which he expected to be back he drove off; and soon the brougham with its occupants was moving swiftly onward out of the villa park, down the descending road, and on toward Florence.

Obed rode inside along with Gualtier all the way. During that drive his mind found full occupation for itself. The discovery and the capture of this man made a startling revelation of several most important yet utterly incomprehensible facts.

First, he recognized in his prisoner the man who had once visited him in New York for the purpose of gaining information about Lady Chetwynde. That information he had refused to give for certain reasons of his own, and had very unceremoniously dismissed the man that had sought it.

Secondly, this was the same man who in disguise had penetrated into his villa with all the air and manner of a spy, and who, by thus following him, showed that he must have been on his track for a long time.

Thirdly, this very man had turned out to be the long-sought Gualtier—the one who had betrayed Miss Lorton to a death from which she had only been saved by a mere accident. This was the man who had won the affections of Miss Lorton's friend, Hilda, who had induced her to share his villainy and his crime; the man who had for so long a time baffled the utmost efforts of the chief European police, yet who had at last been captured by himself.

Now about this man there were circumstances which to Obed were utterly incomprehensible.

It was conceivable that the man who had sought him in New York should track him to Florence. He might have an interest in this affair of Lady Chetwynde deep enough to inspire so pertinacious a search, so that the difficulty did not consist in this. The true difficulty lay in the fact that this man who had come to him first as the inquirer after Lady Chetwynde should now turn out to be the betrayer of Miss Lorton. And this made his present purpose the more unintelligible. What was it that had brought him across Obed's path? Was he still seeking after information about Lady Chetwynde? or, rather, was he seeking to renew his former attempt against Miss Lorton? To this latter supposition Obed felt himself drawn. It seemed to him most probable that Gualtier had somehow found out about the rescue of Zillah, and was now tracking her with the intention of consummating his work. This only could account for his twofold disguise, and his persistence in coming toward the villa after the punishment and the warning which he had once received. To think that he should run such a risk in order to prosecute his inquiry after Lady Chetwynde was absurd; but to suppose that he did it from certain designs on Miss Lorton seemed the most natural thing in the world for a villain in his position.

But behind all this there was something more; and this became to Obed the most difficult problem. It was easy to conjecture the present motive of this Gualtier—the motive which had drawn him out to the villa, to track them, to spy them, and to hover about the place; but there was another thing to which it was not so easy to give an answer. It was the startling fact of the identity between the man who had once come to him in order to investigate about Lady Chetwynde and the one who had betrayed Miss Lorton. How did it happen that the same man should have taken part in each? What should have led him to America for the purpose of questioning him about that long-forgotten tragedy, and afterward have made him the assassin which he was? It seemed as though this Gualtier was associated with the two chief tragedies of Obed's life, for this of Miss Lorton was certainly not inferior in its effect upon his feelings to that old one of Lady Chetwynde. Yet how was it that he had become thus associated with two such events as these? By what strange fatality had he and Obed thus found a common ground of interest in one another—a ground where the one was the assailant and betrayer, the other the savior and defender?

Such thoughts as these perplexed Obed, and he could not find an answer to them. An answer might certainly have been given by the man himself at his side, but Obed did not deign to question him; for, somehow, he felt that at the bottom of all this lay that strange secret which Miss Lorton had so studiously preserved. Part of it she had revealed, but only part, and that, too, in such general outlines that any discovery of the rest was impossible. Had Obed questioned Gualtier he might have discovered the truth; that is, if Gualtier would have answered his questions, which, of course, he would not have done. But Obed did not even try him. He asked nothing and said nothing during all that long drive. He saw that there was a secret, and he thought that if Miss Lorton chose to keep it he would not seek to find it out. He would rather leave it to her to reveal; and if she did not choose to reveal it, then he would not care to know it. She was the only one who could explain this away, and he thought that it would be, in some sort, an act of disloyalty to make any investigations on his own account with reference to her private affairs. Perhaps in this he might have been wrong; perhaps he might have strained too much his scruples, and yielded to a sense of honor which was too high wrought; yet, at the same time, such was his feeling, and he could not help it; and, after all, it was a noble feeling, which took its rise out of one of the purest and most chivalrous feelings of the heart.

While Obed was thus silent, thoughtful, and preoccupied, Gualtier was equally so, and at the same time there was a deep anxiety in his heart, to whom the other was a stranger. To him, at that moment, situated as he was—a prisoner, under such circumstances, and in company with his watchful, grim, and relentless captor—there were many thoughts, all of which were bitter enough, and full of the darkest forebodings for the future. He, too, had made discoveries on that eventful day far darker, far more fearful, far more weighty, and far more terrible than any which Obed could have made—discoveries which filled him with horror and alarm for himself, and for another who was dearer than himself. The first of these was the great, the inexplicable fact that Zillah was really and truly alive. This at once accounted for the phantom which had appeared and stricken terror to him and to Hilda. Alive, but how? Had he not himself made assurance doubly sure? had he not with his own hands scuttled that schooner in which she was? had he not found her asleep in her cabin as he prepared to leave? had he not felt the water close up to the deck before he left the sinking yacht? had he not been in that boat on the dark midnight sea for a long time before the mutinous crew would consent to row away, so near to the vessel that any noise would have necessarily come to his ears? He had. How, then, was this? That yacht *must* have gone down, and she *must* have gone down with it—drowned in her cabin, suffocated there by the waters, without power to make one cry. So it *must* have been; but still here she was, alive, strong, vengeful. It could not be a case of resemblance; for this woman had penetrated his disguise, had recognized him, and at the recognition had started to her feet with wild exclamations, hounding on her companion to pursuit.

But in addition to this there was something still more strange. However she may have escaped—as she must have done—by what wonderful concurrence of circumstances had she met with Obed Chute, and entered into this close friendship with him? That man was familiar with a dark past, to which she was related in some strange way. How was it, then, that of all men in the world, this one had become her friend and protector?

But, even so, there was another mystery, so strange, so dark, so inexplicable, that the others seemed as nothing. For he had discovered in her the one whom Lord Chetwynde was seeking with such zeal, and such passion, and such unfailing constancy. How was it that Lord Chetwynde had found her, and where had he found her? and if he had found her, how had he known her? Was he not living with Hilda on terms at least of respect, and acting toward her as though he believed her to be his wife? What could be the cause that had brought him into connection with Obed Chute? Obed Chute had been the confidant of Lady Chetwynde, and knew the story of her shame. How was it that the son of such a mother could associate so habitually with the man who so well knew the history of that mother? If he were not acquainted with his mother's history himself, how could he have found out Obed Chute for his friend? and if he were acquainted with it, how could he have tolerated him as such? From either point of view the question was unanswerable, and the problem insoluble. Yet the fact remained that Lord Chetwynde was in the habit of making constant visits to the house of the man, the very man, to whom the history of Lord Chetwynde's mother was known as a story of shame, and who himself had been the chief agent in helping her, as it appeared, from the ruin to which she had flung herself.

Then, again, there arose the question as to what might be the position of Zillah. How did she happen to be living with Obed Chute? In what way was she living? How did it happen that Lord Chetwynde was carrying on a series of clandestine visits to a woman who was his own wife? Hilda's story of that passionate interview in the kiosk at the Villa Rinalci was now intelligible in one sense. It was no phantom that had terrified her, but the actual form of the living Zillah herself. Yet, making allowance for this, it became more unintelligible than ever. For what could have been the meaning of that scene? If Zillah were alive and his wife, why should Lord Chetwynde arrange so elaborately this interview in the kiosk? why should he be at once so passionate and so despairing? why should he vow his vows of eternal love, and at the same time bid her an eternal farewell? What was the meaning of his information about that "other whom he hated worse than death," which Hilda had felt like a stroke of death? And why should Lord Chetwynde remain with his false wife, whom he hated, while his true wife, whom he loved, was so near? Why, in the name of Heaven, should he treat the one with even civility, and only visit the other by means of clandestine meetings and stolen interviews? Could such questions be answered at all? Were they not all mad together, or were he and Hilda madder than these? What could be the solution of these insoluble problems?

Such were the questions which filled Gualtier's mind as he drove along—questions which bewildered his brain, and to which he could not find an answer. At one time he tried to think that all these—Zillah, Lord Chetwynde, and Obed Chute —were in alliance; that they understood one another perfectly, and Hilda also; and that they were weaving together some deep plot which was to be her ruin. But this also seemed absurd. For, if they understood her, and knew who she was, why should they take any trouble to weave plots for her? That trouble they could spare themselves, and could arrest her at once whenever they chose. Why did Lord Chetwynde spare her if he knew all? Was it out of gratitude because she had saved him from death? Impossible; for he habitually neglected her now, and gave up all his thoughts and his time to Zillah. Was it possible that Zillah could have been saved, found out her husband, and was now inciting him to this strange course from some desire to get fresh proof against Hilda? No; that was impossible, for she must already have found out proof enough. The withdrawal of her money would of itself be enough to show Hilda's complicity; but her assumption of the *rôle* of Lady Chetwynde was too audacious for a true wife to bear unmoved or unconvinced.

But these things were inexplicable. He could not find even a plausible solution for such difficult problems. His excited brain reeled beneath the weight of puzzles so intricate and so complicated. He was compelled to dismiss them all from his thoughts. But though he dismissed such thoughts as these, there were others which gave occupation to his whole mind, and these at last excited his chief interest. First among these was the thought of Hilda. That very afternoon she might be coming out to carry out her plan of visiting Obed Chute, and confounding Lord Chetwynde. She would go out knowing nothing of that one whom she had doomed to death, but who was now there to confront her. She would go out, and for what? What? Could it be aught else than ruin, utter and absolute?

This was his last dark terror—all fear for himself had passed away. He feared for her, and for her alone. His love for her, and his devotion to her, which had been so often and so conspicuously tested, which had sent him on such tedious and such perilous enterprises, now, when all was over with himself, and not a ray of hope remained, made him rise above self and selfish considerations, and regard her prospects and her safety alone. The thought of her going out to the villa in utter ignorance of this new and terrific truth was intolerable. Yet what could he do? Nothing; and the fact of his own utter helplessness was maddening at such a time as this. He watched through the window, scanning all the passers-by with feverish anxiety, which was so manifest that at length Obed noticed it, and, supposing that he was meditating some new plan of escape nearer the city, sternly reprimanded him, and drew the blinds so that nothing could be seen. And thus, with close-drawn blinds and in silence, they drove toward the city; so that if Hilda had gone along the road, Gualtier could not have seen her.

At the same time Obed, in thus shutting out Gualtier from all sight of the outside world, shut out himself also. And though Lord Chetwynde may have passed on his way to the villa, yet he could not have been seen by the occupants of the brougham, nor could he have seen them.

At last they reached Florence, and Obed drove up to the prefecture of the police. There he made his statement, and Gualtier was handed over to the authorities, and put in prison on a charge of attempted murder committed in Italian waters.

Gualtier was put into a small chamber, with whitewashed walls, narrow iron-grated window, and solid oaken doors, in which there was a small round opening. There was an iron bed here and a chair. Gualtier flung himself upon the bed, and buried his head in his hands. He felt as if he had reached the verge of despair; yet, even at that moment, it was not of himself that he thought. Far above his distress and his despair arose the power of his love, and thus turned his thoughts toward Hilda. Was she on her way out? Was she going to ruin? Or was she still at her hotel? She had not said for certain that she was going to the villa on that day; she said that she was going on that day or the next. Perhaps she had postponed it, and reserved her visit for the next. It seemed probable. If it were indeed so, then there was yet time to make an effort to save her. How could he make such an effort? How could he gain communication with her?

He rose from his bed, and watched through the opening of his door. There was a guard outside, who paced backward and forward solemnly. Gualtier's knowledge of human nature, and of Italian human nature in particular, suggested to him a way by which he might send a message. After some delay he signaled to the guard, who, after looking around cautiously, came up to his door.

"I want to send a message," said Gualtier, in the best Italian that he could muster. "It is very important. It is to a friend. I will pay well."

The guard looked interested.

"Where is your friend?" he asked.

"In the city. Can I have the message sent? I will pay two hundred piastres if I get an answer."

The guard hesitated.

"Wait," said he, after a few moments' thought; "I will see."

He went away, and was gone for about twenty minutes. When he returned he exchanged a glance of profound intelligence with Gualtier, and said:

"I think it can be done, signore."

At this Gualtier went back, and, tearing a leaf out of his pocket-book, penciled the following words:

"A miracle has happened. *She has come to life again.* It was no phantom, but *herself* that appeared to you and me. I am in prison. Do not go out to the villa. Fly and save yourself."

Folding this up, he took it to the guard.

"If you bring back an answer to this," said he, "you shall have two hundred piastres. If you don't find the person, you shall have fifty."

Gualtier then told him the name and address of Hilda, and wrote it out for his information, charging him that it must be delivered to herself, and no other. The guard said that he could not go himself, but would send his younger brother. This satisfied Gualtier, and the guard again departed.

After some time he returned, and paced up and down as before. An hour passed. Gualtier became impatient. Then two hours elapsed. He then beckoned to the guard.

"He is gone a long time," said he.

"Perhaps he is waiting," said the guard; "if it is possible he will deliver the message."

Gualtier waited.

Three hours passed.

The guard at last came back to his door. He handed back to Gualtier the letter which he had written.

"The lady," said he, "was not at home. She had gone away. My brother waited all this time, but she did not return. Shall he go back and wait?"

"No," said Gualtier.

He gave a hundred piastres to the guard. He took his note, and tore it up. All hope faded away within him, and despair, black and dark, settled down upon his soul.

CHAPTER LXXIII.

OBED'S NEW ADVENTURE.

AFTER leaving Gualtier in custody Obed Chute drove away from the police station with an expression of tranquil satisfaction on his fine face; such an expression as might befit one who is conscious of having done his duty to the uttermost. He drove down the Lungh' Arno, and through the Piazza, and past the Duomo. There was no further need to keep the blinds closed, and as he drove on he looked out upon the inhabitants of Florence with a grand benignity of expression to which no language can do justice. Many things conspired to fill his breast with the serenest satisfaction and self-complacency. First, he had saved himself from being humbugged. Secondly, he had been the victor in two very respectable trials of muscle, in which he, by the sheer power of muscle, had triumphed, and in the first of which his triumph had been gained over a man armed with a revolver, and using that revolver, while he very generously scorned to use his own. Thirdly, this man was the very one whom he had sought for months, and who had eluded entirely the police of Italy, France, and England. Obed also had been merciful and magnanimous in his hour of triumph. He had been too great-hearted to avail himself of any undue advantage in the strife, or to do one single act of unnecessary cruelty when that strife was over, and the victory was won. He had not bound his victim till the new flight of that victim had compelled him; nor had he spoken even one harsh word

to him. He had captured him fairly and bravely too, and in the most quiet and unostentatious
manner had handed him over to the police of the
country.

Of course there were some things which might
have been more agreeable under the circumstances. The mystery which surrounded this
man was not pleasant. It was not pleasant, after having captured him, to find himself still baffled in his endeavors to understand him or his
motive; to find that this man had forced him to
interweave the case of Lady Chetwynde with that
of Zillah, when to his mind those two cases were
as far asunder as the poles. Yet, after all, the perplexity which arose from this could not interfere
with the enjoyment of his triumph. Baffled he
might be, but still there was no reason why he
should not enjoy the calm pleasure which arises
from the consciousness of having well and fully
performed a virtuous action, and of having done
one's duty both to one's neighbor and one's
self.

So Obed, as he drove about before going home,
enjoyed the full consciousness of his own merit.
He felt at peace with himself, with the world at
large, and, for that matter, even with Gualtier.
So long as Gualtier had baffled him and eluded
his most ardent search, he had experienced the
bitterest and the most vindictive feelings toward
the villain who had perpetrated such foul crimes,
and persisted in evading all pursuit. But now
that this mysterious villain had been captured,
and by himself, he felt that bitterness and vindictiveness no longer. He was satisfied that the
law would administer to him the full punishment. which was due to his crimes, and as far
as he was concerned personally he had no feeling against him. He was simply desirous of
justice.

Seated thus in his brougham he drove past
Giotto's Campanile, and past those immortal
gates of bronze which Ghiberti made for the
Baptistery, and which Michael Angelo declared
to be worthy of being the gates of Paradise. It
was just at this last place, as the brougham was
moving leisurely on, that his attention was arrested by a figure which was seated on the stone
steps immediately outside of one of those gates.
It was a woman, elderly, decrepit, and apparently poor. She was dressed in deep mourning.
She was very pale, her hair was as white as snow,
and her eyes looked forth with an eager, watchful, wistful expression—an expression of patient
yet curious vigilance, like that of one who is waiting for some friend, or some enemy, who delays
to appear. It was a memorable face—memorable, too, from its sadness, and from the eager yet
almost hopeless scrutiny which it turned toward
every one that passed. This was the figure that
attracted Obed. He gave it one look, and that
one look was enough for him.

The moment that he saw this woman an
exclamation burst from him—an exclamation
which was so loud that the woman heard him.
She started and looked up. At that moment
the brougham stopped, and Obed, tearing open
the door, sprang out and hurried up the steps of
the Baptistery, where the woman was sitting.
She had seen him. A flush passed over her
pale, ghastly face; a wild light came to her eyes.
Tremblingly and with deep excitement she rose
to her feet, steadying herself by grasping the

bronze gateway, and looked at him with an earnest, wondering gaze.

Obed Chute came toward her quickly, yet with
a certain reverential wonder in his face. The
triumph and the self-complacency had all died
out, and there was left nothing but a mournful
surprise, with which there was also mingled a
deep and inexpressible pity and sympathy.

He came nearer and nearer, still with all this
on his face, while she stood awaiting him and
watching him, clinging all the while to the bronze
gates of Ghiberti.

"Is this possible?" said Obed, as he came
near her and regarded her earnestly. "Is it
possible?" he repeated, in a low, soft voice, with
a deep solemnity in the tones that was far different from his usual manner. "Is this indeed
you—and here too?"

He held out both his hands. His face softened; the hard lines seemed to fade away into
a certain unspeakable tenderness, and in his
eyes there was a look of infinite pity and compassion.

"Yes, it is I," said the woman, in a voice
which sounded like a moan. "I am still alive
—still living on—while so many who are better
are dead and are at rest."

She placed one hand in his, while with the
other she still clung to the gateway. The hand
which she gave was shriveled and emaciated,
and cold also to Obed as he felt it while holding
it in both of his.

"Years have passed," said he at length, after
a long and solemn silence, during which each regarded the other most earnestly—"years have
passed," he repeated—"years—since you left
—since I saw you last. Are you living here?"
he continued, after some hesitation. "I suppose
you are with one of the religious houses?"

The woman shook her head wearily.

"No," said she; "I am by myself. I am
alone in the world. I am now simply 'Mrs.
Hart.' I have come here on important business.
It is more than important; it is a matter of life
and death."

"Mrs. Hart! Is that the name that you
have?" asked Obed.

"That is my name," said Mrs. Hart, wearily.
"It has been my name for many years, and has
done me good service."

Obed said nothing, but regarded her for a long
time in silence, wondering all the while at the
mysterious fate of this unhappy woman.

At last he spoke.

"Have you been here long?" he asked. "I
have been here for some weeks, but I have never
seen you."

"Nor have I seen you," said Mrs. Hart. "I
have been here long, but I have seen no one
whom I know. I am alone."

"And are you able to go alone about this
business of which you speak—this business 'of
life and death?' Have you any help? Is it a
thing which you could commit to the police?"

"No," said Mrs. Hart. "I came here in
seach of—of a friend; but I have not been able
to find him."

"Are you alone, then?" asked Obed, in profound sympathy, while his face and his voice still
showed the deep feeling of his heart. "Have
you no one at all to help you? Is this a thing
which you must do by yourself? Could not an-

"IS THIS INDEED YOU—AND HERE TOO?"

other assist you? Would it be possible for you to let me help you in this? I can do much if you will allow me—if you will again put confidence in an old friend."

Mrs. Hart looked at him earnestly, and tears started to her eyes.

"Oh, my friend," she murmured, "I believe that God has sent you to me. I see in your face and I hear in your voice that you still can feel for me. God bless you! my noble, my only friend! Yes, you can help me. There is no secret of mine which I need hide from you. I will tell you all—when I get stronger—and you shall help me. But I am very weak now," she said, wearily.

Obed looked away, and for a time said not one word. But that strong frame, which not long before had dared the shots of a desperate enemy, now trembled violently at the tears of an old woman. With a powerful effort he gulped down his emotion.

"Where are you living?" he asked, in a voice which had changed to one of strange sweetness and tenderness. "You are weak. Will you let me drive you now to your home?"

For a few moments Mrs. Hart looked at him piteously, and made no reply.

"I think it will be better for you to go home in my carriage," said Obed, gently urging her.

She still looked at him with the same piteousness.

"In what part of the city do you live?" said Obed, as he took her hand and drew it inside his arm. "Come, let me lead you to the carriage."

Mrs. Hart held back for a moment, and again looked at him.

"*I have no home,*" she said, in a voice which had died away to a whisper.

At once the truth flashed upon Obed's mind.

"I have no home," continued Mrs. Hart. "I was turned out yesterday. Last night I slept in the Boboli Gardens. For two days I have had nothing to eat."

Obed Chute staggered back as though he had received a violent blow. "O God!" he groaned, "has it come to this?"

He said not another word, but gently led Mrs. Hart to the brougham. He drove to a café first, and persuaded her to take some nourishment. Then he took her once more into the carriage, and they drove slowly out of the city.

Q

CHAPTER LXXIV.

BEWILDERMENT.

SCARCELY any thing was said on the drive out from Florence to the villa. Tears fell frequently from the eyes of the poor wanderer as she sat wrapped in deep thought. Obed sat in silence, looking out of the window upon vacancy, seeing nothing; or, rather, seeing still that face, with its wan lips and ghastly outline, which had told so thrilling a story of homelessness and starvation. His thoughts were going back through the years —the long-vanished years. And as he thought there came over his rugged face an infinite pity and tenderness; from his eyes there beamed sadness and compassion unutterable. He kept silence thus, all that drive, because he could not trust himself to speak.

It was only when they reached the gateway of the villa that he opened his lips. Then, as they drove through, he turned toward her, and putting his hand on her arm, he said :

"Here is your home now—while you live."

"Oh, my friend!" murmured Mrs. Hart; and she could say no more.

On reaching the door Obed assisted Mrs. Hart out of the brougham, and they entered the hall. There were sounds of voices in the drawing-room, and on crossing the threshold of the villa a gentleman's voice arose in a cheerful and sprightly tone :

"Checkmated again! Really, Miss Lorton, after this you'll have to give me the odds of a pawn; you've beaten me seven games out of our last ten."

"I don't believe it was fair," said a lady's voice. "I firmly believe, and I've said it all along, that you let me beat you. Why, you taught me chess yourself, and how is it possible that I could catch up to my master in so short a time?"

"I don't pretend to account for it, Miss Lorton," said the gentleman's voice. "There, before you, is something better than theory. It is an indisputable fact. There is my king, with your queen immediately in front of him, and your rook in the distance guarding that strong-minded lady. And where is my queen? Why, gadding about with knights and bishops, when she ought to have been standing by the side of her unfortunate husband."

As these words came to her ears Mrs. Hart stood still, and one hand grasped Obed Chute's arm convulsively, while the other was pressed to her brow.

"What is this? Who are *these?* Are *they* here?" she asked, in a thrilling voice. "Am I dreaming? Is this some mockery, or are they both here? Is it some surprise? Tell me, my friend. Did you arrange all this?"

She looked at Obed in a bewildered manner. He thought that her mind was wandering.

"Come," said he, kindly, "you must go to your room now and rest, and then—"

But here a loud remark from the gentleman, followed by a merry answer from the lady, interrupted Obed, and Mrs. Hart prevented him from finishing his sentence; for suddenly she started away from him, and, without a word, hurried into the room from which the voices came. Obed stood for a moment quite confounded, and then, feeling assured that the poor creature's brain was turned, followed her hurriedly.

Mrs. Hart burst into the room, with a white face and eager, inquiring eyes. Roused by the noise of footsteps, Lord Chetwynde and Zillah turned. To the amazement of both they saw Mrs. Hart.

Had the form of General Pomeroy, or of Earl Chetwynde, appeared at that instant before them, they could not have been more confounded. Lord Chetwynde, however, was cool and calm. There was nothing in his secret which was very important, and there was therefore no fear of a discovery to disturb the unfeigned joy that mingled with his wonder at this sudden appearance of his old nurse, blended also with deep and sharp grief at the weary, wan, and wretched face that he saw before him. As to his assumed name and the revelation of his true one, that did not trouble him at all, for he could give his explanation very readily. But with Zillah it was different. Rightly or wrongly, she considered her secret a thing which should be guarded like her heart's blood; and now she saw suddenly before her the certainty of a full and grand disclosure—a disclosure, too, not merely in the presence of Obed Chute, but of Windham also. Yet even this fear, terrible as it would have been at other times, was successfully mastered, and her generous and loving nature turned away from selfish fears, with longing and joy and pity, to this dear old friend ; and these feelings, mingling together at that sudden sight, drove away all others.

But now to these succeeded a new surprise, which was overwhelming. For just as she started, in obedience to her impulse; she saw Lord Chetwynde hurry forward. She saw Mrs. Hart's eyes fixed on him in a kind of ecstasy. She saw her totter forward, with all her face overspread with a joy that is but seldom known—known only in rare moments, when some lost one, loved and lost—some one more precious than life itself—is suddenly found. She saw Lord Chetwynde hurry forward. She saw Mrs. Hart run toward him, and with a low moan, a longing, yearning cry, fling herself upon his breast and clasp him in her arms.

She heard her words — words wonderful, thrilling, and beyond all understanding:

"Oh, my boy! Oh, my own! Oh, Guy! Oh, my little boy! Oh, my darling! My God! I thank Thee for this joy!"

Uttering such broken ejaculations Mrs. Hart burst into a passion of tears, and only Lord Chetwynde's strong arms prevented her from falling.

He upheld her. He kissed her. He murmured words of affection, deep and tender and true. With gentle urgency he drew her to a sofa, made her sit down by his side, and placed her head against his breast, and took her emaciated hands in his. He seemed to have forgotten the presence of others in that sudden, that overwhelming feeling of compassion for his aged, his heart-broken nurse. He was unconscious even of Zillah. In that moment his whole soul and his whole heart were turned to this wan face that leaned against his breast.

He said very little. How could he say much? A few attempts at soothing her—a few loving words—these were all. And these were enough ;

for better than these was the love that was expressed in his strong embrace—the love that sustained her now, and changed despair into rapture.

"My dearest," he said—"dearest old nurse —nurse! mamma! Don't grieve now. Come, look up, and let me see your sweet old face."

His voice was broken with emotion. How he loved that one whom he called his "dear old nurse!"

"Look up, old woman. Look up. Let me see your face. You don't know how dear it is to me."

And Mrs. Hart raised her face, and in her face he read a love infinite, all-consuming, imperishable—a love which now, however, satiated and intoxicated itself in the look that she gave.

She said nothing more, but, clinging to him, she seemed to hold him to her weary heart as though she feared that something might take him away.

"Forgive me, my own; do not be angry, my dearest," she murmured, "with your poor old nurse. I left home long, long ago. I rose from my sick-bed to seek you. I came here, and have watched and watched for a long time. Oh, how long! But you never came."

"You! watching for me! here in Florence!" exclaimed Lord Chetwynde, in wonder. "My poor old dear! why?"

"I will tell you again—not now—I am too weak. Hold my hands fast, my own. Let me see your dear face—oh, how dear!"

And with her hands in his, and her eyes feeding her soul upon his face, she lay upon his breast.

Meanwhile Obed Chute had stood thunderstruck. To account for this amazing scene was so utterly impossible that he did not even attempt it. That was beyond the reach of human capacity. But he noted all that holy tenderness, and that unfathomable love which beamed from that wan, worn face, and he felt that this was not a scene for other eyes. He went softly over to Zillah, who had stood motionless hitherto, and taking her hand he led her solemnly out of the room.

They went into another apartment, and sat there in silence. Zillah was so filled with amazement that it overwhelmed her.

She had seen Mrs. Hart's joy. She had heard her give to Windham the name of "Guy." She had heard him call her those tender, well-known names—the fond names with which the letters of Guy Molyneux used always to be filled. What did all this mean?

God in heaven! Was this a dream, or a reality? Could there, indeed, be truth in this scene? Could this be possibly what it seemed to be? Was Windham Guy Molyneux?

The question was too bewildering. A thousand circumstances at once suggested themselves as that question arose. All the past came back before her, with the scenes and the words of that past. She remembered now Windham's saying that he was married, and that he hated his wife worse than death. What did this mean? Did this not coincide with what she knew of Guy Molyneux? And what was to be the end of all this? Her brain reeled at the thoughts that came to her as she asked herself this question.

For this Windham was *hers*. Windham, with his devotion, his fervid passion, his burning words, his despairing love, his incessant self-watchfulness and strong self-control. Windham, who had snatched her from a dreadful death, and given glory and bliss to that heaven in life which she had known in Marseilles and in Florence; Windham, who had found in her society his highest happiness, and had spoken to her words of frenzied adoration; Windham, who had been the partner of so many stolen interviews; Windham, who once had flung aside even his honor and duty in his mad love, and urged her to fly with him to India! And could this man be Guy Molyneux? There were amazing coincidences which she could now recall. He had come home in mourning from India. He had told her of those very scenes in India of which she had read in Guy's letters. He had said that he was bound to a fate which he abhorred, and she recalled what had been her own conjectures as to what that fate might be.

At such thoughts as these she was filled with a mixture of deep joy and deadly fear. What might the end be? what could the end be?— this was the question now. Windham loved; Guy hated. Could these two men be indeed one? If they were, then how could this love and hate be reconciled? Would Windham cease to love, or Guy give up his hate? To her, also, there was still terror in the thought of Guy; and for Windham to be resolved into that man, from whom she had fled, seemed to her as though he were about to become her enemy. Yet this did not seem possible. Such confidence had she in Windham's love that the thought of his losing it, or changing, appeared the wildest improbability. No; that, at least, could not be. Still he was her own. Not yet could she blend his image with that of Guy. In her bewilderment she clung to this as her only comfort, and hoped that, in some way, all this would be explained.

Meanwhile Obed had been sitting in a bewilderment equal to hers, and keeping a silence that was hard to maintain. At length he could restrain his feelings no longer.

"Can you tell," he asked at length—"can you imagine, Miss Lorton—have you the remotest idea of what in thunder is the meaning of all this?"

"I don't know," said Zillah; "I don't understand; I can't even imagine."

"And I'm—well," interposed Obed, with a blank look of despair, "the English language does not afford a word, not one single word, that can express the idea; so I will resort to the American, and merely remark that at this present moment I'm catawampously chawed up."

"Do you know Mrs. Hart?" said Zillah.

"Of course you do."

"Mrs. Hart?" asked Obed, in momentary surprise.

"Yes—her."

"Mrs. Hart? Oh, I see. Yes, I knew her many years ago. This afternoon I found her in Florence. I brought her out here. She told me that she had come here in search of a friend; but, by the living thunder, the very last person that I should have guessed at as that friend would have been Windham. And yet he was the man —the identical individual. But did you ever see such joy," he continued, after a pause, "as there was in her face at her first sight of him? Well, when I met her she was in as deep a despair. She was crouching on the steps of the Baptistery, looking with eager eyes—hungry eyes—to find some one. And all this time it was Windham. She came here to find him, and him only. She has been here for weeks, perhaps for months, wandering about, in suffering and weakness, looking every where for Windham. She had spent all her money; she had been turned out of her lodgings; she had neither food nor shelter. For two or three days she had not eaten any thing. When I happened, by the merest accident, to find her, do you know what she was doing? She was dying of starvation, but still she was looking for Windham. And I solemnly believe that if I had not found her she would be there at this moment. Yes, she would be sitting there in misery, in want, and in starvation, still looking after Windham. And if she had died there, on that spot, I feel convinced that the last movement of her lips would have been a murmur of his name, and the last look of her dying eyes would have been for Windham. I saw all this in every look of hers, and in every word of hers that she has thus far uttered to me about her fearful experiences. I saw this; and now I beg leave to ask, in the quietest way in the world, Who is this Windham, and what is he to her?"

Here Obed ceased. He had spoken in a way that showed the deep emotion which he felt, and the sorrow and sympathy that filled his soul. As he spoke of Mrs. Hart's miseries his voice trembled. Never in his life had he met with sorrow like sorrow. It was not this last scene in her life which gave him this feeling, but it was his knowledge of that awful past in which she had lived, and sinned, and suffered—that past whose sufferings were perpetuated still, whose lurid shadows were now projected into these later days of her life. All this he felt, and he showed it, and he sought earnestly to solve the problem which these things held out to his mind; but he could not find a solution, nor could Zillah give one. For her part, it was with unfeigned horror that she listened to Obed's recital of Mrs. Hart's sufferings and despair; yet as she listened there came to her mind the same question which had been asked by Obed, Who is this Windham? and what is he to her? Could her old devotion as the nurse of Guy account for this? Or was there some deeper cause? Had she come to save him from something? Yet from what? From danger? Yet from what danger?

And thus to each of these alike there came the same problem, yet to each there came no hope of solution.

CHAPTER LXXV.

DESPAIR.

THE time seemed long indeed to Obed and to Zillah, as they sat there in silence, wondering, bewildered, yet utterly unable to fathom the deep mystery that lay before them. Half an hour elapsed; and at last some one crossed the hall and came to the door. It was Lord Chetwynde. He looked troubled and excited.

"Miss Lorton," said he, "she wants you. I don't understand what she says. It is very strange. She must be out of her senses. Come

in, Mr. Chute. See if you can help me out of my bewilderment."

He offered his arm to Zillah, but she did not take it. It seemed as if she did not see it. Filled with vague fears and apprehensions, she walked into the room where Mrs. Hart was, and Lord Chetwynde and Obed Chute came after her.

Mrs. Hart was lying upon the sofa. As Zillah entered she fixed her eyes upon her.

"I have been too selfish," said she. "In my joy at finding my boy so unexpectedly and so wonderfully, I have not been able to speak one word to my sweet girl. Oh, Zillah, my child, you, I know, will forgive me. But are you not amazed to see me? Yet I am still more amazed to see you. How did you come here? How is it that I find you here—along with my noble friend—in his house? I am all overcome with wonder. I can not understand this. I do not know what to say, or where to begin to ask the questions that I wish to ask. Mr. Chute seems a kind of Providence," she added, with peculiar emphasis in the faint tones of her weak voice—"a kind of Providence, who comes to people in their last extremities, and saves them from despair! Mr. Chute," she continued, "is my savior!" She paused for a time, and looked at Obed with a certain deep meaning in her eyes. Then she turned to Zillah again. "My child," she said, "dear, sweet Zillah! you will have to tell me all about this. Why was it that you fled away from Chetwynde? And oh! how could you have the heart to give me up to strangers?"

Amazed, speechless, overcome by wonder, Zillah could not say a word. She went to Mrs. Hart, folded her in her arms, and kissed over and over again the white lips of the woman who had once been dear to her in Chetwynde Castle.

"I do not understand it," said Mrs. Hart, feebly, and with an expression of deep amazement; "I do not comprehend all this at all. Here you all are, all of you whom I love—the only ones on earth whom I love. Here is my boy, my darling, whom I came to seek! Here is my sweet Zillah, who brightened my mournful life at Chetwynde Castle with her love and tenderness. And here I see my best friend, who came to save me from death and despair, and brought me here to life and joy and hope! What is the meaning of it all? My boy can not tell me. Say, my sweet Zillah, can not you tell me? Do you not know? Do you understand? Say, whose plan is it? Is it your plan? Who has brought us all together?"

"It is God," said Zillah, solemnly. "I do not understand how you came here. Let us thank God that you have found your friends."

She spoke at random; she knew not what to say. In her own dark perplexity she was unable to say any thing else; and when she saw that Mrs. Hart was equally perplexed, and turned to her for information, she could only find an answer in those words which were prompted by her heart. So she spoke, and she could say no more.

Nor could the others. All were silent. That white face looked wistfully from one to the other, with eager eyes, as though seeking from each some explanation; but none could give her that which she sought. In the faces that surrounded her she saw nothing else but a wonder which was fully equal to her own.

Obed Chute had now a fresh cause for bewilderment. For here was Zillah claimed fondly as a dear and loved friend by Mrs. Hart. Who was she? Was her mysterious story bound up in any way with the tragical life of the other who thus claimed her? He had been sufficiently astonished at the meeting between the woman whom he had rescued and his friend Windham; but now he saw his protégé, Miss Lorton, recognized by her as her dearest friend, and called by the most loving names—with an affection, too, which was fully returned by the one whom she thus addressed. What to think or to say he knew not. Of all the mysteries of which he had ever heard none equaled this, and it seemed to become more complicated every instant. He was at once perplexed by this insoluble problem, and vexed because it was insoluble. To his calm and straightforward mind nothing was so aggravating as a puzzle which could not be explained. He abhorred all mysteries. Yet here he found one full before him which baffled his utmost powers of comprehension—one, too, in which he himself was intermixed, and in which he saw Mrs. Hart and Windham and Miss Lorton all equally involved, and what was worse, equally in the dark.

But if Obed's bewilderment was great, what can be said of that which filled the mind of Lord Chetwynde? He saw his old nurse, whom he so deeply and even so passionately loved, turning away from himself to clasp in her arms, and to greet with the fondest affection, that beautiful girl who was dearer to him than any thing else in life. Mrs. Hart knew Miss Lorton! Above all, he was struck by the name which she gave her. She called her "Zillah!" More than this, she mentioned Chetwynde! She reproached this girl for running away from Chetwynde Castle! And to all this Miss Lorton said nothing, but accepted these reproaches in such a way that she made it seem as though she herself must once in very deed have lived in Chetwynde Castle, and fled from it. Mrs. Hart called her "Zillah!" To whom did that strange name belong? To one, and to one alone. That one was the daughter of General Pomeroy, whom he had married, and who was now his wife. That one he hated with a hate which no feeling of duty and no bond of gratitude could either lessen or overcome. Was he not married? Had he not seen that wife of his a thousand times? Had he not associated with her at Chetwynde Castle, at Lausanne, on the road, and in Florence? What madness, what mockery was this? It would seem as though Mrs. Hart had mistaken Miss Lorton for that detested wife who stood between him and his love. But how could such a mistake he made? True, the complexion of each was dark, and the hair of each was black, and the forms and figures were not unlike; but the features were widely different; the large, soft, loving eyes of Miss Lorton were not like those gleaming, fiery orbs that he had seen in the woman whom he thought his wife; and the expression of the face in each was as unlike as possible. Could Mrs. Hart be in a delirium? She must be mad! But then the worst of it was, that if she were mad Miss Lorton must be mad also.

"Where am I?" said Mrs. Hart, rousing herself, and breaking in upon Lord Chetwynde's thoughts. "It seems to me that I have suddenly escaped from a hell, where I have been living, and have come into heaven. Where am I? How is it that I find myself among those whom I hold most dear? Oh, my old friend! my savior! my benefactor! tell me, are you really a living being?"

"Nothing shorter," replied Obed, solemnly, "to the best of my knowledge and belief, though at the present moment I feel inclined to doubt it."

"My boy, give me your hand. Do I really hold it? Am I not dreaming?"

"No, my dear old nurse. I am really alive, and you are alive, and I am really your boy—your Guy—though hang me if I understand all this!"

"Zillah, my sweet child, give me your hand too. You have become reconciled to him, then. I see how it is. Ah! how dear you are to one another! My God! what blessedness is this! And yet I thought that you had fled from him, and left him forever. But he found you. You are reunited once more."

She placed Zillah's hand in Lord Chetwynde's, and Lord Chetwynde held it closely, firmly, in a passionate grasp, not knowing what all this meant, yet in his vehement love willing to take blindly all that might be given to him, even though it came to him through the delirium of his old nurse. He held it tightly, though Zillah in a kind of terror tried to withdraw it. He held it, for something gave him in the midst of his bewilderment that it was his.

Tears flowed from Mrs. Hart's eyes. There was a deep silence around. At last Obed Chute spoke.

"My Christian friends," said he, "it's been my lot and my privilege to attend the theatre in my youthful days, and I've often seen what they call situations; but of all the unparalleled situations that were ever put upon the boards, from '76 down to '59, I'll be hanged if this isn't the greatest, the grandest, and the most bewildering. I'm floored. I give up. Henceforth Obed Chute exists no longer. He is dead. Hic jacet. In memoriam. E pluribus unum. You may be Mr. Windham, and you, my child, may be Miss Lorton, or you may not. You may be somebody else. We may all be somebody else. I'm somebody else. I'll be hanged if I'm myself. To my dying day I don't expect to understand this. Don't try to explain it, I beg. If you do I shall go mad. The only thing I do understand just now is this, that our friend Mrs. Hart is very weak, and needs rest, and rest she shall accordingly have. Come," he continued, turning to her; "you will have time to-morrow to see them again. Take a little rest now. You have called me your friend several times to-day. I claim a friend's privilege. You must lie down by yourself, if it's only for half an hour. Don't refuse me. I'd do as much for you."

Obed's manner showed that same tender compassion which he had already evinced. Mrs. Hart complied with his request. She rose and took his arm.

"Tell me one thing plainly," said Obed, as Mrs. Hart stood up. "Who are these? Is not this Mr. Windham, and is not this Miss Lorton? If not, who are they? That's fair, I think. I don't want to be in the dark amidst such universal light."

"Is it possible that you don't know?" said Mrs. Hart, wonderingly. "Why should they conceal it from you? These are my dearest children—my friends—the ones dear to my heart. Oh, my friend, you will understand me. This is Lord Chetwynde, son of the Earl of Chetwynde, and this girl is Zillah, daughter of Neville Pomeroy—Lady Chetwynde—his wife."

"God in heaven!" exclaimed Obed Chute. "Is this so, or are you mad, and are they mad?"

"I do not know what you mean," said Mrs. Hart. "I have spoken the truth. It is so."

Obed said not another word, but led her out of the room, with his strong brain in a state of bewilderment greater than ever, and surpassing any thing that he had known before.

Lord Chetwynde was left alone with Zillah, holding her hand, to which he still clung—though Zillah in her deep embarrassment tried to withdraw it—and looking at her with eagerness yet perplexity.

"Great Heaven!" he cried. "Do you understand this? Oh, my love! my own! my darling! What is the meaning of it all?"

"I don't know," stammered Zillah, in confusion. "Don't you know?"

"It's a mockery. It's her delirium," cried Lord Chetwynde, passionately. "Some tantalizing demon has put this into her wandering mind. But oh! my dearest, something must be true; at least you know her before."

"Yes," said Zillah.

"Where?" cried Lord Chetwynde.

"At Chetwynde Castle," said Zillah, faintly.

"At Chetwynde Castle?"

"Yes."

"Oh, Heavens! Chetwynde Castle! What is this? Can it be a mockery? What does it all mean? You! you! You of all others! my own! my darling! You can never deceive me," he cried, in piercing tones. "Tell me, and tell me truly, what were you doing in Chetwynde Castle?"

"Living there," said Zillah. "I lived there for years, till the Earl died, and then I left, for certain reasons."

"Great God! What is it that you are saying?" He gasped for breath.

"Only the truth," said Zillah.

Lord Chetwynde held her hand still; his eyes seemed to devour her in the intensity of their gaze. A thousand bewildering questions were in his mind. What! Was not his wife even now in Florence? Was he not familiar with her face? What did this mean? What utter mockery was this! Yet every word of Zillah's went to corroborate the words of Mrs. Hart.

As for Zillah, she saw his embarrassment, but interpreted it falsely. "He is beginning to think," she thought, "that I am the one to whom he was married. His old hate and abhorrence are returning. He is afraid to make himself sure of it. He loves Miss Lorton, but hates the daughter of General Pomeroy. When he finds out who I am he will loathe me." Then while Lord Chetwynde stood silent in astonishment and bewilderment, not understanding how it was possible for these things to be, the thought flashed upon her mind about that last letter. He had loved another. Inez Cameron was his true love.

She herself was nothing. Bitterly came this remembrance to her mind. She saw herself now cast out from his heart, and the love that had awakened would die out forever. And in that moment, as these thoughts rushed through her mind, as she recalled the words of that last letter, the scorn and insults that were heaped upon herself, and, above all, the fervent love that was expressed for another—as she brought these things back which had once been so bitter, one by one —hope departed, and despair settled over her heart.

But Lord Chetwynde clung to her hand. The thoughts of his heart were widely different from those of hers, and her despair was exceeded by his own. Who she was and what she was he could not understand; but the thought that he had a wife, and that his wife was General Pomeroy's daughter, was immovable in his mind.

"My darling!" he cried, in imploring tones, in which there was at the same time a world of love and tenderness; "my own darling! You know well that for you I would give up all my life and all my hope, and every thing that I have. For you, oh! my sweet love, I have trampled upon honor and duty, and have turned my back upon the holy memories of my father! For you I have stifled my conscience and denied my God! Oh! my own, my only love, listen and answer. In the name of God, and by all your hopes of heaven, I implore you to answer me truly this one question. Who are you? What is your name? How is it that Mrs. Hart has made this mistake?"

And as Lord Chetwynde gave utterance to this appeal there was in his voice an anguish of entreaty, as though his very life hung upon her answer. It thrilled to the inmost soul of Zillah, who herself was wrought up to an excitement which was equal to his, if not superior.

"Mrs. Hart has made no mistake," replied Zillah, in low, solemn tones; "she has spoken the truth. As you have asked, so must I answer. In the name of God, then, I tell you, Lord Chetwynde, that I am Zillah, daughter of General Pomeroy, and—your wife!"

"Oh, my God!" cried Lord Chetwynde, with a deep groan.

He dropped her hand. He staggered back, and looked at her with a face in which there was nothing else than horror.

What was then in his mind Zillah could not possibly know. She therefore interpreted that look of his from her own knowledge and suspicions only. She read in it only his own unconquerable hate, his invincible aversion to her, which now, at the mention of her true name, had revived in all its original force, and destroyed utterly the love which he had professed. All was lost! lost! lost! lost! and doubly lost! Better far never to have seen him than, having seen him and known him and loved him, to lose him thus. Such were her thoughts. Already her emotion had been overwhelming; this was the last, and it was too much. With a low moan of entreaty and of despair she wailed out the name which she loved so much. It was that word "Windham," which he had made so sweet to her.

Saying this, and with that moan of despair, she threw up her arms wildly, and sank down senseless at his feet.

CHAPTER LXXVI.

HILDA'S LAST VENTURE.

WHEN Obed Chute came back he found Lord Chetwynde holding Zillah in his arms, pressing her to his heart, and looking wildly around with a face of agony. "Quick! quick!" he cried. "Water, for God's sake! She's fainted! She's dying! Quick!"

In a moment a dozen servants were summoned, and Zillah was plied with restoratives till she revived again. She came back to sense and to life, but hope was dead within her; and even the sight of Lord Chetwynde's face of agony, and his half-frantic words, could not lessen her despair. She implored to be carried to her room, and there she was at once taken. Lord Chetwynde's anguish was now not less than hers. With bitter self-reproach, and in terrible bewilderment, he wandered off into the west gallery, whither Obed Chute followed him, but, seeing his agitation, refrained from saying any thing. Lord Chetwynde was lost in an abyss of despair. In the midst of his agony for Zillah's sake he tried in vain to comprehend how this Miss Lorton could believe herself to be General Pomeroy's daughter and his own wife, when, as he very well knew, his own wife was at her lodgings in Florence—that wife whom he hated, but who yet had saved him from death in Switzerland, and was now living on his smiles in Italy. How could one like Miss Lorton make such a mistake? Or how could she violate all delicacy by asserting such a thing? Clearly somebody was mad. Perhaps he himself was mad. But as he felt himself to be in his sober senses, and not dreaming, he tried to think whether madness should be attributed to Mrs. Hart or Miss Lorton, on the one hand, or to his wife on the other. The problem was insoluble. Madness, he thought, must certainly be somewhere. But where? All seemed to be concerned. Mrs. Hart had recognized Miss Lorton, and Miss Lorton had returned that recognition. Somebody must be fearfully mistaken. What was to be done? In the midst of this his whole being thrilled at the recollection of those words in which Miss Lorton had claimed to be his wife. *His wife!* And she must herself have believed this at the time; otherwise she would have died rather than have uttered those words. But what would his real wife say to all this? That was his final thought.

Meanwhile Obed Chute said not a word. He saw Lord Chetwynde's emotion, and, with his usual delicacy of feeling, did not intrude upon him at such a time, though himself filled with undiminished wonder. The first excitement was over, certainly, yet the wonder remained none the less; and while Lord Chetwynde was pacing the long gallery restlessly and wildly, Obed sat meditative, pondering upon the possibilities of things. Yet the more he thought the less was he able to unravel these mysteries.

At last he thought that a walk outside would be better. A quiet smoke would assist meditation. His brain could always work more promptly when a pipe was in his mouth. He therefore went off to prepare this invaluable companion for the walk which he designed, and was even filling his pipe, when he was aroused by the entrance of a servant, who announced that a lady had just arrived, and wished to see him on very particular business. Saying this, the servant handed him her card. Obed looked at it, and read the following name:

"*Lady Chetwynde.*"

CHAPTER LXXVII.

THE CRYPTOGRAM DECIPHERED.

HITHERTO, and up to that last moment just spoken of, this whole affair had been one long puzzle to Obed, one, too, which was exceedingly unpleasant and utterly incomprehensible. While Lord Chetwynde had been pacing the gallery in a fever of agitation, Obed had been a prey to thoughts less intense and less painful, no doubt, but yet equally perplexing. He had been summing up in his mind the general outlines of this grand mystery, and the results were something like this:

First, there was the fact that these three were all old friends, or, at least, that two of them were equally dear to Mrs. Hart.

Secondly, that on the appearance of Mrs. Hart each was unable to account for the emotion of the other.

Thirdly, that Miss Lorton and Windham had been living under assumed names ever since he had known them.

Fourthly, that Miss Lorton and Windham had hitherto been uncommonly fond of one another's society.

Fifthly, that this was not surprising, since Windham had saved Miss Lorton from a frightful death.

Sixthly, what? Why this, that Mrs. Hart had solemnly declared that Windham was not Windham at all, but Guy Molyneux, son of the late Earl of Chetwynde; and that Miss Lorton was not Miss Lorton, but Zillah, daughter of Neville Pomeroy, and wife of Lord Chetwynde!

The Earl of Chetwynde! Neville Pomeroy! Did any of these, except Mrs. Hart, know, did they have the remotest suspicion of the profound meaning which these names had to Obed Chute? Did they know or suspect? Know or suspect? Why, they evidently knew nothing, and suspected nothing! Had they not been warm friends—or something more, as Obed now began to think—for months, while neither one knew the other as any thing else than that which was assumed?

It was a puzzle.

It was something that required an uncommon exercise of brain. Such an exercise demanded also an uncommon stimulus to that brain; and therefore Obed had gone up for his pipe. It was while preparing this that the card had come. "Lady Chetwynde!"

His first impulse was to give a long, low whistle. After this he arose in silence and went down to the chief room. A lady was sitting there, who rose as he entered. Obed bowed low and looked at her earnestly as he seated himself.

"I hope, Sir," said the lady, in a clear, musical voice, "that you will excuse the liberty which I have taken; but the object that brings me here is one of such importance that I have been compelled to come in person. It was only of late that I learned that you were residing here, and as soon as I heard it I came to see you."

Obed Chute bowed again, but said not a word.

His bewilderment was yet strong, and he did not wish to commit himself. This lady was beautiful, and graceful in her manner. She called herself Lady Chetwynde. The name puzzled him, and, in addition to the other puzzle that had visited him on this eventful day, was hard to be borne. But he bore it bravely, and was silent. In his silence he regarded his visitor with the closest scrutiny. At the first glance he had marked her beauty. A further observation showed that she was agitated, that she was pale, and bore marks of suffering. She was a woman in distress. In the midst of Obed's perplexity the discovery of this aroused his chivalrous sympathy.

This was Hilda's last venture, and she felt it to be such. She had come out with the expectation of finding Gualtier on the road, and of receiving some message from him. She had seen nothing of him. She had waited about half an hour on the road, till she could wait no longer, and then she had gone onward. She thought that Gualtier might have failed her, but such a thing seemed so improbable that she began to fear some disaster. Perhaps he had fallen a victim to his devotion. The thought of this troubled her, and increased her agitation; and now, when she found herself in the presence of Obed Chute, her agitation was so marked as to be visible to him. Yet, as far as he was concerned, this agitation only served to favor her cause in his eyes.

"Mr. Chute," said Hilda, in low, steady tones, "I am Lady Chetwynde. I am the daughter of General Pomeroy, once Captain Pomeroy, whom you knew. He died a few years ago, and on his death-bed arranged a marriage between me and the only son of the Earl of Chetwynde. It was a sudden marriage. He insisted on it. He was dying, and his wishes could not be denied. I yielded, and was married. My husband left me immediately after the marriage ceremony, and went to India, where he remained for years. He only returned a short time ago. My father, General Pomeroy, died, and the Earl of Chetwynde took me to live with him. I lived with him for years. I was a daughter to him, and he loved me as one. He died in my arms. I was alone in the world till his son, the young Earl, came home. Pardon me for mentioning these family details, but they are necessary in order to explain my position and to prepare the way for those things which I have to say."

Hilda paused for a while. Obed said nothing, but listened with an unchanged face.

"Not long after my father's death," said Hilda, "I went to pay a visit to my old home, Pomeroy Court. I happened to look into my father's desk one day, and there I found some papers. One of them was a writing in cipher, and the rest consisted of letters written by one who signed himself Obed Chute, and who wrote from New York. All related to the wife of the Earl."

Hilda stopped again, and waited to see the effect of this. But Obed said nothing, nor could she see in his face any indication of any emotion whatever.

"That writing in cipher," she continued, "disturbed me. The letters were of such a character that they filled me with uneasiness, and I thought that the writing in cipher would explain all. I therefore tried to decipher it. I obtained books on the subject, and studied up the way by which such things may be unraveled. I applied myself to this task for months, and at last succeeded in my object. I never felt certain, however, that I had deciphered it rightly, nor do I yet feel certain; but what I did find out had a remarkable connection with the letters which accompanied it, and increased the alarm which I felt. Then I tried to find out about you, but could not. You alone, I thought, could explain this mystery. It was a thing which filled me with horror. I can not tell you how awful were the fears that arose, and how intolerable were the suspicions. But I could never get any explanation. Now these things have never ceased to trouble me, and they always will until they are explained.

"Yesterday I happened to hear your name mentioned. It startled me. I made inquiries, and found that a person 'who bore that name which was so familiar to me, and about which I had made such inquiries—Obed Chute—was living here. I at once resolved to come out and see you in person, so as to ask you what it all means, and put an end, in some way or other, to my suspense."

This recital produced a strong effect on Obed, yet no expression of his face told whether that effect was favorable or unfavorable. Earnestly Hilda watched his face as she spoke, so as to read if possible her fate, yet she found it impossible. His face remained stolid and impassive, though she saw this much, that he was listening to her with the deepest attention. What was most perplexing was the fact that Obed did not say one single word.

In fact, in this position, he did not know what to say. So he did the very best thing that he could, and said nothing. But the mystery that had begun that day with the advent of Mrs. Hart was certainly deepening. It was already unfathomable when Mrs. Hart had said that Zillah was Lady Chetwynde, and that Windham was Lord Chetwynde. Here, however, came one who made it still more hopelessly and inextricably entangled by calmly announcing herself as Lady Chetwynde; and not only so, but adding to it an account of her life. Which was the true one? Mrs. Hart could not lie. She did not seem to be insane. About Zillah there had certainly been a mystery, but she could not deceive. He began to have vague ideas that Lord Chetwynde's morals had become affected by his Indian life, and that he had a great number of wives; but then he remembered that this woman claimed to be General Pomeroy's daughter, which Mrs. Hart had also said of Zillah. So the problem was as dark as ever. He began to see that he was incapable of dealing with this subject, and that Mrs. Hart alone could explain.

Hilda, after some delay, went on:

"I have mentioned my attempt to discover the cipher writing," said she. "My deciphering was such that it seemed to involve my father in a very heavy charge. It made me think that he had been guilty of some awful crime."

"Your father, General Pomeroy?"

Obed Chute uttered this suddenly, and with deep surprise.

Hilda started, and then said, very placidly, "Yes."

"And you thought that he might be guilty of 'awful crimes?'"

"I feared so."

"Had you lived any time with your father?"

"All my life."

Obed Chute said nothing more, though Hilda seemed to expect it; so, finding him silent, she went on without regarding him; though, if she had known this man, she would have seen that by those words she at once lost all that sympathy and consideration which thus far he had felt for her.

"On deciphering that paper of which I have spoken I found that it charged my father, General Pomeroy, with several crimes, all equally abhorrent. I will show you the paper itself, and my interpretation of it line by line, so that you may see for yourself the agony that such a discovery would naturally produce in the mind of a daughter. I will also show you those letters which you yourself wrote to my father many years ago."

Saying this, Hilda produced some papers, which she laid on the table before Obed Chute.

The first was the writing in cipher.

The second was her own interpretation, such as she had already shown to Gualtier and to Zillah.

The third was the same thing, written out line by line for the sake of legibility, as follows:

Oh may God have mercy on my wretched soul A men
O Pomeroy forged a hundred thousand dollars
O N Pomeroy eloped with poor Lady Chetwynde
She acted out of a mad impulse in flying
She listened to me and ran off with me
She was piqued at her husband's act
Fell in with Lady Mary Chetwynde
Expelled the army for gaming
N Pomeroy of Pomeroy Berks
O I am a miserable villain

Along with these she put down a paper which contained her key for deciphering this.

Finally she laid down those letters written by Obed Chute, which have already been given.

All those Obed Chute examined carefully. The cipher writing he looked at, compared it with the key, and then with the interpretation written by Hilda. As she looked anxiously at his face it struck her that when he took up that cipher writing it seemed as though he was familiar with it. For such a thing she was not unprepared. Obed Chute's connection with this business was mysterious to her, but it had been of such a nature that he might be able to read this paper, and know the fullness of its meaning. After reading those letters which had been written by himself—among which, however, that latest letter which Hilda had shown Zillah was not to be seen—he took up that second paper in which she had carefully written out in capitals the meaning of each line, such as has already been given, where the line is extended by characters which are not interpreted. Over this he looked long and carefully, frequently comparing it with the first paper, which contained only the cipher itself.

At length he laid down the papers and looked Hilda full in the face.

"Did it ever strike you," he asked, "that your translation was slightly rambling, and a little incoherent?"

"I have hoped that it was," said Hilda, pathetically.

"You may be assured of it," said Obed. "Read it for yourself, and think for a moment whether any human being would think of writing such stuff as that." And he motioned contemptuously to the paper where her interpretation was written out. "There's no meaning in it except this, which I have now noticed for the first time—that the miserable scoundrel who wrote this has done it so as to throw suspicion upon the man whom he was bound to love with all his contemptible heart, if he had one, which he hadn't. I see now. The infernal sneak!"

And Obed, glaring at the paper, actually ground his teeth in rage. At length he looked up, and calmly said:

"Madam, it happens that in this interpretation of yours you are totally and utterly astray. In your deep love for your father"—and here Hilda imagined a sneer—"you will be rejoiced to learn this. This cipher is an old acquaintance. I unraveled it all many years ago—almost before you were born, certainly before you ever thought of ciphers. I have all the papers by me. You couldn't have come to a better person than me—in fact, I'm the only person, I suppose, that you could come to. I will therefore explain the whole matter, so that for the rest of your life your affectionate and guileless nature may no longer be disturbed by those lamentable suspicions which you have cultivated about the noblest gentleman and most stainless soldier that ever breathed."

With these words he left the room, and shortly returned with some papers. These he spread before Hilda.

One was the cipher itself—a fac-simile of her own. The next was a mass of letters, written out in capitals on a square block. Every cipher was written out here in its Roman equivalent.

As he spread this out Obed showed her the true character of it.

"You have mistaken it," he said. "In the cipher there is a double alphabet. The upper half is written in the first, the lower half in the second. The second alphabet has most of the letters of the first; those of most frequent occurrence are changed, and instead of astronomical signs, punctuation marks are used. You have succeeded, I see, in finding the key to the upper part, but you do not seem to have thought that the lower part required a separate examination. You seem to suppose that all this mass of letters is unmeaning, and was inserted by way of recreation to the mind that was wearied with writing the first, or perhaps to mislead. Now if you had read it all you would have seen the entire truth. The man that wrote this was a villain: he has written it so that the upper part throws suspicion upon his benefactor. Whether he did this by accident or on purpose the Lord only knows. But, to my personal knowledge, he was about the meanest, smallest, sneakin'est rascal that it was ever my luck to light on. And yet he knew what honor was, and duty, for he had associated all his life with the noblest gentleman that ever lived. But I will say no more about it. See! Here is the full translation of the whole thing."

And he laid down before Hilda another paper, which was written out in the usual manner.

"If you look at the first paper," said Obed, pointing to the one which gave the translation of each letter, above described, "you will see that the first part reads like your translation, while the lower part has no meaning. This arose from the peculiar nature of the man who wrote it. He couldn't do any thing straight. When he made a confession he wrote it in cipher. When he wrote in cipher he wrote it so as to puzzle and mislead any one who might try to find it out. He couldn't write even a cipher straight, but began in the middle and wound all his letters about it. Do you see that letter 'M' in the eleventh line, the twelfth one from the right side, with a cross by the side of it? That is the first letter. You must read from that, but toward the left, for seventeen letters, and then follow on the line immediately above it. The writing then runs on, and winds about this central line till this rectangular block of letters is formed. You supposed that it read on like ordinary writing. You see what you have found out is only those lines that happened to be the top ones, reading in the usual way from left to right. Now take this first paper. Begin at that cross, read from right to left for seventeen letters, and what do you find?"

Hilda did so, and slowly spelled out this: "'MY NAME IS NOT KRIEFF.'"

A shock of astonishment passed through her.

"Krieff?" she repeated—"Krieff?"

"Yes, Krieff," said Obed; "that was his last alias."

"Alias? Krieff?" faltered Hilda.

"Yes. He had one or two others, but this was his last."

"His? Whose? Who is it, then, that wrote this?"

"Read on. But it is not worth while to bother with this block of letters. See; I have this paper where it is all written out. Read this;" and he handed the other paper to Hilda.

She took it mechanically, and read as follows:

"My name is not Krieff. I am a miserable villain, but I was once named Pemberton Pomeroy, of Pomeroy, Berks. I fell into vice early in life, and was expelled the army for gaming. I changed my name then to Redfield Lyttoun. I fell in with Lady Mary Chetwynde. She was thoughtless, and liked my attentions. I knew she was piqued at her husband's act in leaving his party and losing his prospects. Out of spite she listened to me and ran off with me. Neville followed us and rescued her from me before it was too late. She acted out of a mad impulse in flying, and repented bitterly. My brother saved her. Let all know that I, Pemberton Pomeroy, eloped with poor Lady Chetwynde, and that she was saved by Neville Pomeroy. Let the world know, too, that I, Pemberton Pomeroy, forged a hundred thousand dollars, and my brother paid it, and saved me. I write this in cipher, and am a villain and a coward too.

"Oh, may God have mercy on my wretched soul! 'Amen.'"

On reading this Hilda then compared it with the other paper. She saw at once that the lines which she had translated were only fragmentary portions that happened to read from left to right. Doubt was impossible, and this which Obed Chute gave her was the truth. She laid the paper down, and looked thoughtfully away. There were several things here which disturbed her, but above all there was the name mentioned at the outset. For she saw that the man who had written this had once gone by the name of Krieff.

"I think it my duty," said Obed Chute, "to give you a full explanation, since you have asked it. The parties concerned are now all dead, and you claim to be the daughter of one of them. There is therefore no reason why I should not tell you all that I know. I have made up my mind to do so, and I will.

"Neville Pomeroy, then, was an English gentleman. I have seen much of Britishers, and have generally found that in a time of trial the English gentleman comes out uncommonly strong. I got acquainted with him in an odd kind of way. He was a young fellow, and had come out to America to hunt buffaloes. I happened to be on the Plains at the same time. I was out for a small excursion, for the office at New York was not the kind of place where a fellow of my size could be content all the time. We heard a great row—guns firing, Indians yelling, and conjectured that the savages were attacking some party or other. We dashed on for a mile or two, and came to a hollow. About fifty rascally Sioux were there. They had surrounded two or three whites, and captured them, and were preparing to strip each for the purpose of indulging in a little amusement they have—that is, building a fire on one's breast. They didn't do it that time, at any rate; and the fight that followed when we came up was the prettiest, without exception, that I ever saw. We drove them off, at any rate; and as we had revolvers, and they had only common rifles, we had it all our own way. Thirty of those Sioux devils were left behind, dead and wounded, and the rest vamosed.

"This was my first introduction to Neville Pomeroy. I cut his bonds first, and then introduced myself. He had no clothes on, but was as courteous as though he was dressed in the latest Fifth Avenue fashion. We soon understood one another. I found him as plucky as the devil, and as tough and true as steel. He seemed to like me, and we kept together on the prairies for three months—fighting, hunting, starving, stuffing, and enjoying life generally. He came with me to New York, and stopped with me. I was a broker and banker. Don't look

like one, I know; but I was, and am. The American broker is a different animal from the broker of Europe. So is the American banker, one of whom you see before you.

"I won't say any thing more about our personal affairs. We became sworn friends. He went back home, and I took to the desk. Somehow we kept writing to one another. He heard of great investments in America, and got me to buy stock for him. He was rich, and soon had a large amount of money in my hands. I got the best investments for him there were, and was glad to do any thing for a man like that.

"I'll now go on straight and tell you all that you care to hear. Some of this—in fact, most of it—I did not find out till long afterward.

"Neville Pomeroy then had a younger brother, named Pemberton Pomeroy. He was an officer in the Guards. He was very dissipated, and soon got head over heels in debt. Neville had done all that he could for his brother, and had paid off his debts three times, each time saving him from ruin. But it was no use. There was the very devil himself in Pemberton. He was by nature one of the meanest rascals that was ever created, though the fellow was not bad-looking. He got deeper and deeper into the mire, and at last got into a scrape so bad, so dirty, that he had to quit the Guards. It was a gambling affair of so infamous a character that it was impossible for his brother to save him. So he quit the Guards, and went into worse courses than ever. Neville tried still to save him; he wanted to get him an office, but Pemberton refused. Meanwhile, out of a sense of decency, he had changed his name to that of Redfield Lyttoun, and under this name he became pretty well known to a new circle of friends. Under this name he made the acquaintance of the wife of the Earl of Chetwynde. It seems that the Earl was wrapped up in politics, and had offended her by giving up a great office which he held rather than act dishonorably. She was angry, and grew desperate. Redfield Lyttoun turned up, and amused her. She compromised herself very seriously by allowing such marked attentions from him, and people began to talk about them. The Earl knew nothing at all about this, as he was busy all the day. There was a sort of quarrel between them, and all her doings were quite unknown. But Neville heard of it, and made a final attempt to save his brother. I think this time he was actuated rather by regard for the Earl, who was his most intimate friend, than by any hope of saving this wretched fool of a brother of his. At any rate, he warned him, and threatened to tell the Earl himself of all that was going on. Pemberton took alarm, and pretended that he would do as Neville said. He promised to give up Lady Chetwynde. But his brother's advice had only made him savage, and he determined to carry out this game to the end. He was desperate, reckless, and utterly unprincipled. Lady Chetwynde was silly and thoughtless. She liked the scoundrel, too, I suppose. At any rate, he induced her to run away with him. For the sake of getting funds to live on he forged some drafts. He found out that Neville had money in my hands, and drew for this. I suspected nothing, and the drafts were paid. He got the money in time to run off with his victim. Silly and foolish as Lady Chetwynde was, the moment that she had taken the inevitable step she repented. She thought that it would be impossible to retrace it, and gave herself up to despair. They fled to America under assumed names.

"Their flight was immediately known to Neville. He lost not a moment, but hurried out to America; and as the ship in which he sailed was faster than the other, he reached New York first. He came at once to me. Then he learned, for the first time, of the forgery. About one hundred thousand dollars had been drawn and paid. We took counsel together, and watched for the arrival of the steamer. Immediately on its being reported in the bay we boarded her, and Pemberton Pomeroy was arrested. He was taken to prison, and Neville induced Lady Chetwynde to come with us. I offered my house. This privacy was a most important thing. She had been freed from Pemberton's clutches, and Neville showed her that it was possible for her to escape yet from complete infamy. The suddenness of this termination to their plan startled her and horrified her. Remorse came, and then despair. All this preyed upon her mind, and with it all there came a great longing for her son, whom she had left behind. The end of it all was that she fell under an attack of brain-fever, and lingered for many months a victim to it. She finally recovered, and went into a convent. After staying there some time she suddenly left. That is the meaning of those letters which you found. Of course I kept Neville Pomeroy acquainted with these circumstances on his return.

"Meanwhile Pemberton Pomeroy had lain under arrest. Neville went to see him, and took advantage of his misery to exact from him a solemn promise never to search after Lady Chetwynde again, or interfere with her in any way. Soon after that Pemberton Pomeroy was freed, for Neville declined to appear against him, and the case dropped. Neville then went back to England.

"Pemberton Pomeroy remained. There was no more hope for him in England. The money which he had gained by his forgery he, of course, had to refund; but his brother generously gave him a few thousands to begin life on. Pemberton then disappeared for a year or two. At the end of that time he came back. He had gone to England, and then returned to America, where he had lived out West. All his money was gone. He had fallen into low courses. He had taken a wife from the dregs of the foreign population, and, as though he had some spark of shame left, he had changed his name to Krieff. He had spent his last cent, and came to me for help. I helped him, and put him in the way of getting a living.

"But he had lived a wild life, and was completely used up. When he came to me he was pretty well gone in consumption. I saw he couldn't last long. I went to see him a good many times. He used to profess the deepest repentance. He told me once that he was writing a confession of his crimes, which he was going to send to his brother. The miserable creature had scarcely any spirit or courage left, and generally when I visited him he used to begin crying. I put up with him as well as I could, though. One day when I was with him he handed me a paper, with considerable fuss, and said I was not to open it till after his death. Not long afterward he died. I opened the paper, and found that it contained only this cipher, together with

a solemn request that it should be forwarded to his brother. I wrote to Neville Pomeroy, telling him of his brother's death, and he at once came out to New York. He had him decently buried, and I gave him the papers. I had taken a copy myself, and had found a man who helped me to decipher it. There was nothing in it. The poor fool had wanted to make a confession some way, but was too mean to do it like a man, and so he made up this stuff, which was of no use to any one, and could only be deciphered by extraordinary skill. But the fellow is dead, and now you know all the business."

Obed Chute ended, and bent down his head in thought. Hilda had listened with the deepest attention, and at the conclusion of this account she, too, fell into deep thought. There were many things in it which impressed her, and some which startled her with a peculiar shock.

But the one idea in her mind was different from any thing in this narrative, and had no connection with the mystery of the secret cipher, which had baffled her so long. It was not for this, not in search of this interpretation, that she had come. She had listened to it rather wearily, as though all that Obed could tell was a matter of indifference, whichever way it tended. To find that her interpretation was false had excited no very deep emotion. Once the search into this had been the chief purpose of her life; but all the results that could be accomplished by that search had long since been gained. The cipher writing was a dead thing, belonging to the dead past. She had only used it as a plausible excuse to gain admittance to the villa for a higher purpose. The time had now come for the revelation of that purpose.

"Sir," said she, in a low voice, looking earnestly at Obed Chute, "I feel very grateful to you for your great kindness in favoring me with this explanation. It has been hard for me to have this interpretation of mine in any way affect my father's memory. I never could bring myself to believe it, knowing him as I knew him. But, at the same time, the very idea that there was such a charge in writing disturbed me. Your explanation, Sir, has made all clear, and has set my mind at rest in that particular.

"And now, Sir, will you excuse me if I mention one more thing which I would like to ask of you. It concerns me, you will see, even more closely than this writing could have concerned me. It touches me in a more tender place. It is very strange, and, indeed, quite inexplicable, why you, Sir, a stranger, should be interwoven with these things which are so sacred to me; but so it is."

Obed was affected by the solemnity of her tone, and by a certain pathos in her last words, and by something in her manner which showed a deeper feeling by far than she had evinced before.

What Hilda now proceeded to say she had long thought over, and prepared with great deliberation. No doubt the woman whom Lord Chetwynde loved lived here. Most probably she was Obed Chute's young wife, possibly his daughter; but in any case it would be to him a terrible disclosure, if she, Lord Chetwynde's wife, came and solemnly informed him of the intrigue that was going on. She had made up her mind, then, to disclose this, at all hazards, trusting to circumstances for full and complete satisfaction.

"'YES,' HE CRIED, 'I'LL HAVE THIS CLEARED UP NOW, ONCE AND FOREVER. "

"Sir," she continued, in a voice which expressed still deeper emotion, "what I have to say is something which it pains me to say, yet it must be said. I am Lady Chetwynde, and traveled here with Lord Chetwynde, who is the only acquaintance I have in Florence. I hurried from England to his sick-bed, in Switzerland, and saved his life. Then I came here with him.

"Of late I have been suspicious of him. Some things occurred which led me to suppose that he was paying attentions to a lady here. My jealousy was aroused. I learned, I need not say how, that he was a constant visitor here. I followed him to a masquerade to which he refused to take me. I saw him with this lady, whose face I could not see. They left you. They walked to an arbor. I listened—for, Sir, what wife would not listen?—and I heard him make a frantic declaration of love, and urge her to fly with him. Had I not interrupted them at that moment they might have fled. Oh, Sir, think of my lonely condition—think what it costs my pride to speak thus to a stranger. Tell me, what is this? Is it possible, or do I dream? Tell me, do you know that my husband loves this woman?"

The emotion with which Hilda spoke grew stronger. She rose to her feet, and took a step nearer to Obed. She stood there with clasped hands, her beautiful face turned toward him with deep entreaty.

Obed looked at her in a fresh bewilderment. He was silent for a long time. At last he started to his feet.

"Well, marm," said he, as he clenched his fist, "I don't understand. I can't explain. Every thing is a muddle. All I can say is this—there's either treachery or insanity somewhere, and may I be cut up into sausages and chawed up by Comanches if I'll stand this any longer. Yes," he cried, "by the Lord! I'll have this cleared up now, once and forever. I will, by the Eternal!"

He brought his huge fist down with a crash on the table, and left the room.

Hilda sat waiting.

CHAPTER LXXVIII.

"THE WIFE OF LORD CHETWYNDE."

HILDA sat waiting.

Obed had gone in search of those who could face this woman and answer her story. He went first to send word to Zillah, summoning her down. Zillah had been feebly reclining on her couch, distracted by thoughts at once perplexing and agonizing, filled with despair at the dark calamity which had suddenly descended, with a black future arising before her, when she and "Windham" were to be sundered forever. He hated her. That was her chief thought; and Windham's love had gone down in an instant before Guy's deadly abhorrence. A lighter distress might have been borne by the assistance of pride; but this was too overmastering, and pride stood powerless in the presence of a breaking heart. In such a mood as this was she when the message was brought to her which Obed had sent.

The wife of Lord Chetwynde was down stairs, and wished to see her!

The wife of Lord Chetwynde!

Those words stung her like serpents' fangs; a tumult of fierce rage and jealousy at once arose within her; and at this new emotion her sorrow left her, and the weakness arising from her crushed love. With a start she rose to her feet, and hastily prepared to descend.

After summoning Zillah, Obed went in search of Lord Chetwynde. Some time elapsed before he could find him. He had been wandering about the grounds in a state bordering on distraction.

Meanwhile Hilda sat waiting.

Alone in the great room, where now the shadows were gathering, she was left to her own dark reflections. The sufferings through which she had passed had weakened her, and the last scene with Obed had not been adapted to reassure her or console her. The state of suspense in which she now was did not give her any fresh strength. Her nervous system was disorganized, and her present position stimulated her morbid fancy, turning it toward dark and sombre forebodings. And now in this solitude and gloom which was about her, and in the deep suspense in which she was waiting, there came to her mind a thought —a thought which made her flesh creep, and her blood run chill, while a strange, grisly horror descended awfully upon her. She could not help remembering how it had been before. Twice she had made an effort to anticipate fate and grasp at vengeance—once by herself alone, and once in the person of Gualtier. Each attempt had been baffled. It had been frustrated in the same way precisely. To each of them there had come that fearful phantom figure, rising before them awfully, menacingly, with an aspect of terrible import. Well she remembered that shape as it had risen before her at the pavilion—a shape with white face, and white clothing, and burning eyes — that figure which seemed to emerge from the depths of the sea, with the drip of the water in her dark, dank hair, and in her white, clinging draperies. It was no fiction of the imagination, for Gualtier had seen the same. It was no fiction, for she recalled her horror, and the flight through the forest, while the shape pursued till it struck her down into senselessness.

A shudder passed through her once more at the recollection of these things. And there arose a question of awful import. Would *it* come again? Now was the third attempt—the fateful third! Would she again be baffled, and by *that?* She feared no human foe; but this hor-

ror was something which she could never again encounter and live. And there came the terror over her that she might once again see this.

She was alone amidst her terrors. It was growing late. In the great room the dimness was deepening, and the furniture looked ghostly at the farther end of the apartment. It was not long since Obed had gone, but the time seemed to her interminable. It seemed to her as though she were all alone in the great house. She struggled with her fancies, and sat looking at the door fixedly, and with a certain awful expectation in her eyes.

Then, as she looked, a thrill flashed through all her being. For there, slowly and noiselessly, a figure entered—a figure which she knew too well. Robed in white it was; the face was pale and white as the dress; the hair was thick and ebon black, and hung down loosely; the dress clung closely. Was it the drip of the sea-wave— was it the wet clothing that thus clung to the figure which had once more come from the dark ocean depths to avenge her own cause? There, in very deed, stood the shape of horror—

> "her garments
> Clinging like cerements,
> While the wave constantly
> Dripped from her clothing."

It was *she.* It was the one who had been sent down to death beneath the waters, but who now returned for the last time, no longer to warn or to baffle, but to change from victim to avenger!

The anguish of that moment was greater far than all the agonies which Hilda had ever known. Her heart stopped beating; all life seemed to ebb away from the terror of that presence. Wildly there arose a thought of flight; but she was spellbound, her limbs were paralyzed, and the dark, luminous eyes of the horror enchained her own gaze. Suddenly she made a convulsive effort, mechanically, and sprung to her feet, her hands clutching one another in a kind of spasm, and her brain reeling beneath such thoughts as make men mad. In that deep agony a groan burst from her, but she spoke not a word as she stood there rooted to the spot.

As for Zillah herself, she, on entering, had seen Hilda, had recognized her, and was stricken dumb with amazement. That amazement made her stop and regard her, with wild, staring eyes, in utter silence. There had been only one thought in her mind, and that was to see who it could possibly be that dared to come here with the pretense of being "Lord Chetwynde's wife." In her eagerness she had come down in a rather negligé costume, and entering the room she found herself thus face to face with Hilda. At that sight a thousand thoughts flashed at once into her mind. In a moment she had divined the whole extent of Hilda's perfidy. Now she could understand fully the reason why Hilda had betrayed her; why she had formed so carefully contrived and so elaborate a plot, which had been carried out so patiently and so remorselessly. That sight of Hilda showed her, too, what must have been the height and the depth and the full extent of the plot against her young, undefended life—its cruelty, and the baseness of its motive. It was to take her place that Hilda had betrayed her. Out of such a motive had arisen such foul ingratitude and such deadly crime. Yet in her generous heart, while her mind understood this much, and her judgment condemned this vile traitor, the old habit of tenderness awakened at the sight of the familiar face, once so dear. Dearly had she loved her, fondly had she trusted her; both love and faith had been outraged, and the friend had doomed to death the unsuspecting friend; yet now even this last wrong could not destroy the old love, and her thoughts were less of vengeance than of sad reproach. Involuntarily a cry escaped her.

"Oh, Hilda! Hilda!" she exclaimed, in a voice of anguish, "how could you betray your Zillah!"

To Hilda's excited and almost maddened fancy these words seemed like reproaches flung out by the dead—the preliminaries to that awful doom which the dead was about to pronounce or to inflict. She trembled in dread anticipation, and in a hoarse, unnatural voice, and in scarce audible words, gasped out,

"What do you want?"

For a few moments Zillah said not a word, though those few moments seemed like hours to Hilda. Then, with a sudden impulse, she advanced toward her. Her impulse was one of pity and kindliness. She could not help seeing the anguish of Hilda. For a moment she forgot all but this, and a vague desire to assure her of forgiveness arose within her. But that movement of hers was terrible to Hilda. It was the advance of the wrathful avenger of blood, the irresistible punisher of wrong; the advent of a frightful thing, whose presence was horror, whose approach was death. With a wild shriek of mortal fear she flung up her arms, as if to shut out that awful sight, or to avert that terrible fate, and then, as though the last vestige of strength had left her utterly, she staggered back, and sank down, shuddering and gasping for breath, into her chair, and sat there with her eyes fixed on Zillah, and expressing an intensity of fear and apprehension which could not be mistaken. Zillah saw it. She stopped in wonder, and thus wondering, she stood regarding her in silence.

But at this moment footsteps were heard, and Obed Chute entered, followed by Lord Chetwynde.

Obed had but one thought in his mind, and that was to unravel this mystery as soon as possible; for the presence of such an inexplicable mystery as this made him feel uncomfortable and humiliated. Until this was explained in some way he knew that he would be able to find rest neither by night nor by day. He was, therefore, resolved to press things forward, in hopes of getting some clew at least to the labyrinth in which his mind was wandering. He therefore took Lord Chetwynde by the arm and drew him up toward Hilda, so that he stood between her and Zillah.

"Now," he said, abruptly, turning to Hilda, "I have brought the man you wish to see. Here he is before you, face to face. Look at him and answer me. Is this man your husband?"

These words stung Zillah to the soul. In an instant all pity and all tenderness toward Hilda vanished utterly. All her baseness arose before her, unredeemed by any further thought of former love or of her present misery. She sprang forward, her eyes flashing, her hands clenched, her whole frame trembling, and all her soul on fire, as it kindled with the fury of her passionate indignation.

"*Her* husband!" she exclaimed, with infinite passion and unutterable contempt—"*her* husband! Say, Mr. Chute, do you know who it is that you see before you? I will tell you. Behold, Sir, the woman who betrayed me; the false friend who sought my life, and, in return for the love and confidence of years, tried to cast me, her friend, to death. This, Sir, is the woman whom you have been so long seeking, herself—the paramour of that wretch, Gualtier—my betrayer and my assassin—*Hilda Krieff*."

These words were flung forth like lava-fire, scorching and blighting in their hot and intense hate. Her whole face and manner and tone had changed. From that gentle girl who, as Miss Lorton, had been never else than sweet and soft and tender and mournful, she was now transformed to a wrathful and pitiless avenger, a baleful fury, beautiful, yet terrific; one inspired by love stronger than death, and jealousy as cruel as the grave; one who was now pitiless and remorseless; one whose soul was animated by the one feeling only of instant and implacable vengeance. The fierceness of that inexorable wrath glowed in her burning eyes, and in the rigid outstretched arm with which she pointed toward Hilda. In this moment of her fervid passion her Indian nature was all revealed in its hot, tempestuous, unreasoning fury; and the Zillah of this scene was that same Zillah who, years before, had turned away from the bedside of her dying father to utter those maledictions, those taunts, and those bitter insults, which Lord Chetwynde so well remembered.

Yet to Hilda at that instant these words, with all their fury and inexorable hate, came like balm and sweetness—like the gentle utterances of peace and calm. They roused her up at last from that great and unendurable horror into which she had fallen; they brought back her vanished strength; they restored her to herself. For they showed her this one thing plainly, and this above all things, that it was not the dead who stood thus before her, but the living! Had her former suspense been delayed a few moments more she would have died in her agony; but now the horror had vanished; the one before her bore no longer the terrors of the unseen, but became an ordinary living being. It was Zillah herself, not in death as an apparition, but in life as a woman. She cared nothing for the hate and the vengeance, nothing for the insult and the scorn. She cared nothing for the mystery that enshrouded Zillah, nor was it of any consequence to her then how she had been saved. Enough was it that Zillah was really alive. At this she revived. Her weakness left her. She drew a long breath, and all the vigor of her strong soul returned.

But on the others the effect of Zillah's words was overwhelming. Obed Chute started back in amazement at this revelation, and looked wonderingly upon this woman, who had but lately been winning his sympathy as an injured wife; and he marveled greatly how this delicate, this beautiful and high-bred lady, could, by any possibility, be identified with that atrocious monster whose image had always existed in his mind as the natural form of Zillah's traitorous friend.

On Lord Chetwynde the effect of all this,

though equally great, was different. One look at Hilda in her first consternation and horror, and another at Zillah in her burning passion, had been enough. As Zillah finished, he caught her outstretched hand as it was pointing toward Hilda, and there rushed through all his being a rapture beyond words, as a dim perception of the truth came to his mind.

"Oh, my darling!" he cried, "say it again. Can this be possible? Is *she*, then, an impostor? Have I, indeed, been blinded and deceived all this time by her?"

Zillah tore her hand away from his grasp. In that moment of fury there came to her a thousand jealous fears to distract her. The thought that he had been so far deceived as to actually believe this woman his wife was intolerable. There was a wrathful cloud upon her brow as she turned her eyes to look at him, and in those eyes there was a glance, hard, stern, and cold, such as might befit an outraged and injured wife. But as she thus turned to look at him the glance that met hers was one before which her fury subsided. It was a glance upon which she could not look and cherish hate, or even coldness; for she saw in his face a wild rapture, and in his eyes a gleam of exultant joy, while the flushed cheeks and the ecstatic smile showed how deeply and how truly he loved her. On that face there was no cloud of shame, no trace of embarrassment, no sign of any consciousness of acts that might awaken her displeasure. There was nothing there but that old tenderness which she had once or twice seen on the face of Windham —a tenderness which was all for her. And she knew by that sign that Guy was Windham; and being Windham, he was hers, and hers alone. At this all her hardness, and all her anger, and all the fury of her passion were dispelled as quickly as they had arisen, and a great calm, full and deep, came over all her being. He loved her! That was enough. The fears which had tormented her since Mrs. Hart's revelation, the fury which had arisen but a few moments ago at the dark promptings of jealousy, were now all dispelled, and she saw in Lord Chetwynde her own Windham.

Quickly and swiftly had these thoughts and feelings come and gone; but in that moment, when Zillah's attention was diverted to Lord Chetwynde, Hilda gained more of her self-command. All was lost; but still, even in her despair, she found a fresh strength. Here all were her enemies; she was in their power and at their mercy; her very life was now at their disposal; they could wreak on her, if they chose, a full and ample vengeance; yet the thought of all this only strengthened her the more, for that which deepened her despair only intensified her hate. And so it was that at this last moment, when all was lost, with her enemies thus before her, the occasion only served to stimulate her. Her strength had returned; she summoned up all her energies, and stood grandly at bay. She rose to her feet and confronted them all—defiant, haughty, and vindictive—and brought against them all the unconquerable pride of her strong and stubborn nature.

"Tell me again," said Obed Chute, "what name was it that you gave this woman?"

"I am Zillah, daughter of General Pomeroy, and this woman is Hilda Krieff," was the reply.

"Hilda—Hilda—Hilda Krieff! Hilda Krieff!" said Obed Chute. "My good Lord!"

But Hilda did not notice this, nor any thing else.

"Well," she said, in a cold and bitter tone, "it seems that I've lost the game. Amen. Perhaps it's just as well. And so you're alive, after all, are you, Zillah, and not in the sea? Gualtier, then, deceived me. That also is, after all, just as well."

"Wretched woman," said Lord Chetwynde, solemnly, "Gualtier did not deceive you. He did his work. It was I who saved her from death. In any case, you have the stain of murder on your soul."

"Perhaps I have, my lord," said Hilda, coolly, "and other stains also, all of which make it highly inappropriate for me to be your wife. You will, however, have no objection to my congratulating you on the charming being you have gained, and to whom you have addressed such very passionate vows."

"This woman," said Lord Chetwynde, "hardly deserves to be treated with ordinary civility. At any rate, she is not fit for *you*," he added, in a low voice, to Zillah; "and you are too agitated for further excitement. Shall I lead you away?"

"Not yet," said Zillah, "till I have asked one question. Hilda Krieff," she continued, "answer me one thing, and answer me truly. What was it that made you seek my death? Will you answer?"

"With pleasure," said Hilda, mockingly. "Because I hated you."

"Hated me!"

"Yes, hated you always, intensely, bitterly, passionately."

"And why? What had I ever done?"

"Nothing. The reason of my hate was in other things. I will tell you. Because I was your father's daughter, and you supplanted me."

"You! Impossible!"

"I will tell you. In my childhood he was fond of me. I was taken to India at an early age. After you were born he forgot all about me. Once I was playing, and he talked to me with his old affection. I had a locket around my neck with this name on it—' *Hilda Pomeroy.*' He happened to look at it, and read the name. 'Ah,' said he, 'that is a better name than Hilda Krieff. My child, I wish you could wear that name.' I wanted him to tell me what he meant, but he wouldn't. At another time he spoke of you as being my 'little sister.' He frequently called me daughter. At last I found some old papers of my mother's, when I saw that her name was Hilda Pomeroy, and then I understood it all. She was his first wife, though I believe now that they were not married. He, of course, deceived her, and though she thought she was his wife, yet her child could not take his name. I asked him this, but he refused to explain, and warned me never to mention the subject. This only showed me still more plainly the miserable truth.

"Years passed. I found myself driven out from my father's affections. You were the world to him. I, his eldest daughter, was nothing. You were his heiress. Good God! woman, do you think I could help hating one who calmly appropriated every thing that ought to be mine?

"Now you know about as much as you need

know. I began years ago to plan against you, and kept it up with never-failing patience. It was the only pleasure I had in life. I won't go into particulars. I'll only say that nearly all your troubles came through my management. From time to time hereafter you will gradually remember various things, and think with tender regret upon your loving Hilda.

"At last things were all ripe, and I slipped away. I got you out of the way also, and I frankly avow that I never expected to have the pleasure of seeing you again. I also hoped that Lord Chetwynde would not come back from India. But he came, and there is where I broke down. That is all I have to say."

Hilda stopped, and looked defiantly at them.

"Young woman," said Obed Chute, in calm, measured tones, "you are very aggravating. It is well that you have generous people to deal with. I don't know but that I ought to take you now and hand you over to the police, to be lodged in the same cell with your friend Gualtier; but—"

"Gualtier!" groaned Hilda. "What?"

"Yes, Gualtier. I caught him yesterday, and handed him over to the police."

Hilda looked around wildly, and with a deeper despair in her heart.

"You," continued Obed, "are much worse than he. In this business he was only your tool. But you're a woman, and are, therefore, sacred. You are safe. It would be better, however, and much more becoming in you, to refrain from that aggravating way of speaking which you have just used. But there is one question which I wish to ask, and then our interview will terminate: "You say you believe yourself to be the elder daughter of General Pomeroy?"

"Yes."

"Do you know your mother's maiden name?"

"Yes. Hilda Krieff."

"Did she ever tell you about her marriage?"

"I was too young when she died."

"Did you ever see any record of her marriage?"

"No."

"You know nothing definite about it, then?"

"No."

"Well, then, allow me to inform you that you are as much astray here as you were in that other thing. This Hilda Krieff was the wife of Pemberton Pomeroy—married after his elopement business. He took her name. You were their daughter. I saw you once or twice when visiting him. You were then a baby. Neville Pomeroy took charge of your mother and you after your father's death. These are the facts of the case."

"What is all this?" cried Zillah, eagerly, as she heard these names. "Do you know about papa?"

"This lady came here with some questions about a cipher writing which she had misunderstood, and I explained it all. She thought the General was guilty, but I explained that he was the best fellow that ever lived. It's too long to tell now. I'll explain it all to you to-morrow."

"Oh, thank God!" murmured Zillah.

"What! you couldn't have believed it?" cried Obed Chute.

"Never! never!" said Zillah; "though she tried hard to make me."

R

Hilda had no more to say. The news about Gualtier, and the truth as to her parentage, were fresh shocks, and already her strength began to give way. Her spirit could not long be kept up to that height of audacity to which she had raised it. Beneath all was the blackness of her despair, in which was not one ray of hope.

She rose in silence. Obed accompanied her to her carriage, which was yet waiting there. Soon the wheels rattled over the gravel, and Hilda drove toward Florence.

Obed walked out and sauntered through the grounds. There was a twinkle in his eye. He walked on, and on, till he reached a place in the depths of the woods far away from the villa.

Then he gave utterance to his feelings.

How?

Did he clench his fists, curse Heaven, weep, and rave?

Not he; not Obed.

He burst forth into peals of stentorian laughter.

"Oh, dear!" he screamed. "Oh, creation! Ha, ha, ha, ha, ha! Oh, Lord! making love on the sly! getting spooney! taking romantic walks! reading poetry! and all to his own wife! Oh, ho, ho! Ha, ha, ha, ha! And he stole off with her at the masquerade, and made a 'passionate declaration'—to his—good thunder!—his *wife!* *his own wife!* Oh, Lord! oh, Lord! I'll never get over this!"

He certainly did not get over it for at least two hours.

He had at last fully comprehended the whole thing. Now the true state of mind between the quondam Windham and Miss Lorton became evident. Now he began to suspect how desperately they had been in love. A thousand little incidents occurred to his memory, and each one brought on a fresh explosion. Even his own proposal to Zillah was remembered. He wondered whether Windham had proposed also, and been rejected. This only was needed to his mind to complete the joke.

For two hours the servants at the villa heard singular noises in the woods, and passers-by heard with awe the same mysterious sounds. It was Obed enjoying the "joke." It was not until quite late that he had fully exhausted it.

CHAPTER LXXIX.

MUTUAL UNDERSTANDING.

MEANWHILE Lord Chetwynde and Zillah were left together. A few hours before they had been sitting in this same room, alone, when Mrs. Hart entered. Since then what wonders had taken place! What an overturn to life! What an opening into unlooked-for happiness! For a few moments they stood looking at one another, not yet able to realize the full weight of the happiness that had come so suddenly. And as they looked, each could read in the face of the other all the soul of each, which was made manifest, and the full, unrestrained expression of the longing which each had felt.

Lord Chetwynde folded her in his arms.

"What is all this?" he said, in a low voice. "What can it mean? I can not yet believe it; can you? What, my darling, are we not to have our stolen interviews any more? Have we no longer our great secret to keep? Are you really mine? I don't understand, but I'm content to hold you in my arms. Oh, my wife!"

Zillah murmured some inaudible protest, but her own bewilderment had not yet passed away. In that moment the first thought was that her own Windham was at last all her own in very truth.

"And are you sure," she said at last, "that you have got over your abhorrence of me?"

Lord Chetwynde did not understand this question, but considering it a joke, he responded in the customary manner.

"But what possible means could have induced you to leave Chetwynde Castle at all?" he asked; for, as he had not yet heard her story, he was all in the dark.

"Because you wrote that hideous, that horrible letter," said Zillah; and as the memory of that letter came to her she made an effort to draw away from his embrace. But the effort was fruitless.

"Hideous letter! What letter?"

"The last one."

"My darling, I don't know what you mean."

"Don't you remember how you reviled me?"

"I didn't; I don't understand."

"You called me a Hindu, and an imp."

"Good Heavens! what do you mean?"

"But you do not hate me now, do you? Tell me, and tell me truly, are you sure that your abhorrence has all passed away?"

"Abhorrence!"

"Ah! you need not fear to confess it now. You did abhor me, you know."

"On my honor, I do not know what you are talking about, my own darling. I never wrote about you except with respect; and that, too, in spite of those awful, cutting, sneering letters which you wrote for years, and that last one, written after my father's death."

"Heavens! what do you mean?" cried Zillah, aghast. "I sent letters to you regularly, but I never wrote any thing but affectionate words."

"Affectionate words! I never received a letter that was not a sneer or an insult. I came home under an assumed name, thinking that I would visit Chetwynde unknown, to see what sort of a person this was who had treated me so. I changed my intention, however, and went there in my own name. I found that woman there—an impostor. How was I to know that? But I hated her from the outset."

"Ah," said Zillah, "you were then full of memories of Inez Cameron."

This thought had suddenly stung her, and, forgetting the Windham of Marseilles, she flung it out.

"Of what? Inez? What is that?" asked Lord Chetwynde, in a puzzle.

"Inez Cameron."

"Inez Cameron! Who is Inez Cameron?"

"Inez Cameron," said Zillah, wondering—"that fair companion of so many evenings, about whom you wrote in such impassioned language—whose image you said was ever in your heart."

"In the name of Heaven," cried Lord Chetwynde, "what is it that you mean? Who is she?"

"Captain Cameron's sister," said Zillah.

"Captain Cameron's sister?"

"Yes."

"Captain Cameron has no sister. I never saw any one named Inez Cameron. I never mentioned such a name in any letter, and I never had any image in my heart except yours, my darling."

"Why, what does it all mean?"

"It means this," said Lord Chetwynde, "that we have for years been the victims of some dark plot, whose depths we have not yet even imagined, and whose subtle workings we have not yet begun to trace. Here we are, my darling, asking questions of one another whose meaning we can not imagine, and making charges which neither of us understand. You speak of some letter which I wrote containing statements that I never thought of. You mention some Inez Cameron, a lady whom I never heard of before. You say also that you never wrote those letters which imbittered my life so much."

"Never, never. I never wrote any thing but kindness."

"Then who wrote them?"

"Oh!" cried Zillah, suddenly, as a light burst on her; "I see it all! But is it possible? Yes, that must be it. And if you did not write that last letter, then she wrote it."

"She! Who?"

"Hilda."

Hereupon ensued a long explanation, the end of which was that each began to understand better the state of the case. And Lord Chetwynde exulted at finding that all the baseness which he had imagined against his wife was the work of another; and Zillah felt ecstasy in the thought that Lord Chetwynde had never loathed her, and had never carried in his despairing heart the image of that dreaded and hated phantom, Inez Cameron.

"The fact is, I couldn't have written that letter for another reason, little girl. I always made allowances even for those letters which you did not write, and until that last one came I always laid great stress on my father's love for you, and hoped some day to gain your love."

"And that you would have done in the ordinary way if we had met in Chetwynde Castle."

"Would I, indeed?"

"Yes," sighed Zillah; "for I think I learned to love you from your letters to your father."

"Oh no! no, no," laughed Lord Chetwynde: "for did you not at once fall in love with that Windham?"

So the time passed.

But amidst these murmurs of affection, and these explanations of vanished mysteries, Lord Chetwynde caught himself looking to the past few months at Florence.

"Oh, those interviews!" he murmured, "those sweet, stolen interviews!"

"Why, Sir," said Zillah, "you speak as though you feel sorry for all this!"

"No, my darling. My fond recollection of these can not interfere with my joy at the present; for the great meaning of this present is that while we live we shall never part again."

Lord Chetwynde did not go back to Florence that night. There were a thousand things to talk over. On the following day Obed explained all about the cipher, and told many stories about his early association with Neville Pomeroy. These things took up all the next day. Lord Chetwynde was in no hurry now. His Indian appointment was quietly given up. He had no immediate desire to go to his lodgings, and Obed insisted that Lord and Lady Chetwynde should be his guests during their stay in Florence.

To this Lord and Lady Chetwynde agreed, and enforced a promise from Obed Chute that he would be their guest in Chetwynde Castle.

Sometimes their thoughts turned on Hilda. They had no desire to pursue her. To Zillah she was an old friend; and her treason was not a thing which could be punished in a court of justice. To Lord Chetwynde she was, after all, the woman who had saved his life with what still seemed to him like matchless devotion. He knew well, what Zillah never knew, how passionately Hilda loved him. To Obed Chute, finally, she was a *woman*, and now undeniably a woman in distress. That was enough. "Let the poor thing go; I half wish that I could save her from going to the devil." Such were his sentiments.

On the second day Lord Chetwynde drove in to his rooms. He returned looking very pale and grave. Zillah, who had gone out smilingly to greet him, wondered at this.

"We talked about sparing her," said he, softly. "My darling wife, she is beyond our reach now." Zillah looked at him with fearful inquiry.

"She has gone—she is dead!"

"Dead!" cried Zillah, in a voice of horror.

"Yes, and by her own hand."

Lord Chetwynde then told her that on reaching his rooms he was waited on by the *concierge*, who informed him that on the previous day the lady whom the *concierge* supposed to be his wife was found dead in her bed by her maid. No one knew the cause. The absence of her husband was much wondered at. Lord Chetwynde was so much shocked that his deportment would have befitted one who was really a bereaved husband. On questioning the maid he found that she had her suspicions. She had found a vial on the table by the bed, about which she had said nothing. She knew her duty to a noble family, and held her tongue. She gave the vial to Lord Chetwynde, who recognized the presence of strychnine. The unhappy one had no doubt committed suicide. There was a letter addressed to him, which he took away. It was a long manuscript, and contained a full account of all that she had done, together with the most passionate declarations of her love. He thought it best, on the whole, not to show this to Zillah.

He knew that she had committed suicide, but he did not know, nor did any living being, the anguish that must have filled the wretched one as she nerved her heart for the act. All this he could conjecture from her letter, which told him how often she had meditated this. At last it had come. Leaving the villa in her despair, she had gone to her lodgings, passed the night in writing this manuscript, and then flung her guilty soul into the presence of her Maker.

As Lord Chetwynde had not gone into Florentine society at all, Hilda's death created but little sensation. There was no scandal connected with her name; there was no bewildering explanation of things that might have seemed incredible. All was quieted, and even hate itself was buried in the grave of the dead.

The death of Hilda gave a shock to those who had known her, even though they had suffered by her; but there was another thing which gave sadness in the midst of new-found happiness. When Mrs. Hart had left the room, after that eventful evening when she had found Lord Chetwynde and Zillah, she was taken to her bed. From that bed she was destined never to rise again. During the last few months she had suffered more than she could bear. Had she lived in quiet at Chetwynde, life might possibly have been prolonged for a few years. But the illness which she had at Chetwynde had worn her down; and she had scarce risen from her bed, and begun to totter about the house, than she fled on a wild and desperate errand. She had gone, half dying, to Florence, to search after Lord Chetwynde, so as to warn him of what she suspected. Her anxiety for him had given her a fitful and spasmodic strength, which had sustained her. The little jewelry which she possessed furnished the means for prolonging a life which she only cherished till she might find Lord Chetwynde. For weeks she had kept up her search, growing feebler every day, and every day spending more and more of her little store, struggling vehemently against that mortal weakness which she felt in all her frame, and bearing up constantly even amidst despair. At last Obed Chute had found her. She had seen "her boy"—she had found him with Zillah. The danger which she had feared seemed to her to have been averted, she knew not how; and her cup was full.

A mighty revulsion of feeling took place from the depths of despair to the heights of happiness. Her purpose was realized. There was nothing more to live for.

But now, since that purpose was gained, the false strength which had sustained her so long gave way utterly. Her weary frame was at last extended upon a bed from which she would no longer be compelled to rise for the watch and the march and the vigil. Her labor was over. Now came the reaction. Rapidly she yielded. It seemed as though joy had killed her. Not so. A great purpose had given her a fictitious strength; and now, when the purpose was accomplished, the strength departed, and a weakness set in commensurate with the strength—the weakness of approaching dissolution.

She herself knew that all was over. She would not have it otherwise. She was glad that it was so. It was with her now a time to chant a *nunc dimittis*—welcome death! Life had nothing more to offer.

Once again Zillah stood at her bedside, constant and loved and loving. But there was one whose presence inspired a deeper joy, for whom her dying eyes watched—dying eyes wistful in their watch for him. How she had watched during the past months! How those eyes had strained themselves through the throngs of passers-by at Florence, while, day by day, the light of hope grew dimmer! Now they waited for his coming, and his approach never failed to bring to them the kindling light of perfect joy.

Lord Chetwynde himself was true to that fond affection which he had always expressed for her and shown. He showed himself eager to give up all pleasures and all recreations for the sake of being by her bedside.

"MY BOY, HAVE YOU EVER HEARD ABOUT YOUR MOTHER?"

On this Obed Chute used to look with eyes that sometimes glistened with manly tears.

Days passed on, and Mrs. Hart grew weaker. It was possible to count the hours that remained for mortal life. A strange desolation arose in Lord Chetwynde's heart as the prospect of her end lowered before him.

One day Mrs. Hart was alone with him. Obed Chute had called away Zillah for some purpose or other. Before doing so he had whispered something to the dying woman. As they left she held out her hand to Lord Chetwynde.

"Come here and sit nearer," she wailed forth—"nearer; take my hand, and listen."

Lord Chetwynde did so. He sat in a chair by the bedside, and held her hand. Mrs. Hart lay for a moment looking at him with an earnest and inexplicable gaze.

"Oh!" she moaned, "my boy—my little Guy! can you bear what I am going to say? Bear it! Be merciful! I am dying now. I must tell it before I go. You will be merciful, will you not, my boy?"

"Do not talk so," faltered Lord Chetwynde, in deep emotion.

"Oh, my boy!" said Mrs. Hart, "do you know—have you ever heard any thing about—your—your mother?"

"My mother?"

"Yes."

"No; nothing except that she died when I was an infant."

"Oh, my boy! she did not die, though death would have been a blessing."

A thrill passed through Lord Chetwynde.

"Nurse! nurse!" he cried—"my dear old nurse, what is it that you mean? My mother? She did not die? Is she alive? In the name of God, tell me all!"

"My boy!" said Mrs. Hart, grasping the hand that held hers convulsively—"my boy! can you bear it?"

"Where is my mother?" asked Lord Chetwynde.

Mrs. Hart struggled up. For a moment she leaned on her elbow. In her eyes there gleamed the light of undying love—love deep, yearning, unfathomable—love stronger than life. It was but a faint whisper that escaped her wan, white lips, but that whisper pierced to the soul of the listener, and rang through all his being with echoes that floated down through the years.

And that whisper uttered these words:

"Oh, my son! I—I—am your mother!"

A low moan burst from Lord Chetwynde. He caught her dying form in his arms, and a thousand words of love burst from him, as though by that embrace and by those words of love he would drag her back from her immortality. And then, at last, in that embrace and in the

hearing of those words of love, there were some few moments of happiness for one who had sinned and suffered so much; and as she lay back her face was overspread with an expression of unutterable peace.

When Zillah returned she saw Lord Chetwynde bowed down, with his arms clasping the form of Mrs. Hart. The smile was still on her face, but it was only the form of that one who had suffered and loved so much which now lay there; for she herself had departed from earth forever, and found a place "where the weary are at rest."

Long afterward Zillah learned more about the past history of that woman whom she had known and loved as Mrs. Hart. It was Obed Chute who told her this, on one of his frequent visits to Chetwynde Castle. He himself had heard it from the former Lady Chetwynde, at the time when she was in New York, and before she joined the Sisters of Charity.

Neville Pomeroy had known her well as a boy, and they had carried on an unmeaning flirtation, which might have developed into something more serious had it not been prevented by her mother, who was on the look-out for something higher. Lord Chetwynde met her ambitious views, and though he was poor, yet his title and brilliant prospects dazzled the ambitious mother. The daughter married him without loving him, in the expectation of a lofty position. When this was lost by Lord Chetwynde's resignation of his position she could not forgive him. She indulged in folly which ended in sin, until she was weak and wicked enough to desert the man whom she had sworn to love. When it was too late she had repented. Neville Pomeroy and Obed Chute had saved her from ruin. The remainder of her life was evident. She had left the Sisters of Charity, from some yearning after her child, and had succeeded in gaining employment in Chetwynde Castle. Such changes had been wrought in her by her sufferings that the Earl never recognized her; and so she had lived, solacing herself with her child.

The knowledge of her history, which was afterward communicated to her son, did not interfere with his filial affection. Her remains now lie in the vaults of Chetwynde Castle beside those of the Earl.

THE END.

By WILKIE COLLINS.

Man and Wife.

A Novel. With Illustrations. 8vo, Paper, $1 00; Cloth, $1 50.

The Moonstone.

A Novel. With Illustrations. 8vo, Paper, $1 50; Cloth, $2 00.

Armadale.

. A Novel. With Illustrations. 8vo, Paper, $1 60; Cloth, $2 00.

No Name.

A Novel. Illustrated by JOHN McLENAN. 8vo, Paper, $1 50; Cloth, $2 00.

The Woman in White.

A Novel. Illustrated by JOHN McLENAN. 8vo, Paper, $1 50; Cloth, $2 00.

The Queen of Hearts.

A Novel. 12mo, Cloth, $1 50.

Antonina; or, The Fall of Rome.

A Romance of the Fifth Century. 8vo, Paper, 50 cents.

No amount of mechanical ingenuity would, however, account by itself for the popularity of Mr. Wilkie Collins's works. He has several other important qualifications. He writes an admirable style; he is thoroughly in earnest in his desire to please; his humor, though distinctly fashioned on a model Mr. Dickens invented and popularized, is better sustained and less fantastic and affected than any thing which Mr. Dickens has of late years produced.—*London Review.*

We can not close this notice without a word of eulogy on Mr. Collins's style. It is simple and so manly; every word tells its own story; every phrase is perfect in itself.—*London Reader.*

Of all the living writers of English fiction no one better understands the art of story-telling than Wilkie Collins. He has a faculty of coloring the mystery of a plot, exciting terror, pity, curiosity, and other passions, such as belong to few if any of his *confreres*, however much they may excel him in other respects. His style too, is singularly appropriate—less forced and artificial than the average modern novelists.—*Boston Transcript.*

PUBLISHED BY HARPER & BROTHERS, NEW YORK.

☞ *Sent by mail, postage prepaid, to any part of the United States, on receipt of the price.*

www.ingramcontent.com/pod-product-compliance
Lightning Source LLC
Chambersburg PA
CBHW030643030726
47497CB00006B/1926